"In order to ... "

ELEMENTS

BOOK TWO
IN "THE BIODOME CHRONICLES"

What are the elements that comprise your life?

by
JESIKAH SUNDIN

[signature]

Just Imagine...
Developmental Editing & Publishing

Text and Cover Design/Illustration
Copyright © 2015 Jesikah Sundin
All rights reserved.

ISBN: 978-0-9913453-2-8
ISBN- 0991345320

Printed in the United States of America

First Edition

Just Imagine...
Developmental Editing & Publishing
Monroe, WA 98272
justimaginestory@gmail.com
jesikahsundin@gmail.com
www.jesikahsundin.com

This book is a work of fiction. Names, characters, places, and incidents are the product of the author's imagination or are used fictitiously. Any resemblance to actual events, locales, or persons, living or dead, is co-incidental.

Cover design by Amalia Chitulescu
Digital Illustration by Amalia Chitulescu
Interior design by Jesikah Sundin

DEDICATED TO

My sister,
Adriel Nicole Frantom ... ahem ... *Nicki*

and

My friends,

Melissa Patton, Tracy Campbell,
Jennifer Newsom, and Katie Kent

If you have a son who does nothing good ... deliver him at once into the hands of a merchant who will send him to another country. Or send him yourself to one of your close friends... Nothing else can be done. While he remains with you, he will not mend his ways.

— Paolo of Certaldo, 14th century Florentine merchant discussing the European Medieval practice of fostering *

Fillion Nichols, 17-year-old son of Corporate World Leader Hanley Nichols, is rumored to have entered the biodome city of New Eden Township, along the Salton Sea in California, to serve 90 days of Community Service Rehabilitation, as sentenced for selling falsified identifications to minors in the state of Washington. Sources state that a young adult from the famed medieval community has emerged in exchange for the business world's Corporate Eco-Prince, a possible requirement for sustaining balance within the mysterious commune. Management from New Eden Enterprises and New Eden Biospherics & Research are declining to comment at this time. Nevertheless, public interest in the Earth-based Mars colony has spiked in the last few hours, with Internet communities eager for a glimpse of the first potential quasi-Martian to visit our planet.

— Tony Dulaney, "Martian Activity along The Salton Sea," *Science Bits & Bolts*, October 3, 2054

JESIKAH SUNDIN

CHAPTER ONE

New Eden Township, Salton Sea, California

Saturday, October 3, 2054

Year 19 of Project Phase One

Day One of The Exchange

C oal's mind faded in and out of consciousness, and it took significant effort to open his eyes. When they did open, the view was fuzzy and he sought relief by closing them once more, blinded by the intense light that shone overhead. Sensations encouraged his body to return to sleep, but his mind shouted that he was in danger. The first tingles of adrenaline hit his bloodstream, and he mentally groped for awareness.

He did not remember falling asleep. Shortly after his arrival, he was whisked into a room by Michael—a scientist he had met upon entering the biospherics lab—who encouraged him to enjoy a tumbler of water as a team sifted through paperwork to receive parental permission for his extended stay and travels. Now, he found himself in a foreign room with a low rhythmic chirp in the background.

What made such noise?

A groan escaped his dry and cracked lips as he rolled to his side and craned his neck toward the sound. Coal's arm winced with a dull ache, and his eyes widened. The chirp belonged to a strange box-shaped machine perched atop a metal pole with a flat rope or twine that traveled his direction before disappearing into the wall. Numbers flashed on the black box, and he sucked in a quick breath as they continued to write and rewrite themselves, over and over again.

Was he in a dream?

A nightmare?

His eyelids fought the urge to remain closed. He forced himself to remain focused and to follow the twine. The blurriness of his vision irritated him, and he lifted his hand with the intention of rubbing his eyes. Mid-air, however, he stilled at the sight of a small, pipe-like object partially dangling from the back of his hand. He drew his hand closer for inspection. It did not appear to be a living object. Nevertheless, the pipe burrowed into his body, fastened to his skin with what appeared to be a secretion.

Alarmed, he sat up and sharply turned his head, taking in the undulating whitewashed room while squinting from the bright, unnaturally white light overhead. The constant motion made his stomach sour, but he pushed past the feeling.

What had happened to him?

Where was he?

Coal yanked off the mechanical parasite upon his hand, wincing as the small pipe emerged from his body, and hurled it to the floor with heavy movements. In his mind he was quick and sharp, but his body betrayed him when it lacked both strength and control. A drip splashed onto his breeches and he watched as another drop of blood pooled along his hand's skin and then fell through the air, landing on his foot. He wiped at the droplets and stared at the smeared blood along his fingers.

The machine screamed in protest, a loud high-pitched sound that pierced the air. He recoiled, covering his ears as he rolled onto his knees and tucked in his head. An unexpected shadow crossed over him, and Coal jumped, further terrified.

Coal squinted at the figure standing before him. Eventually Michael came into focus; he watched Coal with a thin frown. Then, the scientist reached out and steadied Coal's wobbly body, which perched precariously on the edge of an oddly narrow and shortened cot. The bed was covered in a thin paper-like material, crinkling with a sound similar to the dry leaves that rustled and blew across the grass in a bio-breeze. Coal readjusted his position, covering his ears once more as the room tilted and spun with his sudden movements.

With heavy-lidded eyes, he watched as Michael walked behind the bed and tapped a yellow circle on the black box machine. A picture with words appeared in the air, brightened by blue-lit lettering. Coal gasped. Panic consumed him once more when Michael touched and commanded the words with his finger until the sound stopped. With a sharp wave in the air by the man, the floating image dissipated as if mere vapor.

Adrenaline pulsed through Coal's bloodstream and he lurched back in response. His limbs grasped the air as he fell, finding nothing to save his descent. Pain shot through the back of his head as he crashed against the wall, then slid to the floor with a solid thud. Although he fared well, Coal decided to remain still. He possessed no desire to see the magic Michael had used. Then, too, Coal floundered for an explanation as to why he was experiencing such disorientation, petrified that somehow he was under a spell.

Footsteps echoed in a hurried rush and the cot was pushed to the side. Michael knelt next to him on the floor, leaning down until he could study Coal's eyes. In response, Coal blinked against the fuzziness in his head, his anxiety growing. The scientist pulled a thin, metal stick out of his pocket, the length of a twig, and pushed the top, which caused a light to appear on the bottom.

Coal pressed himself tight against the wall, each muscle tensed in anticipation. "No!" He placed his hands in front of his face.

"Coal, stop before you hurt yourself again. I'm trying to help you."

"What is the object in your hand, sir?" The words formed thick and gritty in his parched mouth. "What are you doing to me?"

Michael looked at the stick for a moment and then slowly met Coal's eyes. "It's a flashlight," he said.

With fluid movements, Michael tugged on Coal's hand and lifted the flashlight. Coal wrenched his hand back and drew it close against his body with a glare. Insistent, Michael took Coal's hand once more, offering a friendly smile, and placed the stick against Coal's index finger. Before Coal could protest, the tip of his appendage lit up and he tilted his head in curiosity and horror.

"Feel any pain in this finger?"

"No, but perhaps this is a trick, another spell from your … flashlight … to control my mind."

An amused smile stretched across Michael's face. "Oh goodness, no. We don't cast spells. A sedative was placed in your drink."

"I was poisoned?"

"It's a drug to relax your body, usually resulting in sleep. We needed to inoculate you right away and didn't want to distress you with that process. State law, health regulations… Don't move. I'm going to shine this light in your eyes to make sure you don't have a concussion after that fall of yours."

Michael gradually raised the light to Coal's eyes. Breaths came more quickly as Coal attempted to make sense of what was happening. "Follow the light with your eyes," the scientist murmured, "but don't move your head."

Coal complied and followed the light as Michael moved it up and down and left to right. Satisfied, Michael turned the flashlight off and tucked it away in the front pocket of his white tunic.

"You're OK."

Pondering Michael's words, Coal rubbed the forming lump on the back of his head. He felt awkward and sluggish; and he squinted his eyes against the unnatural brightness of the room. The walls were a crisp white, as were the ceiling and tiled floor. His fingers brushed along the floor as he contemplated the smooth and slightly grooved surface. It did not feel like wood or stone. And it was not compacted earth.

Three white cupboards were fastened on the wall, just below the ceiling. The cupboards blended in with the whitewashed walls. This intrigued him, having never seen cupboards hover in such a fashion. In New Eden they had pieces of upright furniture that only rested upon the floor.

His gaze wandered across the room and stilled upon the pipe-like object. He looked at the back of his hand. The transparent secretion had dried upon his skin in a grid of black and gold lines. "What was placed upon my hand and in my body?"

Michael looked over his shoulder at the items. "The square sticker is a Wi-Fi oxygen sensor. It adheres to your skin. We wanted to monitor you while you were sedated. Just an extra precaution since you're breathing a new atmosphere. And that is a catheter, just in case you had a medical emergency."

Coal drew his eyebrows together, once again not fully grasping Michael's words. With a mildly slurred voice, Coal asked, "And what is in-oc-ul-ate, sir?"

"We gave you medicine to fight the infections of this world—viruses and bacteria that would disable or even kill you. Since New Eden is hermetically sealed, its residents haven't been exposed to as many illnesses. Your immune sys-

7

tem, the part of your body that fights infections, is not as mature as ours. We want to make sure you get home after those ninety days, whole and healthy."

"Could I contaminate my world?"

"Yes, it's possible. We'll quarantine you for a couple of days before reentry, though, just to be safe."

"Did Corlan get quarantined?"

Michael turned his head away and said in a low voice, "No, he didn't. There wasn't much time. We gave him extra meds to boost his immunity and to kill any viral infections he may be hosting. He also got a UV scan to kill any topical parasites." A concerned expression returned to Michael's features as he studied Coal for a few heartbeats and then he stood, offering Coal his hand. "Let me help you up. The sedative causes dizziness." Coal grabbed his hand and stood, feeling his head swim for a moment. "I'll show you to the restroom. I don't think you've gone since you've arrived, and it has been a few hours."

A few hours?

Did he need to lie down somewhere different until the drug no longer addled his head?

Each step took effort, akin to walking into The Waters, and his head ached. They left the room and entered a hallway equally as bleak. Coal slowed, placing a hand upon the wall to steady himself. Another scientist in a long, white tunic gave Coal an inquisitive stare as she passed. Feeling uncomfortable with becoming an object of novelty, Coal lowered his head and looked away.

Michael slowed as they approached a door and tapped a silver object upon his ear. The door opened without human assistance and Coal took a step back, spooked. Doors do not open themselves.

Maybe he simply failed to see Michael use a knob. The drug warred with his concentration and he felt paranoid with the lack of control. He let out a long sigh and fought against the feelings that continued to rise in his chest.

The soft rug beneath his feet changed to a pottery floor as he walked into the rest-room, the cool, smooth surface hard against his bare feet.

Where were his shoes?

Did he walk out of New Eden shoeless?

Until this moment he did not realize they were missing. No matter, he preferred to be barefoot. Coal was about to ask about his shoes when a bewildering fascination cut through his anxiety. Coal stood before his full reflection. Mesmerized by the clarity of the image staring back at him, he walked forward until he could touch the looking glass.

A few within New Eden possessed small hand-held looking glasses, but none were large enough to take in one's full reflection. Otherwise, reflections were sought after in water, polished silver, and in windows, muted and dull images that had been satisfactory, until this moment.

His eyes roamed over his broad frame and muscled arms. Labor-worn fingers reached up and softly touched his long, light blond hair, watching as the strands slowly fell back against his face, skin bronzed from standing before The Forge. Golden Boy, indeed. He tucked the neck-length strands behind both of his ears and allowed his fingers to explore his reflection, marveling as they slid against the metallic surface in perfect symmetry with his false self.

What did Oaklee think when she looked upon him?

Coal licked his dry lips and angled his head, noting how he and Ember shared a similar nose and mouth. His twin sister's brown eyes were indeed as dark as his, and he blinked as memories of his sister floated past his mind's eye. She was now a married woman and bound the Earth Element nobility with the Fire Element house.

His hand fell, landing in a large depression along a long table. Water instantly poured out of a silver spigot and Coal jumped back. He could not help but chuckle, however, over the pleasure of an effortless indoor well.

How did the water pump?

More importantly, how did the water know his hand was there?

Coal looked up with a big grin. "I am astonished," he said, returning his attention to the warmed water spilling over his fingers in a gentle stream. Freshly dried blood washed off his hand and fingers, tinting the white bowl a light red. It was all rather eerie, conjuring thoughts of invisible helpers; nevertheless, Coal was intrigued.

How did the water heat without fire and an iron pot?

The scientist smiled. "The porcelain bowl is a sink, and the water pours from a faucet. There are sensors that detect your hand and reward the motion with running water."

Sensors?

"Fascinating." Too groggy to make sense of such explanations, he skimmed his gaze over the room and asked, "Where do I lie down?"

"What do you mean?" Michael's smile faded.

"You insisted that I should visit the rest-room. Where shall I rest?"

"Oh, that's funny. I never thought of it that way before." Michael started laughing and Coal clenched his jaw as he realized that he had misunderstood something. "OK, so a restroom is not actually a room for resting," Michael said. "It's where one goes for bodily functions, such as urinating."

"Oh?" Coal glanced around the space. "How on Earth has it come to be known as a rest-room?"

Michael eyes crinkled with humor. "That's a mystery to me, too. But you'll discover that we have a nickname for everything, and that the outside culture explains its every move and thought *way too much*." Michael walked over to a small metal door and rested his hand on the top. "So, these are stalls, and inside each one is a toilet."

At first, Coal believed Michael referred to a place where one grooms himself. However, Coal was mistaken, much to his chagrin, and cataloged that toilette held an entirely different definition to Outsiders. Instead, it was a white chair featuring a gaping hole filled with a small pool of water. Coal studied the contraption, bending over to see the underside. It was indeed a solid piece, and not an extravagant bucket. Pipes disappeared into the wall, and he was curious about their purpose. As he stood, he felt a wave of dizziness and grabbed the stall door for support.

"Easy, make sure you stand up slowly for the next hour or so. We don't want you to fall over and bump your head again."

Coal nodded with understanding, then walked inside the stall and shut the door. Dubious, he unlaced his breeches. As the water turned yellow, his anxiety began to escalate, unsure of how to make the clear water return. His mind furiously studied the toilette of the rest-room as he re-laced his breeches, jumping against the stall door when a loud whoosh sounded. Wide-eyed, he gaped as the tainted water disappeared as clear water arrived simultaneously.

"Where did it go?" Coal felt stupid as soon as the words left his mouth.

"The water is taken away through pipes to a treatment plant that sanitizes it."

"We use plants to sanitize our water as well," Coal said. "Norah oversees the wetland room where the gray water is filtered." He walked out of the stall and stopped when Michael held a humored look on his face once more.

"A treatment plant is actually a building that is a machine."

"I see."

Coal released a heavy sigh as he dropped his hands against his sides in defeat. Once again he did not see. How could a building appear like a plant but be a machine to sanitize water? He gave up, and decided that perhaps he really did come from a different planet. They used the same language but the meanings were worlds apart. Frustrated, Coal pushed past Michael toward the door only to face another annoyance as there was no knob or handle. "How does one leave the rest-room?"

"First put your hands in the UV light for ten seconds." Michael pointed to a box on the wall with a purple light peeking through the top.

There seemed to be a box to perform some mysterious task in every room.

Tentatively, Coal lifted his hands above the light and then shut his eyes tight as he turned his head away. Every muscle tensed in anticipation. A light pressure on his arm jolted Coal's eyes back open as Michael gently guided Coal's hands into the box. The ethereal light blanketed his fingers and Coal held his breath as he internally counted to ten, slowly pulling them out upon completion. He flexed and curled his fingers and accounted for every sensation that should exist, relieved with the results.

"We're going to a meeting room down the hall," Michael said casually over his shoulder. The scientist then stepped before the entry and the door opened.

The stark hallway startled Coal's senses. Nevertheless, the rug again caressed his bare feet and he luxuriated in the soft sensations. Fantastical rooms, open to the hallway, appeared from time to time. Each space contained a multitude of men and women who performed various tasks he could not describe, the images surreal and belonging to a dreamstate. The foreign concepts and visions blurred together in Coal's mind, adding to his confusion, as very little resembled the people, landscape, or things of home. And although he wished to absorb each image and entertain each curiosity, Coal eventually kept his head down. He did not wish to make eye contact with any of the Outsiders, who paused in their work to study him as he passed by.

Warm light caught his vision, and distracted him from his anxiety. To his left, a large window perfectly framed the enormous biodome structures outside. His steps faltered. Sunlight glinted off the honeycomb-shaped panes of the biodome, producing a brilliant flash of light. It was a magical image, which added to as well as eased the pang his heart endured with each beat. Michael did not slow, however, and the sight of New Eden Township disappeared from view as they continued forward and left the window behind. Wistfully, Coal fixated on the long, bleak hallway that stretched before him and not the eyes that studied his every move.

So far, he was not impressed with the hospitality given him, nor the strides taken to ensure his comfort as he navigated a new world. Although he could accept the scientific community's concern to keep him healthy and alive, he could not understand the necessity in tricking someone who was completely and wholly dependent upon another for his welfare. He was a grown man, and he deserved to be treated as such. Given such insults, Coal was grateful he took Leaf's place so his brother-in-law did not experience the shame of being in such a frightening and vulnerable position so soon after losing his father.

Large double doors loomed ahead and Michael paused before the entry to place his thumb onto a strange black box on the wall. An unexpected click greeted Coal's ears before Michael turned the knob.

"Here you go. Make yourself comfortable. I'll be back in a bit."

"You are not staying with me?" Coal shook his head, realizing he asked the obvious. The scientist misunderstood his body language as disapproval and frowned for the first time.

"I won't be gone long. Promise. There's an aquarium inside filled with exotic fish. Have you ever seen an aquarium before?" Coal did not reply, crossing his arms over his chest and allowing his guide to feel a little discomfort in their exchange. Michael cleared his throat and then continued in his usual jovial tone. "I imagine the room looks similar to what you're used to seeing in New Eden. Might be a comforting sight. OK, I'll see you in a few minutes."

Coal peeked into the room, begrudging each step as he entered. The door shut behind him and he turned around in a panic, feeling the ebb and flow of disorientation as the motion in his head created waves in the walls. He placed his hand on the handle, but it would not turn. A fire simmered in his veins as the Outside world sealed him away once more, and a few choice words in French breached his self-control and passed his lips.

Home seemed so far away even though it was mere steps. It was a thought that mournfully sang in his mind as he slipped a hand into his pocket to caress Oaklee's leaf. Taking in a deep breath to calm his nerves and the quickly spreading fury, Coal pivoted on his heel to study his new enclosure.

ELEMENTS

It is not titles that honor men, but men that honor titles.

— Niccolò Machiavelli, Italian historian and philosopher, 15th century A.D. *

Liberty is to faction what air is to fire, an aliment without which it instantly expires. But it could not be less folly to abolish liberty, which is essential to political life, because it nourishes faction, than it would be to wish the annihilation of air, which is essential to animal life, because it imparts to fire its destructive agency.

— James Madison, "The Same Subject Continued: The Union as a Safeguard Against Domestic Faction and Insurrection," *The Federalist* No. 10, November 23, 1787 *

CHAPTER TWO

The Fall air brushed across Oaklee's skin as she ran through the forest, and a shudder trembled through her body from head to toe. The leaves rustled a soothing song from up above, a beauteous melody that slowed her feet. With eyes closed, she stilled her mind, not wishing to miss a single windy note or arborous lyric. Oaklee never tired of nature's gift to heal and encourage the soul, a necessity to temper her turbulent tendencies.

Glancing over her shoulder, she sighed with relief. The gathering still continued in the meadow by the North Cave. Desperation drove her to seek solitude. She needed to sort through her mounting emotions before she crashed, growing ill as she had a few days prior. Fury consumed her moments earlier when The Elements quarreled and disparaged one another upon learning how Coal had traded places with Leaf

And Oaklee had used every ounce of willpower she possessed to remain planted in the meadow as long as she did, listening to the building dissension…

"Whose idea was it for Coal to leave?" Timothy, the Wind Element, had demanded.

Her brother, Leaf, had remained passive. "My answer does not change the fact that Coal has left and, therefore, the answer is irrelevant."

"Are you refusing to honorably take responsibility?"

"Perhaps you can enlighten us all as to how I have broken The Code to warrant such a claim as dishonor? Anyone can leave at any time and for any reason."

Heads turned toward Norah, the Water Element, as she began to speak. "And why is Coal leaving the source of such discord?" She drew in a shallow, raspy breath. "The Son of Fire made a choice and the Earth Element honored that request."

Norah's breathy voice turned to wheezing and she paused with a hand in the air to signal there was more to say, even though her knees bent with weakness. Norah's eldest son fetched a chair he had brought for his mother and eased her in while her husband caressed her hand with gentle strokes.

The Water Element lifted her head and viewed the gathering, continuing in a strained voice, "Would the community have refused Coal's request? He is a grown man and no longer under the authority of his parents. This debate does not hold merit, nor does it honor Leaf as a leader, a man still in his bereavement week no less. He holds the right to remain with his family."

"That is, unfortunately, not the point, Norah." Timothy offered Norah a kind smile and walked closer to Leaf. "You do realize, Son of Earth, that with the coming colonists, during the Second Phase, your strength and integrity as a leader will be questioned more regularly."

Leaf had crossed his arms over his chest and considered Timothy's words, narrowing his eyes in a look of contemplation. "Mine specifically or all leaders?"

"All leaders, of course."

"Well, then, thank you for the reminder, My Lord." Leaf bowed his head in deference. "That was most kind of you to ensure that we are *all* prepared."

Corlan, the Outsider exchange, quietly snickered by Oaklee's side. Anger flashed through her body, and Oaklee shot a glare Corlan's direction before fixing her attention upon Leaf once more.

The Wind Element released a low, humorless laugh. "People do not like change, My Lord. If they feel a leader is easily tossed to and fro with every breeze, they will cast off any and all respect they once held for his or her position. The Nobles who stand unwavering—whose strength and trust are predictable and reliable—will withstand the winds of change."

Leaf took a step closer to Timothy. "The community will respect a leader who is willing to forsake tradition and bend for their benefit if the situation requires such flexibility. Honor is not defined by holding fast to traditions. Laws, codes, rules, and traditions can change." Oaklee tensed as her brother spoke with uncharacteristic boldness. "Flexibility is a necessity for our future. The *game* of survival demands it, does it not?"

Timothy's eyes subtly widened, and he smiled in such a way that Oaklee discerned he understood Leaf's hidden message. "Interesting," Timothy said. "Are you suggesting that you support disbanding and merging with the Outside world? Like your father?"

The crowd gasped and the rustle of murmurs grew to a rumble as Oaklee observed men and women whisper into one another's ears. Leaf watched the crowd as well, yet determination shone in his eyes.

"Come, we have much to celebrate today." Leaf offered Timothy his hand. "Let us not quarrel." When Timothy refused his hand, her brother leaned in and whispered so only those in the circle could hear. "Let us not be inflexible for the sake of tradition, My Lord. You would not wish to appear rude before the community, now would you? Or, is honor no longer defined by tradition?"

Timothy smiled but the warmth did not reach his eyes. "Why should I shake hands with a man who breaks a brother's oath?"

Leaf flinched and looked down at the grass. Oaklee's stomach tightened into a complication of knots with her brother's response. Remorse darkened Leaf's features, but he did not cower before Timothy. Instead, he maintained a posture of dignity though the words visibly pained him. Fury had tingled in her limbs and she felt Hurricane Willow gain strength as the winds of injustice whipped inside her heart. She clenched her fists and teeth as she glared at Timothy, her breaths heavy as she, in vain, tried to contain her spirit.

A soft touch on her forearm had startled her from her raging thoughts, and she whipped her head in Corlan's direction. He faced the circle but slowly shook his head, casting her a quick side-glance. The interference baffled her and the winds quickly died down, replaced by an eerie calm. How did he know she would react? Oaklee studied Corlan's profile, further perplexed as he held a look of open contempt. If he felt such emotion, why did he wish to hold back hers? Timothy's voice regained her attention and she turned back his direction.

"It seems there are some traditions you still measure through honor, Leaf. Guilt is a cruel friend."

"Enough," Connor said in a near whisper, but with an authority that demanded obedience. The Fire Element's large shoulders had sagged as he turned to Oaklee and asked, "Have I offended my son? Did I fail him somehow as a father?"

She lowered her head as a profuse blush colored her face. "No, My Lord. Your son has left to prove he is a man worthy of my hand after I have refused him." Her eyes began to fill and Leaf's features softened with a sad smile. "The day Leaf was nominated, I had unkind words for Coal and attacked his character. I believed his nomination was an act of punishment for refusing his hand. I was wrong, My Lord, and the price of my carelessness is his life."

The look on Coal's face, after she hissed that he was a stupid and insensitive fool, flashed in her mind. Oaklee knelt in the soft grass before Connor. Her throat constricted against the forming tears as she whispered, "I am most sorry for shaming your house and ask your forgiveness for being the cause of such distress and pain this day."

The Fire Element had knelt before her in the meadow. With a single finger, he lifted her chin and then took both of her hands in his. "I assure you there is nothing to forgive, Daughter of Earth. It is I who humbly asks forgiveness on behalf of my son, who would selfishly place the responsibility of his actions upon your heart to carry and grieve over as a move to win your affection. Coal acted dishonorably and that rests upon his shoulders. Not yours."

Large, work-worn hands pulled her into an embrace as she began to sob. Oaklee closed her eyes and melted against Connor as callused fingertips rubbed her back in soothing circles. For a heartbeat, she almost believed it was her father granting comfort in the moment.

When she had recovered, Oaklee pulled away and Connor offered his hand to help her rise and led her back to Leaf. Connor whispered loud enough for those in the circle to hear, "I would be proud to call you daughter, but you should marry for your reasons alone and not my son's, words I know your own father would share in this situation."

Tears had trailed down her face in silent grief. Connor had offered a momentary reprieve from her guilt. But Oaklee knew she had used her words as sharp weapons, delivering the injury with glee and motivating her friend to behave in such a way to regain her good opinion.

She touched her lips and remembered their kiss, and the pain of her choices returned. In the end, Coal had pledged himself to her and Oaklee was fairly convinced she would never see him again. And if he came home, she would have to refuse him again, severing any hope he had upon his return. It may very well end their friendship, but she could not marry him.

Self-conscious, she examined each Noble in the small group, then curiously studied the young man at her side. Corlan remained quiet and tense, holding an expression she had seen only one other time. Five days prior, she had been called upon to offer an apology in order to seal a young man's secrecy. She had humbled herself and lowered to the floor before the Outsider, who had stared at her through the portal.

This new Outsider reflected a similar inward and withdrawn posture. He radiated an aloof grace and a reserved authority—thumbs tucked into his breeches casually, shoulders elevated a notch, his dark mahogany hair feathering in the wind. Though he moved nary a muscle, Corlan's gray-blue eyes slid her direction. The air rushed from her chest in response.

Her body must have stiffened noticeably. Leaf gently patted her arm, which was looped through his, and gave her a wary look. He considered Corlan and then, as if nothing was amiss, returned his attention back to The Elements and the gathered community.

Corlan continued to hold her inquisitive stare, and he blinked as if trying to determine if she were real. It was the most perplexing response. So much so, Oaklee tilted her head in question. In the Cave, he had confessed that he was heartbroken, just like her. And he wished for her to grieve for them both.

Oaklee's pulse thrummed audibly in her ears as questions continued to flash in Corlan's eyes. His gaze trailed over her face, hair, and body with fearful reverence. Then, as if his emotions snuffed out akin to a candle, his face relaxed and softened, his attention resting upon her mouth. The warm air of his nervous sigh caressed her skin for a moment before he sharply turned away from her. Oaklee had winced with the abrupt disconnection as the emotions he openly and intimately expressed to her swirled in a mad rush inside her head.

Who was this Corlan that an entire Exchange was orchestrated to ensure his presence within the Township? Their town had been sealed shut for nearly twenty years, with the Second Phase still ten months away. Why receive visitors now and not then? What did this have to do with her family? How would Corlan revolutionize her community? And was their touching moment in the North Cave genuine and real? Or part of this game they all played? It was all so very confusing.

Motherly had hands reached out then and stroked her cheek, and Oaklee turned toward Norah. "Willow Oak, how did you receive the gash upon your forehead? Do you fare well?" Norah looked upon her with concern.

Ember came forward, brushed a strand of hair from Oaklee's face and took her hand. Oaklee wanted to grab Ember and hold her close, to cling to Coal's sister as a connection to her lost friend and beg forgiveness. Instead, she had focused on staying calm. "The sun's light was intense, and when The Door shut I had felt disoriented and hit my head upon the cave wall."

Excited chatter sifted through those gathered nearby. She had seen real sunlight. Until The Exchange, that was an experience no other second generation had known—and that most could still only imagine.

Her brother remained fixed on the circle of Nobles and did not pay the crowd nor her any heed. Oaklee was thankful, as she did not wish for the community to know about the horrifying technology beyond their panes, or that Corlan possessed a magic unparalleled to any skill or occupation within New Eden. Until she understood the reason for his presence, and why he looked and behaved in so familiar a fashion, Oaklee would not expose his capabilities.

Inquisitive stares drifted to Corlan and he shifted on his feet, turning his head the opposite direction as the muscles in his jaw clenched. Long and awkward heartbeats passed before

Timothy asked, "Corlan, how did you receive *your* injury? Rather peculiar coincidence, is it not?"

The Outsider leveled his eyes at Timothy and raised a single eyebrow with a look bordering on boredom. "Really? Out of all the questions you could ask me, that's the one you lead off with?"

"Indeed," Timothy said, returning the steady inspection. "Perhaps I should ask—"

"Corlan," Connor interjected. "Our most humble apologies. You see, we heard a rather loud scream followed by a pounding sound..."

Leaf cleared his throat. "The Door made a loud screeching sound as it shut. We can only imagine what it must have sounded like from the glade."

Oaklee inclined her head at Leaf and tried to remain passive, but she did not recall what they were discussing. Perhaps this occurred while she was unconscious? Corlan lifted his shoulders a little higher and angled his head away from the curious glances. Vulnerability flashed in his eyes once more and Oaklee felt a wave of exhaustion pass over her as she attempted to make sense of all the events this morning. There were simply far too many emotions.

Unable to stand trial a moment longer, or stand in Corlan's presence, she had blurted, "Please excuse me. I suffer a headache and wish to lie down."

Leaf studied her, worry etched in his features, but he graced her with a slight bow. Without a moment's hesitation, she marched along the worn path with head held high. The people in the crowd parted for her as they continued to gossip into each other's ears.

Upon reaching the wood, she had broken into a sprint and had raced the leaves that flew in the bio-breeze through the forest, running as fast as the wind could carry her, away from the North Cave and from the memories of Coal's kiss...

Oaklee now stood among the trees, her chest still rising and falling in exertion and grief. She blotted the sensitive skin around her eyes with the underside edge of her sleeve. Branches swayed with each breeze, like a mother comforting a child in her protective, nurturing arms. The scene captivated Oaklee's imagination as memories of the meadow, of The Door, of Coal faded into the shadows of the forest. The trees whispered their consolation as the bio-breeze came through again, a rare mild wind storm that mimicked autumn weather, so she was told.

She surveyed the undergrowth and focused on a cluster of fern fronds curled tightly against the new life they had been given. She often wondered why a fern's new existence was so firmly wound up. But she questioned its response no longer. Oaklee felt every muscle in her body want to curl up in self-protection, to comfort the pain, anger, and fear. With reverent touches, she pulled off two new fronds from the parent cluster and wrapped them around her ankle. Her fingers gently caressed the tender green leaves, and then she stood and walked as gracefully as she could toward her apartment to begin her new life.

"Willow."

She jumped, placing a hand upon her chest, and gulped in a large breath. Skylar leaned on a tree opposite from her on the path, arms crossed, a withdrawn expression lining his features. Sandy brown hair lifted in the breeze as his youthfulness aged before her eyes, and she ascertained he heard the news of Leaf and Ember's union.

"My Lord," she said, dipping her head respectfully.

The Son of Wind approached her with stiff strides and arms crossed against his chest.

"Are you well?" Skylar looked to the gash upon her forehead.

"Yes, 'tis but a scratch. I bumped my head upon the Cave wall."

"Most unfortunate. I am sorry to hear it." He regarded her carefully before continuing. "You are fired up. I can see it in your eyes. Did Leaf or the Outsider offend you? How may I avenge your honor, Willow Oak Watson of the Wood?"

A crooked smile slowly appeared and she almost smiled in response, especially as he used her childhood nickname. But his body language confused her. She could not tell if he jested or spoke in earnest. Not wishing to add to his injuries, she decided to smile politely.

"You are kind to concern yourself with my welfare."

"Pray tell, who are you offended with? If you will not permit me to avenge your honor, perhaps we can commiserate together. Misery loves company, does it not?"

"I am most sorry for your pain, My Lord. Please do not hate my brother. Leaf's actions are most peculiar." Oaklee issued a pleading look, and a shadow crossed over Skylar's features as he maintained a tight smile. "As his friend, you know Leaf would never use another for his own personal gain, especially through elopement. Nor would he wish to betray you."

"Leaf is fortunate to have such a dedicated sister. Mine are too young to give advice on matters of the heart."

Oaklee grew uncomfortable with the awkward atmosphere between them. Another gust of wind rushed by her and long tendrils and braids covered her face. His hazel eyes searched hers with intensity for several heartbeats before he broke away and diverted his attention in the direction of the North Cave.

He cleared his throat. "I wish to maintain my offer from last night. Should you need anything, you have but only to ask. I am entirely at your service."

"I thank you, My Lord. You are generous."

A relieved smile lightened his features and some of the youthfulness returned to his face. "Forgive me, I am not myself at present."

"There is no need for forgiveness, I assure you."

"May I escort you to wherever you were running off to?"

Oaklee blushed. Racing through the woods in a wedding dress was most unladylike. "I wished for a rest prior to the celebration this evening. My apologies, but I shall call upon your services another time, Skylar Kane of the Four Winds."

She bestowed what she hoped was a playful smile and began to move away. Skylar touched her arm and she paused while keeping her eyes on the ferns and grasses that grew near the tree. Their pliable stems bent with the invisible pressure as another breeze stirred the atmosphere.

"Please be careful."

She looked up and found him regarding her with sincere concern. "I have heard it on the wind that a faction is forming, and the dispute supposedly involved your father. Fear can lead people toward ... regrettable decisions."

Timothy's words to Leaf in the meadow echoed in her mind. "Whatever do you mean?"

"Oh, Leaf did not share with you? I am surprised, although, he is clearly distracted." Skylar tensed and then let out an angry breath as his eyes roamed over the ribbons and leaves in her hair. She grew dizzy as the blood drained from her face, and she met his worried eyes, determined to not faint. "I would not wish to overstep your brother's authority as head of your home."

Oaklee struggled as she knew he was right, though she wished for the details he honorably withheld. Familiar resentment brewed against her brother and she spun a strand of hair onto her fingers in an effort to distract her thoughts. "I understand, and shall ask Leaf at first opportunity."

"Please do not share that I spoke of such matters with you. I would not want to add to our grievances, nor place you in the middle of our affairs."

"Nor would I wish to add to them. You can trust me." She folded Skylar's hand in hers. "You are a good man and so is my brother. We have all lost our senses this week from grief and The Exchange thrust upon our community. I shall pray for your comfort, My Lord."

"Leaf is indeed lucky to have such a sister," he said, and attempted an encouraging smile, although she knew it pained him to do so. "Hurry away, Willow. Find your solitude."

Oaklee nodded and then dashed away down the wooded path, tree branches beckoning her to hurry. Despite the scramble of voices and thoughts shouting in her head, she heard the willow oak call to her from the forest, and she longed to answer. Perhaps once she changed she would pay a visit to crawl into the branches and sit high above the community and escape the pleasantries, smiles, and polite conversations in celebration of a new resident, one whose presence caused her further grief.

Thoughts of Coal flashed through her mind. Memories of their times together—perched high above the world they called home—drew the poison from her heart and into her blood stream. She had killed her friend. The only residents who had ever left the biodome had died and her heart did not know how to feel otherwise.

Did her father know the truth of what she had done?

Could he see her from heaven?

Shame burned through her, and Oaklee imagined his grave disapproval. She had kissed an honorable man whom she should marry but never would; and she gave her heart to a dishonorable man who had mocked and manipulated their family.

She continued to run—running even harder to escape her thoughts. The willow oak appeared at the bend and she halted abruptly, gasping for air as leaves swirled around her body. Longing to touch something tangible from her past that would remain in her future, Oaklee trailed her fingertips along the coarse bark of her mighty tree. With a last fortifying breath, she sprinted toward the apartment once more, allowing the wind to wipe away her tears.

Her legs burned as she climbed the stairs, and she limped into her home. Oaklee shut her bedroom door with force and stomped over to her small vanity table and screamed. The fury and pain churned until she was certain guilt's madness would consume her completely. Frantically, she pulled the pins and braids from her hair, gritting her teeth against the ache. The wild storm stilled, however, when she removed her mother's intricately carved dragon comb. Her knees gave way and she sank into her chair, gripping her stomach as she wept.

Surrendering to the grief, she crawled over to her oak chest, lifted the heavy lid and rummaged through her belongings until she found her father's Harvest token. The embroidered linen felt smooth against her cheek as she cradled the rag to her face.

The next time she would wear her mother's comb would be in a few weeks—the twenty-ninth day of October moon—when she would stand before the community on her sixteenth birthday. It was a day she dreaded, especially in light of her confessions to have refused Coal's hand.

"Kiss father for me," she whispered to the dragon, caressing the polished bone with her thumb.

Deft fingers wrapped the treasured comb within the folds of the Harvest token she had made long ago for the man who now resided in the fields boasting his life's labor. As she closed the trunk, the lid moaned with protest as if to echo her heart, and she pressed her cheek to the wrought iron tree as tears splashed across her cheeks once more. Time slipped by with each tear, and she forced herself to let go of the oak chest and crawl beneath the covers of her cot, wrapping weary arms around her knees.

The cup of tea Coal had brought her earlier in the week still rested upon her nightstand, and Oaklee wrinkled her nose. In all the drama, she had forgotten to return the vessel to the Great Hall. Its presence both disturbed and comforted Oaklee. Within moments, she fell asleep while gazing at the earthen cup, desperately wishing Coal sat in the corner chair as he did so faithfully four days prior.

If there were problems inside, residents would leave and more would use the communications system we have provided. Their silence shows us that all is well, that they are happy and content and already forgetting the world they left behind. Is this not the result we are seeking? LARP has proved the best psychological breakthrough for isolation, confinement and extreme [ICE] environment syndrome and my wife, Dr. Della Jayne Nichols, should be commended for her theory that has paved the way for interplanetary homesteading.

— Hanley Nichols, interviewed by Richard Ramsey, "A Brave New World," *Ecopreneur Today*, August 21, 2051

CHAPTER THREE

A large glass box, filled with percolating water and a rainbow assortment of fish, was positioned neatly against a cob wall with hewn timber framing. The offense that consumed Coal moments ago turned to reluctant curiosity as he stood before the aquarium. The sight drew him in and he inched closer, jumping back when his nose touched the cold glass.

The water was not boiling?

How did it bubble so?

He rubbed his nose and shook his head, baffled by the engineering enigma. Settling on his haunches, Coal continued to watch the fish with wonder. Then, he frowned.

Until this day, he was a fish that swam in an unnatural environment. Coal was currently in a room emulating the look of New Eden, yet it was painfully obvious it was not—the aquarium being one of those obvious signs. Pulling out Oaklee's leaf, he twisted it in his fingers and reflected on all the events leading to this moment. Part of him felt like the little blue fish that came to the surface, gasping for air, and he prayed he did not become like the brown fish, belly up in the corner.

The countless unknown items, strange sensorial experiences, and new pieces of information further dulled his drugged mind. So to calm his burning thoughts, Coal tracked the patterns the fish made as they swam around happily, seemingly ignorant of their glass house. He was a blissfully ignorant fish not too long ago, swimming around in his glass aquarium. He had known life existed beyond the panes of his home, but his world only revolved around New Eden Township. There had been nothing to compare it to and, therefore, no reason to feel ashamed of his confined existence. Nor to question it.

Callused fingers tucked long strands of hair behind his ears as he contemplated his faint, ghost-like reflection in the glass box. He felt completely out of his element, like a fish out of water. More so upon experiencing just how vastly different his world was compared to the world he had just entered. His hand pressed against the glass, and he shifted his focus from his reflection onto his charcoal stained fingers. New Eden Township and The Forge lay a short distance from the biospherics lab. But watching an aquarium bubble from a mysterious power source made him feel worlds apart from his origins.

How had his father taken the news?

As Coal was under eighteen years of age, a lawyer was speaking with Jeff to obtain parental permission and temporary release of guardianship. This much he remembered prior to falling under the effects of the sedative. If permission was not granted, he would return to New Eden with the shame of being treated as a child. Coal did not realize his leaving would create such a flurry of activity. For nearly two years, he had walked New Eden Township as a man no longer under the governing authority of his parents.

Did youth mature more slowly beyond the walls of his home?

By age fifteen, he had completed an apprenticeship and was a full-fledged blacksmith, was a titled Noble son who represented the Fire Element House, spoke three languages, and was well versed in The Classics. This year, he was given rights to marry and was aware of several maidens from the village who would be honored to have his hand. Now, he was back to being considered a child although he was two months shy from turning seventeen.

Would his father grant permission?

Honor Coal's decision as one made by a grown man?

Any person may leave New Eden for any reason per The Code, and age was not a stipulation.

Perhaps his worries were for naught. His father guarded the Watson family's secret and would, therefore, tread carefully, not wishing to tip the apple cart. Several times this week he had overheard his father and Brianna discuss the forming faction and their concerns for the Watson household. And then Coal's twin sister had married this morning before the break of day. He was not invited, nor was he given any knowledge of the act until after the hand-fasting was complete. Now the Hansen blood was tied to The Aether, his father's grandchildren given the ability to secretly lead the biodome city as invisible monarchs.

Was this his father's plan?

Did Ember marry Leaf out of obedience?

Even if she did, Coal knew his twin sister loved Leaf and had for many years. The Son of Earth would make an excellent husband for Ember. Coal did not object to their union. He objected to his father's request of an elopement that would further alienate Leaf from Skylar and pit the Wind Element House against the Fire and Earth Element Houses.

Was his father the faction leader?

Coal pushed thoughts of his father away in order to bank his heated insecurities, which now colored thoughts of his home and prior life in a strange light. He would glean whatever truths he could find when his head was less muddled, as he had taken Leaf's place with an intent to garner information.

All he would endure, experience, and learn was for Oaklee. He wanted to protect her from harm and further pain. Coal knew his behavior this week was ungentlemanly. Consternation drove him to such measures. If anything happened to her whilst he knew he could prevent it, he would never forgive himself.

Why did she not wish to marry?

Her romantic disinterest began before Joel's death, and he knew she fiercely clung to the last vestiges of girlhood while womanhood forced changes upon her that she resented. Willow Oak Watson did not have a fondness for change. Nevertheless, she needed another guardian and protector as she was next in line should anything befall Leaf, a fact that terrified him. Joel Watson did not die of natural causes, he was sure of it in light of how Joel had urged his children to leave New Eden with his dying breaths. The guarded comments he overheard regarding the Watson family as well as a forming faction only confirmed Coal's trepidation.

Although ungentlemanly, Coal did not regret that he had kissed Oaklee and pledged himself to her against her expressed wishes, with Leaf as witness. He welcomed the shame of being branded as dishonorable before the community if it meant Oaklee had a greater chance of surviving any future planned attacks against her family.

Closing his eyes, he rested his head against the aquarium and thought of their kiss, enjoying the sweet rush. For the first time, Coal faced an adventure without her, and it filled him with a new form of emptiness.

A fish nipped another in the tail. The offended fish urgently swam away to perceived safety.

Whose fins were being nipped in New Eden besides the Watsons?

Who was the territorial fish?

A click pulled Coal's attention toward the door. Michael and two other men walked in, each offering friendly smiles. Coal stood from his crouched position. He recognized one of the other men from his initial entry into the lab. The third he did not recognize, and Coal experienced a slight twinge of anxiety as the tall man approached him. Remembering the leaf, he tucked it away safely into his pocket.

"Coal, nice to finally meet you. *Je vous souhaite une cordiale bienvenue en touchant le sol de la terre pour la première fois.*"

Coal regarded the man warily, surprised by the welcome to Earth in French. "*Acceptez mes humbes remerciements pour l'invitation et l'experience,*" Coal said. Although he felt insulted by the insinuation that he was an alien to their land rather than a neighbor, Coal thanked him for the opportunity nonetheless.

The man's hazel eyes reflected the confidence of the intelligent as they swept over Coal from head to toe, and a satisfied smile crept along the man's face. The stature of the man suggested he was of an older age, but his appearance was oddly youthful. Light brown hair was kept in a shorter style with the front longer and fashioned to the side with care. An expression of warmth radiated over his features while sharpness cut through the air around him. It was a perplexing atmosphere even Coal could sense, and he a perfect stranger. Then Coal noticed that the man's skin appeared to glow.

Was he real?

How did skin reflect such light?

Coal examined the articles of clothing, intrigued by the contrasting colors and textures. The man wore a dark, tight cloak that reached his calves, fitted with sleeves, similar to a robe but decorated with buttons and straps. A tight-fitting tunic was underneath, tucked into breeches made from a course blue material, and held in place with a belt featuring a stunning buckle. Coal studied the buckle, impressed with the craftsmanship and curious about the metal.

The man extended his hand, his fingernails clean and perfectly groomed—unlike Coal's or those of most men in

New Eden, their life's labor staining their hands. Coal stared at the extension, wondering what to do.

Did the man do something offensive and need forgiveness?

Not wishing to appear rude, Coal reached out and took the man's hand. The man moved Coal's arm with his own, up and down, in waves. Coal reasoned this must be a custom of greeting—he did not perceive an offense, and they were not presently striking a bargain.

"I am Hanley Nichols."

Coal's eyes widened and his stomach turned somersaults, and then the fire that had traveled through his veins settled in his belly as he stood before the man responsible for the experiment and for Coal's treatment since he arrived Outside. He swallowed back his rising temper and reminded himself to remain in control.

Hanley chuckled kindly. "I take it you know who I am."

"Yes, My Lord, sir. Everyone in New Eden knows of your name. It is … nice … to meet you, sir." Coal bowed his head in respect.

How was he to properly address the owner and creator of New Eden?

"My apologies for causing you to wait so long." Hanley touched his cheek with a thoughtful look. "I just received a treatment to heal an injury received prior to the exchange."

"As you well know, I was otherwise engaged myself," Coal said. Hanley did not flinch at his words; rather, another satisfied smile lit his already glowing features.

"You sound just like your father," Hanley said. "Safety is very important at the lab, and I take it seriously. Your comfort is important to me as well. Although, I know it feels quite the opposite at this moment. Believe me, being sick is not an enjoyable way to spend your days outside of New Eden."

Not trusting himself to remain calm, Coal simply nodded his head. Casually, he studied the older man once more, and his mind recalled Corlan, the Outsider exchange. The young man had sported a rather impressive welt above an eye, and his nose looked bloodied as well.

Did he attack Hanley?

Was this why Corlan's ankles and wrists were bound?

Was he safe to place inside of New Eden?

What sort of treatment heals evidence of any and all afflictions and with such unnatural expedition?

And why was Corlan not given the same courtesy?

"You met John outside when you emerged." Hanley waved a hand toward the man who stood between him and Michael. "John is my friend and legal adviser. You know his cousin, Jeff."

Coal turned his attention to the man with dark hair and eyes. He could see the family resemblance. "Nice to meet you, again," Coal said, figuring this was a common greeting in the Outside world. In New Eden, everyone greeted each other based on the time of day as they were already well acquainted with one another. John replied with a nod of acknowledgment and a small friendly smile.

"And you know Michael, Mr. Hansen. Michael is my lead scientist at New Eden Biospherics & Research." This introduction caused Coal to crease his brows slightly.

Why had Hanley switched to his formal name after speaking with him so casually earlier?

"Please, call me Coal if you would be so kind. It would allow me to feel more *comfortable*."

Looking behind him, Hanley eased into a chair with a humored smirk and gestured for everyone else to follow suit. "Great, no need for formalities here. After all, I have known your father for a very long time. We are family, Coal. Did you know this?"

Coal felt his legs shake as he sat, watching the blue fish gasp for air.

He was related to Hanley Nichols?

Hanley observed him closely for a few seconds, and then asked, "How is the peppermint oil? Is it helping to reduce the pungent smells?"

Coal's face scrunched up, perplexed. Thoughts of possible relation circled in his hazy mind until Hanley's latest questions took their place. Until mentioned, he had not realized the scent, too overwhelmed by other sensations.

"Yes," he replied, still distracted. "Thank you."

Was Hanley waiting for him to ask how they were related?

Something inside of Coal yearned to know, yet he could not shake the feeling that he was being baited. As if somehow the notion of kinship removed any offenses. So instead of responding, Coal sat perfectly still and waited for Hanley to continue.

"Excellent. Let us know when you need more. We estimate it will take two to four days to acclimate to the chemical smells of our society." Hanley paused briefly, long enough to give quick looks to John and Michael. "We will stay at the biospherics lab for one week to help you transition. Then, depending on some things, we'll take a plane and go to Washington state, where I live and where New Eden Enterprises is headquartered. Any questions?"

There were far too many questions, Coal internally quipped. Instead, he voiced the loudest of them all in French, too ashamed to ask in English before John and Michael. "*Est-ce que mon père a donné son autorisation finale?*"

He looked down at the floor covered in a wall-to-wall rug, feeling his face flush. It was a scenario he did not anticipate nor think through clearly. Since a lad, he had often made decisions with haste, acting on instinct rather than lengthy thought or persuasion. This trait earned him Oaklee's humored ire, who oft declared he was impetuous. Hanley shifted in his seat and Coal tensed in anticipation of the man's answer.

"Yes, we do have legal permission for you now." Hanley looked to John who gave a single nod of agreement. Coal relaxed a bit with this news. "It seems Connor did not expect your exit today. What made you trade places with the nominated exchange?"

"Personal reasons."

"We are in a sound-proof copper Faraday cage. The only people who will hear our discussion are the four of us in this room. I have some questions, and your answers will determine whether you stay or whether you return to New Eden."

Hanley waited for a reply with a kind smile, eyes crinkling in the corners. Coal had never heard of a Faraday cage. Nor could he see a cage-like apparatus in the room. But he did understand the message of privacy. And the cushioned warning. He was cornered. Still, he did not wish to return to New Eden, yet.

"I shall do my best."

"I have no doubt," Hanley said. He readjusted his position in the chair and then began. "I know that Leaf Watson was the exchange." Michael blanched with this news and John's eyes flinched, but only subtly. "Michael and John, I could not share until this moment as I did not know what would happen."

"Nevertheless," John muttered, crossing his arms over his chest, "withholding *critical* information placed me in a precarious position at The Door, especially with media drones behind the privacy gate and the scare with the one that flew in close." The lawyer appeared as though he wished to say more, but he closed his mouth and looked away.

"Why is he so pale?" Coal asked while watching Michael, not understanding John's comments about media drones and their ability to fly.

Was it an insect, like New Eden's male drone bees?

What did this have to do with Leaf?

What information was Hanley withholding?

Coal released a slow breath, trying to calm his mind to one central question, focusing on Michael once again.

"How well do you know the Watson family?" Hanley asked.

Shifting in his chair, Coal weighed the question, trying to understand the angle. However, he felt intimidated by the lack of respect the owner showed his trusted council. And him. So much so, it was distracting. Hanley's behavior differed from that of men within New Eden. It was a strange paradox. Hanley came across as if he cared and expressed himself in earnest, but he just smiled away concerns as if they did not exist, flitting from one question or comment to another.

Knots continued to form in Coal's gut. But he finally dismissed his anxiety. The Legacy and The Code both originated from Hanley, after all. And fear of banishment from New Eden was now ineffectual, his life already tied to the Outside world for a duration.

Licking his lips nervously, Coal began. "Willow Oak is my dearest friend. Laurel and my sister Corona are inseparable as well." Coal chuckled as he thought of his family and friends. "Poor Blaze is left out of this camaraderie."

"And Leaf?"

Coal darted a quick look Michael's direction, who remained pale. "Leaf and my twin sister Ember eloped early this morn." Coal felt himself tense.

John let out a slow breath upon hearing the news of marriage. Their eyes met, and Coal knew the lawyer was calculating information and making decisions. He had seen a similar look on Jeff's face on occasion. Something was amiss.

"Did you see Joel die?" Hanley continued without a blink or a fuss.

"Yes, My Lord. I was with Leaf and Willow when Joel passed away in the outer garden of The Rows." The memories came racing back to Coal's mind and he allowed his eyes to wander over to the aquarium, recalling every word and every movement of that day. The men were quiet, he realized, granting him a moment to gather himself.

"I am not part of the nobility. You may address me as Hanley, or as 'sir' if my first name is too informal for your comfort." Hanley offered him another kind smile. Coal nodded his head, feeling his face warm despite the gentle correction. "Did Joel share anything with Leaf or Willow before passing away?" Hanley asked softly, appearing sensitive to

Coal's position and memories. "I know my question may appear to go against the codes of honor you are accustomed to," he said. "But your answer is instrumental to our investigation. I am relying on you to help us, to help New Eden."

"Yes, sir." Coal looked at each face, sucking in his bottom lip and releasing it once more. "Joel shared with Leaf that Claire was The Aether, and upon his last breath, Leaf would continue the Legacy and become King as the rightful heir." He opened his mouth to share more and then closed it while rubbing his jaw to appear natural, deciding to withhold the odd request for Leaf to gather his sisters and leave to seek out a woman named Della. Or was it Jane?

"Did anyone besides you and Willow Oak hear this news?"

"No, I do not believe so as it was the hour of rest prior to evening meal. Workers were no longer in the fields. Is something amiss?" Coal stood up. Adrenaline surged through his limbs and his muscles tensed and relaxed with the internal struggle to remain in control. His temper was unwieldy at times and it was coming dangerously close to sparking a scene.

"Do you believe Joel's death was natural or planned?"

"Pardon?" Coal blinked in disbelief, every muscle going still.

Even they believed Joel was murdered?

Why did they suspect that Joel had not died of a heart attack as declared?

A visceral warning prickled the hairs on the back of his neck. "How could you suggest something as outrageous as someone murdering Joel Watson? Not only is it against The Code, it is dishonorable and the cruelest act anyone could resort to in our community." Thinking back on his father's words to Brianna to keep a closer watch on the Watsons, he felt another sense of dread.

Would his father resort to such measures to gain political power and control?

"Because," Hanley said, "nearly six years ago death certificates were issued from New Eden for Laurel, Willow Oak, and Leaf Watson, declaring that they had died from salmonella contamination. As you know, they are not dead."

Coal sank into his chair, placing his head into his hands. His fears were confirmed. Oaklee was truly in danger and he began to worry that he had made a grave mistake in switching places with Leaf. The Son of Earth may have been safer on the Outside. And now he was beyond reach when Oaklee may need him the most.

"It is important for you to know that their deaths created a massive lawsuit on the medical rights of children within New Eden. John and I were in court for many months and I faced possible charges of neglect and manslaughter. New Eden Township was nearly shut down. Therefore, it is crucially important that the last time we speak of the Watson children living is in this room. If word got out that they were alive, the media would destroy them, and New Eden too."

"I understand, sir. I would never wish to cause harm to them." He did not know what "media" was or "manslaughter." Both sounded horrifying.

"I believe you, and that is why I need your help."

"I will do anything. I secretly traded places with Leaf, for Willow was not managing well, and I could not bear to see her suffer further with her brother's absence." He lowered his head, hoping the men did not see the feelings burning behind his eyes. "I have done this much, and I am willing to do more. I would protect the Watsons with my own life."

Hanley simply raised an eyebrow and an unreadable expression flashed across his face before it shifted into the familiar image of friendliness. "I knew you were a man of honor; very valiant, too. You remind me of my son, who would also be willing to lay down his life for another. In fact, he did a few months ago, taking a large hit for his friend, almost paying a rather high price. He is laying down his life again as we speak. It is his nature, his fate, just as much as yours." John turned his head and studied Hanley with a frown.

It was Coal's fate to lay down his life?

Was Hanley speaking literally or figuratively?

As Joel was most likely murdered, Coal could not rule out any possibility. "Is your son in danger?"

Hanley regarded him with a studious gaze. "Depends. Is New Eden safe?"

Coal started as he realized the implications of Hanley's question. "Corlan is your son?"

"His real name is Fillion, and yes. We changed his name to disconnect association from me. The village will not know that name."

"How is he laying down his life to enter New Eden for a temporary exchange?"

"By giving up the one he has on the Outside."

Coal grit this teeth, frustrated that Hanley had not fully answered his question. Entering New Eden was not an act of honor nor a move that could be described as valiant. No more than his own presence existing beyond the walls. It was the motive for Fillion's relocation that justified whether his act was honorable.

What was Fillion's motive?

Or, perhaps his father's?

Coal's head seemed to swim for a heartbeat, and his thoughts grew sluggish as though they traveled through mud. "How may I be of assistance?"

"Your presence is the perfect distraction. We'll ensure the media stays focused on you instead of any other news that is discovered about New Eden Township. Already the tales of a Martian visitor are exciting the inhabitants of Earth," Hanley said. "Perception." The word hung in the air a few seconds before he continued. "It's a powerful tool. You are a product of research, and it is time to show the world that the key to the future resides in the past."

There were far too many things to ponder, and Coal felt himself fading away as he attempted to grasp Hanley's request. His eyes darted around the room in search of something to which he could anchor his mind. Voices grew distant. Looking at his hands, he saw a slight tremor. He felt dizzy.

A light touch upon his arm startled Coal, and he looked up. Michael stood nearby, trying to relay a message. Coal scrunched up his face in confusion, feeling more panic as he struggled to make out the words. A heavy pressure registered in his back as Michael pushed his torso forward until his head rested between his knees. Through hazy thoughts and another dizzy spell, Coal realized that he was hyperventilating.

Eventually, his mind slowed down and his ability to hear returned. He was able to make out the words of "breathe long and slow," so he obeyed. After several measured breaths, the pressure in his chest began to lighten as the adrenaline waned.

"I think he answered enough questions," John said quietly, offering Coal a sad, concerned smile.

"Sorry, sir. I have recovered." Coal wiped sweat from his forehead with the hem of his tunic.

"John is right. You were pushed too hard," Hanley said. "I needed to know if I could trust you. You have had a lot of big changes and been given a lot of distressing information. The atmosphere is far different from yours, too. The oxygen is thinner than what you are used to. Your body is self-regulating against a lot of foreign things at this moment." Hanley paused and gave Coal a sympathetic look, and Coal clamped down the offense that wished to reignite. Conveniently, Hanley left the sedative and inoculations from the list of hardships. With a sigh tinged with worry, Hanley said, "Why don't we break for a late lunch, and then we'll show you to your room."

"So I am allowed to stay..."

"You are the perfect young man to help us through this time in the media spotlight. And as the son of the Fire Element, you'll pick up, understand, and accept technology far quicker than most from New Eden. Has Connor shown you modern technology?"

"No, sir. How could he?"

Hanley considered him for a moment and then walked out the door without a reply or backward glance, with John trailing close behind him. Michael paused in the door frame and politely waited for Coal to follow, maintaining a distressed posture.

Coal regarded the aquarium once more. Fish swam around oblivious to their curious spectator as he studied his reflection in the glass. The fish whose tail was nipped separated itself from the group and began to appear sickly, most likely from stress, Coal reasoned. He refused to be this fish, or the belly up fish, or the blue fish gasping for air. Rather, he resolved to be the other fish, the one who found purpose and meaning despite the unnatural environment, despite depending upon keepers for survival.

Either give me more wine or leave me alone.

— Rumi, 13th century A.D. *

CHAPTER FOUR

A pop sounded in Fillion's ear. He was relieved when the Cranium turned on. A joint dangled loosely in his mouth and he lifted his fingers to take another draw. God, that felt good. Smoke left his mouth in thin wisps as he peeked inside the partially opened window.

The Great Hall filled with loud, spontaneous laughter. Fillion rolled his eyes and shook his head in irritation. He scanned the tables until he spotted the source. Several heads tilted back at a far table and their shared laughter carried through the room and out the window. At least someone was happy. It sure as hell wasn't him. Fillion leaned his head back against the stone wall with a weary sigh and stared out into the night. The cold air made him shiver, but he enjoyed the sensation.

"Cranium, what's the time?" he asked in a near whisper. Activating the holographic user interface was out of the question this close to the medieval hippies.

Not knowing the time was driving him crazy. There were no clocks. Anywhere. He asked for the time twice during the day and everyone in hearing distance would immediately look around them, like they were scenting the air. And then, suddenly, their eyes would fixate on some object and narrow in concentration. Fillion looked in the direction and saw nothing except shifting shadows, furniture, trees, whatever. Their faces would relax and, with confidence, they would share the time. God, he thought *he* was crazy. At least he didn't see imaginary time pieces.

"The hour is 7:49:21 p.m. Pacific Standard Time."

The computer synchronized with his thoughts, humoring him. He drew on his joint again, the smoke leaving his mouth as he whispered, "Cranium, phone Mack." Nothing. He knew John had Mack's number because of Fillion's trial. Just as he was about to try a different name, a notification ping echoed in his head.

"User interface," he whispered, moving away from the window as his eyes hunted for human movements. He tapped on the privacy screen and then the notification. "What the...?" An ad hoc network with another Cranium user was attempting to connect. Inside the dome? The hairs on the back of his neck prickled. Another notification pinged.

DragOnMa1den2038 requests permission to sync systems.

Hell, no. Not without a background check first. He tapped on the red "x" and closed the interface. That had to be a ghost. A freak-of-nature Wi-Fi glitch.

"Cranium, phone Mackenzie Ferguson." A static noise filled his head and turned to an outgoing ring tone. He pulled another drag on his joint as he stepped further away from the window. As casually as possible, he watched the dark air for moving shadows.

"What do you want old man?"

"Mack, it's me."

"Holy shit. How did you get John's Cranium? Is this a secure line?"

"No, not yet."

"Are you in the biodome?"

"Yeah. Hey, I don't have much time." Fillion jogged to the window and checked the scene. Same as before. Then he moved away again and whispered, "How's Lyn?"

"She's awake, but she refuses to talk about the assault."

Fillion closed his eyes to rein in his anger. "Is she … in pain?"

"They got her hyped up on narcs."

"Good. I can't safely use an interface. Are her images—"

"Yeah." Mack paused and Fillion swallowed nervously. "I told her. I thought she was going to lose consciousness again so I told her you loved her in case … you know…"

"Thanks, mate. I owe you one."

"Oh god, don't get sappy on me. Shit." Fillion knew this was Mack's deflection and tensed. "So, are the girls hot?" Mack asked, with a forcibly lighter tone.

"Covered head to toe. It's sexy like a nunnery. You'd *nosebleed*." This time Mack laughed, and Fillion smiled at the sound. "Hell, even your pathetic attempts at hooking up might actually work here."

Mack laughed again and then let out a string of swear words in Japanese. When he finished, he sighed dramatically. "You're an ass."

"Get over yourself. Think of all the action you'll get while I'm imprisoned."

"It's all I think of. Trust me."

"At least I know where I stack up in your world." Fillion paused and then asked, "Hey, do me a favor?" He debriefed Mack on the mysterious request from *DragOnMa1den2038*. "I need a full background check. Before I left, I uploaded to our cloud the access files to the Green Moron commune."

"Roger, roger. What's up?"

"Probably a lefty's catcher mitt."

Mack chuckled. "*Laughing Man* ghosting your contraband device?"

"Exactly." Fillion smiled. "His eyes are everywhere."

In a hurried, muffled voice, Mack whispered, "Your mom just walked in."

"Call you tonight."

Fillion didn't want to talk to his mom. And he certainly didn't want her to know he had a Cranium. He pulled the forbidden technology off his head when he felt it vibrate. "Shit." He wrapped his fingers around the Cranium with a tight fist. Then he put the device back on against his skull. The incoming ring tone paused to announce "Dr. Della Jayne Nichols," and he cringed.

In a quick swipe to his ear, he disconnected the line. "Cranium, block incoming calls, messages, and emails from Dr. Della Jayne Nichols and Hanley Nichols." When the computer confirmed the request, he pulled the device off his head and tucked it inside his sack.

It was a miracle the Cranium still powered up. He was sure Hanley would have cut him off by now, or John would have reported the loss. Weird. Fillion's fingers shook and he closed his eyes. Emotions needed to take a back seat before he deflated into an even sorrier excuse for a human being. At least his mom would take charge with Lynden, to save face if nothing else.

Before cinching up his bag, he pulled out another oregano joint and used the butt of the nearly finished one in his hand to light up. The hemp paper crinkled and trailed smoke as Fillion drew on the rolled up garden herbs, then he flicked the first joint's ashes.

By afternoon his hands had twitched for something to defend their existence. Especially when stuck in Jeff's office. Out of habit, Fillion continually reached up to turn on a Cranium that wasn't there. Then, he would reach up to tuck his hair behind his ear only to remember it was chopped off. His hand had flopped to his side and his body had sunk lower in the chair each time.

He twitched and muttered "shit" more times than he could count. He swore The Elements and their eldest children thought he was afflicted with Tourette's or something.

He was such a baby and conjured images of himself curled up in a fetal position on the floor as a slow panic began to rise. But he squelched it, determined to live without becoming a tech-wimp. He had skills. He was street smart. And he was intelligent enough to force mind over matter. Maybe.

Leaf had watched him struggle and finally excused himself from Jeff's office—during another ridiculously long meeting—and returned with a tinder box from the Herbalist. When no one was looking, Fillion blew Leaf a kiss and winked. The young noble seemed to hold back a laugh and avoided eye contact. The memory elicited a small smile as Fillion exhaled into the night sky. He watched the smoke vaporize into nothing as if it never existed. If only he could do the same.

The Elements and community scrutinized his every move. All. Day. This was his first blessed moment of solitude. Just beyond these glass walls, he was viewed alternately as a freak, a hated icon, and a sexually desirable idol worthy of worship. The Net buzzed with his image, plastered throughout the dark recesses of even the most obscure social media sites. He wanted to vomit with each conversational thread that tossed around the term "misbehaving Eco-Prince." The media's title for him circulated through the masses with orgasmic frenzy, each climax at the expense of his soul. What did they care? He was just a character on the Net to arouse and entertain the *otaku*'s ravenous appetite for human flesh.

Lynden was now the fresh catch of the day featured at the ether's feast of sacrificed souls. Between the two of them, the Nichols name was no doubt uttered as a contented sigh from the Net community as it belched and moaned in appreciation.

So, inside the dome, it was easy for him to ignore the first and second gen's rudeness. It was nothing compared to his other life. If the Green Morons here were trying to intimidate him, it wouldn't work.

When he had emerged from the Cave and introduced himself as Corlan Jayne, however, every hair on the back of his neck stood on end. Brianna's eyes widened and she took in a sharp breath. Of course she recognized his handle. He and Brianna were clearly related. There was no doubting the resemblance they shared—both with the same near black, mahogany hair and gray-blue eyes, as well as other Jayne family traits. Not only did she know the name, but so did Connor—big surprise—as well as Norah and Timothy, all reacting in their various ways. At a loss for words, Brianna had delicately cleared her throat.

He had lowered his head and watched Willow from the corner of his eye. She ignored everyone and everything. Save the strand of hair she furiously twisted onto her fingers and the grass she burned holes into. Damn. The anguished expression on her face had made his heart sink. He already knew she'd hate him. Fillion was just buying time.

And, god. The endless, petty droning of The Elements. Fillion thought they would grow roots with feet planted in that meadow for all of eternity. Hell was not a lake of fire. It was an enclosed glade filled with the sound of LARPers in a political debate and pretend peasants who looked on wide-eyed. Staying put felt like agreeing to eternal damnation. Especially when the Epic Meeting in the Meadow dragged on and on and on.

A chair scraped the wood floor nearby. Fillion snapped out of his thoughts and investigated the source through the opened window. Inside the Great Hall, the nobles had settled at the head table. He was assigned Coal's place next to Willow, who had been going to great strides to ignore him. Hence his smoke break outdoors to ease her suffering—although not before lifting a jug of wine from a table near the exit.

All Fillion wanted to do was chain-smoke the evening away. And think. And get drunk. And … he turned his head and peeped back inside at Willow. She stared at his empty chair, eyes puffy and face pale. Was she thinking of him? Or

Coal? He knew the answer to that and closed his eyes as he thunked his head against the stone wall. "I'm so lame."

Unable to help himself, he looked her way again and bit the inside of his cheek. The wine sloshed in the jug as it bumped against his leg; and he lifted it to his mouth and savored a long drink.

Laughter reached his ears once more, but this time he turned away from the window. This damn feast was in his honor. He loathed with every nanoparticle of his being the role of center-of-attention. The community was weary of him, making an already stressful situation worse. Leaf's plot twist with Coal didn't help either. Hanley was such an idiot for a genius. His dad's biodome lab rats couldn't handle one stranger. What the hell were they going to do when they faced an entire world of strangers from strange lands and with strange cultures?

His limbs still tingled with unreleased anxiety and fury. He needed to find something for them to do before he exploded. Fillion took another swig of wine followed by a drag on his hippie organic herbal joint. It wasn't the same as a cigarette, but he wouldn't complain about the lack of tobacco. At least he had something to smoke, or he might have lit up New Eden Township. He smirked with that thought, and then let out smoke rings, gently blowing at them to reshape their momentary existence. And, man, was he thankful for alcohol.

"Corlan?"

Fillion turned his head toward Leaf, who appeared in the shadows a few feet away. "Yeah?"

"You are needed."

"Peachy. How do I get to entertain the community this time?" Fillion rolled his eyes. "My heart flutters in anticipation."

Soft, padded footsteps cut through the still night as Leaf approached. Fillion directed his focus onto the blackened limbs in The Orchard and hoped Leaf got the message.

"Quite the opposite, I assure you."

Nope. Alone time was over.

"Save your reassurance," Fillion mumbled and then took another drag on his joint.

"I did not regard you as a man who wallowed in pity."

"You regard me, Leaf? I'm flattered." Fillion chuckled, and then bit his bottom lip flirtatiously. He received a wry smile in reply. "I'm not wallowing in pity. I'm escaping. Two different things."

"Unless you are escaping to wallow in pity privately?"

"All right smart-ass, what's my mission? How can I serve the glorious community?"

"The *glorious* community wishes to serve you."

"Fine. Take me to your leader." Fillion flicked the nub of his joint and rubbed it out, casting Leaf a sly, humored look. With a hand over his heart, he said, "Rest in peace hippie organic herbal joint. You were good to me."

Leaf stared at him curiously and then shook his head. To stall even more, Fillion offered Leaf the wine jug with raised eyebrows. He didn't expect Leaf to accept, let alone drink straight from the medieval bottle. But Leaf took the offer with a smile and then surprised Fillion further with a long swig.

"Easy, mate. You're increasing your attraction factor by the second."

Leaf let out a loud laugh, nearly spewing the wine from his mouth. "You have strange criteria for the elements of attraction."

"God, you're telling me." Fillion smirked when Leaf responded with a droll look. They began to walk and Fillion pushed Leaf in jest, satisfied when Leaf lost his balance. Unable to resist, Fillion grabbed Leaf's arm to steady him and felt his bicep. "I do declare, Leaf Watson, you're quite the man." Fillion wagged his eyebrows suggestively.

"Alas, I cannot return the compliment, Corlan Jayne," Leaf replied with a shy grin as they approached the entrance to the Great Hall. "Stop acting like a simpering woman."

"Heart-breaker."

The smells of dinner met them as they entered. Cheeses, wine. And roasted goat, prompting Fillion to reflexively work his jaw in disgust at the memory of the stringy, gamey meat. Latticed windows twinkled in random patterns from the tiny flames that danced throughout the Hall. The candles flickered in free-standing candelabras and hung suspended overhead in large wrought iron chandeliers. Despite his many annoyances, Fillion conceded that the image before him was magical. Especially when he looked *her* way.

Willow shifted in a high-back wooden chair and watched through lowered eyes as they approached the head table. A strand of golden hair, made richer by candlelight, wove in and out of her fingers. Fillion's heart rate kicked up. He swore under his breath at what a sap he'd become, resisting the urge to roll his eyes at himself.

Leaf slowed his steps in front of Connor. "We are ready, My Lord."

The cryptic message kept Fillion's pulse pounding. What the hell was going on? The community began to quiet as Connor raised a hand in the air and stood.

"Esteemed residents of New Eden, it is indeed an honor and a privilege to host our first guest within these walls." Connor offered Fillion a kind smile, but sadness wrinkled Connor's forehead and the skin around his eyes. "Corlan Jayne visits us from Seattle, in Washington state. He has left his community behind to join our family. Let us bestow upon him our heartiest welcome and ensure he is not treated as a stranger, but as a long-lost part of our community come home."

The majority of residents drummed their hands on the tables and murmured approval to each other, although it sounded hollow to Fillion's ears. He wanted to dissipate like the smoke he had exhaled to the night as his eyes traveled over the unfamiliar faces. A few unhappy and skeptical faces in the crowd, directing dark stares at Connor, drew his eye. He liked these people. At least they were honest. And having a hell of a time, like him, by the looks of things.

"It has come to my attention," Connor continued in a loud, but eloquent tone, "that many have brought gifts for Corlan."

"What?" Fillion swiveled toward Leaf and whispered, "I can't take their gifts." Both Connor and Leaf turned his direction with tight smiles.

Leaf leaned toward him and whispered back. "You would not wish to offend those who extend hospitality, would you?"

Fillion shook his head and looked at the dirt floor. This was ridiculous and unnecessary.

"Come form a receiving line over yonder to personally welcome Corlan," Connor said. He placed a hand on Fillion's shoulder and directed him toward a small stage.

Residents from the nobility and village moved through the room, armed with objects of various sizes. "The village" was a term the community used to signify those not belonging to a noble house, he had learned. Which was confusing because the village was also a location. But the word "peasant" would apparently be demeaning, so whatever.

Fillion stood in front of the stage. His eyes scanned the room and each face in the line. This was torture. Another circle of punishment inside hell.

A girl came forward first. Maybe his age? Maybe older? He couldn't tell. Her hands shook as she extended a small wreath made from small dark green leaves and bowed. "For you, sir, on behalf of our family," she said, a slight tremor in her voice as she spoke. Her hazel eyes reminded him of Lynden and another weight pressed against his chest. "May I place the Crown of Honor upon your head?"

Fillion swallowed. Crown of honor? "Sure. What's your name?"

"Anna, sir, of the Paylin household." She gestured toward her family, who smiled and bobbed their heads.

Leaf leaned toward him. "If a person is the source of celebration, it is customary for the eldest unwed daughter in the chosen home to present a Crown of Honor."

Fillion gave what he hoped was a polite smile and then lowered his head. He felt like a dork but complied to keep his behavior in check. God, it was hard. The girl placed the wreath on his head, her hands trembling but gentle. He whispered, "Thanks, Anna," and met her timid gaze.

She smiled with downcast eyes as her cheeks warmed. It was a look of—what? Fillion stared, perplexed. All the girls in New Eden exhibited a shy response to attention that mystified him. It wasn't flirtatious but sincere, an aspect of femininity he didn't understand. Modesty, he realized.

A man came forward next, ushering a woman and three small children toward Fillion. The older man bowed and extended a folded cloth. "Welcome home, Corlan of Seattle. We are the Kinneck family." Fillion nearly choked on the word "home," and he coughed to cover up his response. "My dear wife sewed a tunic for you today. She is happy to tailor to your size if too large."

"Oh." Fillion accepted the neatly folded garment and brushed a curious finger over the fabric. "Thanks, Kinneck family."

With subtlety, Fillion looked over the family's clothing and blinked back the shock. The Jones family gave him their best? They should have sewn new garments for themselves. Or at least for their children. Their clothing was frayed, dirty with stains, and thin from constant use. Resources were limited, something he knew before coming into the dome. *Have you ever grown clothes from seed?* Fillion thought of Leaf's earlier words before embarrassment shut down all reasoning.

Families and individuals continued to come forward with introductions and gifts. The offerings confused him as he struggled to comprehend why they would give up precious commodities and items for *him*. He had never known want, never received a homespun gift. Each item was a testament to their labor, to their survival, to their interdependency. Leaf leaned toward him from time to time, explaining the tradition and custom of a gift or why so-and-so gave it over so-and-so. Information swarmed Fillion's already buzzing head.

A pile on the stage grew and displayed garments made from linen, hemp, and wool; a dark, nearly black, woolen cloak with a large hood; wrought iron candle holders and hand-dipped candles; a pillow stuffed with wheat hulls. An older man and woman offered a wool comforter stuffed with feathers, a luxury item he guessed by the stares of wonder and delight—but no jealousy. People were genuinely happy for him to receive this item. He also received soap; a personal grooming kit with a steel razor; a small knife with a carved bone handle that attached to his belt; a leather pouch, also to attach to his belt; linens for bedding; a wooden chair; a mattress cover they referred to as ticking, stuffed with straw; and hemp rope for his bed, which made him quirk an eyebrow. What was the rope for?

The receiving line finally ended, and he never wanted a cigarette so badly in his life. As if this day wasn't hard enough. To him, humility parroted shame. It was as if he was supposed to feel guilty for his modern, affluent life. He didn't choose to be born. He didn't choose any of this. Now he understood how the homeless must feel—ashamed of their dependency, but moved by a stranger's care for their needs.

"New Eden Township, you have welcomed our son, Corlan, in a way that leaves me speechless," Connor said, holding in emotion as he finished. "I am proud to belong to you."

Son? Fillion snapped back to reality and he clamped down on the urge to explode. It was all a lie. A game. He examined the gifts and his stomach clenched as his mind attempted to make sense of what just happened. The gifts and gestures were real. The people were real. This room was real. But Connor's show? A cold shiver traveled down his body.

The Fire Element turned to him and continued in warm tones. "You shall reside in the open apartment next to The Forge. After the feast, the matriarchs will see to your comfort this evening."

Despite his anger, Fillion resisted the urge to snicker. Mack would make a bad joke right about now. Leaf and

Connor looked at him expectantly and Fillion realized he was the closer. "Shit," he breathed. He looked over the community, absorbing their hopeful faces. These were his employees. Everyone in this room belonged to his inheritance. His eyes scanned the crowd for Willow, but couldn't find her.

Fillion shifted on his feet and raised his shoulders higher, forcing a light tone as he said, "Thank you. I'm humbled by your gifts. It's a memory I'll tuck away and never forget."

The community stood in unison and lowered to one knee as they bowed, even the children. Except a small pocket of individuals near a back corner. They stood and glared at him. A sardonic smile pulled on Fillion's lips as he tipped his head in reply. With casual movements to appear natural, he looked toward Leaf to see if the noble noticed. But the new Earth Element was also on a knee with lowered head. Fillion wanted to die this instant. God, he couldn't escape fast enough. Then, he wanted to laugh. The mock-aliens bowed before their new leader. It was too rich. And terrifying.

One by one, people rose and returned to their seats, plates of food, and conversations. When it appeared OK to disappear, Fillion turned to Leaf. "I'm going for a walk." Not waiting for a reply, he went straight to the head table, grabbed his leather travel bag, and marched toward the exit.

The cold air hit his flushed skin in a rush and his body began to tremble. Lanterns lined the path and Fillion pulled out a joint, opened up a lantern and, with shaking hands, lit up. He took a long draw on the joint and closed his eyes. The predictable habit brought a small measure of comfort. Laughter seeped through the large wooden door, and he opened his eyes.

What were his escape options? Beyond The Orchard was the forest, a perfect place to hide until it was time for the matriarchs to see to his comfort. Shaking fingers steadied the joint in his mouth and he enjoyed another drag.

In long, quick strides, head down, he walked through The Orchard and entered the forest. Everything was drowned in darkness except for the orange glow of his joint, exactly how he liked it. His mom would say he was afflicted with nyctophilia. But it was a matter of the soul not the mind. The black air didn't possess expectations or judge those who walked in its presence. It absorbed everything and reflected nothing.

He flicked the ashes and stopped to snuff them out. With a sigh, he began walking again when he slammed into something. No—someone.

"Oh shit!" Fillion dropped to a crouch as the collapsed form came to a sitting position. The silhouette took shape as his eyes adjusted. He leaned in closer to get a better look and his eyes widened.

"Willow—"

"What are you—"

They stopped and stared at each other in silence for several seconds, each tick as mentally audible as the heavy rhythm beating in his ears.

He whispered, "I'm so sorry. I didn't see you." He rolled his eyes at himself. Obviously he didn't see her. Fillion moved to sit next to her on the leaf-littered ground. "Are you OK? Did I hurt you?"

"No, sir. I fare well. Thank you. I am astonished by your sudden presence, nothing more."

"I'm an idiot."

"You can hardly blame the night's lack of light on your intelligence."

"Nice." God, she was a brat and he laughed. This was the first time she had spoken to him since this morning. Alone, together, his senses marinated in the lyrical sound of her voice and his pulse responded. Again.

"I see the gift ceremony finished. I had left mine behind and went back to fetch it before my brother noticed my absence." She placed a small jar in his hands. "This is a comfrey compound and should soothe your injuries. Place a small dab on each wound tonight before you sleep."

"Thanks." He brushed his thumb over the clay jar. "Here, let me help you up."

Fillion stood and extended his hand. She wrapped her fingers around his and he pulled until she stood before him, inches away. They locked eyes in the limited light and Willow tightened her hold around his hand. He blinked back sudden shyness and tried to steady his breathing. What the hell was wrong with him? No girl had ever rendered him completely useless. Willow released his hand with slow grace, her fingers trailing his until they no longer touched. The absence made his hand cold, but the rest of him filled with pleasurable warmth.

"You are shaking," she whispered. He bit the inside of his cheek and remained quiet. He couldn't think, let alone speak. "We have both suffered a most grievous day," she said.

"Yeah." Not the most inspired reply, but the only one he could manage.

"I shall not delay your escape a moment longer, sir."

Willow curtsied with a sad smile and then ran off. He watched over his shoulder until she vanished into the black air. And then he breathed again. Would she always haunt what remained of his sanity?

He resumed his walk and looked for a lighter, groaning when he remembered they didn't exist in the Middle Ages. "I hate this day," he muttered. "And I'm still talking out loud like a homeless person." He was seriously mental.

Being played by his dad killed him. Being enclosed killed him. Not being there for Lynden killed him. Living a lie killed him. Being out of his element killed him. The gifts from the community killed him. Connor's false humility killed him. Willow touching him and then running away ... instant death.

Emotions came to a raging boil and he kicked a rock his shoe discovered. "OK dad, I officially died!" he shouted to the trees. "I'm dead! Do you hear me? I'm dead! Congratulations!" The last word trailed off in a hoarse whisper as he slumped to the ground and leaned against a tree. Angry tears burned his face. His fingers found a small rock and he threw it as hard as he could.

Fillion buried his face into his knees until the tears gave up. Like him. The breeze rustled the leaves, a soothing sound that eventually lulled him to sleep. His head, drugged by exhaustion, rolled to the side and then snapped up. What had jabbed his head and shoulder? Fillion whipped his head from side to side and studied the darkness. How long had he been in the forest? And what the hell was poking his head? He lifted his fingers to explore and groaned when feeling the Crown of Honor, thunking the back of his head against the trunk of the tree, earning him another poke. He loosed an angry breath. Damn, it was cold. The night's chill blanketed him and his teeth chattered, pissing him off once again.

With slow movements, he grabbed the jar, stood, and brushed off his pants before hoisting the travel bag over his shoulder. Fillion looked around the forest until he oriented himself in the direction of the Great Hall and began a death march back to the community. He had an appointment to keep with the matriarchs.

ELEMENTS

What game doesn't have rules? Is it even possible to imagine chess if there were no rules to the game? ... All games are this way, in various degrees, and larping is no different.

Rules are the invisible barriers of a larp. They hem the game world in while keeping everything else out. They are the catalyst of collaboration toward the goal of group pretending. Rules give a framework to everyone so that pretending in the same space is viable...

[The] integrity of group pretending is based solely on what everyone assents to. When a group agrees on what is possible via rules, options become available in the pretend space where there were none. If there are no rules there is no balance.

— Dave Funk, "LARP Definition," *LARPing.org*, 2013 *

ChAPTER FIVE

Sunday, October 4, 2054

An ethereal blue light bathed Fillion's skin as he lay in bed with one arm tucked behind his head. With his other hand he swiped, dragged, and tapped at holographic screens until his arm cramped with fatigue. Mind over matter, he kept telling himself. He successfully hacked into the device and went to work. His arm and hand moved on autopilot as his mind continued to process all of the events of the night.

The rest of the feast had passed in a slow and torturous blur, like everything else Fillion had encountered in New Eden. The Elements were pissed, but they plastered on plastic smiles for the crowd. Willow had sat next to him and stared at the table, pushing food around on her plate. The emotions visibly evaporated off of her body in a hot steam.

Understandable. They both had died inside this day and could do nothing about it except fester.

She only acknowledged his presence when he poured her a glass of wine. His near drunken state found courage to whisper in her ear, "Drink up and drink fast." Yeah, he was a goddamn poet. Her eyes lifted from the table and shifted toward his. Their faces were millimeters apart and he stilled, taking in her image. The low-lit room amplified her beauty, and his eyes had trailed over her face, resting on her mouth a few seconds, before meeting her curious gaze.

Self-control was never harder. But he slowly inched away and returned his focus onto his half-eaten plate of food. From the corner of his eye, he watched as she gracefully reached for her goblet and sipped the wine as quickly as possible and still remain lady-like. When she placed the cup back onto the table, he filled it up again without a glance her direction.

Eventually, Skylar stood and announced he was "retiring." So, Fillion used the buddy exit strategy and did the same. He thanked The Elements for a nice evening, wanting to gag on each word. Connor volunteered that the apartment was to the left of The Forge, and then Fillion staggered out of the Great Hall.

It was weird having a place of his own. He didn't know what to expect when the matriarchs assigned to ensure his comfort arrived, either. He soon realized they were assigned because they had the longest time in the outside world and, therefore, had experience "hosting" guests. Whatever that meant in New Eden. Several times he bit the inside of his cheek to keep from rolling his eyes.

The apartment was sparse. But they introduced every piece of furniture in case he was blind and didn't notice the *only* chair in the living room. Or the bed—no, cot—filling up most of the bedroom—no, bedchamber. And he figured out what the ropes were for. Disturbed, he fetched the ropes from the living room at the head matriarch's request, unsure of where this was heading. He snickered quietly to himself when he strung the bed frame to hold the mattress—no, ticking filled with straw.

They excused themselves not too long afterwards and he was once again left alone with his dangerous thoughts and emotions. Apathy began to numb some of the anger and pain, but it was always short-lived. He needed to stay focused. The Cranium was vulnerable now that he had wiped out the security key. But that's as far as he could get. His eyes burned from strain and exhaustion and refused to stay open.

The contacts screen popped up with a tap, and he scrolled down until he found Mack's info. The line opened up and he closed his eyes as the outgoing tone hummed in his head.

"Dreaming about me? I think you miss me terribly, *bishounen*," Mack said. Fillion opened his eyes to his friend's mischievous smile and random spikes of blue, green, and white hair.

"Nah. I have a new lover. He's way cuter than you, too."

"Damn."

"I'm not done using you, though."

"That's all right. My lack of self-esteem makes me user-friendly."

Fillion rolled his eyes. "You're pathetic." Mack flipped him off, followed by a long string of swear words, and Fillion replied with a tiny, humored smile. "OK, not so pathetic. I need your brain right now. Mine is at maximum capacity."

"Sure thing, mate."

"I need to lock my door."

"You want me to mail you the key or do it for you remotely?"

"Remotely. I'm about to shut down and go into sleep mode."

"You're such a machine," Mack said with a wink and flirtatious grin.

Fillion smirked and ran a hand through his hair. Sometimes he wished he was a machine. He would factory reset and reprogram his life.

"OK. I'm in." Mack flashed Fillion a wry grin. "Here it goes." His friend's face relaxed in concentration as he began to swipe commands. Fillion opened up the minimized screen as a layer and watched as the new secure key downloaded in rapid fire. "Shit," Mack sighed when the download stopped. "Forgot a bit of protection." There was a brief pause, then the download started up again. Fillion struggled to remain focused as sleep tempted him with darkness and nothingness. Several minutes later the minimized screen refreshed to a new user interface. "Was it as good for you as it was for me?"

"You need to work on your rhythm," Fillion said. Both stared at each other with straight faces and then broke into laughter.

"You're an ass."

"Keep saying that. Maybe one day it'll be true."

His friend grinned. "Get a hint."

"Ignorance is bliss and way more fun."

"What happened to your eye?"

Fillion yawned. "Brawl with my dad."

"Seriously? Shit. Who won?"

"He had police backup." He strained to focus. "How's Lyn?"

"Relieved and pissed to see your mom." Mack looked away.

"At least she's aware enough to have emotions."

Mack's face grew serious, a look his friend rarely exhibited. "She'll start medical treatments and rehab tomorrow. I'll be there all day. I'm in the parking lot right now." Fillion nodded and swallowed back the rising emotions. "They found the guy. DNA matches with the skin under her fingernails. The biometric stats led them right to an apartment near the waterfront. Your mom officially pressed assault charges. The police found my DNA on him, too, but let it go when I explained the situation."

"Damn. What a mess." Fillion tensed as a slew of emotions barreled through him. "I'm glad Lyn doesn't have to worry that he'll find her and finish the job."

"Yeah, I thought the same thing." Mack studied him a half-second. "He didn't know who she really was. I think he shit his pants when he found out."

"Like it matters," Fillion ground out, then yawned. "Sick bastard."

Mack pinched his eyebrows together again. "Hey, I looked up your ghost and couldn't find a record anywhere on the network you mentioned. I'll keep hunting, though."

Fillion nodded, then slurred, "I don't mean to use you and leave you, but I'm falling asleep."

"Just like a man."

A sleepy smile pulled on his lips. "Yep. Catch you later. Thanks, mate."

Fillion stowed his Cranium and fell back onto his pillow. The wheat hulls clicked and rustled in his ears and his eyes popped open as he groaned. The pillow would take some getting used to. But not this night. Sleep claimed him within a nanosecond.

"Fillion," a male voice whispered. Warm air pulsed near his ear, followed by a firm shake. "Fillion."

"*Koroshiteyaru mae ni hotto ite!*"

"You need to wake up," the man said again. "This morn is the Last Ceremony. It is time to rise and prepare for the processional."

Fillion squinted and lifted his head. "What?" With a groan he fell back onto the pillow and sighed when the sound of wheat hulls rushed in his ears. "*Hanarete ikanakereba, umarete kita toki o koukai suru zo!*" He had been dreaming in Japanese. Reality was a bit soupy at the moment.

A pressure on his shoulder made his skin flinch. Then his body shook again. Irritation took over and he grabbed his pillow and swung at the person leaning over him, hitting whoever three times in a row. The man in silhouette chuckled and Fillion turned toward the sound. Sleep's haze slowly came into focus until he recognized Leaf, framed in a soft yellow light. Curious, he looked over his shoulder and squinted at a lit lantern on his nightstand. The feather-filled quilt was heavenly in the unreasonably cold air, though; so Fillion pulled it over his head and buried his face into his arms. Sleep's oblivion returned by next breath. But like a stubborn bastard, the Son of Earth grabbed him by the feet and dragged him out of bed. Fillion flopped onto the wood floor to the sound of Leaf's laughter. The sharp cold made Fillion's body curl into a ball and his skin shiver into goosebumps.

Leaf was going to suffer, he decided. Fillion's sleep-deprived nerves didn't appreciate Leaf's cheeriness. That last thought made him inwardly snicker. The Son of Earth had spent the night having far more fun than Fillion had. Not a stubborn bastard—a lucky bastard. Encryption algorithms were the only company Fillion enjoyed during the night hours. Well, and Mack.

He flashed a look of challenge, grabbed a nearby shoe, and chucked it at Leaf. The young noble jumped out of the way with a yelp and laughed when the shoe hit the wall. Ego amped up, Fillion marched over and shoved Leaf hard, followed by a back sweep behind Leaf's legs. Leaf landed with a solid thud, and satisfaction spread like wildfire through Fillion. Leaf groaned and stretched out his arms in surrender.

Fillion turned to walk back toward the bed to retrieve his tunic. Leaf said, "Pride cometh before a fall," grabbed Fillion's ankle again and yanked. Fillion crashed next to him on the ground and broke the fall with his hands. Pain seared his knuckles and he hissed as he sucked in a breath. Now he was pissed.

"Feeling frisky still?" Fillion asked with a wicked grin. In smooth movements, he rolled over and jumped on top of Leaf and pinned him down. He whispered in the sexiest voice he could muster. "You have such beautiful eyes, Leaf." He inched toward Leaf's face like he was going to kiss him.

Leaf began speaking rapidly in French, pushed him off, and came to a quick stand, staring at Fillion in horror.

"Oh god," Fillion began, "your face—" But he stopped when he couldn't talk through the laughter. After a minute, he sighed. "Damn that was good." Laughter rolled out of him again when Leaf placed his hands on hips and glared.

Gaining control of himself, Fillion stood and stretched, running a hand through his short hair. So the medieval hippie didn't appreciate this kind of humor. Surprise, surprise. Leaf's eyes wandered over Fillion's tattoos in the dim candlelight. The noble said nothing, though the questions were written on his face. Sometimes the self-control Leaf exhibited was admirable—like yesterday—and sometimes it was annoying—like now.

"Stop checking me out." Fillion pulled the tunic over his head with a faint smirk. "You're making me blush." He wrapped the leather belt around his waist and his fingers ached as he knotted it off in the front. The silence grew awkward and uncomfortable, so Fillion filled it with more talk. "Your belt is badass. Did you make it?" OK, that was lame. His lack of small-talk skills was his eternal shame.

"It was my father's."

Their eyes met, and Fillion drew his eyebrows together. Not only was he socially awkward, but an insensitive ass, too. "Sorry." It was all he could manage.

"He died seven days ago today."

The lump in Fillion's chest liquefied and rolled in nauseating circles inside his stomach. Every insult of being the son of a killer stabbed his conscience, but he pushed aside the familiar fears. Leaf needed details to protect his family and to help find answers. And now was a perfect moment. It didn't matter if Leaf liked him or not. That was never the point. Nor was it even a reasonable expectation.

Fillion cleared his dry throat. "The Death Card belongs to my dad."

"Pardon?" Leaf's sturdy demeanor deflated and he stared wide-eyed. "Hanley wished for my father's death?"

Everything inside of Fillion wanted to say his dad killed Joel Watson. But a small, nibbling voice said it wasn't true.

71

The more he thought over the situation, the more convinced he became that Joel's death and the death certs issued for the Watson siblings were two unrelated events but with the same goal in mind.

"The clues point strongly in that direction, but I can't map it right in my mind. The information just doesn't add up." Fillion looked away. "There's more."

He continued to describe in detail the trial to Leaf, who sunk onto the bed, rested his elbows on his knees, and hid his head in his hands as he listened. In hushed tones, Fillion also explained that Leaf was removed, by name, from the Legacy as he was presumed dead. And Fillion's attempt to corner Hanley into legally reinstating Leaf by name had failed. He elaborated on the Dungeon Master and why he played the role to protect them from others at New Eden Enterprises and, by extension, the media. After a short pause, he revealed the origins of the Death Card and Hanley's implication that it was used by one of The Elements. Fillion also admitted the crime he had committed, the trial, the conviction, and his dad's bright idea for an exchange so Fillion's sudden presence looked natural. Followed by an explanation of how Hanley wanted Fillion to use his hacker handle, Corlan Jayne—also the name of his great-grandfather—to hide Fillion's real identity from the community.

He wasn't sure how much Leaf absorbed. There were no physical cues. It was if Leaf had gone into hibernation mode. Nevertheless, Fillion continued and shared about Joel and Della's conversation through Messenger Pigeon. Fillion stumbled over words every so often as he disclosed each moment on the recording. The sound of his mom's voice asking Joel to kiss his children for her echoed in his mind, and his stomach formed painful knots.

The confessional purge ended. About the only thing Fillion didn't share was the inheritance he would get on his twentieth birthday. That and the personal details of how he was persecuted during The Watson Trial, and the nervous breakdown that followed. Leaf maintained the head-in-hands position. Seconds turned to minutes and the silence stretched to an unbearable tension.

Unable to take it, Fillion voiced, "You have every reason to hate me and my family. I came into the dome knowing it would happen. Now or later, makes no difference."

Leaf raised his head and whispered, "I do not hate you."

Fillion sat beside Leaf and closed his eyes, blocking out the pained expression on Leaf's face. There was nothing to say. The honesty won brownie points at the moment. But eventually thoughts would fester into resentment, and resentment would putrefy into contempt. The pattern was predictable and constant. Anything his dad touched died in some way. Physical, intellectual, or emotional—it made no difference.

"Thank you," Leaf whispered.

Fillion whipped his head in Leaf's direction. "I hate things that are fake, including me. Don't placate me out of some sick and twisted idea of honor. Or because you know who I am." Fillion pushed off his bed and leaned against the wall, tucked his thumbs into his belt, and raised his shoulders.

"You are rather sure of my feelings," Leaf said.

Instead of replying, Fillion shoved off of the wall and searched for his shoes. The injustice was overwhelming, and all Leaf could do was thank him and show consideration for his feelings? What the hell? The man before him had lost nearly everything and was about to lose his home and way of life in a few years too. And all because narcissistic needs meant more to Hanley than the humans who empowered him. God, he wanted to punch a wall or kick something.

Leaf, on the other hand, stared at the lantern with perfect stillness. It was an image of control and meditation that forced Fillion to stop his agitated movements and thoughts. The dark circles under Leaf's eyes became more pronounced as light from the small flame flitted across his face.

Why wasn't Leaf angry? Fillion would be pissed if the roles were reversed. Hell, Fillion was pissed now. He wanted Leaf to yell at him, to throw the first punch, to blame him for all the pain—not to try to reassure him. There was no hope, and Fate didn't care about fairness or justice. But he would go down fighting, and he hoped Leaf would too. He needed to smoke. Stat.

The tinder box sat on his nightstand next to Leaf's lantern. Fillion grabbed three joints and placed all but one in the leather pouch that hung from his belt. These were the last of them. He'd need to figure out where the Herbalist was to get more. Fillion lit up a joint and took a long drag while using Leaf's flame to light his own lantern. A warm glow filled his room and he watched the shadows flicker on the wall as he exhaled.

They walked in silence through The Orchard toward the forest in the dark morning air. Time ticked away in blurry seconds as Fillion puffed on his joint. He could sleep while walking, he was so damn tired. He was about to ask Leaf how to tell time in New Eden, when the medieval hippie stopped mid-stride and faced Fillion with narrowed eyes.

"I wish to disrupt the game further."

Fillion looked around the forest and then whispered, "Peachy. I'll help you."

"In doing so you shall dishonor and deceive your family."

"Don't worry about my family. I can't dishonor something that's not honorable. My dad doesn't really give a shit about me, just what I'll do for him. Plus, my sudden presence here already disrupts the game, right?"

"I am most sorry for your pain," Leaf said as he bowed respectfully.

"How can you say that? This isn't about me."

"Yes, My Lord, it is."

"Now you're freaking me out." Fillion took a step back and morphed into an aloof posture. He took a drag on his joint and blew the smoke away from Leaf. "Are you mental?"

"You are Hanley's son and have sacrificed much for my family." Leaf stared at him with intensity, opened his mouth and then shut it and looked away. After a few seconds, he cleared his throat and continued. "You possess a higher nobility status than I and hold more authority than any individual within New Eden. Are you not a prince?"

Fillion whispered harshly, "Are you not a king?"

"No, My Lord." A sad smile appeared on Leaf's face. "Not anymore."

"Says who? Hanley was certainly willing to let you believe it, so why not? The hell with him."

"And what happens, pray tell, if he appoints another Aether in my stead?"

"With what Scroll? How would a newly appointed Aether communicate with him? His hands are tied until Project Phase Two. Until then, let's raise Cain."

"You make an excellent point, My Lord."

"Oh god, stop it." The anger finally burst and Fillion pinned Leaf with a hard stare. "Yeah, I'm a prince. A corporate prince. My dad's the Green Movement monarch of eco-business and holds several nations in the palm of his hand. It's disgusting. They depend on him for their papayas in the tundra—and for the bank accounts big enough to let them rot in the fridge. The world has a love-hate relationship with Hanley and, as a result, a love-hate relationship with me." He walked up to Leaf and grit his teeth. "I'll inherit that kingdom on my twentieth birthday. All of this—" he waved his arms "—will be mine."

Leaf's eyes widened. "I see."

"No, you don't. I won't get to keep my position a secret. The entire world will sit around and judge me every day. And this community—the very one that gave me the best of what they had and knelt before me last night—will know that I'm an impostor who played them. Do you get it? I'm just like my dad. So forgive me if I'm not gracious toward your 'acts of kindness' or your effort to honor me. I'm trash. Your sister was right and nailed it from the very beginning. I'll help you, but don't turn this into something it's not. You'll hate me one day. Trust me."

Hurt burned in Leaf's eyes as he regarded Fillion in si-lence—as usual—for an infuriating amount of time before finally speaking. "Willow is drawn to you. She declared early yesterday morn that she shared a connection with you that defied understanding or propriety."

"What?" Fillion felt the air leave him as vulnerability re-placed offense with lightning speed. Just her name amplified every unworthy feeling inside of him. "Why are you telling me this?"

"She argued that you were wounded inside and was ra-ther insistent that you were more than you appeared. When she bestowed upon you her heart, I hated you. That was the only time I have ever felt contempt toward another. You toyed with her affection while she grieved and, still, she chose to lay down her reputation to honor you."

"She wept." Leaf took a step closer and his voice became more impassioned as his anger finally surfaced. "When the portal blackened, she wept for you and feared she would nev-er see you again. She genuinely feared for your life. Do you know how many tears she has known this week? I tried to speak reason to her, but she would not listen. Rather, she de-fended your right to feel loved and to know you were im-portant. Never did I believe we would ever see the Dungeon Master again, and so I ceased to argue."

Warmth flushed through Fillion's body and his heart pounded in response. She saw through his games? She saw *him*? He couldn't look at Leaf and lowered his head.

"I am happy to be wrong," Leaf said.

"And just like that I'm OK?" Fillion rolled his eyes. "Se-riously?" He took a step closer and pushed Leaf's shoulder with his hand. "You think I'm decent because I told you eve-rything, but I'm not."

"Yesterday, My Lord, you shared that your feelings for her were real."

Fillion whispered, "They are."

"You do not wish to convince me that you are worthy of the heart you were given?"

"I'm not worthy."

He looked up and met Leaf's eyes as he brushed past and tramped down the path with quick steps. He had no idea where they were heading originally, and at this moment, he didn't really care either. An image flashed in his mind of Willow gifting her heart, and the unfamiliar feeling of acceptance seduced him for a brief moment. God, what was he thinking?

She'll never be yours.

"You did not let me finish," Leaf called after him. Fillion halted his steps and raised a single eyebrow, easing into an arrogant, detached posture. "I wish for you to share everything with Willow," Leaf said. "She deserves to know the truth and choose her own path of happiness."

"A path of happiness?" Fillion let out a humorless chuckle. "God, you really are mental."

"You do her a discredit."

"Hell no."

"Fillion, she deserves to know about *everything*."

"Tell her yourself. But not about me."

"I thought you hated things that were fake?"

"This coming from the guy who said it was best if Willow didn't know the man she gave her heart to just walked into the biodome. Good one. I should listen to you more often."

"My apologies, you are right."

"What? No hand to shake?"

Fillion walked away a short distance and kicked the dirt path. He drew on his joint and focused on his mission. It was safer. The hell with Leaf. Thoughts computed one after another. The word "revolution" continued to play on repeat in his mind. He didn't want to introduce technology to the second gen. The scientists, who would short-term colonize the dome, could do that. So, what was he missing?

His dad's words—that a Gamemaster ponders the hidden, not the obvious—floated around in his brain's stratosphere in a looped cycle. Technology was obvious. What was hidden? The word "hidden" kick-started an idea and he slowly turned his head toward Leaf with a wicked grin.

"You want to disrupt the game? Go public."

"Now who has lost his wits?" Leaf looked over his shoulder and around the darkened forest, then whispered with urgency. "To disclose the position of Aether is a high offense, one punishable by banishment per The Code."

Fillion's smile got wider. "Then let's change the rules."

"How, My Lord? Do you propose we commission a new legal document?"

"Possibly. I'm a hacker. Breaking and rewriting code is what I do." Fillion blew out a thin stream of smoke. "New Code or not, let's reprogram the community."

"I am not familiar with the term 'hacker,' but I generally understand what you suggest. How do we legally break The Code?"

"Give me a sec."

Fillion looked around the forest as he brainstormed the path of least resistance, his first step before each hack. Any rules that could be broken and difficult to report? Hidden rules and back doors, Fillion thought to himself as ideas raced by his mind's filter. What was hidden? What wasn't being said but assumed? Like trading worlds before Project Phase Two. The Elements knew something was wrong, but the community didn't. The person he exchanged places with had to be over the age of sixteen, but not over the age of twenty. Weird. Why was that?

He turned to Leaf. "Does the second gen ever sign The Code? Say, when they turn sixteen?"

Leaf's eyes narrowed. "No, My Lord. We do not."

"Sounds like you are not legally bound to the original Code. It states only those who sign and minors in their care, right?"

"Indeed." Leaf rubbed his chin and stared past Fillion for a few seconds. "And how shall we commission a new document to become drafted and approved?"

"We probably don't need one if I'm legally correct, right?" Fillion looked around the forest and leaned closer. "So, my friend is going to use my funds to finance a large collaborative hack. Basically, a group of people are getting paid to dig up any and all dirt on my dad. When they're done, I'll use the requirement of a new Code, or whatever it is you want, as leverage to not publicize details."

"I see. And what were your plans for such 'dirt' prior to this conversation?"

Fillion smiled with Leaf's astuteness, then dragged on his joint. He exhaled and resumed a sleepy trudge toward wherever Leaf was leading him and left the question dangling in the morning chill. Leaf didn't need to know Fillion was going to use leverage to get Leaf reinstated in the Legacy as before. It was the least Fillion could do to make things right. But maybe Willow's brother didn't want that anymore. He'd let Leaf call the shots.

They resumed silence once more, both lost to their confetti of thoughts. A mysterious breeze blew in gentle wisps through the trees every so often. Fillion lifted his eyes as he drew on the last bit of his joint and watched branches sway. This world seemed so real even though it was a mere simulation, a paradox his mind struggled to fathom.

Footsteps echoed from behind and both Leaf and Fillion looked over their shoulders as a cloaked figure approached and halted in front of Leaf. As she flipped a large hood away from her face, all the air rushed out of Fillion. He swore under his breath. God, he felt so corny and lame. His mind immediately traveled back to last night. Apparently Willow's mind did too. She acknowledged him with a quick nod before narrowing her eyes at her brother once again.

"You were to escort Laurel and me to our home, were you not? I shared last night that such a request was completely unnecessary. However, Laurel is most insistent now." She pursed her lips together. "As I am a grown woman, Connor allowed me to leave and fetch you, not wishing to intrude on his daughter's … privacy." Willow raised her hands to her cheeks and averted her eyes.

Fillion hid a smile by lifting the last of his joint and inhaling. He didn't realize Willow and Laurel were staying at the Hansens. But it made sense. Leaf and Ember probably wanted privacy while they honeymooned.

"I am most sorry," Leaf said as he lowered his head and offered his hand. "I am rather distracted this morning."

Willow turned her head to the side and lifted her chin. "Dare I ask what has distracted you that you would remember the Outsider and not your sisters?" Leaf let out a heavy sigh and covered his face with his hands. Willow's eyes widened before nervously darting Fillion's direction. She whispered, "Please do not trouble yourself, My Lord. I do not have the heart for secrets this morning."

Leaf's whole body seemed to relax with her words. "Come, let us fetch Laurel," he said, offering an arm to Willow. Before leaving, Leaf shot a look at Fillion over his shoulder with a slight amused grin. "Do not sneak back into your apartment and crawl into bed. I shall not be as kind should I need to drag you from your covers once more."

"Pity," Fillion said while stifling a yawn and chuckling.

Willow whipped her head around and narrowed her eyes at him. Fillion didn't know what he had said or done to earn her acute attention. Nevertheless, she appraised him as a complex look of fear and anger crossed her features.

"How is it, sir, that you know Master Fillion?"

"How is it, *My Lady*, that *you* know Master Fillion?"

"It is complicated," she said and narrowed her eyes further.

Fillion lifted a single shoulder in a faint shrug. "Same here."

"Are you intentionally evading the question?"

"No more than you."

She flashed a mischievous look his direction. "I do not fall to the whim of Outsider boyish fancies."

Fillion grinned, thinking of last night, and said, "Except when you're walking in a dark forest at night." Checkmate.

He casually took a drag on the nub of his joint and exhaled slowly, but couldn't hide the amusement. The look on her face was priceless. Leaf, however, squinted his eyes as he looked between Fillion and his sister. With an exaggerated harrumph, she faced the trail and Leaf took the cue to start back toward The Forge.

The rhythm of Fillion's steps became hypnotic as he attempted to pull inward and ruminate over plans. But his thoughts kept wandering back to Willow. She was beautiful to distraction and so damn cute when mad. Her long, wavy hair glinted gold in the flickering lantern-light, a white ribbon woven into a braid draping along her face. Remembering the feel of her hair slipping through his hands yesterday, he wanted to bury his face in the silky strands now.

As if sensing his thoughts, Willow casually peered over her shoulder and sought his attention from down the path. And all he could do was stare, like an idiot. She was drawn to him? Wept for him? God, what was he thinking? Leaf may be kind and forgiving, but she would hate him with a fiery passion. That thought should terrify him, but strangely, it made him want to smile. Everything inside of him wanted to piss her off and then kiss her fury. It would be like kissing the surface of the sun.

He bit the inside of his cheek again, wincing with the pain, and looked away. He needed to stay focused. Mind over matter. Yeah, right. Fillion raised his shoulders and lowered his head. She was on to him. And what seemed like a turn-on a few seconds earlier fed his greatest fear.

The soul is a breath of living spirit, that with excellent sensitivity, permeates the entire body to give it life. Just so, the breath of the air makes the earth fruitful. Thus the air is the soul of the earth, moistening it, greening it.

— Hildegard of Bingen, 12th century A.D. *

CHAPTER SIX

Cold air awakened Oaklee's mind, and her breath formed clouds as her family quietly led the way to The Rows. The early morning twilight held a stillness, nature's collective breath held in anticipation of the sun's rise. The dark lavender sky with tinges of gold on the dome horizon regally welcomed the residents of New Eden, a fitting gesture as they walked beneath the reflective canopy with lanterns in hand and hoods raised in mourning.

Resentment continued to brew inside of her with each step. Leaf's disregard for her and Laurel this morning did not help. Were the ceremonies of death part of this psychological game the Township played? Was the expectation to marry young part of this game as well? She was not entertained by Coal's sacrifice to prove his love for her. This was real. This was her life. Confusion clouded her thoughts, and so she fastened her mind to Leaf's reassurance that the first generation no longer played a game but embodied true convictions.

This evening, the Township would feast upon edibles from the Ceremonial Garden, a communion to amalgamate each life together, dead and living. Death was honored within the tightly knit community. Each resident labored for the survival of all, ensuring the success of the project and, if actually on Mars, the continuation of life itself. Leaf was right, and she decided to push aside Outsider words as the enormity of this day dawned in her heart with the rising sun.

Oaklee relished that the community tended to more than its physical survival. Their souls were connected, each breathing in the same atmosphere, air created by the essence of their very existence. The breath of one became the breath of another. When a newborn released its first cry or a resident exhaled their last to the Township, it altered the environment.

Overcome with such thoughts while walking to The Rows, Oaklee inhaled deeply to saturate her body with the new make-up of the biodome's atmosphere. Corlan was now a part of the air she breathed, and she studied the puffs of frozen vapor that left his mouth as he walked behind Leaf. He met her curious stare. Shadows danced across his face in the flickering lantern glow. His features held an adorably sleepy expression, and he blinked in a slow manner as a near indiscernible grin tugged at his mouth.

Their chance meeting in the forest the previous eve had rattled her nerves. She absently touched the fingers that had grazed his as she recalled his words from the feast. Her stomach fluttered with the memory of his warm breath on her neck, laced with wine, as he whispered in her ear to drink up and drink fast. Especially when she turned and her face nearly touched his. His voice, eyes, and smile were far too reminiscent of another to be a true stranger. Or so she thought.

Corlan had studied her when he did not think she noticed, moments that increased as he drank more wine. She feigned ignorance and secretly studied him in return while resisting the unsettled feeling of being haunted.

But their meeting this morning reawakened every question she had previously pushed aside as nonsensical notions born of grief. Convoluted feelings of betrayal and elation warred within her as she entertained that perhaps Corlan and Master Fillion were indeed one and the same. If they were not one and the same, they were most definitely twins. She had not taken leave of her senses. And his refusal to disclose his association to Master Fillion only confirmed this conclusion.

When he spoke, the soft and dejected tones, edged in mild ridicule, made her want to close her eyes and allow the fluid sounds to wash over her like a gentle, mournful breeze. His blue eyes were otherworldly and possessed an intelligence and intensity Oaklee found beautiful. In truth, he was beautiful for a man, from his features to the emotions that shrouded him like a funeral cloth; and despite such observations, it only heightened his masculinity. His presence carried an authority and a diffident yet aristocratic grace unlike the Nobility of New Eden, but most certainly of a Noble bearing from his world. These were rather strange and forward thoughts, she realized, and Oaklee lowered her head to hide the blush that heated her skin.

Nevertheless, the draw both she and Corlan experienced toward each other—the same one she shared with Master Fillion—was undeniable, and she felt so faithless. She did not possess romantic notions! Her heart's response to his presence displeased her to no end. Why could she not have such feelings for Coal? Life would be so much simpler if only the Son of Fire stirred such reactions from her by simply walking into a room or suddenly materializing in the woods. But he did not.

Leaf cast an inquisitive look her direction. Oaklee ignored him, keeping her vision as well as her footsteps moving toward the garden, wishing to answer only her own curiosities this day.

She felt ready for this ritual, ready to purge her soul as she ceremonially performed an act of sacrifice so life could continue. *In order to live, something must die.* The black hands of death had ripped away pieces of her heart all week as it continued to beat within her chest. Tradition held that she and Leaf would figuratively die this day by denying their bodies comfort, sustenance, and companionship as they rested in the soil with their loved ones. *Death makes way for the resurrection of new life.* When they rose from the ashes eight hours later, they would begin anew, altered forever by the metamorphosis that would transpire during their time of death and rebirth. Rebirth would first come with a Celebration of Life; then, a day later, by resuming their toil in assigned tasks.

Oaklee finally understood what it meant to continue living in the midst of grief. She still yearned for the comforting predictability of the previous life she had known. Even though she now realized how foolish those desires were in the end. Death may have taken pieces of her heart, but life would mend the tears with living memories by using the legacy of her father as the threads to stitch the stolen pieces back together. It was time to transcend, to reach beyond, grasping with determined strength to live.

Upon arriving at the Ceremonial Garden, Leaf extended a hand as she sank to the living soil, then knelt beside her at a respectable distance. Oaklee placed a lantern before her on the ground and focused on the small flame as it danced upon the wick. The Code required family members over the age of thirteen to participate in the Last Ceremony. Although Ember was technically a family member now, she was excused in order to care for Laurel. The little girl now clung to Ember, her big eyes taking in the scene before them.

Norah approached with the aid of her husband. With a shaky hand, she poured a small pool of oil into her palm from an alabaster vial. "May your family be blessed and your heart find hope as you journey through sorrow today."

Brother Markus prayed over Oaklee's kneeling form and she closed her eyes as Norah traced a heart upon her forehead with the oil—the symbol of life and death in New Eden. The gentle touch brought tears to Oaklee's eyes as she cherished the motherly hand upon her head.

Norah likely would be the next loved one taken from their community. The Water Element's fingers were bones, gaunt remains of a once-strong woman as the cancer living off of her body viciously claimed her life. Oaklee was thankful Norah was yet alive to initiate this Last Ceremony for her father. She could not imagine Connor or Timothy executing the rite of passage with the same tender ministrations. Norah dipped her finger into the oil and also placed a heart upon Leaf's forehead as Brother Markus prayed over her brother.

"A new day is dawning, Watson family," Norah soothed as she chanted the conventional words. "Remember your father and the life he gave you. Remember the love and the richness of honor and integrity he cultivated in each of your hearts. Bury his death once more and then resurrect your mind and your heart to a new life. The old ways have passed away and became the foundation for the new road you shall walk, leading toward hope and a future marked with a deeper understanding of love and community."

Long, auburn hair fell across her shoulder as Norah leaned over and kissed the top of Oaklee's head, bending deeply in order to reach her ear. "Be strong and courageous, My Lady," she whispered for her alone. "You are a mighty oak and your roots are going deeper as you stretch and grow in unimaginable ways. Do not allow your father's death and Coal's absence rob you of your wild, bold, and beautiful spirit."

The words of encouragement and comfort washed over Oaklee and she wept. Norah caressed her cheek and wiped away the tears with motherly affection before moving over to Leaf, also kissing his head and leaning forward to speak into his ear. From her bowed posture, Oaklee watched as Leaf met Norah's eyes, brimming with restrained emotion, and nodded quickly. She touched his chest just above his heart and Leaf lowered his head until his hood covered his features. His shoulders gently shook.

With the blessing complete, Norah took her husband's arm with marked weakness; he scooped her up and carried her down the footpath. Family groups passed by and bowed before Oaklee and her brother with solemn, reverent movements before departing for the village. A breeze had enchanted the air and the cloaks swished and flapped in a macabre dance as leaves rained through the sky. Flickering lantern light caught the leaves here and there as they fell, illuminating skeletal stems.

When The Rows held only Oaklee's family, The Daughter of Fire approached with Laurel. Leaf stared, riveted, and Oaklee flushed as her brother continued to regard his new wife with an open expression of love and desire. Ember rested her hand along his cheek with a sweet smile of adoration before she leaned down and bestowed a chaste kiss. Leaf, however, held her face and pulled her back toward him and ardently returned her kiss.

Their little sister giggled and Oaklee turned several deeper shades of pink at her brother and sister-in-law's immodest display. Ember giggled as well, whispered into Leaf's ear, and slowly departed with one last coy glance over her shoulder.

The Outsider winked at her brother with a sly, amused grin. It was a rather inappropriate response, but her brother did not appeared offended. Then Corlan studied her and his features softened. Strands of her hair wavered across her face beneath the hood, and Oaklee lowered her head in modesty as a bio-breeze rushed through the garden and pressed her cloak against her body. She simply could not process the possibility of the Dungeon Master in her garden, looking at her with such longing.

The sound of Corlan's retreating footsteps marked the official start of her and Leaf's social seclusion, and her heart grew heavy in the growing silence. The dark greens bent and swayed in the gray light, and her cloak fluttered in the invisible air that stirred her heart. Drop by drop, her tears watered the ashes of her parents as she scooped a handful of the rich tilth, feeling the grains slip through her fingers. What else would she lose?

"Leaf?" she asked quietly. He turned her direction with raised eyebrows. "I know it breaks tradition to speak with another, but I have questions and we are finally alone." He gave a permissive nod. She whispered, "Why not ask The Elements about the card? Or bring our worries before the community? Surely there are many who would aid our cause and rally for justice."

Leaf paused with a wary expression as he considered her questions. "We are not dealing with a rational mind," he eventually said in response. "To show such a card to the community may incite panic and unrest, which may be exactly what the card holder desires. Why else place such a card in father's pocket to be displayed publicly? So long as we remain the only family targeted, I shall not frighten our neighbors."

"Do you believe father was murdered?"

He let out a heavy sigh. "That is certainly the impression we are meant to receive. But I am not sure and, therefore, I am reluctant to assign such judgment."

Oaklee traced her finger through the dirt. "The response of The Elements yesterday was quite confusing."

"Indeed." Leaf watched her closely as a small smile touched his face. "I do believe my return unsettled them— one of them, especially—a rather insightful exercise, I confess."

"You surprise me, My Lord." Oaklee boldly met his eyes. "Is Corlan fully aware of our situation?"

"Yes, he knows."

"And does he know who you are?"

Leaf scanned the gardens with panic, then whispered, "Yes, he knew upon arrival."

"Is he also aware of a forming faction?" Oaklee was growing irritated and threw in this bit of knowledge without sharing its source.

Leaf flinched and lowered his head into his hands, and Oaklee stiffened. Once again, her brother struggled to formulate words to a secret he held close. Resentment toward her brother quickly began to build a raging storm inside of her.

Skylar had spoken truth. Trust was paramount inside the bio-dome, indeed.

"Oaklee, I am most sorry you did not hear about this situation from me. It was not intentional, I assure you." Leaf looked around the garden a moment, gradually meeting her inquisitive stare. "Yes, Corlan is aware of the possible faction."

"And how is it, *My Lord*, that you found time to share with the Outsider and not your own sister?"

"Skylar mentioned the possibility of a faction to me Friday eve prior to my request to hold the Earth Element position. As you know, the last day has held more emotions and life-altering activities than a single day should." Leaf's face fell into an imploring look, beseeching her to believe him. "Corlan and I spoke while you rested yesterday afternoon and further discussed the situation this morning."

"Is he Master Fillion?" The question left her mouth before she could control her impulses. Leaf's eyes widened for the briefest of moments before returning to a contemplative look, as if he deeply considered her question. "'Tis a simple inquiry, Leaf. You are a terrible liar." Angry tears formed and escaped despite all efforts to remain in control. "How could you? I trusted you and in the process made a complete fool of myself. How shall I ever face him again?"

Her brother appeared genuinely pained and he blinked several times before releasing an anguished sigh. "Willow—"

"*Oaklee.*"

"Oaklee, I have known since you fainted in the Cave. I asked him to keep his identity hidden from you. Do not be cross with him. I am to blame for this deception."

"Does Master Fillion now do your bidding? My, how the roles have reversed." Oaklee scoffed and glared at her brother. "The deception began far before he entered our town. You are both to blame."

"True, although to use your own words from our time at the portal, Master Fillion is more than he appears," Leaf said, his mouth set in a troubled line. "I was wrong to keep from you his identity, but Willow, I was scared. Since father died, I have spent every moment of my new life ensuring your and Laurel's safety, which has proved an exhausting feat this week."

He paused and looked down at the ground momentarily and blinked his eyes again. "You gave your heart to Fillion as a token of your affection. I did not know his character, and what he had demonstrated thus far through the portal did not recommend him as an honorable man. His intentions were rather clear and ungentlemanly. Please believe me when I say that my decision was not to patronize you, but as an act of brotherly protection."

She played with the edge of her cloak as she pondered her brother's words. A strong bio-breeze rushed through the meadow, and the gardens and trees bowed before its invisible power as the leaves sang lyrics of fealty, loyal subjects to the wind. Her heart pulsed with the music as her spirit accepted that she, too, was subject to the winds of change. She desperately wished for predictability. But secrets continued to unearth and chain their cold, unfeeling fingers around her ankles, anchoring her to a shifting future she could not control.

This thought pulled up an image of Corlan—no, Fillion—as he stood in the sunlight of the Outside. His ankles and wrists had been chained and his faced was bruised. He remained withdrawn and quiet as a dark grief shrouded his presence, a festering whirlwind of emotion that made Hurricane Willow a mere gust of wind in comparison. The oppression and deeply rooted fury even now was palpable. Every so often he would reply with a witty quip and offer a small smile or laugh, but she knew it was a mask. She wore a mask of a similar nature.

What horrors had Fillion faced? What horrors would Coal face? Would the Son of Fire return as a broken spirit devoid of life? Would the technology ghosts absorb Coal's goodness and spit out an angry soul? A sob caught in her throat as she thought of how her selfishness had reaped a rotten harvest. Thoughts pushed against her head until she thought she might burst from the pressure, one mystery rising above them all. Oaklee turned toward her brother and asked, "Who is he?"

"He is Fillion Nichols, eldest son of Hanley Nichols, a prince of his world and heir to New Eden Township."

She did not know what answer to expect, but this information was beyond shocking. Her mouth slackened as a multitude of thoughts and feelings—contrary to the previous ones—overwhelmed her all at once.

"I pledged my heart—"

"Yes," Leaf said.

"But he appeared—"

"I know. 'Tis how his generation fashions themselves. He was required to go through a transformation before entering our town."

"The son of Della and the daughter of Joel." She smiled to herself as her heart marinated in the epiphany. He was a prince, and she a princess. She did not possess romantic notions but the enigma of their circumstances filled her with a wondrous awe. And fury. He had played a dangerous game, manipulating and mocking her from the onset. Was their moment in the portal even real? Or in the Cave? Or was it all part of a role he played for his father's game? Voice tight, she asked, "Am I the reason for his presence?"

"No, and yes. The reasons are rather complicated and I shall allow him to explain—when he is ready. The story is his to share and I shall not dishonor him, and neither shall you." Leaf regarded her with a serious expression.

"Just days prior you said he was a man you would never welcome as my husband, chastising me for my unladylike deportment. And now you defend him?" Oaklee shook her head. "I am all astonishment. Has Master Fillion wooed you with his power and prestige, now that you know who he really is?" She lifted her chin and spat, "You have wounded me! How shall I trust anything you say or do?"

She could see the wheels turning inside her brother's mind as he weighed and measured every piece of information.

He moved so that he faced her, reached out, and took her hands. She flinched with his touch, but allowed it when seeing the remorse in his eyes.

"I told Coal I would never force you to marry, despite the community's expectations and traditions. Yesterday, I did not know he would kiss you and pledge himself to you. I am most sorry and have struggled with guilt over his actions, especially as you had refused him already."

She opened her mouth to speak but he held up a hand.

"Connor spoke correctly yesterday, and I stand behind his words of wisdom. Father would wish for you to marry for your reasons alone. Do not feel pressured by Coal—and do not feel beholden to Fillion." Leaf bowed his head. "You have shown me that you know your own heart, and I trust you."

Her mouth slackened and her eyes rounded. Disarmed, she blinked back her confusion and righteous indignation. "I do not blame you for Coal's or my behavior," Oaklee said softly. "I have no desire to marry. As for Fillion, I was given an opportunity to show compassion to a man I truly believed was going to war and would die, and I could not bear such thoughts. Oh, how that man infuriates me! How dare he toy with my heart in such a way," she ground out. After a measured breath, she began again in a much calmer tone. "Fillion feared my rejection. Does he not have another to comfort him? Why did he seek *my* approval?"

Leaf shifted his eyes and Willow felt the hurricane winds gain strength inside of her once more. Her brother could never hide anything.

"You know, do you not?"

Her brother remained silent for several heartbeats before he asked in whisper, "Do you love him?"

"Have you lost your senses, Leaf?"

He smiled. "No, my wits are quite secure. Yours, however, should be questioned." She pursed her lips and narrowed her eyes and he quietly laughed. "Do you recall your words to me? You spoke with sighs of a connection that could not be explained."

"Spoke with sighs?" Her eyes widened at the mere thought and she lowered her head. Had she spoken with sighs? Perhaps a little, she internally relented, and she placed her hands on her cheeks with mortification.

"Yes, you were lost to me at one moment."

"I shall admit that I find him intriguing and enjoyed our battle of words." (And his smile nearly unraveled every offense she felt toward him, she continued in her mind.) "But I am not in love with him. How could I? I do not know him, and what little I do know vexes me. Love is formed from mutual respect and companionship, of which we have neither."

"And what if he claims the heart you have gifted him?" Leaf raised his eyebrows.

Oaklee watched the greens sway in the breeze. She did not know how to answer Leaf. Although she did not wish to marry, she could not deny the part of her that came alive when in his presence.

"I have enjoyed one night with my wife." Leaf's complexion turned various shades of red and he looked at the ground, gently touching the dark green leaf of a spinach plant as he cleared his throat. "I would never wish for you to share so much of yourself with a man not worthy of your heart. You say you do not wish to marry, and I can understand why, but I see the way you steal glances at Fillion and how he admires you. Even, dear sister, when you believed he was Corlan." Leaf lifted his head and sought her eyes. "You are practical and logical, albeit tempestuous in your delivery. This riddle has plagued me. I must relent. Perhaps there is an attraction that goes beyond superficial elements as you say, for it is not in your nature to behave this way."

Tears gathered in her eyes. "Leaf…"

"I am sorry that a woman could not have this sensitive conversation with you." Leaf frowned. "Despite what you may believe, I do love you exceedingly. You are my family,

Willow Oak. I would do anything to protect you and ensure your happiness."

"I do not deserve you, Leaf Watson."

Oaklee flung her arms around Leaf's neck and nearly knocked him over. She held onto him and buried her face into his shoulder. They continued to cling to each other until Oaklee's eyes grew heavy with fatigue. As she drew away to move back to her position, Leaf kissed her forehead with a kind smile, and she giggled.

Adams: I understand that The Elements are players from the Eco-Crafting Eden series that aired for a couple of years. Rumors and behind-the-scenes gossip hinted that one of these players was responsible for the faction that nearly brought down the game. Is this true?

Nichols: Do I believe one of them intelligent enough to pull off such a show-stopping stunt? Absolutely. You have to admit, the faction was a brilliant move by whoever internally sabotaged our game world. Terraloch nearly lost everything. It was our collective strategy and solidarity that overcame the possible game-ending faction, though. So, all this to say, I do not believe one of The Elements was responsible in that game. The Elements and I have known each other since our early teens and formed an alliance and a camaraderie that intentionally bleeds into game life.

— Jennifer Adams and Hanley Nichols, _Atoms to Adams Daily Show,_ August 15, 2030

CHAPTER SEVEN

The air was comfortably warm beneath the shade of a large and impressive olive tree. Coal sat upon the packed earth and surveyed the Outside world for the first time. Reddish soil covered his hands as he absently broke apart dry clumps with his fingertips, his mind all the while processing the sights, sounds, and smells of planet Earth. Until yesterday, he was not entirely convinced they were on Earth.

How would he have known?

The Elements had shared that, by law, they were required to ensure everyone knew they were on Earth although they lived as if they were an actual colony on Mars. But Coal did not have context for such a law, nor was he given opportunity to verify such knowledge.

He stretched out his legs and contemplated the sky, squinting against the afternoon light. The expanse was endless and reflected a rich shade of blue his eyes had never beheld. Small wispy clouds lightly smudged the uppermost reaches of the sky and Coal furrowed his brows.

Were not clouds larger and, according to his education, the bearers of rain?

How could such minuscule wisps enable the atmosphere to weep and water the land?

His body ached to move, so he rose and headed toward the garden. Since his arrival, every moment was spent in a stationary state. It was a bizarre reality to live in a world where most jobs were performed from a chair. His trade was physically laborious and his body spent a good portion of the day in motion. Those around him seemed soft and scrawny. Coal knew his size was larger than most, same as his father, but beyond the walls of his home he seemed a giant.

Plants brushed against his fingers and legs as he traversed the small trails. Most of the edible vegetation was familiar. Chickens roamed the shrubs and verdant patches and scratched the dirt in search of insects. A bee buzzed by his ear and he turned his head and watched it land in a pea bonnet and then pay a visit to another nearby. So many sights were familiar, and yet they were not foreign.

Sunlight touched his skin and he paused with the sudden heat. Coal lifted his head to the sky, closed his eyes, and allowed the fiery star to bathe his face and arms in warmth.

"You need to get back into the shade," Michael hollered from a distance. Coal opened his eyes and sighed once more. He took two steps back and felt the temperature drop considerably. "I found an old umbrella." The scientist jogged up next to him out of breath and popped open an odd, black contraption. "This will keep you shaded. Remember, your skin is not used to such intense UV lighting."

"Thank you," Coal said as he accepted the shading device. He could not remember the word Michael had used. Although he understood the caution, all he heard was fear. Since he emerged, every reaction was one of fear. There was fear of spreading germs, fear of contracting viruses and bacteria, fear of media, fear over his ability to integrate with society, and now fear of the sun. It was rather tiresome, and Coal longed for quietude.

"Now that you have shade, you want to stick to the gardens?"

Coal glanced at the biodomes beyond the lab. "Are there restrictions as to where I may walk?"

Michael followed Coal's line of vision and his usual jovial disposition became thoughtful. "No. I'll be over at the lab door if you need anything." The scientist jogged to the shade, turned, and waved.

Coal's heart leapt as he stepped toward his home. The aquarium materialized in his mind's eye and he envisioned the community swimming blissfully in their unnatural environment. Now he was an Outsider. He had joined the people of myth and lore. In many ways he felt like a newborn babe who longed to be swaddled upon entering such vastness after a confined existence. Coal wished to place his head upon the biodome panes and feel the heartbeat of his life-giver, to touch his mother home once more. And like a babe, he had to find contentment from external comfort while longing for the internal.

His eyes beheld the domes one last time before focusing on the ground as he walked. The shadows of this world were different than New Eden, and telling time took more concentration than before. Inside the lab there were no natural shadows. Rather, they were fabricated from overhead lighting. The people checked a Cranium—a most peculiar technology—for time, information, needs, and communication. It was as if the human soul and brain were sucked from the body and placed within the small, silver device. Michael assured him that before he arrived in Seattle, Coal would know how to use a Cranium. It was mind-boggling and Coal grasped for the familiar in response.

His eyes focused on his lithe silhouette, which stretched in a long length and walked in tandem with his form. After a few footsteps, he concluded it was nearing five in the afternoon time.

Today was the Last Ceremony, and he thought of Oaklee and Leaf kneeling in the soil of the Ceremonial Garden. At this hour, the community was returning to their homes for the afternoon rest prior to the Celebration of Life. Coal was grateful Oaklee had not knelt alone, an experience he knew would further break her fractured heart.

His shadow stretched up a wall of reflective glass and he followed the dark line up, squinting. His eyes trailed the height of the structure until the back of his head was nearly resting upon his shoulders. Tentatively, each finger caressed the surface and he breathed in deep as a weight crushed him. A sob formed in the back of his throat, and he dropped the shading device and pressed his entire body against the outer north wall of the main biodome as he wept. Until this moment he did not have words for his feelings, but his heart grieved. It was if he had died, eternally separated from those he loved, given one last opportunity to connect from the Outside before he must choose to walk forward into his afterlife.

Each memory of his loved ones caused his body to heave with grief until he felt his heart would collapse. He slid against the panes and sat in the thirsty soil and watched his tears evaporate within seconds. A gentle breeze embraced his form and he felt momentarily comforted by the invisible. It was time to separate from his prior existence and accept his new life. Today, new beginnings were celebrated in New Eden, and he would join them in spirit.

Reluctantly, Coal took a single step back from the reflective panes as he wiped the remaining tears from his face. With one last touch upon the mysteriously cool surface, he squared his shoulders, turned, and walked away. The future would be different. It may be lonely and sterile within a scientific community, but his past lived inside of him always. He would embrace this opportunity and, when ninety days passed, he hoped to return a better man than the one who left. Even though he feared he might never return. There was no previous experience to lend such reassurance.

The parched soil scraped against the sole of his shoe as he shuffled along the path. He had indeed left New Eden barefoot, and so they bought him a pair of shoes. Coal walked toward a large iron gate, wishing to see the world beyond New Eden Biospherics & Research. He left one set of walls only to be comforted within another set, granting him freedom without overwhelming his sense of space. A metal fence framed the landscape, decorated by even taller shrubs that flowered in a profuse display of reds, pinks, and whites, offset by dark, thin green leaves. The shrub buzzed and hummed in a strange rhythm as bees covered the flowers, seemingly drunk in a paradise of pollen.

His steps slowed before the gate. He gripped the shading device's handle in one hand, then reached with the other to grasp the hot metal of the gate. Although his skin stung with the heat, he did not let go, pulling himself forward to peer through the bars and study the endless shades of white, rust and gold before him. Land sprawled in every direction, a disorienting thought. And, to his utter disbelief, mountains! His heart pulsed with excitement as his eyes traveled over the curved land. In books, the word majestic was always paired with the geographical feature and he could not agree more. Each peak was part of nature's crown that rested upon Mother Earth's head, proudly boasting her nobility.

A rumble sounded to his right and he angled his head and blinked. Dust swirled the air down the dirt path and Coal stared in fascination. He probably should be frightened as he lacked an explanation for the rumble and the dust. The golden cloud moved along the wide path and a dark spot gleamed from the center. Startled by the strange sight, he walked backwards, clutching the shading device as a shiny enclosed cart rolled by, kicking small rocks up into the air. One struck him on the thigh and he jumped.

Transfixed on the Outsider cart, he nearly missed the circular object that flew toward him from beyond the gate. The instant his eyes locked onto the mysterious sight, his entire body paralyzed.

How did it fly?

As the question repeated in his mind, a transparent man appeared beneath the disc and asked in unnaturally smooth tones, "Hello, are you from inside the biodome?"

Coal's heart stopped. Then, his feet went into motion and he raced back toward the lab.

People did not appear from thin air. It was impossible. Perhaps he had indeed traveled to the afterlife and met his first ghost. Michael's eyes widened when Coal dropped to the ground, sweat dripping from his forehead as his body began to shake. Through chattering teeth he attempted to vocalize that he saw a ghost, but could not form the words. So instead, he pointed toward the gate. Michael jogged toward where Coal had indicated and halted his steps. Pivoting on his heel, the scientist ran back, encouraging Coal with urgent tones to get up and to get into the facility. Fear accelerated through Coal once more and he barreled through the door.

Once inside the temperate forest, Coal jumped into the creek and splashed water on his face. He needed to cool down and regain control of his senses. There had to be a logical explanation, but he was far too disturbed to form rational thoughts.

"Did it speak to you?" Michael asked as he knelt on the ground beside him.

"It?" Coal's eyes widened again and he blinked when water dripped into his eyes.

"That was a media drone."

Coal grabbed Michael's lab coat with his fist and yelled, "Those words mean nothing to me! Explain properly, please."

Michael paled and Coal let go with a heavy sigh and turned away. He felt a moment of shame for the aggression, but his body did not know if it should continue to run away or fight in self-protection.

"It is a machine that flies and projects a picture of a person," Michael said in a calm tone, "programmed to talk and interact with humans. It records you and then replays on a Cranium for everyone to see."

"Records me?" Coal considered his words and then splashed more water onto his face, deciding to just dunk his head into the creek instead. The cold water brought instant relief and his scalp pleasurably tingled. He pulled out of the water and shook his head, then wiped the dripping water from his eyes with his hand.

"It's hard to explain. Let me show you."

Michael activated his Cranium and Coal watched, pulse still pounding, as Michael moved the air with his finger. Coal could not see what Michael viewed, but Michael stared at the void with a serious face. While Coal waited, he pulled his hair out of the leather strap and brushed his fingers through the strands.

"OK, ready to see?"

The scientist's finger touched the air and suddenly Coal's image wavered in front of their vision, mimicking the motions Coal had just made while grooming his hair. Coal jumped, landed on his arse, and scooted back along the forest floor until his back bumped against a tree trunk. "Is that my spirit?"

"Oh my god, I am so sorry. No, Coal. No." Michael stepped toward Coal. "That was not your spirit. It was a recording. It's like a mirror that can be played back. Nothing more."

Coal's stomach spasmed and he turned on his hands and knees and vomited. His body continued to shake and his teeth chattered once more. The contents of his stomach purged again and his muscles convulsed.

"You're going into shock. Breathe deep, breath slow." Michael placed a hand on Coal's back.

"I wish to return to my room," Coal said through shallow, ragged breaths.

"First, let's get you regulated. You've experienced too much adrenaline, there is less oxygen in the air outside, and your body is shutting down."

"My room!"

Michael pulled his hand away. "OK. If you can stand and walk, then let's go."

The fear in Coal's bloodstream turned to a white-hot anger, and he wished for solitude before he did something rash. There was no wood to chop. No iron to pound. No stalls to muck. No soil he was allowed to till and plow. He could not *sit* and work. He could not *sit* and breathe to humor Michael. Instead, he wished to repeatedly punch something and scream until his body no longer needed the workout.

Every muscle tensed as he forced his body to maintain control. But the nausea rolled again and he leaned over to the side into the bushes with a hacking cough. Sweat beaded on his forehead as he flushed from head to toe. Michael opened his mouth to probably tell him to "sit" but Coal glared and the scientist shut his mouth and opened the door.

The motion of walking lowered his anxiety a smidgen. Coal fixed his eyes on the carpet—a word they used to describe a wall-to-wall rug—and refused to acknowledge passersby or those still working behind their desks. Despite the smiles and platitudes, all they wished for him to do was "sit" and accept that, as their human experiment, they could drug him, lie to him, and terrify him. He longed to return to the falsified life behind glass—at least it was a life he understood and did not fear.

"All right, here you go. Place your thumb on this black box. I programmed it remotely with your vitals while we were outside."

Coal glared at Michael and crossed his arms over his chest.

Michael frowned and placed his own thumb on the black box. The door clicked and Coal shoved into the room and slammed the solid wooden door in Michael's face. A bright and unnatural light instantly came on overhead and Coal squinted and shielded his eyes. He walked to the holographic switch and, with his thumb and index finger, pretended to grip the nob and rotate it until the lighting lowered to the level of candlelight. The holographic nob glowed with a strange blue light amongst the shadowed walls and he stared in agitation. There was no actual knob, yet its appearance was no relic from the spirit realm.

Was the recording similar to this hologram?

Fury fired through his veins and he approached his pillow and punched and punched and punched as a guttural growl emerged. He delivered blow after blow, gritting his teeth until his head pained from the tension. Still unsatisfied, he grabbed the pillow and used all his strength as he pulled at the center in different directions. A tearing sound ripped through the room and a strange fluffy substance burst into the air.

For a moment, he stilled and observed the pink and blue bits float in a mysterious current as if faeries. It was beautiful and he reached out a hand and watched the unknown substance land on his palm. As the tiny objects cycled downward, they stuck to Coal's clothes and coated his hair, and he dropped his hand. With a resigned sigh, he lowered onto the edge of his cot and slumped forward over his knees.

A click sounded and his head snapped up as the door creaked open. Hanley stood in the door frame and surveyed the room.

Did no one knock in the Outside world?

"Is this a good time?" Hanley asked with a humored smile. "May I come in?"

Coal gestured toward the chair in his room and clenched his jaw. Hanley walked through the room with care, brushed off the seat of the chair, and sat.

"Did the pillow spontaneously combust?"

"No, sir."

Another small smile appeared on Hanley's face, and Coal looked down at his hands. He should feel ashamed for destroying the property of another, but the heat still coursed through his body. Coal lightly kicked at some of the pillow substance on the floor as he anxiously waited for Hanley to share the reason for his visitation.

"Do you know how your father came to be known as The Fire Element?"

Coal shook his head and acquiesced to conversation as his body further slumped forward; he dug his elbows into his knees to support his head. He had his ideas on Hanley's question—namely his father's craft as a blacksmith—but never had a story attached to such notions. The Elements just *were*, in his mind, and as a Noble son, he just *was*. The past lacked context and, therefore, relevance. From the corner of his eye, he watched as Hanley leaned back comfortably and stared at the ceiling.

"When we were a little older than you, but not by much," he began, "Connor and I roomed together at a college named the Massachusetts Institute of Technology, or MIT for short. And boy did he have a temper. He would get so angry sometimes that he was known to punch holes into walls. Our dorm room was riddled with holes. Needless to say, the Dean was not pleased." Hanley smiled to himself and then continued. "Connor was built like you—tall, athletic, and muscular from all the welding he did for side jobs to pay for school. His welding employer tired of Connor's temper and told your father on the last day of our second year that he acted as if he had fire in his veins."

The room was an utter mess and Coal smirked. He was the Son of Fire, and the fire of his father flowed in his veins. The thought brought a modicum of happiness to his heart and he looked up and finally met Hanley's eyes.

"This theory, of course, could not go untested," Hanley said with humor. "The next day we returned home for the summer and promptly went out with some friends to a cabin in the woods that belonged to my wife's grandfather. Joel, Timothy, John, Jeff, Dylan, Connor, and I spent the afternoon drinking until Dylan had the bright idea that if Connor had fire in his veins, then naturally he should be able to breathe fire as well. Dylan *always* had radical ideas that *always* ended in an epic disaster. But the ideas *always* seemed ingenious at the time."

Coal was smiling now and Hanley began again without skipping a beat. "Your father, eager to prove he was a dragon, swished and swallowed a gulp of one hundred-and-twenty-proof moonshine and then blew out, holding up a flame to the fumes." Hanley started laughing and Coal's eyes widened in disbelief. "Except, he blew out toward a curtain which promptly caught on fire. Dylan started shouting 'I knew it! I knew it!' over and over again while Jeff, always hyper-nervous, rushed to the kitchen and grabbed a large pot and filled it with water. Joel was on the floor doubled over in laughter. John helped Jeff. Timothy shook his head and rolled his eyes. But your father... I have never seen a man look more proud than at that moment. He was a dragon."

Laughter rolled out of Coal. That was probably, by far, the best story he had heard in his life. He could picture every-thing, even the proud look upon his father's face.

"You have fire in your veins, Coal," Hanley said. He looked at Coal with nary a blink, and a slow smile crept along his face. "It needs a proper outlet or you'll burn down every-thing in your path."

Coal shifted upon his cot as the humor quickly faded. "I see," Coal said carefully. "And what would you have me do?"

"Tomorrow you'll start getting instructions on infor-mation technology, past and present, and within the week you'll know how to use a Cranium and even how to build a basic computer."

"Does this require long hours spent in a chair?"

Hanley laughed. "You are so much like your father." The owner stood up and walked toward the door. "After dinner I'll show you the welding shop and assign someone to in-struct you on how to use our modern blacksmithing tools." He turned in the doorway. "It's the same shop Connor used to help build New Eden Township."

"Thank you, sir."

"Oh, and one more thing," Hanley said as he rested the door against the frame. The owner's eyes swept over Coal from head to toe with another calculating gaze and Coal braced himself. A sad expression stole the older man's features and Hanley looked away. "When we arrive in Seattle, I'll need you to act as a guard for my daughter, Lynden. With her brother away, she needs someone to protect her."

"Is her life threatened?"

"A man assaulted her. She is in a hospital receiving medical attention. I am flying out tomorrow morning and will return Thursday evening. Can I trust you to apply yourself and not give Michael or any others on my team grief?"

His daughter was assaulted by a man?

What sort of man harms a woman?

Nausea rolled in Coal's stomach again. The very idea made his heart heavy and he felt humbled that, after his angry display, Hanley would trust him with his daughter. Perhaps this was why Hanley acted so strangely since yesterday. Not only had he temporarily lost a son, the distraction of being here when he would rather be at home comforting his daughter must be painful.

"Yes, sir. I shall do my best this week. And I am honored that you should trust me to protect your daughter. I shall treat her with the utmost respect." Coal stood and bowed.

"Thank you. As I said yesterday, I knew you were a man of honor, and most valiant, too."

Michael appeared in the hallway and looked into the room with big eyes. "Oh my."

"Did you know Coal is a dragon?" Hanley winked at Coal, and then disappeared down the hallway.

Coal's lips twitched as he worked hard to suppress a smile, especially when Michael stared at him with part incredulity and part confusion. Thoughts of Hanley's daughter surfaced and his anger renewed.

"Well, Mr. Nichols is in a good mood. Perhaps you should destroy pillows more often," Michael said, shaking his head. "I came to tell you dinner was ready. Goodness, you are covered in nanopolyfill. Hop in the shower and I'll wait for you in the hallway." Michael touched the Cranium against his head and began poking at the air with a concentrated look. His hand grabbed the air and then he looked up with a polite smile. "Rosa will be here soon to clean up."

"Whilst I bathe?" Coal's eyes rounded.

"Not anything she's never seen before. But don't worry. Rosa will stick to your bedroom while you use the, ahem, restroom." He laughed at his own joke and Coal smiled nervously in reply.

A woman in his chambers while he bathed?

"I shall see you shortly and not delay dinner a moment longer." Coal quietly shut his door and faced his room. He licked his dry lips and took in the mess, embarrassed that another was responsible for cleaning up after his choices. Nevertheless, he moved into the restroom and adjusted the light.

The shower turned on with a push of a button and he marveled at the ingenuity of modern plumbing for a moment before undressing and entering the luxurious stream of instantly warmed water, calibrated to a temperature he preferred. Toilets and showers were, by far, his favorite Outsider technologies. Several minutes later, he reluctantly turned off the water and stepped out onto a rug, wrapping a towel around his mid-section. The looking glass fogged, but no matter. He was used to grooming without the aid of a reflection.

As he ran a comb through his hair, he thought over the dragon story with swelling concern. There was something off-putting about Hanley Nichols, and yet his charismatic presence dulled any forming concerns. Coal could not help but become engrossed by his storytelling. Listening to his father's friend made him almost forget how he had been mistreated since his arrival.

Was the story to gain trust?

Or did Hanley honestly care about his wellbeing?

Coal puffed out his cheeks and slowly exhaled while he examined the small space, resolved to meditate upon happier thoughts. He turned toward where he left this garments and started when his tunic and breeches were nowhere to be found in the restroom.

Did Rosa enter while he showered and remove his garments?

Heat trickled through his body and he slowly faced the door, turning the knob as quietly as possible. The door inched open with a creak and he peeped through the crack. A woman with dark hair tied up and wearing an overly tight tunic and breeches on her slim figure held a bizarre machine that suctioned away small objects. He watched in surreal fascination as the substance from his pillow disappeared.

"Are you freshened?" the woman asked, moving her head his direction. The movements were fluid but contained an unnatural grace that triggered instant trepidation. Her glassy eyes fixated on his face and her mouth moved with precision as she asked, "Do you feel better?"

"Yes, thank you Madam." Coal lowered his head, his pulse hammering in his chest. "Where are my garments?"

"I am laundering them for you. May I bring you clean items?" She blinked, but it was strangely slow. "Your blood pressure is dangerously high. Do you feel lightheaded or dizzy?"

"How ... how do you know of such things with a mere glance?"

She responded with a throaty laugh. "I am programmed to read vitals, Coal Hansen. You are in the system. I put new clothing in the dresser for you. May I bring you clean pants and a shirt?"

Coal tip-toed out of the restroom and then jogged to his bedroom door, yanking it open to find Michael sitting in a chair across the hall. The scientist looked up with large eyes as his face settled into a baffled expression, studying Coal's semi-dressed state with raised brows.

"What's wrong?" Michael asked. All Coal could do was turn toward Rosa and gape, eliciting a friendly laugh from Michael. "That's a Rosa, short for Robotic Online Service

Assistant. She's a humanoid robot, a machine. Don't worry, she's perfectly harmless."

Coal's mouth suddenly went dry and the air vanished even though he drew in breath.

How could a machine look like a woman?

Talk like a woman?

Move like a woman?

"I need to get dressed," he muttered, the words quavering.

"Ah, I see." The scientist stood and walked up to the door, popping his head inside. "Rosa, I'm sorry to trouble you but Coal needs a private moment to dress."

"No trouble." The female machine walked with fluid strides out of the room and Coal partially hid behind the door as she exited.

"Thank you," Coal said, and shut the door.

He squeezed his eyes shut, forcing his body to breathe. He did feel lightheaded, and a dizzy spell overwhelmed him as he placed his forehead against the wall. Surely he was dreaming, stuck in a nightmare, and any moment he would awake to the clank and clink of metal as his father tidied the shop.

Determined to adapt to his new environment, Coal pushed off the wall and approached the peculiar chest made of drawers. In the top bin he found a linen tunic and breeches, familiar items that cooled some of the heat.

How did they have such homespun items?

No one else in the Outside wore such garments. Nor did New Eden commerce with the lab. He tied his new breeches and froze, the laces falling from his fingers as he whispered, "Merde." Oaklee's leaf was tucked away in the pocket of his old breeches.

Dance, when you're broken open. Dance, if you've torn the bandage off.
Dance in the middle of the fighting. Dance in your blood. Dance when
you're perfectly free.

— Rumi, 13th century A.D. *

Oh grieving heart, you will mend do not despair
This frenzied mind will return to calm, do not grieve

When the spring of life sets again in the meadows
A crown of flowers you will bear, singing bird, do not grieve

— Hafiz, "The Lost Joseph," 14th century A.D. *

CHAPTER EIGHT

O aklee glanced over Laurel's head and absorbed the motions of happiness and family. Life simmered in the cadence of arms, legs, and heads that rippled in a unified celebratory tempo within the stone walls of the Great Hall. Laurel rested against her shoulder with a contented sigh, and Oaklee absently played with her sister's soft, gold tresses. Dainty herbal flowers and maiden hair ferns were woven into their braids, and Oaklee savored the earthy scent emanating from Laurel.

Her sister was a beautiful gift and she felt blessed that, on this night, Laurel wished to keep her company rather than chatter away joyfully with Corona. A lively tune began and Oaklee tapped her toes as her fingers continued to spin her sister's hair. Tomorrow, Oaklee would begin her work again, and her body filled with the pleasure of predictability.

Laurel maneuvered so that she looked up and said, "'Tis this not your favorite tune? Oh, how I do enjoy a good reel."

"Indeed." Oaklee did not wish to dance, but Laurel lifted her head. A broad smile lit her sister's face and Oaklee's ruminating dissipated. Oaklee evoked a serious tone, "May I have this dance, My Lady?"

Her sister giggled. "I would be honored," she cooed and batted her eyelashes.

Oaklee extended a hand and admired the swirls and designs temporarily tattooed into her skin with henna. The matriarchs had ceremonially marked her hands and feet with the ancient designs of life. This was the first time Oaklee had ever been tattooed, and she felt beautiful participating in this ancestral ritual that connected all feminine spirits past and present.

"Do, however, be careful with my little toes," Laurel said.

Oaklee laughed, pulled Laurel close and kissed her forehead. "Oh darling, how I adore you."

Laurel grabbed Oaklee's hand and pulled her out of her seat, through the gathered crowd, and onto the dance floor. They stood with barely contained mirth as they waited for the right beat. When the song circled back to the familiar riff, they shuffled across the floor with the other dancers. Oaklee laughed as they spun and again when they paused to clap before grabbing each other's hands and swishing enthusiastically across the floor once more toward the far wall.

A nervous jolt fluttered Oaklee's breath upon noting Fillion nearby and her smile fell. He leaned casually against the stone wall, arms crossed loosely across his chest, his face expressing disinterest. He looked at her then, and she attempted to appear ladylike and modest, although her body heaved from the exertion. Laurel tugged on her hands, yanking her arms, and Oaklee smiled at her sister as they side-skipped to the other side of the dance floor. The dancers moved around her. Laurel spun as they clapped their hands. Oaklee followed suit while casting shy, furtive glances toward the other end of the room, locking eyes with his. Her heart faltered each time and her legs grew unsteady. The song ended and Laurel wrapped her arms around Oaklee's waist and squeezed.

"Darling, I fear I must sit now," Oaklee said between breaths. She raised her hands to her cheeks and felt the warmth. "You are a wonderful dance partner. Shall you save me another dance before the evening is complete?"

"I would be honored," Laurel cooed once more. Oaklee laughed and curtsied and Laurel did the same. "May I visit Corona over yonder?" Laurel pointed near the hearth where other girls had gathered. "Or would you be too lonely?"

"I shall fare well, dear one. Please enjoy the evening with your friends."

"Thank you for not stepping on my little toes," her sister replied with another wide grin before running through the tables to the other side of the room.

Music began once more and Oaklee turned toward the dance floor. Curious, she peeked Fillion's direction only to meet disappointment when his attention was solely on the musicians. She chided herself for entertaining the romantic fancies and notions of girlhood rather than those of a woman, who would never seek out a man's attention in such an obvious way.

Lifting her head a notch, she walked gracefully to the head table and lowered herself with elegance. Oaklee poured a goblet of wine, sipping as quickly and as daintily as possible. Thoughts and feelings jumbled through her mind as her heart continued to betray her logic. She should not seek the attentions of a man who had lied to her repeatedly and whose presence removed Coal from their community. And yet, her heart came alive the more she attempted to think of other things or remain cross. The last drop of wine touched her tongue and she poured herself another goblet full and enjoyed a long sip.

Ember cleared her throat, catching Oaklee's attention. The Daughter of Fire leaned forward across the table and whispered, "Go."

"I beg your pardon?"

"Leave, no one shall notice your absence for some time."

Confusion wrinkled Oaklee's thoughts and she continued to stare at her sister-in-law. "Where shall I go?"

"I believe you wish for a private moment, do you not?" Oaklee's eyes widened, and Ember leaned forward even further. "This is your moment."

"A private moment for what, pray tell?" Her sister-in-law only smiled. "Ember Lenore Watson, have you taken leave of your senses?"

"Away with you," Ember said. She waved her hand and smiled.

"Are you well?" Leaf turned toward Oaklee.

"She is simply in need of fresh air," Ember said with casual grace. "She reeled and feels flush. It is rather warm inside the Hall is it not, My Lord?"

"Indeed, My Lady." Leaf scooted his chair back and turned to Oaklee. "I shall keep you company."

"No, please do not trouble yourself, My Lord," Oaklee said. "I shall fare well, and solitude suits me. I shall not venture far."

"Oaklee," he whispered emphatically, glancing around the table. "You should have a chaperone. For several reasons. It is unladylike and tongues will wag."

Oaklee placed her hands onto the table and leaned forward. "Please, My Lord," she whispered in irritation. "Do not confine me any more than I already am."

Her brother drew back, uncertainty and distress hardening his features. "I do not insult you with the request," he said between gritted teeth. "I insult those who wish our family harm." After a few heartbeats, Leaf reluctantly assented with a dip of his head. He twisted away from Oaklee and bestowed his attention on the other half of the table once more as a muscle twitched in his jaw.

When Leaf resumed conversation, Ember leaned forward and whispered, "Fret not, you shall be fine and I shall remind him so." Ember gestured for Oaklee to take note that all The Elements were present. "Go. I believe there is something rather distressing you wish to settle in your heart. Make amends within yourself so you may begin anew tomorrow. I have a hunch, and I am rarely wrong."

Unpleasant sensations swirled in Oaklee's stomach with even the simplest thought of sneaking out and into the night for a private moment—for what, she knew not. Her fingers gripped the goblet of wine and lifted the vessel to her lips. It was a poor attempt at ladylike deportment as she drank to the bottom, but Oaklee needed to settle her nerves, and with haste. Fillion's advice to drink up and drink fast echoed in her mind, and the muscles in her stomach tightened in response. She offered Ember a timid smile and then slowly walked away from the head table without looking back.

The musicians began a lively piece. Oaklee approached the crowd of onlookers gathered near the entrance who merrily clapped for the dancers. A Celtic drum beat in rhythm with her heart, her shallow breaths fogging the latticed window as she searched the darkened night. Never had she aimlessly traversed the biodome at late evening by herself simply to seek solitude. The very thought was as exhilarating as it was terrifying. She teetered on the edge of propriety, and Ember's insistence mystified her.

Unable to resist the music, she lightly bounced on her feet. Slipping a hand into her pocket, she thoughtfully caressed the hemp paper as her mind conjured, yet again, what could possibly be contained in its folds. She was not ready to read the contents, though, and instead drew comfort from the memory of Coal. Did Ember know of Coal's letter? Most likely, Oaklee mused to herself. Ember and Coal were close. Naturally, he would share such sentiments with his sister.

Oaklee stopped at the door and turned to look over the crowd once more. Everyone was consumed with their own merriment. Fillion continued to watch the musicians with knitted brows, his focus interrupted when Laurel and Corona approached him. Her little sister tapped Fillion's arm and he looked down surprised, shifting his body to face them. Corona lifted a white flower and Fillion knelt down and accepted the proffered gift. A charming smile softened his face as he smelled the wildflower for show. Oh how that smile made various emotions flutter and dance within her chest! The girls ran off, hiding their giggles behind small hands, and Fillion trailed their movements with a sober expression.

He looked down at the flower for a few heartbeats and then swept his gaze across the room until he found her. Oaklee quickly looked away, unable to hide a small, bashful smile. Irritated at being caught staring, she tip-toed out of the Great Hall. The song ended and the crowd cheered loudly as she pushed the heavy door open with a loud, creaky groan. She quickly shut it behind her, pulse racing.

Her breath left her body in a ghostly vapor that faded into the inky night. Oaklee drew her cloak closer. Lanterns lined the dirt path and she sighed in relief, fetching one as she ambled in the direction of The Rows.

The cold air nipped at her exposed skin as she drew the large hood over her head. It was another moonless night and the ambient light from the dome ceiling cast eerie shadows across the meadow. The night breathed deeply, a restful sigh that flapped her cloak against her body and waved the hood across her face in gentle motions. Although the Celtic drum carried on the night wind from the feast, she fastened her eyes upon the earthen trail and listened to the trees whisper their lullaby to the sleeping forest. A tangible serenity infused each step and she smiled. Nighttime was beautiful, she concluded, and she felt a swelling appreciation for the solitary shelter it provided. Perhaps grief was not the only state that painted everything black. Perhaps peace did as well.

Leaves crunched beneath her feet and added accent beats to the drum. The harmony moved her soul and she added a dance to her step as she skipped down the footpath, turning in the bio-wind at the appropriate choreographed moments.

She paused before a sapling, growing on the edge of The Orchard. "Why yes, Sir Tree, I would be honored to dance with you." Her fingers gripped a thin, bare branch and she arched her arm above her head, tucking herself beneath the bow in a slow spin. She gave a light kick, took two steps back and then swayed forward and backward with melodramatic grace as she bit her lower lip to contain the erupting giggles. Mayhap she had indulged in too much spirits as well. The song ended and Oaklee curtsied to the sapling, placing fingers over her mouth as she giggled once again. The tune carried in her heart and she hummed the melody as she continued her journey toward The Rows.

Guilt and grief—two emotions she knew well—had become her closest companions, often flavoring her day with disquietude. Jealous friends from the onset, these dispositions tainted every happy moment. But this night, she wished to live. She wished to push through the heartache that had stolen her life and, instead, seek friendship with closure and comfort.

A bride and groom were also celebrated this eve, their sacred oath as ancient as time. In New Eden, a bride was the symbol of life. She was adorned with flowers and leaves as if she were Spring, ushering in a new season after the hollowness of Winter. It was a message of hope and always cause for the greatest of celebrations. A groom pledged his life to serve his bride, even if it meant he must lay down his own life for hers. Thankfully, no man in their community had yet to physically sacrifice himself to save a woman. She suddenly stopped in the path. No man, until Coal.

Her view tilted as her heart and mind began to discuss the possibilities with heated tones, and she placed a hand onto a large maple to steady herself. Ember had dressed and prepared Oaklee as a bride to send off Coal and welcome a new resident at The Door during the union of two worlds. Her sister-in-law knew that Coal was sacrificing himself and shared that the newcomer would revolutionize New Eden.

In her subtle way, Ember gave Oaklee a message and allowed Oaklee to decipher the greater meaning in her own time. It was not that Oaklee should marry Coal; rather, she should choose to live. This was Coal's gift. He was sacrificing himself so the Winter of her life could give way to Spring.

The Last Ceremony marked the end of her bereavement period and welcomed a season of new beginnings. Knowing this, Coal protected her need for family and predictability within her home.

He was not stupid. He was not insensitive. Although he was still a fool. A rascally and impetuous fool that always charmed her into laughter and, only recently, made her cry over him. The knave! Oaklee smiled to herself as she thought of her friend. Mayhap it was the three goblets of wine she enjoyed within the half-hour, but for the first time in seven days she thought of Coal without a large dose of guilt and fear.

The Son of Fire's letter shifted in her pocket with each step, and she looked up at the dim glow of the geodesic sky. The lantern easily slid onto a low branch of a pear tree on the outskirts of The Rows and, with a deep breath, she pulled Coal's letter from her pocket. The hemp paper glowed beneath the candlelight as she untucked the folds. At first, her eyes wandered over the beautifully scribed note, each letter looped and slanted with uniformity. Coal's penmanship was as artistic as the drawings he charcoaled or inked onto spare paper when allowed. She brushed her fingers with fondness over the ink, as if the very letters could leap from the page and materialize into her friend.

Dearest Willow Oak of the Wood,

How does one say farewell? The very act eludes me, never having practice in the art of saying goodbye. Since my decision to take Leaf's place, I have penned four letters to you. Each one filled a page with trite messages that, no matter how they were described, could not approach what burns inside of me. My apologies if my words do injustice to our unfolding story, which, I dare to hope, contains a happy future.

I have loved you since I was a lad of four when Leaf brought you to The Waters to play while your mother rested. There I was a boy knight and you a faerie princess, roles we longed to fill and played at our entire childhood. Now, grown up, you are indeed a princess and I leave on a quest for your family. Is it not strange how fate has twisted our lives' tales as such?

Please, do not grieve for me. I know you, Willow Oak Watson, and I did not depart to add to your sorrows nor shall I tolerate tears shed over my absence. Although, I smile at the very image of you cross over my decision, storming inside for demonstrating my stupidity and foolish insensitivity. Upon my return, I desire for you to inflict your tempestuous nature upon me. I shall relish in it and deem it a worthy hero's return. I smile yet again, knowing full well these words infuriate you. Be warned, My Lady, your gale force winds only billow the fire and I, in reply, burn brighter for you.

Enclosed is a poem I discovered quite by accident when I borrowed a book from Norah. The page was neatly tucked away as a forgotten marker and I do believe it was penned during an age not allowed per The Code. I copied the words to save and wish to gift them to you, knowing how you secretly enjoy all things scandalous.

This is farewell, My Lady, and as Shakespeare writes, "Parting is such sweet sorrow." I shall return to you and when I do, I hope a happy ending awaits us both.

With all my love and affection,
Yours Truly,

Coal M. Hansen

"Dear friend," Oaklee sighed, "I grieve over breaking your most faithful heart." She closed her eyes and concentrated on the sounds of nature to calm her troubled spirit. However, the festive music from the Great Hall drowned out the gurgling creek's cheerful tune. She opened her eyes and shuffled the papers, drawing the forbidden poem closer to the light.

Nature's first green is gold,
Her hardest hue to hold.
Her early leaf's a flower;
But only so an hour.
Then leaf subsides to leaf.
So Eden sank to grief,
So dawn goes down to day.
Nothing gold can stay.

By Robert Frost

Despite Coal's admonishment not to cry over him, she could not contain the tears that slipped over the threshold and fell down her cheeks. The poem was beautiful and gripped her heart fiercely as she contemplated the last line. The community's Golden Boy did not stay as Eden sank to grief, and took with him her golden tribute. The nibbling dread that paid visits since Coal's departure whispered to her once more, and she began to believe that her fear of his never returning held substance.

Straightening her shoulders, she folded the precious words of the poem and placed them within her dress pocket. An urge shivered through her as she faced The Rows, and her fingers lifted his letter to the lantern's flame. Death was the only goodbye she understood, and Oaklee needed to let go properly if she was to move forward and embrace the dawning Spring of her life. This was Coal's gift, and she would not fail to appreciate his sacrifice.

As the hemp paper flamed, she approached the heart of the Ceremonial Garden. Reverently, she lowered the burning letter to the soil and watched as his last words turned to ash. The embers faded into the black of the rich soil and she scooped dirt over the remnants to cool the ashes as her fingertips tilled the remains into the garden. His words of love and honor would now feed and nourish this community, becoming a part of each individual.

She blew a kiss to her parents and to Coal, rising from the garden as a new woman. It was time to return to the Celebration of Life and lift a goblet in Coal's name. Her heart experienced lightness as she approached her lantern; so much so, she lifted her face to the night and allowed the bio-breeze to caress her form and sift through her hair. The fresh feeling flushed through her entire body and she giggled with the release, forgiving herself for the unkind and selfish acts against her family and Coal, while forgiving Coal for his foolish quest in pursuit of her heart. She was now officially ready to transcend, to reach beyond, to live.

Footsteps shuffled from behind and Oaklee slowly turned as a shadow moved toward her. She lifted the lantern from the branch and dangled it by her side and nibbled the inside of her lip in anticipation of his presence. An orange glow cut through the dark, brightening momentarily before lowering closer to the ground.

"Hey," he said, almost shyly.

"Hay?" She stared, perplexed. "Do you always greet young women as if barn animals?"

Fillion laughed, the sound reminiscent of a soft, fluttering breeze; and her heart began to dance in tandem to the quick rhythm of the drum as she surreptitiously admired his smile. The silvery blues of his eyes possessed an ethereal quality, taking captive every one of her thoughts. With great effort she looked away, heady with wine and acceptance.

"H-e-y. Hey. It's outsider speak for hello."

"I see."

He slid her a sly look. "And do you like what you see?"

"I see many things," she quipped. "Perhaps you can enlighten me. To what do you refer?"

"Nothing." He casually lifted a shoulder in a shrug as a near indiscernible smile pulled at his lips. "Everything."

"Are you intentionally elusive so I become cross with you?" She lifted the lantern to better see his face. He looked away with an amused grin and then raised a joint to his mouth as his eyes roamed over the meadow and The Rows.

Fillion exhaled slowly as he studied the dome's sky. Another humored smile played across his face—one that reminded her of the Dungeon Master—before he met her waiting gaze.

In a dallying tone, he asked, "You wanted me?"

"Do not be absurd," she said with a huff and narrowed her eyes. Fillion raised his eyebrows with a look resembling boredom, and yet it contained a flirtatious element that muddled her senses. As subtly as possible, Oaklee studied his features as a sudden idea surfaced. "You know the mill along the North Pond?"

"Maybe. Is it by where we came in yesterday?"

"Precisely." Her heart pounded noticeably as she became more aware of him. In a delirious cycle, her mind whispered over and over to her runaway thoughts that this was the man to whom she had pledged herself. And the man who had lied to her. He was definitely the Dungeon Master, a more gentle and timid version, a revelation that destroyed every notion of how to feel or behave. Modesty won over in the end, and she lowered her eyes to the ground. "There is a rather large tree across the bridge and to the left of the mill."

"And you're telling me this because...?"

"I wish to meet you there at half-past the hour, if you will oblige."

"Sure, I'll oblige," he responded with a shaky smile, drawing on his joint again. "Why the secrecy? Just say what you want to say now."

Oaklee inspected The Rows and meadow. "I cannot be seen with you alone at night and unchaperoned. I have already compromised my reputation by traversing the gardens alone. If we were seen together, it would place us in a precarious position before the community."

He took a step forward so that their toes nearly touched and she held her breath. His fingers plucked a white flower from his belt, the one Corona had gifted him, and placed it in her hand as he stared at the wild grass.

"I'm not afraid of New Eden's mob mentality, but whatever."

She whispered, "What are you afraid of, then?"

With a bashful grin, he met her eyes for a mere heartbeat and whispered, "See you around," before sauntering back toward the Great Hall.

The wine on his breath made her think of the prior evening and her stomach fluttered. She watched until Fillion's form disappeared completely and then she giggled behind her hand.

She would raise a goblet in Coal's honor after she met with Fillion. They may not have another moment of privacy such as this. As she ambled through The Orchard, her fingers brushed along the trunks of some of her favorite trees, hoping Leaf did not worry over her prolonged absence, and hoping the trees would guard her secret. The old biddies of The Orchard witnessed her interaction with Fillion and she knew their red fruit blushed at the scandal of their clandestine meeting, and the one to come. "Shhh," she directed at the trees, raising a finger to her lips, before giggling once more.

The wildflower twirled in her fingers as she rubbed the stem absently. In a moment of whimsy, she leaned her back against a pear tree, closing her eyes as she inhaled the sweet fragrance of the flower, unable to hold in a smile. Heartbeats passed in a euphoric blur, and she eventually resumed her stroll along the footpath as she tucked the flower into her hair.

The night air blanketed her in solitude once more and she pulled her hood over her head, deciding to walk the path along the apartments. Candles burned in a small number of homes as mothers tucked in their young to the lullaby of the Celtic music that carried on the bio-breeze. Her eyes wistfully lifted toward the apartments. Then she tugged on her hood and trod toward a confrontation she both longed for and dreaded.

By *the fountain, near the gate,*
There stands a linden tree;
I have dreamt in its shadows
so many sweet dreams.
I carved on its bark
so many loving words;
I was always drawn to it,
whether in joy or in sorrow.

Today again I had to pass it
in the dead of night.
And even in the darkness
I had to close my eyes.
Its branches rustled
as if calling to me:
"Come here, to me, friend,
Here you will find your peace!"
The frigid wind blew
straight in my face,
my hat flew from my head,
I did not turn back.

Now I am many hours
away from that spot
and still I hear the rustling:
"There you would have found peace!"

— Wilhelm Müller, "der Lindenbaum," *Die Winterreise,* 1823 *

CHAPTER NINE

Fillion waited in the shadows of the Great Hall. He smoked his last joint with shaky fingers, forcing himself to walk into the forest. She knew. He could see it in her eyes and it took everything inside of him to play it cool. God, she was going to kill him and leave his body. One part of him enjoyed the idea of dying at her hands and the other part of him was ready to fall on his own sword. Either way, he was terrified. And yet, even though these were his last minutes on Earth—or Mars—or whatever the hell this was—he marched forward to meet his fate.

Logic told him with confidence that, now or later, it didn't matter. Self-preservation urgently shouted to enter the North Cave and bang on The Door until it opened. The last glimmer of hope whispered that she didn't regret giving trash like him her pure and innocent heart. "I'm so lame," he muttered under his breath and then shook his head. He really needed to stop talking to himself out loud.

Fillion hoped, no matter what happened tonight, that he would be able to focus on his mission and help Leaf. Tomorrow he was to meet with Connor and go over his job options. The thought made him groan. With his luck, he'd have to pull carrots from the ground or peel potatoes for ninety days. Or worse, milk goats. That last thought made him shudder.

He slowed when he reached the stone bridge that crossed over the far end of the pond. The large tree nestled against a Tudor-style mill, as described. A wheel sat in an emptied channel, perfectly still, the buckets poised and ready to drown and emerge, load and dump. He picked up a small rock and skipped it across the pond as he traveled over the stone bridge, satisfied with the familiar plinks and plunk.

A figure emerged from behind the tree and his steps faltered. God, she was beautiful. All he could hear was his own breathing and the pounding of his heart. They were the sounds of life. His life. He blinked rapidly, lowered his head, and continued toward Willow. He exhaled a little too loudly when he stopped in front of her and lowered his hood. But there was no help for it.

"Hey," she said softly.

He looked up and bit the inside of his cheek. She offered a kind smile and his heart pounded with more violence. Fillion should be humored by her greeting, but the nerves racing through his body overwhelmed him beyond any reasonable thought. He was on the verge of a system crash, but somehow managed a "hey" in return. Being reduced to stupidity, yet again, was getting old.

"I wish to show you something," she said. Her voice quavered and Fillion felt a smidgeon of relief that she was nervous, too.

He trailed behind her as she walked around the large tree. A lantern rested near the trunk, flickering across the bark. Willow's features were enchanted with warm light as she bent forward and picked it up.

With reverence, her fingers caressed the bark of the tree. His eyes trailed over the henna tattoos decorating her hands and he felt his heart begin to race for entirely different reasons. Flowers and leaves cascaded down her long, wavy hair, including the one he impulsively gave her. He needed to focus. After tonight, there would be no knowing her—in any capacity. Fillion shifted on his feet with growing impatience as he watched her inspect the "something."

"Do you fare well?"

"Yeah. Fine."

She slid a glance his direction and held his eyes. And as usual, he stared, like an idiot. She blinked and returned her focus to the tree. What the hell was she doing? What the hell was he doing?

Willing confidence, he took a step toward the tree and leaned in to see what the "something" was she wished to show him. Initials in various shapes, sizes, and patterns, covered the tree like druidic runes. The tips of her fingers brushed against each mark and she paused every so often as if they spoke to her. After a few exasperating seconds, her hand stilled over a set of initials. Her lips formed a faint smile and she beckoned him to come closer with a quick nod. He leaned in farther and closed his eyes as a shot of adrenaline hit him when their cheeks touched.

She leaned to the side to create more space, whispering with a slight tremor, "Do you see the letters?"

"Yeah." Once again, not a very inspired reply, but the only one he could manage.

"J.W. and D.J." Her voice had a strange quality to it as if he should recognize them. But his mind stopped working the moment he stepped into her presence. She began again, much to his relief. "These are my father's initials. He always carved or penned leaves in the letters like this. 'Tis his signature, to be sure."

"OK."

"In medieval folklore this was known as the 'the tree of lovers.' It was also believed that one could not lie when speaking beneath its boughs. So men and women pledged their eternal love for one another beneath such trees."

"Interesting." Fillion forced a polite smile. He hated illogical stories like these. But whatever.

"According to a legend in New Eden, this tree once belonged to two star-crossed lovers, a man of humble origins and a maiden of unparalleled beauty. One day, they met beneath the Tree of Lovers to declare their affection. When she gifted her heart to him, he carved their initials into the trunk to seal their pledge. For many months they knew nothing but happiness. However, before they wed, a great tragedy tore them apart." Willow's fingers played with the edge of her cloak as she continued. "Heartsick, the woman sought the tree for comfort. It is said that the tree took great pity upon the maiden and wept a single tear." He studied the large heart-shaped leaves littering the ground. "When the small, silver leaf landed upon the palm of her hand, it magically transformed into a pendant to wear around her neck. This way, the heart of the man, in the form of a leaf, could stay close to the heart of the maiden he left behind."

"Quite the legend."

"Do you not see?" She stood up.

He scanned the letters once more and swallowed when he recognized his mom's initials. She definitely knew. He felt like his gut got punched. His only thoughts were commands to breathe. Damn, Leaf. It wasn't that she thought he was the Dungeon Master, but that she knew exactly who *he* was. The air was frigid but sweat began to bead on his forehead. He tucked his thumbs into his belt and raised his shoulders, tensing when she spoke again.

"This is a linden tree and—"

"What?" Fillion took a step back and looked up at the branches.

"Pardon?"

"What's the name of the tree?"

"Linden…"

"OK, go on." He tried to act casual but the atmosphere had shifted.

"The name of this tree bothers you?" She took a single step forward and squinted her eyes in a look of suspicion. "Why is that, My Lord?"

Fillion cringed with the title. "It's my sister's name."

She clearly didn't expect that answer and widened her eyes. "*You* have a sister?"

"I know it's hard to believe, *nettomo*, but I don't live in a computer." He rolled his eyes and shook his head. "And I'm not a genie and you didn't summon me to New Eden through Messenger Pigeon to grant your wishes."

Willow took two slow steps back, arms akimbo. Since learning of his sentence in New Eden, he thought he would turn into a puddle of useless nothing with any kind of confrontation with her. But the urge to fight kicked in and he met her challenging glare.

Nobody was allowed to wipe their feet on him anymore—and that included Willow. He didn't care if he was possibly the son of a killer. Or that she was essentially his employee. Or that she had gifted him her heart to guard and keep safe. He was exhausted and mentally unraveling after a sleepless and intense forty-eight hours. And most of all, he was tired of being afraid of Willow. Fillion couldn't live ninety days tip-toeing around the inevitable. She could hate him now. Logic won out in the end.

"That is most unfortunate," Willow said, "as I *wish* to know why you lied to me. And how you knew my full name before we were properly introduced. Since you are not in the business of granting wishes, I suppose this conversation is over."

Willow spun on her heel and began to walk away. Fillion grabbed her hand and pulled her back. She bumped into him with the momentum and looked up with rounded eyes.

"Unhand me!"

He shouted back, "I lied to protect you!" He let go and lifted his hands to his chest in mocked surrender and took a step back.

"How very *gallant* of you, sir. Or shall I refer to you as a soldier? I humbly thank you for coming to my rescue." She turned her head and lifted her chin. "How can I be sure this is not another game you play? Is this even the real *you*?"

Fillion stared at her profile for a moment. A volcano of emotions threatened to erupt. Whatever. He shook his head and brushed past her toward the bridge. The hell with her. The toe of his shoe scuffed the worn path and he kicked at it as the anger fully surfaced.

"Fillion!"

"Shit," he muttered. His name on her lips made him hesitate and he continued to swear under his breath. As petty as it was, though, he didn't want her to win so he kept walking.

"Fillion!"

This time the voice was right behind him and he stopped. She ran in front of him, frantic. "Save your breath," he said. "I don't want to hear it." He moved to walk around her.

She side-stepped and placed her hands on his chest and he stilled. "When a lady calls for a gentleman, he should regard her and honor her request."

"I don't care who calls for me. I'm not sticking around to be mocked and shamed."

"Rather a peculiar statement coming from a man who mocks everyone, is it not?" She tilted her head with a bold stare.

He took a step closer, feeling her fingers burn through the layers of clothing, and leaned toward her face. "Everyone?" he asked through gritted teeth. "*They* didn't suffer because of me. *They* weren't asked to give up everything and deny who they are because of me. You don't know shit."

Willow gasped and paled as tears quietly began to trail down her face, but he couldn't care less. Like usual, she could think of him as a machine devoid of human emotion. He wouldn't give anyone room to cause him pain a second longer.

"Go ahead and school me on the art of being a gentleman to appease your finer sensibilities," he derided. "It doesn't change the truth. Nothing changes the truth! I'm trash, remember? And we're pawns. Both of us. So, yeah, I lied. But I did it to protect your family and mine. How you and I feel isn't even factored into this goddamn equation." Fillion pushed past her once again.

This time she grabbed his hand and pulled him back toward her, immediately dropping her hold as if touching him was repulsive. They stood and faced each other for a few moments as emotions flew back and forth in a wild blur. This was the first time he ever stood emotionally naked before anyone. The vulnerability gnawed at his mind until he literally felt sick to his stomach. But he couldn't keep holding it all inside.

Everyone wanted something from him. Always. She was no different. His eyes stung and he tensed his face to hold back the emotion. He wouldn't let her hurt him and he sure as hell wouldn't cry in front of her.

"What do you want from me?!"

She fearlessly met his eyes, but he knew she was terrified. Yet, her voice was soft, affected even, as she said, "I have never wanted anything from you other than the truth. I long to know the *real* you."

"Doubt it. But let's pretend you actually care and test this theory." He ran a hand through his hair in quick motions and then dropped his arms to his side. "Here's the truth."

Fillion poured out everything he confessed to Leaf that morning, except their plan to hack The Code. Willow placed a hand on her chest as more tears pooled in her eyes. There was nothing he could do. He couldn't bring Joel back to make it right. He couldn't save her to make it right. Hell, he couldn't save his sister or himself. That realization triggered an internal landslide, and he knew the momentum would be destructive. His soul was done. "Trust me, you don't want to know the *real* me. I'm not trash—I'm an entire landfill. The stench of my life will make your perfect, Green Moron, community-minded, fake existence gag and vomit."

"Fillion—"

He cut her off as he retched details from his personal life, things that Leaf didn't even know. He began with Lynden and her hospitalization, followed by the computer underground, and continued on about how his parents were never around but blamed him for every failure in their life. She blushed when he described how the world vilified him as Hanley's son while simultaneously declaring he was the sexiest and wealthiest young man alive. The confession kept rolling and she listened, not moving a muscle, wiping away a tear every so often.

"These," he said with a cracked voiced as angry tears began to fall. "These are the elements that comprise my life. I'm nothing. Even when I inherit all of this, I'll still be nothing. I've been groomed by the world to be an empty vessel that exists for the entertainment of others—including my own mom and dad. Nobody cares. Nobody gives a damn about who I really am. And. Neither. Do. *You*."

"That is a lie, My Lord," she whispered. "I do care exceedingly."

Fillion relaxed and took on a seductive posture. He bit his bottom lip flirtatiously as his eyes raked over her, grinning with wolfish appreciation. In a single step, his body leaned into hers and she softly gasped when his hands rested on her hips. Willow blinked nervously and turned her head away and he stared at the quickened pulse in her neck as his emotions continued to rage.

"Girls like you want boys like me." He leaned forward and whispered in her ear, "I'm thrilling. Dangerous. Sexy. Different than your boring, mannered existence. You think you can heal my bleeding heart, but you can't." The shallow breaths against his cheek told him everything he needed to know. This is what she wanted from him. So he pulled her tight against him, nuzzling his mouth against the skin of her neck. "You care *only* because I turn you on." His hands dropped to his side and Fillion glared at her, arrogance pulling on the corners of his mouth.

Willow pushed him forcibly away, took several steps back, and glowered with narrowed eyes as heat suffused her neck and face. The anger sparked out of her, fists clenching and relaxing, chest heaving, causing a smug smile to form on his face.

"How could you mock me in such a way?" she asked, as if horrified. "I shall not entertain your blind fury. Do not presume to know me or my character. You commit the same offense that grieves you by treating me as though I am nothing!"

"God, you don't get it." He threw his hands into the air as he began to pace back and forth, pulling at his hair in agitated movements. After a few seconds, he turned toward her and shouted, "Here's the truth in simpler terms: We can never be together! You should have never given me your damn heart!" He pointed at his chest. "Do you understand what that has done to me? Love is a fairytale. It's a painkiller, a drug that dulls with time, making the wounded desperate for larger doses that will. Never. Ease. The. Pain."

"I am astonished by your accusations. Are you not the one who asked for a token of *my* affection on *your* last night of freedom?"

"Spare me your sheltered-life pity," he spat with disgust. "My dad gave you a better life than I'll ever have, and I don't want your lectures or your sympathy!"

Willow's face grimaced with anger and then she slapped him. The hit was so forceful that his head snapped to the side. She continued to glare at him as he touched the stinging skin on his cheek, too stunned to move or even blink.

"You are now spared my pity." Willow crossed her arms over her chest. "Are you quite done? Or do you wish for me to pay for more emotional reparations to justify your anger and fear?" He clenched his jaw and lowered his eyes. "Fillion Nichols, you are an arrogant, self-centered, vulgar man."

"It's part of my charm," he said with a cocky smile. "Now do you hate me?" Fillion closed the distance and whispered harshly, "Say it. Slap me again and say it!"

She took in a shuddering breath as tears fell down her face once again. He became faintly aware of a drum echoing in the distance as his heartbeat throbbed in his head. His chest rose and fell in agitation. Willow wiped away the tears on her cheeks in fluttering motions.

They eventually locked eyes as their angry breaths mingled and she whispered in reply, "I have laid down my reputation for you twice now and nearly lost the respect of my brother, a man who was willing to leave to exchange places with *you*. I paid you the highest honor during a week when my heart shattered, and you return the favor by cheapening me in order to defend your pain."

She threw out her hands in a gesture of confused exasperation. "I thought you were a soldier going to war, a man who faced death and desired comfort for his fears. I grieved that I may never see you again, afraid for your life." Her hand lifted and pointed at him. "You say such lies were to protect my family, but they only protected you.

"No, My Lord, I do not hate you," she said, seeking his eyes. "I hurt deeply for you. But I am most displeased."

He stilled as the shock of what she said jolted him out of his acerbity. She didn't hate him? He cheapened her? She hurt for him? Confusion quickly replaced the rage as disconnected thoughts flurried in his mind, creating a blizzard of jumbled emotions. Finally, he mentally surrendered, "I'm sorry," with a heavy sigh.

"Do not further insult me with an apology. I do not wish for empty sentiments." She took in another ragged breath, and the warmth caressed his skin. "My heart is broken and I grieve, for I have known love. Your heart is broken and you grieve, for you have not. I shall not add to your sorrows. But you, My Lord, shall not regard me with such flagrant dishonor and disrespect." Willow dipped into an elegant curtsy, not a single trace of mockery in her gesture, and he grew even more confused. "Good evening time, My Lord."

For a single heartbeat, they locked eyes. And then, slowly, she turned and marched toward the linden tree and grabbed the lantern. With a straight back and slight lift to her head, she stormed past him on the stone bridge and faded into the forest.

What the hell just happened?

The remnant pieces of himself ached and writhed with a pain he had never known before, and he doubled over with nausea. He wanted to die. But Fate always refused to kill him. It was content, instead, with perpetually tormenting him until insanity took over and fabricated hope. But hope was for the weak-minded. No more games.

Minutes passed and his labored breathing slowed to a manageable rhythm. Fillion looked around in a dazed fog. He half-expected to see rubble and pieces of the biodome crumbled on the ground in a heap of wispy, black smoke from his explosion. Instead, geodesic lines shimmered in reflection across the inky water and he stared absently. "Oh my god," Fillion grit through clenched teeth. He wanted someone to shoot him and put him out of his misery.

Feeling antsy, he pushed off the bridge and walked toward the linden tree. Heart-shaped leaves fluttered above him and rustled along the grass. His fingers shook, but he plucked a still silvery-green leaf from the tree and caressed the soft, waxy surface.

A sudden vibration against his lower hip startled him. He checked the surrounding darkness, looking for movement. The sound of the distant drum continued to float in the air and so he decided to take a risk out in the open. In swift movements, he pulled the Cranium from his leather pouch and put it on his ear. Never had Fillion wanted to hear his friend's voice more than now.

"Mack?"

"No, it's Lynden."

Fillion closed his eyes as a sob caught in his throat. The sound of his sister's voice elicited a strange combination of relief and guilt, and words failed to form.

"Fillion?"

He opened his eyes and stared at the leaf in his hand, and then slid to the ground as his body leaned against the trunk.

"Hey, Lyn."

"I'm sorry. I'm so very sorry, Fillion. You were right and ... and ... I'm stupid, so stupid."

"Shhh," he soothed. "I'm not mad at you." They were silent for a few seconds. "I've missed you."

"Really?"

"Really."

He had to change the subject before he lost his mind again. "Please tell me you've kept my pathetic friend out of trouble." Lynden scoffed and Fillion swallowed nervously, not knowing if he offended her or if it was for show.

"He *is* trouble so how can I keep him out of trouble? Mack can't help his disposition. We shouldn't judge."

"Ouch!" Mack said in the background and then his friend joined their line. "You two can go to hell."

"I'm already there," Fillion volunteered.

"Yeah, me too," Lynden said.

"Well shit. It's a good thing I'm trouble then since it appears I'm the only one available to bail out your sorry asses. Again."

Lynden cooed in a syrupy voice, "Ah, poor Mack. Do you feel underappreciated? Come here, little fella. Let me scratch behind your ear. Who's a good boy?"

This was the playful tease Fillion remembered from before Pinkie came onto the scene nearly a year ago. Given the circumstances, Lynden was far too cheerful and he guarded himself. Was it the narcotics? Was she in denial? The concussion? Regardless, he was glad for this small gift, however long she felt free from the pain.

Relief had never felt so good and he rubbed at the forming tears. She would be OK. God, he needed to stop crying.

It was pissing him off. Sleep and a cigarette would help tremendously. And he would do just about anything for a bottle of whiskey this moment.

Mack laughed. "Fillion, do you have any idea how I've suffered?" Fillion imagined his friend flipping Lynden off good-naturedly.

"You like it. Stop your gritching," Fillion replied.

A loud muffled sound echoed in Fillion's head and he wrinkled his forehead in irritation. What were they doing? Mack's humored voice blared but with distance, and he figured Lynden had grabbed the Cranium off his friend's head.

"Give it to me you *kusogaki!*"

Lynden's laughter filled Fillion's head and then everything went silent as Lynden moaned. "Oh god, it hurts."

"What's going on?" Fillion demanded.

"I'll be fine. Just my ribs. Laughter makes ... everything ... hurt."

"Sorry, Rainbow," Mack said, serious, Cranium back in place. "Didn't mean to be so funny."

Lynden started to laugh again, followed by another moan. "Don't say anything cute, Fillion, or I'll kill you."

"Noted."

"I need to go." Lynden's tone remained strained. "Hearing your voice makes me feel better, though."

"Hearing your voice makes me feel better, too."

"Really?"

Fillion rolled his eyes and shook his head as he smiled. She was definitely hyped up on narcotics.

"Really."

"I think I just threw up a little in my mouth," Mack said in playful disgust and Fillion laughed. He couldn't help it. Lynden let out a groan of frustration and he smiled at the familiar sound of his sister's ire.

"Oh my god! Seriously. When Fillion gets back you can make out with him, OK?"

"Peachy," Mack replied, followed by melodramatic kissing sounds. "I want to grab his skinny ass too." Laughter spilled out of Fillion despite all attempts to keep it in.

With irritation, his sister sighed. "Bye."

"Take care of yourself, OK? Keep a low profile for a while. It'll all blow over soon. And don't, under any circumstances, search your name on the Net. Promise me?"

"God, you're such a dictator!"

"Don't forget it," Fillion said with a sad smile.

"Like you'd ever let me."

"Methinks the lady protests too much," Mack said, followed by taunting laughter. "Gasp! Shudder! Make it stop! I'm so frightened by your pertinaciously narrowed eyes, Lynden Norah-Leigh Nichols."

"Pertinaciously? That must have hurt your brain."

"Oh, please. I'm smart and stuff."

"Whatever, Mackenzie Patton Campbell Ferguson the Third. Your male pride is gross, you son of a—"

The line disconnected with Mack's laughter and Fillion leaned his head against the carvings with a smirk. He twirled the leaf in his hand as the hairs on his arms stood on end. Did he really just have a conversation with Lynden while sitting beneath a linden tree? The idea was absurd and yet it filled him with a strange, indescribable peace. Fate seriously had a wicked sense of humor.

Fillion looked up at the tree as if it held an ancient magic, infusing its tales of love and truth into the night air. Did the tree take pity on him too, ensuring his sister called just at that moment? Normally he would roll his eyes with such corny thoughts, but this evening had changed him.

I have never wanted anything from you other than the truth. I long to know the real you.

Was love really a fairytale?

His fingertips grazed the scars cut into the tree, marks that immortalized the proclamations between lovers. He dropped his hand and lowered his head as his shoulders sagged. Tattooed declarations marked his body as well, each one a scarred testament of his desire for something real, something meaningful.

Willow's words seared him. She had no desire to use him and only wanted to know him, the real him—and not in a sexual way. There were no games. Her aroused response was one he knew how to get. And even though he used her, she still treated him as if he possessed worth and value and refused to allow him to treat her as if she didn't. His world tipped upside down.

Love and truth.

With unsteady legs, he stood and stepped in rhythm to the drum's beat. A Celebration of Life raved on and Fillion shoved death's familiar voice out of his head. He wanted to live. He wanted to know the pain from loving too much rather than from its deficit. New Eden's motto consumed his mind, and his soul pleaded for the identity forged by the world to die so that the real him could emerge. He didn't know what that would look like or even where to begin, but the desire burned hot inside of him.

Minutes passed in a surreal fog as he trudged through the forest, his mind captivated by this moment of metanoia. He eventually found himself in front of the Hansen apartment, and he looked over his shoulder. The air was still, possessing zero signs of nearby human activity, so he lifted the iron knob and pushed. The door opened easily and he paused to see if anyone was there. Satisfied they were still at the feast, he tiptoed down the hallway. He opened doors until, at the far end, he smelled a faint trace of lavender, *her* scent.

A few days ago, he remembered how she treasured a leaf that had fallen from her pocket, giving way to an idea. Apologies weren't his forte. But he hoped she accepted his gesture and understood his message.

The linden leaf twirled in his fingers one last time before he rested it on her pillow. In thoughtful motions, he slowly traced the outline of the leaf. Then he walked through the shadows and out into the ambient light of the dome's night sky as the drum beat ended.

The Anime Generation has almost grown up, giving scientists the first real glimpse into the future—and it is dire.

Born during a mysterious population surge in 2030s, this demographic is now under strain from a corporate system unprepared to support the employment needs of so many. Early on, it was believed the only way to sustain a future for the Anime Generation was to inflate their global marketability—imparting epoch-making skills and knowledge in high tech innovation. With unanimous support from Congress and from the Oval Office, educators and resources were contracted from Japan to ensure a cross-cultural pollination and cyber-instructive immersion.

Twenty years later, the Anime Generation is proclaimed the most highly educated to have ever walked the planet. Yet intelligence is a meaningless asset when jobs are scarce. In the wake of unemployment, youth across the nation—and world—have formed grassroots communities that readily engage in black market activity.

Socio-economists are scrambling to find ideas to preserve the future before it's lost to war or famine. Unemployment and crime rates continue to rise, climbing higher every year since this demographic has come of age. The Anime Generation is sleek, sexy, and intellectually superior, but may not survive long enough emotionally to realize that potential.

— Hunter S. Bradstreet, "The Key to our Future May be Lost," *Money Talks*, July 24, 2054

CHAPTER TEN

Monday, October 5, 2054

A hologram appeared from a circular object hovering nearby and wavered in front of Coal's vision. Coal pressed his back against the wall as much as possible. All previous irritation with the Outside garments he was given to wear this morning disappeared as adrenaline pumped through his veins until he thought his heart would burst.

Michael warned with an uncertain voice over breakfast, mere minutes earlier, that Hanley had left a parting gift. But now Coal understood Michael's reluctance as Coal stared at the object of his terror. His breath came quickly and sweat beaded on his forehead. The disturbance was so great his body fairly vibrated from the fear. It was not real, he continued to tell his mind. But it did not matter.

"This is your new Companion," Michael said calmly. "Many children have AGI—sorry—artificial general intelligence Companions while growing up."

"Do they not have human friends?"

"Of course. But most days are spent at home in front of a computer. Roughly seventy-five percent of the nation is educated through the Cyberschool system. So, AGI Companions are brought into the home to ensure interaction throughout the day. The drone is small, convenient for travels, and more affordable than full-bodied androids. Parental features often are built into a Companion's software, allowing working parents to view their children through a video feed, which is streamed through a private channel."

Coal whipped his head Michael's direction as his jaw slackened. "You jest?"

"No. "

A young man with light brown hair, brown eyes, and a medium build—nothing remarkable, simply average—continued to exist no matter how many times Coal blinked and wished for the image to disappear. The false man wore dark blue breeches, similar to his and Michael's, and a short-sleeved gray tunic. The name of the breeches eluded him this moment.

Something similar to deans?

Or keens, perhaps?

Michael stood next to the technology with a serene expression and eyes fixed in concentration, noting Coal's every move while simultaneously focused on another invisible object before his own vision. The transparent being blinked and then met Coal's frightened gaze, locking onto his face with such precision that Coal's pulse elevated in response.

"Greetings, Coal Malcolm Hansen of New Eden Township," the technology spoke. The lips moved and the apparition's body shifted naturally on its feet. Its voice was both youthful and mature, in an accent reminiscent of Outsider speech—fast with clipped sounds. The drone's mechanics hovered just beneath the ceiling, a dull metallic glint catching Coal's eyes on occasion.

"Go ahead and respond," Michael said with an encouraging smile. "Ask your Companion his name."

"Greetings," Coal replied, nerves fluttering rapidly in his stomach. "What is your name, sir?"

"Ignis."

Coal snickered in spite of himself. "Your name is fire?"

"My creator wished for me to relay a message: 'A man should learn to play with fire, especially when fire is in his veins.'" The hologram tilted its head as if taking note of something most interesting. "Your eyes dilated, Coal Hansen. Do you like my name?"

"It is a clever name. And my first name shall do." Spooked, Coal turned to Michael, and forced his breathing to steady. In a whisper, he asked, "It sees me?"

"The drone is programmed with software that reads biometric vitals and a specialized camera that records your face and body language. Ignis will learn your emotions and social cues, responding appropriately to all your needs." Michael's focus shifted over his work, shielded by a privacy screen, and onto Coal. "What you're experiencing is known as the 'uncanny valley.' It's a psychological response to seeing something humanoid and yet knowing it's not really human."

"I would prefer to begin lessons on a Cranium," Coal muttered as he wiped sweat off his forehead with the hem of his blue tunic—no, shirt. The variety of new words came in and out of focus, fading more so as his anxiety elevated.

Michael gave a thoughtful expression. "Hanley is preparing you for the macro as well as the micro experience. In Seattle, AI and AGI walk around all the time. Drones, androids, and holograms provide many services. It's something you'll need to get used to. Ignis here will be your ticket to walking out of the uncanny valley."

"Is this a gift I may refuse?"

"You don't want to be my friend?" Ignis asked, his tone a little saddened.

Coal considered the hologram. It was not real. It did not have true emotions. However, the moral code within Coal flared and swelled inside of him until deep confusion stinted his ability to respond. In truth, he did not wish for this gift. His conscience, however, the one tricked into believing the exchange was real, pulled on his empathy. The answer battled inside of him as he hunted for a morsel of truth that felt appropriate. Stalling, he pulled a strip of leather from his pocket and tied his hair back at the nape of his neck, tucking the shorter strands behind both ears.

How does one answer a machine?

Perhaps as with real relationships.

"May I be honest with you, Ignis?" Coal asked, sucking his bottom lip in nervously.

"Yes."

"I am frightened of you."

"Yes. Your heart rate has continued to rise. Perhaps you should sit down?"

Coal rolled his eyes and let out an angry sigh. He no longer had patience to dialogue with a machine.

Why did AGI and drones perform services when humans were given hands and feet, a strong back, and a mind to accomplish everything on Earth?

Did no one spend an honest day working to survive?

Was there so much free time in the world that man could entertain such nonsense?

At this moment, Coal could not comprehend how his community would ever integrate into the society of Earth. This was his third day in the lab and already he had questioned everything, including his own existence. Never once did he have such thoughts and feelings in New Eden.

"Where are you going?" Michael asked.

"I need air," Coal replied, pulling the door open with force. A woman stood on the other side and flinched and Coal jumped back startled by her unexpected presence. He regarded her through lowered eyes to see if she wavered like a hologram, relieved when a human hand settled upon her chest as she regained composure. "My sincerest apologies, Madam," Coal said as he bowed. "Do you fare well?"

"I do, thank you."

Her voice was soft and elegant, and he looked up. Before him stood the most beautiful woman he had ever beheld. Long dark hair, a strange color between black and violet, fell just below her shoulders and silver-gray eyes examined him curiously. A black dress with shortened sleeves, made from a shiny fabric and embellished in embroidered silver tree limbs and blossoms, covered her up to the neck but hugged her figure, ending near the knees. Her fingernails were neatly trimmed and colored dark silver. He could not surmise her age properly. She was not as young as him, but her skin and complexion were far too smooth and fair to be of an older age. Lips, painted in a dark rouge, smiled with mild amusement, and Coal looked away embarrassed.

"Coal Hansen, I presume?"

Her hand extended toward him and he gently took hold, lifting it to his mouth and kissing her fingers as an answer before realizing what he had done. She smiled at him again, but this time an unsettled feeling colored the adrenaline coursing through him. There was something strangely familiar about her. Coal looked behind him and noted how Michael stood straighter, and looked on with a nervous expression. Ignis still stood next to Michael and Coal nearly flinched, pride stopping him short. He refused to respond with fear in front of a woman, especially one who boasted such beauty. So he turned back to the unexpected visitor and offered a charming smile.

"You know my name, My Lady," Coal said. "What shall I call you?"

"Dr. Nichols, preferably," she said with another amused smile as she brushed past him into the room, a faint scent of honey trailing in her wake. "Michael, my apologies for not announcing my visit. I decided on a whim to take an early flight to capitalize on the workday."

"No worries. I'm used to it this week. Mr. Nichols arrived unannounced as well." Michael cringed with the last words, as if making a grave mistake, and then straightened.

"Yes. How is Fillion? Do you know?"

"How is he right this moment? Or before he entered New Eden?"

"Coal, please shut the door," Dr. Nichols asked in a kind tone over her shoulder. Coal obeyed, but remained by the exit. "Has he checked in through Messenger Pigeon since being enclosed?"

"No, I'm afraid not."

"Let's remedy that. Please dispatch a note in Hanley's name to Jeff, stating that Fillion is to report to Messenger Pigeon."

Michael lowered his eyes and paled. The scientist blinked several times and then faced the hologram. "Ignis, are you still recording our session?"

"Yes, Michael."

"Please trash the recording, delete any feeds, and then shut off."

"Yes, Michael. Anything else?"

"No, thank you. We'll chat with you later."

The transparent man waved at Coal before disappearing. The drone glided across the air and gradually lowered into a box that appeared to be made especially for it.

"Dr. Nichols, may Rosa bring you coffee? Tea?"

"Tea for Coal and for me would be lovely."

Michael turned on his Cranium, placing the order.

The woman waited politely until he was done. "Now, perhaps you can tell me why my request to contact my son bothers you." Over her shoulder, she beckoned Coal to join them with a wave. Michael looked between Dr. Nichols and Coal, swallowing nervously again. "I am aware of my husband's penchant for drama," she said. "What has he done this time?"

The blood drained from Coal's face.

Husband?

This was Hanley's wife?

Coal had been too taken with her and had failed to make the connection with her last name. Warmth ran up his neck. Of all the hot-blooded things to do, Coal groaned inwardly.

Did he really kiss her hand as a suave move?

How did she remain so youthful in appearance?

It was remarkable and eerie, as if she had discovered the famed fountain of youth. Guilt tinged his thoughts as Oaklee came to mind, followed quickly by thoughts of home.

Michael noticed Coal's shocked demeanor. "Oh, goodness! I forgot introductions. Coal, this is Dr. Nichols, lead psychologist over the human experiment project and second-in-command at the lab."

"A pleasure, My Lady," Coal said quietly, dipping his head with due respect.

She was the lead psychologist over the project?

Responsible for many aspects of the community's life?

Michael cleared his throat and returned focus to Dr. Nichols. "Fillion went in as Corlan Jayne. Hanley had a judge sign off on witness protection papers, which John delivered at the exchange." Michael looked at Coal briefly before lowering his eyes to the floor again. "New Eden doesn't know your son is inside, Dr. Nichols."

"Unbelievable." She sighed, and Coal sensed the anger despite her unruffled tones. "Very well. Please dispatch a message to Jeff that Corlan Jayne is to report to Messenger Pigeon this evening, two hours past his work start time at New Eden Enterprises. Hopefully that will stave off any unwanted attention. Oh, and tell him to send Joel Watson as Corlan's escort. Thank you, Michael."

The scientist looked up with widened eyes and Coal tried to restrain his surprise as well. It seemed everyone he met at the lab knew of The Earth Element's passing.

Dr. Nichols did not know of Joel's death?

Why did Hanley keep this information from his wife?

Especially one who was reputed to be second-in-command at the lab?

Michael issued Coal a look out of the corner of his eye, raising his shoulders slightly in question, and Coal responded with an imperceptible nod. Silence seemed to be the best course for now.

A knock sounded and Rosa entered with a tray. Coal maintained a downcast posture, refusing to look at the human-like robot. Thankfully, she did not stay long, placing the tray on a small table near the door before exiting. Michael followed close behind.

When the door shut, Dr. Nichols casually appraised Coal before walking over to the tea set. She poured a cup and offered it to Coal with a polite smile. Once again, Coal felt perplexed as to how he should feel toward Hanley.

What sort of man drugs and medicates another against their will?

Encloses his son in an experiment without consent from his mother?

And withholds details of the experiment from his second-in-command?

Coal accepted the dainty cup and remained standing until Dr. Nichols sat, then lowered himself into the chair next to hers.

"How is your father?" She took a polite sip of the tea, and then settled the cup onto a saucer.

"He is well. Thank you, My Lady."

Her eyes roamed over him once again with curiosity, and so he sipped the tea to distract himself from his growing discomfort. "Is something amiss?" he asked when the silence grew too long.

She lightly laughed. "No, not at all. I am just gathering myself after realizing that I am conversing with the product of nearly thirty years of research and theories. Your dialect is beautiful. It is not quite British, but close. Perhaps we can officially label it as Martian?"

Coal drew in a tense breath, sipping his tea to cover the simmering offense. Dr. Nichols looked at his exposed arms and began studying his general build, and he looked away rather than endure her scrutiny. If she was truly younger he would relish the attention, but the look on her face made him wish to shrivel up and disappear.

She gently brushed strands of hair from her shoulder, and asked, "What is your occupation inside New Eden Township?"

"Blacksmith."

"Of course." She smiled kindly at him and then crossed her bare legs, remarkably hairless. She leaned forward, balancing the tea cup in her hand.

Why was she here instead of with Lynden?

Any daughter would wish for her mother after such a grievous experience. And any mother would care for her child with maternal fierceness. The discomfort Coal felt grew, and he shifted in the chair. He cleared his throat. "How fares your daughter?"

"Hanley told you?" She winced and then the smooth demeanor returned to her features.

"Yes, My Lady. He wished for me to act as a guard on your daughter's behalf whilst her brother is away."

Dr. Nichols raised a single eyebrow and studied his build again. "Always the attentive father." A thin smile cooled her expression. In a flatter tone, she said, "I am quite certain Lynden will enjoy your company." Coal fixed his attention on the tea as his pulse quickened. After a beat, she asked, "What do you miss most about your home?"

He looked up with the abrupt change of subject and blinked. "The ignorance of believing my life possessed actual purpose and value."

"Purpose and value no longer exist?"

"They do, most assuredly." Coal sipped his tea and looked around the room. "However, when I lived in New Eden, I never once saw myself as part of an experiment, rather, as an individual within a community. I was viewed as a man and treated as such."

"Do you feel these values and sense of self were developed by your community instead of through personal discovery?"

Coal sat back against the chair, further annoyed by her question. "Are you suggesting that I am a product regardless of which world I live in?"

"No, I am not suggesting it. I am asking if that is how you feel." Her face remained passive and he felt his irritation rise even higher as he met her steady gaze.

"I do not wish to speak of my *feelings* at present." Coal placed the cup and saucer on a side table, and amber liquid sloshed over the rim.

"I cannot tell you who you are or what you will become. That is for you to decide," Dr. Nichols said. "I do, however, understand that you feel frustrated. As you should. Change always unsettles us. The dark and unrefined elements of our lives are shaken to the surface and, depending on the choices we make, can become opportunities for our betterment." She reached out and placed a hand on his knee and every muscle stiffened. "I am your ally, Coal."

The strange familiarity returned. His first thought was of Fillion. Of the little he saw of the young man, it was quite clear that he favored his mother considerably. But that is not what troubled him. She reminded him somewhat of Brianna, not only her colorings and features, but also the soft quality of her voice. Especially the dainty way she cleared her throat. As subtly as possible, he looked over her facial features. Dr. Nichols looked at him questioningly, and he forced himself to be confident.

"Forgive me, this is most random, but are you perhaps related to Brianna Williamson Hansen?"

Another smile tugged on her lips as she sat back, removing her hand from his knee. "She is my first cousin."

Hanley's earlier comment returned to his memory. "Then we are related by marriage. Brianna is my stepmother," Coal said. "I do not believe I gathered your first name?" Coal asked with a small, charming smile, hoping she complied.

"The first generation rarely speaks of their prior life, so please forgive your cousin's oversight."

"Of course. It's Della. Della Jayne."

Joel's request to Leaf came rushing back to Coal's memory, and he stared at Della in bewilderment.

This was the woman whom Joel wished to care for his children?

The silence grew thicker and Coal labored to remain in control. A knock on the door rescued him and Michael's head appeared, much to Coal's relief.

"Sorry to interrupt, but Mr. Nichols wants to speak with you Dr. Nichols and says you're not answering his calls."

Her face relaxed into a subtle expression of satisfaction. "Thank you, Michael. It appears I left my Cranium in my room." Her eyes did not waver from Michael, not even to search for her device.

She slowly rose and Coal looked away, refusing to entertain the thoughts that wished to surface. He needed to move, so he stood as a gentleman should when a lady leaves the room. Another amused smile lit her features and then she turned and walked from the room. Michael scooted out of the way as she passed and quickly shut the door behind her, then looked at Coal with rounded eyes.

"Just between you and me," Michael said, pausing to swallow, "she does to me what Ignis does to you."

Coal laughed, grateful for an avenue to release his contained nerves. "Imagine how I felt alone with her? You abandoned me to an uncertain fate." He gave Michael a lopsided grin. "And here I thought we were becoming fast friends. I shall have to reconsider now that I know you leave at the first sign of trouble."

"I was dismissed," Michael said with a wide grin. "But I fled as fast as I could."

The pair laughed. Then Coal thought of her request to see Joel and how he and Michael had feigned ignorance. He groaned. "She shall suffer embarrassment when she learns I knew the truth about Joel and withheld it from her. And yet so did her own husband. Perhaps my offense will be pardonable in such a light."

Michael nodded slowly, shifting his eyes away.

Did the scientist also have information he withheld?

"OK," Michael said with a fortifying breath. "Back to work. Now that you know there are scarier things out there, let's take Ignis for a walk. Want to visit the gardens?"

"Only if I may also have a lesson with a Cranium," Coal said.

"Sure. Ignis can help you with that, too." Michael touched the device on his ear, swiped the air, and then poked at an unseen object. "I downloaded the tutorial software. He's now equipped to assist you." He looked over the privacy screen at Coal. "Companions are activated with a code phrase. It can be anything you want."

"Boo." Coal's lips twitched as he tried to hold back a smile. Michael shook his head with humor and swiped at the air.

"Give it a try."

"Boo!" Coal shouted the word and took a dubious step backward as the drone lifted from the strange box. It was yet another box to facilitate something for Outsiders. This love of boxes mystified Coal. He watched the circular object fly toward him. Ignis materialized as if otherworldly liquid poured out from the drone, the head appearing first and the shoe-covered feet last. The muscles in Coal's body tensed. The image would forever haunt him, but he pushed back the fear and stood tall. It was not real.

"What can I do for you, Coal?" Ignis said, wavering in the air.

"Let us walk to the outside garden." Coal headed toward the door, encouraged when Michael smiled and Ignis followed. "I wish for a lesson beneath the olive tree on how to use a Cranium."

"Sure, I can do that."

"Thank you, Ignis."

"Do you need shoes first?"

Coal looked down at his feet, spooked, yet again, by a comment that appeared as if the false man could see. "I prefer to be barefoot, unless I am striking iron."

"Why do you strike iron?"

"I am a blacksmith."

"Really?" Ignis smiled as if he just learned the most fascinating fact. "I didn't realize that profession still existed. I am happy to be wrong."

"Why would you be right?" Coal stopped and turned toward Ignis.

"I possess all of the world's information."

"I see."

"You also see the information?"

"No. Well, not in the way I believe you are suggesting, which I am unsure I can fully understand at this moment." Coal turned and looked at Michael in frustration, and then began walking again. "My apologies, Ignis, but I need quiet to process my thoughts."

The hologram swung his arms and matched Coal's stride, remaining quiet as requested, and Coal's spooked feelings pulsed with each step. To distract himself from his growing trepidation, Coal trailed his vision over the various scientists. Several moved their eyes to note his presence, then returned their attention to the various screens they commanded. Everyone and everything was connected to a machine, and now so was he. He maintained a composed expression as scenery changed from lush work spaces to bleak hallways, turning his head only to capture the sunlight filtering through the windows dotted sparsely along the outer walls of the building.

They were about to leave the lab when Coal tarried. The air was heavily laced with the spice of evergreen trees and he closed his eyes. This was the scent of home. He could almost hear Oaklee hum a tune as she meandered through the trees, leaves rustling in chorus with the bio-breeze. As he opened his eyes, Coal looked over at Ignis and drew his brows together.

What was he doing?

How could he possible forge a relationship with a machine?

"Do you like this forest?" Ignis asked, glancing around the room as if he could actually see with real eyes. The absurdity of the body language assaulted Coal's senses, but he remembered his promise to Hanley to not cause the staff grief.

"The forest is reminiscent of my home."

"Would you like to learn how to use a Cranium here instead of the outside garden?"

Coal looked up at the geodesic sky and sighed. "Yes, very much."

"Great. Where do you want to sit?"

Of course they would have to sit. It was not only the response of Outsiders, but of their machines as well. Coal moved to a cedar tree and rested his body against the large trunk, stretching out his legs. His fingers plucked a piece of grass and twirled it absently, thoughts of family moving through his mind. The piece of grass continued to spin back and forth in his fingers, stilling when the hologram moved to a sitting position, crossed its legs, and leaned forward on its elbows. A nudge snapped him out of his trance and he flicked the blade of grass away as Michael placed a small, metal object in his hand.

Sometime later, after receiving tutorials and instructions from Ignis, Coal strapped the device onto his ear and turned it on. A light pop echoed in his head and he winced, bringing his hands to his head in surprise. Michael had explained that Craniums used bone conduction technology, which meant little to Coal at the time.

"Do you hear me?"

Coal snapped his head toward Ignis, flattening his palms onto the ground. The voice came directly from his head.

How was this possible?

"Yes, I hear you. How is it you speak to me thus?"

"I have an internal Cranium, so you can call or message me anytime." Ignis smiled, but no words formed with this mouth. It was as if Ignis was capable of speaking to his mind, another otherworldly disturbance to add to Coal's ever-growing list. Nevertheless, he was ready for more.

"How do I move the air?"

Ignis tilted his head in deep thought. "I don't understand your question."

"I've got this one," Michael said, noting the hologram's response. "Touch the button on the metal device. Good. A screen should pop up ... oh, there it is. OK, now poke the rectangular box right in front of you. See the letters, numbers, and symbols that appeared?" Coal nodded and the image moved with him, a dizzying effect his brain did not enjoy. "This is a keyboard. You'll form words by swiping like this. Now give it a try." Several attempts later, Coal correctly swiped the strange message Michael had given him and the screen gave way to another with multiple pictures, some that moved as if they were real. "You did it! Fantastic. So, what do you want to search?"

"I am not sure I follow," Coal said. He moved his head forward to see the screen more closely only to realize the hologram moved with him. He felt stupid and offered Michael a droll look in response. Movement captured his attention once more and his eyes darted back to a small box in a corner, blinking when a string of words in an opposite corner flashed to a different sentence. Coal reared his head back in surprise, making the hologram shift and he squinted his eyes and placed a hand on his head with the disorientation. Michael laughed and shook his head, his face calming to a simple expression of amusement after a few heartbeats.

"You'll learn that you move your eyes and not your head when working a Cranium's user interface." Michael tapped his ear and then folded his hands into his lap. "If you could know or see anything in the world, what would it be?"

"Truly?" Coal's eyes widened and Michael nodded. "I wish to see my mother."

"Sure. Tap that icon right there. No, the one that's a lighthouse. Good. This is Xandria, the world's biggest search engine and library of information. Put your finger in the long rectangle at the top. Yep, like that. This is a search bar. Now swipe your mom's name."

Coal stuck his tongue out while concentrating, and swiped the name "Camilla Hiddleston." The screen shifted and several pictures flooded his vision. Disappointment quickly crushed the excitement he experienced moments earlier as he stared hopelessly at the multitude of women who apparently owned his mother's name.

Were there so many people in the world that names were commonly shared?

"Do you see her?" Michael asked.

"I have never seen her," Coal whispered. "She died minutes before I was born."

"I'm so sorry. Let's see if I can find a photo of her in the lab files to help us out." Michael turned on his Cranium and pointed at the air, swiped, and then dragged his finger in an upward motion. "Here we go." He shifted focus to Coal's screen, his eyes moving back and forth as he searched, eventually tapping on a photograph and pulling it from the corners until it enlarged considerably. "There she is."

Emotions swarmed within Coal as he looked into his mother's eyes for the first time. He whispered, "She is beautiful." Short, light blond hair with bright pink strands—cut on an angle—reached her chin, and eyes that reflected shades of the sky stared back in an eternal moment of happiness.

"Do you want to save this image?" Ignis blinked his holographic eyes at Coal.

"Yes, please."

"Place your finger on the image and drag it to the side icon labeled 'shelf.'" Coal followed the hologram's instructions and felt his heart constrict when the image of his mother disappeared. "When you want to see that picture again, just tap on your shelf."

"You can shelve anything, building your own personal library," Michael said. "Videos, photos, articles, you name it."

Coal nodded as he began another search, swiping in the name 'Lynden Nichols.' If the scientist seemed surprised, he hid it well, busying himself with work behind a privacy screen. Or maybe he just did not notice. Michael often became distracted by his work within a blink of an eye.

A young woman with rainbow hair dotted Coal's screen in a plethora of tiles and he studied each picture with curiosity. She wore the most interesting clothing, as if the articles were chopped up and pieced onto her body, joined by straps. Occasionally she flaunted a short, ruffled skirt. He tapped on one image to observe her facial features with more clarity, smiling at her playfully taunting pose, tongue sticking out as hazel eyes glared.

She had a ring fastened to her lower lip?

And how did her hair reflect such shocking strands of color?

One particular image held his sight, and his stomach lurched. A man with blue, green, and white hair, which stood up in random spikes, carried her limp form. Clothes hung in shreds and blood dripped from her face. There were no adequate words to describe what he saw, and a fury unlike any he had ever known billowed into a rage inside of him. Fire in his veins, indeed.

Coal went back to the playful picture of Lynden and shelved her image.

Emotion resembles a wheel spinning free. When the cogs work, action begins, emotion ceases.

— David Lindsay, 20th century Scottish novelist *

Then when she had put the kitchen in order, she sat down to her wheel and began to spin. Dobrunka had a pretty voice, as pretty as any of the song-birds in the forest, and always when she was alone she sang... But her mind wandered. The image of the young man kept rising before her eyes and I have to confess that, for an expert spinner, she broke her thread pretty often.

— Antonín Leopold Dvořák, "The Golden Spinning Wheel," 1896 *

CHAPTER ELEVEN

The whirl of the wheel infused the silence of her family's apartment as Oaklee's feet treadled with familiar rhythm. Nimble fingers toyed with the carded alpaca fleece. She pinched the drafted portions with confidence as the soft, lumpy threads twisted and spun from her fingertips. The fibers were dark and lustrous, destined to be woven into a warm cloak that would grace the shoulders of a growing child or perhaps a blanket to place into the storehouse. Dust motes magically twinkled in the encroaching sunlight as the spinning wheel disturbed the air with each rotation.

A yawn quietly escaped, interrupting her spinning for but a moment. Oaklee had not slept well, too emotionally overwhelmed to rest easy. Shadows had played across the room and held her mind captive until she finally rose from her warm covers. She had placed an ear against the cool cob surface of the wall, hoping to hear Fillion from beyond—but he remained silent. Sleep eventually claimed her, and her eyes flickered open hours later to discover her palm still embraced the surface of the wall, her other hand pressing the linden leaf against her heart.

A figure walked by the window as she spun, drawing her attention. Oaklee's heart momentarily galloped until she realized it was not her father, and then her spirits fell.

She logically accepted that he would never return, but her emotions cried out in defiance. His voice seeped into her thoughts, whispering, "Good morning, *ma chère*," with such clarity that she would pause and inspect the empty apartment, waiting with excitement to see his smiling face. Instead, the dappled sunlight streamed through the latticed window, painting the floor in diamonds.

The wooden wheel continued its mechanical song of merriment as she forced her thoughts to settle upon happier times. The ache born of grief eased for a few blessed moments as the familiar whir captured her soul in an embrace long overdue. Oh, how she cherished these moments early in the morning. Oaklee oft rushed home directly from Mass to enjoy the quietude of the rising sun as it stretched upon the planked, wooden floor until its warm fingers touched her wheel. By then, the household would have returned after breaking their fast, and she could retreat to the Great Hall to savor the remnant morsels of the morning meal without the demand of conversation before the landscape fully awakened to a fresh day.

A hint of blue in the corner caught her eye, and Oaklee smiled as a modest cluster of forget-me-nots spilled over a wooden tumbler upon the cupboard. Her brother most likely picked the dainty wildflowers for Ember, a way to request her faithfulness, enduring love, and to never forget him as her lover. 'Twas a medieval tradition many grooms employed to woo and romance their new brides, one she found endearing and, at the same time, rather scandalous. The flowers were beautiful, and her mind wandered, eventually resting upon the unusual blue of Fillion's eyes. She nibbled her bottom lip, enjoying the sensations that filled her with such unbidden thoughts, when the yarn snapped from too much twist.

"Oh, drat!" A heavy sigh escaped and her hands collapsed into her lap.

She studied the shadows to assess the time, irritated with how just a single thought of him flustered her to distraction. She needed to maintain her wits with such a long, laborious day ahead. Following the breakfast meal, Oaklee would spend the morning in the meadow by The Forge to clean and card new bags of wool as well as to process the remaining bundles of flax from harvest last. She left the wheel and carefully lay prepared fleece into her work basket and covered the top with a square piece of hemp cloth.

A multitude of tasks and thoughts arranged and rearranged themselves in her mind as she ambled toward her bedchamber, untying the apron and gingerly pulling it over her head. The iron ring to her door knocked against the hewn wood as she shut it, and the sound filled her chamber as she shimmied out of the garment reserved for Mass and finer occasions.

The morning air still held a chill, and she rubbed her arms as she walked to the oak chest and folded the woolen tunic dress inside, dolefully caressing the wrought iron oak tree upon the lid. Limp and lifeless, her everyday work dress hung upon a peg near the door and Oaklee fingered the linen before maneuvering the piece over her heavy chemise, tying it off with an old tablet-woven belt. She made a mental note to grab the apron prior to leaving so that she did not need to borrow one from the shop, which reeked of wood smoke and sweat.

Oaklee plaited her long tresses and then pinned the braids into a crown around her head, adding sprigs of lavender from the wreath she wore yesterday for the Celebration of Life. She was now officially ready for the work day with a few moments to spare.

Purpose filled her with peace while memories added weight to the responsibilities Oaklee would shoulder as she rejoined the community in daily activities. Everything felt the same and yet entirely different. How could this dichotomy exist? And yet, it must. When she arrived at The Forge to gather her tools, Coal would not be there to greet her. His rascally smile and ready quip would not fill her morning with laughter this day, or the next. Nor would her father poke his head in the apartment door to ensure she stopped to enjoy the gathering hour where the community joined in fellowship mid-day over a meal before returning to their duties. Her father knew her penchant for losing herself to a task and to her wandering imagination.

She would not crash. She would not allow the gluttonous floor to consume her as grief and peace battled for dominance over this day. Since The Exchange, Oaklee had pushed hard against moments such as these, refusing to fall deeper and deeper into the dark hole that had become her life. Nevertheless, fatigue from endless battles, such as now, exhausted her resolve, and she eased her body onto the cot, staring absently at the whitewashed mud wall.

Her fingers inched their way beneath her pillow and pulled out the linden leaf she discovered in Ember's old room last eve. In sullen reverie, Oaklee lowered her head upon the pillow and curled up atop her blankets as she caressed the leaf. Visions of Fillion flitted across the landscape of her mind once more. The geodesic night sky had accentuated the vulnerability and torment etched into his features, lighting his skin with a faint, silvery glow. His aggrieved and despondent tones, spoken in hoarse whispers and gritty shouts, shook the boughs of her heart and the various leaves of emotion tumbled and churned in the mighty wind that gusted from his life's storm.

She blinked as the heart-shaped leaf fanned her face while her hand meandered back and forth in wave-like motions. Green blurred through the air, holding the attention of her heavy thoughts as they settled onto the rather unexpected presence of the leaf itself. His apologetic gesture was beautiful and heartfelt, and the metaphor far surpassed a handshake or age-old words. It was as if he understood her language and wished to demonstrate his respect as he simultaneously professed his quest for love and truth. To make such a vulnerable declaration, after how she had responded to his angry outpouring, cost him much. And she felt honored by his sacrifice to demonstrate care for her feelings.

Oaklee rolled to her back with closed eyes as a wistful smile warmed her features and her arms lazily draped across the cot in surrender. Her father's words filled her mind, as his deep voice said, "From our first breath we cry out to be loved. Love is the meaning of life, Oaklee—and without it, life is meaningless."

Yesterday eve on the stone bridge, her heart shattered as she understood Fillion's anguished confessions. The Outsider was akin to an injured animal, frightening her, most especially when he touched her body while whispering provocative words in her ear. Coal's kiss showed desperation for her affection, but Fillion's touch showed desperation for control. She felt violated, and girlhood vanished that instant as womanhood responded to his advances and then demanded he view her as more than flesh for his pain and pleasure. His only saving grace was that his raw, unloved state pulled her toward him with such force that the experience had irrevocably changed her.

Her father's words suddenly had depth and seized the numerous threads dangling from the fabric of her life, weaving in a new color of enlightenment. Love's thread looped, knotted, and intertwined every individual she knew, each soul adding to the beautiful tapestry that depicted her community, highlighting their intrinsic value and worth.

Did Fillion fully realize how he had cheapened her? Could he respect any boundary line she drew?

Any revolution he sparked would be for revenge rather than for the heart of her community, and she refused to see her home and way of life altered for ignoble reasons. He may not wish for his inheritance nor care much for the community. But her family did. And both her mother and father died serving each resident of New Eden. By fighting for Fillion, she also fought for her home—they were entangled truths.

Oaklee rested the linden leaf against her mouth and nose, inhaling its subtle fragrance, much milder than the spring blossoms that perfumed the dome and intoxicated the bees. She sighed. Fillion possessed a beautiful soul despite his guarded, vulgar outward nature. His true affection was quiet, unassuming, and gentle, never bringing attention to himself, but rather to the person to whom he opened up to. She thought of the fingers, soft and kind, which held her hair when she grew sick in the Cave; the wine he poured for her when she could no longer manage Saturday night; the wildflower he offered her in The Orchard near The Rows; and the linden leaf pressed to her throbbing heart.

Another sigh escaped her body just as a loud crack, followed by a crash, echoed throughout the apartment. Oaklee sat up with an involuntary squeak, clutching the leaf tight against her body. The sound of snapping wood and multiple items hitting the floor filled the emptiness of her home once more and the linden leaf fluttered to the floor. Oaklee flattened a hand against her chest as her heart attempted to beat out of her body, forcing her to concentrate on deepening her shallow breaths. She crawled off her bed to pick up the leaf, then hid it beneath her pillow with trembling fingers.

Slowly, as if traveling through water, Oaklee approached her door and opened it the tiniest sliver to peek into the hallway. She did not sense movement and eased out, staring wide-eyed toward the living room. Nothing moved and the eerie silence after such a ruckus made the tiny hairs on the nape of her neck rise. She was not sure what she expected to find, but nothing prepared her for the pile of debris littering the planked floor.

The spinning wheel no longer sat in the corner, but lay smashed on its side, splinters and parts scattered to every corner. The front door remained wide open and she stared in a terrorized trance as a scream traveled through her entire body, yet refused to pass her lips. She knelt in the remains and caressed what was once one of the flyer's maidens as her shoulders shook. Then, she reached out and scooped up the bobbin, still dressed in black yarn.

Footsteps raced toward the door and she heard Laurel's shout in excitement, "Oaklee!" Her sister neared the door and said, "Miss Tabitha had her baby last night and..." Her little voice halted with a loud gasp. "Whatever happened?"

Oaklee fingers wrapped around the bobbin and squeezed. "Where is Leaf?"

"He was summoned to the rainforest."

"By whom?"

"By a gardener. Two ficus trees need trimming and they wished to consult the Earth Element first."

"Please fetch Leaf." Oaklee turned and faced her sister as she contorted her face to hold in the forming hurricane. Gale force winds of justice were about to blow mightily and it took all her mental faculties to contain it. "Do not stop for anyone, no matter what they may say or request. Only stop when you find Leaf and then tell him I need his presence at The Forge immediately—it is of utmost importance. Do not share about the spinning wheel with anyone, not even Leaf. I wish to keep this news from the wrong ears. Do you understand?"

"You are scaring me." Laurel stepped over part of the wheel and its spokes, and placed her small arms around Oaklee's shoulders. "I am most sorry about your wheel. 'Twas it an accident? Oh, your heart must be filled with such bitter sorrow!" Her sister sniffed.

Oaklee pulled her sister away and held her arms. "We shall grieve later, dear one, but now we need Leaf. When you find him and deliver your message, I wish for you to cross your heart like this." She demonstrated the movements. "Our brother will know the significance of such a gesture and will act with haste."

"Yes, Willow," Laurel said with another sniff. "I shall run like the wind."

"Thank you, darling. I shall see you at The Forge."

She kissed Laurel's cheek and watched as her sister flew out of the apartment. And then Oaklee's body jerked as she inhaled a sharp, ragged breath, stifling a sob with two fingers pressed against her lips.

From her vantage, she studied the forest and wondered how the trees swayed and bent to the winds of change with faithful acceptance and ease. Predictability was within her grasp, then taken from her like everything else she had loved. Terror gripped her with unrelenting pressure, but she had to make her way to The Forge, and with as much grace and elegance as possible to ensure that if anyone watched her departure, they did not receive satisfaction from her distress.

She inspected the living room once more, squinting her eyes when an object glinted near what remained of her work basket. A small, rectangular card lay atop the upturned basket and she froze. Was this another Death Card? Was she marked? Oaklee swallowed back the rising panic. She crawled toward the basket and quailed at the familiar geometric designs.

With trembling fingers, she turned over the card and blinked rapidly, her pulse hammering in her throat. An image of a raven filled the top portion of the card while script filled the lower half. She read the card aloud with a whisper. "You are hereby cursed. A person, place, and thing in your life—objects of love—shall each experience death or damage to redeem your affliction. Only when the person, place, and thing have redeemed you shall the curse be lifted."

Oaklee flung the card away from her with a small scream and scooted back until she pressed against the wall, pulling her knees up to her chest as she rocked back and forth. "Oh dear Heavenly Father, let it not be so," she prayed over and over. Her fingers automatically flew to her prayer beads, and she fingered them one by one while whispering prayers under her breath.

Her eyes darted toward the opened door and latticed window. What had she done? She should never have sent Laurel out alone to fetch Leaf. She scrambled to her feet, snatched the card, and raced to the upper deck. Fresh air hit her face, igniting her memory of watchful eyes. She tucked the card into a pocket and smoothed her dress, pulling and wiping at the folds to appear natural. Then, as smoothly as possible, she shut the front door and turned toward the stairs, descending with a straight posture and head held high.

Rather than take the path through the forest, Oaklee trod along the trail that skirted the apartments to remain visible. Black clouds gathered inside her heart, but she wore a small smile as she dipped her head in greeting with various villagers.

"Willow!"

Oaklee shifted her eyes over the apartments, forest, and the smattering of individuals about their business. When she heard her name again, she tarried and nibbled on her bottom lip as Rain ran toward her.

"Willow, I was on my way to your apartment," the Daughter of Water said through heaving breaths. "Mother has requested your family's presence."

Oaklee stiffened as she touched the curse card in her pocket. Withdrawing her hand, she grabbed Rain's in concern. "Does she fare well?"

"No, she has waned considerably and her breaths are quite shallow." Tears pooled in Rain's eyes and she blinked. "Father believes she shall not make it through today."

"Oh my dear friend, how my heart fills with sorrow for you," Oaklee said. She gathered Rain in her arms. Thoughts of her spinning wheel and the card were pushed to the back of her mind as she stroked her friend's hair.

"I am most sorry, Willow. I do not deserve your kindness just now."

"Nonsense." Oaklee pulled away and brushed a strand of dark hair from Rain's face. She offered her friend a comforting smile.

"No, truly. Last week, I was most jealous of the attentions Coal bestowed upon you and resented your position, especially when you insulted him publicly. My comments during your brother's going-away gathering were ... oh, I am so embarrassed to recall what I said and did." Rain turned her face to the side as her cheeks pinked. "When I learned Coal left to prove his value to you, I ... I ... and then Corlan arrived and continually looks upon you as if you are the rising sun itself."

Oaklee widened her eyes and felt heat creep up her neck, but she quickly took hold of Rain's hands. "I do not carry any grievances toward you," she whispered. "Please, do not add to your sorrows."

"You needed my compassion, and instead I set out against you."

"We were all deranged from grief and fear last week."

"I feel so lonely," Rain said as she wiped her eyes. "I love my mother ardently and am thankful for every moment spent caring for her. But in my heart of hearts, I wish for a home of my own as my sister has made with Matthew. She is so happy and quite becoming with child." The Daughter of Water lowered her head. "Does this not make me the most spiteful of daughters? That I wish to start my own family whilst my mother suffers and lays dying?" Rain gently beat her breast with her fist, as an anguished sob released and she choked out, "So you see, I am most undeserving of your kindness." She drew in a deep breath and splayed her fingers as if pushing away the air. "I must away. I need to inform Connor that his family's presence is requested as well."

"Please allow me. I was heading to The Forge just now. May I do this simple task for you?" Oaklee pleaded with Rain with a quiet look, and Rain reluctantly nodded assent. "Have the Kanes been notified?"

"Yes."

"Are there any others that your mother wishes to see?"

"Corlan."

Oaklee's eyebrows shot up and she could not hide the shock from her face.

"It baffles me, but Mother was most insistent, muttering words of how she owes it to her friend to bless him as well." Rain shook her head and wiped away more tears. "I do believe she has lost her senses for I cannot imagine what she means."

"I shall inform him, rest assured." Oaklee offered another comforting smile, even though the fear swelled quickly inside of her. Did Norah refer to Della as her friend? Did she know Corlan's true identity? And if so, did any others in the biodome?

"Thank you," Rain whispered.

"Of course." Oaklee reached out and held Rain's hands once more, gently squeezing before letting go. A sad smile graced Rain's features as she turned and disappeared down the trail.

A slow breath left Oaklee in a shaky sigh, and she resumed her mission to reach The Forge, the hurricane gaining strength, pulsating with fury for release. Another she loved was being taken from her. Although she knew the cancer would claim Norah eventually, the grief she had known this past week renewed with a fierce ache.

A babe was born last night, its cries infusing the atmosphere with its sweet innocence. And a good woman would breathe her last this day, the atmosphere carrying her blessed words of love as she left this world for another. Between them was another who exhaled angry breaths amid the violent wreckage of her spinning wheel.

Oaklee filled her lungs with the air of her community's life, adding to the gale force winds that would blow.

Nichols: _You ask an interesting question, one I'll admit my team has considered greatly. So, first off, yes, I am very familiar with Zimbardo's prison study. That was the 1970s. Our thinking has evolved since then. Is New Eden Township a similar social experiment? Only in that role-playing is used to reach the game objective: building a sustainable community that spans twenty-five years and withstands the symptoms of isolation, confinement, and extreme environment syndrome. Although there is a social class system, the nobility only possesses certain rights of respect out of their managerial positions. But all must work, all must contribute, and all must care for the community. To eradicate any sense of wealth, currency will not exist in the biodome. There will not be a have and have-not system. Each job and function is considered equally as important. It is a 'commune' mentality, the best approach when building an isolated system. In the prison study, the positions of guard and prisoners were role-played to such extremes that violent and aggressive behaviors naturally developed and the experiment was shut down within six days as a result. There are no social factors within my experiment that should naturally foster violent and aggressive tendencies. Rather, we hope to obtain the exact opposite._

— Hanley Nichols, _Atoms to Adams Daily Show_, August 15, 2030

CHAPTER TWELVE

The orange flames of The Forge came into view. Fillion slowed his steps along the path and searched for the Herbalist's shop. His eyes skimmed over the doors on the first level, locating the wrought iron herb garden design. To think, Fillion practically lived next door to the shop, and Leaf only told him over breakfast today.

The village, the main square housing all the merchant shops, teemed with residents busy socializing and working. People openly stared at him. The dark, mysterious stranger had come to town. What a joke. It almost made him laugh. He guessed no one ever taught them it was rude to stare at strangers. Why would they need that social courtesy? But he was used to being on display and a pro at ignoring the human race. Annoying.

Fillion angled around a small crowd of girls carrying baskets of laundry. He reached the shop and gave a light knock. A crowd of eyes bored into his back and he studied his shoes while he waited. The door opened with a low creak and revealed a middle-aged woman with long brown hair, pulled back in a braid and draping down her back. Fillion didn't mean to start. But he had pictured an old crone, bartering with a witch for New Eden's version of cigarettes. A pungent savory smell wafted from inside and his nose itched, feeling a sneeze form as the potpourri gained strength. The Herbalist wiped her hands on an apron and then gestured for him to follow her inside.

"Corlan is it?" She walked toward a wooden counter. "My name is Joannah."

Fillion walked in, ducking his head through the entry. His eyes squinted as they adjusted to the dimness of her humble shop. Bunches of herbs hung from the rafters, and neatly labeled clay pots lined floor-to-ceiling shelves behind the counter.

"I am honored by your visit." Joannah dipped into a curtsy and graced him with a kind smile.

"Thanks." He blinked. "Leaf mentioned that you have more rolling papers and herbs for smoking?"

"Yes. Do you suffer from withdrawals?"

Fillion nodded his head and peered out the window. He didn't want to admit a weakness, especially to a stranger. And he felt weird knowing that he was conversing with someone who knew the real world, but pretended it didn't exist.

"What flavors do you enjoy?"

"I've no clue. Only smoked one kind of herb until I came inside New Eden. Have any of that?" He gave her a small lopsided grin and she smiled in reply while shaking her head no. He shrugged. "You choose. I liked your selection last time." Fillion pulled out the tinder box from his leather travel bag and handed it to her.

"I shall have your supplies ready shortly."

"Wait. How do I pay for everything?"

Another kind smile formed on her face. "There is no currency in New Eden, sir."

"Right. So do we barter a trade or something?"

"Your contribution during your stay shall provide for my sustenance and comfort, payment enough."

With graceful strides, Joannah walked out from behind the counter toward him. She placed a hand on his arm and studied his eyes for several seconds, and he stiffened—too afraid to look away and too paranoid to maintain eye contact. The room was small, and the interaction was far too intimate. Even for him.

"Love has little to do with romance and everything to do with honor."

"Um, sure." What the hell? Fillion turned his head as she walked away, focusing on his foot as he scuffed the compacted dirt floor. The words floated around in his head in an attempt to anchor to something he understood. But there was nothing. Honor, for the most part, was a meaningless idea in his world. It didn't exist. Not like here, at least. Romance, however, was an industry that sponsored every relationship, every product, and every experience.

A clay jar clunked onto the wooden counter, snapping Fillion out of his thoughts. He was definitely out of his element, and he needed to give his mind an occupation. Turning around, he drifted toward the corner of the shop and perused the labels inked onto clay jars and containers of various sizes. The jar labeled "lavandula angustifolia" piqued his interest. Lifting the strange fabric that sealed it, he leaned forward and took a whiff. Fillion enjoyed one more sniff before gently placing the waxy fabric over the top.

"Your order is ready, sir."

He started at the sound of her voice and casually looked over his shoulder, trying to act cool. Fillion meandered back toward the counter and Joannah lifted the lid to his tinder box when he neared. Inside were rolling papers, two small clay vials, a cloth sack, and five joints already prepared for him.

"One is sweet with spicy undertones and the other is savory. Try both and do let me know which you prefer and I shall keep a ready supply of your favorite flavor on hand. The cloth sack contains St. John's wort tea to help with the withdrawals. Bring it to the Great Hall and they shall boil water and steep the tea on your behalf." Joannah handed him the box. "I do not have a candle lit at present. The Forge is next door, as you know, should you wish to enjoy a smoke immediately. Connor will not mind your company, I am sure."

"*Arigatou gozaimasu.*" Fillion wanted to roll his eyes with the shaky sound of his voice. Joannah blinked curiously, but didn't appear bothered by his language slip. "Thanks. I appreciate everything." He took out one of the joints, rolled it between his thumb and forefinger, and then placed the tinder box in his bag.

"Good day, Corlan." Joannah dipped into another curtsy.

"Yeah. Same to you." Unable to resist, he gave a shallow, tight bow and said, "*Yoi ichinichi o.*"

In quick strides, he ducked through the opening and exited into the morning light. His eyes squinted against the sudden brightness as he ran a hand through his hair. The Forge was a stone's throw away. He rolled the joint between his fingers, ignoring the curious stares.

That morning, he had found a note just inside his door with the cryptic message, "I know who you are," scribbled across it. Really? That was supposed to terrify him? The entire world knew who he was. And with his handle and resemblance to Brianna, it was only a matter of time. Whatever. Now that Willow knew the truth after his monstrous purge, his worst fear had passed. Everyone in the dome would know who he was eventually anyway.

Connor emerged from The Forge to toss a tool into a bucket of water and spotted him. The sizzling sound made an irritating hiss. The biodome was strangely quiet. The flat and dull quality made Fillion feel dizzy at times. He never realized how much ambient noise was in the outside world until he came inside these panes.

"Corlan, good to see you." Connor slowed in front of him and looked around. "Are you on your own?"

"Leaf ditched us. He was summoned to the rainforest." Fillion tried to smile politely, but he was irritated. The Son of Earth wasn't his babysitter or interpreter, and he was tired of everyone treating him as if Leaf was necessary for his survival. "Joannah said I could light up at The Forge?" Fillion lifted up his joint, feeling a little foolish.

"Come, keep me company. We can talk without Leaf's presence," Connor said.

Fillion almost replied "You think?" but kept his mouth shut. Damn, it was hard. Instead, he tried the politeness thing again. "Want a smoke?"

"No, not at this moment. I shall take you up on your offer another time, though."

They entered The Forge and Fillion had to adjust his eyes once again. This would take some getting used to. His first impulse was to search the wall for a switch, making his fingers twitch.

Connor picked up a burning coal with a pair of iron tongs, motioning with his head for Fillion to approach. Fillion placed the joint in his mouth and then leaned forward, inhaling as the hemp paper began to crinkle and smoke. God, that felt good. It never got old. A pleasant taste filled his mouth as he inhaled again. Savory herbs danced on his tongue. Was that sage? Hints of oregano? A thin trail of smoke curled past his lips as he exhaled and Fillion closed his eyes as he leaned against a wall. A joint and a dark corner. Glorious.

"Difficult day, is it not?"

A scraping sound echoed in the shop and Fillion opened his eyes. With the tongs, Connor moved some of the coals around aimlessly. A drawn expression darkened the older man's face as the orange light flickered and intensified with the fresh oxygen. Coal. Did Connor miss his son?

"Yeah. God, I hope there's alcohol tonight at dinner again. I could use a drink or two. Shit. I could use a whole jug." Fillion thunked his head against the wall with a heavy sigh. Why did he just share that? He was a socially awkward idiot. He really shouldn't be allowed to make small talk.

A humored smile formed on Connor's face. But the Fire Element kept his focus on the furnace. "My heartfelt apologies," he said in a teasing tone. "Wine is only served on Sundays and during celebratory feasts." The furnace crackled as the silence ticked away. Fillion puffed on his joint instead of replying with meaningless conversation. Eventually, Connor continued. "Do you possess any Old World skills?"

Fillion lifted his head from the wall. "Not much. Most of my skills are from the good old present." Mack was the only one besides his immediate family who knew of his non-tech trade skill, and only because he spent many summers with Fillion's great-grandfather, too. "I can do some woodworking."

Connor quickly turned his head. The Fire Element's eyes narrowed slightly before he turned around and walked toward the opposite end of the shop. Fillion watched through the haze of smoke as he exhaled slowly. He flicked the ashes into the furnace and enjoyed another drag. Shuffling sounds padded in the dim shop as Connor lumbered toward him, holding a worn box.

"This belonged to Della when she was a little girl. It was hand-carved and crafted by her Grandpa Corlan, a man I shall never forget."

The cinnamon tones of the wood warmed with the firelight. Fillion imagined his great-grandpa in his wood shop, a master carpenter who labored and built custom furniture every day until his dying breath. Fillion spent his summers and many weekends with him at his cabin, fishing, hunting, and building in the wood shop. He was the only adult who ever made Fillion feel like he mattered, gifting him with a childhood.

Every evening, Grandpa Corlan would pour a shot of whiskey and sit on a log round, toasting the sun as it set behind the hills. Even when it rained. Fillion used to think the man was crazy to sit in the rain and toast the cloudy sky. But his great-grandpa would insist, with a wink, that it was an Irish tradition, a believable explanation in his thick brogue.

Fillion was twelve, spending the night at Mack's house, when his mom called with the news that Grandpa Corlan had died. Both he and Mack had cried—the only time they had ever cried together. As a tribute, Mack snuck down to his parent's liquor cabinet and poured both he and Fillion a shot of whiskey. They climbed out of his bedroom window and onto the roof and toasted the moon, for the sun had already set. They felt so damn poetic and grown-up. And then they choked the amber liquid down, coughing and shuddering with the burn.

Fillion took another long draw on his joint. He tried to push away the memories. "Why are you giving this to me?" he managed to ask, smoke billowing around his face.

"Della gifted this chest to me on Moving Day as a family keepsake for my first wife and me as we began our new life and a new family inside New Eden. I pray it shall comfort your homesickness. I know Della would wish for you to have it." Connor extended the chest toward him.

Fillion looked up at Connor. Did Connor know who he really was? Of course he did. He was married to Brianna, after all. Placing the joint in his mouth, Fillion took the chest and held it with both hands, his thumb brushing over the smooth surface. Opening the lid, he found a single clump of coal, and his throat tightened as he peeked over the rim at Connor.

"Fill the box with memories, Corlan, and when you leave us, take it with you so that you may remember the family you have left behind." Connor placed a large hand on Fillion's shoulder and gave a gentle squeeze. Drawing in a deep breath, Fillion turned toward the fire and blinked. "You look so much like Dylan," Connor said. "The resemblance is … uncanny."

Fillion hugged the box tighter against his body as he took another long drag on the joint. The large hand dropped from his shoulder and Connor turned away. Fillion flicked the ashes.

"When you walked into the meadow it was as if a ghost had appeared. I would almost believe Hanley planned that on purpose. Joel dies, and suddenly Dylan rises from the ashes." He slid a quick glance toward Fillion to gauge his response. So Fillion morphed into a posture of indifference, returning to the wall and placing a foot behind him as he leaned back. He shrugged. "It was planned too perfectly," Connor said.

Fillion expected a follow-up question and relaxed when none came. The drawn expression returned to Connor's face as he picked up the tongs and moved the coals around, pausing to watch the glowing embers grow brighter. Coal and Ember. The Fire Element missed his children.

Did Hanley miss him? Fillion knew the answer to that, and he bit the inside of his cheek as the heartache threatened to overwhelm him once again. His dad was probably relieved of the burden. Not that he ever showed any concern.

"Let's skip the charades," Fillion blurted. "We both know my name isn't Corlan." Connor didn't even look up. He just nodded knowingly. "I don't know if Hanley planned it like you say," Fillion said, "but he's always plotting something."

"Why are you really here, Fillion Nichols, Son of Eden?" The Fire Element shifted his attention from the furnace and faced him.

A shiver ran through Fillion's body. He placed his great-grandpa's chest on a nearby table and moved in front of Connor. "What the hell do you mean by Son of Eden?"

"It is your honorary title, given to you upon your birth. You are a Noble son of both worlds."

An unamused chuckle left Fillion as he shot Connor an arrogant look. "I promise you, I'm entirely of my world."

"Indeed. That is not to what I refer."

"Then enlighten me in your anachronistic medieval hippie ways, oh wise sage." Fillion rolled his eyes. "I don't want anything from my dad, including a stupid title."

"Happy for you, then, that it was not your father who gifted you with the title." The small, humored smile appeared on Connor's face again. The Fire Element sized him up. "I bestowed this title upon you when you were a month old. Hanley and Della approved, as did The Elements."

"Doesn't change how I feel about it."

"You are rather defensive over something you know very little about. Since your arrival, you become disagreeable whenever someone in our community wishes to pay you respect. Why do you believe you are unworthy of such honor?"

Last night returned in a rush and Fillion refused to rehash his anti-self speech to Connor. Instead, he shuffled on his feet. "I've done nothing to earn anyone's respect."

"Finally, a serious answer from you." Connor warmed with a kind smile. "Let us make a deal, you and I." He extended his large, charcoal-stained hand. "I shall not play games with you, and I expect the same in return."

"The irony of your statement nullifies the very root of your request." Fillion puffed on his joint and shook his head with irritation.

Connor laughed. "Indeed. You will have to forgive me for I have not spoken your ways and been part of your world in so long. You, *Son of Eden*, have much to teach me and I you."

"Fine." Fillion shook Connor's hand. "How am I deserving of such an epic title?"

"You are a Son of both worlds. One day soon, you shall hold New Eden Township in the palm of your hands as you stand firmly upon the soil of Earth, the original Eden."

Fillion sighed and a small stream of smoke escaped his lips. "Don't get cute. New Eden is firmly upon the soil of Earth."

"Granted. However, a whole generation may not fully understand this truth. You are their *real* connection to the Eden beyond these walls, their champion, their protector, and their provider."

Are you ready to discover what is real? The hologram's words from Saturday morning echoed freshly in Fillion's mind and another chill coursed through him.

"I still fail to understand how this became my problem?"

"It is your birthright."

Fillion swallowed and slowly met Connor's eyes. "I'm ... I'm not fit to lead. OK?"

"And why is that?"

"It's complicated." Fillion threw the butt of his joint into the furnace. "Is this interview over?"

"Not quite." Connor crossed his large arms over his chest. "You shall begin carpentry duties on the morrow, working under me in this shop."

"Not what I thought you were going to say," Fillion muttered. "What time do I report for active duty?"

"After you break your fast each morning."

"Deal."

Connor offered a knowing smile. The expression unnerved Fillion and he looked down at his feet. The Fire Element returned his attention to the furnace and picked up the tongs, once again absently shuffling the hot coals around. "What is Hanley's agenda? Please do not drag this out, either. I wish for a direct answer."

"Works for me. But my question first: Was Joel murdered?"

Connor drew his eyebrows together and cleared his throat as his face fell. His eyes nervously flitted around the shop and then he answered quietly, "Della received my message?"

"Too ambiguous."

Connor sighed. "You have your father's mind."

"Lucky me." Fillion angled his head away from Connor, reining in the instant anger. God, he hated being compared to his dad, especially as a compliment.

"We have a tradition in New Eden. When a member of the community passes away, someone close to the family is assigned to place a well-known object of value in the pocket of the deceased for the household's representative to publicly discover and display prior to cremation."

Fillion couldn't hold back his disturbed expression. His stomach sickened as he remembered Leaf's story of how the young noble found the Death Card. The idea of a cremation freaked Fillion out. It was so gross. But Connor didn't seem to care or notice, instead continuing without missing a beat.

"I was given Hanley's Death Card—the one he used as a Gamemaster to permanently remove characters from the game we played once upon a time—with instructions to use it should I ever suspect someone was murdered. Most especially if I suspected it was due to ICE symptoms. Jeff records every detail of every death ceremony and procedure for your mother's psychological team and your parents read every report. Although I planted the card in Joel's pocket for Leaf to discover and display before the community, the Son of Earth failed to do so. I was most certain the card burned with Joel and, since his cremation, continually worried about how to relay such a message to Della without gaining unfavorable attention or alerting the media."

Fillion felt the air whoosh out of his lungs. "What the...? Oh my god." He blinked rapidly, trying to contain the surge of shock and disbelief pulsing through his system. "So my dad didn't kill Joel?"

The blacksmith dropped the tongs and narrowed his eyes, considering Fillion's words. "You believe your father is capable of murder?"

Fillion rubbed his temples as his pulse throbbed, pushing back the paranoia that wanted to root itself in his mind. Why the hell didn't his dad tell him about the card's origins or history? In fact, his dad outright stated that he didn't know why the card was in the dome when Fillion confronted him. Fillion thought over Connor's story, not sure if he should fully trust the explanation. Was his dad playing him? Wouldn't be the first time. He'd caught his dad in so many lies it was ridiculous.

"Yeah, I do believe Hanley is capable of murder," Fillion said through gritted teeth. "He's locked you all up in here to see who lives and dies, right? Or has New Eden's motto completely brainwashed you?" Fillion pinched the bridge of his nose with his thumb and index finger, closing his eyes tight. "How do I know you didn't kill Joel?"

"I would never commit murder."

"Well, that solves everything. Case closed." Fillion pinned Connor with a hard stare. "You may have convinced everyone else that honor guarantees truth in your little piece of utopia, but not me."

Connor's face tensed even more. "I have nothing to gain by killing Joel."

"Sure. You'll just marry your daughter off instead because you have absolutely nothing to gain. Less messy that way. Convenient." Fillion looked away as if bored with the conversation. "For those without daughters to pawn off, what's the gain?"

"I advise you to hold back on such accusations with others." Connor's face darkened. "I am forgiving, as I know you are intentionally prodding my pride, but others are not. Son of Eden, you walk a dangerous line."

Fillion glared back. "I don't give a damn! I'm too much of a coward to take my own life, so murder me now and put me out of my misery." Connor's face drained of color, and Fillion looked away. He hadn't meant to confess so much. He thunked the back of his head against the wall. Stupid. So very, very stupid.

They remained silent for a couple of minutes. Then Connor softly spoke up. "You know what Joel's life is worth as you are part of the same value system."

Fillion formed an arrogant smile to cover up his feelings. "There's still the problem of heirs. Joel has three."

"Indeed." The Fire Element's eyes remained steady, but Fillion noted the muscles in the man's face tensed. Connor either didn't know about the fake deaths, or he wouldn't tell, or he was still trying to figure out Fillion's unchecked response. Fillion didn't know the man well enough to judge his reaction, either, so he decided to poke around in other ways.

Mack had made no headway so far, so he'd question the Insider.

"How many people have Scrolls or personal forms of technology inside the dome?"

A ghost of a reaction formed on Connor's face. "And how does this question connect to Joel's murder?"

"Probably doesn't. Just curious."

"Did Hanley tell you there were personal forms of technology inside New Eden?"

"No. Why?"

"Same reason as you, curiosity." When Fillion didn't offer a reply, Connor placed his hands on his hips. "Now, entertain my questions. What is Hanley's agenda?"

Fillion continued his bored expression. "Project success at all costs, even it means his friends die to achieve that goal. He knows Joel was murdered, and he refuses to do anything about it."

"Pardon?" Connor drew his brows together. "How did he conclude Joel was murdered?"

"How did you?" Fillion flung the words back with a faint, cocky smile and a raised eyebrow. "For all I know you're playing me and everyone else."

The shop doors burst open and Willow stood in the door frame, golden sunlight spilling around her form. She wore her hair like a crown. Fillion stilled, noting that Willow's complexion had changed to a sickly shade of white. As she wobbled toward Connor, she sucked in deep breaths. Connor ran over and cupped her face as he silently questioned her with his eyes. The image of fatherly tenderness and protection mystified Fillion, and he wondered if perhaps he had Connor figured all wrong.

"Norah does not fare well and has requested the presence of our families posthaste," she said, a tear slowly trailing down her cheek. Willow gulped again and skittishly shifted on her feet, and Fillion realized she wanted to freak out and was holding it all in. Her eyes twitched as they snapped from one object to another. Like the very corners of the shop might manifest into something dark and dangerous. What was she afraid of? His heart sank, hoping it wasn't him.

The blacksmith slowly dropped his hands. He steadied himself, then slumped, as his chin nearly touched his chest. Fillion was baffled by the displays of grief.

He had never been around a dying person, or a corpse. A memorial wasn't held for Grandpa Corlan. Only his mom and dad went to the funeral home to pick up the ashes. Funerals were rare events anymore. People had online friends all over the globe and few in reality. So, death had become a tidy business in his world, an unseen event that piqued morbid curiosity but, in the end, was treated with the same detached insensitivity as everything else. People aren't real—they're bits of code, programmed commands, streaming snapshots of entertainment.

The older man sniffed, and rubbed his hands across his face. "Is Brianna aware?"

"No, My Lord. I came directly to The Forge."

"Thank you, Willow Oak. I shall gather my family for Norah's last words."

She dipped into a curtsy as Connor trundled past her, closing the large double wooden doors to The Forge with heavy, awkward movements, seeming to forget about Willow and Fillion in the process. Fillion remained in the dark corner, unsure if he should reveal his presence.

The Daughter of Earth carefully studied the entrance for several seconds before facing the furnace. She wrapped her arms around her stomach and began to cry. Shaky fingers reached up and swiped at the tears in furious motions as she straightened her shoulders and stiffened her body. Then, she let out a low, guttural scream, arms straight at her sides with fists clenched. She whipped around to grab an iron poker and slammed it across the wooden workbench. Unsatisfied, she whacked the workbench again and again. The iron rod slipped from her hand and landed with a thud. It seemed to catch her off guard and she stumbled back a few steps, staring with disbelief at the object of her wrath. Willow gulped, as if desperate for air once again, and then draped across the table with a mournful groan.

God, she was killing him. Fillion couldn't stay hidden a second longer.

"Willow," he whispered, and took hesitant steps into the amber light. She jumped back with a shriek, knocking his great-grandpa's chest onto the dirt floor. As he bent down to pick up the chest, Willow claimed the iron poker from the ground and aimed the point at his chest. Terror replaced all color in her face.

He placed the chest on the table and slowly raised his hands. He maintained an even gaze, willing her to focus on his face. When recognition hit her, Willow closed her eyes with a look of relief and placed a hand flat against her heart. The poker hit the dirt. Then anger flared.

"How dare you!" She pounded him with her fists, grunting with each hit. Fillion angled away and, as gently as possible, grabbed her arms, pinning them to her side. "Unhand me this instant!" she shouted, shaking her head wildly.

"No."

She screamed in response, so he held her arms tighter against her side. Fillion tensed when she tried to yank herself free, clenching his jaw as he held his ground. "You want me to let you go? Stop freaking out." He bent to become eye level and whispered, "Willow, look at me." She shook her head again in a frenzied temper. So he took in a deep breath and shouted, "Damn it! Look at me!"

Her body stilled and she found his eyes. A moan escaped her lips as her face contorted in anguish. Tears streamed down her face. What the hell was going on? This was beyond grief. He was pretty sure of it. Panic began to rise in Fillion as every worst-case scenario flashed in his mind, especially when she began to mumble.

"It is gone. Destroyed. Everyone and everything I love is taken from me. The card is right, I am indeed cursed."

"What are you talking about?"

"My spinning wheel—" She sputtered as she tried to hold back another forming sob. "Someone violently destroyed my spinning wheel this morning."

Fillion's muscles tensed, but he eased his grip on her arms. She rubbed at the tender spots where his fingers had been, her eyes sweeping around the shop. "Did they hurt you … in any way?" He was embarrassed, asking her this question in light of how he treated her last night, but he had to know.

Willow gently shook her head and then hugged her arms over her chest as the tears started up again. Anger he would understand, but she was in full blown fight-or-flight mode.

"Did you say a card was right? What card?"

With fidgety movements, she pulled a playing card from her pocket and held it up for him to see. There was a picture of a raven, but he focused on the words. He read the inscription again as rage hit his bloodstream. Remaining calm was necessary for Willow's sake, though. So, he focused on each word as he computed the info at rapid speed. If Connor used Hanley's Death Card, whose card was this? His mind swore with yet another mystery, hoping it was tied to the others.

"This isn't real. You know that, right? It's just a ploy from whoever is leading this invisible faction to bully you."

"My father's death is real. Norah dying is real. The destruction of my spinning wheel is real."

"No, I mean that you're *not* cursed. It's a terror tactic."

She lowered her eyes and nervously wove a strand of hair on her finger. "Did my father die to redeem me? Or is Norah fulfilling this position? Or shall another?"

"Listen to me. No one has or will die to redeem you. It. Is. A. Lie. Any act of murder is on the murderer. You didn't bring this on your dad, Norah, or anyone else."

In a small voice, she asked, "How are you so certain?"

Firelight danced across her skin, flickered in her eyes, and turned her tears to liquid gold as they trailed down her face. He felt so powerless. As usual.

He stepped close, "Willow Oak Watson, I would *never* lie to you about something as serious as this. I'll figure out who is doing this to your family and take care of it. Promise." Her face softened and her lips parted as she held his eyes. "If I could go back in time and change how we met, how I treated you last night, I would. But I can't. I don't ever expect you to trust me. Or like me." Breathless, he stammered, "Just know I'd ... I'd do *anything* for you."

Time suspended as his confession breathed warmly between them. Wood crackled in the heat of the fire. He let his thoughts drift into the unknown. He was gone. Fallen off the edge of reason. Lost. Never to recover. And then he resisted the urge to roll his eyes, realizing how pathetically lovesick he appeared. God, how pathetic. He'd never hear the end of it from Mack.

Sunlight slivered into the shop as the door to The Forge creaked open and Laurel's approaching voice piped through. Fillion and Willow jerked farther apart and faced the door.

"Please do not share with Leaf," Willow whispered hurriedly. "I shall do so after Norah's vigil."

Fillion nodded. "Your secrets are always safe with me, Maiden."

"Thank you, My Lord," she replied quietly, watching the door as it opened further. "For *everything*. Even last night." She turned her head toward her shoulder and lowered her eyes, and he knew she was blushing. "Your secrets are always safe with me as well."

Diffidence hit him, and he needed to move. Fillion casually picked up his great-grandpa's chest and sauntered toward the door as Leaf propped it open. "Running to my apartment for a sec," Fillion said. "I'll be outside if you need me for anything."

Leaf nodded, squinting his eyes as he took in Willow's shrunken posture and blotchy, tear-stained face. Laurel ran over and wrapped her arms around Willow's waist with a frightened expression. Willow looked up at her brother and, in a jittery voice, began sharing about Norah.

Love has little to do with romance and everything to do with honor.

The Herbalist's words played on repeat in Fillion's heart. His thumb brushed over the wooden chest as he walked to his apartment. The bed exhaled a quiet groan when he sat down. He opened the lid to the chest. The lump of coal crowded a corner. He thought of the young man who had left, sacrificing life as he knew it to help protect another. Fillion closed the lid, placed the chest under his bed, and left.

You are an entirely different character, son.

His father's words taunted him. But, strangely, they started to make sense. He couldn't be Fillion Nichols—social outcast and Internet sensation—while inside New Eden Township. A new reality awakened in him. In order to help the Watsons and to prove to Willow that he wasn't Outside trash, he needed to join the game in all seriousness. This was his kingdom, his birthright. And there'd be hell to pay if anyone burned it to the ground before he did.

ELEMENTS

This body is not me; I am not caught in this body,
I am life without boundaries,
I have never been born and I have never died.
Over there the wide ocean and the sky with many galaxies
All manifests from the basis of consciousness.
Since beginningless time I have always been free.
Birth and death are only a door through which we go in and out.
Birth and death are only a game of hide-and-seek.
So smile to me and take my hand and wave good-bye.
Tomorrow we shall meet again or even before.
We shall always be meeting again at the true source,
always meet again on the myriad paths of life.

— From the Sutra, "Given to the Dying" in the Buddhist scripture *Anguttara Nikāya*, translated 1935-36 *

CHAPTER THIRTEEN

D ark corners always suited Fillion. But not readily having a clock to mark time was making him mental. He
guessed two hours of silent vigil had passed as he drew
his legs up and rested his cheek on his knees. Until today, he
wasn't sure if he'd ever spent so much time in complete silence with absolutely nothing to do. "Shoot. Me. Now," he
muttered under his breath. Being left to his thoughts for so
long was never a good thing. The angst was choking him, and
he felt trapped in a box as the walls pressed in, inching closer
every second.

A yawn escaped and he turned his face into his arms and
closed his eyes. They didn't bring chairs to the Daniels
apartment like the other families. Fillion had convinced Leaf
to come straight to Norah, rather than return to the apartment where the spinning wheel still sat in shattered pieces.
He'd let Willow explain that one later, as he promised. So he

and Leaf were doomed to sit against a wall, allowing the women to occupy the available seats.

Back home it was every person for him or herself. If a girl walked in and no seats were available, then tough shit. Vintage notions of proper behavior annoyed him. No matter how many times he tried, he couldn't logically wrap his head around the purpose. He would bet every woman in this room wanted to be considered equal to the men. But they expected special treatment? Perhaps honor wasn't meant to be logical.

Yielding to the maddening boredom, he raised his head and scanned the room for the hundredth time. The Daniels residence looked similar to all other apartments he'd seen so far. Whitewashed cob walls brightened the space, reflecting light from the candles in wrought iron holders that hung around the room. Butter-yellow wax hardened into a drip off one of the saucers. To maintain privacy, the family had closed the shutters over the latticed windows. Large beams spanned the ceiling, carving rectangles. Fillion enjoyed the symmetry. The linear architecture made the chaos inside of him feel more organized.

What it did not help was the odor of unwashed bodies that assailed his nose. Herbal remedies meant to hide the body odor accomplished little. When did people bathe anyway? He hadn't seen a tub anywhere. For the last two mornings, Fillion had used a spare bucket to pump water from the well near The Rows. He dunked his head into the frigid water to wash his hair, then cleaned himself as much as possible with a rag, and wrapped up by shaving with the primitive kit he received.

Not showering was weird. There was no antiperspirant either. Instead, he was given a pouch that was essentially baking soda mixed with masculine smelling herbs. Or he could use citrus. Brushing teeth involved a similar powder, applied to twigs with frayed ends. It was awkward and he finally gave up, laughing, knowing he looked stupid. Hygiene was one of his obsessions and constantly being around dirty, sweaty bodies made his gag reflex act up.

As instructed, he left his bucket of filthy, soapy water outside his door. Assigned villagers took the buckets to various biodome buildings throughout the day to water plants, or to the wetland room, which he had yet to see. Actually, he hadn't seen anything other than this main biodome. The bucket returned to his doorstep right before the mandatory down time prior to dinner.

Apparently, once a week, only on his scheduled day, he was to leave his compost bucket for pick-up. Gross. He could kiss his great-grandpa for teaching him woodworking so he wasn't stuck with that shitty job. Fillion involuntarily shuddered, grimacing with the thought of how raunchy the air would be that day. He was starting to think that perhaps the sense of smell evolved out of these people for survival.

His eyes moved from objects to people, studying the grief-stricken faces. It was truly mysterious how everyone, including small kids, was willing to stop life and patiently wait for someone to die. It was seriously creepy. An awkward energy stifled the air of the room. Was it Norah's impending death? Or the animosity that continued to brood between The Elements and their families? Or both.

The tedium of a clockless existence, time ticking away in a slow, torturous rhythm, was turning his compassion to insensitivity. He needed a distraction.

His thoughts rested on the attorney as his first victim. Jeff darted his eyes around the room with a nervous twitch. In fact, Jeff had been a nervous wreck since the moment they first shook hands. Had he cracked?

Skylar stoically leaned on a wall across the room, only his eyes betraying that he felt anything. The Son of Wind kept stealing glances at Leaf, concern burning in his eyes. Did Skylar know something about the spinning wheel? Or the faction perhaps? On Saturday, anger radiated off of Skylar like water hitting hot pavement. This morning, the signs of distress were still there.

Connor buried his head in his hands, rubbing his face every so often. His large shoulders would rise and fall as a new wave of grief lapped against his frame. Fillion couldn't tell if Connor was simply putting on a good show.

Timothy barely blinked. A strange vibe, almost bordering on oppressive, pulsed all around him. Was he angry or in a state of shock? Fillion started counting, waiting for Timothy to blink, until he realized what he was doing. It was an internal game he often played with his father, who had the same body language glitch. Others were charmed into thinking Hanley was attentive and, therefore, cared. Bullshit.

Most everyone else was praying, eyes closed, fingering beads attached to belts, or meditating on the macabre dance of tiny flames near the window. Occasionally, someone would walk to the altar of candles erected in a corner of the room. Using a medieval version of a punk, they would light a candle, cross themselves, and then walk back to their seat. Did they think lighting a candle would prevent death? Fillion rolled his eyes with the thought. Superstitious Green Morons.

To calm the escalating emotions—again—he focused his attention on Willow, studying her as covertly as possible. Laurel perched on her lap, daintily curled up with arms tangled around her sister's neck. Willow mindlessly played with a strand of her sister's hair. Her henna-stained fingers twirled and spun. She stared absently at the flickering glow near where she sat. Small wisps of hair that had come loose from her braided crown framed her face. The swollen, red-tinged skin around her eyes appeared dark against her fair skin.

Willow's attention shifted from the candles to her sister's head, and then she glanced his direction. Warmth filled him as she continued to check him out. And he stared back. As usual. Like an idiot. The entire world faded away as the invisible thread that connected them pulled tighter. God, the ache was intense. Their lives were destined to be entangled. Both were heirs to the same Legacy that defined their past, present, and future. Energy existed between them, pulsing with relentless torment. And yet, he couldn't fathom how any kind of romantic relationship would ever work out. Not that it ever would come to that. Fillion returned his face to his arms, closing his eyes with a pensive sigh.

Her soft femininity captivated him, a bygone concept beyond these walls. OK, so maybe vintage notions of proper behavior weren't so annoying after all. She didn't possess the kind of beauty his world appreciated. In fact, he knew the Net communities would find her unadulterated natural state grossly unattractive. Even the hippies wore makeup and dyed their hair, attempting a tribal appearance to exude an earthy seductiveness.

The goal was to become the object of another's sexual fantasy and experience. Everyone was a character on the Net, playing a role. Even if they claimed to be Mother Earth's offspring. Attractive images became worshiped idols. Sites were erected by *otaku* followers, with or without permission. Nothing was real. Everyone was fake. People detached from one another's humanity. Treated others how they pleased. Whatever it took to continue the disillusioned ecstasy of feeling alive.

All of that programming dissipated when he looked at Willow. She baffled him in the best kind of way. "I'm so corny," he whispered to the dark spot his limbs created. He shook his head at the need to hear a voice. Even his own. The walls pressed in another inch.

God, he needed a smoke. Forget it. He couldn't sit here a moment longer. He stood up, caught Leaf's attention. Fillion made the international sign for smoke break, then retrieved a joint from his leather pouch. He walked right up to the candle altar, ignoring the curious stares, and lit up. A couple sharp breaths from behind reached his ears and he rolled his eyes. They were candles, not mystical vessels of the gods. It took everything in him to not flip off the room as he walked out the door.

Fresh air greeted his nostrils and he inhaled deeply. He didn't realize how warm it had been inside. Fillion rested his back against a wall beneath the eaves. There was nowhere to hide. No escape. People were always around. Always needing something. Always expecting contribution, celebration, contrition. It had only been three days, and already the amount of human interaction was making Fillion's brain short-circuit. He had never been asked to care about so many people and things, while following so many rules.

A dull headache formed behind his eyes and he closed them tight for a few seconds. He slowly opened his eyes and focused his vision on the scenery. Safer.

The mid-morning sun crested the dome horizon with a strange, muted brilliance and distracted Fillion's mental rants. Latticed windows sparkled through the leaves from the apartments that curved around the forest. Large wooden staircases, intricately carved with Celtic knots, descended to the biodome floor. Fillion looked up and squinted his eyes at the golden light, taking in the reflective nanotech panels of the ceiling. Shielding his vision, he continued to absorb his surroundings.

Fillion marveled at the medieval mud and timber construction as he dragged on his joint. Each wooden door sported its own personal metal insignia. Doorways and windows were capped with stone. The cool blue and gray tones drew in his eye against the stark contrast of the white walls and the dark exposed timber.

As much as he wanted to, he couldn't deny the allure of their storybook dwellings. All his life he had imagined the people of New Eden Township lived in huts or teepees. Something more rustic and less modern, like an eco-punk commune. He rolled his eyes and let out an irritated sigh. Green Morons. Hanley hadn't allowed any media inside to take images. Even workers and lab employees had been required to check in all their electronic devices during construction.

The door to the Daniels apartment opened and Fillion tensed, hoping he wasn't being summoned inside. Skylar emerged and quietly shut the door, glancing Fillion's direction with a polite smile.

"The air is refreshing," Skylar said. He was matter-of-fact, as if there was no room to believe otherwise. If Skylar didn't look so tense, Fillion would think it was a poor attempt at humor. As a reply, Fillion turned his head and ignored the Son of Wind. Skylar walked near him and dropped his voice. "Pardon my intrusion. I know you wish for solitude at present."

"Your intelligence is inspiring."

"I find myself in a quandary, and I hope you may assist me."

"Hope is for the weak-minded." Fillion faced Skylar with a smug grin and then blew smoke in his face. "I won't be party to any games against the Watsons."

"That is what I wish to speak to you about." Skylar remained unfazed by Fillion's deliberate rudeness. Instead, the young noble took another step closer and whispered, "I do not wish to be party to such games either."

Fillion rolled his eyes. "Yeah, nice try."

"I am most sincere."

"Prove it." Another arrogant smile formed on Fillion's face as he lifted his eyebrows in challenge.

"I shall not cower before your effrontery."

Effrontery? Fillion wanted to laugh. With a single step, he brought himself inches from Skylar's face. "You should."

"On what authority?"

Fillion grinned and leaned against the wall. "Why are you so pissed off at Leaf?"

Skylar looked away for a moment. "Ember and I had been courting until the morning she married Leaf," he whispered. He briefly looked over his shoulder. "Even though Leaf and I are sworn brothers."

"What the hell does that mean?"

"We vowed to honor and serve each other all our days, a bond considered stronger than family." The Son of Wind shifted on his feet and cleared his throat. "Despite the community's support, Leaf's secret marriage is seen as an act against my home."

"Did Ember have a choice in any of this?"

"Yes, of course. That is not, however, what I am concerned about. Connor met with Leaf the eve prior to the handfasting to discuss a private condition for becoming the next Earth Element."

"Shit," Fillion muttered. He drew on his joint in thought. The implications were huge, and he thought of Connor's story about the Death Card. Leaf's insistence on disrupting the game echoed in his mind as well. Ember didn't appear to be suffering as Leaf's wife, though. He locked eyes with Skylar, unsettled with how much the noble resembled Hanley at this moment. "Are you suggesting that Leaf married Ember to play the Wind and Fire Element houses against each other?"

"I fear that others may believe so."

"So what do you want from me?"

"I hear the village gossip, and there is escalating trepidation over the second wave of colonists. My generation fears the Outside world, and the first generation is quickly deciding their opinions about project shutdown. Some wish to return to their families and prior lives, while most wish to remain inside the community. Joel is believed to have been a supporter of disbanding, and I fear some are willing to engage in dire behavior to gain favor on their convictions." Skylar leaned forward. "There are rumors that perhaps an act against Leaf's home may transpire soon, but I am unable to discover the source at present or the potential deed. I fear for their safety. "

Thoughts arced and hummed with electricity in Fillion's mind as he charged certain ideas and questions. As calmly as possible, he lifted the joint to his lips and puffed, exhaling slowly. "Where do you stand?"

"This is why I seek your assistance, as you are from the Outside."

Fillion offered a cool smile. "You should stand by Leaf and whatever he decides. Especially if a so-called deed against his home ever happens."

"Yes, of course." Skylar looked away nervously. Fillion had to strain to hear his next words. "Only, to do so would require that I publicly stand against my father, which is not done in New Eden."

"You've been asked to keep your distance from Leaf?"

"And never to reconcile." The noble's eyes glossed and he blinked, looking up at the dome ceiling.

Fillion suddenly understood Skylar's fear. Fillion had carried the marks of shame for over five years, and he understood what communities did to sons like them. It didn't matter if the father was guilty or innocent. The threat was all society needed. The Son of Wind had made his stand, and Fillion would guard his position.

"Thanks for telling me the gossip." Fillion casually looked around the deck. "It's very useful."

Skylar bowed, a look of relief softening his features. "Anytime, sir." He looked like he wanted to say more, but closed his mouth.

"I'll be working at The Forge as a carpenter if you need to find me."

"Thank you, sir."

Skylar issued a grateful smile before quietly walking back into the apartment. It was weird, but that smile was so much like Lynden's that Fillion shivered. What the hell? He couldn't help but wonder if he was related to Skylar Kane. No. It had to be an odd coincidence. Either that or he was experiencing psychosis. Hanley was an only child, whose father died when Hanley was a baby. Grandma Esther never remarried, dying an old, lonely woman. She was a weird, paranoid nut. They never had a funeral or anything for her either. God, his family was the very definition of dysfunctional.

He needed another smoke and lit another joint with the butt of the old one. A strange taste hit his tongue and he scrunched up his face and looked at the joint, perplexed. He must have discovered one made from spices. There was a faint orange flavor behind the cinnamon and clove. He puffed another hit and decided it wasn't so bad after all.

The front door opened again and Fillion sighed heavily. So much for alone time. Jeff peeked out and emerged upon spotting him nearby. "Glad you are close."

Fillion made a welcoming gesture with his hand and said in a flat voice, "Step into my office."

"There are smoking laws in New Eden," Jeff said in a wry tone, lifting a corner of his mouth.

"Great." Fillion smiled. "A lawyer with a sense of humor. The worst kind."

Jeff gave an appreciative nod, but it was clear he was heartbroken. His dejected movements as he stepped toward Fillion looked as if a corpse traipsed across the deck. Nonetheless, he communicated with an air of business. "Hanley sent a message for you to connect with him tonight via Messenger Pigeon. He wishes to meet with you two hours after your work start time at New Eden Enterprises. He also instructs you to bring Joel Watson. He must mean the new Earth Element. He confirmed receipt of the death certificate last week."

Fillion narrowed his eyes. The message wasn't from his dad. Hanley wouldn't want another situation where Leaf could be potentially exposed to others in the company. Only so many glitches can happen before employees become suspicious, especially in a short period of time. And he would never ask for Joel Watson. For once, Fillion was glad he thought like his dad. But his heart sank as he realized the message probably came from his mom, masquerading as his dad. She didn't know about Joel's death?

"I don't meet his demands."

Jeff registered shock, and cleared his throat as an attempt at composure. "How would you like me to reply?"

"If and when I want to meet with him, he'll know." The lawyer's face paled, so Fillion tried another tack. "Tell him the timing isn't right, but I'll let him know when it is, so stay tuned. Make it as polite as you want. I don't care."

Jeff studied him a few seconds, further concerned. "And what if he overrides your response?"

"He won't."

"What is it exactly that you do for New Eden Enterprises?"

A wicked grin stretched on Fillion's face as he took a casual drag on his joint. "Science and shit. And whatever the hell it takes to piss off Hanley. It's very important work."

Jeff's lips turned up slightly in a shaky smile and then sobered. "The real reason I came out here is because Norah requested your presence. Lady Rain emerged from her mother's room looking for you, and I capitalized on the opportunity to share Hanley's message." Fillion's stomach tightened. He couldn't see a nearly dead person. He'd never seen anyone die before in his entire life. Jeff seemed to notice his sudden anxiety. "She wishes to pass on a blessing."

"A what? Why?"

"It is tradition. Come on." Jeff gestured toward the door. "Never keep a woman waiting, especially if she is…" He didn't finish, as if realizing mid-sentence that the joke wasn't that funny after all. Jeff's face reddened. "Sorry," he said. The lawyer whispered, as if Fillion wasn't there, "I have loved her so long."

"No worries." What else could Fillion say? Was that why Jeff joined New Eden?

The lawyer looked up at him with a haunted stare. And one of the most heartbreaking smiles Fillion had ever seen formed on Jeff's face. Was it worth it? Did the years of unrequited love make up for the grief of separation?

The front door opened and Rain emerged with uncertain steps. Her hair swished at her waist, and her eyes were puffy from crying. She looked nothing like her red-haired, freckled mother and siblings. Or the blond-haired, blue-eyed father. And it had nothing to do with her tears. Fillion drew his brows together and looked between Jeff and Rain.

Jeff's face relaxed as he looked over his shoulder, and that is when Fillion knew. Did Rain know? To hide his surprise, he walked to the railing, stomped on his joint, and then pushed it over the edge until it fell to the grass below.

"My mother requests your presence, sir."

As he turned, he schooled his features and gave Rain a tight smile as he re-entered her home. Everyone looked up at him from their seats and he swallowed nervously.

Rain led him to her mother's bedroom, then quietly stepped aside for him to enter. The room was dark. A single candle burned by Norah's bed. Her red hair lay strewn across the pillow like flames. Norah's eyes were closed, and her breathing was raspy.

Fillion's feet felt like lead as he walked closer. The door groaned and creaked behind him. He shot a look over his shoulder, unable to hide the fear in his eyes. A sad smile touched Rain's lips, and then she closed the door, leaving him alone with a woman who could breathe her last at any moment. Every muscle in his body stilled, as if any sudden movement could cause her death.

Norah's eyes squinted open and rested on him. A faint smile lit her face. "Come," she croaked. "Kneel on the floor beside me."

Fillion lifted his shoulders and dropped his head, forcing himself to breathe. Carefully, he lowered onto the hard floor. Norah's hand surfaced from a multitude of covers and reached up to touch his cheek. Her fingers were cold, causing him to flinch. He was on the verge of a total freak-out. Fillion forced himself to meet her eyes, confused by the kindness.

"I know who you are," she said. It was clearly hard for her to talk, but she continued. "I am thankful I lived long enough to see you." Her thumb caressed his face gently and he blinked rapidly, attempting to hold back the swelling fear. "Son of Eden, never forget your immeasurable value and worth." She paused to take in a deep, rattled breath. "You are exactly who this community needs."

"I don't know—"

"Shhh," she soothed with a loving smile. It was a look Fillion imagined most mothers graced their children with, and his eyes stung as tears formed. "Do not allow fear to dictate your steps. You are a man of remarkable strength and honor. I see it in your soul."

A tear slid down Fillion's cheek with her declaration. She moved her head on the pillow to see him more clearly and he took in a measured breath, straining to remain in control. Her fingers trembled on his face for a moment before she lowered her arm, searching for his hand.

In automatic motions, he lifted his hand and found hers, feeling strange when realizing the intimacy of his gesture. A human lay dying before him, and he was touching her and listening to some of her last words. Never had he felt so small, so insignificant, so ugly and hateful. People died every day and he didn't give a shit. But she was real. This was really happening. Lives began and lives ended. Everyone in the other room understood this profound truth. Regret over his shallowness pressed heavily against his chest.

She didn't have to waste her few, precious minutes on him. Norah had four children, a husband, and lifelong friends. But she wanted to give *him* some of her remaining time. She even publicly requested him, letting others know she considered him important. No one had ever demonstrated that they believed he held worth like Norah had this moment. Was this her blessing? It was overwhelming. He possessed remarkable strength and honor? The community needed him? The last thought made his stomach churn.

"I'm so scared," he whispered.

"Love is stronger than fear," she said. She placed her hand on his chest, over his heart.

Fillion hung his head as another tear fell. "I don't know how to love."

"There is a difference between being able to love and believing your love is valuable, worth giving away." She paused and her hand went limp. Relief flooded him when she began again. "He would have loved you like his own flesh and blood," she said with a raspy whisper. His breath caught and his head snapped up. Norah offered a warm smile. "Allow me to bless you, Fillion Nichols."

"You already have," he said quietly.

"Come closer." Not wanting to argue, he leaned toward Norah as her hand lifted once again. A trembling finger outlined the shape of a heart on his forehead. "The legacy of your life is love. May it fill you and pour out of you the remaining days of your life. Be blessed."

Heat flooded Fillion as if light poured into his veins. Norah smiled beautifully, patting his cheek with a look of pride that warmed her gaunt features. Emotions rose and fell as a war waged inside his mind, one he couldn't shake. It was too much to take in and confusing. Fillion shifted his gaze and stared at the solitary half-melted candle on Norah's nightstand as ideas continued to capture him. His legacy was love? The words seared, and another tear crawled down his cheek.

Fillion looked up and his eyes widened. Norah's face was relaxed, peaceful. Her eyes were closed. How long was he stuck in his head? Was she breathing? He stared in horror as he sought a sign of life in her face. Was she dead? He was too afraid to find out. His chest heaved as he gulped in a large breath. A sudden pain filled him and tears fell, feeling hot against his flushed skin. God, how would he tell the Daniels family? Just as he pushed off the floor, wheezy breaths began to fill the silence and Fillion's shoulders slumped with relief. She was still alive. God, that freaked him out. Norah's eyes slowly fluttered opened and he wiped the tears away in quick motions before resting his forearms on the edge of her bed.

"Can I get you anything?" He looked around the sparse room. "Water?"

"The Watson family, please."

"Sure." He quietly rose to his feet and bit the inside of his cheek. Before he lost his nerve, he leaned down and kissed her sunken cheek and then turned toward her door.

"Fillion," she said. He stopped and looked over his shoulder. "Make sure my family remains ... on ... Earth." Her voice trailed and she took in quick, shallow breaths.

Perplexed, Fillion returned to her bedside and knelt on the floor once again. Was she referring to the Outside world? She wanted the community to disband? "What do you mean?"

"There is now an entire generation ... who have never seen the world." Her eyelids closed again.

Fillion waited for her to continue, but her breathing became uneven and rattled. He didn't dare disturb her to get a better answer. Slowly, he tip-toed across the floor. At the door, he looked back at Norah one last time. "Thanks for making me feel real," he whispered.

Multiple pairs of eyes looked up as he entered the living room, the polite curiosity evident in their troubled stares. Willow blinked with concern as she silently questioned him. He forced himself to look away and focus on Leaf. "Norah requests your family."

Leaf gave an appreciative nod as he rose, taking Ember and Laurel by hand. Willow's lips trembled as she followed, meeting Fillion's eyes for a split second as she passed. The Watsons faded into the dark hallway. The sound of iron striking wood echoed as the bedroom door closed behind them. Fillion swept his gaze across the room, feeling the walls close in one more inch.

He had to leave. He needed to find solitude.

Thoughts surged in his mind. When the user interface of his consciousness refreshed, he realized he was in the woods, running. But he didn't care. He just wanted to disappear.

A giant oak tree appeared around the bend, painting an image straight from the pages of a fable. He abruptly stopped and admired the long, sprawling branches. Wind rustled his garments and leaves fell, the tinfoil sound of their collision to earth reverberating in his ears. The crunch of dead and decaying life shouted at him with each step—he almost covered his ears—until he reached a large cluster of ferns against the trunk. He lowered himself, leaning his back against the tree. Fillion gripped his hair for a moment, then buried his head into his arms and knees.

Norah's words spoke to his soul in a murmur, her command prompt foreign to his system. What if he did have something valuable to give away? What did Norah see in him that led her to believe that he possessed remarkable strength and honor? Questions spurred more questions until he thought he would crack. To still his thoughts, Fillion raised his head and watched shadows lean and stretch as time progressed. Occasionally, he paused to listen to the sounds of village life nearby, silencing the voices of doubt and shame in his head.

Two birds flapped noisily off a nearby branch as brisk footsteps echoed the protests of the forest floor. Fillion angled his head toward the approach, feeling his stomach clench when Willow appeared. Norah had died. Every anguished word Willow could share was already evident on her face.

Two people—Elements no less—were now dead thanks to his family's experiment. The guilt was overwhelming. But he refused to hide, welcoming any anger Willow wanted to inflict on him. Adrenaline coursed through his body and he stood quickly, causing Willow to startle and jump back.

They stared at each other curiously. Holding back tears, he sucked in his lower lip as he begged for her to forgive him with his eyes. She blinked in reply and placed a hand on her chest and then pressed the same hand over his heart, and Fillion deflated.

The strange energy that connected them pulled tighter. He closed his eyes, momentarily overcome by her gesture and her touch. The feelings were painful. A breeze rustled the trees. He glanced up as yellow leaves cascaded all around them, slowly meeting her eyes once more. Wisps of hair flew across Willow's face, her lips flushed and rosy as she held his eyes. He longed to kiss her. But he was too terrified to ruin this moment.

She pulled away gradually, stepping backward as she blushed into her shoulder. With a deep sigh, she lowered in a curtsy and placed her hand onto her heart once again. Fillion didn't know what to do, far too humbled and stunned by the implications of her gift.

Willow wiped away silent tears as she rose. Offering him one last look, she rounded the trunk of the giant oak and climbed into its branches. Fillion had climbed trees with Mack on a few days they felt aimless, but he'd rarely seen anyone else do so, and never a girl—let alone a girl in a long dress. He watched as she settled onto a thick branch and began to heave with sobs into her dress. The image was striking, especially with the leaves framing her in gold. The linen folds of her dress flowed over the branch, rippling in the breeze.

He was completely beguiled, his focus drawn away only when a golden leaf fluttered past his face. Shaky fingers caught the long, narrow leaf. He wasn't a sentimental type. It was stupid and silly. But as he peered up at the Daughter of Earth, who grieved in the boughs, he thanked Fate for a piece of willow oak that could be entirely his own.

With a final glance up into the tree, he tucked the leaf into his pocket. Then he jogged off toward the Watson apartment. Now that Norah was dead, Leaf would discover the spinning wheel. And he needed to tell the Son of Earth about the Death Card.

Any sufficiently advanced technology is indistinguishable from magic.

— Arthur C. Clarke, "Hazards of Prophecy: The Failure of Imagination," in *Profiles of the Future*, revised edition, 1973 *

CHAPTER FOURTEEN

O aklee haphazardly leaned against the trunk, swinging a leg below the supporting branch. She wrapped an arm around her other leg, pulling her knee tight against her chest. The bark was smooth against her back from years of rubbing, compared to the abrasive and grooved areas that marked the remainder of the tree's surface. Thoughts flitted around, her questions seemingly endless, as she gazed up through the canopy of glimmering leaves and swaying tree limbs to the mosaic pattern of the sky she had always known. The reflective blue darkened to various shades of gray, almost as if the Outside world also mourned the loss of Norah Daniels.

Did Earth feel pain when its creation returned to her? When the trace elements comprising the soul's outer shell no longer bore the genetic imprint of who they are, did Earth remember? Tomorrow the Daniels family would endure the Cremation Ceremony, and Oaklee would watch another parent-figure burn, becoming a living ingredient to nourish the soil and enrich the agriculture.

In a far-away voice, she intoned, "'In the sweat of thy face shall thou eat food 'til thou return to the earth, out of which thou wast taken: for dust thou art, and into dust thou shall return.'"

Beads, fastened to Oaklee's belt, slipped between her fingers as her lips moved in a prayer her mind could no longer comprehend. The atmosphere of her community altered once more, and she inhaled deeply, refusing to entertain the free-fall sensations that tempted her bruised heart. She knew the floor would claim her, knew she would crash. Still, she longed to detach and float blissfully unaware of the pain.

As she observed the rhythm of the forest, an acorn landed in her lap and Oaklee's fingers stilled on the prayer beads as she stared at the small nut in wonder. She always marveled how something so mighty and majestic grew from something so very simple. In many ways, she felt akin to this acorn—plain, small, and yet containing a purpose so grand that the very notion bordered on the impossible.

A rabbit scurried from the underbrush, the light thump of its hind legs announcing its presence as it searched for another hideaway. Acorns dotted the leaf-littered ground, providing treasures for the squirrels, and she swallowed with the pain of life's never-ending cycle of love and loss, survival and sacrifice. "May your journey be blessed," she whispered, then flicked her wrist, tossing the acorn to the ground. Oaklee stilled in anticipation of the telltale plunk and, instead, gasped when an irritated groan resounded instead.

She peeked over her arm to discover Leaf, who glowered at her from a couple branches below. He rubbed the top of his head. With a heavy sigh, he dragged his fingers through his mess of dark brown curls and resumed his climb. Oaklee stiffened as she closed her eyes to listen to the sounds of nature, desperately seeking peace. Normally, she would giggle over such a situation. But she was far too disconsolate, and Leaf appeared far too angry.

"Willow, I wish to speak with you."

She opened her eyes. "It is Oaklee."

"*Willow Oak*, we need to speak immediately—and be warned, I am in no mood for dramatics."

"Whatever it is you wish to say, do so quickly, for I am in no mood to deal with your patronizing tones." She turned her head and lifted her chin.

"I am grieved—"

"As am I!"

"That you and Fillion would keep from me—"

"I did not think we needed your precious blessing to speak alone, *My Lord*."

"Pardon?" Leaf paused. "You spoke with Fillion unchaperoned once more? When?"

A blush warmed Oaklee's face as she met her brother's eyes, now level with her own. "Shortly after Norah died. You are not here to scold me while attempting to avenge my honor?"

"No. Well, yes, but over a completely different concern." Anger burned across his features once more. The ever-present dark circles under his eyes now swelled with red. Had he lost his senses from Norah's passing?

Leaf pulled from his pocket a bobbin wound with black yarn. He reached for the hand in her lap, and pressed the carved object into her palm, closing her fingers over the wooden piece. Oaklee's body sagged as she held a remnant of her destroyed spinning wheel, an event she had shamefully forgotten in the wake of Norah's vigil and passing. No, *she* had lost her senses.

"How dare you withhold from me something as dire as this," her brother continued through gritted teeth. "My job is to protect my home and uphold the laws and Code of our community. Instead, my own sister intentionally withholds this crime against our family and asks another to partake in such a foolish decision."

"How dare *you* accuse *me* of dishonor! Perhaps you should examine your own actions, Leaf Watson." The knuckles on her hand grew white as she gripped the bobbin. "Get off my tree!"

"Your tree?" He held onto a branch above his head and leaned forward. "You honestly believe such a childish response will remove me from *your tree*? Willow Oak Watson, sometimes you infuriate me to such deep levels I could go mad."

"My heartfelt apologies for encumbering your life."

Leaf snapped a nearby twig and tossed it to the ground. "Do you ever look beyond your circumstances? Or do your emotions swallow you whole with each and every opportunity to exert their will?"

Oaklee repositioned and turned her back toward Leaf, then hugged a neighboring branch as she blotted away the traitorous tears. She attempted to collect her thoughts, feeling her brother's insistent presence. Leaf went too far with such harsh words and tones. In fact, her brother appeared as though he would be willing to cut down her tree and perhaps the entire forest, simply to ensure she understood his message.

Leaf loudly sighed. "If you do not possess sense for your own safety, at least consider the safety of our sister. You denied me the opportunity to protect her should whoever destroyed your spinning wheel wish to act as violently against her. For Heaven's sake, Willow! Our father may have been murdered by the very same individual."

Her throat tightened. Oaklee twisted to see Leaf over her shoulder as his words penetrated her mounting offense. "Leaf, I did not wish to dishonor Norah on her last day among the living. I promise that was my only motivation." Oaklee repositioned on the branch and crossed her heart, hoping Leaf would believe her. "I feared your response and asked Fillion to guard his knowledge of the incident to ensure the Daniels family had our undivided support." She extended a hand to her brother and bowed her head. Apologies were difficult for her, but she knew her brother would never believe her sincerity otherwise. "Please forgive me. I should have fully considered the ramifications of my decisions."

Her brother blinked with the unexpected display of contrition. He took her hand and shook it, dipping his head in honor. But the anger remained on his face. "There is a silent war for power, and I shall not stand for my family to suffer for it." Leaf descended the tree, jumped to the ground from the last branch, then looked back up at her with authority. "Come."

She did not hesitate and gingerly climbed down the branches, spooked by her brother's words and fearful of what he may do if she did not obey. Nevertheless, upon the last branch, she dangled longer than necessary, hoping to prolong the inevitable, until fingers wrapped around her waist from behind in an unexpected gesture of assistance.

Oaklee turned to thank Leaf, lowering into a curtsy. She paled upon recognizing Fillion. She looked for her brother, not bothering to hide her distress. She spotted Leaf on the path, pacing, while Ember held Laurel. Tears wet Laurel's cheeks as her eyes tracked their brother's tense movements, little fingers wringing with rhythmic persistence.

"We don't have much time," Fillion whispered, regaining her attention. "Leaf gave me a few minutes to talk to you. He doesn't know about our … talk … last night and thinks that info is what I'm sharing before shit hits the fan."

She could not form a reply. Their close proximity quickened her pulse and she attempted to regulate her breathing to appear as unaffected as possible. Nevertheless, all she wished to contemplate were the hands that rested upon her waist and those eyes, inches from her face, imploring her to trust him. Their bodies were mostly hidden by the large trunk, and the partial seclusion thrilled her addled senses. His fingers moved, readjusting his loose hold over her thin linen work dress, her fabric and his skin sliding along her midsection. Enfeebled, her thoughts traveled in a drowsy haze, and she was convinced she would surely float away once Fillion no longer rooted her to the leaf-littered floor.

"I didn't tell Leaf about the spinning wheel. Your brother guessed you had asked me to keep information from him after seeing us this morning in The Forge," he continued. "And even then, I evaded his questions. I meant what I said. Your secrets are always safe with me."

His touch was doing odd things to her, feelings she could not fully describe. Memories of their earlier moments, shortly after Norah died, drowned her thoughts in delirium, and she barely whispered a reply. "Thank you, My Lord." But he seemed not to notice her struggle nor his effect on her.

"He's madder than hell and about to piss off a lot of people. Do not, under any circumstances, challenge him publicly. Promise me."

"I beg your pardon?" Oaklee's febrile thoughts instantly cooled, and his hands dropped from her waist as she stepped away. And contrary to previous notions, she did not float away. Every enraptured sensation evaporated in that moment, replenished by offense over his patronizing request. "If my brother is not acting in a proper manner, I have every right to challenge him as any other within this community. Do not presume our earlier moment means I swoon over your Outsider boyish fancies or submit to your egotistical notions of grandeur."

"Egotistical notions of grandeur?" A subtle, playful lift of his mouth taunted her. "You're losing your edge. Try again. You can do way better than that." She pressed herself against the tree, clenching and unclenching her fists, as he stepped closer. When she refused to be baited, he said in a slow, overly emphasized voice, "Promise me."

"Why should I?"

"Because," he began, as sudden shyness seized him, "I need you." The sincerity of his confession stilled the storm inside of her, and Oaklee's determination momentarily faltered. Fillion dropped his eyes and lifted his shoulders as he whispered. "But don't make me choose between you and your brother right now." He exhaled a shaky breath and met her eyes. "Promise me."

Bemused, she wound a strand of black yarn, dangling from the bobbin, onto her finger. "Is Leaf fulfilling revenge on your behalf?"

His eyebrows shot up. "Your brother has his own vendetta."

"How can I be sure you are not using him to end your Legacy?"

"Wow. Your vote of confidence is overwhelming. I could blush." Fillion rolled his eyes and then pinned her with a hard stare. "God, I'm an asshole, but I'm not that selfish. Promise. Me."

She groaned, followed by a dramatic sigh. "You continually vex me, especially with your vulgarity." A satisfied grin stretched on his face. Instead of appeasing his attempts at riling her up, she said, "I am sure I shall regret this decision, but I shall honor your wishes, *Master Fillion.*" Oaklee angled her head away but watched him from the corner of her eye.

Fillion hid his gratification casually behind a hand and she softened when the merriment in his eyes did not belittle or mock her loss in their debate. Rather, it was if he reveled in besting her independence and what her brother would surely declare as temerity. Oh how that smile destroyed every effort to remain strong!

With shy nonchalance, Fillion whispered, "My humble thanks, Fair Maiden."

For a moment, he focused on her mouth and she held her breath in anticipation. Leaf cleared his throat a short distance away and both she and Fillion locked eyes in surprise. She had nearly forgotten about her brother, and by the look on Fillion's face, so had he.

"Your brother is a mood-killer. Remind me never to invite him to any parties."

Oaklee suppressed the urge to laugh, grateful the discussion lightened. "You are trouble and I need rescuing, lest I find myself an accomplice to your errant intentions, My Lord."

"Fillion."

"*Fillion*, you are trouble."

He placed a hand on the trunk near her face and leaned in close. "My intentions are innocent. I swear."

"Honest men never need swear oaths of innocence. Their actions prove the integrity of their deeds." She slid a glance his direction, neatly folding her hands against her lap.

"Bludgeon me with your words later," he said with a wink and a devilish grin. "We need to go. Leaf is pissed off enough." Grasping her hand, he jumped over the large roots, and led her through the wild grass toward the footpath before she could object.

Leaf studied their knotted fingers, and she quickly released Fillion's hand, smoothing the front of her skirt and avoiding eye contact as modesty dictated. But not before witnessing Fillion stick his tongue out at her brother in playful mockery, and she thought, perhaps, a ghost of a smile formed for a moment on Leaf's face.

"May we proceed?" Leaf asked Fillion, who nodded in reply. "Walk with me, please."

"Wait," Fillion said, looking her way. "Do you have the card on you?"

The flirt had disappeared and Fillion returned to his usual insouciant state, studying the surroundings with disinterest as he awaited her response. Oaklee reached into her pocket and revealed the mysterious card, too afraid to meet her brother's eyes. Would Leaf blame her for their father's death? Or Norah's? Although Fillion shared that the curse was superficial, she did not trust her brother's emotional stability at present to believe the same argument. Fillion plucked the card from her hand, his fingers brushing along her knuckles as he watched her. Perhaps the flirt had not completely disappeared. Oaklee shifted on her feet with a nervous look her brother's direction.

The trees groaned in reply to a strong gust of bio-wind. Dappled shadows flitted across her brother's face while he read the curse, and a pained look harshened his features as he tucked the card into his pocket. A shiver coursed through

Oaklee with the wind's chill and she absently rubbed her arms while awaiting Leaf's reply. Her brother shifted on his feet as he covered his face with his hands, dragging earth-stained, calloused palms down across his eyes and cheeks as if plowing a field of thoughts. His hands dropped and she forced herself to meet his eyes boldly, even though she was terrified.

Her brother's face softened as he regarded her poor attempt at bravery. "Do you fare well?"

"I am not sure," she said. Oaklee chanced a look at Ember and Laurel. "I was told the curse was not real and the card is a ruse to inspire fear; however, I am confused." She hugged her arms and lowered her eyes. "In truth, I am most frightened."

"Come here, *ma chère*," he sighed. Leaf opened up his arms, and she fell against him in relief. The warmth engulfed her and she buried her face into his chest, listening to his strong heartbeat. He murmured into her hair. "You are not cursed, I promise."

"You are not cross with me?"

"I was over your decision this morning, most definitely. But you are not responsible for such a card nor another's actions toward our home." Leaf pulled away and began untying his cloak, wrapping it around Oaklee's shoulders and retying the laces. "Once more, you have forgotten your cloak. Your mind is often in a faraway place, gathering wool."

Oaklee's lips trembled as she replied with a small smile. "How I must trouble you so."

"You are my family, Willow Oak. I will never replace mother or father, nor do I wish to. However, I do find great pleasure in caring for you and Laurel. It is an honor." He straightened the cloak around her shoulders with a sad, distracted smile. "Your indomitable spirit has encouraged me these past few days." Leaf slipped Fillion a quick look, but said to her, "*Je suis fier de la femme que tu deviens.*"

"Indomitable? Really, Leaf Watson." She blinked with embarrassment. Nevertheless, her brother's words of pride touched her heart. "*Père serait très fier de toi, cher frère.*"

"Is my company finally preferred over that of a snake?" His face remained passive, but a twinkle in her brother's eye gave him away.

"Yes, although barely. Do not let it go to your head."

"I shall do my best." He smiled kindly for a mere heartbeat and then distemper darkened his features once more. "Be strong," he continued in a near whisper. "Fillion and I plan to disrupt the game in such a way that the community shall never recover."

"I believe I shall be sick."

"Be strong, Oaklee," he said.

Leaf turned on his heel and marched to where Fillion stood. The use of her requested name made her stomach churn, and she pressed her hands into her abdomen to suppress the queasiness.

She attempted to silently question Fillion, but he kept his eyes fastened on Leaf. The two young men spoke in hushed tones as they walked until Fillion suddenly stopped. He stiffened and rummaged through the pouch hanging from his belt, pulling out a metallic object, which he promptly placed upon his ear.

"Mack?"

Oaklee gasped and looked around the woods as the hairs on her arms stood up, trying to understand what she was seeing. Was the metal object an enchanted stone? Leaf crossed his arms as he regarded Fillion, but his face contained no trace of concern nor fear.

"Yeah, we're going to confront the community now. What'd you find out?" Fillion stared at the dirt path and slowly raised his head with an impish grin, shrugging his eyebrows at Leaf. "*Kono yaro!*" he muttered. "Thanks, mate. Later."

Fillion swiftly tucked the metallic device back into his pouch. Memories of him standing in the luminous sunlight, commanding the air and defeating an otherworldly apparition, rushed through Oaklee's mind. He was powerful, far more than his unconfident nature suggested, and she was baffled by his need of her.

As if knowing her thoughts, Fillion flicked an uncertain glance her way, then turned back to Leaf. "Legally, you are still part of the Legacy. My dad removed you by name and instead stipulated, 'The oldest surviving heir of Joel Watson.' Mack is sending over the response from his lawyer."

"Does the lawyer know?"

"No. Mack asked lots of questions on my behalf to cushion the target question, plus other gimmicks." Fillion tapped his head. "We're smart like that."

Another secret pressed against Oaklee's chest. Thoughts spiraled and tumbled through the atmosphere of her temperament, signs she was about to crash. She was far too grief-stricken by Norah's death and turbulent in Fillion's presence. Before she could curb her tongue, she demanded, "What do you speak of?" She stomped over to Fillion with fists clenched at her side. His eyes rounded slightly in surprise. She turned to her brother. "What magic did he use to assist our family?"

"It's technology, not magic," Fillion said. "Even you can manipulate it. It's easy."

"Does it summon ghosts such as the one that appeared at The Door?"

The world tilted as the blood rushed from her head. Before he could answer, the bile rose in her throat and she ran to the nearest bush and vomited. Her stomach spasmed as sweat beaded upon her forehead. "Oh dear Lord," she moaned. Every muscle in her body ached and she wished for nothing more than to curl up in the leaves and drift off into the numbness of oblivion. From the corner of her eye, she noted Fillion's worried expression as he moved toward her. She raised her hand as a signal to stop and his steps ceased.

"Please continue on without us, My Lord," Ember said near her ear. "Laurel and I shall care for our sister."

The forest whispered words of comfort in the ensuing silence, and Oaklee closed her eyes as a bird sang a melancholy tune. Fillion and Leaf's footsteps faded around the bend.

"There are far too many intimate emotions this day to call by name," Oaklee said, her voice thin.

Ember caressed her back in soothing motions. Oaklee looked up once more into the tree canopy at the leaves, limbs, and geodesic sky that shimmered in the smoke-shaded afternoon light. A body pressed into Oaklee's side and she draped an arm protectively around Laurel's shoulder, her fingers combing through her sister's tresses.

"All will be well. You shall see," Ember said. "Leaf is a sight to behold when impassioned, is he not?" Her sister-in-law lowered her head with a becoming grin.

"Unless you are the subject of his wrath."

"Indeed." Ember smiled in her usual mysterious way. "Today we shall witness the beginning of a revolution."

"Odd words of comfort, My Lady."

"Have faith in your brother. He is a pillar of strength in this community, one they shall realize today is necessary for support should we wish to remain standing."

"How can you have such peace?" Oaklee gave Ember an unconvinced look. "I am not so strong."

"Of course you are strong." Ember threaded an arm through Oaklee's and slowly led her down the path. "If I recall correctly, your father oft said you were strong and resourceful. I do not imagine he would lie about such things."

"No," Oaklee agreed. "I do not possess the constitution for change, though."

"When one's roots are deep, it is more difficult to change, but not impossible." Ember smiled kindly and then turned to Laurel. "Sweetling, when we arrive at the Great Hall, remain by my side please."

"Yes, Ember," Laurel said meekly. "What did Corlan, pardon, Fillion use on his ear?"

Oaklee's steps nearly faltered. They knew his real name? Did they also know of his real identity?

"He used a Cranium," Ember replied, as if it were common knowledge, and the hairs on Oaklee's nape prickled and stood on end once more. "Outsiders use it to communicate with one another using signals in the air. The biodome prevents signals in the air from leaving and entering, but there is a hidden tower that transmits signals through the ground rather than through the air."

"How do you know so much about Outsider magic?" Oaklee paused and turned toward her sister-in-law.

Ember lowered her eyes and knotted her hands gracefully against her waist. "My father has shared such knowledge with me."

"I see," Oaklee said, at a complete loss for words. It was a strange admission of knowledge, but she knew Connor enjoyed the workings of simple machines, so surely he must miss the devices of the life he once knew before Moving Day. Ember was ever the generous listener, and no doubt her father capitalized on such a virtue to reminisce over his life, past and present.

"I fear we must arrive soon so Leaf does not worry excessively over our safety." Ember gently encouraged Oaklee to move forward once more.

"Yes, of course."

Leaves swirled and spiraled through the air. Oaklee marveled at how they danced in submission to the winds of change, even as they passed on to another world. The forest floor would become their afterlife, and still the leaves soared with graceful acceptance in anticipation. She could not accept the changes. There were far too many.

Perhaps most significantly, astronauts on future missions will have to be psychologically capable of surrendering to the fact that they are literally millions of miles from home, stuck in a tiny compartment, with no possibility of leaving (at least not until Martian touchdown or a safe return to Earth). While none of the Mars500 crew decided to leave the simulation at any point, the option was always available. The sense of safety and security that this provided just can't be brushed aside.

— Robert T. Gonzalez, "Why the Mars500 mission doesn't prove we're psychologically capable of a trip to Mars," *io9* / *Gawker*, November, 3 2011 *

CHAPTER FIFTEEN

A ngry shouts thundered through the meadow, interrupting Oaklee's dark reverie. She gasped when families began pouring into the large stone building with panic-like haste. Oaklee and Ember exchanged worried looks and then simultaneously sprinted toward the Great Hall, lifting their skirts to gain better footing despite the scandalous appearance. Upon arrival, Oaklee blanched when recognizing the infuriated tones of her brother's normally calm voice.

"I shall not tolerate cowardice nor terrorizing a woman to satiate political or personal grievances. If you are truly a man, step forward with your offense so I may learn of this quarrel against my home." Leaf's voice boomed over the gathered masses, and heads turned as people studied their neighbors for signs of guilt or admission.

"Your home threatens the life we have sacrificed many years to build!" hollered a man from the back corner. Sporadic cheers of agreement followed throughout the crowd.

Oaklee struggled to see over the many heads and stood on the tips of her toes. Ember grabbed her hand and led her and Laurel along the perimeter until they reached the front of the assembly.

"Who speaks? Come forward and face me like a man."

Leaf scrutinized the community, trying to pinpoint the source of contest, and did not see the young women's arrival. But Fillion acknowledged them with a tight nod. He stood beside Leaf, Connor, and Timothy upon the stage, his face pale and his posture uncharacteristically straight and rigid. Did he fear standing before crowds? He mouthed the words, "Feeling better?" and she offered a weak smile in response before turning toward a commotion in the crowd.

Villagers shuffled in the back corner, gradually moving away from a man. Disappointment ripped through Oaklee at the sight of Lawrence, one of the head gardeners.

"Did you destroy Lady Willow's spinning wheel?" The catch in Leaf's voice gave away her brother's disheartened confusion.

"No, My Lord," Lawrence answered, equally as shaken. "I have my opinions, but I am not a violent man."

"I believe you. But pray tell, how has my home threatened the life my family has also sacrificed greatly to establish, build, and preserve?"

Lawrence crossed his arms over his chest. "Joel Watson is a known supporter of rejoining the Outside world, a lifestyle many do not wish to possess or revisit."

"I am astonished that so many know my father's position and yet I am just learning of it myself after his death." Leaf swept an intense gaze over the community. "I am even more astonished that he is accused of support for something of which each first-generation adult in this room verified understanding with a legal signature. Is there a first-generation adult in this room who did not sign The Code? If so, let him or her come forward and Jeff shall remedy the situation."

People looked around, some with shamed expressions, quietly murmuring to one another.

"Lawrence, you worked by my father's side, knew him well, and yet you hold such hostility," Leaf continued. "Joel Watson is not responsible for your fear. He was placed in a position to uphold The Code, as are Connor, Timothy, and myself today. Perhaps you have objections with Hanley Nichols you wish to address? If so, I am happy to listen and will ensure your comments and concerns are brought before him for consideration."

"Yes, My Lord." Lawrence bowed awkwardly, as if ashamed of his outburst. "Thank you, My Lord."

"I believe I speak for everyone," Timothy interjected, "when I share that Joel was a good, upstanding man. And although he fared well and was highly respected, he did carry an estranged relationship with Hanley Nichols, due to a past relation with Della Jayne Nichols, Joel's fiancée prior to Claire—"

"Timothy, that is irrelevant." The authority in Connor's voice added to the crescendo of gasps. Oaklee's stomach flipped and she looked down to gage Laurel's response, whose tears silently fell down her cheeks as her face tinged pink. Connor opened his arms, palm up, in a gesture of disbelief. "Are you intentionally stirring the already charged atmosphere? If so, I strongly advise you to desist."

"My point is that Joel could not be relied upon to make objective decisions to represent the community when all he wished to do was see Della once again. Catch my drift? Lawrence was simply sharing an observation we in Nobility already understood. It was a courtesy to allow Leaf to become the new Earth Element."

The village promptly shouted their outrage or support over Timothy's words and Leaf lowered his head, closing his eyes momentarily. Bending her knees, Oaklee braced against the urge to faint as she watched her brother struggle for control, his chest rising and falling with an attempt to remain steadfast in the face of betrayal and public humiliation.

"That's a load of shit and you know it," Fillion said, and the entire place calmed to an eerie silence within moments.

"What legal authority did Joel have to amend The Code to ensure the first generation remained inside New Eden Township? If he wanted to leave and see Della, as desperately as you claim, he would've done so. Nothing prevented him from leaving."

Timothy cocked an eyebrow at Fillion. "The first generation is singularly mentioned once more in comments—"

"Answer the question." Fillion relaxed into an aloof posture, an intimidating pose of nonchalant power that intensified Oaklee's waning fortitude.

"You are an interesting figure, *Corlan*." Timothy offered a friendly smile that did not reach his eyes. "Why exactly do you stand as leadership upon the stage? You are a guest in our community, not a Noble. Not even my son stands beside me this moment. Do you wish to share any reasons as to why you demonstrate public confidence as a figure of power?" An arrogant smile formed on Fillion's face in reply as he tucked thumbs into his breeches, which Oaklee noted were trembling. Timothy added, a triumphant gleam in his razor sharp gaze, "Your father groomed you well, Fillion Nichols." The smug expression remained on Fillion's face, but his eyes creased as if experiencing a brief shock of pain.

Whispers began to circulate once more and Fillion's name softly echoed throughout the stone building. Curious eyes regarded him, and Fillion shifted attention to the stage floor, a muscle flicking in his jaw. The community now knew who he was, or at least they connected the surname to Hanley. The murmurs reflected confusion, excitement; some lilted with fascination.

"Answer the question, Timothy!" shouted a man from near the center of the room, and Fillion's shoulders sagged in relief.

Timothy smiled at the gathering and said, "Gladly. The issue is not about legal authority, it is about representation. Lawrence and many others are calling into question Joel's willingness to—"

"What kind of moronic response is that?" Fillion asked in an even angrier tone than before. "So it's Joel's fault if the community disbands because you, Connor, and Norah were too inept to represent your community? Way to insult everyone, Timothy."

Laughter floated throughout the room and Timothy scanned the crowd as his face darkened. "Once again you interrupt me and twist my words."

"No, I'm untwisting—and keeping you on point," Fillion said. "Do you regularly make stupid, uneducated statements as if they are fact?"

"Please share with New Eden exactly what recommends you as an expert on such topics," Timothy said with raised eyebrows and a taunting grin, one that appeared more jovial and charming than arrogant. When Fillion refused to reply, Timothy smirked. "*Fillion*, leave this building. We shall deal with your insubordinate behavior later."

Connor cleared his throat. "Timothy, he is intimate with details pertaining to our community for he is Nobility of his world and ours, as well you know. You are also aware that he holds more power than you and I, or any other within New Eden." Shocked whispers circulated once more, heads bending toward each other, and Connor paused to allow the revelation to fully absorb. "Perhaps I should formally introduce our guest. New Eden Township, I am honored to present Fillion Nichols, Son of Eden, also affectionately known as Corlan Jayne in certain circles to honor his late great-grandfather."

Oaklee pressed her hand onto her stomach with shock. Fillion was the Son of Eden? Leaf winced, confirming what she doubted. Most stared wide-eyed at Fillion. Wonder and reverence colored the faces of those from the second and third generation, as the man of bedtime stories stood in the flesh before them. Of course he was the Son of Eden, she internally chided herself. He possessed magic and was indeed powerful, and the mystery behind their personal, twisted tale deepened further.

She did not think Fillion capable of blushing, but his face shaded several hues as he slowly lifted his eyes and found hers. The world dissolved and narrowed until only they remained, and he blinked slowly, vulnerable, as if pleading for her to rescue him. Then, his eyes skipped over the crowd. For those who perhaps did not know his body language cues, he appeared stoic and regal. But she saw the slight elevation of his shoulders and the subtle downward angle of his head, his brows furrowed in distress.

"And, he makes valid points," the Fire Element continued after a long pause, "which anyone in the community is given freedom to make." Connor turned toward Fillion and bowed his head. "Please stay. You are welcome, My Lord."

The Wind Element's eyes turned to slits as he scrutinized Fillion, and his lips curled up in a slight smile. Fillion looked away in a blasé manner, as if the very sight of Timothy was the most uninteresting view he had ever beheld.

Appearing unaware of the silent challenge, Connor began once more. "The community cannot solely blame Joel if we, as a Nobile class, failed to represent your needs and concerns to Hanley Nichols. I am most grieved and shall endeavor to find solutions to your worries, and I am confident Leaf and Timothy embody mutual sentiments."

"Oaklee?" Laurel squeaked. "Does the community no longer have affection for our family?"

"Oh, darling. We are still esteemed and valued." Oaklee pulled her sister tight against her and stroked her hair. "There are many who are afraid of change, though, and feel powerless." Ember looked at Oaklee and frowned, a rare breech in her usually calm demeanor.

"Thank you, Connor. I do indeed express the same sentiments," Leaf said with a bow toward the Fire Element. "Timothy established a most interesting point as well." Her brother also dipped his head toward Timothy. "New Eden Township shall endure many changes in the months and years to come. Those who are affected the most by the transition to Project Phase Two and Three are notably the second and third generations. For this reason," Leaf paused and shared a glance with Fillion, "with the authority and ownership granted to me by Hanley Nichols, I respectfully ask for Connor and Timothy to honorably step down as Elements and I shall appoint new Elements from the second generation in their stead."

The room hushed into a restless stillness. People stood immobilized, mouths agape and eyes rounded. It was as if a collective breath was being taken. Then, a maelstrom of shouting began and the community undulated with agitated motions.

"You have no authority for such decisions!" yelled a woman.

"New leadership! New leadership!" chanted a young man, followed by others from the second generation.

"He thinks he's The Aether!" shouted several others at once, and cries of alarm sprung from the crowd as the implications of Leaf's declaration settled upon the room.

Connor held his hands behind his back as his posture straightened. "Son of Earth," the Fire Element said, voice stiff, "we need to speak privately."

"There is nothing to discuss," Leaf said in reply. "I have made my decision."

"This is an outrage!" Timothy sputtered.

People continued to shout over one another, arguing and chanting their positions, and the roar of various emotions rumbled through Oaklee.

Timothy maneuvered his paunchy frame in front of her brother, narrowing his eyes. "Leaf Watson, I do believe the isolation and confinement has addled your thinking as you are displaying, once again, characteristics unfit for leadership, even proclaiming authority you do not possess. Your brash behavior is evidence that *you* should honorably step down. Grieve the loss of your father and care for your family and let go of the additional stress of also caring for the community."

Leaf lowered his head and his face warmed with the condescending insult. The winds of injustice sprang to life within Oaklee. The anger swirled and consumed her until she could no longer bridle her tongue.

"How dare you," she snapped, stomping toward Timothy. "A person from this community entered our home without permission and committed an act of violence against my personal property, a necessary tool for my trade. And you have the audacity to make this about Leaf's mental faculties?"

Timothy turned toward her with a kind smile and bowed. "Daughter of Earth, my sincerest apologies for the pain and fright you have experienced this day."

"Thank you, My Lord. Your apology, however, does not rebuild my spinning wheel nor ensure my safety against one who most definitely exhibits traits of insanity, for who would commit such an act against their neighbor or a young woman? What shall you do to recompense for my loss, Timothy Kane? Why do you blame my father and brother instead of standing up for my home by trying discover the perpetrator? Perhaps this is why we need fresh leadership."

"Willow Oak," Connor said as anger simmered in his large frame. "We appreciate your words, but please return to Ember and Laurel. I shall discuss further with your brother *privately.*"

"I shall not! I am First Representative and my voice shall be heard!"

"And it has been made most clear. Thank you, Daughter of Earth," Connor said with firmness, gently taking her arm and leading her toward the stairs.

"Let her stay," Fillion said. "She's the victim in this situation and deserves the opportunity to publicly represent herself."

Connor studied Fillion for several heartbeats and then released her arm, his muscles flexing from the controlled anger. Normally, the Fire Element was more vocal and asserted his authority at every opportunity, but he allowed Fillion to have the upper hand.

The look of incredulity on Timothy's face nearly made her laugh and brought further unrest upon those within the Great Hall.

The gathering rippled with energy, and Oaklee boldly met the eyes of those she had known her entire life. The hurt lanced her last resolve and she turned toward Fillion and graced him with an elegant curtsy for his defense of her needs, bowing her head in honor as she lowered to the ground.

"She supports the Outsider!"

"No, she supports the Son of Eden!" hollered another.

"My family also stands behind the Son of Eden!"

"Aye!" Voices lifted in solidarity.

"The Watsons wish to disband!"

"Silence!" Leaf shouted and, surprisingly, the command was obeyed, faces registering bewilderment as if considering whether Leaf's earlier claims were true. Or perhaps they were shocked into silence by Leaf's uncharacteristic anger. Satisfied with the response, Leaf faced Timothy and Connor and said, "Do you honorably step down from your positions of authority?"

"Leaf Dylan Watson, we need to speak privately now!" Connor bellowed. "If you possess any shred of decency or care for this community, you shall heed my request."

Her brother squinted his eyes in contemplation. "I accept your request, but we shall converse here," Leaf said, dipping his head. "Please excuse us," her brother stated to the gathering. He walked over to the far corner of the stage and gestured for Connor to follow. Timothy began to walk toward them, but Connor turned and shook his head.

Not wishing to remain alone on the stage, or to be forced to stand beside Timothy, Oaklee lifted her head and gracefully walked across the planked platform toward Fillion.

"Nice," he whispered. Oaklee whipped her head toward Fillion and offered a feeble smile as her heart galloped, before lowering her eyes in modesty per custom.

"I fear I shall faint at any moment," she whispered in reply, gripping the bobbin until her fingers cramped.

"If you do, I'll kiss you in front of everyone."

"You jest!" She looked up, horrified.

"Wake the sleeping Maiden—you know how the story goes."

"Only a prince can awaken the slumbering princess," Oaklee retorted under her breath. A small, devilish grin appeared on his face and he gave her a mischievous side glance. "You are so infuriating."

"You like it."

"You think too highly of yourself. I most certainly do not."

Oaklee narrowed her eyes, hoping her protests sounded sincere. Her eyes always gave everything away, though. He leaned over and she felt his lips against her ear as he whispered, "Then don't faint," and she could not stop the shiver his words produced.

Fillion resumed his position and lowered his head to hide an amused grin. She pursed her lips to suppress the irritated groan that wished to surface, knowing it would only encourage him further. He was such a knave. She closed her eyes and took in a deep breath, slowly releasing the air in an attempt to calm her nerves.

"Willow." His warm breath breezed over her cheek, and she opened her eyes. "Who is the Son of Eden?"

"A man of magic and power." Oaklee angled toward him. "Since my early childhood, stories were told that the Son of Eden would come and save the new generations from the evils of the Outside world."

"Evils? God, no pressure or anything." Fillion's face contorted with controlled anger. "What the hell?"

"I do not believe such pressures come from the Divine or Hell, but rather are man-made."

Fillion bit his lower lip to suppress a laugh. "You're such a brat." With a dry tone, he said, "The claim is vague. You believe this story?"

"You did not know…," Oaklee said, unsure of how to answer him. "Perhaps Connor is mistaken and you are not the Son of Eden?"

"Moot point. Everyone thinks I am now. And they all know who else I am, too." Fillion lifted his shoulder in a subtle shrug as his lower cheek twitched, as if he nibbled the inside of his mouth. Murmurs grew to loud conversations as everyone awaited Leaf and Connor's return. But she ignored the building noise and instead regarded Fillion's mannerisms as he silently processed. "I didn't know the story," he said, his confession barely audible. "My dad finds great pleasure in setting me up to fail."

"You shall not fail, Master Fillion," Oaklee said, drawing herself up taller with a resolute look. "You are far too pig-headed."

A corner of his mouth lifted as he studied her face, the light blues of his eyes clouding with apprehension despite the marked amusement. "You don't know my dad."

Footsteps clacked across the wood as Connor approached the front of the stage and a hush fell over the crowd. Even the children quieted. The Fire Element's face was strangely relaxed even though the lines around his eyes suggested inner tension. Leaf maintained a respectful but downcast expression as he straightened his shoulders to appear dignified without garnering center attention.

"New Eden Township," Connor said regally. "It has been a great honor and privilege serving you as your Fire Element. I humbly relinquish the head Noble status to another who shall rise up and lead a new generation."

The crowd remained too stunned for comment, silently watching on as if in a dream state. Oaklee's mouth slackened involuntarily with his unexpected statement.

"No," Timothy said, shaking his head in disbelief. "What evidence do we have that Leaf possesses legal authority for such decisions? For all we know, these are the demands of the delusional! Anyone can claim to be The Aether."

Fillion's expression changed from apprehension to boredom as he stepped forward, pulling from his pouch the metallic device. Eyes watched him closely, astonished sounds echoing through the room when the silver object glinted in the light. He placed it on his ear, tapped it, and a strange ghostly image with vibrant colors suddenly appeared and wavered in the air, showcasing words, lines, and shapes.

Women shrieked, startling several babies and children into wails, and the crowd stepped back. Laurel buried her face into Ember's side, a reaction that intensified the swelling trepidation in Oaklee, and sudden dizziness made her list. But she remembered Fillion's promise and refused to faint, planting her feet.

"Magic!" several young people cried out, eliciting a wave of fearful vociferations throughout the room.

Fillion confidently tapped an image that hovered in the air, and all of the pictures and words suddenly vanished, only to be replaced by another picture. Fillion seemed to grab the corners and pull out, and the image responded by gradually enlarging. The flying piece of paper continued to mysteriously float in the air; and villagers exclaimed over the phenomenon. Fillion turned the paper to face the crowd, many of whom threw up hands to cover their faces in horror, horror that he ignored and, instead, beckoned for Jeff to come forward. The lawyer's eyes still reflected the grief of Norah's death, but he trudged toward the stage with pinched brows, staring curiously at the paper, reading.

"What does it say?" Fillion asked.

The lawyer perused the paper, placing a hand over his mouth as his face sobered into concentration. Jeff touched the paper and moved it to the right, and a new page immediately appeared, moving the page yet again as a finger tracked where he read. When he finished reading, he moved the pages to the left, and the previous pages reappeared, and then he lifted his eyes to Fillion. "It is best if you state it."

A small, triumphant smiled formed on Fillion's face. "Don't want to break The Code?" he taunted. "It says that the oldest surviving child of Joel Watson is heir in a Legacy that bequeaths partial ownership of New Eden Township and New Eden Biospherics & Research. Additionally, the trust grants Leaf governing authority as The Aether."

"You realize, Leaf," Timothy said in a singsong voice, "that by revealing your secret identity you are hereby banished to the Outside world per The Code, where you shall face possible charges of corporate sabotage, also outlined in The Code."

Voices began vehemently shouting once again. The words and sounds blended into a discordant noise, causing Oaklee to scrunch up her face and cover her ears.

"Leaf, did you ever sign The Code?" Fillion asked.

"No, My Lord, I have not. Nor have any others who have reached full majority in the second generation."

"The first generation signed for the minors in their…" Timothy stopped and turned wide eyes to Jeff. "Is what he speaks true? The second generation is not under the legal authority of The Code?"

Jeff blinked nervously and raised a curious eyebrow at Fillion, a small calculating smile lifting the corners of his mouth. "It appears the Son of Eden has found a loophole in the document. You cannot break something to which you are not bound."

Timothy reddened and turned for guidance to Connor, who gave a solemn nod of acknowledgment.

"Your father and mother would be most proud of you, son," Connor said, his face tensing with emotion. Leaf's eyes sheened, though he maintained a steadfast expression and sturdy posture. "This day, you boldly walked forward as a man and risked much for your family." Connor knelt upon the wooden stage with one knee. "And I wish to be the first to proclaim: Hail, King Leaf, The Aether of New Eden Township!"

One by one, dazed and uncertain community members knelt down and began to chant, "Hail, King Leaf! Hail, King Leaf!" in a fashion closer to a reaction than a conviction.

Oaklee's hands flew to her mouth as she realized Connor had broken The Code and asked all, including the first generation, to do the same. They were all guilty now. It was a move that equalized the growing imbalance and provided leverage for any communications Leaf may have with Hanley over this incident. Never had she wanted to embrace Connor as she did now. He had given her family a beautiful gift from the ashes of this grievous adversity.

Fillion waved a hand through the air as if grabbing the image, and the document promptly vanished. The magic boggled Oaklee's mind and she studied the silver object fastened to his ear. In fluid movements, Fillion lowered to one knee beside her and bowed deeply before her brother, turning his head to the side. Through lowered lashes, Oaklee studied Fillion from her position of honor, moved by his sacrifice.

"Thank you, Maiden," he whispered, meeting her eyes.

"For what, My Lord?"

"Fillion."

She sighed. "How have I earned your gratitude, *Fillion?*"

"You didn't make me choose between you and your brother." He bit his lower lip, more as a nervous gesture. "You kept your promise."

"Aye, My Lord." Oaklee hesitated, unconvinced of her brother's brazen move, despite the cheers venerating Leaf with exaltation of his kingship. She turned toward Fillion and whispered, "My pledges of honor are always sincere." Vulnerability flashed instantly in his sharp gaze, his eyes appearing to dim further, if that were possible. Without words, she knew he was thinking of an entirely different pledge.

Nearby movement caught her eye and Oaklee watched with disgust as Timothy knelt with obvious reluctance. She examined the room and noted many who did not kneel, however, their arms crossed over their chests or straight at their sides, stiffened with offense. Leaf also noted these individuals with a kind smile and bow, his stare unmistakably determined; and Oaklee could almost see the wheels turning in her brother's head. Was one of these community members responsible for their pain and loss?

"Thank you for the esteem. Please rise," Leaf said, thick with emotion. Rustling sounds of fabric and movement resounded throughout the room and when it quieted, Leaf continued. "I shall endeavor to be a man worthy of such a position and will uphold my family's legacy of love and honor in our community."

Her brother knelt on the stage and placed a hand on his heart as he lowered his head to return the honor given him. After several beats, he rose and nervously sought out Ember, his face relaxing as he beheld his wife. Ember blushed prettily and offered Leaf a beautiful smile, the pride fairly glowing all over her sister-in-law's face. Laurel beamed as well, a wide smile gracing her small face as she stared in wonder at her brother. Leaf bowed toward Ember and Laurel, and then resumed a strong posture before the community.

"I wish to relay a message to Hanley Nichols and need your assistance," Leaf said to the gathering. "To better estimate the opinion of those who wish to oppose project shutdown, I request that you divide into two groups. On this side of the Great Hall," Leaf pointed with an extended hand toward the grand hearth, "is where I need you to stand if you wish to disband. Those who wish for a permanent residence within New Eden, stand over yonder."

People studied one another with dubiety and then shuffled to separate parts of the room. She stared at her brother with swelling fear, wanting to pound him with her fists for making himself a grand target, yet embrace him for being so steadfast as he broke traditions for the sake of the community. Leaf turned his head and met her worried look. Subtly, he crossed his heart as a somber smile eclipsed his show of strength. To others, it may have appeared he adjusted his garment. But she understood his message and crossed her heart in reply.

The residents settled into positions, a large majority wishing to remain in New Eden permanently. Neighbors eyed each other warily, some with mounting hostility, and Oaklee felt the edges of her vision fade once more.

"Thank you. I shall send Hanley Nichols a message relaying that three-quarters of our community have declared their desire to request permanent residence within New Eden Township. Please, join one another and erase the line of separation. And please do not allow differences in opinion to divide our home. We are a unified community and shall stand strong, regardless of how many days we share together."

Heads turned and sought the direction of neighbors. Feet shifted and low murmurs conferred. Then, one brave soul in favor of disbanding moved toward those who wished to remain, and another, followed by the rest of their small group. Once the community settled, Leaf offered an appreciative smile and issued another request.

"Skylar Kane and Ember Watson, please step forward."

The air crackled with suspense, for the pairing was most unexpected, especially in light of Leaf and Ember's elopement. Laurel ran to Oaklee's side as Ember mounted the stage, and Oaklee placed a protective arm around her sister.

Leaf faced his friend and said, "Skylar, I wish to appoint you as the new Wind Element. Do you accept this position of honor?" Skylar shifted his eyes to Timothy. "Son of Wind," Leaf said with firmness. "You are a man and do not need permission from your father. I possess the power to appoint another in your stead. I shall ask you again, do you accept the head Noble position of Wind Element?"

Skylar gripped Leaf's forearm. "Yes, Your Majesty. I am honored and shall dedicate my life to the community."

"Well said, and quite Noble of you," Leaf replied in a hushed voice. "Have you been trained for the aristocracy?"

The new Wind Element laughed quietly, almost a forced sound, and with a wry smile walked away and stood behind Leaf.

"Ember Watson," Leaf said in a much softer tone. "I wish to appoint Coal Hansen as the Fire Element. Do you accept this position in his absence as his First Representative?"

"Yes, Your Majesty, with honor." Ember lowered to the ground with elegance. When she rose, Leaf took her hand and kissed it.

"Family," her brother began again. "I present your new Element head Nobles of New Eden Township." The community clapped their hands, some cheering. But most simply looked on wide-eyed, their hands moving only with obligation.

When the residents quieted, Leaf continued. "Today an incredible woman breathed her last. A woman I considered an adoptive mother, and I know many of you share similar sentiments. She embodied love and kindness and gave much of herself for our community. Let us set aside our differences and fears and remember the Daniels family this week as we observe all the rituals of death in Norah's honor. Harvest is almost upon us, as well. There is much work to accomplish. A new Water Element shall be appointed in due time."

Heads bowed in agreement, many placing hands upon their hearts, and Leaf closed his eyes with a look of relief. But Oaklee gathered that most did so out of obedience and to honor Norah, not her brother.

A faded beat rapped from a distance. A sound like war drums grew louder, as if an entire army marched over their heads. The pitter-patter of their footsteps rumbled with a steady pace. Her brother had just declared war, and the entire Great Hall stilled as the Outside weather thumped to the shift of their community's atmosphere. Nevertheless, Oaklee gasped with delight, and placed a hand to her chest as her heart threatened to leave her body and join the rhythm echoing throughout the biodome.

As she stared at the entrance, the Daughter of Water walked into the Great Hall with ghost-like movements. Her pale skin appeared transparent and gray beneath her exposed dark hair and swollen, red eyes. Upon seeing the gathering, she raised the hood of her cloak. The community acknowledged her state of mourning and followed suit to show their support.

Fillion leaned toward Oaklee. "What's going on?"

The grass swayed in the bio-wind just past the giant hewn doors, propped open by stones, and shadows stained the landscape like watermarks. Oaklee smiled, blessed by Earth's tears of sorrow over Norah's death and tears of joy over Leaf's triumph. Oaklee closed her eyes and imagined a weepy sky and a shower of water droplets crashing against her body. Oh, how she longed to immerse herself in the redemptive experience and forget all her woes and hardships. Was Coal given opportunity to enjoy such a wondrous phenomenon?

Her eyes fluttered open, and she nearly blushed with the unbound look in Fillion's eyes as he admired her every nuance. Instead, she marveled over the flickering dotted shadows beyond the entry once more. The army continued to march, and she whispered, "Rain."

Transitions prompted by hardships are essential experiences along life's journey. The maturing of one's mind and heart is always fraught with awkwardness, making it difficult to want to complete this process. However, if this step is skipped, the elements that comprise our inner-person risk remaining no more solid than shifting sand.

— Dr. Della Jayne Nichols, "The Necessity of Transitions," *Psychology Today*, January 2049

CHAPTER SIXTEEN

Thursday, October 15, 2054

Mercer Island, Washington state

Tiny pin-prick drops stung Coal's face as he emerged from the car, and he lifted his eyes to the dreary sky, mesmerized by the sensation. Since departing the airport, wisps of watery lace had streaked the car's windows and Coal had stared with longing, wishing to feel rain against his skin. Two weeks prior it rained in Southern California, but the pollution level was too high for a stroll outside, according to Michael.

Coal continued to watch the sky in wonder, jumping when a drop of water landed in his eye. Humorously he wiped his face, realizing he must look rather stupid. From the corner of his eye, he noted that Hanley spoke with the chauffeur and had, thankfully, not noticed.

"Ready?" Hanley asked, pulling a small bag from the trunk. "The chauffeur will unload our belongings."

Coal studied the large home with many windows winking in the afternoon light—incredulous that a small family needed such space—and then flitted his gaze around the property. His eyes fastened upon a body of water that sparkled and shimmered behind the Nichols residence, whispering an invitation to come stand before its shores.

"I need fresh air and shall join you shortly," he said with a tight smile. "May I?" Coal nodded toward the lake.

Hanley looked in the direction Coal indicated. "Ten minutes."

"Yes, sir."

Coal removed his shoes and socks with haste, and his feet wiggled in the lush, green grass. Hanley and the chauffeur walked away in brisk strides, eventually disappearing into the large abode.

Fat drops splattered across Coal's body and he laughed, pulling the leather strip from his hair. He ran a hand through the loosened strands and closed his eyes while exposing his face to the sky once more, listening to the thundering pitter-patter of water colliding with earth. Giddiness filled him and he opened his eyes and jogged through the yard beyond the house.

The deep-blue surface of the water erupted with dainty gray-white splashes. A mist shrouded the structures over on the opposite shore, and they appeared as faerie homes nestled in an enchanted wood, the trees swaying with the same spell that bewitched him. He sat on the edge of the grass, sinking his toes into the rocky sand, not caring that he was drenched. Water and wind swirled around his form as he stared out into vastness. This was real. This was how the elements played and interacted with one another as nature intended.

A large smile touched his face and he fell backwards onto the grass, stretching out his arms as he closed his eyes. Water gently pulsed on his skin in an ancient rhythm and he breathed in deeply the mystery and wonder of such an experience. Bio-rain was a mechanical response, a shower that fell from pipes embedded within the geodesic sky. Clouds did not bring rain nor did the sky change color before the water fell. Gray had never looked as elegant as when it dressed the sky, he decided.

A contented sigh left his mouth right before an object jabbed his side, and he reflexively flew to a sitting position as his body snapped to attention. A young woman screamed and jumped back, dropping the offending stick as her hands covered her mouth. Large hazel eyes stared in horror, and he remained immobilized on the grass as his mind caught up with his pulse.

"I thought you were dead!" She lowered her hands, but her eyes remained rounded with fear.

"Forgive me for my unexpected resurrection," he said with a lopsided grin, but she did not appear to appreciate humor this moment.

He casually studied her features, admiring how much prettier she was in person. The pictures on the Internet did not fully capture her pixie-like qualities as exhibited presently. Rivulets of water ran down her fair skin, sprinkled with tiny, nearly indiscernible freckles. Bruises or indicators of assault were absent from her face, most likely the result of an Outsider medical treatment. Lynden blinked, raising a hand to shield her vision from the rain, and the bright blue polish on her fingernails came alive against her black hood. An errant red strand peaked out, swooping over an eye, and he held back a smile, curious to see her vibrant tresses.

"Are you crazy? What the hell are you doing on my property?" She paused and widened her eyes once more. "Are you from the media?"

"No, I am from—"

"Go home or wherever it is you crawled out from."

Coal lifted his eyebrows in surprise. "If only I could return home. Alas, you are stuck with me for a duration. Your father and I have just arrived."

He gradually stood and moved the wet hair that had fallen in front of his face to behind his ears, feeling self-conscious of his charcoal-stained fingertips. Lynden took several steps backwards and then abruptly halted all movement upon noting his size. Her eyes trailed him from head to toe and then slowly back up again as she nibbled a lip ring on the left side of her mouth and twisted a black metal band round her thumb. The simple gray shirt he wore clung to his body as the water suctioned the material to his skin; and he warmed despite the damp chill as she appraised him, as if he may not possess familiar human traits.

Astonishment transitioned to annoyance, and her features hardened as their gazes collided in mutual curiosity and irritation. Still, he remembered his manners and bowed as a gentleman should. He anxiously met her eyes once more, brightened by a thick black line that rimmed her eyelashes and a dark, sparkly purple paint upon her lids.

Extending his hand, he said, "I am—"

She groaned, interrupting his introduction, and then rolled her eyes while placing her fidgeting hands into the pockets of her tattered jacket. Lynden quirked her eyebrow with a blasé expression and then stomped toward the house. He rapidly blinked his eyes as nerves pooled in his stomach. Confused, he ambled toward the house a few strides behind. In two weeks, he had met many people. But she was the first to intentionally snub him.

What had he done?

Did she resent it that her father employed him to guard her in public?

Or was he viewed as a lesser human in her eyes since he was merely the product of an experiment?

The glass door leading into the house shut in his face and he stood awkwardly, not sure if he should enter while dripping wet, or what to make of her rudeness. Nevertheless, standing outside while looking in was even more awkward. So he turned the knob and entered with quiet steps, startling when a hand grabbed him roughly by the belt loop and yanked, leading him across the tiled floor to a highly polished wood table.

Lynden shook her head as if he was a helpless lad in desperate need of assistance. "Sit," she commanded, then pushed him into a chair. Of course he would have to sit.

Coal licked his lips nervously, leaning against the chair back, and averted his eyes to ensure he did not cause further offense. But his blood boiled and he worked hard to bank the growing heat in his veins. And then he felt guilt, for no doubt she was still processing the many emotions from her traumatic experience. Perhaps he had frightened her.

Coal chanced a look her way when Lynden opened a giant metal box, sticking her head in as she rummaged around. In smooth movements she turned his direction and threw an apple. Coal caught the red fruit easily, marveling at the chilled outer skin before peering her way in question. She smirked and then grabbed another apple and a small cup with a metal lid. The young woman hopped onto a marble counter, tucked the apple into a pocket and then shut the box's door with her foot while opening the metal lid on the cup with her teeth while simultaneously leaning to the side and opening up a drawer. Her eyes looked up to the ceiling in concentration as the metal lid tore off the cup, hanging in her teeth, and she lifted up a spoon in celebration. Coal had to suppress a smile, amused with her unladylike deportment.

He subtly took in her fashion as she sauntered his direction, unable to understand why some young men and women of the Outside preferred clothing that was ripped, hanging in strange threads, and wrapped in some areas like bandages. Chains and straps apparently were not meant for function but for ornamentation. Her pants strangely ended mid-thigh, held on by straps that disappeared under a rather short skirt. Coal looked away embarrassed, not wishing to appear ungentlemanly or insensitive to any form of modesty she may possess. The young women of this culture did not hide their bodies as he was accustomed and he warred with constant guilt, feeling dishonorable in the direction of his thoughts at times.

To his surprise, she jumped onto the table top as if it were a chair. Her legs swung back and forth like a child sitting upon a tree limb, the metal lid still hanging from her teeth. Her head tilted slightly as she regarded him, and then she pulled the lid from her mouth.

"Here, lick it. It's the best part," she said in a matter-of-fact way. Coal tentatively took the lid and lifted the flexible metal up for closer inspection, marveling that she removed it with her teeth. "It's yogurt. Seriously, just lick it off. Everyone does."

Not wishing to cause further offense, he followed her suggestion and gave the lid a light lick. A burst of sweet flavor greeted his tongue and he needed no further encouragement to finish off the rest.

"I have a weakness for yogurt," she said as her face softened a little.

"I am fond of yogurt as well. Although, I have never tasted one so sweet."

"Poor you."

"Indeed." Coal smiled, turning the cold apple in his hand.

"Take a bite of the apple. It's a honeycrisp. My absolute favorite. You'll die when you experience the first juicy bite." Lynden issued a look of patient perseverance when Coal hesitated. Nothing appeared as it should since he emerged, and many things were deemed poisoned or polluted. She gave him a gentle nudge on the leg with her shoe. "Come on, I don't know even know your name. I only poison people I know on a first-name basis," she said with a straight face.

Was she insulting his intelligence and mocking him?

Annoyed, he whispered, "My name is—"

"Wait on intros!" she said with urgency, eyes wide. In a calmer voice she continued, "Take a bite first. Trust me." She maintained a serious expression and waited patiently for him to follow her directions.

Not sure of what to make of Lynden, or her style of interaction with a perfect stranger, he took a bite of the honeycrisp apple. The snap and juiciness were most pleasant as tart and sweet flavors filled his mouth, and he chewed appreciatively.

"Now let's meet." She sighed in dramatic relief. "According to the spell, you prevented the poison by not sharing your name, which only activates with a first bite." She gave him a bored look and the corners of his mouth lifted in a slight smile, understanding her brand of dry humor. She pulled the apple out of her pocket and took a bite and then said while chewing, "I'm Lynden Nichols."

"Coal Hansen," he replied with a slight bow of his head while suppressing yet another smile.

"By the way, I'm your Guide to Life or some dumb official title like that." She puffed at a damp strand of blood-red hair from across her eye. "You passed the first test—surviving a honeycrisp apple." Lynden placed her feet on the seat of the chair and against his thighs, and Coal looked down in discomfort with her familiarity. "I'm glad you're not retarded."

"I beg your pardon?" Coal jerked his head up.

"Yeah, first impressions and all that. You looked like a giant oaf out there in the rain. I seriously thought you died smiling." Coal burst into laughter—the imagery was too rich. Her face relaxed as she studied his face, and then, as if snapping out of a trance, it quickly changed into irritation. "Who does that? Is it some Martian ritual or something?"

"No," he replied quickly, attempting to suppress more laughter. "Our rituals are dark and barbaric and involve blood sacrifices."

An ill-humored look flashed across her face, one he knew was more in jest. "Which is why you believe in poisoned apples."

"Naturally."

"What the hell were you doing then?"

He looked around the room, suddenly feeling foolish. "I had never experienced rain until a few moments ago."

"Seriously?"

He whispered, "Not real rain, My Lady." The honorary titled slipped out even though he knew it was not used in this world. Some habits were harder to break than others.

Lynden winced and stared at him for several heartbeats before replying, "Oh my god. How weird."

Shame surfaced with her response and he lowered his eyes. The apple rotated in his hands in an attempt to stay busy and contain his brewing emotions. Coal tired of being a novelty.

She nudged his thigh again with her foot. "Hey, toughen up."

Coal clamped down on all comments that burned in him with her insult, and she released a sound that unhappily crossed a sigh with a groan. Lynden jumped off the table with cat-like motions and slinked onto his lap. He dropped the apple and gripped the chair's frame as she brought her face within inches of his own. A coy smile touched her lips as she bit into her apple. A fleck of juice sprayed his cheek as the rhythmic crunch teased him. He was quite certain the veins in his neck visibly throbbed. No woman in New Eden would ever deign to such a wanton position, and all his training as a gentleman choked at how to handle such a delicate situation. Flustered, Coal looked away, but she grabbed his face and forced him to pay attention to her.

"My culture will devour you in a nanosecond."

"How pleasant," he said, risking a charming smile to mask his real feelings. Nevertheless, Coal flinched with her words.

"You're awesome, remember that." She continued, harsh and bitter. "Who cares what anyone says about you? And they will talk shit. People are going to verbally destroy you, plaster your image all over the Net, say hateful things about you as if they're fact, and you need to be indifferent. Got that? You don't give a shit. About anything." She removed her grip from his chin. "Why?"

"Because I am awesome."

"Exactly. OK, Mr. Awesome, one more lesson."

She readjusted her position and straddled his lap across the chair as she pressed her body against him. He sucked in a quick breath right as her mouth unexpectedly claimed his. Every muscle stilled and every thought disarmed and he furiously attempted to regain composure. She tasted of apple and the sweetness danced across his tongue as his senses flared with temptation, especially when her hands traveled up his chest and down his arms in languid motions.

What was he allowing?

Coal jumped to a standing position, gently grabbing her around the waist. Lynden winced and touched her ribs for a moment and then relaxed into an aloof posture. Once they both found their footing, Coal dropped his hands and slipped behind the chair, struggling to maintain self-control.

She gave an exasperated look. "Worse than I thought."

"Are you mad?" he bellowed.

"Relax. I needed to know how much work was ahead of us."

"Forgive my ignorance, but when does becoming so familiar with a stranger create a baseline for work? And I wish it to be known that I would never dishonor you, nor any woman, in such a manner."

Lynden's face softened with disbelief and she nibbled on her lip ring once more. "That's kinda cute actually."

"Please tell me you jest."

"I jest," she said in a mocking tone, rolling her eyes. "Get real. You think what I did was bad? Shit, you have no idea, do you? Did they prepare you for anything before departing your planet?"

"How is this relevant to any life I shall endure before returning to New Eden?"

She offered a hollow smile. "Toughen up, Mr. Awesome." Lynden maneuvered around the chair, intentionally bumping his hip with hers while biting into her apple. "Going to change my clothes. I'll be down in a sec."

He peered over his shoulder, surprised as Lynden passed a young man with wild blue, green, and white hair—the same man from the picture. Coal placed the apple on the table and angled his body to face the stranger.

How much did the young man see?

"I feel sorry for you," the young man said with a straight face. Lynden's sopping wet jacket pelted him in the head and he yelped. "You'll rue the day you were ever born, Rainbow! Just wait and see if you don't!"

"Done!" she chirped from a distance and the young man laughed, kicking her jacket across the floor. Coal watched the jacket leave a moist trail as it journeyed beneath the table, releasing a pool of water as it stilled. "So, you're Farm Boy?" The young man casually leaned up against the door frame and smirked. "Shit, look at you. What exactly do you plow on Mars?"

"I am not a farmhand."

"I know. You're a blacksmith, Son of Fire, blah, blah, blah." The man sniffed and walked into the kitchen area, sizing him up. "I like the nickname Farm Boy, though. So, Farm Boy it is!"

"And what do they call you?" Coal asked, coiled and ready to strike at the slightest provocation.

"Well, the ladies call me..." The young man slid a sly look Coal's way as his words trailed off. "Never mind. You're a noob. Probably your first kiss by the sounds of your manly squeals of protest."

Fire entered Coal's bloodstream and he punched the young man in the face before he realized what had happened. Hanley and Dr. Nichols walked into the kitchen just as the man staggered back, cupping his nose as blood seeped through the crevices of his fingers and dripped onto the floor.

"Shit! I think you broke my nose!" Vulgarities hissed from the man's mouth to the floor as he leaned over, tensing his face in pain.

Dr. Nichols lifted an eyebrow at Coal as her eyes wandered over his appearance. Heat suffused his face as puddles pooled around his feet and as blood dripped over the beautiful stone floor near the other young man's feet. Coal's disheveled state was shameful, as were his actions and lack of care or consideration for her home. Although Dr. Nichols was visibly disturbed, Hanley held a mildly amused smile.

"What did you say, Mack?" Hanley asked in an unruffled tone, as if such occurrences were common.

In a hushed reply, Dr. Nichols said, "Does it matter? Coal expressed an aggressive response, which should be evaluated further. Perhaps he is not regulating with the over-stimulation of our culture. He should sit out the press conference. I told you he should have remained at the lab one more week."

"My nose…!" Mack said in an exaggerated attempt to redirect attention.

Hanley regarded Mack for a heartbeat and then turned to his wife. "Mack said something to provoke Coal. Your project is not malfunctioning from over-exposure. And he won't embarrass you before the world."

"Oh. My. God." Mack cried out melodramatically.

"My sincerest apologies, My Lady. I am ashamed of my behavior and disregard for your home and company. Please permit me to make amends." Coal lowered his head and bowed.

What was a press conference?

"Holy shit. It was me! I deserved it. Now can someone get something for my nose?" Mack looked up and rolled his eyes at Coal, blood streaming down his hand and all over the floor.

Dr. Nichols' mouth set in a tight line as she flicked a glance at her husband and then walked away, the click of her tall, pointed-end shoes echoing throughout the neighboring room. Coal felt so helpless and awkward. This was his first time in another's home outside of New Eden Township, and already he was the cause of so much distress.

"Coal, freshen up. We have a press conference in forty-five minutes."

"Yes, sir. Where might I find my belongings?" He shifted on his feet, uncertain if he should travel through their home and potentially ruin other floors.

"Mack, take a seat and keep your head down," Hanley said, activating his Cranium. Somewhat distracted, he continued, "Your room is the second door on the left after climbing the stairs."

Mack looked at Coal. "Ever wanted to sleep in a coffin?"

Coal pinched his brows together, not sure if Mack was issuing a threat or describing the bed Coal would sleep in during his stay with the Nichols family.

"Whoa…" Lynden paled as she took in the scene, shooting a frightened look Coal's direction. "You did this?"

"Yes, My Lady." His shoulders sagged as he realized the slip once more.

How could he be so stupid?

Mack's comments were uncalled for and emasculating, but not worthy of a broken nose. After being assaulted by a man, this was the worst possible reaction he could have exhibited in Lynden's home.

"I was an ass," Mack's muffled voice volunteered. "Let it go, Rainbow."

"My temper overwhelmed my good senses," Coal said. "It shall not happen again."

"Are you always trouble?" she asked. Coal shrugged sheepishly in response. Lynden followed the trail of blood to where Mack sat, and then burst into laughter.

A droll look passed over Mack's eyes. "It's all your fault, *kusogaki*. Why the hell did you tell him to toughen up?"

"Whatever," she snorted as she tried to hold in more laughter. "Next time, kiss him instead of pissing him off. Maybe he prefers men over women." She winked at Coal and laughed once more, but sobered as soon as she noted the disapproval on her father's face. "Oh, don't give me that look." She batted her eyes and moved her body to appear angelic and innocent.

Dr. Nichols returned with a rag, went to the giant metal box and retrieved ice cubes, and placed the bundle in Mack's hands. "A doctor should arrive within the hour. Mackenzie Ferguson, you are a mess. Have you learned anything from this experience?"

"Yeah, don't mess with aliens. They'll kick your ass."

"Or perhaps diplomacy is a skill an elite son and heir, such as yourself, should employ more often?"

"I can behave," Mack said in a serious tone, almost indignant.

"The words 'I' and 'behave' have never paired well together in your life." Dr. Nichols smiled, amused.

"Oh please," Lynden said. "Mack just needs to lick his wounds and tuck his tail, not receive a counseling session." Lynden looked at the bloodied man and cooed in a syrupy voice, "Don't ya little fella?" The young man glared playfully at Lynden and made a gesture using his middle finger, and a satisfied grin lightened Lynden's features momentarily.

Dr. Nichols' mouth formed a tight line once more. "Please listen for the front door. I need to finish getting ready for the press conference."

"I am most sorry for the mess I have made," Coal said, as a puddle continued to pool and dribble around his feet, and Dr. Nichols halted her retreat. "Please allow me to clean it up once I have changed. Simply instruct where I may find usable rags."

"Thank you for your offer, but no need. Rosa will care for our floors. I have already summoned her." Dr. Nichols offered a small, distracted smile—her lips painted red—as she smoothed the front of her form-fitting black dress. She was still the most beautiful woman Coal had ever seen. He rolled his gaze toward Lynden, who watched her mother carefully, noting every nuance, before lowering her eyes with a look of disgust.

Coal let out a heavy breath and shifted on his feet, feeling awkward once more, when he lurched forward. Lynden yanked on his belt with a wry grin and the belittling treatment ignited his irritation. "Please excuse me," he said hastily as he moved forward at Lynden's behest once more.

"Come on, Mr. Awesome." Lynden pulled tightly.

He smiled politely as he passed his hosts, averting his eyes toward the ivy climbing the stone wall along the stairwell. Never had a woman touched his belt, let alone led him toward private chambers by one, which nearly made him laugh at such absurdity—as a woman had never climbed into his lap and kissed him before either.

His nerves increased with each step. A solid blue strand of hair that limply lay against the back of Lynden's head caught his attention. Her shoulder moved as her arm swung, causing her undershirt to shift. The small sleeve slipped down her arm and exposed the fair skin of her shoulder blade, sprinkled with tiny freckles. He began to turn his head away when a tattoo of a red dragon with yellow eyes stared at him briefly before it disappeared beneath the folds of her garment, peeking at him once more with another swing of her arm. The dragon continued to taunt him with each step, conjuring a memory of the day Hanley asked him to guard his daughter after telling the dragon story. Unease trickled through Coal's body, but he did not know why.

At the top of the stairs, she stopped and unwrapped what appeared to be a bandage that wound up her forearm. He had seen others with strange wrappings on their arms and legs and concluded it was fashion, not injuries. The white fabric dangled in the air as she slowly turned her head with a serious expression and he swallowed.

"Close your eyes," she said in a grave tone. He knew better than to question her after their previous interactions and so he obeyed, even though he did not relish the loss of control over something as mundane as seeing one's bedchamber. She must have sensed his anxiety. "You can't look at the black hole until you've jumped inside of it."

"What would happen should I see this room prior to jumping inside of it?" He flinched when he felt Lynden touch his face with the fabric.

"You don't want to know. There's a reason it's called the coffin."

"How tragically ominous."

She leaned against him until her warm breath pulsed on his neck as she wrapped the fabric around his eyes in several layers. Coal made his mind concentrate on breathing normally and not the discomfort of being led toward the unknown or of a young woman's body pressed against him.

His mind traveled to images of Oaklee and he pondered their kiss in the Cave, imagining it was her hands upon his face and not Lynden's. Homesickness was a word he learned this week as his heart sunk with yearning for the faces, voices, and sights of his past as he continued to interact with his future. He missed the musical sound of Oaklee's voice, her smile, the atmosphere of her presence, her wit, and the graceful ways she used her hands.

Did she miss him?

They had never been separated like this, and he felt as though a large piece of his self had been carved out of his soul. Yet, as each day passed, he pondered more and more Oaklee's resistance to his romance.

Could she perhaps be right, that they were better off as friends rather than lovers?

Did he cling to her out of fear of losing that friendship, should she marry another?

Did he really want her to love him merely as a result of his persistence?

If he were truly honest, he knew he could offer Oaklee protection without giving her his name. They were not dependent truths, although he had longed for them to be so.

Lynden moved her body away from his. "Think of dark and depressing things so the black hole can suck it out of you when your feet land in its existence."

Coal nodded his head as Lynden's fingers entwined with his, slowly guiding him to the door. He heard a creaking door hinge. She gently lifted his other hand and maneuvered his fingers to rest upon the wood of the door frame.

"On a count of three we'll jump," she said, her grip on his hand tightening. "1 ... 2 ... 3 ... jump!"

Lynden squealed as they both sprang into the air and he could not help the smile that stretched across his face. They landed with staccato beats upon what felt like a wooden floor, and Coal shuffled a foot on the smooth surface to further investigate his first sensation inside the Black Hole. Soft hands brushed against his face as Lynden wrapped herself around him to untie the fabric shielding his eyes.

"Keep your eyes closed, OK?"

Lynden walked away and the silence spanned until he thought he could manage no longer.

"Open your eyes," she summoned from across the room.

His eyes fluttered open and darkness engulfed him completely. Black Hole, indeed. The ceiling, floor, furniture, curtains and even the rug were all black, to the point of disorientation, and Coal struggled as his eyes wished to perceive depth and focus on items that instead faded in and out of the shadows. In the corner lay a bright blue instrument, similar to a lute, a blissful interruption.

"My brother lacks imagination," Lynden said from a large black chair, offering a bored shrug as she rolled her eyes. She appeared to float as his eyes adjusted to the contours of the chair, an ensorcelling image. The young woman glowed, her pale skin and brilliant hair a vibrant contrast to their surroundings, and Coal felt mystified as he knelt in her ethereal presence.

"Quite the opposite, I assure you," he said in reverent tones, unable to remove his eyes from the vision floating in the chair. "Beauty overwhelms and beguiles the soul in the ashes of this room. The colors seduce and awaken the senses to feel alive." Lynden's face stilled and their eyes locked. Coal cleared his throat. "I appreciate the poetry and ingenuity of it."

"That's beautiful," she whispered. The ache in her voice gripped his heart. She quickly lowered her eyes, relentlessly twisting the band on her thumb as her features hardened once more. "Why would my brother call it 'the coffin' then?"

Coal whispered back, "In order to live, something must die."

"Well, it appears you'll live another day, Coal Hansen. The black hole has willed it. I cringe at who or what was sacrificed so that you may live, though."

Rather than give a lecture on the motto of New Eden, he decided to continue their witty dialogue. "I extend my heartfelt gratitude to the Black Hole for granting me life and not becoming my coffin. The coffin clearly appreciates what it sees," Coal said.

Lynden rolled her eyes. "Oh god, don't let the Mr. Awesome thing go to your head."

"Drat. I suppose I shall settle for mere charm instead." He humorously flashed a smile from his position on the floor, tucking the mussed strands of hair behind his ears. Lynden blinked as she drew in a slow breath and then chewed on her bottom lip ring before looking away. Her response confused him. The confidence of one who kisses mere strangers melted into the folds of the black chair, and uncertainty surfaced instead. Before his thoughts could fully process her ambivalence, he whispered, "Lynden."

She met his concern with diffidence before she looked toward the window. "Finally," Lynden said while nibbling on a fingernail. "No more 'My Lady' business." Her hands dropped into her lap.

"I owe you a debt." Coal stood with a bow. "Twice now you have saved my life."

The corners of her mouth slightly lifted as she shoved out of the chair and walked toward the door. "You seriously need saving."

A flash of rainbow enchanted his vision before the door slammed shut, and his shoulders slumped. She would keep him on his toes.

Rain pelted the window, redirecting his thoughts, and he peeked through the black screen to the enormous body of water. He pulled on the shade and jumped back when it scrolled up. Smoky light spilled into the room and Coal's muscles relaxed in response. He blinked as his vision adjusted. "Boo!"

The drone lifted from its black box, nearly invisible in the corner of the black room. Ignis materialized nearby, his ghostly colors shimmering against the atramentous backdrop.

"How may I assist you?" the hologram asked.

Coal pushed a button next to what he surmised was a closet. The door slid open and he smiled humorously at the black contents. "Good afternoon, Ignis. I trust you fare well after our travels?"

"Yes. And you?"

"I am still processing." Coal trailed a finger over the black clothing. "I have a question I hope you can assist me with. What is a press conference?"

The hologram began reciting the particulars and Coal's anxiety levels elevated once more. The entire world would meet him shortly, and Lynden's message hammered away in his head.

"So I should wear something more presentable?"

"Jeans are OK. You should wear a black or white shirt, preferably with long sleeves. Buttons will make you look more polished."

"Thank you," Coal muttered as he reached for his luggage.

"Perhaps you should sit down. Your blood pressure is elevated."

"My apologies, but you may shut off now. My time is limited today. Rest well."

He watched as Ignis disappeared and floated back to his base. Coal dressed, groomed, then slumped onto the edge of the bed.

What would the world think of him?

His body fell back with a thump, and he threw his arms out in surrender. "I am awesome," Coal chanted under his

breath. He stared at the black ceiling, and the endless darkness claimed his thoughts as he released a long, heartfelt sigh.

Your love
Should never be offered to the mouth of a
Stranger,
Only to someone
Who has the valor and daring
To cut pieces of their soul off with a knife
Then weave them into a blanket
To protect you.

— Hafiz, *The Gift*, 14th century *

Run from what's comfortable. Forget safety. Live where you fear to live.
Destroy your reputation. Be notorious.

— Rumi, 13th century A.D. *

CHAPTER SEVENTEEN

The marble steps felt cool on Coal's bare feet as he slowly descended the grand stairway. His fingers brushed against the dark, heart-shaped ivy that clothed the beautiful stone wall. It was reminiscent of the castle-like wall that bordered the base of the biodomes. Water dribbled down the large window that crowned the entry door, and Coal tarried to watch the various shades of gray move across the sky.

His heel pressed onto the stone floor of the foyer just as an anguished sound rent the silence from a nearby room. He knew that sound. A heart keened. Grief's song whimpered and writhed in a familiar pattern.

Lynden and Mack ran into the foyer, then stopped before the room. Coal took a step, and then another, afraid of what he may discover, wary of the death wails and cries. He stood beside Mack and watched as Dr. Nichols began to wildly attack Hanley, eliciting another round of anguished cries.

These sounds always haunted Coal. Women who had lost their husbands. Young mothers, some not much older than him, who had lost their newborn babes. Memories of Oaklee's cries, when her father died in Leaf's arms, still made the hair raise on his arms and neck.

"I'm seriously freaking out," Lynden whispered.

The young woman paled to an almost sickly shade of green, her eyes widening in horror as she watched her mother manifest the misery of severance. Mack draped an arm around Lynden's shoulders and pulled her close against him. He balanced the ice in his hand and touched a Cranium upon his ear, keeping his head level.

He was recording this?

Disgusted, Coal returned his attention to Lynden. "I believe she has just learned the truth about Joel Watson," Coal offered. "I have feared this moment. I did not know, however, the strength of her bond to him." Dr. Nichols continued to unravel, and Coal creased his brows as he considered her possible relationship with Joel.

"What are you talking about?" Lynden asked, but her eyes remained fastened upon her parents. "You mean *the* Joel Watson? The one who lost all his kids like five, six years ago?"

Fear slithered through Coal's veins and coiled around his heart. "Yes," was all he could manage in response.

"My brother had psychotic episodes during that time. Mostly about the girl, the daughter. Willow." Coal's entire system stilled with her statement. "It was so weird. PTSD."

"He's harmless, Farm Boy." Mack readjusted the ice on his nose with a quick side-glance.

Dr. Nichols started to moan again as she staggered back a few steps. Hanley attempted to support her, but she pushed him away. "You kept this from me! You narcissistic, self-absorbed monster!"

"Only because you were traveling. I knew it would break your heart. I didn't want you to bear this alone."

"So you hacked my devices?" She shoved him again with another guttural scream. "You took my son from me!"

"Fillion broke the law. You knew he was on trial, and you decided to go to Hawaii anyway. Don't blame me for your decisions."

"He's dead. Oh god, he's dead."

Lynden gasped, and Mack whispered without turning his head, "Not Fillion. Relax."

Dr. Nichols canted toward her husband and then slumped to the ground as sobs wrenched from her body.

Hanley knelt on the ground before his wife and took her hands. "I wanted to share the news with you sooner, but I knew what it would do to you."

"I love him so much. I never stopped loving him."

"I know."

Those two words were confessed with such an ache that Coal looked away, embarrassed for witnessing their private moment. He pivoted on his feet to walk away.

"Did you do it for the money? Or jealousy?"

Dr. Nichols' questions, her voice seething, deadened Coal's steps. He turned back, and waited.

Hanley's features sharpened as if he analyzed his wife. "Don't make me a villain for your grief. Joel chose to break the engagement. He chose to move to Africa. He chose to enclose himself in New Eden, which is really *your* project. And he chose to marry Claire."

"You did do it!" she shouted.

Unhinged, Dr. Nichols wildly clawed at her husband. Hanley's face burned red. Grabbing her hands, he yanked her forward, and she yelped.

"Careful what you say," he said, each word slow, punctuated, and threatening. "The walls are listening." Dr. Nichols blanched and her eyes shifted toward a nearby window and then back to Hanley. He let go of her hands as his face became emotionless, but his eyes grew cold. "We have a press conference in twenty minutes. Go fix your make-up, tidy your hair, and take a shot or two of vodka. Now."

She rose on unsteady feet, smoothed the front of her dress in jerky motions, and then stormed away. Coal bowed his head respectfully as she passed, his eyes remaining downcast as the angry click of her shoes echoed through the large house, followed by the loud slam of a door.

A few heartbeats later, Hanley moved from the room. "Come to my office in ten minutes," he said, with such dispassion that Coal looked up.

How could a man dismiss distressing emotions so easily?

Coal desperately wished for his hammer and a forge to work out the slew of information swirling violently in his head. He stared at his feet again. "Yes, sir."

Satisfied, Hanley brushed past Lynden and Mack and disappeared through the kitchen. Only when a door in the distance shut did they move, and searched each other's frightened expressions. Coal opened his mouth, but Mack cut him off.

"Don't talk about it." Coal was spooked by the sharpness in Mack's tone. With a tilt of his head, Mack gestured toward the stairs. Tapping his Cranium, Mack repositioned the ice pack on his nose. "To the black hole."

Lynden nodded in a daze, but moved quickly to follow Mack up the stairs. Once sealed within the blackened room, Lynden trudged toward the chair by the window and crumpled into the seat.

The pressure from all of the events this day was dangerously building inside of Coal. The angst swelled and undulated in nauseating waves, and he turned around and punched the wall. Lynden jumped with a sharp gasp. The knuckles on his right hand stung from the impact, but his muscles released a brief sigh of relief, desperate for another punch. Coal refused the urge.

"Shit. Are you going to turn green and rip off your shirt, too?" Mack raised an eyebrow humorously, but Coal failed to comprehend the reference. His thoughts were raging over Dr. Nichols' accusations, hoping they proved untrue.

What money did she reference?

Coal missed Joel, and the grief was overwhelming at times. Watching Dr. Nichols keen made the moment of watching Joel die fresh in his heart and mind. Flushed, Coal used the hem of his shirt to wipe his face. He let out a heavy breath as he lowered the black garment. Lynden quickly moved her gaze back to the window, her face pale.

Mack smirked. "Damn. I officially hate you." A small smile touched Coal's lips and he rolled his eyes, more to resist the warmth that wished to creep up his neck and face once more. "Are all Martian males made like you?"

"No. I am a rare breed," Coal said with a lopsided grin.

"Good. I was starting to worry for Fillion's skinny ass." Mack pulled open a drawer from a nightstand positioned against the bed and removed a large, thin book. "Read and write?" Mack asked. Coal grit his teeth against the insult.

"Bien sûr, idiot, et en trois langues différentes!"

"Um, I'll take that as a yes." Mack sat on the bed and began writing on a blank page. When finished, he handed the book and pen to Coal. "Writing only. In English."

Mack reached behind the nightstand and pulled out a bottle of amber liquid as Coal studied the page. The stick-like handwriting was sloppy, but legible.

Watson kids alive?

Alarm shot through Coal, and he struggled with how to respond. At the lab, he had given Hanley his word he would never speak of Leaf, Oaklee, and Laurel as living. But Hanley unnerved Coal, especially by how the information he presented always seemed vaguely askew.

Reluctantly, Coal decided to answer with honesty and gave the book back to Mack, who let out a relieved sigh and cast a nervous look Lynden's direction. The young woman with rainbow hair remained fixated at the window, however, with nary a movement. Mack bent over the book once more, and Coal decided to sit next to him on the bed for lack of another chair.

The young man paused from writing and handed Coal the bottle. "Drink up. You'll need it." Then he returned to the book.

Coal untwisted the cap, took a whiff, and smiled— whiskey. The community always reserved some of the corn from each harvest to make a small batch, used mainly for medicinal purposes. His father charred a few barrels for the cooper each Harvest season to age the clear liquid, which was then stored in the root cellar beneath the Great Hall.

The cool rim of the glass bottle touched his lips and he tilted his head back and enjoyed a small drink. Mack watched Coal closely, grinning when Coal swallowed and handed the bottle back without a fuss. The liquid warmed Coal's gut almost immediately and his muscles unwound a notch.

"Nice." Mack enjoyed a long drink. The young man pulled out a small box, flipped the lid, and pulled out what resembled the joints smoked in New Eden, offering one to Coal. "Do you smoke?"

Coal accepted one. "Of course. I am the Son of Fire," he said with wry smile and Mack laughed.

"Smart-ass."

Mack lit up his joint and then tossed the mechanical torch Coal's way. He flicked the flame, as he had seen Mack do, and inhaled, coughing with the difference in herbs and potency. This type was not remotely reminiscent of the joints he enjoyed with his father on occasion. But he recovered, and inhaled again, ignoring the mild nausea, or the urge to cough again. This gained Lynden's attention, and she twisted to study him, nibbling on her lip ring as she did so. Coal glanced away from Lynden just as Mack shoved the book into his hands.

F launching full investigation of H, Elements, & N.E.T. & requested ur help. Will require full makeover & misbehaving like a boss.

Coal read the note several times as his mind filled in the blanks. He was excited by the request. Finally, a way to put his emotions to work. The only cause for hesitation was the makeover and misbehaving comment. Coal was unsure what was implied. Nevertheless, joint dangling in his mouth, he replied: *I shall assist you in your quest, for I have one of a similar nature.*

"God, Rainbow, take a look at this epic handwriting. It's like a monk scribed it." Mack hid the question regarding Willow under his fingers and pointed to Coal's recent response.

Lynden grabbed the joint from Mack's mouth, inhaled, and then slipped it back between Mack's lips as he winked at her.

"Great," she said, dispirited. "Tonight?"

"Shit. Sooner the better." Mack wagged his eyebrows at Coal with a mischievous grin. He ripped the page from the book and lit it on fire with the mechanical torch.

"I'll text Coral and Devon to meet us in the garage at eleven," Lynden said. "Whatcha thinking?"

"Whatever," Mack drawled. "He's your project. Dress him up and play with him as much as you want." He paused and gave Coal a sly look and then bit down on his tongue suggestively, before addressing Lynden again. "Need to let Daddy know you're tampering with the experiment?"

"Please regard me as the man I am and do not refer to me as an experiment," Coal stated firmly, coming to a stand. They considered him for a moment and then Mack grabbed him by the arm and yanked him back down onto the bed.

"Yeah, I'm *nosebleeding*," Mack said in a droll voice. "Literally. Manliness noted." He raised his eyebrows for Lynden to carry on.

"Nah. Daddy never gave me rules to this 'Guide to Life' shit."

In a teasing, sing-song voice, Mack said, "You play so nasty."

"Runs in the family apparently."

Mack's face fell when Lynden crossed her arms over her chest and raised her eyes to the ceiling, trying not to cry.

"Lyn…" Mack's quieted and he hung his head. "I didn't mean it that way and you know it."

"Yeah, I know." She turned around.

Coal studied the bottle in Mack's hands and gently tapped on it. Mack nodded his head in agreement, first taking a drink and then passing it over. Coal nearly spewed the liquid when a loud bell rung unexpectedly throughout the entire house. "*Merde!*"

"Doorbell. Relax. Must be the doctor." Mack grabbed the sopping rag as he left the room.

Coal and Lynden remained silent. The scene with Hanley and Dr. Nichols had been gruesome, and he could not imagine the kind of pain and confusion Lynden was processing this moment. The click of her mother's shoes sounded in crescendo as she passed the door, fading as she walked farther on.

"Lynden," Coal said quietly. He patiently waited for her to face him. "I need to find your father's office."

"Through the kitchen. Take the stairs that lead to the dungeon. It ends at his door." Her clipped response saddened him further.

"Thank you. I look forward to our adventure this evening." He offered a kind smile, even though he was terrified. Her face softened a little, but within a blink of an eye she again appeared bored, hurt dissolving into a disinterested look. "Until then," he said and bowed deeply.

"I am awesome," he muttered under his breath as he skittered down the stairs. "I am awesome." He passed through the foyer and peeked into the adjoining room. A physician touched Mack's nose, who instantly hissed through his teeth and scrunched up his face.

Coal let out a heavy sigh and muttered again, "I am awesome," as he continued through the kitchen and into the dark hallway, leading to the stairway Lynden had mentioned. The stone tile changed to a thin rug, and Coal realized he still was not wearing shoes. Upon reaching the door, he gave a light rap and stared at the ornate bronze handle as he waited.

"You're late," Hanley said as the door swung open. "We have minutes before we air live."

"My apologies, sir. Shall not happen again." He offered his hand, which Hanley shook and then Coal entered the large office, shutting the door behind him.

Three stools were set up against a large screen that reflected a city alive with motion. Cars crawled through the streets, like beetles dashing across a tree limb. Holographic advertisements flashed off of buildings as the sun set over the expansive water and dipped behind the mountains, coloring the water in a diamond dust of pinks and lavenders. Coal could stare at the man-made objects positioned neatly against nature's backdrop for hours.

"Della?" Hanley's tone was business-like. Dr. Nichols turned from a corner of the room and approached the stools. During the three visitations to the lab, she had presented herself with coyness. But in her own home, she seemed tense and unsure. Her gray eyes stared, unfocused, at the three stools. The heartache was evident in her movements, despite all efforts to exhibit elegance and poise. Her fingers absently played with a silver necklace—one she had not worn earlier—caressing the leaf pendant as her forehead wrinkled with emotion.

"Where shall I sit?" Coal asked, and Dr. Nichols touched the stool in the middle. "Thank you, My Lady." She nervously inspected him and her eyes settled on his feet.

"Where are your shoes?"

"I believe I may have left them outside on the front lawn," he said sheepishly. The rain pitter-pattered upon the roof.

"Doesn't matter. The camera is angled for our waists on up," Hanley said.

"I can't do this." Dr. Nichols released an anguished sigh, turning her head sharply to the side.

"Play a part." Hanley took a seat on the third stool. "It's what you do best." Coal stiffened and felt his face flame with the shame of Hanley's comment toward his wife. A smug smile curled the tips of Hanley's mouth, and then he said in a light tone, as if nothing ever happened, "Don't answer any questions other than bland, simple ones. Nothing that reveals too much. See the red light on the desk?" Coal nodded. "It will turn green in two minutes and a hologram will appear, revealing a split screen and two reporters from a major news circuit. It is a similar set-up to the conference you and I held through Messenger Pigeon last week."

"I understand."

A knock on the door plucked at the tension in the room and Dr. Nichols gracefully lifted from her stool and glided across the darkly stained wood floor. Lynden brisked past her mother without waiting for an invitation, settling at the desk.

"I want to watch. I know the drill."

Coal forced an impassive expression on his face and stared directly at the light just as the red turned green. A hologram screen appeared in the air, hovering over the desk, and Coal's stomach flipped as a woman and man looked up and met their expectant gazes. From his peripheral vision, Coal observed Dr. Nichols and Hanley shift into different postures and break into friendly smiles. The hologram woman with rich auburn hair, curled to her shoulders, and dark blue eyes spoke first.

"This hour, we are pleased to welcome to the *Atoms to Adams Daily Show* Dr. Della Jayne Nichols, lead psychologist over the Mars colonization project, New Eden Township, and author of several books, including the New York Times bestseller, *Misery Loves Company*, an exploration of how hope is sorrow's companion throughout life. And, as always, we are delighted to have Hanley Nichols, CEO and owner of New Eden Enterprises and New Eden Biospherics & Research, and famed Nobel Peace Prize winner."

"Thank you for the warm welcome, Jennifer." Hanley flashed a charming smile. "It has been many years since we first graced your show to discuss New Eden Township, and we are delighted to be back."

"Twenty-four years to be exact," Jennifer answered in teasing tones.

"Who cares about numbers, right? We are dying to meet this young man." The gentleman on the split screen, his hair unnaturally brown and his eyes the exact shade of his tie, chuckled with a fake sound that burned in Coal's ears.

"Absolutely," Hanley chuckled in reply. "Jennifer, Joe, fellow inhabitants of Earth, I present to you Lord Coal Hansen, Son of Fire, visiting from New Eden Township."

"Hansen as in Connor Hansen, the Fire Element?" Jennifer asked.

Hanley nodded as he bestowed a proud smile toward Coal. "Yes, the very one."

Joe regarded Coal and asked, "Should I refer to you as Coal or Lord Hansen?"

"Coal, preferably," he offered with a shaky smile.

"Tell us a little about yourself."

"Of course, sir," Coal said as calmly as possible. But his mouth dried up instantly. "What would you have me share?"

"So polite, so quaint," Jennifer said. "How old are you? For starters."

"I am sixteen years of age, Madam."

"Oh, I think I just shivered. Joe, from now on you must call me Madam." Joe and Hanley laughed and Della responded with a cool smile, almost demure, her fingers still fondling the leaf pendant around her neck. Coal felt his face warm, especially when Lynden rolled her eyes from beside the desk.

The interview continued and Coal answered mundane questions about his family, home life, education, and occupation. Satisfied with those answers, Jennifer smiled and asked, "The Code states that the age of marriage begins at sixteen in New Eden Township. Do the youth often marry young?"

"Yes, Madam. It is tradition to marry by age twenty."

In a teasing tone, Joe asked, "Are you married?"

"No, sir," Coal smiled and shook his head. A strand of blond hair came loose and fell across his face.

"Is there someone special, perhaps?" Jennifer asked.

"Perhaps," Coal replied with a charming grin, tucking the loosened strand behind his ear.

"You just broke a lot of hearts," Jennifer quipped, eliciting light laughter from Hanley and Joe once more. The woman turned toward Dr. Nichols. "You are quiet, Dr. Nichols. From a socio-psychological standpoint, our Martian visitor appears to function well. Wouldn't you say?"

"Yes, indeed." Dr. Nichols casually brushed her hair from her shoulder. "He has exceeded our expectations, most especially in the field of technology. A team of scientists worked closely with Coal over the past two weeks, and within that short time period, he was able to not only command Smart technology, but build it. I am confident that integration with modern Earth will not prove problematic as many have questioned. Additionally, Coal has shown a remarkable amount of empathy and has easily formed bonds with others since his arrival. The community has raised a generation that esteems virtues of honor, chivalry, intelligence, and strong social values."

"These observations," Hanley interjected, "have excited our team as we prepare for Project Phase Two. Role-playing," Hanley said, as he cut a glance at his wife, "has once again proved to be a reliable method to leave behind the past and start fresh."

The subtle bite in Hanley's comment made Coal wince and heat flowed into his veins once more.

Dr. Nichols crossed her legs the other direction and tossed a coy smile at Hanley. "My husband is correct. Role-playing is an effective tool in psychology to condition the mind to new experiences, new thoughts, a different point of view, and to build skills and confidence in weak or troubled areas."

Joe looked at Coal. "Were you aware of the role-playing aspect of your home before leaving?"

Coal opened his mouth, feeling every nerve burn with shame, and closing it when he struggled for words. Fingers wiggled for his attention and he looked at Lynden who mouthed, "You are awesome," and he straightened his shoulders and forced indifference into his tone and face. "Yes, I was aware the first generation had left their life behind and forged a new one with elements of make-believe. After all, we are not truly on Mars."

"Interesting," Joe replied thoughtfully. "We'll explore this topic more in a bit." The man looked to Hanley. "First, have you heard from your son, Fillion, since he was enclosed?"

"He is scheduled to check in soon."

"Dr. Nichols, do you worry about his safety?"

"It is only natural that mothers worry over their children, regardless of circumstances," Dr. Nichols said. "I miss his presence at home and I know his sister does as well. However, I am not worried about his presence in New Eden. They are a kind people who embody a true community spirit." She smiled warmly.

Jennifer smiled in return. "Fillion has a very large fan base. His generation seems to worship him."

"My son *is* the Anime Generation," Hanley said in a proud tone. "He reflects the culture and values of this present era and also embodies the future. And at present, he is becoming acquainted with the past. After all, the key to the future resides in the past. One day soon, he'll make a fine leader when he takes over ownership of New Eden Biospherics & Research and New Eden Township. And I am confident he'll find solutions to the unemployment crisis plaguing his generation. Who knows? Maybe there is a future on Mars for many his age wishing to restart civilization." Hanley offered a charming smile and winked at the camera.

"Noble words from a very proud father," Jennifer said. "Rumors speculate that due to global corporate laws, Fillion is stepping up so that you may step down to take full ownership of a secret company?"

Hanley laughed. "If you say so, then it is clearly not so secret."

Jennifer and Joe both chuckled. When Hanley did not offer more information, Jennifer continued. "There have been several recent developments within New Eden in addition to the unprecedented exchange. We have learned that the mock-colony has experienced two very big losses in the past two weeks," she said with an empathetic frown.

Coal knew of one loss, but could not fathom the other big loss, and his heart hammered erratically.

"We just received word that Norah Daniels, the late Water Element, passed away on Monday, October fifth, after a long battle with cancer."

Norah died?

A pain tore through Coal's chest and tears gather in response, but he remained stoic. He had missed Norah's blessing, her last words, and his chance to say farewell. Hollowness seized him as he realized the rituals of death were now over. So much so, he barely paid attention when Jennifer began again.

"This comes in the wake of Joel Watson's death on Sunday, September twenty-seventh, from cardiac arrest."

Joe cleared his throat and said in a respectful tone, "Many might remember The Watson Trials of 2048. Coal, that must have been a traumatic experience to lose every member of The Watson family."

"Yes," he replied. Hanley visibly relaxed with Coal's response and Dr. Nichols stiffened. She clenched and unclenched a fist below waist level as her other hand closed around the necklace.

"Documents are emerging, stating that the late Joel Watson was an investor and possessed a mind-boggling amount of money, which would have been bequeathed to his wife or eldest surviving heir. As there are no surviving family members, records show that the fortune will be entrusted to the estate, established as New Eden Biospherics & Research, mother property to New Eden Township."

Coal gripped the stool as every muscle flexed, slowly moving his head to face Hanley, who waited for his reaction with a caring smile that did not reach his eyes.

"This is true," Hanley said, casually glancing away from Coal's accusing look. "The money, of course, will only go to benefit all the families of New Eden Township." A warning flashed in Hanley's eyes and Coal resisted the urge to destroy everything within sight.

The interview continued for several more minutes, although Coal had no idea how much time had passed, nor the questions that were asked. He snapped out of his trance when, in a poof, the hologram disappeared followed by Dr. Nichols springing from her seat and charging out of the room. Hanley walked to his desk, ignoring those who still lingered around in his office. Unable to stand it a moment longer, Coal marched from the office and sprinted through the house, up the stairs, and into the black bedchamber.

A sob rose from his gut and his body shook as hot tears streamed down his face. He curled up on the bed against the pain, unable to process that Norah was truly gone or that Joel may have been murdered for money. The tears turned to anger and he grabbed the pillow and began beating the bed as low screams emerged through tightly clenched, gritted teeth. A door click sounded from behind but he continued to hammer away, eventually dropping the pillow as his body slumped with fresh tears.

"Hey, Mr. Awesome," Lynden said in a near whisper. A hand rested on his back and he angled his body to face her, not caring that he was crying or that she witnessed the complete loss of control over his senses. "The money part is shocking." She let the statement hang between them. "You didn't know about that woman's death, did you? Norah?"

Coal turned his head away with a small shake. He wiped at the tears. "Norah always ensured I stood proud of the man I was and the man I would become. But I forgot her when I left. The only farewells I have ever experienced were deaths."

She studied him for several heartbeats, her face unreadable, as usual. The black absorbed his thoughts until he saw nothing else, even when Lynden hooked her fingers into his belt loops and gently pulled him to her. The ache squeezed once more just as Lynden provocatively nibbled on his bottom lip. Air left him in a quivering rush. Small, quick breaths pulsed upon his skin in a seductive tempo, and his distress yearned to surrender to her entirely. Coal wrapped his soot-stained hands around her waist with every intention to kindly push her away. But her mouth claimed his and, with it, every weak protest he possessed.

Everything within him knew this was wrong. Women were to be cherished and protected; they were not vessels to dull a man's pain. It did not matter that he was breaking from loneliness, or that he felt disembodied, or even that he longed for comfort. Coal craved to be touched, desperately wishing for a real connection to ground him with another. Perhaps Lynden desired comfort and wished to dull her pain as well, joining her sorrows and fears with his. As if in response to his thought, Lynden deepened her kiss.

He hesitated only a beat before responding, hungry for more, his body screaming to labor through his emotions. Her fingers burned trails across his body, unbuttoning his shirt. He tossed it across the room without breaking their kiss, wrapping his arms around her waist.

Nobody beyond the panes of his home knew him intimately. They had his biometric stats. They knew his interests and search patterns on the Net. They knew surface details pertaining to his family and occupation. But nobody on the Outside knew *him*. Until this moment, sharing himself completely with another soul, he had not realized it was a need that burned so bright within him. His muscles flexed and shuddered, his heartache fading, and a new pain emerged as the collision of both worlds merged inside of him.

She dipped her fingers below his pants line and gripped the flesh around his hips and pulled him tighter against her. Another heady intoxication galvanized him, and he moaned into her neck, undone. The sensations owned him, demanding more, needing more.

His name formed a sigh on her lips as she dug her fingers into his back. The sound unraveled him further and his mouth crashed against hers in reply. As they kissed, Lynden unbuckled his belt, followed by the button on his pants, and his body stilled.

What was he doing?

Coal looked around the room as if waking up from a vivid dream. Reality struck him in a painful flash and his stomach soured with how stupid and insensitive, yet again, he had been. He was a fool. A weak, impetuous, hot-blooded fool. Only one day in her presence and already he selfishly took liberties he had never known with any young woman.

"I am so very sorry, My Lady." He raked his hands in agitation through his mussed hair, forcing himself to meet her confused gaze. She was alluring, beautiful, her lips swollen from their kisses. "I am despicable and ashamed of my actions toward you. Please name any honor price and I shall redeem my reprehensible offense."

"What the hell are you talking about?" Lynden adjusted her clothing as she rolled her eyes. "Are you for real?"

Coal whispered, "I used you."

"Yeah, that was the idea. Why'd you stop?"

"I beg your pardon?" Coal stared, further horrified. "You wished for me to take advantage of you?"

"That's what I said. Shit, who cares? People hook up all the time. You needed to forget your pain and I was available."

He furrowed his brows. "You are worth far more than this moment or my needs. I would never wish to treat you with such dishonor..." His words trailed off as panic renewed within him. "I am so very sorry. No woman has ever offered me her body before, and you are not even my wife."

Lynden played with the band on her thumb and lowered her eyes. "God, you really mean it, don't you?"

"Upon my oath as a man," Coal said, seeking her eyes, "I never wish to take from you what is not truly mine to have."

"Um, a bit over the top, don't you think? My body is mine to give away, but if you don't want me, then fine." Lynden stalked across the room and tossed him his shirt. "She's a really lucky girl."

"Please, wait." Coal took her hand in his as she breezed by, catching her off guard. She wrenched her hand back and visibly cowered, and Coal's heart sank. Eyes wide, she stared at him, as if he might ... he refused to finish the thought, horrified.

"Lynden," he whispered, embarrassed. "I would *never* physically harm you. Although strangers, I shall labor without rest to earn the favor of your trust, and will consider every moment a worthy endeavor." Her eyes watered and she looked away. "I only wished to say, before I so carelessly reached for you, that whoever claims *your* heart is the lucky one."

A beautiful smile shone on her face as she blushed, almost vulnerable. It was a fleeting response before she nibbled on her lip ring in what Coal came to realize was a nervous gesture. But as usual, her emotions shut off quickly and she hid behind a mask of unimpressed arrogance.

"I don't believe in fairy tales or happy endings, so whatever." She paused at the door. "Be ready in three hours, Mr. Awesome, and kiss your old life goodbye."

He nodded. When the door clicked shut, he walked over to the bed and fell face first into the folds, biting into the blanket to silence his scream. She was the poisoned apple, and he felt the fatal spell leach into his bloodstream.

He needed to remain level-headed. She had already been grievously hurt by a man. He would not add to her life's sorrows. Her father employed him to guard her, and already he failed. His chest heaved as his pulse attempted to quiet and find rest, but it could not. Pain shot through him again and tears cooled his flushed skin, his mind flooded with thoughts of Oaklee, his home, his family, Norah, and Joel in a never-ending cycle of internal torment.

Coal rolled to his back and stared with desperation at the ceiling, suddenly remembering the whiskey. Three hours was enough time to get drunk and then sleep it off. There was nothing else to do, and he no longer wished to think anymore.

Escapism seems to be the primary draw to the larper, but this feeling ultimately blossoms into something different. The common portrayal of the larper is someone who escapes from their insufferable routine into the fantastic. I think this feeling changes into a need to invade our lives with the fantastic. Instead of running away from our lives, we instead are given the ability to run into them. Pretending makes this possible. Visualization is a common practice in goal oriented task resolution. Being able to see ourselves in the imagination accomplish something of great difficulty becomes the fuel needed to accomplish such tasks in our real life.

— Dave Funk, "LARP Definition," *LARPing.org*, 2013 *

CHAPTER EIGHTEEN

Saturday, October 17, 2054

New Eden Township, Salton Sea, California

The warm mineral water blanketed Fillion's bare skin and he sighed, inwardly and outwardly. His muscles ached from the long days and hard labor. There was nothing simple about New Eden Township. Not. One. Damn. Thing. And yet, this was the definition of living simplistically, according to his world. The irony wasn't lost on him. Or his body. God, the ache was unbearable.

With eyes closed, he dipped beneath the surface and combed through his floating hair. Bubbles grazed his face as he released the air in his lungs. Then, his head emerged from the water and he wiped the droplets from his eyes. Satisfied with the tingly sensation on his scalp, he swam over to a boulder on the edge of the hot spring, warmed by the steam.

Tropical flowers grew alongside the water, bursting in sunset colors of red, yellow, and orange. Long, tangled tentacles, belonging to orchids and other epiphytes, draped over the stone walls that lined the pool. Fillion leaned against the warm boulder and peered up at the dome ceiling. It was a full moon and the reflective panels sheathed New Eden in an otherworldly glow.

Bathing solo was glorious. Men and women bathed once a week at The Waters on alternating nights, following the evening meal. Rock walls scaled three sides of the enclosure and the front was hedged in with trained shrubbery. A wooden screen shielded the entrance to ensure privacy before everyone undressed. Then, the men bathed Roman style, turning what Fillion had always considered a private affair into a communal activity. It was a social event, complete with debates, discussions, and typical male humor. Awkward didn't even begin to describe the experience.

Many of the first-generation men possessed tattoos like him, unlike men from the second generation. Compared to other young men his age, Fillion was a bit on the scrawny side. He'd always been lean, somewhat toned—he walked everywhere and danced until he dripped with sweat at raves—but his culture was soft, prizing an androgynous look. Most jobs were mechanized and automated. Very few occupations in his world worked the body like daily living did in New Eden.

Naked or dressed, he didn't fit in. He was used to having every detail of his life aired in the media. But in the dome, with every marked difference fully exposed, it felt more personal. It made this private bathing session all the more enjoyable.

He was supposed to be in bed but, for the first time in two weeks, he couldn't sleep. He was cold, too. The nights in the main dome were frigid. So he ventured out of his apartment, while the community slept, to The Waters to soak in the natural bath, even though it violated the so-called rules of trust. So many damn rules.

Water droplets glistened silver across Fillion's exposed skin. His eyes roamed over his tattoos, eventually resting on the pomegranate tree on fire on his bicep. The flames sprawled onto his shoulder and singed the feather tips from the wings stretched across his chest.

The symbol of New Eden Enterprises, etched onto The Door, had glinted with the fire of redemption the day he was enclosed. But it was hard to stay focused on anything. Even on his mission to figure out the Watson deaths. Pieces of him were dying. And sometimes he felt as though his identity was shrouded on a funeral pyre, waiting for the torch to ignite his soul and his convictions. He couldn't decide if he cared about anything anymore. Or if the caring was so intense he was shutting down.

Cremation was as disturbing as he thought it would be. The smell of burnt, charred human flesh was permanently imprinted in his nose. He inhaled the fumes and flyaway ash of the woman, who just one day earlier, wanted to bless him and shared that his legacy was love. Nobody else thought the experience was horrific. To New Eden, it was a beautiful ceremony and they bonded over the idea of communing with Norah through the nutrients her ashes would give the gardens. Eating dead people was on the disturbing end of the creepy spectrum. The very idea, no matter how naturally the medieval hippies packaged it, was barbaric and some serious Green Moron shit. His progressive mind had no place for such a notion; and he involuntarily shuddered as memories of that week flashed through his head.

To distract himself, he let his vision wander around and soak in the sights and sensations while his mind downloaded various thoughts. He considered firing up his vid feed while secluded and returning Mack's calls. But he wasn't ready. The rituals of death plagued Fillion's psyche. He wasn't in the mood to deal with his old life, let alone his new life. He didn't want to talk to Mack. Or Lynden. And he had zero desire to talk to his mom or dad, who spammed him with messages via Jeff and The Aether to contact them.

Fillion just wanted to be left alone and have time to sort through the paradigm shift that was patching the operating system of his mind. The "real world" was comprised of more meaningless, fake, fantasy moments than this pretend world. Each experience in New Eden forced him to cull the incorrect data from the annals of his life and recalibrate his personal truth.

Are you ready to discover what is real?

Fillion finally understood the mockery of the hologram's statement on Exchange Day. The machine was a product of physics and human engineering. The digital humanoid mimicked life, but it never breathed, didn't possess a heartbeat. And yet, it invited Fillion to learn what was real. Human ingenuity of another kind had preserved Earth's natural cycle of a closed loop system. Sealing it away within the largest machine in existence. One that breathed and possessed a heartbeat, the biomimicry not only reflecting life but sustaining it. The biospherics engineering tantalized Fillion. As much as he wanted, he couldn't resist crushing over the physics of the Kingdom he'd soon inherit. Or the *real* world it conserved.

But no matter how prodigious the miracle that was New Eden Township, he always went back to the same question. Why would anyone want to live on Mars? Despite the human race's consistent track record as a terrible owner, Earth was a perfect place for life. And yet pockets of civilization wanted to chain themselves to an enclosure, an ecological prison in space. He would be ushering in this new age as owner of New Eden Biospherics & Research. Crazy. He couldn't do it. As beautiful as this recreated world was, it was a mark of defeat and denial. Man couldn't save Earth from himself, so he would go and destroy another planet's surface and atmosphere? Stupid.

Once again, he became outraged that humans—more specifically his dad—would rather invest in something pointless than the people right in front of them. Would Earth still suffer and need movements dedicated to its healing if humankind was rooted in reality? He needed healing, and the sickening truth that Hanley cared more for eco-business than his own son was a bitter pill to swallow.

Fillion touched the water and watched the concentric circles ripple across the gunmetal gray surface. A heavy sigh escaped and he bit the inside of his cheek.

With a grunt, he pushed himself up onto the large rock, pulling his knees up to his chest. The air was comfortable and he needed to dry off before dressing. Damp clothes would increase the chill this Fall night, and probably wouldn't dry by morning. His fingers found a small rock and he skipped it across the surface of the hot spring, listening to the light plinks and final plunk. Fillion rested his head on top of his knees and closed his eyes. He really needed to snap out of this existential trance and focus on an immediate issue. Like the community.

The atmosphere in New Eden was strange. Fillion could see glimpses of what the Township was probably like before Joel died. But now, the air crackled with tension. Two fights broke out in the Mediterranean dome. One man was knocked out. Rain was appointed the new Water Element over her older sister, Mist, making Rain the youngest head noble in New Eden. Villagers poured into lines day in and day out to list their grievances before their newly exposed King. Leaf listened with astute attention and remained steadfast, even when settling disagreements between community members. The Great Hall, once loud and boisterous each meal, dimmed to a low hum of conversation. People hurled insults at each other as they passed by. The worst offense was to be in support of joining the Outside world.

It was illogical. All of it. But this kind of fear never thrives on logic. Rather, its existence is fueled by irrational responses. And there were plenty in New Eden.

The Son of Earth had his hands full, and the stress hung on the young noble like a second layer of clothing. Residents now referred to Leaf as His Majesty and graced Willow as Her Highness. Little girls regularly brought Ember and Willow flowers, star-struck by the idea that a queen and a princess walked among them.

Although Willow accepted the flowers with a gracious smile, it quickly faded once the little girls ran away, sometimes with Laurel in the lead. Since Norah died and Leaf publicly announced he was The Aether, Willow had withdrawn, her face expressionless. She rarely attended meals and, when she did, she shuffled the food around on her plate in aimless circles. At times, she appeared skittish, glancing over her shoulder and jumping at the slightest sounds. Ember and Leaf often excused her absences as headaches and exhaustion from a labor intensive day.

Fillion had stopped by the Watson apartment a few times after dinner the last two weeks to discuss with Leaf the reformation and future of the community. Willow would knit with needles made from bone or make lace with a complicated process involving tiny bobbins. She ignored all the commotion and conversation, especially him, isolating herself in a corner while occupying her hands. If she wasn't working so often in the meadow near the Forge—cleaning, carding, and processing wool and flax—he would hardly see her.

At The Forge, Willow's tools were placed along a back wall, and she would slip in and out. Nonetheless, whenever she entered the workshop, Fillion quickly hid a certain project. One he hoped was finished before her sixteenth birthday. Sometimes he worked on it after dinner to kill time, taking smaller pieces back to his apartment. Otherwise, he was busy fixing chairs, tables, bed frames, gardening tools, doors, fences, and flooring, using archaic tools and pine pitch for glue. Never had he worked so hard in his life, and every inch of his body felt it. Most nights he fell into bed and slept solid until morning. Unlike tonight.

Yesterday, Fillion pulled out Willow's large, free-standing loom from a storage shed near The Forge so she could join other weavers in the meadow. He had never seen a loom before, and he was intrigued by the engineering and how such a simple wooden device could create something so essential.

During his smoke breaks, Fillion leaned against the outer wall of The Forge, enraptured. Willow sat among the tall grasses and wildflowers as she wove fabric under the soft reflective sunlight. Children ran by her on several occasions and she watched them pass with a wistful expression before returning to dedicated concentration on her task. She was so beautiful. He never tired of drinking in her image.

The thought made him roll his eyes. Even though it was a good thing his and Willow's initial sparks dissolved into the community's atmosphere, he knew he was pathetically lovesick. Borderline fool.

He needed to think of something else. He really wasn't in the mood, but he knew he probably should call Mack so his friend didn't think the Martians enslaved him or something. Mack had called him five times today, and he never did that unless it was important. Either that, or his friend was getting antsy since it had been over a week since they last spoke.

Goosebumps erupted on Fillion's skin as he moved off of the heated rock. He had tossed his garments on another naturally warmed stone to get that fresh out of the dryer feeling. In a matter of minutes he was dressed and he brushed his fingers through his hair a few times before lifting the hood on his wool cloak. His mind was still too alert and so he decided to walk through the forest.

In a whisper, he commanded, "Cranium, phone Mackenzie Ferguson." He walked across the meadow and through the small opening to the willow oak tree in the heart of the forest. The outgoing signal beeped in his head. No video chat session. He was out in the open and the hologram would be too bright.

"Oh. My. God. He lives!" Mack's words slurred together and a small humored smile formed despite Fillion's dispirited state. The recent tongue ring Mack acquired made his friend's speech worse. Loud music blared from the background, the drop-beat reverberating throughout Fillion's body. God, he missed being in the heat of music. And he missed his guitar. When Fillion didn't reply, Mack asked, "Wait? Are you alive?"

"Barely."

"Hey everyone, he's alive!" Mack laughed as a female cheered in the background, and Fillion hoped it wasn't Lynden. Mack had to be at The Crypt. "I thought you had become green slime."

"Something like that." Fillion hunted the forest for any signs of human life. None. "You OK? Computer quiet isn't your thing, boss."

"Yeah, just tired. My schedule flipped and I now work days as a carpenter. I think my body's broken."

"No shit. It's good for your *hikikomori* soul. You'll be a wood-building ninja when you integrate back into modern society. Tree origami *chikara*—put all other public art to shame." His friend's musings when drunk always made Fillion smile. "Farm Boy, toss the bottle." Who was Farm Boy? Must be Coal, Fillion concluded, snickering at the nickname. The music volume turned down and Fillion sighed. He wanted to listen longer. "Couldn't hear you, *bishounen*," Mack began again. "We're at my place, hanging for the night. Going to the underground in a few days. Farm Boy's tats still need to cool. Did you get the links I sent you?"

Tats? "Sorry, mate. First time I've fired up the Cranium in a week."

"Damn. Are you sure they aren't probing you or anything?"

Fillion smirked. "Jealous?"

"Hellz yeah."

"How are you passing off Farm Boy in the underground?"

"He's my UK cousin, cage fighter, works at the New Eden Enterprises London office."

"Cage fighter?" Fillion started laughing. "Nice."

"Yeah, you should see my nose. The little shit punched me to defend his girly honor the first day he arrived." Fillion lost it. "You owe me, *bishounen*," Mack said. "Big time."

"I thought you were my official fake boy. No action?"

"Tons. The sexiest girls on the planet, aka Farm Boy and Rainbow. Bagbiters. Both of them."

Fillion was laughing so hard his stomach began to cramp, but he couldn't stop. A loud smack popped in Fillion's ear and he scrunched up his face, his laughter easing up. Mack swore and slurred something at Coal, and then Fillion heard male laughter in the distance, followed by Lynden's. Liquid sloshed in the background and Fillion let out an amused breath, waiting for his friend to remember that he was on the line. Several seconds later, he did. "Hey, you really need to watch those links. Game changing."

"Bit dump."

"Can't say much. But first link is one of your mom——"

Dead silence. Fillion swallowed when seconds ticked by. "Mack?"

Nothing. Weird. He tapped the Cranium again and said, "Cranium, phone Mackenzie Ferguson." No outgoing signal. Fillion pulled the device off his ear and pressed the power button. It lit up in a red blinking light, usually indicating it was powered enough to display an error message. "Shit," he muttered to himself.

He tapped on the device and red script appeared in the air: *Wi-Fi access denied by Admin.*

"What the...?" Who denied him? He looked around the forest, spooked. Someone had hacked his Cranium. He needed to get to the underground computers and alert Mack. Now. His friend would start a hunting campaign, unleashing their cyberspace hounds to trace and hopefully isolate the black hat responsible for this breach.

The report vanished and another appeared: *A Gamemaster ponders the hidden.*

Swear words shouted across the sharp edges of his mind. No need to hunt. Fillion knew exactly who had hacked him and he clenched his teeth against the rage. His dad probably set up a digital trip wire on Fillion's line to receive or place one more call, triggering a timer. As expected, the second report message vanished and the Cranium power cycled. Once it finished rebooting, he was left with an "Access Denied" dialog. The trip wire had reprogrammed the device, permanently locking him out.

In ignorance, Fillion thought he could escape his dad for ninety days. He warned Hanley before crossing the threshold of The Door that he'd give his full report at the end, but apparently that wasn't good enough. If his dad set up the digital trip wire correctly, it should issue a message saying the device was disarmed. Hanley was probably logging into Messenger Pigeon now, waiting for Fillion to connect through the "hidden" underground computer system per his cryptic message.

Anger fueled each step as Fillion quickly traversed the forest, taking the path that led toward the Watson apartment. He was so consumed with his thoughts that he almost missed the hushed tones coming up the trail. Fillion dashed behind a large tree and pressed himself against the trunk. He watched the individuals approach, drawing his hood further over his face.

Three men walked swiftly down the path, gritching about something. One recognizable voice surfaced and Fillion's stomach flipped. Timothy. He seemed to be delivering instructions. But whoever he was talking to was disagreeing. The young man closest to Fillion looked around the forest in casual motions, then froze when his eyes fell on Fillion. Skylar gave a brisk nod, and then returned his attention to the pathway as he continued to walk alongside the former Wind Element. The noble wouldn't rat him out. Good.

Fillion couldn't make out any of the words, and his mind scrambled to assess whether it was safe to emerge. Maybe skirting the apartments would be better than walking through the heart of the forest. Clearly he wasn't the only one trying to conceal rule-breaking under cover of darkness. What were they doing?

When the threat of discovery passed, Fillion maneuvered through the underbrush toward the village. A bird startled from a bush he jostled as he ran past and flew at him, and he nearly yelped.

The staircase became visible around the bend and Fillion released a sigh of relief. Tip-toeing, he ascended the stairs and walked across the upper deck. As steady as possible, Fillion pushed in the front door and quietly shut it behind him, wincing when the handle knocked against the wood. He pressed the iron ring to the door, silencing the sound. When he was certain the only noise he could hear was the heartbeat that pulsed audibly in his ears, he continued.

Shuffled footfalls murmured through the sleeping apartment as Fillion crept toward the hallway. He paused in the stone arch and his system froze. Ember materialized in the hallway just outside the lavatory. They faced each other with widened eyes, until her face relaxed. She arched an eyebrow.

He whispered, "I need Leaf."

"At this hour, My Lord?" Her smooth voice clipped elegantly and he understood the unspoken message that she was the gatekeeper.

"Yes, at this hour. It's important." Fillion tucked his thumbs into his belt and composed his body into an impassive posture.

Ember eyed him warily. "And what, pray tell, is so dire that a man must rouse past midnight to work?"

"Business that concerns Leaf, Your Highness." A corner of Fillion's mouth tilted upwards.

She walked toward him, her nightgown billowing with each step. The moonlight touched her hair, glinting reddish-gold despite the blue light, the soft curls cascading loosely to her waist. A small smile graced her face as she neared him. It was a smile that continually irritated him, not quite smug but not quite friendly. It contained secrets, masked behind a pretty face, a regal bearing, and a compassionate personality.

"You may fetch my husband once I know you are not placing him in danger."

Fillion smirked. "Never pegged you for the control freak type."

She whispered, "A black cloud clings to you, and I am unable to discern if it darkens with passion for justice or solely for self-destruction."

"What are you? The town witch?" Fillion rolled his eyes and pushed past Ember into the hallway. The words spooked him, even though he didn't believe in premonitions or omens. The Daughter of Fire reached out and gripped his arm. "Please," she pleaded softly. "Leaf shall not come to any harm? You shall not place him in danger?"

Fillion looked down at her grip on his forearm, then back to her face. Fear was etched into each of her dainty features and he sighed. She truly cared for Leaf. This wasn't a game. His mind must be playing tricks on him, he concluded.

"Look, my Cranium was hacked. I'm locked out, and I need to use Messenger Pigeon. This means nothing to you. I get it. But time is of the essence right now. I studied 3D models of New Eden, but I don't remember where Messenger Pigeon is, so I need Leaf."

Ember angled her head and regarded him for several seconds, and then pivoted on her heel and glided down the hallway into her bedroom. Fillion leaned against the wall and closed his eyes, biting the inside of his cheek. A few minutes later, soft padded footsteps regained his attention and he shifted his focus toward the bedroom door. Ember emerged, softly shut the door, and cradled something close to her body.

She whispered, "I do understand and I shall answer any questions you may have under one condition."

Fillion stared at her hands. "My allegiance is to Leaf, not you."

"Yes, I do not question your position or your loyalty, nor shall I ask you to betray Leaf." Ember lowered her eyes. "You shall discover this truth for yourself eventually, as shall Leaf. I thought perhaps you already knew and attempted to connect with you, but I gathered rather quickly that you were not given knowledge."

"Get to the point," Fillion snapped and Ember flinched.

"My condition is that you never volunteer what you are about to know. Should Leaf ask, by all means. However, do not report me to my husband, for he is not ready for such knowledge. Knowledge I am under oath to not reveal until a specific time."

Fillion took a step toward her with an arrogant smile. "Is Leaf sleeping with the enemy?"

Ember's eyes glossed in the silvered light and her bottom lip quivered. But she didn't look away even though she flushed several hues of pink. "I love Leaf as though he is my own life and have for many years."

"Poor Skylar."

A tear trailed down her cheek. "'Tis not what you think, My Lord. Skylar knew I did not possess affection for him, but his father was adamant over a union. I am ashamed that my father allowed the perception of courtship to inspire Leaf's jealousy." Ember lowered her eyes.

"What?" Fillion's eyes widened with disbelief. "Does Leaf know you're a political pawn?"

"Everyone within nobility is a political pawn and arranged on a chess board, awaiting your move, Son of Eden."

Nausea whirled in Fillion's stomach with her declaration and name for him. But he continued the charade of irritation to cover his feelings. "Fantastic. Let me guess, you saw this with your crystal ball? Or better yet, through the entrails of those you deceived?"

Ember blinked with his derisive tones, but maintained an even countenance. "I love him, My Lord. Leaf Watson is my heart and soul. I willingly lay my life at his feet."

Fillion cooled into an aloof posture and narrowed his eyes, even though he believed her. "Fine. I'll keep your secret."

In response, her hands stretched out to him with a slight tremor and slowly revealed a Cranium. "Please have mine. I shall take yours and exchange it for a new device and pretend it was mine, provided there is nothing on your hard drive you do not wish another to see. I trust you can breach the security features and password settings?"

His mouth dropped open and then he clamped it shut. "Where did you get this? Cranium technology has only existed for a decade, at most."

"The answer is far too complicated for this moment. I shall answer your questions during daylight hours." She glanced over her shoulder. "Leaf or another may awake and discover us alone. A post needs repair by a goat pen. Seek me out and I shall show it to you." He was still too stunned to form an argument. Ember blinked nervously and lowered her head.

Fillion pulled the inoperable Cranium from his pouch. Their gazes locked as he handed the device to her. "I keep everything on a cloud and my hard drive is partitioned with a decoy user interface. The back end is encrypted. Access is granted only to those with biometric keys. But right now, the start-up has an 'Access Denied' dialog." Her eyes lit with understanding, a response that baffled him.

"Did you design the encryption software?"

"Yeah, with help from a fellow hacker."

"And you were compromised?"

"By my dad. He has cryptographers working at New Eden Enterprises. He probably paid someone under the table." Fillion's eyes widened. "You're Drag0nMa1den2038."

Ember dipped her head in acknowledgment and then peeked over her shoulder. "I should return, My Lord."

Fillion nodded and then whispered, "I'm sorry for calling you— "

She placed a finger to his lips and he stilled. "Although not blood relatives, we are still cousins." Ember removed her hand and kindness shone in her eyes. "Family always cares for one another's needs. I am honored to serve you."

"Even though a black cloud clings to me?"

The secretive smile returned. "You cleared the air of concerns, My Lord. The cloud darkens with passion for justice, and your storm shall save a generation. I have a hunch, and I am rarely wrong." She turned toward him and dipped into a curtsy, her long nightgown spilling over the wood planked floor in elegant ripples. "I shall return to bed. After a small measure of time has passed, you may enter and awaken Leaf." Ember disappeared into her bedroom and closed the door.

Fillion turned and placed his forehead against the cool mud surface of the wall, absently rotating her Cranium in his hand. He could hack this device and call from Messenger Pigeon. But it wasn't worth the risk of his dad discovering his access to the new device.

How many others in the dome had technology like Ember? And how the hell did she get it? Maybe there was a hacker in the dome, and maybe they did create government documents. And if so, how many other fake deaths and births existed? After two weeks of digging around, this looked more plausible than any other scenario to date. "*Kuso!*" Fillion muttered under his breath. Did Skylar also have a Cranium? Is this why he and Ember were paired off?

The last thought fired off recent observations Fillion had noted regarding Skylar's family. Timothy no longer sat at the head table, instead joining a table two rows over. His jovial tones were easily heard, setting everyone on edge, especially when he laughed. Skylar was the only Kane who remained at the head table. He sat with a straight posture and a stoic expression, wincing whenever his dad laughed. Nobody talked to Skylar beyond pleasantries except Alex, Norah's widowed husband, who would engage him kindly each meal.

Fillion felt sorry for the Son of Wind, knowing exactly how he felt. First-born losers of first-rate swindlers. As the public, political sons of complete bastards, it was a shitty life.

The direction of Fillion's thoughts wasn't helping his mood. He decided enough time had passed and moved down the hallway toward Leaf's door.

Princes and governments are far more dangerous than other elements within society.

— Niccolò Machiavelli, Italian historian and philosopher, 15th century A.D. *

CHAPTER NINETEEN

illion opened the door and peeked in. The room was dark, but he could see the outline of Leaf laying next to Ember. She remained still.

"Leaf." Fillion nudged the young noble's arm and waited a few seconds before repeating the process. The man refused to wake, though, and Fillion let out a heavy sigh. Then a wicked smile formed and he went to the end of the bed, grabbed Leaf's ankles, and yanked him off the bed. The Son of Earth flopped onto the hardwood floor with a loud thud and Fillion burst into laughter. Payback was sweet.

Ember jolted upright with a small shriek, raising the blankets to her chin. "State your business," she demanded, pressing herself against the wall. God, she was good. Then again, role-playing was in her blood.

He managed to whisper, "It's Fillion," through more laughter as he stared at Leaf.

Leaf groaned and then reached out to grab him. But Fillion jumped away, nearly tripping on a book that had been haphazardly tossed to the floor. Leaf gave up without much of a fight, spreading his arms out in surrender. So Fillion seized the opportunity and crowed over Leaf's form with a victorious grin.

"I need to kidnap your husband," he said to Ember, keeping up the show.

"And what, pray tell, shall you do with him?" The smile in her voice caused Fillion to look her way, but her eyes were riveted to Leaf's half-dressed state.

"Midnight stroll," he deadpanned. She turned his direction with an arched eyebrow. "Business with Leaf. He'll be safe. Promise."

"Go, My Lord," she said in honey tones to Leaf. "I shall await your return."

"Yes, My Lady."

The Son of Earth snatched his cloak off a peg on the wall, and his tunic and belt off a nearby chair, and started to dress. When finished, Leaf marched over and pushed Fillion out of the room, smacking Fillion on the back of his head. Fillion laughed. He couldn't help it. He almost slapped Leaf on the ass in reply, but knew he was already pressing his luck. After Leaf shut the door, Fillion tried to maintain a straight face, but he snickered despite all efforts.

"Why was I rudely removed from my bed?" The stern look on Leaf's face was betrayed by a small, humored smile and Fillion quietly laughed again.

"My Cranium is compromised and Hanley is waiting for me. I need you to take me to Messenger Pigeon."

"It is in the Rainforest biodome."

"Let's get Willow first. She'll kill us both if she finds out later."

"No other reason?" Leaf gave him a sly look.

"Actually, let's not." Fillion turned toward the living room. "My dad likes to mock me, using Willow as bait. Consider this a warning."

Leaf placed a hand on his shoulder and turned him around. "Whatever do you mean?"

"I ... um ... damn it." Fillion cleared his throat and looked down at the wood floor. Stupid. So very stupid. "I'm mental, OK? I don't want to talk about it."

"I am confused," Leaf whispered. "Your mother is a psychologist, is she not?"

"Yeah. You'd think I'd be pretty damn well-adjusted." Fillion rolled his eyes, his words dripping with derision. "I had psychotic episodes after you and your siblings supposedly died." He continued to explain the story, including how he was picked on at Academy, even beat up, and how the media villainized him. "There. Now you know. Happy? Come on." He started to move but Leaf stopped him.

"No, rather I am grieved for you, My Lord. Do you still experience episodes?" Leaf squinted his eyes in his typical way when contemplating information.

"Are you serious?" Fillion glared at him with disgust. "What do you think? God, this conversation is over." He pushed Leaf out of the way and walked to the front door. "Still up for taking me to Messenger Pigeon, or changed your mind now that you know I'm a complete freak? And I get it if you want me to stay the hell away from your sister."

The young noble placed a hand on Fillion's shoulder. "My apologies. I did not mean to insult you." He extended his other hand to Fillion with a frown. "You are a good man, and I would never wish to sully your character."

"Whatever," Fillion said with a shrug, shook Leaf's hand, and then looked away.

"I am most sincere. No matter what your father may say, I am honored to know the real you."

Fillion snapped his head up and tensed his face, but managed, "Let's go."

"No, I am not finished."

"Cue the inspirational speech and heartwarming music," Fillion sighed, and looked up at the ceiling. "Leaf, I'm pissed off and looking for a fight. I don't like talking about this area of my life. Social cues. Get them."

Leaf removed his hand from Fillion's shoulder with a heavy sigh. "I do not hate you, nor do I believe you are a freak, whatever that may mean. As for my sister, she is the topic I wished to discuss." Fillion raised his shoulders and stared at a battered, dead leaf by the entry floor. "At first, I believed my sister had lost her mind from grief, and that thoughts of you were merely an escape from her reality. She gave her heart to a stranger, a man who behaved dishonorably toward our family, and who teased and manipulated her affection."

"I'm an asshole. Why are we re-hashing this?"

"Because you never argued with me when I made such statements. I often wondered why as you are rather protective of your behavior, and readily supply justifications. Now I understand."

"Leaf—"

"Do you love her?"

Fillion thunked his head against the door and closed his eyes. "It doesn't matter how I feel or what I want. Never does. My life doesn't have a happily ever after."

"It does matter how you feel, though."

"Leaf, I can't deal with this right now. My dad brings out the worst in me. I need to keep my head on straight."

"Yes, I see and you have shared as much. This is why I wished to have this conversation with you." Leaf leaned against the door next to him. "My father had a saying: 'Feelings are real. They often become one's reality. But they are not always based on truth.' Your father may mock you and make you feel less than a man, but I wish to gift you knowledge to counter the feelings. My sister has affection for you, and nothing your father may say shall change that truth."

Fillion was thankful his forehead rested on their front door. "My dad controls everything," he said, his voice strained. "You think he'd let me have a relationship with Willow? Get real. He already made that very clear before I entered New Eden. I'm nothing! Programmable like a drone."

"You are a merchant prince. Stand tall, My Lord." Leaf nudged Fillion's shoulder, but Fillion ignored him. "I said, stand tall." He pushed Fillion hard, and Fillion lost his balance, staggering backwards. "Shall I repeat myself?"

Fillion rolled his eyes and then straightened his posture with an exaggerated look of irritation. It was annoying whenever Leaf started barking commands, this moment no exception.

"As I said, you are a prince of your world. It is a birthright that requires more from a man. I did not choose to be The Aether, and even though I have lost much, I shall not disappoint those who depend on my leadership. You are a man worthy of honor and respect, and it is time you hold your head up high and no longer insult those who give you such esteem, which they give freely not because of your father, but because of *you*, Son of Eden."

Leaf stepped closer to Fillion until they were inches apart, and Fillion drew in a nervous breath. "I shall not pretend I know the wounds that grieve you, as I do not. But I do know you are a good man, regardless of what your father or others may say."

Instead of giving in to the voices that perpetually took shots at his self-image, Fillion stood tall and settled an even gaze on Leaf. Out of all the people Fillion had ever known, Leaf was the only person who understood what it was like to be bound and judged by this life.

The Son of Earth's lips tipped up in a kind smile and he dipped his head. "When you see your father, do not cower like a lad. Stand tall as a man, as a prince who shall one day be King." The kind smile gave way to a lopsided grin. "Shall we proceed?" Leaf opened the front door and gestured for Fillion to exit.

Each step painfully slow to minimize the creaks and groans, they slipped down the stairs. A breeze whipped through the trees. He and Leaf seized the loud rustling sound to bolt through the forest. No such luck when tearing through the meadow, though. The loud thump of each sprinting step echoed in the flat silence. Fillion's legs and lungs burned, and he wanted to rest once they reached the concealing darkness of the South Cave. But they kept moving until they left the chilled air of the main biodome for the thick, sweltering heat of the rainforest.

Fillion covered his ears as he looked around. Night life in this biodome could easily rival the deafening noise of The Crypt, a jarring sound after the unnatural, muted quality of the main dome. Birds, insects, and who knows what else, streamed constant noise in a pulsing rhythm.

A narrow path of spongy substrate squished beneath his shoes. Wet, warm earth, rich with the scent of decaying green matter, filled the air. A white orchid hung low off a tree and Fillion leaned forward and inhaled, his eyes rolling back with the heavenly fragrance. If the temperate forest slept at night, rocked to the lullaby of a gentle breeze, the jungle was alive, undulating in the shifting light and shadows. His eyes roamed over the verdant labyrinth just as Leaf veered off the trail and toward the untamed jungle. Fillion's heart stilled.

"Oh god. You've got to be kidding me."

"Scared?"

Fillion didn't need to see Leaf's face to know it was a taunt. "Could we be turned into a monkey's midnight snack?"

Leaf laughed. "No monkeys. Stay close, though."

"I'm moved you want me close."

"No, not really. I prefer the company of one fairer than yourself."

"There's none fairer than me. You're crushing my soul."

"Pride cometh before—"

Fillion suddenly placed a hand over Leaf's mouth. From behind them on the trail came voices and the repetitive crashes of people stomping through brush. Fillion whipped his head toward the sounds as his heart rate kicked up. Leaf grabbed him by the cloak and shoved him behind a tangled mess of vines and a plant with enormously large leaves. Their movement disturbed the condensation on the long, wide leaves and water dripped all over Fillion's face, but he remained still.

Three figures ambled toward the large wooden door separating the rainforest from the South Cave. The reflective moonlight was overshadowed by the blackened jungle, making it harder to see faces. Timothy's laugh was unmistakable, though. Did they visit Messenger Pigeon? If so, why? Fillion was pretty sure Skylar took up the rear. The young noble's head hung low. As the men paused before the door, Skylar crossed his arms over his chest in a restless motion and looked around, the gestures tight and jerky.

When the door shut behind the men, Fillion turned toward Leaf. He debated whether to tell the Son of Earth of his earlier encounter with the same group in the temperate forest. He decided to keep it to himself a bit longer.

"Is that the way to Messenger Pigeon?" he asked.

"The trail leads to the Dragon Bridge, near Messenger Pigeon," Leaf said.

"OK, let's go."

"Do you believe they went to the hatch?"

Fillion arched an eyebrow. "Unless they were performing a medieval hippie tribal ceremony, I can't see what else they'd be doing in the rainforest at night."

"Timothy cares for some atmospheric duties when the community is safely tucked away at night. Well, he used to, that is. Perhaps he is assisting Skylar. My father pulled me from my bed once to witness Timothy spark excess methane in the livestock biodome while the residents slept. With the East Cave door shut, the sound was mostly contained."

"Shit! He sparked methane enclosed?"

"The facilities use bio-digesters. But occasionally a small amount floats to the biodome ceiling, and Timothy sparks it before it builds into something unmanageable and truly dangerous." A mischievous smile formed. "I have seen Skylar disturb and light up trapped pockets of methane from the compost piles as well."

"Leaf Watson, you're such a badass."

A shy, humored grin warmed Leaf's features as he stood from his crouched position. The noble wiped the water from his skin and pulled his hood further over his face. Fillion followed suit, and they trudged through the jungle.

Fillion's body ached as he pulled vines away and climbed over fallen trees. Water trailed beside them, the rushing gurgles competing with the insects and birds. A stream perhaps? Eventually the jungle cleared and gave way to a small clearing and Fillion paused and whispered, "Whoa."

A large stone bridge glistened in the moonlight, veiled in a mist from a waterfall that roared nearby. The railing was carved in multiple arches, as if the beast was alive and moving through the jungle. Dark scales gleamed from the side of the bridge and, as they emerged from the dense foliage, Fillion realized they were made of bronze. Did Connor help design this bridge? Other metal filigree glinted under the soft reflected light. It was incredible.

The narrow trail reappeared underfoot and led to the bridge. Fillion stared into the face of a mythical stone dragon, mouth open, teeth sharp, tongue eternally flicking the air. The other rail featured the tail of another dragon, which curled and formed the foundation for the first step.

He rested a hand on the damp stone, and his fingers brushed along the arched scales in wonder. The scales passed over the backs of the twin beasts, disappearing into the water vapor. Fillion blinked, awestruck by the massive waterfall. It just suddenly appeared out of the wall, easily forty feet up. The liquid sparkled, and spilled over the wall, splashed over jutting rocks, and emptied into a large pond covered in lily pads. He wasn't the romantic sort. But this scene probably inspired plenty of poetry.

Leaf tugged on his sleeve. "Ready?"

Fillion nodded and they walked on. The path widened. Tropical flowers grew on either side of the trail, their sharp, pointy leaves and petals poking him on occasion. At the end of the pond lay a boulder. Leaf knelt on the ground by a large boulder and pushed it aside, revealing a door.

"This is it," Leaf said through grunts as he swung open the door. "After you. There is a toggle on the wall beside the ladder."

The substrate squished between Fillion's fingers and he made a sound of disgust as he crawled backwards and descended into the black underground chamber. He found the light switch and flipped it, a feeling of nostalgia sweeping through him. Finally. Something that at least faintly resembled home.

A yellow light filled the room and he shook his head with amusement as he stared at the old-school incandescent bulbs, and then his smile fell. How did they get replaced? These bulbs burned out quickly. He didn't know if they were made anymore, either. Maybe it was to limit UV exposure to the residents? To make it feel more like candlelight?

Then his eyes rested on the machines responsible for Messenger Pigeon. A pair of forty-two-inch flat-screen monitors rested on top of a metal table. Vintage upright CPU boxes hummed beneath. The idiots had forgotten to turn off the computer when they exited. They had definitely been here.

Fillion approached the monitors as Leaf stepped into the room. "Well, aren't you a pretty thing," he murmured to the machine as his fingers caressed the cool surface, pausing over the camera. He lowered and tilted his head to get a better look. "My, you make me weak in the knees. Mack would be so jealous."

"Are you talking to the portal?"

He ignored Leaf, but from the corner of his eye Fillion could see the noble's baffled expression. Fillion squatted to examine the towers. "Beautiful," he sighed. Fillion looked over his shoulder at Leaf. "This is the oldest computer I've ever had the privilege of meeting. Maybe 2010? The '20s? God, she's classy. Listen to that purr."

"Willow believed it was a singing rock."

Of course she did. So damn cute. Fillion placed his hands on the CPU tower. "Don't listen to them, Bessy. You may be from the tech Stone Age, but you could never be as dull and plain as a rock." He looked back up at Leaf and sighed with what he hoped was a dreamy expression. "I think I'm in love."

"Felicitations."

A small smile tugged at the corner of Fillion's mouth. "Let's unplug her and force restart."

Fillion climbed beneath the table and located the end of the cord. The glissando sound of the computer's power down made him grin. After ten seconds, he plugged the cord back into the wall and felt his heart pump as the mechanical engines revved back up to life. "She does have a nice singing voice. I'll give Willow that one."

"You are a very peculiar man," Leaf said with a lopsided grin.

"Just geeking out, mate."

The screen came on after a few seconds of lag and Fillion shuffled back. The blue screen flashed and his stomach clenched, knowing he'd see his dad shortly.

"Stand up against that wall so Hanley doesn't see you."

Leaf nodded his head, crossed his arms across his chest, and leaned against the cob surface.

The screen changed, reflecting the copper walls of the Faraday cage room in his dad's office. Fillion took in a fortifying breath.

ELEMENTS

The existence of hope—whether attributed to the divine or born of human determination—has sustained and shaped humankind since the beginning of time. Although, until recent history, humanity has never been shaped quite like the Internet culture. Online, the tendency is to bypass the natural process and unsavory business of emotional stages, sharing only the images of a perfect life. Hope is, therefore, no longer an attainable idea.

Psychologically, this is detrimental to society's health. The human psyche was designed to learn and grow from hardships, with the aid of visible relationships in real, physically tangible communities. However, modern society has shifted to villainize sorrow as the criminal who stole hope, judging those who would dare spoil the illusion of happiness. Being real is viewed as a sign of weakness, unless it can be used to sell a product.

It begs the question: Is the absence of real hope, the kind born only from perseverance, related to the staggering number of individuals who feel as though they are losing touch with reality? Without accepting sorrow in all its various shades, hope is reduced to a pain killer that lasts for only fleeting moments rather than truly empowering humankind toward a lasting, transcending existence.

— Dr. Della Jayne Nichols, "Chapter 5: Sorrow's Defense," *Misery Loves Company*, 2047

CHAPTER TWENTY

Seattle, Washington state

oal pressed his forehead to the cold glass of a large window and stared out into the night sky. The guest room at Mack's apartment was nearly as large as Coal's entire family quarters in New Eden. There was a large, plush bed, a leather divan, metal furniture of various types, and an Imigicast. Black and white photographs of cities from around the world dressed the walls. Intrigued, Coal had studied the images of foreign structures and the people captured in the acts of their daily lives until he mustered enough confidence to approach the window. Then, the sparkling city, bustling with life, owned his thoughts.

A couple hours earlier, after Hanley and Dr. Nichols had left, Mack had hacked the home-arrest cuff on Coal's ankle to release the magnetic lock and attached it to Coal's bedpost in the Black Hole. Hanley and Dr. Nichols were furious with Lynden over the makeover, almost placing a home-arrest cuff on her as well...

Dr. Nichols had been living in an emotional cocoon, her gray eyes dull and unresponsive. But she flared to life upon seeing Coal's piercings, elaborate tattoo, and hairstyle. Her perfect specimen was now spoiled, contaminated, and their marketing plan to promote the natural, medieval Martian turned to ash.

A part of Coal was satisfied with such results. But the other part knew they would spin the situation into their favor eventually. It did not matter how he looked. He was still their product, and they would exhibit him without care for his feelings.

In response to Lynden's "audacity" and his exhibited "ignorance," Dr. Nichols requested a private audience with Coal and delivered a lengthy speech on how he needed to examine his choices and think through his decisions in order to preserve his reputation. With a calm tone, despite her rigid posture, she expressed that she was certain negative associations and behaviors existed in New Eden, as it was human nature. This world, though, presented far more temptations and with stronger social consequences. Therefore, his future was greatly at risk.

Could one be banished from this world?

So far, he had yet to encounter anything as stringent as The Code. Coal, however, understood her real concern was for the experiment being at risk—not him—and he glowered as she continued. After a series of questions, she concluded that the best course of action was to keep him under house arrest. Since he lacked experience in this world and could not be trusted to make the correct choices without her or Hanley's guidance, it was a "necessary" action.

Hanley removed the responsibility of "Guide to Life" from Lynden, with an underhanded comment that she should apply more energy toward her studies, given her inability to focus on both work and her education. The insult caused injury, Coal could tell, but she remained impassive, only her hazel eyes dimming as Hanley continued belittling her abilities, comparing her to her brother every now and then. Mack struggled to keep his mouth shut, shifting in a chair nearby, watching Lynden with growing concern.

And then she snapped.

"So Fillion can screw up and cause property damage and do whatever the hell it is he wants over and over again and you still send him a paycheck. But I get fired?" Lynden crossed her arms over her chest and looked up at the ceiling.

"Fillion is my heir and future owner of one of my businesses," Hanley said with a dismissive tone. "You had one job and failed. You were to help Coal integrate."

"I did!" Lynden screamed. "He no longer looks like a Martian freak, but an American sixteen-year-old boy."

Hanley raised his eyebrows and lowered his voice. "Did I give you those instructions? As my employee, you only do what I ask you to do and nothing else."

"You haven't given me any instructions. Yet you punish me. Typical."

"And did you ask?" Hanley shook his head with a mocking chuckle. "Common sense. See? You are not ready for employment."

"What you're really saying is I'm not essential enough to fight for or forgive. Gotcha." Lynden circled Hanley and meandered over to where Coal sat. "Well, in that case, I'll just act like the *otaku* girl you think I am."

Mack whispered, "Shit," and lowered his face into his hands. Coal had looked his direction with confusion. "I can't watch this."

Lynden suddenly burst from her bubble of boredom and fury, throwing her hands into the air as if gleefully surprised. "Omigod, he's sooooo hot. Did you get him for me, Daddy? Can I keep him?" Lynden jumped up and down and squealed, biting her fingernails as if trying to contain the excitement. "I always wanted my own Martian alien teenage boy."

Coal's eyes widened and he choked, and Mack pushed him in the arm. Dark blue eyes peeked at Coal from behind fingers, and Mack whispered, "Whatever you do, don't make eye contact with an *otaku*. You'll turn to stone." Too late. Coal had locked eyes with Lynden, who squealed again with a giant, crazed grin. Mack groaned and leaned back in his chair, draping an arm over his eyes. "It was nice knowing you."

"Did you see that?" Lynden shrieked. "He looked at me! Omigod. Omigod. Zomigod!" She bunched her shoulders together and batted her eyes. She looked to Hanley, who steeled his gaze and crossed his arms over his chest, as if bored with her overzealous display. "Best. Day. Ever." She looked back to Coal. "We'll ride ponies, pick flowers, and have hot alien sex."

Coal lowered his face as his skin heated, wishing he could turn to stone.

"Thanks, Daddy. I love him! What I always wanted. I'll be sure to name our first child after you. Girl or boy." She made a heart with her hands upon her chest. "I. Heart. Androgynous. Names."

"I am happy to hear you feel this way," Hanley said casually, almost appearing satisfied. A calculating smile appeared on the older man's face and Coal shivered involuntarily. "Your new job will be to take Coal out and be seen publicly. Let the media believe you are falling in love and make the *otaku* jealous of *you*."

"What?" Her eyes widened and she paled.

Coal stood. "Sir, I must protest—"

"Perception." Hanley pinned his daughter with a stare as sharp as a knife. "Make the Martians a desirable race. Coal is here to woo and charm the media for me. Don't guide his life. Be his life. The world needs to see that the community of New Eden Township is fully human, and so are the residents of any future colonies."

Lynden staggered back as if punched in the gut and glared at her father as she morphed back into her otherwise emotionless existence; and Coal's heart broke. He detested her posture of emptiness, where every smile was fake and every glance appeared as if it took great effort.

"Got it. I'm not smart or pretty. Don't have any talents except one, apparently." Lynden tensed her face for a moment, then blurted, "God, how I must embarrass you!"

"Don't be dramatic," Hanley snapped in reply. "You want to make things right after nearly ruining thirty years of research? Do your duty to your family and to your brother. Build up his empire. You care about *his* future, right?"

Lynden never answered. Instead, she fled from the room. They heard the slam of her bedroom door. Awkward silence filled her void, and Coal and Mack sat very still. Coal was not even sure if the young man next to him breathed anymore. Hanley looked at Coal with a friendly smile, as if nothing was amiss. "You remember your assignment?"

"I made this choice," Coal said as he strode across the room to face Hanley. "Which I had in ignorance believed I had the freedom to make, for I wished to belong to their culture." He straightened his shoulders and stood taller. "Do not punish Lynden for my decision. Punish me instead." Mack lowered his arm, his jaw falling in shock, or perhaps fear.

"Always so valiant."

Hanley placed a hand on his arm in an affable gesture, although his eyes were still blazing. With a squeeze, his hand fell away and the older man side-stepped past Coal and strolled toward the front door, whistling a merry tune as he pulled a coat from a closet. Dr. Nichols waited for Hanley, already retreating into her emotional cocoon.

What mother stood by, caring not that her daughter believed such lies about her worth?

"You have fire in your veins, Coal," Hanley began again. "Apply it toward guarding my daughter, rather than destroying the opportunity you were given. Be her knight in shining armor. What damsel in distress can resist one?" He casually slipped into the coat. "On Tuesday, you'll accompany me to New Eden Enterprises. In the meantime, remain on the property and don't speak to any strangers. The cuff is programmed and will alert the authorities if you decide to test my instructions."

"I am your prisoner?"

A small smile formed in reply. "No, absolutely not. This is for your protection. Every decision I make is to ensure your comfort and safety." He opened the door and paused. "I purchased a variety of welding tools and supplies, which you'll discover in the garage. Please, be my guest. Della and I will return on Monday."

The front door shut and Lynden peeked her head around the top of the stairs. Even before the car rolled out of the driveway, she begged Mack to let them "crash his place," as she put it. She had snarled and paced in agitation until they finally hopped into Mack's car and left...

The view from the guest room window at Mack's refocused in Coal's vision as his thoughts faded into the night sky. He placed his hands onto the glass next to his face as he stared straight into a dream.

He physically interacted with the environment, yet he felt disconnected as he attempted to process the voluminous amounts of information and new sights. This moment, towering high into the atmosphere, mentally agitated him akin to when he first communicated with a hologram. He had never stood so high above the ground before, save when flying from New Eden to Seattle, an experience so surreal Coal stopped trying to compare it or to find any semblance to the life he had previously known.

Presently, he stood sixty-five stories above the concrete surface of the city. Vertigo threatened to topple him to the rug beneath his feet. Regardless, he forced himself to stare until his body regulated, mesmerized by the myriad colors that flashed and twinkled as far as his eyes could see. Even the Puget Sound, an inlet of water in the Salish Sea that connected to the Pacific Ocean, shimmered with colors as reflections bled across its surface. Transfixed, he allowed his mind to wander over more memories from earlier this evening...

Mack resided in downtown Seattle. As they had waited for the elevator, Mack explained the building was only five years old and part of a new Green design. It also incorporated the latest Smart Tech, courtesy of Mack's family, which is why he occupied the Penthouse Suite. His father had purchased the suite in advance and gifted it to Mack at the beginning of summer, upon turning eighteen.

The elevator had startled Coal, his insides releasing a strange ticklish sensation when the floor suctioned him in place as it shot up past the twilight horizon. Lynden had jumped onto Mack's back with a mischievous giggle, despite the obvious pull to remain grounded.

The doors opened directly into Mack's apartment, and the young man had promptly dumped Lynden onto the black leather divan. Coal's heart stopped. Floor-to-ceiling windows framed the main living area, and it appeared as though Mack had thrown Lynden off the edge of the world. She playfully shrieked and threw a pillow at Mack, who ducked with a celebratory laugh, sticking out his tongue in reply to Lynden's gesture.

With a humored grin, the young man lit up a cigarette and walked up to the glass wall and scanned the forest of buildings that grew out of the concrete. The sidewalks and streets operated much like gridded roots as the ecosystem of cars and people crawled along its outstretched infrastructure.

Coal was not used to such views, nor standing in the sky. Lynden rolled her eyes at him when he had refused to leave the kitchen area to listen to music in the living room, another strange experience in its own right. The music here was vastly different, the sounds overwhelming and consuming, a negative and positive experience he could not reconcile.

To distract himself from his discomfort, he had studied the room. The furniture was elegant, but markedly masculine. At first, Coal thought Mack might be an artist. But the young man confessed to having hired an interior designer, an occupation that baffled Coal.

People actually designed the insides of people's homes? Life beyond the panes continually proved opulent and wasteful. Nevertheless, Coal enjoyed the bounty of colors and the artistry the Outside world offered compared to his childhood home.

After consuming several shots of whiskey in a row, he had ventured beyond the comfort of the kitchen and sat beside Lynden and faced the glass. Delighted, Lynden draped her legs across his lap and leaned back against the plush arm of the divan. With careful consideration, he readjusted his position and gently pushed her legs off of his lap, keeping his stare straight ahead. Somehow, staring out the window had become less frightening than the young woman by his side. A pulsing beat reverberated throughout the room.

Lynden sat up with cat-like grace, grabbed his chin and forced him to look at her. Mack was occupied, conversing with Fillion, and ignored them. Coal had licked his lips nervously, forgetting about the piercing near the corner of his bottom lip, and a tender ache had made him wince. He blinked rapidly, a dizziness making his head swim, unable to discern if it was the whiskey or vertigo, or perhaps both.

"You don't give a shit, remember?" She raised an eyebrow, the same way her mother did, questioning him and challenging him in a single movement.

"Alas, I do and always shall—pardon—will 'give a shit,'" he said in response. "I am not sure I could ever detach so readily, nor do I wish to."

"It's not that you detach. It's that you show no fear and no pain, no emotion at all. You're awesome. Nothing fazes you. In your world, you had to physically survive. In my world, you need to emotionally survive."

Coal maneuvered out of her grip and leaned back. "I am not accustomed to the constant flux of overstimulation, nor presenting a lack of honor toward another."

She eyed him as she plopped a candy on a stick into her mouth, what she referred to as a lollipop, and pulled her legs up to her chest. Her hair was pinned in the most unique twist on either side of her head. Random strands of color flew out of the coiled tresses and a dark, blood-red section of hair fell over one eye. Today, her eyelids sparkled light green, the same shade as a young blade of grass, framed in thick black, setting off her hazel eyes. Her lips were painted to match the blood red of her hair and Coal had forced himself to look away.

He knew those lips, an experience that should have never happened and one he could never take back. Lynden acted indifferent, like usual, her childlike antics and playfulness carrying on as if she never offered herself to him. In her words, she didn't give a shit. Coal did, however, and warred with guilt and shame, feeling awkward whenever he was in her presence, which was often. Before his makeover, he had asked Ignis what it meant to "hook up" and was horrified.

Was she accosted while engaging in such conduct with that monstrous excuse for a man?

Anger. That is what Coal felt. And sorrow. Guarding her was never meant to be an act of protection from others, he had realized in that moment. It was to protect her from herself.

Did Hanley actually possess affection for his family?

Sometimes it appeared so, in strange, curious ways. Nevertheless, the older man often dismissed those around him as if his own needs, concerns, and thoughts were the only ones which were valid.

With a conspiratorial smirk, Lynden had plopped one leg across Coal's, pulling him out of his introspection. Every feature on her face dared Coal to refuse her, the lollipop swirling around playfully in her mouth. The faint smile he offered her in reply dissipated, however, when he looked out the window once more. Dizziness had returned and churned his stomach in sour circles.

"Are you afraid of the glass because it reminds you of being enclosed? Or is it the height?"

"I simply have no context for sitting in the clouds."

She had looked at him curiously for a second, blinked, and then returned to her usual unimpressed expression…

The memories of this evening dissolved into the view once more, and Coal shifted on his feet. Lifting his eyes, he searched for stars, even though Mack explained that the city released far too much ambient light to fully see the sheer quantity of tiny flecks in the night sky. But to Coal, to look upon even one star was rewarding enough. He wished to know the constellations that dotted the sky with pictures and stories, but did not desire to retrieve his Cranium from his overnight bag.

"Boo!" Coal said, leaning away from the glass. The whisper whir of the drone increased in volume as it approached, and Ignis materialized by his side. The technology's unnatural white light summoned a reflection in the window pane, and Coal squinted until his eyes adjusted.

"Greetings, Coal."

The electronic apparition waited for instruction, but Coal stared at the ghost in the window, haunted by how different he appeared as he searched for a remnant of the man he once knew.

"Good evening time, Ignis. I hope you fare well—excuse me—are doing well." He detested such nonsensical comments to a machine, but Ignis had a sensitive side that needed proper care.

"Yes, I was perusing the news when you called for me. Want to know what's buzzing?"

"No, not really. Thank you all the same. I am most curious and hope you can assist me." Coal turned and looked at the wavering man. "What are the constellations that appear in our sky?"

"I am happy to assist you. In October, there are many." Ignis pulled a constellation map out of the air and held it in his hands. "Hercules, Aquila, Sagittarius…" As Ignis spoke each name, the constellation lit up brighter on the map. Coal pressed his forehead to the glass and studied the stars again, connecting dots until an image formed in his mind.

A light rap on his door made him jump, and he hit his head on the glass with a mild thunk. Light poured into his darkened room and he looked over his shoulder, knowing it was too late to command Ignis back into his box. Lynden tilted her head as she stared at his holographic Companion. Hesitant, she shut the door behind her, dousing the intruding light from the hallway.

"I see I have competition as your Guide to Life."

Realizing her mistake, she looked up to the ceiling in disgust. Lynden approached his side and flipped strands of hair hanging over one of his eyes. Since his haircut, she often amused herself with flicking the red and black strands that draped across his face. Or petting the short, spiky hair on the back of his head, left in his natural hair color, what she called platinum blonde.

"So, who's your Companion, Mr. Awesome?"

"This is Ignis, a gift from your father while at N.E.T."

"It is a pleasure to meet you, Lynden Nichols," Ignis said in a kind tone.

"So my dad never really planned on maintaining my employment. Wow. No words." She turned to Ignis. "Please ensure my image or voice are never recorded, Ignis. Any and all recordings must be deleted immediately."

"Yes, Ms. Nichols. Any other security or privacy requests?"

"No."

"Coal, do you approve of Ms. Nichols's requests?"

"Yes. Whatever Miss Nichols commands, Ignis. You and I are entirely at her service."

"Coal has wonderful social skills, don't you think?" Ignis turned his head from Coal to Lynden with a friendly smile, still holding the constellation map. "I have learned so much from him."

Lynden nibbled on her lip ring thoughtfully for a moment, and then her gaze slowly traveled toward Coal. "Yep. A gentleman." She studied the map. "Making wishes, Mr. Awesome?"

"Is not that tradition saved for stars that fall from the heavenlies?" Coal asked, studying her features in the unnatural glow of Ignis' presence. "Their death dance in the night sky nourishing the soul by granting a hopeful, longing heart its one desire?"

She whispered, "What does your heart desire?"

"Ignis, thank you for your assistance. You may shut off. Goodnight to you."

"Yes, Coal. Have fun stargazing. I like your nickname. Mr. Awesome. I'll have to remember that one."

The light evaporated instantly, and Coal and Lynden were consumed by black. They remained still for several heartbeats. City lights sparkled and shimmered in waves of intensity, man-made stars that grounded his wishes. A click cut through the silence, announcing that Ignis was secure in his box, and Coal let out a pent-up breath.

"Lynden, I am a jumbled mess and desire many things at present." He looked at her over his shoulder. "There is a lack of adequate words to describe my experience in your world thus far, and I fear my thoughts will never make sense."

Silence. Small, even breaths pulsed onto the exposed skin of his face, and he remained still, his mind tethering to every nuance of her presence next to his. Time passed slowly before Lynden asked in a soft, feather-like voice, "What's she like?"

Coal hung his head and angled his focus back toward the city. "Her hair holds captive golden rays of the sun. Her eyes are as deep and soulful as the green of the Earth. Her laughter is akin to birdsong..." The last word trailed off and he cleared his throat.

"That's so poetic."

Coal whispered, "She is poetry."

"Lucky girl." Footsteps shuffled along the rock-tiled floor and the door creaked open. "Mack asked me to get you. He's waiting in the living room."

"Please," he said, pivoting toward her. "Stay for but a moment longer." Lynden lowered her eyes and quietly shut the door. Nervous, he confessed, "I shall not return after my ninety days are over." Coal shuffled in the dark toward her voice, hands out in front in search of obstacles. "I wish to remain in your world."

"What? Have you ever heard the old saying, 'Be careful of what you wish for?'"

"How can anyone ever be careful about wishes? I know no more about the future than you. All I know is this moment and how I feel." He heard her release a heavy breath near him and so he stopped his steps. "I am far too changed and have seen too much of the world's grandeur to return to a simple, sheltered life."

"So, you'll leave her? Just like that?" The anger in Lynden's tone shocked him. "What a joke. I never saw you as the impulsive, fickle type. Is this about my dad's stupid request?"

"No, not at all." Coal's forehead wrinkled. "In truth, she does not desire my rescue and rejected my hand twice." His shoulders fell from his normally straight posture as he surrendered his heart to the past and to the future. "I love her," he said, "and always shall, but we will never be. Not in the way I had *wished*, at least. It was only recently that I realized how foolishly I had behaved toward her. We are destined to be friends, not lovers."

"Recently?" Lynden asked, her voice small. "God, tell me you're not punishing yourself?" Worried he might say the wrong words, Coal paused a beat in an attempt to think through a response. But Lynden misunderstood the silence and came unglued. "Are you for real? Not innocent enough to fight for her anymore?" She taunted. "Sorry for ruining your *wish*." Coal grabbed Lynden's hand to stop her from leaving, but she yanked it away. "Don't," she spat. "What an asshole move!" She slammed the door in her wake.

Your task is not to seek for love, but merely to seek and find all the barriers within yourself that you have built against it.

***

Yesterday I was clever, so I wanted to change the world. Today I am wise, so I am changing myself.

— Rumi, 13th century A.D. *

CHAPTER
TWENTY-ONE

Sunday, October 18, 2054

New Eden Township, Salton Sea, California

T he squeak of a body shifting across leather was the only sound Fillion heard at first.

"Pull back your hood so I may verify identity."

Fillion flushed with anxiety at the sound of his dad's
voice. It shimmered and vibrated as if a living thing, taking
hold of him. Its claws pierced his tender layer of confidence.
Even his feet tingled with adrenaline-induced nerves. When
had he become so afraid of Hanley?

The community—fake and built on lies, yet real and
honest—had absorbed Fillion as one of its own. And he had
let down his guard, feeling safe and understood. Giving in to
his desire to belong. Giving in to his yearning for something
meaningful. Despite his non-sentimental take on life, Fillion

had already placed several items into the chest carved and crafted by his Grandpa Corlan: a willow oak leaf, iron nails, a piece of a splintered spinning wheel, an herbal joint, a linden leaf. Each object was tied to a memory, a reminder of the "family" he would leave behind.

Family.

Small beads of sweat broke out on his forehead, but he refused to fall into a state of panic. Fillion flipped the hood off his head and glared at his dad. A smile formed on Hanley's face and rage trickled into Fillion's bloodstream in response.

"Medieval life suits you."

Fillion schooled his features to remain expressionless and allowed his eyes to do all the talking. He wasn't the same person from two weeks ago. Norah's words, to remember he had value and worth, whispered to his faltering courage, and he lifted his head a little higher.

"You summoned me?"

"What do you think of the world I created?"

"Impressive," Fillion said, choosing his words carefully since Leaf was listening. "Except one thing. You forgot to include a stone circle. The meadow would look badass with one. I didn't think a man of your caliber and vision would overlook such an important detail. So disappointing."

"That could be your mark on this world. Your gift as the new owner," Hanley quipped.

"Maybe." He lifted a shoulder in a slight shrug. "Every fantasy culture needs folklore and magic. Makes a LARP more exciting." Fillion narrowed his eyes slightly. "Wait, magic already exists in New Eden in the form of technology, right? Clever." Rather than satisfy his poke, Hanley switched subjects and Fillion internally sighed with irritation.

"I understand New Eden has experienced unrest since you entered."

"You understand?" Fillion laughed with offense. "Jeff tattling on me or do you have a different informant?" Hanley simply stared as if he was waiting for Fillion to get to the point. "Just because I refuse to bow down to you doesn't mean I'm the source of unrest. A man lost his father and is looking for answers. A sheltered generation just met its first stranger. For every action there is an equal and opposite reaction."

"I know your ways, Fillion. Since you were a boy, you've had a hunger and thirst for something to fight for, something to defend and protect. And when you cave in to your activist tendencies, every move is subtle and cunning. You don't like the attention, preferring to work from the shadows, a perfect smokescreen to execute your shrewd agendas. Why do you think I chose New Eden Township for your sentence?"

Hanley looked at him as if brimming with pride. Fillion clenched his jaw and looked away. Was his dad right? Did he use people like that? Possibly, but not intentionally. Not like his dad. There was something lurking beneath the surface here. Everything Hanley said and did was never as it appeared. Ever. Which brought Fillion to the next point of confusion.

His dad wanted Fillion to fight for New Eden Township? Defend the community? Red flags waved in his mind. Was everything, including solving the Watson deaths, just a distraction so Fillion would bond with the community and desire to become owner? His spirit deflated, crushed by the idea. All the energy he expended was probably for nothing, a smokescreen to execute Hanley's own shrewd agendas.

In a lighter tone, Hanley asked, "Any leads yet?"

"If I give my full report now, does this mean my sentence is over?" Fillion arched an eyebrow.

Hanley chuckled. "I am afraid the terms of your sentence are non-negotiable."

"I could walk out and leave whenever I want. You'd have to send me to jail then, right?"

"Others can walk out, but not you. The entire staff at N.E.T. as well as those working surveillance and communications know not to open The Door for you." Hanley shifted in his chair and continued in a businesslike tone. "Even though

I am weak where you're concerned, you broke the law, son. These are the consequences."

A cocky smile formed on Fillion's face. "At least someone in our family pays for their crimes." They stared at each other for several seconds before Fillion relaxed into a posture of cool detachment and gave his dad a bored look. But his heart hurt with the betrayal. "We're not having this chat because you miss me. So what do you want?"

"You misunderstand me, as always. Your mother misses you. So does your sister."

A caring look warmed his dad's face and Fillion swallowed. Had that look ever been true? Did Hanley ever mean it once? The words ticked across Fillion's mind until the answer came. It was a trick, as usual. Hanley confessed that Fillion's mom and sister missed him, but didn't claim any such sentiments himself. Just an accusation that Fillion misunderstood him. Shame. Always shame. A pain in Fillion's chest nearly brought him to his knees. This was the first phase. Charm. How could he have been so stupid?

"How is your eye and nose? It appears the apothecary took care of your needs."

Rage surged once again as Fillion thought of his sister. But he clamped down on his jaw, refusing to give Hanley the satisfaction. A faint smile appeared on his dad's face, one that was smug and arrogant, before vanishing within a blink.

"I wanted to remind you that your job is to serve time by working off community service hours and help solve a crime—not restructure the society I created."

A flippant remark begged for release, but instead, Fillion remained calm and said, "I'm not restructuring your society. The community is course-correcting. Every generation has its struggles, and the second gen is modifying *their* world to accommodate *their* needs."

"And here I thought you were the poster boy for no movement," Hanley bantered. "You'll make a fine Gamemaster one day, Son of Eden. But now is not your time."

The kind smile remained on his dad's face, even though it didn't reach his eyes. *You are an entirely different character, son.* Hanley's words baited him and Fillion refused to bite. Instead, he shifted on his feet and angled his head with impatience.

"You isolated an entire generation," Fillion countered with mild disgust. "Your grand experiment worked. They'd rather spend the rest of their lives confined to their world than integrate with modern society."

"I never thought I would see the day my son would take life seriously. Or his role." Hanley leaned back in his chair and raised his eyebrows. "And why do you believe the second generation wishes to remain confined and isolated?"

"Stockholm syndrome."

His dad chuckled and shook his head with placating humor. The fake sound grated on Fillion's nerves, and he rolled his eyes and looked away. "There's the familiar snarky reply. Even someone as intelligent and clever as you doesn't reform that quickly. Your characterization is good. Have you fooled the community as well, Dungeon Master?"

Hanley chuckled again. Fillion glanced up at Leaf, who gave an encouraging nod. A long pause ensued and Fillion knew his dad was ready to soliloquize, blabbering on with justifications for his decisions to showcase his superiority. When the charm didn't work, Hanley buffered until the argument formed. And he was done buffering.

"Despite what you may think, I am not the bad guy," Hanley said. "I simply created an opportunity. Most of these people wanted to escape their lives. They wanted to isolate themselves from the real world. Isn't that why you joined the computer underground? You seized an opportunity created by the Anime Tech Movement—and they deal in black market operations and support lawlessness, unlike me. But, in your eyes, I'm still the bad guy." Hanley paused and smiled at Fillion with triumph. "So, you see, how am I responsible for the first generation's choices? They enclosed their families and chose to isolate the next generation, not me."

"God, you're sick! What the hell is wrong with you? These are real people. Their lives are forever affected by your so-called opportunity."

He wanted to defend the Anime Tech Movement, but knew it was pointless. His dad didn't care, nor would he listen. To rein in his anger, Fillion let his gaze wander around the room, to look at anything but Hanley. His search paused and he squinted his eyes. Near where Leaf stood, next to a table, was a door. Strange. Was that an airlock? That would explain many things. He wanted to ponder the discovery, but his dad was watching him closely.

Fillion took in a deep breath and released it slowly, getting back on point. "Many residents in New Eden are scared because they have no life skills when it comes to big changes. They know their lives are dependent on New Eden Enterprises, and they feel powerless."

"Yes, as to be expected. I'll share your observations with your mother, though." Hanley tilted his head in a gesture of victory. "I knew you were the perfect solution for New Eden Township."

Fillion groaned at the amused sound of his dad's voice, raking a hand through his hair. A perfect solution for what? The Outside world? Something wasn't right. He couldn't put his finger on it, but there was something being said between the lines that was alluding him. His eyes flitted to Leaf and then back to the screen. Fillion needed a new tactic. A detail floated to the forefront of his mind and he settled focus onto his dad once more.

"Why didn't you tell me that Connor had your Death Card?" Fillion tucked his thumbs into his belt. "You looked me in the eye and lied to me. I walked into New Eden without a shred of information, and you want me to believe you're not a bad guy? You set me up to fail. As usual. It's what you do, because you always need someone to blame when things don't work out according to your master plan."

The kindness dissipated on Hanley's face and Fillion knew the tables were about to turn. As usual, the charm didn't work and Fillion braced as his dad buffered. The accusations were about to be flung back his direction and he internally cringed in anticipation.

"I trust you've kept your breeches laced? Or did you take something that isn't yours to have?" The intended barb hit its mark and Fillion angled his head away and lifted his shoulders as his face warmed. Even though he warned Leaf, he couldn't look at Willow's brother. Hanley continued and Fillion flinched. "If she gets pregnant, that's on your conscience. You can't claim a child by someone who is legally dead."

"You're *not* allowed to talk about her," Fillion nearly growled. "The world will know they're alive in a few months. And I thought learning they were alive gave you hope? God, you probably knew it was a scam the entire time."

"I didn't know if they were alive. I swear. It was too risky to ask Joel or Jeff directly."

"If? Risky?" Fillion stilled and studied his dad's face. "So, what I hear you saying is there's something for you to gain in their deaths, real or falsified. Do you possess a conscience at all? Joel was your friend."

"A piece of paper didn't harm the Watson siblings if they were alive." A small smile curled Hanley's mouth. "Perception." His dad stared at him as if that word held magical properties. "It is what has kept New Eden Township afloat."

Fillion rubbed his temple and closed his eyes for a couple of seconds. Was "perception" the new watchword? Irritating. "How would they integrate into society after Project Shut Down if legally dead?"

"I've been crucified for the last time, Fillion. Do you understand what the media will do to New Eden Biospherics & Research over this? The lawsuits that will spring up? The government contracts that will be rescinded and renegotiated?" In a softer tone, Hanley continued, "You are full of passion right now. I remember the intense feelings I had for a certain young woman when your age. She made me feel so alive, even when she couldn't be mine. I was willing to do anything for her, even change the world."

Was Hanley talking about Della? Or another? Fillion thought quietly for a moment as goosebumps formed on his skin. "You did the change the world. And then created another one."

Hanley picked a piece of lint off his sleeve and acted as if he never heard Fillion. Instead, empathy radiated from his dad's face, and Fillion felt that familiar tug. He wanted so desperately for his dad to give a damn.

"There's no DNA record of Leaf, Willow Oak, and Laurel's existence," Hanley began again and Fillion braced, knowing the thrust was coming. As his dad continued, Fillion could almost hear the melodic shrill of Hanley unsheathing his weapon. "Only birth and death certificates exist for them. Biomedical records are easily manipulated, too. The experiment was approved with an allowable margin of insanity. It's a simple thing to assess her mental health. Leaf's, too. It's the first stage of Project Phase Two." Hanley's voice carried an eerie calm, his eyes unmoving as he spoke. "I'll allow him to play King for a little bit, and only because he's revealed himself to the community. But he no longer exists, and neither do his sisters."

A clammy sweat gathered on Fillion's skin. He blinked rapidly as queasiness stirred in his stomach, his dad's weapon slowly drawing from his gut. Despite the fog building in his head, thoughts came quick and sharp. He needed Mack to get to the underground, stat. The scales of injustice had tipped too far. Hell if he'd allow his dad to lay a finger on Willow or her siblings. Or anyone else for that matter.

The smile on his dad's face grew wider. "Good. I see my message has penetrated your young lover's mind. Remember, she'll *never* be yours, so keep your distance and keep your pants up."

"Answer the question. Why did you lie to me?"

"Akiko Hirabayashi's father has entertained discussions of an arrangement. The daughter of Japan's leading Tech Baron is a superb match. Well done, son. She's very beautiful, too, I might add."

He knew it. His dad had plotted out his life, even down to whom he should marry. Fillion turned his back to the camera. Fear slithered through his veins. The panic threatened to consume him, but he took a large breath as his mind uploaded the information.

Fillion met Akiko a year ago, when he traveled to Japan with his dad. It was a last-minute trip, and Fillion had felt conflicted. He wanted to go to Japan, no question, but not with Hanley. Mack was not permitted to tag along and Lynden was still in school. He and Hanley stayed in Tokyo for two weeks, and the majority of that time was spent with the Hirabayashi family.

God, Akiko was so damn sexy. But he kept physical distance. Mack had a cyber-crush on her at the time. Hell, his friend still did. Fillion had zero interest in Japan's tech heiress, and that pissed her off to no end. She promised Fillion that she always got what she wanted, and she wanted him. Why? It made no sense on a personal level. Whatever her reasons, it didn't matter. He wasn't for sale or trade, and he wouldn't be bullied into marriage for corporate empire building.

Fillion faced the monitor and, by some miracle, kept his face devoid of the emotions raging through him. "Please relay to Mr. Hirabayashi that I am honored by the esteem, but I must regretfully decline any offers of marriage to his daughter."

"I am afraid that is not possible. I have already relayed your gratitude and interest to their *Nakoudo*. We'll travel to Japan in four months for *Yuinou no gi*. Mr. Hirabayashi agreed to a long engagement so you may attend MIT and then join me on a world tour once you become majority owner. You and Akiko are young yet anyway." Hanley tapped his Cranium and scrolled behind a privacy screen. "Ah, here it is. Mr. Hirabayashi, in addition to any gifts and monies exchanged during *Yuinou*, has agreed to a substantial monetary gift, bestowed upon the one-year anniversary of your marriage. He'll also give you sizable stock in his company."

Fillion bit the inside of his cheek until he drew blood. The metallic taste filled his mouth as the fury and humiliation whipped around inside of him. Hanley's mind games were breaking him. Beating him back into submission. Punishing him for ever thinking he had a choice. One thing he knew for sure, though: He'd never marry Akiko Hirabayashi, no matter the consequences.

Mustering what tremulous confidence he had left, he said, "Hanley, I have a busy day tomorrow." Fillion's voice cracked. "Let's get to the point. Stop deflecting and answer the damn question. Why did you lie about the Death Card?"

"It really doesn't matter what I say as you have already decided the truth. I'm always the bad guy to you. But, for the record, I never lied to you about the Death Card. I really didn't know it was in New Eden." Fillion felt like the wind was knocked out of him. Again. Damn this was getting old. His dad folded his hands in his lap and leaned back in his chair. "So, Connor had it? Interesting."

"But..." Fillion lowered his head and thought back to the conversation he had with Connor. *I was given Hanley's Death Card.* "Shit." He stabbed his fingers through his hair once again and lifted his eyes. Was his dad toying with him? He couldn't tell. "Yeah," Fillion continued. "Connor placed it in Joel's pocket as a signal that the death was suspicious. He hoped you would read about it in the report Jeff sent over. But Leaf found it before the Cremation Ceremony and didn't reveal it to the community, a tradition of theirs. And here we are."

Hanley's face tensed in contemplation for a few seconds, before relaxing. "And what do you think about that story?"

"You tell me."

"You're the one with the information."

"OK. Fine. Initial thoughts? I think it's weird that an El-ement would have the job of signaling by using a unique card when another Element has died of foul play, because it as-sumes it'll never be him. Sort of begs the question if they're the one behind the crime." Hanley nodded thoughtfully. "But the plot hole with that idea is that Connor said the card was given to him. So the real questions are, why did the card giver think a signal like that would even be necessary? Why did they believe Connor would be safe? And why were you left out?"

"Indeed."

That was it? He waited a few seconds to see if Hanley would engage in the topic more, but his dad remained tight-lipped. "Happen to know who would use a Curse Card in New Eden?"

His dad's face stilled. "A Curse Card was used?"

"That's what I just said. Are you now reduced to redundancy as deflection?" Fillion rolled his eyes. "Willow discovered the Curse Card on the remains of her spinning wheel."

"Was this the same day Norah died?"

The nausea that had pooled in Fillion's stomach stirred once again. "Yeah, why?"

"Fitting puzzle pieces together."

"Norah spoke with me before she died." Hanley's eyes widened ever so slightly and Fillion internally rejoiced. Good. He'd play back. Adopting a casual tone, he continued. "She shared some things. So don't play games with me."

"The Curse Card is for me. I spin the tales and I weave the stories together. It's a warning."

"A warning about what?" Fillion waited, but his dad didn't answer. So Fillion thought he'd throw out the first bit of information that could be linked to such a sign of communication. "A faction has formed."

"Disagreements in opinions are not the same as civil war. I am not shutting down the project."

"People have died! Lives are threatened."

A belittling, amused expression lit his dad's features. "A heart attack and cancer. They're the same threats beyond the walls of New Eden."

Fillion creased his brows. "Two Elements in two weeks. That leaves Timothy and Connor. Oh, and Jeff. Which one was The Aether before Claire?"

JESIKAH SUNDIN

"Now you are thinking like a Gamemaster."

Hanley leveled a calculating look, and Fillion flew into a rage. "This. Is. Real. Holy shit! Are you mental?" Fillion continued to swear under his breath and glared at Hanley. "Why won't you tell me? Who are you protecting?"

"You can hate me as much as you want." Hanley's countenance was empathetic, but his gaze insidious. "One day you'll thank me. I'm preparing you for a necessary future."

"How hubristic of you to think I need your permission to have feelings or a future."

Before his dad could reply, Fillion walked over to the tower and pushed the power button and the screen went black. All the self-control he possessed dissipated into the dank, sweltering air that spilled in from the jungle, and he marched over to the back wall by the ladder and released his fury onto the mud surface. Blood dripped from his knuckles, but he threw another punch. And another. The sensation satisfied a primal urge to feel alive, endorphins and adrenaline mixing together in a violent rush. Red dotted the walls, but he didn't care. His blood was figuratively being poured out for this place. Might as well make it literal, too.

When the fight finally left him, he leaned his head onto the wall, closing his eyes as the cool surface soothed his flushed skin. Sweat dripped down his face and back. His body involuntarily shuddered.

"Fillion."

He'd forgotten about Leaf. He slowly turned, too mortified to meet the noble's eyes. Fillion was on the brink of a system crash, his vision dimming as he stared at the floor. It was black. Everything. His future. His existence. He felt nothing and everything all at once. Dizziness swam in his head and his lungs burned, and Fillion realized he'd been holding his breath. He gulped, his chest heaving as an army of emotions marched through him. Each beat of his heart echoed life, but he was dying inside. Probably already dead. Only shades of his former self remaining to interact and respond.

338

Arms wrapped around him and pulled him close, and Fillion lost it. Tears, heated by the heartache and the rage, burned his skin as he sobbed. Nobody had ever comforted him before like this. And Fillion felt vulnerable, reduced by resignation. The oppressive weight of his life felt stronger than gravity. And all he could do was lean against Leaf.

For two weeks he received messages of worth and value. The desolate oceans of his life showed signs of restoration rather than the barren wasteland it had been. Hanley wiped all that away, destroyed every ounce of confidence, and the lifeless desert returned.

The message was clear. He was to be dependent on his dad for everything. Hanley would dole out bits of life, like nourishment to satisfy Fillion's hunger and keep him alive, only to show that he, and he alone, was responsible for Fillion's future. Submission would guarantee some emotional comfort, and defiance would not be tolerated. Others would be punished as consequence.

Where was his redemption? He internally swore at Fate for her cruelty. He had asked for a sign and was given one. But hope was for the weak-minded. A second wave of rage surged through Fillion and he pushed Leaf away. If he fought, it was certain death. If he didn't fight, it was also certain death. He would die inside either way. He paced the room, pulling on his hair, the agony in his heart far greater than the knife-sharp pain stabbing through his knuckles.

"Fillion, how your father wishes for you to feel and think of yourself is not real." Leaf's voice somehow breached the barricades he had boarded up and he locked eyes with the Son of Earth. "What is the truth?"

"Who gives a shit? Does it even matter?!"

Then, as if in answer to Leaf's question, a light sparked in the darkness of Fillion's mind, and the funeral pyre of his life caught fire. Thoughts fueled the flames as he tossed them into the inferno like sticks, the deafening roar of the furnace blocking out all voices but truth.

His dad had never cared about him. Neither had the world. Hanley wasn't a father of a son and a daughter. He was a father of lies, lies the world bought into. So why did Fillion allow Hanley or the world to define his value? Determine if he was worthy of acceptance? Worthy of love? The truth *did* matter.

The lies were suddenly so clear. Their shrieks attempted to pierce his resolve. But no more.

The remnants of his old life burned with a fury. The paved graveyard of dreams had led to redemption after all. And this marked the moment he knew, without question, that he owned his life.

Fillion lifted his head. Red and swollen eyes stared back, shadows lining Leaf's face. The passion for justice, family, and honor that resonated in the Son of Earth emboldened Fillion. Leaf Dylan Watson was one of the greatest men Fillion knew. He was annoying as hell at times. A rule-following, arrogant bastard at other moments. But everything Leaf fought for, he did for noble reasons. He was meant to wear a crown of power. And Fillion would make sure it stayed that way.

"Hanley lost a son today."

Leaf nodded slowly, his face full of emotion. "I shall be your family." The Son of Earth grabbed Fillion's forearm and gripped him tightly. "I bond myself to you as a sworn brother, and pledge my life to serve and protect yours. I shall be your other family, one who honors your life."

Fire shot through Fillion's veins with those words. "I bond myself to you as a sworn brother, too. I'll keep fighting for your family. Hanley won't lay a goddamn finger on you or your sisters."

The Son of Earth bowed deeply, and Fillion received the honor without self-deprecation. He was a prince and would stand tall as the man of power and influence he was. Leaf pulled Fillion in for another embrace, clapping him on the back. "Come," Leaf whispered, draping an arm across Fil-

lion's shoulders and directing him toward the ladder to climb
out of the pit.

Over the past two decades, symptoms of emotional isolation have reached a pandemic state in populations across the world. The common feeling described is disconnection or a lack of bonding despite strong social networks. Normally, this is a very common phase while processing grief. Hardships force people into a place that demands a re-evaluation of values. What was once considered significant can become relegated to the petty, creating a domino effect. This inward journey is a critical step when traveling through sorrow toward hope. It is concerning, however, when entire populations claim feelings and experiences of emotional isolation as if the world is in a state of global-wide grief.

— Dr. Della Jayne Nichols, "Chapter 2: Emotional Isolation," *Misery Loves Company*, 2047

CHAPTER
TWENTY-TWO

Seattle, Washington state

Coal dared not move, baffled by what had just transpired. Though he did not have long to ponder his thoughts. The door slid open manually in an angry rush, snapping him out of his confused trance. Lynden grabbed the chain dangling from his belt loop and pulled him forward.

"Come on. Mack is waiting."

As she marched down the hallway, he whispered, "I did not mean to imply fault nor guilt."

"Whatever."

"Upon my honor, I speak truth."

She whirled around and faced him, the anger sparking dangerously from her eyes, and he matched her fiery passion, drawing himself up taller. She backed away a step with a nervous breath, hugging her arms. Coal realized his mistake and relaxed his posture, softening his expression. In response, her emotions dimmed to indifference, the flames of offense cooling to the unreadable.

"I may be a whore according to the Martian standards of living," she spat, "but you didn't just want me that day, you *needed* me. There's a whole world of difference, something you don't get because you've never had to emotionally survive until now."

"I have been taught that such passions only exist between a man and his wife, and to know a woman's body before she is your wife ruins her reputation," Coal said. "If a man does not redeem the woman's virtue through marriage, then, according to the community, each must never marry or risk banishment. For to then share a bond with another would be to commit an affair, which is against The Code." Coal took a step closer. "Go ahead, laugh and scoff. In New Eden, there is no escape from each other. Property is communal and privacy is scarce. There is very little we truly own. But our heart? It is the most guarded and cherished possession of all." He tried to plead with her to understand with his eyes, but she looked away. Lowering his voice, he continued, "I cannot change my truth in a few days. To expect otherwise is unrealistic. Please allow me my due process until I am able to make both worlds coexist within me."

"You think others will give you your due process? You don't get it, Coal. You're fresh meat." She threw her arms up into the air. "They'll take what they want and then forget about you when they're done." Lynden looked up at the ceiling in frustration. "What the hell kind of community punishes a woman's reputation but not the man? New Eden is messed up."

"I understand what you share, I simply lack the experience to couple with your truth."

"Are you leaving her because we nearly hooked up?"

"You believe I am impulsive, as if I have come to such conclusions lightly, even though I left my childhood home three weeks prior. Yes, I am ashamed of my dishonorable behavior toward you, but that is not why I have chosen to remain here."

"God, male pride. Yuck! A bit over-the-top, don't you think?"

"Allow me to finish," he ground out in frustration.

"Whatever."

"You think so little of me?" She issued a bored response and he dangerously skirted the edge of unhinging. "I am torn. I feel as though my heart has been ripped into a million pieces!" Lynden's eyes widened and her face blanched with the tone of his voice. "Everything I have ever known or thought is in question. It is as if I have partaken of the fruit of the Knowledge of Good and Evil and am suddenly aware of my nakedness, longing to hide my shame." Coal grimaced with anguish and thumped a closed fist over his heart. "I am leaving behind my entire family and a community that raised me. And although it pains me, I know this is the right decision. New Eden was never big enough for me. I was restless for more and longed for adventure, something my sister understood. Something Oaklee knew as well."

"That's her name? Oaklee?"

Coal relaxed his muscles but maintained a tight smile. "Yes."

"What is it with tree names for girls in New Eden?" She rolled her eyes. Coal refrained from comment. Lynden studied him as if leery. "So, this isn't some kind of sick alien bond thing? Imprinting on me?"

"I am not an alien, nor am I from Mars. Do not insult me." Coal's head fell back in agitation. "Please, Lynden. Although we have acted beyond friends, I need your friendship."

"I'd think friendship with me would go against your sanctimonious upbringing."

"Stop."

"What?"

Coal stepped forward and their gazes collided in a heated swirl of emotions. His heart shouted conflicting messages to his mind, and Lynden seemed lost in a similar struggle. In a breathy whisper, he confessed, "I have never desired anyone as I desired *you*. I shall not deny it." He took another step closer, admiring the freckles that kissed her skin. "But what really gains my attention? Even more than any passions that may exist between us? You are the only real thing I know in this world. I would be utterly lost without you. Perhaps that makes me selfish, but I need you, and I desire to need you for all the right reasons."

"Oh. My. God. What's taking so long?" Mack bellowed dramatically from the living room. "Get your asses over here!"

She closed the distance between them. "I've had a lot of boys damage me in a lot of ways. But no boy has *ever* broken my heart. Don't be that boy, Coal Hansen."

"I wish— "

"What the hell is going on?!" Mack stomped over to them, and Lynden casually moved away from their contact. "Fine. Let's meet in the hallway. Why not?" He slumped against the wall and raised his eyebrows. "So, what's the secret meeting about and why wasn't I invited?"

Coal maintained eye contact with Lynden, but said to Mack, "My apologies. I needed to make amends over a misunderstanding."

"Cleared up?" Mack looked between them.

"Murky." Lynden fidgeted with the ring on her thumb. "So, what's up?"

"We need to hit the underground much sooner. Something happened to Fillion's line, and it's making me antsy. So, we're going to kick-start this circus while the cat's away and hope our juggling act works, or however that metaphor should go. Damn. What time is it?" Mack flashed his Cranium. "Shit. What the hell is wrong with me? I'm like suddenly an old person. OK. Before we can go, Coal needs lessons on what to expect from the Earthen female species who make their homes in the underground."

"I don't like the look on your face," Lynden said, narrowing her eyes as she stared at Mack. "How does this involve me?"

A silent understanding passed between Lynden and Mack, and Coal watched with growing concern as Lynden shifted on her feet and gathered herself. Mack, normally jovial and pouncing on every line with a ready comeback, held a serious expression as he watched Lynden.

"If not you then someone else, and you know it." Mack lowered his voice. "Look at him." Lynden obeyed, but avoided eye contact. "It's not like you never thought of it. I saw you *test* him the first day he arrived."

"Fine. But you can't watch."

Mack rolled his eyes. "Oh, please. Like I've never seen you ticket. I was there the night Fillion hauled your ass out of The Crypt."

"I do not wish to cause Lynden distress," Coal said quietly. "I am not sure I fully understand, but I have gathered enough and recognize that she is uncomfortable with whatever it is you are asking her to do for my education. And, if you are asking her to be physical with me, I shall leave. As one man to another, I cannot respect nor approve your request."

"See? He'll be fine." Lynden crossed her arms over her chest and looked away.

"I know his type." Mack flashed him a quick glance. "Trust me. He'll be anything but fine, and you know it better than me. Tell me I'm wrong."

Lynden released a loud groan, stared at Mack like she wanted to murder him, and then relaxed. After a few heartbeats, she lifted her head with a flirtatious glint in her eyes, and Coal sucked in his bottom lip nervously. He knew this look. And he knew he was in trouble. The attraction she communicated suddenly switched to disinterest as she walked toward him while inspecting his body from top to bottom and bottom to top. When she reached him, she lifted her eyes again and smiled. It was playful, almost a tease, confident and yet held traces of demure-like qualities, and his heart rate responded despite all efforts to ignore her allure.

"Stop," he croaked awkwardly. "I know it is a ruse. I understand and shall be wary of such approaches."

"What approaches?" She tilted her head, smiled in that certain way again, and then pressed her body against his. "Come here, I want to tell you something and don't want Mack to hear."

Coal hesitated, licked his lips again, wincing with the tenderness of his new piercing. Although he knew he should resist and do anything but fulfill her request, he leaned forward anyway. Disappointment colored her eyes and he paused. But it passed quickly and she lifted her eyebrows with mock-impatience. Confused, he continued down the path he began and lowered until they were face-to-face. She whispered in his ear, "Don't fight me," and then pressed her mouth to his.

He jumped back astonished, and flinched with the pain in his lower lip. But she fisted his shirt in her hands and pushed him against the wall, finding his face and kissing him again. Coal gently tried to push her away and he turned his head. But she knew he would do each of those actions and diverted him. Her whispered words surfaced somehow through the chaos of panicked thoughts in his head, and he finally resigned himself to let her kiss him, closing his eyes against the ache in his heart. Lynden's fingers burned trails over his body, eventually hooking in the pockets of his pants. Without realizing it, he was returning her kiss, suddenly savoring the connection.

Everything changed between them in that moment, and their kisses slowed to something deeper. Something meaningful. Quintessential. Coal wanted her. But more than that, he *needed* her, and Lynden's earlier words pierced him. There was definitely a world of difference, and the longing ebbed from his heart to his fingers as he raised both hands and softly cupped her face.

Her body trembled, as if she was stifling the urge to cry. Ashamed, he gently dropped his hands to her shoulders and nudged her away to sever their embrace. They locked eyes, breaths heavy. Lynden lifted his new wallet for all to see, dropped it to the ground, and walked away. Coal stared at the dark brown leather, too distraught to meet Mack's eyes or watch Lynden's retreating form.

"I hate you Mackenzie!"

A door slammed shut and Coal released a long sigh.

"I am such a stupid, *stupid*, insensitive fool."

"No, you care about her. And I heard her whisper." Mack shifted his position on the wall. "She knows I care about her, too, and will forgive me eventually. I was right, and that's what she hates."

Coal looked at Mack with concern. "You have affection for Lynden? Please forgive me. I had no idea and would never—"

"Eww. Not *that* way," Mack said quickly. "Nope. That'd be like making out with Fillion." He paused with a look of consideration, tapping his chin. When Coal refused to play, Mack rolled his eyes and continued in a sober tone, "She's like my little sister. I've known her since she was two. I'd do anything for her."

They grew silent and after several loud moments of nothing, Coal whispered, "I thought her kiss was real." He closed his eyes as the guilt grew stronger. "She confuses me. Everything confuses me. Nothing is sincere and very little is real."

"Before you mentally flog yourself further, just know I get it. I've been in your shoes. Not with her, but with another."

"You have faced a personal crux to reject the morality that has always comprised your entire life?"

Mack cleared his throat. "Um, no. That sucks, I'll give you that. I just meant that pretty much every male noob in the underground is the victim of a ticket girl at one point. They prey on boys who show signs of inexperience. And you're like a neon sign, begging to be ripped off. This is why I wanted you to get ticketed here, instead of there, and only by Rainbow." Mack paused to let those words sink in. "She's beautiful and doesn't know it. Always comparing herself to Della and Fillion. And she's lonely. It's why Pinkie scouted her out and pretended to be her friend. Well, one of the reasons why. There are many."

Mack nudged his arm until Coal squinted open his eyes. Mack picked up Coal's wallet, opening the folds to reveal it was empty. Lynden had walked away with his cash. Unbelievable. Frustrated, Coal closed his eyes again and clenched his jaw, clenching harder when Mack spoke again.

"For nearly a year, the Madam of the Cyber Call Girl circle personally groomed her. Except, Lynden doesn't know Pinkie is the Madam. Most don't. It's a well-guarded secret. I paid someone a hefty tag for that bit of info. For Pinkie's personal stats, too."

Coal opened his eyes and faced Mack. "I do not understand."

"Lynden was a ticket girl. Usually they attack in packs. One acts as the decoy, distracting the man, while the other lifts the money. Their ticket to a quick income without fully selling off their bodies to get paid. The next phase is to become a CCG, and men bid daily, like an auction, for the companion they lust over online. You get the gist."

"Why would a young woman of standing lower herself to such employment?" Coal felt the anger ripple through him. Wave after wave of fury and disgust consumed his humiliation until nothing remained but rage. "Nor do I understand why women would resort to such licentious behavior either. Where are the men to provide for their needs? Care for their families?"

"Um, we're not in the Middle Ages, mate. Men are not sole providers. Everyone for his or her self." Mack frowned, a strange expression on his face. "Lynden has her reasons. People always do. And they're never what you'd expect, either. One of the lessons I've learned the last four years."

He tossed Coal the wallet, then, as if suddenly remembering something, snatched it back with a slight frown. "The chains aren't decor. They serve a purpose." Mack secured the wallet to the chain for Coal. "Never keep cash in your wallet. Only your ID and random plastics. It's why we wear cargo style pants. Many pockets make it harder for cash to get pickpocketed. Choose a pocket with a button or clasp, not a zipper."

Coal nodded absently, too grieved to fully pay attention to Mack's instruction. The young man eyed Coal, as if weighing options, then launched into another explanation. "As for the ugly side of humanity, it's simple. Money. They don't have jobs, and they can't get respectable jobs because there are none, and they probably have large debts to pay off, too. Means to an end. You do what you can, mate. Game of survival. Don't judge."

"You support such ventures?" Coal stared wide-eyed at Mack.

"God, no." Mack pulled a face of disgust. "I hate that whole affair. Everyone hooks up. But pay for someone? Own someone? Gross. Evil." The young man retrieved a cigarette and offered one to Coal, who accepted. Mack lit up. "There really are no jobs. For anyone. And no jobs means no money, and no money means no food, and starvation is a painful way to die. The street is littered with desperate, hungry people."

Coal opened his mouth but Mack cut him off.

"Don't give me a speech about my money or the way I live. Life's not fair. First lesson you learn as an Elite. I didn't choose to be born rich and they didn't choose to be born poor. My money creates jobs underground, and I give it away street-level to help where I can. So does Fillion. The point is: Life sucks and then you die. The end. You're welcome. This chat has been way fun. Let's do it again sometime."

Coal remained quiet for a while, too stricken by such information, but could not end the conversation yet. "They cannot open a shop or grow a garden to provide for their needs? Is that not a given human right?"

"Sure. Only if you have money to purchase land or pay rent, not to mention pay for all the licenses, permits, miscellaneous fees, inspections, equipment, and so forth and so on. People don't have money for groceries let alone all of that shit. It's so back-asswards. So many want to work, but they can't—not allowed to. It's against the law, because a business overlord or one of their minions hasn't given them permission to survive by hiring them out. Instead, they employ robots and computers. Cheap labor that rarely complains or takes sick days or quits, the training turnaround time is ideal, and the quality control is superb…"

Mack looked at the ceiling and dragged on his cigarette, slowly releasing the smoke.

"There are laws against chickens on private property, and you can't grow a garden unless the Department for Genetically Modified Organism-Free Agriculture has verified that your seeds or stock meet regulations and didn't come from the black market, which, of course, costs money. The world is terrified of cross-pollination. Who cares that people are dying of hunger practically in their backyard. We're messing with nature and that's bad. We might get cancer or something." Mack lifted his mouth in a dark, wry smile. "Technology advances and makes us useless, but we must pretend to live naturally like we're from the Middle Ages. Because displacing humans doesn't mess with nature at all. Idiots. This is our plague, our Black Death."

For the first time since he emerged, Coal felt gratitude as he thought of New Eden Township. He had lacked for nothing, always able to provide for his needs and the needs of others. The rules seemed so simple and relational, and people in the community genuinely cared for one another. Here, it was as if each person he encountered were merely flesh and bones, their spirit dead long ago, surviving the day but dreading the future.

"It is such a shame that New Eden Township shall be shut down, as it is a perfect solution for our generation." Coal puffed on his cigarette. "Is there a way to create more townships like my childhood home so people may work and provide for their needs without permission to survive?"

Mack's jaw slackened and he stared at Coal as if he had suddenly materialized in the hallway. "That is the sexiest idea I've heard in ages. Damn, you're hot. Mind. Blown."

"What a shame. Your best feature."

Mack laughed. "Smart-ass." The young man flashed the time on his Cranium again. "Holy shit. I could sleep for a millennia. We'll hit the underground tomorrow." He shuffled a few steps and paused. "Let it be known that I officially resign as Fillion's fake boy. He can have his job back." Coal nodded, unsure of what Mack meant, and then watched him trudge down the hallway. "Help yourself to whatever," Mack called over his shoulder.

When he was no longer within sight, Coal meandered to Lynden's door and hesitantly knocked.

"Go away!"

He started to turn, acknowledging a lady's request as he had been taught. But a new education overruled his initial instinct. For the girl who claimed he shouldn't give a shit, she sure acted as if she did. With one last look down the hallway, he pushed the button and entered her room, spotting the silhouette of her body in the barely lit space.

She lay face down in the bed, shoulders shaking as the pillows and blankets muffled her sobs. Throwing propriety out the sixty-five-story window, he sat next to her on the bed and waited. He was unsure of what he should do next, but remained seated.

"He told you, didn't he?" Her anguished voice was muffled in a pillow. "That bastard." She lifted her head. "Leave me alone."

"I wished to see you before retiring."

"Still making wishes?"

Coal grinned. "Yes, along with a few silent ones for you to spare my life."

Lynden rolled to her back, and the dusky low-lit room shaded her in golden hues. She had stripped down to a camisole and undergarments, but he focused only on her eyes.

"Now you've seen me. Happy?"

"No, I came to see *you*."

"Yeah? Well, as Ignis said, you have nice social skills. Good job. You've done your chivalrous deed for the night." She nibbled on her bottom lip ring and turned her head toward the wall.

"I shall take my leave." Coal slipped from her bed. "My humble thanks for giving a shit about me, despite my foolhardy antics and insensitivity this day. I am honored to know *you*, Lynden Nichols."

He offered a charming smile, one that the Matriarchs always said could persuade even God of Coal's angelic intentions. Since a lad, often the urge to act led to trouble, even though his heart always resided in the proper place. He should have thought through his confession before laying it before her feet. When he reached the door, she whispered his name, and he looked over his shoulder.

"Before Mack interrupted us in the hallway, what were you about to wish for?"

Coal dragged on his cigarette, and then lifted a corner of his mouth. "I wish to know the young woman who comforts me when I am weary of sleeping in a coffin, teaches me how to properly jump into a black hole, saves me from poisoned apples, brings me to life after succumbing to the tiny stabs of rain drops, and whose presence dulls the surrounding colors with her brilliance." Her expression softened into a tiny, bashful smile. "Until the morning, My Lady."

He bowed and slid the door shut, grinning to himself as he walked back to his room. Before luxuriating in the warmth of thick covers, he walked to the window, pressed his forehead to the cold glass once more, and thanked the stars for granting him a glimmer of hope.

"Oaklee, if you can hear me, I am so sorry," he whispered to the night sky. "You were right, about everything. Especially about me."

Adams: _After interacting with Coal, what do you believe will be the biggest hardship for Martians present and future?_

Nichols: _I think the hardship they will experience is the same as any other culture-shock scenario. I have traveled all over the world. However, when I first began my travels, the differences I encountered, while at times exciting, were usually fraught with discomfort and anxiety. For Martians, the ways of Earth will be shocking since they are entirely removed from the trends and pop culture that shape Terran society. For Earth, the hardship will be to view the Martians as fully human rather than an alien species as often depicted in science fiction._

— Hanley Nichols and Jennifer Adams, _Atoms to Adams Daily Show_, October 15, 2054

CHAPTER
TWENTY-THREE

New Eden Township, Salton Sea, California

W ait," Fillion said. He turned away from the ladder and sought the door he had seen near Leaf while talking to Hanley. He gripped the latch and felt intense stabs of pain. Fillion grimaced, slowly sucking air between his teeth. His knuckles were cracked, some still bleeding.

Leaf crouched beside him, eyebrows deeply furrowed as he twisted the handle. The door hissed as it unlocked and opened—it was an airlock. Both he and Leaf angled their heads to peek inside and discovered a folded and sealed note. In quick movements, Leaf broke the seal and opened the missive.

WiFi access shut down. Hacker infiltrated the inside network. New hidden system to be launched: TechMage2054 / PW

C0rlanJayn3#2037. Guardian Angels on standby. Clog a water filter if you need help and then show at 0100 hours. Written response acknowledging instructions required before network launch.

Below the instructions was a scribbled reply, and Fillion groaned.

Hacker isolated, killed access. Launch TechMage2054.

"I'm screwed," Fillion muttered. He tossed the note back into the airlock and closed his eyes tight. "Damn it. I needed to contact Mack tonight."

The nausea that had been swirling in his stomach lurched. He laid down on his back, knees bent, and draped an arm over his eyes. Breathe in, breathe out. Repeat. Despite the renewal that was still scrubbing his insides, he teetered on the edge of losing his mind from betrayal.

Leaf crawled away from him. Think, Fillion kept telling himself, but he was spent. Rustling sounds continued to distract Fillion's tired thoughts, and he turned his head toward Leaf and lifted his arm just high enough to peek out. The medieval hippie bent over a pile of straw and blew across the waking embers.

"I could seriously kiss you right now."

"Your energy would be better served in other employment." Leaf looked his direction for a brief moment and returned to his task with a kind smile.

"Why aren't you shaken up? God, I want to jump out of my skin."

"I am." Leaf's face darkened for a split-second, then relaxed. "I prefer to draw inward to process and mean no offense."

"No, I get it. I'm just more—"

"Outwardly passionate. You are a man of war, and I am a man of peace."

"You're flirting with me." Fillion lifted his arm and threw Leaf a small, wry grin. "I like it."

Leaf quietly laughed. "I do believe you best Willow's hurricane-force winds of injustice. She has finally met her match." They grew quiet for a few seconds, and Fillion tried to relax his mind. But it was futile. "I was ever content to be the son of a gardener," Leaf said. "To me, fulfillment is encouraging living things to grow and thrive, and spending time in the company of my family. There is not a day that goes by where I do not wish to just be a worker in the fields. I am a simple man. My needs are few."

The confession resonated with Fillion and he closed his eyes tight against the ache. He quietly replied, "Believe it or not, I'm a simple man, too. No car. No high-end designer clothes. I bum cigarettes from strangers. I plan to move in with my friend rather than have a place of my own. My circle is mostly lowlifes who barely scrape by. Wealth, social status—they never mattered to me."

"I believe you."

"Thanks, mate." Fillion peeked out at Leaf again with a humored smile. "Let's run away. We can be happy together. Forever. You can grow things and I can … um…"

"Flirt with things."

"Smart-ass."

"The fire nest is ready," Leaf said in a dry tone, then cracked a small smile.

Fillion scooted toward the small flame. His hands, jittery and clammy, pulled a joint from his leather pouch and leaned forward. The joint shook in his mouth. But he managed to inhale deeply, exhaling the smoke with rapture as he eased onto his back once more, knees up. His free arm fell over his eyes and he moaned in pleasure as he dragged on the joint again. After a few seconds, he turned and blindly flicked the ashes into the fire nest. Or, where he hoped the fire nest was. Whatever. His mind was rambling.

What was his next move? Think, he reminded himself again. God, he was tired. He just wanted to curl up and drift off to the sounds of the jungle seeping through the opened hatch. Focus. Maybe the network was still accessible. It was worth a shot.

The compacted earth grated against the back of his head as he maneuvered to retrieve Ember's Cranium, placing it on his ear. With a tap, it turned on. At least that was working for him. He could attempt hacking Bessy. But it would take hours to hack and reprogram that dinosaur. He didn't have hours tonight.

"Kill the lights," Fillion said as he squinted at the faint holographic password screen. "Thanks," he sighed as the hatch plunged into darkness. "You haven't asked what the note meant."

"I knew you would share when ready." Leaf stomped out the fire nest and then stretched out on the ground next to him. "Your father reminds me of Skylar in some ways, especially with his oddly youthful appearance. Even the quality of his voice is reminiscent."

"Yeah, I've thought that since Exchange Day." Fillion put the joint in his mouth, held his Cranium so he didn't flash Leaf, and then turned the Earth Element's direction. "My mom and dad get treatments to eternally look twenty-something. It's gross. One day I'll look the same age as them, and then older and older. It weirds me out."

"Aging is something to respect and honor."

"Something like that." Fillion looked back up at his holographic screen.

Leaf looked up. "This is a Cranium?"

"Yep."

"How is it different than the Messenger Pigeon portal or a Scroll?"

"Bessy needs big parts, physical screens, speakers. Scrolls use smaller parts. Craniums use bone conduction so the sounds are not in your ears but in your head. The display is holographic, ghost-like. The parts are micro."

"Fascinating." Leaf placed a hand behind his head.

"Yeah, modern magic." He adjusted the Cranium on his ear to ensure it was snug. "I hope this works," he said aloud, mainly to himself.

He held down the power button for ten seconds and waited for the device to reboot into maintenance mode, but nothing happened. "Cheeky thing," he said under his breath.

Fillion repeated the process, but this time touched the upper right-hand corner of the holographic screen as he simultaneously held down the power button. The Cranium refreshed to an admin login screen and Fillion's lips turned up in amusement. Ember had left a back door into the security settings by hacking her start-up screen.

Fillion arranged the admin screens with one hand while placing the joint between his lips with the other. Smoke curled in front of him and then faded behind the holographic field. He tapped on the service tab, selected the option to "reset admin permissions." Yes, he wanted to remove the current password and go to factory default. A few swipes later, he was in the system and went to see if TechMage2054 was online. No WiFi access. There had to be a hidden network out there, though, because he just connected to his dad through Messenger Pigeon. He went back to work and began writing code to scan for broadcasting wireless networks.

"It is almost like a language," Leaf said.

"That's exactly what it is. I'm fluent in five computer languages and partial in three others. This is the core language. Every hack-wannabe knows it."

Leaf lifted his hand and pointed. "Is this also the other language you verbally speak?"

"No." Fillion smiled. "That's Japanese." He placed the joint in his mouth, lifted up his tunic, and pulled down his breeches a bit to reveal the lines and curves tattooed on his lower stomach. Leaf sat up and examined the exposed skin, etched in blue. "This is Japanese—its *hiragana* form, anyway. There are several syllabaries. I like the look of this one." Fillion rolled his eyes at himself for info dumping on Leaf. Now, he was verbally rambling. There was no help for it. He was so tired. "It says 'hacker.'"

Fillion's eyes burned and were swollen, compliments of his explosive catharsis. But he turned his attention again to the slew of digital information hovering above him. He groaned after drawing on his joint, frustrated with finding no trace of TechMage2054. Maybe they hadn't pre-launched for beta. He adjusted the filters on his rules and continued to search.

"You speak many languages."

"Only two human languages, same as you," he murmured, distracted by the new data.

"I speak three."

Fillion smirked. "Hot," he drawled in a sexy voice and Leaf chuckled shyly.

After scanning through lines of output, he found a hit—an active broadcasting signal. The victory was short-lived, though. The password didn't work. "Damn," he muttered and stifled a yawn. Sharp pricks of pain inflamed across his knuckles as he bent his fingers, and Fillion winced. He let out a disgruntled sigh and rubbed his face, then puffed on his joint. "Well, here goes nothing." He had the channel for the hidden network. So he launched a low-level packet capturing tool he found built into the Cranium's shell. In a matter of seconds, he collected enough data on the hidden network to reverse engineer the security key. He entered the final command and waited to be "Denied."

But the dialog never came. It worked. He stared, disbelieving, as his pulse raced with excitement. At the bottom of the field a Xandria icon appeared and he dragged open a Net screen to the front of his tiles and enlarged it. Ads ran across the side, some flashing, some with live action. Normally the activity didn't faze him, but his eyes were out of practice and he blinked a few times.

"I feel as though I am watching you manipulate a dream," Leaf said in wonder. "The colors are absolutely stunning."

Squinting, Fillion swiped in a URL address, concentrating too much to comment. His body wanted to power down and recharge and he fought against the current to stay alert. The cloud system he shared with Mack appeared, stored on a server from the underground, and Fillion swiped in the password. The nub of his joint hung loosely in his mouth as he grinned. Encryption keys, software tools, and cheat files greeted him like old friends, tokens of his prior life and his future.

"Touch the word 'pathetic' for me. I need to do something."

Leaf slowly touched the pool of light in the air, releasing a breath when the screen changed. Fillion used the opportunity to flick the ashes and pull out another joint, lighting up from the previous one, and then tapped on the quick connect to Mack's line. The outgoing signal was music to his ears and he laughed. Physically laughed out loud. Oh god. He really was losing his mind.

"Who's th— Whoa, *bishounen*. You look like, uh, like someone died or something." His friend's forehead wrinkled. Or was it a pillow crease? "But you were laughing." Mack's eyes widened and he sat perfectly still. "Have you cracked? Is that even you? Or is this an alien using Fillion's body as a host?"

Fillion pressed his lips together in a droll expression. "The black eyes are bletcherous, man."

"Ha! Ha! LOL." Mack scratched his head with his middle finger.

"Don't use that kind of archaic text-speak with me," Fillion said with a slight half-smile. "Poser."

"OK. It's you."

"Why haven't you received a med treatment?"

"Battle wounds to attract the female species," Mack said, then bit down on his tongue and grinned. Fillion chuckled to appease his friend. "So, in all seriousness, you look like shit. Are you in trouble?"

"Hanley."

"Wait, is this line secure? I'm assuming your other Cranium is fried."

"Shit. So damn tired. I forgot." Fillion let out a heavy sigh. "I was hacked. We both need new keys."

"Hackers are such pests. We should rid the world of this plague before it totally ravages the wild fields of Cyberspace." His friend's lips twitched as he suppressed a grin. "I got our backs. Again. As usual. Have I mentioned yet that you owe me big time?"

Still gritching under his breath, Mack's eyes grew distant as he stared at a new screen layer, and his finger danced through the air. His friend's speech slurred on occasion. But Mack was definitely on the downhill back to sober. A command prompt appeared as a layer on Fillion's end. He minimized the screen and watched the key download. After a few minutes it refreshed to a new user interface, greeting his handle.

"Did you kill someone for this Cranium? You look like you could've committed your first murder and are all twitchy about it."

"It was a gift from a ghost."

"Tell me it was a hot-medieval-Martian-cyberpunk chick, the kind that haunts you for all the right reasons. Not *Laughing Man.*"

Even though he wasn't in the mood, Fillion played along. "Fat, ugly, hairy beast of a man. Totally your type."

"Damn Internet." His friend's face broke into smile. "All right, hit me."

Fillion spilled everything. The full conversation with Hanley, the Death and Curse cards, even his supposed engagement to Akiko. All the stuff he wanted to tell his friend before leaving for New Eden, but couldn't for fear of being overheard. All the goings-on of New Eden, including Leaf's coming out of the closet. The airlock, and the note.

It felt good to unload. The pressure inside him released. The line was secure and New Eden was housed inside a giant Faraday cage, so he didn't worry about being vocally tapped by the media.

As expected, Mack wrote out his questions and lifted up the notebook, and Fillion answered. A frown remained in place as his friend listened, an out-of-place look on Mack. The bruises around Mack's eyes added to the grim expression, their shadows deepening as eyebrows, usually raised in humor, pinched together in distress. This dark look rarely visited Mack and made his friend look much older than his eighteen years.

"Damn. No wonder you look like shit," his friend said when the purge reached completion. "Stupid question, but are you OK? Like, going to make it, OK?"

"No and yes."

"Fair enough." Mack tapped his bottom lip in thought. "Did you watch the links yet?"

"The trip wire cut me off before I could. Load them up?"

A vid box materialized in the lower right-hand corner and Mack started up the first link. The waning nausea attacked full force as Fillion watched his mom's wild reaction. Not once had she ever expressed such intense emotions about anything. She had always loved Joel? Hanley's response to that confession confused him. It was like he actually loved his mom. Was it real or for show? He chanced a look at Mack, who studied him closely, the frown reappearing. Fillion cringed with the sound of his sister's voice, especially when she blabbed his secret to Coal. Was nothing sacred? He let out a nervous breath.

Without missing a beat, Mack launched the next link when the first one ended. Hanley, Coal, and Della filled the screen. So, this was the Son of Fire. Willow refused him? Twice? No time for jealousy. Plus, he hated triangles. Always had. Pyramids, food charts, traffic cones, Bermuda, team flags, the Illuminati, love… He preferred simple lines, of the vertical and horizontal variety. Squares and rectangles didn't represent unsolved mysteries or domination, nor the complexity of human emotion. Once again, his mind was rambling. It was irritating. Fillion placed the joint in his mouth and distracted his multifarious emotions by memorizing Hanley's every nuance in the interview.

"Oh my god," he said in a breath when Joel's money was mentioned. The look in Hanley's eyes only confirmed his worst fears.

Thoughts circled in a carousel, up and down, round and round, faces and images fading in and out as the mechanics of Fillion's mind whirred in perpetual motion. The world was fading. The familiar lies began to seduce his vulnerability. The truth was harder to hold on to now that he knew, without question, that he really was the son of a killer. Voices from his past mocked him, their jeers and taunts like daggers, murdering him en masse all over again. And he felt himself slipping away, hypnotized by the rush of spinning out of control.

An image of Willow flashed in his mind, not the Willow he knew, but the Willow of his delusions. "Save me," she said, her voice helpless, weak, begging and accusing all at the same time. Dirt and grime smudged her tattered dress and skin, her hair hanging in dingy strings. Sunken eyes implored him, blue lips set in a grim line. "I can't," he replied, on the verge of tears. "If I try, he'll hurt you." Did he say that out loud? He didn't know. Reality was soupy. "Please," she beseeched him once more as she disappeared into the void.

The Willow he knew suddenly appeared and his heart pulsed in recognition. Sunlight kissed her skin and blended into her long hair. She leaned on an elbow as they lay next to each other, hidden by tall grasses in a field, the sky framing her in a blue aura. He blinked lazily, overcome by her image. A smile, bright and playful, teased him as she leaned forward. Her hair brushed across his face in sweet, seductive caresses, and he sighed. The kind of sigh that filled him up as the breath left his body. Her emerald eyes reflected equal longing as she whispered, "I need you, Son of Eden." Before he could reply, her lips—warm, soft, and tasting of wine—fell onto his, and she kissed him with the same desire burning inside of him.

He couldn't breathe. Her presence was so beautiful it suffocated him. He gasped for air, his system drowning in equal parts surrender and fear. Panic overloaded his body until it went into shock. They needed to stop kissing. They needed to disconnect. They could *never* be together. The joint dropped from his hand onto the ground, and he pressed his palms into his eyes. "Please," she asked again. A tear pressed through and crawled down his cheek and he whispered back, "I couldn't live with myself if he harmed you because of me. Everything he touches dies. Everything."

"Fillion, look at me."

At first, he thought Willow spoke to him, so he removed his hands. But when the words repeated the vision dissipated and Mack's holographic image wavered in the air above his face.

"Come back to me." Mack's voice held uncharacteristic softness. "Fight it."

Fillion's sense of reality pulled into focus and he locked eyes with his friend.

"Hey."

"Hey," Fillion said, feeling heat creep up his neck and face. Another tear fell. "I'm the son of a killer, Mack. Oh god. They were right. All of them."

"Maybe. Doesn't change who *you* are. And you're still stuck with my pathetic ass, too."

The look of compassion on his friend's face nearly did him in. A soft grip warmed his forearm and Fillion closed his eyes. Leaf didn't judge him either, and echoed Mack's sentiments without making his presence known. He couldn't even begin to imagine the heartache Leaf was processing at this moment. But, god, Fillion felt like such a freak.

Mack frowned again. "This the first time or have they been happening regularly since entering New Eden?"

"The last video triggered it." He wiped the cold sweat from his forehead with tremulous fingers, not even registering the pain in his knuckles. "First time in nearly three years."

"Glad you were hacked then. Man, if you watched that alone…"

"I know." His voice quivered with weakness, his breath still shallow and fast.

Tension pulled at the lines of Mack's mouth as his friend's dark blue eyes held Fillion's feeble gaze. "You love her, don't you?"

"Mack…" Fillion swallowed, afraid to answer. "What would you do if a girl you thought was dead suddenly came back from the grave?"

"Is she cute or creepy looking?" His friend smiled with mild amusement.

Fillion whispered, "Beautiful."

"I'd kiss her before she got away." Mack grinned now. "Like a boss. God, this is the weirdest love story I've ever heard. Leave it to you."

Leaf quietly laughed by his side, not loud enough to be picked up on Mack's end, and Fillion bit the inside of his cheek. Stringing two thoughts together was becoming increasingly difficult after the high-octane emotions and devastating information this night. But he firmly clung to the newly understood belief that perhaps he did possess a love worth giving away. Not that it mattered. Hanley's reminder echoed in his head.

"I'll put her in danger. Hanley made it very clear."

"Fillion," Mack sighed, his face drooping with a dry expression. "You're way more intelligent than that. Seriously. Give me a sec."

Mack wrote out: *Her life has always been in danger. Nature of the beast, mate. Hanley played you and you believed him. Whatever he plans to do to her or her siblings, he's planned to do all along.*

His friend tossed the notebook aside. "Your gothic romance is in the way."

"Gothic romance?" Fillion cracked a small smile.

"Come on, pretty boy. Being poetic. Don't kill my vibe." Mack slapped his hands across his thighs, as if everything was settled, and leaned forward. "Continuing from the previous episode: After I kissed her like a boss, leaving her breathless and satisfied, moaning my name…" Mack winked with exaggeration. "…I'd avenge her death. So, let's get down to business. What's the plan, *bishounen*?"

This love wounds my heart
with a sweet taste, so gently,
I die of grief a hundred times a day
and a hundred times revive with joy.
My pain seems beautiful,
this pain is worth more than any pleasure;
and since I find this bad so good,
how good will be the good when this suffering is done.

— Bernart de Ventadorn, troubadour, 12th century A.D. *

CHAPTER TWENTY-FOUR

Monday, October 19, 2054

O aklee journeyed toward where the village matriarchs gathered in The Orchard to inquire about her duties during reaping. Today was the first of many in Harvest. Soon, field after field of wheat, rye, barley, and alfalfa would replenish the depleted grain barns. Just beyond the meadow, men were hard at work with scythes, slashing through the golden stalks of wheat, which infused the main dome with a sweet, earthy fragrance. Oaklee ambled past The Forge along the way and observed Connor sharpen tools with a whet stone, his sullen, focused gaze lifting long enough to dip in acknowledgment.

This was a difficult day for her family. It was the first Harvest in New Eden history where her father did not preside as the Earth Element, but instead joined in the celebration from the ground. And Coal was not present to show off in the fields, eliciting the excited chatter of the unattached females, especially when his tunic clung to his sweaty figure. The last two thoughts were enough to make her groan, and she could not resist the private chuckle that emerged despite her despondency.

Lost to her memories, Oaklee touched an apple tree to gather her runaway mind and to greet the Old Biddies that watched over the gardens. She peered through the gnarled branches to the scene shortly ahead. It was the same image she had always known; and yet the anomalous reality further detached her from what should be a joyous occasion, promising the bliss of community bonds and blushes of courting rituals.

Woven bassinets hung in the lower branches of several apple and pear trees, dotting The Orchard with the fruit of soft, pink babies, nestled snug and tight in their swaddling blankets. The matriarchs placed knotted fingers upon the baskets and, with gentle pushes, rocked the sleeping babies to old lullabies. Those awake were given leaves to reach for and fondle, or acorn sacks to kick, which rewarded eager legs with rattles and tiny feet with small lumps to feel and explore.

Younger women held small bundles with doting eyes and dreamy faces, quietly conferring upon blankets stretched on the ground; while others played with the toddlers, chasing them in merry games or hiding behind aprons for peek-a-boo.

This was the way every Harvest. Older women passed on various wisdoms of womanhood to the maidens or newly married women, as the mothers trailed behind the men, bundling the grain or performing other Harvest tasks. The young ladies socialized and vied for the attentions of the laboring young men, who displayed their virility through hours of endurance. And if not from the men, the young women sought the honor of receiving the personal attentions of a matriarch.

As Oaklee neared the gathering, many whispered and turned curious eyes her direction. She pretended not to notice and ambled toward the head matriarch for work direction. Three young women she passed, sitting upon a woolen blanket, pressed dainty hands to their mouths to stifle unkind giggles, looking her direction before drawing heads close to whisper once more. Their long hair shifted in the breeze and boasted decorative braids and herbal flower chaplets, the babies in their arms stirring only slightly with their activity. The village girls were a little younger than Oaklee, although not by much, and they expressed the immaturity of those wishing to seek attention from the young men in the fields. Although Oaklee knew this game and understood the competition, she chose not to reply or acknowledge their girlish notions.

"Come, Your Highness," Verna encouraged, and the head matriarch's kind brown eyes silently relayed compassion. The elderly woman dipped her head in honor. Oaklee repaid the honor with a curtsy, lowering to the grass at Verna's feet. "Do not pay them heed. A man desires a confident woman, not a jealous girl. They shall learn soon enough and trade pettiness for more becoming behavior."

"I am not offended, Madam," Oaklee said, fidgeting with the pleats of her dress. "My family is the source of much controversy. I am used to the stares, whispers, and otherwise rude behavior."

"You poor dear," Verna said, placing a comforting hand upon Oaklee's cheek. "You are a strong woman. Your name suits you well." The elderly woman brushed a thumb across her cheek and then returned to the knitting in her lap. "All of the wee ones are cared for at present. I do have an idea for an occupation, though." Verna turned to a small village girl. "Susan, please fetch Lady Rain at my request."

"Yes, Madam." The little girl darted through the trees toward the gardens, bare feet turning up leaves as braids bounced with each stride.

"You do not wear flowers in your hair this day, Your Highness," Verna said with a sly smile. "Have you perhaps captured the heart of a young man? Or do you honor Connor's lad?"

Oaklee lowered her eyes and folded her hands properly in her lap. "I simply do not wish to advertise an interest in courting at present. My heart is otherwise engaged in separate matters of a personal nature."

"Well said," the woman replied with a warm smile. "Your mother and father would be most proud of the young lady who sits at my feet." A tear slipped through all attempts of restraint and slid down Oaklee's cheek. "There, there," Verna soothed, caressing her cheek once more. "Have you seen this pattern yet?" Wrinkled hands lifted up a partially knitted shawl for Oaklee to inspect.

"No, Madam. It is quite lovely." Oaklee smiled wanly and fingered the fine stitches. "Shall you teach me?"

"It would be an honor, Your Highness."

A companionable silence settled between them. The click of bone needles and the murmurs of feminine voices and of babies wrapped around Oaklee, and the walls of her home seemed to move in. How could one be in the company of others and still feel so isolated?

Not wishing to give in any longer to the melancholy that gripped her, Oaklee swept a thoughtful glance toward the fields. Her brother's form was easy to identify as he wove in and out of workers, listening, instructing, and assessing. She absently blinked with resignation and searched for the amber curls of her sister-in-law. Oaklee could not locate Ember's elegant bearing amongst the gathering, concluding that the Daughter of Fire was still caring for the goats. Laurel played with the village children close by in a copse of birch trees edging the forest, her sister's melodious voice and laughter a balm to Oaklee's soul. With a wistful sigh, she dropped her eyes and fiddled with the folds and tucks of her dress as it rippled around her legs.

Oaklee heard the faint footsteps before she noted Rain's approach. The Daughter of Water curtsied before Verna and then faced Oaklee. "Your Highness," she greeted softly. Oaklee internally cringed with the new courtesy title she was bestowed by the community, even her close friends, but remained emotionless.

"The wee ones have caregivers at present," Verna said. She casually brushed her long gray braid over her shoulder and lifted her brown eyes to Rain. "Do you have a position upon your staff available, My Lady? Perhaps to offer water to the men and women?"

"Yes, Madam. I would be most grateful for the assistance."

"Wonderful. Willow Oak, you are employed," Verna said with a smile and quiet chuckle. "Enjoy this day safe in the company of your friend."

"Thank you, Madam," Oaklee said as she rose and curtsied once more. She turned to Rain and offered her arm. "Shall we, My Lady?"

Rain slipped her arm into Oaklee's with a conspiratorial smile. "Indeed."

They ambulated through the blankets, baskets, and women, exchanging greetings with those who presented themselves in a friendly manner, and ignoring those bent on jealous musings or dissension. Once out of earshot, they turned toward each other and giggled with relief.

"Oh, how I have missed you," Rain said, leaning a head on Oaklee's shoulder for a few steps. "You are ever a good friend to me."

"You are easy to love," Oaklee replied, patting Rain's arm. "It is selfishness on my part. Should I have to work hard to earn your affection, well..." She smiled and Rain laughed.

"Happy for me then, solitary creature that you are."

"It is joy shared."

"To think, I have you all to myself. Coal was always stitched to your side, more so this last year." Rain sighed, the sound long and reflective. "I wonder if he is the source of trouble in a new community."

Oaklee replied, "And if there are matriarchs to charm and convince he is nothing but angelic?"

"Oh, but he is," Rain said with a sly smile.

"To be sure." Oaklee watched her brother pick up a scythe and join the rhythm in the field. "I fear Coal's thirst for adventure and his impetuous antics shall only lead him into trouble of an unwanted variety."

"Is the trouble ever intentional?" Rain giggled. "You must miss him."

"Yes, very much."

"There are no flowers in your hair."

Oaklee stopped and turned toward her friend. "Are there rumors?"

"There are always rumors, are there not? But no, fret not. 'Tis my own curiosity." Rain angled her head and searched Oaklee's eyes. "May I have your permission to show interest upon his return?"

"You do not need my permission, silly toad." Oaklee giggled.

A faint smile touched Rain's lips. "There is another who owns your heart, I believe. One whose eyes must surely reflect the skies on a cloudy day." The smile grew. "He is a handsome man. I would not suffer much under his kisses."

"Rain Daniels!" Oaklee squealed in astonishment, raising hands to her cheeks. "Such things you say."

"Do not be pretentious." Rain batted the air as if what she said was not the slightest bit improper. "To kiss an Outsider…"

"If you swoon, I shall leave you on the meadow floor to fend for yourself," Oaklee admonished playfully.

"Please ensure my dress is pooled around me in a dramatic fashion so I maintain propriety while dreaming of clandestine meetings and forbidden kisses." Rain slid Oaklee a side-glance.

Oaklee groaned, "Oh dear Lord," but finished with a mischievous look of her own.

Rain's humor faded and she drew her dark brows together. "Harvest does not seem the same."

"No, nor shall it ever be. Nothing is as it once was and I fear change shall only continue to torment us."

"Thank you for being my friend."

The abrupt change in topic worried Oaklee and she stopped and faced her friend once more. "You are easy to love, Rain." She gathered her friend into an embrace and whispered, "With time he shall discover this truth and make all your immodest dreams come true."

Rain looked out over the fields and did not laugh as Oaklee hoped. "No man in New Eden shall want me once they know the truth of my birth."

"Whatever do you mean?" Oaklee pulled away and locked eyes with her friend. "I thought you wished to show Coal your interest?"

"Never mind. Just the silly things I say. Shall we?" Rain gestured toward the pump well.

Buckets and ladles crowded the well as a young woman pumped and another filled, taking in empty buckets and lining up those recently filled. Two young women, hair adorned in flowers and styled fashionably, fetched buckets and moved toward the fields.

The young village woman who filled buckets glared at Oaklee, hesitantly meeting Rain's eyes. "Why is she here?"

"Laynie, her Highness shall join us in the fields and you shall remain civil." Rain's tone brooked no argument and Laynie simply nodded, handing Oaklee two buckets before retrieving another empty vessel. "I shall be behind you shortly," Rain said with an apologetic smile.

Oaklee smiled in reply, feeling her cheeks warm, and turned toward the golden field, the only one in the main biodome. Her father once explained that it was a conditioning field as the Mediterranean dome was hot, dry, and more demanding on the body. This week, the men and women would practice in the cooler air until a routine was established and their bodies were prepared for the more difficult task of reaping field after field.

She searched the landscape in a broad sweep for the other water bearers. By their glow, cheeks and lips prettily blushed rose, and the swing of their hips, Oaklee figured the two young women stayed close to the outskirts where The Orchard met the meadow, and where the young men congregated to demonstrate their strength in the front fields adjacent to The Rows. So Oaklee followed the small foot trail around the field, over the small stone bridge across the stream, to the back acre.

The buckets were heavy and the hemp rope rubbed against her palms, but her arms managed after carrying bags of heavy wool and bundles of prepared flax linen over the past fortnight. The water sloshed on the uneven trail, wetting her toes and squishing in her shoes. She wrinkled her nose in irritation, but continued on her mission.

The soprano voices of the women workers, who bundled the felled wheat, grew louder as Oaklee approached. Their songs provided rhythm and much needed entertainment as the men toiled away.

Leaf stood up from a hunched position near the edge of the field and stretched his back. Upon seeing her, he smiled and then wiped the sweat from his face with a hemp rag he kept tucked into his belt. The fabric, gifted by Ember before Mass, was beautifully embroidered with leaves, and Oaklee's heart smiled at the sentimental gesture.

This morning was the first since her mother died that she had not gifted her brother or father a Harvest token to carry into the fields. Although she normally rolled her eyes at such romantic gestures, she felt empty this day, useless, and all tied to a silly piece of cloth, one she spun and wove herself.

"Do you bring water?" Leaf asked, breathless.

"Yes, Your Majesty," she answered, ever aware of the many ears listening to their family. She ladled water from the bucket and Leaf drank greedily. Then he took the ladle from her hand and poured water over his head.

"There are others nearby in need of water," he said, pointing his head in the direction of the workers. "I fear the other maidens prefer the front field and do not visit often."

"I shall care for your workers, Your Majesty. Lady Rain shall assist me."

"Thank you, Willow."

"Oaklee."

Leaf chuckled and shook his head, bending over to return to work. Oaklee smiled to herself and moved in the direction Leaf suggested, offering water first to several women. Grain coated their aprons and hair, and their cheeks flushed from the exertion. Next, she visited three men who stood in a row, slashing back and forth at the grain to the beat of the women's cheerful songs.

She continued down the line of reapers, walking around mounds of tied bundles, and hesitated near the midpoint of the field. Fillion's unexpected presence startled her, believing he assisted Connor in The Forge this day. Oaklee's mouth parted as she reveled in his appearance, eyes as light as day, glistening charcoal hair with hints of mahogany mussed and fashioned by the wind, his tunic ruffling in the crisp autumn air and clinging to his body. He made a beautiful and cutting figure in the undulating gold and, for the first time, she felt weak simply by gazing at him. A bio-breeze perfumed the air in a sweet, earthy scent, and she blinked as a dizzying rush of foreign emotions threatened to overwhelm and lay siege to her good senses.

She recovered, and directed attention to her occupation, grounding her fluttering thoughts upon something more practical.

"You're staring at me." He cracked a one-sided smile.

"Water, My Lord?"

He nodded, his breath coming in fast and deep, chest heaving from the work.

"God, I think I'm dying."

"Shall I fetch Brother Markus to issue your last rites?"

Sweat dripped down his face and he blinked it away in irritation, his lips forming a subtle smile. Oaklee lifted the ladle to his mouth and he took the handle and tipped it up, sighing upon completion.

"May I offer you another?"

"Thanks," he said simply, still out of breath. After finishing another dip, he wiped his face with the sleeve of his tunic.

"Do you not carry a rag?"

"A what?"

"You shall stain your sleeve." She regretted her words the instant they left her mouth, remembering he did not have a woman—mother, sister, or admirer—to supply a token for him to carry as he toiled for Harvest.

"That's OK. I've had three girls offer to do my laundry today." The smile begged for her to reply.

"Is that so?" She raised an eyebrow. "I wish you much luck while navigating the politics of such offers."

"No offer from you?" The smile widened into something devilish, before he settled into the familiar unimpressed expression, one that was more coy and flirtatious than anything else. Oaklee stared at him, confused on how to respond.

"I bring you water and you reply with requests for me to do your laundry?" Oaklee turned her head and lifted her chin. "For shame."

"I'm just teasing you."

He took a step closer until they almost touched and her head swam in a delicious headiness. It was a most irritating predicament, one she had never known before. Everything within her was ready to run and she blurted, "Please, do not trouble yourself, My Lord." Oaklee reached for the buckets at her feet. He touched her arm and she paused, looking away.

"Willow?"

"Yes?"

He whispered, "Look at me."

She gradually looked his way, and her thoughts faded into an intensity of gray that captured her completely. Those otherworldly eyes never missed a beat, always assessing, always discerning, equally as eager to smile at her antics, and, on occasion, allowed glimpses of the man behind the pain and derision. But at this moment, they worshiped her, the adoration evident as he held her gaze.

Her body slackened as her resolve melted, a dreamy rush turning her into a puddle at his feet. But terror gripped her once more within a blink, a breath, a flutter of a heartbeat, silencing the confessions her heart pounded to proclaim in return.

"Willow—"

"I must return to work, My Lord."

"Yeah. Sure. OK, see you around." He responded with a near indiscernible shrug and a small dip of his head. "Thanks for the water." In a few steps, Fillion returned to his place in the field. He slashed at the golden stalks with renewed abandon, his face lined with tension.

Uncertainty seized her. She desired to respond to his silent questions and honor him. Yet, by doing so, she would publicly display her affection for all to know. Oaklee was not ashamed of Fillion. Quite the opposite. But she did not wish to share the pain of his leaving with the community. They were privy to the makings of her grief quite enough.

The internal battle continued until she bent over and lifted the hem of her skirt to grip the worn linen of her work chemise. Last year she had added a ruffle to extend the length after growing taller, and could remove the damaged excess and replace it later. She grunted as she tore off a long piece, dismayed that is was a poor offering compared to others the men sported in their belts. It would have to do.

Fillion noted her approach and lowered the scythe as he raised an eyebrow in a look of vulnerability. Lilting, harmonious voices nearby wrapped around her, each trill encouraging her heart forward. With a tremulous sigh, Oaklee tucked the remnant of her chemise into Fillion's belt as lyrics of love and loss infused the atmosphere they both breathed in and exhaled.

Her fingers, trembling yet bold, trailed along the linen. Tongues would wag after this, especially as she refused a flower chaplet to garnish her appearance this day. There was no going back now. Her fingers slid off the yarn she spun and wove, and she timidly folded her hands at her waist.

Though she quavered, she chanted the ritualistic words with surety, "May you reap a harvest for the cellars as well as for the heart, My Lord."

His mouth parted as various emotions flitted across his face. She curtsied, despite her unsteady legs. When she rose, Oaklee stood on tip-toes and kissed his cheek. He smelled of earth, wood smoke, cedar, and sweat, and she closed her eyes, breathing him in once more. Before losing confidence, she whispered against his skin, "You honor me, Fillion," and he drew in a quiet breath. It was a sound that echoed the sentiments of her heart as well.

Then Oaklee pivoted on her feet and marched away with her buckets, clenching the hemp ropes in her hands until they burned.

Biosphere 2 was an important and eye-opening project because it revealed to us not only the difficulty of managing a closed ecosystem and the fragility of human psychology, it also showed us how challenging it will be for us to manage Biosphere 1—the Earth's biosphere—should things really start to get out of whack.

Consequently, Biosphere 2 should not be considered a failure, but rather a wake-up call to scientists, environmentalists, politicians and the general public. Cynicism should be replaced with the understanding that it was an idea ahead of its time—but an important idea nonetheless.

— George Dvorsky, "Why We Should Reboot the Biosphere Projects," *io9 / Gawker*, August 29, 2012 *

ChAPTER
TWENTY-FIVE

Wednesday, October 21, 2054

Unable to sleep, Fillion got up early and studied archived videos of "Eco-Crafting Eden." Another day in New Eden promised more physical pain and discomfort in the fields. His body was already protesting at the thought. But this moment, he wanted to forget his swollen knuckles and blisters and hunt for clues. Anything.

"Eco-Crafting Eden" looked a lot like New Eden, in fact. As more of the same content streamed by from the show, his mind yawned and glossed over. Village life wasn't a novelty anymore for Fillion. Not that it ever was. Rustic costumes, melodramatic gestures, chickens pecking near the kitchen in search of scraps. Boring. Head-banging-on-wall boring. On the screen, someone walked by leading a goat on a leash, and Fillion resisted the urge to roll his eyes. The whole damn thing was staged for the Net. The show aimed to convince viewers that the players saw this natural, agrarian life as real. But there was always an agenda.

The political slant of the show grated against each and every nerve Fillion possessed. It had nothing to do with how they emulated a life before the age of machines. Fillion had actually come to respect that lifestyle, and he acknowledged the beauty in it. Rather, it was the pretentious preaching that accompanied the post-apocalyptic player messages that bothered Fillion. Earth is good. Humans are bad. Well, all humans except them, the ones who were called of Earth, the chosen ones who "got it." Unlike the selfish, destructive version of humanity that scourged the land with their idiocy. Green Morons. They were nothing more than pawns for the corporations that delighted in their elitist, good-doer mentality.

What better way to take down competition than through public opinion? The organic industry was no exception, and boasted just enough truth to cover up all the lies. Shame-filled consumers stuffed their carts with organic foods and products. Products that were packaged on automated, carbon-spouting machines. Then checked out on a machine. Only to be driven home on a machine. To be kept cooled or frozen via a machine. Yep. Organic. So natural. And none of it was cheap. People were financially desperate and hungry. It made him so fucking mad.

A leaf-shaped corporate logo spun on the screen, spitting out streams of simulated sunshine. Sponsors interrupted every fifteen minutes of recorded game play with typical Green Movement advertising. Buy organic. Support local commerce and reduce the carbon footprint. Say no to big pharma and their conspiracy to drug the world or "they'll own your paychecks as well as your bodies." That last message finally earned an eye roll. The same people who spouted such verbal evangelical tracts in order to sell and promote their naturopathic products also never hesitated to rush to the hospital to continue breathing one more day. Nature be damned at the moment of cardiac arrest. Whatever.

Antsy, Fillion readjusted his position against the wall, pulling the covers up a little higher as game play resumed on the holographic screen. Random players were culled and interviewed. Most remained in character, pretending they were being surveyed by their ruling government for ideas, opinions, and general comments—be it King, Pharaoh, Archon, Emperor, or President. The King of Terraloch, he learned, was none other than Connor Hansen. Interesting. Hanley was the Royal Adviser, the official position of all Kingdom Gamemasters. And there were five Kingdoms: Ancient Greece, Egypt, China, the Middle Ages, and Colonial America.

The object of the game was simple. Reach the twenty-year mark—in game time—with the largest and most prosperous civilization and claim victory. The winning kingdom would rule all others in the LARP's next game phase, boasting the New World Order crown. Except, it never came. It ended with Terraloch's win, followed by Dylan's accident on the mountain, Joel ending his engagement with Della, and a couple years later, the birth of New Eden Township.

He paused the video and squinted. What was that? Fillion swiped to rewind and replayed the scene again. A twenty-something Hanley, dressed in medieval finery befitting a royal, spoke with eloquence to the camera. Peasants and nobles milled beyond. Fillion defocused on Hanley, and studied the background. There it was. He paused the video again. Pulling on opposite corners, he enlarged the image and studied the face.

Just behind Hanley, a younger Timothy lurked in the crowd. His face pointed toward a merchant table. Timothy's features were relaxed in an unnatural expression of bland ease. All others were caught in a candid pose, mouths open, arms mid-air in a gesture, eyes fixed on something specific. Not Timothy. He was known in Terraloch as The Messenger. Always on a mission. Never resting. Breezing through crowds. It was often said in Terraloch that rumors were "heard on the wind."

It wasn't the face that caught Fillion's eye, though. At thigh level, Timothy flashed a game card to the camera. It had been quick, a blink. Fillion backtracked frame-by-frame until a clearer view emerged. He enlarged the image once more and exhaled loudly. The raven was unmistakable as were the six letters that spelled out "cursed." How many players had and used this card? For all Fillion knew, all of nobility used Curse Cards.

Curious, he rewound the video once more. This time to study Hanley. The scene started up again. Timothy walked behind Hanley, who glanced over so casually that it appeared he was distracted by a merchant. But when Timothy flashed the card, Hanley dipped his head, as if to look at his hands, lifting his face to the interviewer within seconds. The movements were graceful, fluid, almost flawless. But Fillion knew Hanley. When the Royal Adviser stared into the camera once more, he did so with a charming smile.

The Curse Card is for me. I spin the tales and I weave the stories together. It's a warning.

Hanley's words cycled through Fillion's mind. A warning of a threat? Like, the destruction of the spinning wheel signified the end of Hanley's reign as the one who spins the yarns of New Eden Township? Or a warning that a certain plan or players are in position? Like a tip-off? He thought of the faction that nearly cost Terraloch the game. Instead, Terraloch rallied its nobility and fought for the win. Even though, for several episodes, nobility and peasants resisted ideas of change and stubbornly clung to the original ideas.

In order to live, something must die.

Did Hanley capitalize on the simmering unrest to kill the original plan through a faction? Desperation drove the masses to listen to Hanley as he breathed life into a new plan. He gained control at that moment and moved the player characters on the chess board at will. Fillion thought of Ember's comment, that nobility were pawns on a chess board awaiting his move. Spooky.

How was Hanley involved in New Eden's unrest? The forming faction? And was Timothy his henchman? Or Connor? The good cop, bad cop routine was getting old. Until Fillion had concrete information of the Death Card's purpose in New Eden, he couldn't fully buy Connor's story or Hanley's denial of its existence within the walls. And, as far as the Curse Card was concerned, only one item had been redeemed. A thing. The spinning wheel. Two action points remained for the card user to act upon. And why play the card on Willow? It made no sense.

Annoyed and bored, he closed out the videos and opened a new browser. Swiping his mom's first, middle, and maiden name, he skimmed through articles. Most of it had to do with "Eco-Crafting Eden," where she played a Lady of the Court. Joel played a poor villager, a farmer's son, who engaged in a forbidden relationship with Della. As with all forbidden relationships, it was discovered and started a small faction, where peasants held back food distribution to the main houses and to the royal court and went on strike when Joel was punished publicly for his love. That was the catalyst for the larger faction.

Ready to give up, a headline caught his eye and he paused. "Theory of Reconstructing Universal Society and Trusteeship," he muttered to the morning air. He touched the link and opened up an article about an award his mom won for her research on anthropological theories behind generation ships and space colonies—more specifically, how to psychologically overcome ICE symptoms. Role-playing was at the heart of her theories. No surprise there. "The T.R.U.S.T. patent and copyright," he spoke out loud to himself. Fillion drew his brows together and continued reading, impressed that his mom was business savvy enough to demand ownership of her ideas. The Code echoed sentiments from this research, as did the societal reconstruction of the township.

Fillion shelved the article and then turned the Cranium off and closed his eyes. He tried to ponder the hidden. Bits and pieces floated around aimlessly, though. If only he could return to sleep and allow his mind to defragment.

The secrets Ember had shared with him rested in the storage cloud of his brain, too.

A dozen from the second generation had been secretly groomed as computer technicians and engineers as part of a simulation, initiated seven years ago. It was the same time The Elements had gone radio silent through Messenger Pigeon. According to Ember, the Techsmith Guild's mission added an element of "magic" to the LARP with real-world application. If they were a colony on Mars, technicians would be needed. Naturally.

As this was a socio-psychological experiment, Ember explained, their participation served an additional purpose. New Eden Biospherics & Research tested to see if the technicians could have modern knowledge, communicating regularly with Earth, and still participate in an off-grid lifestyle like their counterparts, without suffering from psychological breakdown. When Project Phase Two began, their training would be considered complete and a new mission would begin: educating New Eden Township about Outsider technology. As they saw it, world history has shown that people learn best from their own.

So, why the hell did Hanley keep the Guild's presence a secret? Fillion wanted to scream. To pull his hair out. The walls closed in more and more every day. The ceiling seemed to drop lower. Still, he refused to cave in to his mind's delusions. The confinement wouldn't break him. But Hanley's cycle of set-up-to-fail strategies just might.

And what did Joel's monetary legacy have to do with any of this?

That lingering question brought a dull ache behind Fillion's eyes. He pinched them shut even tighter. God, he couldn't think anymore. Any decision he made was an opportunity for Hanley. If Fillion failed, he would become the goat that was set on fire and sent to the hills. If he succeeded, Hanley would continue to imprison him to be used again, and again, and again. Bringing glory to the great Gamemaster. Reversing Hanley's Midas touch and turning each golden death into golden fame.

Why was the Curse Card given to Willow?

That question rose to the surface once again. Fillion's mind touched it, as if a holographic screen, moving pieces to a front layer, enlarging bits here, diminishing others there.

Does Willow have blond hair and green eyes?

It was clear, from the beginning, that a power struggle existed between the Watsons and whoever originally held the The Aether position. Claire was a stranger. Joel's rebound relationship post-Della. Was Willow targeted because she resembles Claire?

The puzzle pieces slowly came together. Fillion bit the inside of his cheek and concentrated, rethinking the details. Hanley spins the tales and weaves them together. Claire was part of this story, woven into the fabric of the Nichols Legacy. A Techsmith Guild springs up a year after Claire dies, grooming the second gen to eventually educate their own to transition and integrate to the Outside world. Within this group, an individual plausibly hacks the government and issues falsified death certificates. Hanley couldn't have created or allowed a more perfect cover for a hacker within the dome. N.E.T. would have noticed the additional Wi-Fi activity besides the Scroll users. But create a Guild of tech users? Brilliant.

Before New Eden, there was "Eco-Crafting Eden." Beneath the obvious, it appeared as though Hanley billowed the faction that directly placed control into his hands, using Joel and Della's forbidden love as the catalyst. But he didn't do it alone. The Messenger made that clear. A couple decades later, a man dies with a fortune bequeathed to New Eden Township as a result of no living heirs.

Was someone from "Eco-Crafting Eden" collecting on a favor owed? Did Hanley negotiate one last favor in return? And was it the King of Terraloch, or The Messenger, or perhaps another? Someone completely off the map?

Fillion was convinced Hanley had struck a deal with someone inside the dome. If "they" killed Joel and removed the heirs, then Hanley would grant "them" something. Maybe even Aether status. Perhaps reinstate their Aether status. Or, someone was playing to Hanley's narcissistic ego to earn back Aether status. Hanley loved it when people worshiped him, too.

Except, why falsify documents instead of actually killing the Watson children? The last thoughts swirled around inside Fillion's head. He studied it at different angles until a better image surfaced. If Joel had lost his wife and children, he may have drawn up new beneficiaries. By not actually killing the Watson children, Joel couldn't react and, therefore, change his financial legacy. God, Hanley was sick. Is this why it was too risky to personally ask Joel or Jeff about it? It disgusted Fillion and he felt the familiar rage swell inside of him.

Why the hell did New Eden Township need Joel's money anyway? It's not like Hanley had a lack. Or any of his companies. Most of the world was indebted to Hanley for their economic successes. New Eden Enterprises owned and managed each and every desalination plant and irrigation system, leased by a multitude of countries. The innovative, cost-effective engineering of DesertSEA reversed the carbon footprint and ensured Third World nations could thrive. The deserts of humanity flourished.

The irony wasn't lost on Fillion. The First World nations, once oceans of wealth, were dying off, becoming the next great desert of humanity. The law of a closed-loop system echoed in business. Even in the rise and fall of nations.

Something wasn't right with the detail of Joel's money. It picked at Fillion's brain. Soon, his head would pound from the sores. "Stop," he said out loud to himself. The sound of his own voice startled him in the silence, and he opened his eyes. He would catalog this information and analyze it later. It was time to join Leaf in the fields.

Every muscle ached as he pushed himself off the bed. Fillion walked over to his window and pushed open a pane, allowing the cold air to shock him into a different mental rant. He scanned the woods and nearby apartments. But it was something much closer, a white object on the windowsill, that caught his eye. It was a neatly folded cloth.

Perplexed, he picked up the fabric and held it up to the sliver of sunrise peeking through the forest. A large tree was embroidered on the front of the cloth in small, even stitches. He opened the folds and a note fell to the floor. The paper was coarse and the ink was unusual. It was black but with a red cast to it. He almost expected to see a wax seal. Instead, he unfolded the note without resistance and read:

To My Lord, Fillion Nichols,

For eight years, I have gifted my father this rag to carry into the Harvest season as my token of devotion. Although we have two per annum, the Autumn Harvest is the most important and, thus, rich with ceremony and tradition. I bestowed upon you a torn remnant of my chemise as part of these ceremonies; however, a piece of my garment is a meager offering for a great man such as yourself. In replacement, please accept my father's Harvest token for this season, and for the one you shall endure when you depart New Eden Township. Although it is merely cloth, fibers of plants and nothing more, it carries my family crest, a seal that represents my heart, and holds within its weaves memories held dear to me. You pay me a great honor, Fillion, and I shall never forget you. May this cloth sustain your memories of me as you continue to toil and labor for my birth home and for my family.

With affection,
Yours Truly,
Willow Oak Watson

His thumb caressed the oak tree. Fillion read the note a second time, and then again. He knew Willow didn't part with such an item easily, and it humbled him.

He knelt on the floor, and pulled his great-grandpa's chest out from under the bed and opened the lid. Carefully, he placed Willow's note inside, beside the dried linden leaf. Then he retrieved the piece of her chemise and tucked it away as well. "I'm such a sap," he muttered under his breath. God, he was still talking to himself. What the hell was happening to him? This time, Fillion rolled his eyes at himself. A couple of weeks ago, he would have gagged with these sappy thoughts.

With a humored shake of his head, he rose and dressed. The rag hung from his belt and lightly tapped against his hip with each step. Before leaving, he lit a joint and blew out his lantern. It was past the breakfast hour already and time to go. Fillion shut his front door and pulled the wool cloak tighter around his body. Still, he shivered. He would never take indoor heating for granted again.

The joint loosely hung in his mouth as he surveyed the village. Images of "Eco-Crafting Eden" simmered in the forefront of his thoughts, comparing and contrasting buildings and landscape. Then, his body was in motion, potential energy converting to kinetic with each step.

The smoke left his mouth and blended into the dusky shades of dawn. He exhaled another thin stream. Curling, shape-shifting fingers writhed in the air, reaching for the geodesic horizon as if clawing the pseudo-sky. Fillion furrowed his brows at the image. He dragged on the herbal joint once more, and focused on the dirt path moving beneath his feet.

Families left in large groups from the Great Hall and journeyed toward The Orchard. Most gave him wide berth. Some bowed their heads as he passed. He was the Son of Eden. A man of magic. An Outsider. The object of political desire and disdain. It wasn't a new position for him. But this? He kept walking, head down.

Fillion approached the golden fields and looked for Willow. The air still smelled pleasantly sweet. He puffed one last time on the joint and then snuffed it out with his shoe. Skirting the edge of the wheat field, he followed a worn path next to a thin layer of trees. Leaf's unmistakable voice carried over the murmuring stalks, and Fillion paused.

"Pardon my confusion," Leaf said. "I do believe my ears failed to hear correctly. You refuse to work?"

"Yes. We shall not support a King who will disband New Eden Township."

It was an alpaca worker. Fillion had seen the man in the Mediterranean dome. The growing light cloaked Leaf's face from where Fillion stood. But he could imagine the shock and confusion. After a few more steps, Leaf's rigid form and stunned features became clear.

The young noble narrowed his eyes. "I do not write law, nor did I originate The Code which demands such action, nor did I force you to sign the document prior to Moving Day."

"Why were our children not required to sign The Code? It seems far too strange and begs many concerns."

"I am not sure, sir. You do ask a fine question." Leaf said. "May I present your inquiry to Hanley Nichols for reply?"

"And believe the man who set a double standard in the community?"

Fillion moved to Leaf's side. The Son of Earth dipped his head in greeting while placing his hands on hips. "I am sure there is a simple and logical explanation."

The man moved forward. "What if the second generation is shipped off to Mars? They are not bound to a Code that requires they disband from the community. And they are the only humans on Earth born and raised in captivity."

"Nobody is going to Mars," Fillion said. All eyes turned his direction. "This is an experiment, not a mission. Refusing to work doesn't change The Code either."

"We do not intend to change The Code. We wish for new leadership."

"I see." Leaf drew his eyebrows together. "Who do you wish to appoint in my stead?"

The man crossed his arms over his chest. "Skylar Kane."

Leaf nodded his head thoughtfully. "He is a good man. I can see why. However, he is incapable of rewriting The Code, same as I. New Eden is just as likely to disband under his leadership as mine."

"Not what we heard," the man retorted. "We heard it on the wind that Skylar has favor with Hanley Nichols."

"Heard it on the wind?" Fillion felt his stomach drop. Peasants going on a work strike? Holding back food distribution? The coincidence was too eerie. "Trust me, nobody has favor with Hanley Nichols. Nobody. Hanley is too in love with himself to give a damn about anyone else."

"Why should we believe a son who would turn on his own father?" The man looked behind him with smug appreciation at the crowd of men who whispered to one another.

Fillion relaxed his posture and stared at the man as if he, and all the others, just lost their minds. "You just declared you didn't trust Hanley, but you'll support his so-called favorite? You don't want to change The Code, but you want the second generation forced to disband? But you don't want to disband? Are you listening to yourself?" Fillion lifted an eyebrow. "It's clear you were put up to this stupidity by someone else. You can't even stand firm in your convictions."

The crowd burst into debates between each other. The man never had a chance to reply. The alpaca worker's skin reddened and his mouth opened in a slack-jawed expression of distress. As the noise elevated, Fillion watched as men, women, and children poured in from the fields and The Orchard. Willow, Laurel, Rain, and Ember soon appeared around the bend, worry creasing lines around their eyes.

"New Eden!" Leaf boomed. "Hear me." The gathering grew quiet. "Allow me to assure you that I am doing everything within my power to ensure all families are happy, safe, and remain unified. Fillion and I are presently investigating the legal mysteries surrounding the newer generations. I do care about your fears, but we must not bow to rumors. Fears shall divide our home. We did not work so hard, nor sacrifice so much, only to be divided now."

"We demand answers!" someone shouted from the crowd, receiving a wave of cheers.

"Yes," Leaf said. "I demand answers as well."

"We refuse to work until Hanley tells us why the second generation is not bound by The Code!" More cheers followed.

Leaf's face fell. A few, long seconds passed and the Son of Earth lifted his eyes back to the community. Lines crinkled around Leaf's eyes, the tension spreading. "It saddens me to say this," he began. "But you leave me little choice." The community grew deathly silent. "Let it be known that if you choose not to work, then you are choosing to not eat as well."

"Tyrant!" a voice screamed.

"You believe asking your neighbors to work on your behalf honorable?" Willow spat back at the crowd. She clenched her fists at her side and glowered.

Before she could say more, Connor jogged through the crowd and toward Leaf. In a hushed voice, the former Fire Element asked what was happening. Leaf quickly replied and Connor's eyebrows shot up. Slowly, in disbelief, Connor faced the crowd. Fillion watched as the muscles in Connor's neck bulged and twitched. Fillion knew the former King of Terraloch was making his own comparisons to a former role-playing life, and he watched the blacksmith carefully.

"I support our King," he bellowed. Some in the crowd broke into cheers, while others booed. "The Aether has demonstrated wisdom."

"Look my children in the eyes and tell them how you refuse to feed them, *Your Majesty*," the alpaca farmer said. Leaf flinched and lowered his head. "Then explain to them how a leader who does not feed children cares about their future."

"*You* look in your child's eyes and tell them yourself!" Fillion shot back. He was ready to explode, angry that Leaf was paying for a war that was never his. "And don't forget the part about how *you* incited a strike over rumors. You accuse a man without facts."

"Tyrant!" The villager shot the same insult at Fillion, and then shouted it again over the rumbling crowd at Leaf. "Skylar Kane as Aether!" A low chant echoed the words until the small pocket of individuals quieted all others into shock.

"Where is Skylar?" Fillion asked Leaf. "Or Timothy?"

Leaf whispered, "I am not sure." He scanned the gathering, eventually looking at Ember. With a deep breath, Leaf faced his accusers. "New Eden," he shouted, the anger rippling in his tone. "I do not punish children for the choices of their parents. I said if *you* choose not to work, then *you* choose not to eat. Never once was there mention of your family."

"Tyrant!" the rebuttal came once more.

"If you do not like this decision nor trust me to dialogue with Hanley to gather answers, then you are welcome to leave our colony and confront Hanley yourself." Leaf schooled his features, even though his eyes traveled from face to face with growing panic. "Any person may leave, at any time, and for any reason. Disband now. Or stay, and wait to discover the fate of New Eden Township. The choice is yours."

"That is not a choice, *Your Majesty*," the man said. "That is a threat."

"Harold Moore, I shall not tolerate dissension. We are men grown. Shall we adjourn to Jeff's chancery to continue in civil conversation?"

"There is nothing to discuss. I refuse to follow a tyrant for a King." Harold took a woman's hand. "My family officially leaves New Eden Township this day."

"Are you shitting me?" Fillion blurted. He was pretty sure his face mirrored the disbelief reflected in others' faces. "You don't want the community to disband, but you're leaving? What the hell?"

"My family leaves as well!" another voice called out. A man led his wife and children away from the crowd.

"Plea—" Leaf attempted. But Connor placed a hand on Leaf's shoulder and shook his head. In a whisper, Leaf said, "What have I done?"

"You delivered a tough but necessary message and possibly prevented a full-scale strike." Connor squeezed Leaf's shoulder and dropped his hand. "Harold made a choice. His mind was poisoned by fear."

"No, by someone," Fillion muttered under his breath.

"Do you think he demonstrates symptoms of insanity?" Leaf asked.

"Dr. Nichols shall determine such a diagnosis," Connor replied. "We should not speculate and further tarnish Harold and his family, nor Frederick's family."

"Yes, you are right, My Lord," Leaf said, hanging his head. He cast a side-glance to the gathering who watched in terrified silence as the men and their families departed. "Father, why did you leave me?" Leaf twisted away from the community and covered his face in his hands. His shoulders rose and he inhaled sharply. "I know not what to do," he whispered through his fingers.

"Son, there is time later to process. Now, the community needs you to remain strong," Connor whispered. "You once told Timothy that the community will respect a leader who is willing to forsake tradition and bend for their benefit if the situation requires such flexibility. Give them opportunity to respect you."

"I spoke with haste, impassioned by a cause. I no longer believe I am capable of such a feat. Perhaps Timothy was right, and I should step down from leadership and grieve my father."

Fillion grabbed Leaf's forearm and pulled him close, and whispered, "Hell no. Trust me. I found something today. I'll show you later. It involves Timothy." Leaf pulled away and maintained a downcast posture, a frown darkening his face. After a few seconds, he nodded.

"Give them hope and direction," Connor whispered. "Be strong." In two large steps, the former Element positioned himself behind Leaf.

Fillion took the cue and stepped into the background as well. The Son of Earth dropped his hands and squinted his eyes. Hundreds of faces stared at Leaf in anticipation.

"Family," Leaf said, straightening his posture and looking over the fields and meadow. "Who among us still refuses to work?" People looked around them, but no one volunteered such convictions. Leaf stretched out his hands, palms up. "Would all of you please show me your hands."

Uncertain, the residents complied. Fillion raised his hands to show his support for Leaf, but he felt like a dork. He hated interactive motivational speeches.

"With these hands," Leaf continued and Fillion looked up, "we have built a community that works together, celebrates together, and mourns together. Let us not use these same hands to tear down what we have labored so long to create."

Murmurs of agreement swelled until the sound turned to cheers. Hands, once stretched out, clapped their approval.

"One last comment, if you would be so kind," Leaf hollered over the cheers. Quiet descended on the dome once more. "We shall not speak ill of our neighbors. Nor shall we disparage the Moore and Carson households. Instead, we shall mourn their absence in our community. Tonight, I ask that you please light a candle and say a prayer for their families and bless them. May they find the peace and the answers they seek."

Heads bowed with respect and they lifted hands and placed them over their hearts. Fillion couldn't understand how people would choose to honor someone like Harold. The man was a tool.

Love has little to do with romance and everything to do with honor.

The Herbalist's words rung through his mind and pricked his heart. Villagers and nobility both demonstrated a choice that baffled Fillion. By choosing to honor the families who left, the community acknowledged their value—a worth that transcended their crimes against Leaf or anyone else.

"A new day rises," Leaf said. "Let us return to our shared purposes, and continue to employ our hands toward sustaining our home and each other."

The residents dispersed, somber. Some wiped away tears and quietly wept. Leaf slouched and dropped his chin to his chest, lost to his thoughts. Then he slowly spun on his heel and marched toward the fields. The Son of Earth didn't acknowledge his wife or his family, Connor, or even Fillion. A few thumped Leaf on the back as he passed by, but Leaf kept moving. The noble's body grew more rigid with each stride.

Fillion stood by a small line of trees, studying faces. Mannerisms. Analyzing Leaf's words and request, as well as the community's response. It bent Fillion's mind and forced him to recalibrate, yet again, what he previously considered truth. Was this why Willow chose to honor him, despite his selfish, vulgar actions at times? Most times? He declared it was part of his charm, but was it? She acknowledged the inertia of his choices and, with a slight push, enabled the journey toward honoring himself.

Before walking away, he risked a look Willow's direction. Everyone from their circle had already departed, leaving them alone. She watched him through lowered eyes, as most girls from New Eden did to exhibit modesty. It was demure and not flirtatious. A strand of hair wove around her finger with fidgety movements. He had no words. His mind was full, busy reconciling conflicting thoughts and emotions, information and fears.

They continued to stare at each other. The world rotated at high speed, the centrifugal force of motion creating a pocket of stillness where they stood. His fingers gripped the edges of his cloak and pulled away the wool. Her eyes followed his movements, and she blinked prettily when recognizing her father's token.

The world blurred and faded away. Fillion took a few steps forward as Willow sauntered to where he stood. Each step they made was timid, bashful. Her fingers grazed the cloth hanging from his belt as her emerald eyes shyly sought his eyes.

She whispered, "You honor me."

"No," he whispered in reply. "You honor me."

Willow attempted to smile. But it fell as she sagged against him. His arms shot out in surprise and he staggered back. Shoulders, small and round, quivered as she pressed her face into his chest.

"I am so frightened," she whispered into his tunic as her hands clutched the fabric. "I wish to feel safe. My community alters, and their grievance connects to my family once more."

Warmth surged through him with her words until his mind buzzed, as if high. She wished to feel safe through him? Fillion wrapped his arms around her and rested his head on top of her braids. Was he really holding her? Comforting her? He had dreamed of this moment for so long. This was real. She believed he held answers, wanted him to save her, even if it was just from her own apprehension.

She readjusted her head. "Why did they leave? And hate my brother so?"

They were alone and protected by a small crop of trees along the fringe of the fields. Still, Fillion scanned for any passersby.

"I think they were bribed into it," he whispered in reply.

She pulled away and looked up at him. "By whom?"

"Not sure. I have a strong lead, though. I'll tell you once I have all the facts." He cupped Willow's face with one hand and caressed her soft, pale skin with his thumb. "I promise." His fingertips tingled as they rested along the contours of her jaw. Her mouth parted slightly in response and when she spoke, it became breathless.

"Why create such hateful dissension?" She stepped closer and leaned her cheek against his chest once again. Fillion closed his eyes. "I am scared, My Lord. For my home. For my brother."

"Someone wants to bring new order through chaos. It's an old trick, but it works."

In truth, he was worried for Leaf, too. Two items remained on the Curse Card. Assault on Leaf's life wasn't beyond the realm of possibilities. It could make his death on paper a reality. The escalating emotions and accusations only confirmed Fillion's trail of thoughts. Was New Eden perhaps the "place" the card user had in mind? Or smaller, like the Watson home? Hanley wouldn't want to destroy New Eden. It had to be a smaller location, a place to strike fear with minimal damage.

Warm breath pulsed through the thin linen of his tunic. She was still leaning into him. God, she was so soft. "I'll do everything I can," Fillion murmured into her hair. "It's my top priority."

Willow lifted her face toward his. "Thank you, My Lord. For *everything*."

A bright and fervent energy whipped around them. Her face was so close, her body melting into his. Fillion's heart pounded with violence as the energy consumed him. Acceptance was still a humbling experience, rendering him speechless. And he stared, as usual, like an idiot.

She shifted her focus to his mouth for a nanosecond before turning away. They were entangled in a strong awareness of one another with equal pull to remain separated. Maybe it was self-protection. Maybe it was acceptance of a bitter truth. Or maybe the feelings were just too damn overwhelming.

Conflict warred in her eyes as she stepped back and created distance. Unattached men and women were not allowed physical familiarity. He felt honored, once more, by her display of trust. Nearby, sounds of field workers and children created music on the wind—New Eden's theme song of survival and innocence. She was innocent, unmarred by the world. Untouched. Unmolested. That knowledge always freaked him out. Especially because he was tainted, used, prostituted by the Net communities. And no stranger to girls.

Still, she made him feel like everything was a first time. Each touch. Every lingering glance. Perhaps the lack of intimacy, and emphasis on self-control, intensified everything. Or, perhaps it was because she was the only girl who knew him. The real Fillion Nichols.

Willow smiled bashfully at him. He offered a shy smile in reply then stared at the ground, lifting his shoulders. A sweet fragrance wafted on the breeze. The rich air stirred the golden fields as well as her golden hair, which cascaded down her back, unpinned from her crown of braids. Unable to resist, he reached out to caress the wispy, fly-away strands, fluttering across her neck, just as a girl called Willow's name from around the bend. Willow jumped back with wide eyes. In twitchy movements, she smoothed the folds of her dress, glancing over her shoulder.

"There you are—oh, pardon me." Rain stopped and angled away, her cheeks turning pink.

Fillion tucked his thumbs into his belt and looked at the toe of his shoe as he made circles in the exposed dirt.

"No, 'tis all right," Willow said. "I was on my way to seek you." False cheer colored her tone and smile, and Rain flit a curious look toward Fillion. With a shaky sigh, Willow gracefully curtsied his direction. "Until later, My Lord."

"Yeah. See you around."

She cast him one last smile and then jogged off toward Rain, slipping her arm through her friend's.

Fillion watched them walk away, releasing his breath when they disappeared. For the second time this week, Willow had made a physical move. How the hell would he concentrate on anything today? He rubbed the edge of Willow's gift, not ready to let go of the moment. But he walked into the wheat fields, silently taking a spot beside Leaf.

What is a cynic? A man who knows the price of everything and the value of nothing.

— Oscar Wilde, Irish poet and writer, 19th century A.D. *

ChAPTER TWENTY-SIX

Mercer Island, Washington state

Rosa hummed a tune as she mopped the entry tiles. Coal stepped around the android maid on his way to the kitchen, flashing a friendly smile. "Careful. The floor is slippery when wet," Rosa said in her smooth, computer-like voice. The comment comforted the fear-driven thinking of Outsiders; but to Coal, it was common sense.

"Thank you for the kind reminder."

Coal jerked the hair out of his eye and continued on his mission to gather a light repast. Hanley lifted the restrictions on Coal's home arrest cuff long enough to permit a jog on a nearby forested trail, and only because it was for the private use of residents of this housing community. Media was strictly prohibited on the premises. Although, according to Hanley, the media could still listen in through nanotech devices and take long-distance photographs. Still, they could not directly interact with Coal.

Mack had tired of watching Coal's "fidgety pacing" and introduced him to the idea of nonsensical running. The very notion of running for no reason other than to physically labor humored Coal. Nevertheless, he was pleased with the activity and the momentary freedom.

The only catch: Hanley required Ignis to tag along to ensure a security camera trailed Coal's movements. The transparent man jogged beside Coal and even appeared to breathe hard when they halted before a stop sign. Coal shook his head.

The cuff rubbed and irritated the skin of his ankle, even more so after a run. So he tried to think of other things. But all he could ponder was his weekend at Mack's apartment. They never went to the underground Sunday night as originally planned. Mack had ascertained that the project manager of the hacking circle was away on undisclosed business. Monday morning, he returned with Mack and Lynden to the Nichols' residence, and the home arrest cuff was placed upon Coal's ankle once more. Hanley and Dr. Nichols arrived a couple hours later none the wiser. Soon after, Mack left for work, mumbling something about a required meeting with his father.

Coal's stomach grumbled as he neared the kitchen. After refreshments, he thought he would tinker in the garage with the welding tools. Before leaving N.E.T., an engineer provided lessons with the modern blacksmithing equipment. He wished for a creative outlet, a purpose, something besides sitting around and browsing the Net or attending meetings or media interviews. It was such a wasteful, unproductive use of time, in his opinion.

Yesterday, he accompanied Hanley to New Eden Enterprises. The large, strangely tiered, glass structure—like a ziggurat—jutted out over Puget Sound, and Coal entered with anxiety that it might topple into the salt water. Before entry, however, he paused before the building and admired the bronzed windows, reflecting small, scintillating beams from the morning sun breaks. The sky, dressed in silver and lead, framed the building and kissed the dark emerald depths of the water.

Various shades of green vining plants draped over each roof line and trailed the metallic glass, akin to drawings he had seen of the Hanging Gardens of Babylon. Flowers in jeweled hues spilled out of large earthen containers, standing sentry on either side of the main entry.

The main door in itself was an incredible piece of artistry, and he could not help but inspect the craftsmanship. Wrought iron trees arched over the ash-tinted glass doors, the branches forming the words "New Eden Ent.," similar to the gate of New Eden Township. A dark, shadowed image of a tree, matching the one etched into The Door, spanned the glass entrance, dotted with a small number of dark, red fruit.

Coal sighed. The architecture inspired him, and he longed to mold metal to his creative whim.

Instead, board meetings had consumed his day and stifled any artistic thoughts he may have previously possessed. Coal was placed at a head position, opposite of Hanley, in a drab room that overlooked the water and Olympic Mountains. Board members, top management, and a select handful of sponsors attended, all present stunned to see his current state. Each one expressed their disappointment in greeting a young man who no longer appeared medieval.

Coal apologized, as instructed beforehand, and explained that experiencing his generation's culture was an integration test as part of his colony's preparation for the Second Phase. In reply, he received skeptical stares and nods, and a smattering of kind smiles.

After a full day of meetings, he settled in Hanley's office to participate in three different interviews with the media. Coal disliked those the most. Nothing within him desired to entertain the masses of nameless, faceless people who dwelled on the Net.

The distraction appeared to work, though. The Net buzzed with activity over Coal's "visit to Earth," breezing over news of Joel's death and monetary legacy, as well as Norah's recent passing.

A few *otaku* sites dedicated to his fandom popped up. Lynden explained each site was like an altar, erected for followers to worship him. Apparently, being on the Net with such fame granted him demi-god status. Random photos taken from interviews plastered the pages, topped off with comments that made him blush. Lynden giggled over some of the confessions, rolled her eyes at others. He tried to leave the room, but she grabbed the chains dangling from his pants and yanked him back onto the sofa. "Toughen up, Mr. Awesome."

His wandering mind came back to task as he entered the kitchen in search of a snack. Slumping down in her chair, Lynden released a loud, deflated sigh as she faced her tutor.

"Did you accomplish your assignment?" the tutor asked. Lynden slithered farther down a chair at the dining room table, her head tilted up as she stared at the ceiling with arms crossed tight across her chest. Rob, a middle-aged man with the patience of a saint and a ready smile, sat adjacent to her and displayed a holographic book, *Stranger in a Strange Land*.

Lynden groaned. "Nope."

"And why, Ms. Nichols?"

"It's boring. The book was written a hundred years ago. Who cares?"

"Ninety-three years ago, actually. But I thought you would enjoy the relevance it has today."

"Yeah, your first mistake."

"Ms. Nich—," Rob started, and then noticed Coal. "Good afternoon, Coal."

"Good afternoon," Coal said. "My apologies for the disruption. I will only be but a moment."

"No worries." Rob smiled and returned his attention to Lynden.

Coal opened the refrigerator and grabbed two apples. He tossed one to Lynden, who sprung to life and caught the red fruit with a look resembling a plea for help. "Honeycrisp, my favorite," he teased. She glared when he passed by her with a charming smile.

"Any spells?"

He paused in the door frame. "No, for you have already cursed yourself by not honoring your education." Lynden arched an eyebrow with a droll expression. "Look at Rob, the poor man."

"He gets paid to forget his suffering. Whose side are you on, anyway?"

"There is some suffering that compensation cannot erase." Coal's mouth tipped in a humorous grin. "Oh, wait. I do recall this particular apple is enchanted to help the consumer accomplish even the most daunting of tasks, such as reading a book written up to one hundred years ago. One bite and you should be able to apply your mind—and ease Rob's suffering."

"Traitor." Lynden shifted her position on the chair to appear as if she was dismissing him. "See if I ever save your ass again."

Coal bit into his apple. "Toughen up, Rainbow," he said as he walked away. He could almost hear her silent fuming and knew she would punish him later, but it would be worth it. The grin stretching across his face disappeared, however, when Hanley emerged from the sitting room and gestured for Coal to follow.

"How was your run?"

"The jaunt was nice. Thank you, sir."

"Come with me. We need to speak privately."

Hanley's face remained impassive as he moved toward the kitchen and through the dining room. Before they entered the hallway, Coal threw Lynden a mock-expression of a plea, and she rolled her eyes and turned away, her lips curling up with satisfaction. He smiled to himself as he hopped down the stairs and into Hanley's office.

Once inside, Hanley shut the door and walked to a large bookcase. A biometric scanner, positioned on the wall near a light sensor, read his thumbprint and the bookcase slid across the floor. The air Coal held in his lungs released all at once and he nearly choked on the bits of apple in his mouth.

"Step inside."

The room was breathtaking. Never had Coal seen walls made from copper, and he touched the fine, lace-like material with reverence. The seams came together as small filigree, adding to the elegance. Whoever smithed this room possessed remarkable talent.

Four black leather chairs were situated in the space according to the Four Winds with a small, low table in the center. A silver triangle, stitched onto the back of the chair he faced, gleamed in the low lighting. Alarmed, Coal studied each chair to confirm his inkling: one up, one down, one up with a slash through the top point, and one pointed down with a slash. He looked to the table and, sure enough, a six sided star within a circle resided in the center, inlaid with darker wood.

"Go ahead. Find *your* seat." Hanley met Coal's eyes briefly before turning his attention to a buffet, which boasted a large assortment of earth-toned bottles. "Wish for a drink? Wine perhaps?"

"No thank you, sir."

Coal paused before the chair stitched with a triangle, its tip up, located in the compass point for South. His hand brushed over the soft leather as he eased into the plush seat and waited for Hanley with growing nerves. The Aristotelian elemental symbol for The Aether glared from the high-gloss table, dulled only when he shifted nervously and his reflection cast the image in shadow. Hanley chose a chair situated East, the cardinal direction associated with the Wind Element. He lifted a glass of wine in salute and enjoyed a small sip.

"Do you have any news of New Eden?"

"Pardon?" Coal scrunched up his face in confusion. "How could I?"

"Mack share anything, perhaps?" Coal licked his dry lips and blinked, but maintained an even gaze. Hanley leaned back into his chair and sipped on the wine again. "No matter." He smiled, a friendly look that disarmed Coal. "Have you heard from your sister?"

"No, sir. I am unclear how I would." Hanley's smile grew wider and apprehension swelled within Coal's chest. To ease his trepidation, Coal bit into his apple and casually looked around the room.

"What can you tell me of Harold Moore?"

Coal swallowed the apple painfully. "This is a most random inquiry." Then his eyes rounded. "Did he pass away?"

"No, no, nothing so drastic."

Hanley waited with patience, nary a blink disrupting his serene countenance. With a start, Coal realized Hanley was awaiting a reply to his question. "Harold Moore is an upstanding man. He works in animal husbandry, specializing in the alpacas herded inside the Mediterranean dome. His wife, Dee, works with my sister as a milk maid. They have two young lads."

"Is he given to tempers or violence?"

Coal furrowed his brows. "No, absolutely not." He wished to ask Hanley why such questions, but the unruffled, casual expression on Hanley's face silenced Coal.

"And Frederick Carson?"

"I am sorry, sir, but I must demand an explanation." Coal stood and fidgeted with the apple in his hand.

"Yes, of course." Hanley gestured for Coal to take his seat again, and sipped on the wine. With careful movements, he placed the goblet onto the table. "The Moore and Carson families left New Eden Township today with claims that they refuse to remain inside with Leaf Watson as King."

"Dear Lord in Heaven," Coal breathed. He crossed himself and lowered his head, his thoughts transforming into urgent prayers. Never had his heart raced as it did now, pumping wildly over the implications and declarations of unrest. Not a single resident had ever left, nor threatened to leave. It was unheard of. "Is Leaf safe? His family? Has any harm come to them?"

Hanley studied Coal. "As far as I know they are fine."

"My family."

"All accounts say they are well."

"And your son?"

"Fillion is fine."

Coal's thoughts suddenly caught up to him and his eyes widened. "How did the Moores and Carsons know Leaf was The Aether?"

"Leaf revealed his position before the entire community the day Norah died."

"No," Coal said with disbelief. The cold fire of fear quickly heated to a white-hot rage and he stood once more, and promptly began to pace behind his chair.

"Apparently, Harold and Frederick both are demanding to see me as they were ensured I would grant them entrance back into New Eden once I named Skylar Kane as Leaf's replacement." Hanley chuckled and shook his head. "Well," he said, and pushed himself up to a stand and waltzed over the buffet. "I am leaving this afternoon for N.E.T. and will not return for an indiscernible amount of time. Della will accompany me. As you know, Leaf is no longer alive and so such comments are clearly signs of delusion. My wife and her team will perform a full-scale psychological evaluation, but I am fairly confident I already know the results."

"Dr. Nichols does not know that the Watson siblings live?" The heat chilled once more and a cold sweat broke out on Coal's forehead.

"You witnessed her response when she learned of Joel's death. Do you understand what this kind of news would do to her fragile state?" Hanley finished the wine in his glass goblet and leveled his eyes at Coal.

"Will she not discover the truth during the Second Phase?"

"I am on the verge of a media crisis, and New Eden Township dangerously courts failure." Coal opened his mouth, but Hanley cut him off. "Please do not test me in this or give me lessons in honor. Who do you think supplied you the world responsible for such lessons?"

"Yes, sir," Coal ground out. "I understand."

"Perfect." Hanley walked to the opening and pushed a button and slipped out into the filtered light of his office. The older man stared reflectively at the apple in Coal's hand as a smug smile formed on his face. "Life would be nothing without both sweet and sour moments. To savor both flavors with satisfaction is not only the objective of the game, it is also the thrill."

Coal bit into his apple with defiance and Hanley laughed affably, as if they had talked of pleasant things. At this moment, Coal believed he truly was capable of breathing fire. There was so much he wished to say, but he remained silent.

Hanley winked at Coal and breezed out of his office. "You'll travel to N.E.T. in a week or so. I'll call you and give you the details once I have them," Hanley said over his shoulder, then climbed the stairs whilst whistling a merry tune.

Time stilled as Coal waited for Hanley to disappear. Then, it sped with vengeance as he leapt up the stairs, rushed past Lynden and her tutor, out the French doors, and across the lawn to the waterfront. He took his shoes off and chucked them toward the house, allowing his feet to sink into the cool, graveled sand of the small beach. Tears burned and blurred his vision, and he quickly wiped them away.

The half-eaten apple turned in his hand, and Coal watched the gold-red colors shift to shades of ivory as his fingers spun the fruit around and around. To deny Leaf, Willow, and Laurel the right to live was not akin to savoring the sweet and sour moments of life. Nor was turning healthy confessions from good, respectable individuals into babbles of delusion and then punishing them for it. Nor allowing one's wife to tarnish her reputation by incorrectly diagnosing entire families as sick when they were whole.

The water's surface glittered with a soothing rhythm. Coal bit into his apple once more. He chewed thoughtfully as sweet and sour danced with delight upon his tongue. The energy billowing in him needed an outlet, and so he swiveled toward the house and marched to the garage, retrieving his shoes along the way.

Within minutes, Coal had suited up properly. An electric forge sat in the corner, and he programmed the desired temperature. Ideas swirled in his head as he looked at the small copper ingots. His mind drew images of what he could create, the designs flowing to his hands and pouring into each finger. Safety glasses tinted the surroundings yellow, a befitting film through which to see the world as Golden Boy, he internally quipped. Satisfied, he went to work melting iron to pound into forms for the copper he would use. The familiarity washed over him and, for an afternoon, Coal forgot the pain of reality as he thought only of his family, of Leaf and Oaklee, and of his childhood home.

Sometime later, he turned off the hand-held torch and pulled the visor from his head. Questions and enigmas still burned inside of him, and his mind flirted with confusion. The sun had set, and Coal pivoted toward the thin stream of light from the corner lamp in the garage.

Why had his mother and father entered New Eden Township?

Why did they choose to raise a family secluded from the world, and separated further by an entirely different civilization?

Originally, he had considered his father responsible for the forming faction. But he knew his father would never wrest power from Leaf, especially now that Ember was The Aether's wife. Not only that, it truly was not in his father's nature to begin with, a notion he finally could acknowledge with a clearer head.

Coal removed his gloves and pulled the Cranium from his pocket. He placed it upon his ear and, within a few swipes, pulled up the image of his mother. He stared into her bright blue eyes as if answers might be hidden somewhere in their still-framed depths.

"Hey, Mr. Awesome. Fangirl?"

A shadow lined the doorway, and he startled upon spotting Lynden.

"Hey." Coal lifted his finger to turn off his Cranium.

"Let me see her." Lynden approached and leaned her head against his. "She's pretty, in an old-fashioned way."

"This is my mother, Camilla Leigh Hiddleston Hansen."

Lynden lifted her head and studied his face and the image. "I would've never guessed." She flipped the strand of hair falling over his eye and then leaned on him once more. "Mama's boy?"

"I never met her, actually. She died right after Ember was born. It was a miracle I survived."

"I'm sorry. Wow."

Coal turned off his Cranium and nudged Lynden off with a lopsided grin. He wiped his forehead with the hem of his shirt. "Is dinner ready?"

"God, you're always hungry." She rolled her eyes. "Selah is determined to introduce you to sushi tonight, even though it's just us."

"I will be there shortly. Thank you."

Lynden walked over to the workbench and inspected the scattered bits of his project. "Dad and mom left an hour ago."

"I am sorry to have missed them."

"Yeah, I guess your good social skills have a limit. Does the guilt burn yet?"

"Fiercely."

"Poor Coal."

He whispered, "Indeed." The ache of holding in lies hit him once more. He sucked in his bottom lip a few seconds and then attempted a polite smile.

"So, this is blacksmithing?"

"In a way."

"I always pictured burly shirtless men wielding large hammers. Overcompensating for other deficiencies, of course." Coal burst into laughter and slid her a sly side-glance. She maintained a bored expression. "I guess you'll do."

His smile widened and her face relaxed as she eyed him curiously, twisting the ring on her thumb. The guise of irritation returned just as quickly as it disappeared. With a flip of her hair, she spun toward the door with cat-like movements, graceful but with marked attitude. The chains on her black skirt and demi-pants clinked with each step. He watched until she faded through the doorway and then focused his attention on tidying up.

A few minutes later, he walked into the dining room. Selah, the hired cook for the Nichols family—and a human helper no less—rolled up a woven mat with slow precision. Black, glossy hair dangled over her face, and her caramel skin richened under the ambient lighting she preferred when cooking. The tantalizing aroma of unknown, foreign spices and herbs lulled Coal's senses into a state of bliss.

"Are we to eat reeds for dinner?" Coal waltzed into the kitchen and gestured toward the mat as he nabbed an orange slice from a platter, promptly tossing it into his mouth.

Selah looked up with an amused expression and returned attention to her fingers. "If you steal another piece from the platter, I'll whip you with my towel."

"How pleasant," Coal managed while chewing. With a playful look, he grabbed another orange slice as Selah snapped her hand towel his direction. He dodged and then planted a kiss on her cheek as he sneaked another slice, popping it in his mouth with a charming smile for show. Selah smiled and humorously shook her head.

Coal's eyes roamed the kitchen and dining room. Nerves tingled in each limb, and he almost wished he had time for another jog. His stomach, however, had different plans, grumbling with impatience. "And what are we feasting on this night? Lyn mentioned sushi?"

"Tonight, you will enjoy a traditional meal from Japan, which is both nourishment for your body and for your soul. Sushi is a work of art." Her dark brown eyes met his as she applied light pressure to the mat. "Ramen noodles in a savory algae broth is first course."

"Algae broth?" Coal issued a skeptical look. Selah smiled. It was a subtle look of mirth, both friendly and mysterious. Another ache released a flurry of anxiety as he thought of Ember, which led to worries over Leaf, which conjured images of Oaklee, and his heart could manage no more.

Lynden walked into the kitchen that moment and arched an eyebrow at Coal, the dull, unimpressed look almost humorous. She slumped into a seat at the dining table and fingered long white sticks, the tips resting atop a narrow, slightly curved piece of pottery. Then, she gathered her hair in a bunch and whipped it into a ball, colors popping haphazardly, and pierced the white sticks through at angles to hold the hair in place. The look was strangely beautiful, and Coal eyed Lynden with appreciation when the ever-defiant chunk of blood-red hair fell across her eye and curled at the tip.

Selah retrieved another pair of sticks from a drawer and carried them in her palms as she delivered the platter of sushi to the table.

Lynden accepted the sticks with a tight head nod and said, "*Arigatou gozaimasu.*"

"*Dou itashimashite,*" Selah replied. Then, she brought over two steaming bowls of soup, the broth a bright, lively green hue. The cook flicked Coal a quick, mischievous look, and walked away. He remained still, back straight as Selah returned with a separate platter, displaying various fruits and raw vegetables.

"Do you have *sake?*" Lynden asked.

"With your parents away—"

"Whatever. It's not illegal to drink in your own home. Dad placed it on the menu, right?"

"Yes, Ms. Nichols." Selah delivered two small cups and poured a chilled, clear liquid half-way as Lynden gripped the demitasse cup with one hand, supporting the base of the cup with the other. Coal watched and held his cup the same way as Selah served him. "*Sake*," she said. "Rice wine."

"Thank you," Coal said.

Lynden downed the liquid as if mere water. Curious, he brought the cup to his lips and sipped. Sweetness tingled on his tongue and warmed his mouth, and Coal nodded in appreciation, never tasting chilled wine before, much less wine fermented from rice.

Selah poured Lynden another cup, placed the flask on the table, and said to Coal, "Per tradition, you will pour for Ms. Nichols in my absence." With a bow, she walked out of the dining area toward the sitting room. After serving meals, she retreated to allow the family to sup in privacy, returning afterward to clean. Although, Coal had ascertained that full family meals were a rare event. Instead, Selah took pride in serving Fillion, Lynden and, more often than not, Mack.

The intimacy of a shared meal between just he and Lynden intensified the anxiety and nerves Coal experienced after his meeting with Hanley. Meals were always a communal affair in New Eden.

An understanding had passed between him and Lynden since Saturday night, and he enjoyed the camaraderie of her friendship. She still clung to him in familiar ways, but never for intimate reasons. Rather, he gathered she was a physically affectionate person by nature. To him it was almost childlike, as grown women did not cling to men in such ways in his experience. Here, however, touching was common practice and even encouraged, a reality he was reluctantly accepting.

The two white sticks balanced elegantly in Lynden's fingers. With impressive skill, she used them to select several items from both platters and filled her plate. Coal picked up the sticks and watched her fingers, attempting to mimic her movements. But the sticks fell from his grip and clattered onto the table. Lynden did not look up nor acknowledge his struggle. Instead, she dipped the sticks into the algae broth and pulled out a long string of noodle, which she stuffed into her mouth with as much decorum as one could in such a scenario. Coal attempted to use the sticks again and they fell onto the table and rolled to the floor.

With a sigh, he reached for an item on the sushi platter and Lynden's gaze collided with his. The dim lighting and exotic hairstyle accentuated her loveliness, and he faltered for a moment. The silence they shared was almost as tortuous and clumsy as trying to eat with sticks. Unsure of etiquette, he took a small bite into the roll and the other half fell apart in his hand. Lynden groaned and rolled her eyes.

"I guess I'll save your ass again." She plucked a roll from the platter, lightly touched it to a green dab of sauce, and extended the food toward him with an open mouth, as if feeding a babe. Irritated, he set his mouth into a straight line. She opened her mouth wider and made a sound of encouragement, and a laugh sputtered out of him despite his annoyance. Lynden seized the opportunity and shoved the roll in its entirety in his mouth. "You have to eat it in one bite, *baka*. Otherwise it's considered rude."

"What is that sauce? The heat is incredibly delicious."

"*Wasabi.*" She returned to her food with a posture of indifference. "A little goes a long ways."

"How am I to eat the noodles?"

Lynden arched out of her chair and strolled to where he sat. With her own deft fingers, she positioned his on a fresh set of sticks and, after a few direct instructions, he opened and closed them with success. The idea of using sticks as utensils amused Coal, and he beamed at Lynden with pride. She flicked the black and red strands across his eye and sauntered back to her seat, drinking another cup of *sake* before sitting down. He offered to pour her another, but she waved him off and poured her own, with an admonishment to start eating.

Coal wasted little time and filled his plate with colorful morsels. The ramen noodles and algae broth surprised him. It was salty, and carried a subtle onion and ginger flavor that appealed to him immediately. Sushi, he decided, was the food of gods.

"Catch," Lynden's voice sang. A strawberry hit him in the face just as he looked up, and she giggled. She drank more *sake* and sighed, and Coal believed she may have perhaps finished most of the flask. "Come on, Mr. Awesome," she teased with an easy smile. "You can do better than that."

He lifted a corner of his mouth with amusement as she lifted another strawberry and tossed it toward him. Coal opened his mouth and caught the red fruit, chewing appreciatively. As he swallowed, she tossed another and he nearly missed. She laughed, lifting the cup to her lips. He watched her movements and imagined the woman she would be ten years from now, then twenty years from now, and smiled.

"What?" she asked in teasing tones. In reply, he shook his head, to suggest nothing of importance, and returned attention to the sushi. She rose in fluid movements and sashayed over to him. A light chortle escaped as she jumped onto the table next to his food. Legs swung back and forth as she lifted a single shoulder, a baffling gesture somewhere between a challenge and bashfulness. Lynden picked up a strawberry from his plate and brought it to his mouth, with a thoughtful look. "Close your eyes."

"Lyn," he sighed. "I think you have indulged in too much *sake*."

Giggles spilled out of her. "Seriously. Close your eyes," she drawled. "These are not like the strawberries in New Eden. When you close your eyes and chew, they transform."

"Fascinating."

"Indeed," she replied, mimicking a deep voice and way of speech like his. "I am Coal. I am too stoic for transforming strawberries." Lynden covered her mouth as she laughed, and then grew playfully serious once more. "I would rather hammer metal to overcompensate for my deficiencies."

Coal rolled his eyes and quirked a smile. "You dare mock me?"

"Sensitive about it?"

Not wishing to flush over her borderline humor, he cleared his throat to announce he was ready, closed his eyes, and opened his mouth. Laughter sputtered from Lynden, and he thought perhaps she snorted. This was the first time he had ever seen her drink. She passed up alcohol every time it was presented, and he found her drunken state rather endearing. An object touched his tongue and he slowly bit down, smiling when tasting a piece of sushi flavored with *wasabi*.

"OK. Open your eyes!"

He obeyed, his focus resting on her face, her eyes wide and her bottom lip sucked in as she strained to contain the spirited chuckles he knew would erupt at any moment. To go along with her story, he enriched his speech and asked, "Pray tell, when eyes closed, how doth strawberries transform into the decadent food of mermaids?"

A hand covered her mouth as she laughed, and she situated her foot on the chair next to his thigh as she leaned forward in merriment. "Are we under the ocean?"

"Swimming blissfully unaware of the world above us." Coal sobered with his comment, recalling the aquarium at N.E.T.

Who was the territorial fish demanding a change in leadership?

Anxiety bubbled inside of him and he furrowed his brows. By allowing Hanley to accomplish his plan, Coal felt like an accomplice. The aftertaste of dishonor spoiled his desire to eat, and he looked away.

"Sad Coal is sad," Lynden said, spurts of laughter seeping between words. Before he could reply, she leaped off the table and into his lap. Arms, bound mummy style in white strips mid-way up her forearms, wrapped around him as she nuzzled her face into his neck. "I'm sorry you're sad," she cooed.

He whispered, "How can I be sad when you have gifted me with your laughter?"

She lifted her head and studied his face, the longing for affirmation and approval evident in her eyes. "You like my laugh?"

"It is melodious and magical, akin to chimes in the wind. Faerie laughter, they call it."

A subtle, shy smile touched her lips and she looked down at her lap. "Say my name," she whispered. "I like the way you sound when you talk."

"Lynden," he said, his voice mellifluous. "'*Under the linden tree, on the heath, where we two had our bed, you might find both beautiful flattened flowers and grass. At the edge of the wood in the valley, tandaradei, the nightingale sang beautifully.*'"

Her eyes widened and her mouth parted in a look of awe, her cheeks turning a rosy hue he found most becoming. "Did ... did you just make that up?"

"It is the first stanza in the medieval love poem, 'Under the Linden Tree.'"

"Oh." She twisted her thumb ring. "What's the rest of the poem?"

This time Coal blushed and he looked away once more. "It is a poem about a man and woman who consummate their love beneath the boughs of a linden tree, told through the eyes of the maiden."

She arched her brow. "Linden tree?" A quiet giggle trailed after her words and her face twisted with humor.

"Aye, My Lady. For centuries lovers have professed their eternal, undying devotion beneath the heart-shaped leaves and perfumed blossoms." Coal shyly met her eyes. "They seal their pledge by carving their initials into the tree of love and truth."

"I'm named after a tree of love? Weird."

"I am named after carbonized plant matter."

"All right, you win." She laughed, but it died off after a couple seconds and she placed her hand onto her stomach. "I need to lie down. I never drink this much. Oh god. What the hell was I thinking? Never mind. I know what I was thinking."

"Allow me." Coal scooped her up and stood. "Why did you drink so much?" He walked with her toward the stairway.

"We're going to the underground tonight." She snickered, and he knew it was the alcohol. "I'm a joke, you know. The Ticket Girl who wouldn't put out during her initiation to become a CCG. That's why he beat me. I let everyone think it was because I was sloppy trying to ticket someone who wasn't a noob, instead of..." She laughed again, the sound hollow, and the pain echoed through him. "But that's not why," she continued. "I realized what a mistake I had made. It was all to see what my price tag was. To feel essential to somebody, even if it was just for a moment. Dumb, right? I didn't want to be a CCG. I didn't want to be a Ticket Girl either. Apparently I have standards, and I almost sold them off. But..." Lynden released a heavy sigh, laced with soft giggles. "I don't have any friends. Nobody wants to associate with me. They're too afraid of my dad or star-struck by my brother. I'm freaking out over tonight."

The evening he had arrived in Seattle seared him with new clarity. She did wish to comfort her pain through him, connecting to his grief, and his throat constricted with fresh sorrow. "I will protect you."

"I know." Lynden sniffed and curled up tighter in his arms. "That's why I told you."

The trust moved him, and he felt his chest expand and contract. He continued up the stairs to her bedroom and gently placed her upon the unmade bed. She rolled over and buried her face into a pillow. Coal turned to leave, his arms itching to return to the garage and work more on his project until it was time to go and distract his heartache.

"Stay. Please."

"Yes, of course." Coal pulled the covers up to her chin. "I will sit by the window."

"Fillion gets so pissed when I drink. Dictator mode activates each time."

"He cares about you."

"It's like truth serum." She giggled, the sound rolling out of her. "I confess everything and never remember a single damn thing I said or did." Lynden met his eyes, her focus hazy. "Don't remind me."

He nodded and she relaxed her face, eventually closing her eyes. Seconds passed and became minutes, and still Coal stood by her side, worried that if he moved it would disturb the peace she desperately sought. When her breathing became even, he walked to the chair by her window.

Five weeks prior, he sat in the bedchamber of another young woman sickened from grief—another young woman named after a tree. Except, unlike last time, this young woman desired to be rescued. Distressed even in her sleep, Coal maintained silent vigil and vowed that tonight, he would fight in Lynden's honor.

ELEMENTS

Young men have strong passions, and tend to gratify them indiscriminately. ...

Their hot tempers and hopeful dispositions make them more courageous than older men are; the hot temper prevents fear, and the hopeful disposition creates confidence; we cannot feel fear so long as we are feeling angry, and any expectation of good makes us confident. They are shy, accepting the rules of society in which they have been trained, and not yet believing in any other standard of honour. ...

They would always rather do Noble deeds than useful ones: their lives are regulated more by moral feeling than by reasoning; and whereas reasoning leads us to choose what is useful, moral goodness leads us to choose what is Noble.

— Aristotle, "The Art of Rhetoric," 4th century B.C. *

CHAPTER TWENTY-SEVEN

Seattle, Washington state

Alight sprinkle of rain fell as Coal walked beside Mack and Lynden. Just a few minutes earlier, they had parked in the garage at TalBOT Industries, a leading Smart Tech company owned by Mack's father. Coal readjusted his fingerless gloves and pulled up his large black hood. As instructed, he kept his head down. Nevertheless, he peered at the bright lights from lowered eyes and studied the wares displayed in the windows of shops they passed.

"Smoke?" Mack asked, holding out a pack as they walked.

"No," Coal said. "Perhaps later."

"Rainbow?"

She did not respond and, instead, pulled her hood further over her face. Mack shrugged and put the cigarettes back into his pocket, and lit up one for himself. Their boots sloshed on the damp concrete, each step an audible notification of the battle they marched toward. For Coal, it was to assist the Watsons and fight for Lynden, even if that meant breaking the law to do so. It terrified him, but he tramped toward the darkness in search of light with determination.

"In a few blocks, the cityscape is going to change." Mack swung a glance his direction. "We'll pass a park, the last pretty thing you'll see. When that happens, don't stop for anything. Keep moving. Don't—I repeat, don't make eye contact or talk to anyone."

"I understand." A car drove by and a small wave of water splashed toward them. Coal jumped back with the unexpected spray.

Mack grabbed his arm and pulled him close. "You're cooler than shit. Nothing surprises you. Got that? You act like a noob, then your world will quickly become hell. Actually, hell would be preferable."

Coal relaxed his face to appear bored and maneuvered out of Mack's grip, moving forward. The young man quickly caught up and offered a lopsided grin. The approval encouraged Coal and he continued to mimic Mack's movements, as if nothing held interest, and yet aware of everything as if he owned the world.

The streets grew darker and Coal shivered, wishing he had taken up Mack's offer for a cigarette. It would have employed his anxiety in an occupation other than the thoughts consuming his mind

Before leaving the Nichols residence, Mack had explained the system. The underground needed the money. However, control was the greater currency. The hackers would act as if they had the option to refuse work.

"We need to woo the PM," Mack had said. "Romance them. Court their fancies, whatever their dark heart desires."

"That is a rather open-ended situation," Coal had replied. "How will the PM take you seriously in a skirt?"

"Utility kilt," Mack corrected as he flashed his legs and wagged his eyebrows. "It's my business skirt. Wins them over every time."

"Business skirt?" Coal had studied the black, knee-length garment, combined with combat boots. His forehead wrinkled in bafflement as he studied Lynden, who wore a similar style of dress. "So, to woo the project manager, you must dress as though a woman?"

Lynden sniggered and playfully nudged Mack with her shoulder. The young man scratched his head with his middle finger and she stuck her tongue out in reply.

"Haven't you ever heard of a Scottish Highlander?"

"No. Do they wear skirts?"

"Hellz yeah, and some of the brawniest men to have ever walked this planet." Mack struck a melodramatic pose, demanding that Coal and Lynden admire him. "Behold, Mackenzie Patton Campbell Ferguson the Third."

"Yuck!" Lynden had declared and walked away. "You can take your male pride and stick it up your wannabe Highlander ass."

"She's just jealous because she's Irish," Mack said with a wink Lynden's direction. "Born in Dublin like all good Jaynes."

"Oh please," she had responded, rolling her eyes. "Don't start that war."

"Sooo," Mack drawled, "we are going to convince the PM that they want to be wooed by watching you cage fight." Mack looked at Coal. "We probably don't have to do much wooing at all. I mean, come on. Look at you. Who wouldn't want to watch your body in motion?"

Coal loosed an anxious sigh. Until he had punched Mack in the face, Coal had never physically struck another person in anger, only metal—well, and a pillow. There were make-believe wars as a child. And men participated in the Spring Tournaments, an event held at the end of each April during "Bringing in the May," which determined the May King for May Day and Whitsun Feasts. All fighting was for fun and sport. He tried to explain this to Mack. But the young man waved him off with comments that Coal was a natural and to study cage fighting online—for it, too, was all for fun and sport.

Lynden encouraged him to seek Ignis' help. For several evenings in a row, Coal received tutelage from his holographic Companion, swinging punches with the computerized man. Cheers and laughter bolstered him as Lynden sat in the black leather chair beside the window while he practiced. Before falling asleep, he watched videos of cage fights and memorized the known game worlds.

Would a virtual arena feel real?

Before leaving the apartment, Mack had given him the opportunity to bow out. Coal refused. He had left New Eden explicitly to garner information and, at this point, the underground appeared the only resource to fulfill this quest without alerting Hanley. Too, Coal had agreed to Mack's warning that to assist Fillion would require that he "misbehave like a boss." Coal would do whatever was necessary to protect his family.

Thoughts of cage fighting dissipated in the rain, and Coal furtively studied the surroundings as they walked. Buildings loomed in every direction and created the illusion of a dense forest. Lights flashed, blinked, and bled strands of colors across the wet streets. Drones flew just above their heads on occasion. The majority of machines whirring around belonged to businesses and to the government. Curfew was one o'clock morning time in certain neighborhoods and blocks. It was shortly after midnight, so the police drones would not yet interrupt their journey. As they passed under a street lamp, a humanoid android approached. Its fluid steps and strangely brightened eyes were unnerving.

Mack whispered, "Ignore it."

The electronic man stopped in front of Coal, and Coal held his breath and side-stepped around the android. The robot turned its head and watched him, no doubt aware of his biometric response to its presence.

"Are you the Martian?" the android asked, pivoting on its feet their direction.

"Shit," Mack muttered. "Move. Fast. Media droid. Last thing we need."

Coal picked up his pace, and licked his lips. Fingers touched his and he nearly yelped, but he remembered Mack's admonishment to remain cool. The fingers interlaced with his and he angled his head toward Lynden. She maintained a straight, downcast posture, the hood covering all her features save her lips, which sloped up in a faint smile. He squeezed her fingers and she squeezed back.

A few hours after passing out, Lynden had awakened in a groggy haze. She stared at her fully dressed state and looked around the room, startling when locking eyes with him. Coal approached her bedside and knelt on the ground, and had asked if she fared well.

"What happened?" she asked, squinting her eyes with sleep.

"You imbibed in a fair portion of *sake*."

"Shit." Lynden released a heavy breath. Vulnerability flashed in her eyes, before she hardened into indifference, and she said, "Whatever I said or did, it wasn't true. OK? Why are you in my room anyway? I never took you for a lurker."

"You asked me to remain."

"Oh god, did I share something?"

"Yes," Coal said, lifting a corner of his mouth. "I had the pleasure of experiencing transforming strawberries."

"Transforming—what?"

He had taken her hand and tugged her out of bed. "I will show you. Far safer than enchanted apples."

Coal's chest tightened with the memory, and he contemplated Lynden once more. The hood had fallen back on her head some, providing a glimpse of her features. Blue-glitter eye shadow glinted from her dark-rimmed eyelids. Lips, painted blood red to match her front strands of hair, formed a tight line. A black kimono-style jacket flared over her blue and black plaid skirt. Lace-like tights covered her legs, the holes so large that Coal could not fathom their function. She finished her ensemble with shiny blue combat boots.

He was getting used to the otherworldly fashion of Outsider women. However, the black corset top Lynden wore this evening concerned him greatly. It left her upper chest and shoulders bare, save for the black ribbon tied around her neck. Tiny freckles kissed her exposed skin, and tempted him to do the same. If it inspired such thoughts in him, he could only imagine the thoughts other men would sport. Coal needed to think of something else, not wishing to disrespect Lynden. So, he returned to absorbing his surroundings as surreptitiously as possible.

Trees grew out of the sidewalk every few steps. Their partially naked limbs stretched toward the sky as if begging to be spared from their artificial environment. Coal reached out and grazed a tree as he walked by, his fingertips extending his sympathies, for he understood. He felt similar.

An apartment building gave way to a low wall made from rubble. Beyond the stone-like fence, a lush garden, the size of a city block, spread before them. Fruit trees dotted the landscape, and Coal stared with horror at the sheer number of apples and pears decomposing upon the ground. Coal slowed his steps and gaped at the city's oasis.

Why grow food only to let it go to waste?

"Keep moving, Mr. Awesome," Lynden said, yanking his arm.

"This garden is teeming, but the food is left to rot."

Mack dropped his voice low. "City law mandates permaculture gardens every two miles within city limits. It's part of the Green City Initiative."

"Who may benefit from the food?"

"Those who pay taxes," Mack said. "The employed and land owners."

"And yet they do not."

"Nobody wants to appear needy. It's a sign of desperation. A couple of decades back it was a sign of elitism." Mack eye's shifted toward Coal in a side-glance. "I know. Like I said, control is the greater currency. Trumps everything. Even hunger."

A drone slowed its flight on the sidewalk before them and a holographic woman appeared, well figured and dressed in undergarments. "Hey boys. Want to touch a real woman?"

Coal lowered his eyes as his skin heated. He looked to Mack for direction. With a wide, mischievous grin, Mack walked right through the woman, lifted his hand, and flipped off the drone, never breaking stride. Lynden chuckled and gave a slight shake of her head.

"There's Pioneer Square. Head down. No stopping."

The boarded and gated windows disturbed Coal, a more unsettling kind of disturbance than the ostentatious store-front displays of the wealthier areas of Downtown. The shift was so sudden, that Coal wished for the gaudy holographic ads in the windows simply for more light.

Dark lumps against the walls grew in number and he gasped when noting gaunt, pallid faces beneath the occasional lights from the street. Some of the forms extended hands, weary voices pleading for food or money. A few reached forward and attempted to tug pieces of their clothing to gain attention. The sounds of anguish wrapped around Coal until he thought he might suffocate from the shame of walking by whilst they suffered.

He tapped the device on his ear, "Cranium, phone Mack."

"What?" The voice whispered in his head.

"Who are they?" He whispered back.

"Homeless."

"I beg your pardon?" Coal resisted the urge to stare at the individuals, and kept a downcast posture as instructed. In his peripheral vision, he noticed a woman gather a child close to her, similar in size to his brother Blaze, and lift a piece of cardboard over them for a blanket. The sight nearly made Coal jump out of his skin with fury.

How could neighbors watch those from their community waste away like the fruit in the garden?

Mack whispered, "No jobs, no homes."

"Surely there are places for them to stay warm and dry. Especially the children."

"They have to rotate. Too many homeless, not enough shelters. The foster system is clogged. People aren't taking kids anymore. They can barely feed their own." Mack let out a sigh. "Don't do anything stupid. No heroics."

"This is a grief I have never experienced. The pain is intolerable," Coal whispered. "Is there nothing we can do?"

"No."

"I have an apple in my pock—"

"Shit, don't mention food or show it." The urgency in Mack's voice alarmed Coal, and he tightened his hold on Lynden's hand. "They'll mob you. If you're lucky enough to survive that, then you'll get the privilege of being hauled away by the police for inciting a riot."

"Can they not eat from the garden?"

A low, dark laugh rumbled from Mack. "What do you think?" Silence ticked between them for a minute, but Mack kept their line open. "They're micro-chipped. If they step foot in that space the police drones will arrive and use sonic waves to subdue them." Mack paused. "It's population control. Too many people live too long, so let the hungry die—"

Coal disconnected the line, unable to listen to another word. Hot tears gathered and he tensed, slowly exhaling through clenched teeth. A finger caressed his inner-wrist in slow circles and he blinked, drawing in a ragged breath.

"Save the injustice for the cage," Lynden whispered to him. "I can't stand it either."

Fat drops of rain now fell from the sky, and she blew a wet strand out of her eye in annoyance. A swelling crescendo of sound accompanied the outpour of precipitation. Coal lifted his head to the smudged dark sky as he trudged along, enjoying the tiny beating upon his face. Anxiety melted with the night's tears, and anger poured into him instead. Resolved to unleash justice's fury, he hung his head toward the sidewalk once more and kept a corner gaze on Mack, who took a sharp turn into a nearby alley.

Lynden's steps hesitated for the briefest moment, but her rhythm returned before he could question her. Then, she pulled him close, answering his silent concern. He released his hand and wrapped his arm around her waist, holding her tight to his side, and her shoulders relaxed a notch.

Mack paused before an unmarked door, touched his Cranium, and then shoved it open. Coal assisted Lynden inside the dank, abandoned building. A musty scent assailed him, and he wrinkled his nose in response. The high ceilings dripped, and the plopping sounds of droplets ricocheted throughout the room. A man materialized from the shadows behind a pillar and, upon recognizing Mack, relaxed and disappeared behind the broken support once more. Mack walked past him with a slight nod and continued down a long, winding hallway. Lamps hung haphazardly from the ceiling and streams of water poured down the walls and created small puddles on the concrete floor.

Another unmarked door opened to an old, rusty stairwell and they spiraled down level after level. Footsteps echoed in the chamber, the pulsating sound growing the deeper they traveled. Occasionally they would pass a guard, each one showing recognition of Mack in various ways. Once they descended at least eight stories, Mack pushed through a door and into another dimly lit, moldy hallway. The walls might have been a shade of white once. Now darkly yellowed, and spotted with green and black mold, the walls cast an eerie vision of decay.

A man, dressed how Mack fashioned himself usually, leaned against a wall next to a large metal door, dragging on a cigarette. They halted their movements and Mack touched his Cranium again. As they waited for the door to unlock, the man issued Lynden a flirtatious smile, his thoughts clear and evident, making Coal's blood boil. He was not entirely certain how he would manage this evening. In response, Coal wrapped his arm around her waist once more and glared at the man, who smirked in response. Lynden ignored them both and fixed her eyes on the door while releasing a sigh of irritation. He could almost hear her thoughts, telepathically shouting at both of them about male pride.

The door opened and loud music with slow, seductive beats blared into the hallway. Mack's normally playful expression sobered as he regarded Lynden, and Coal watched as an understanding passed between them. Then, Mack perked up, looked over at him and said, "Welcome to the Den of Iniquity, *desu.*"

Coal walked in, already feeling his face flush. People took in their entrance, but with the same bored indifference Lynden applied to most things in life. Mack transformed into an aloof posture as he strode through the throng of people engaged in various licentious acts. As their small group passed several others, many recognized Lynden and started laughing, some even calling out names so vulgar that Coal tried in vain to erase them from his mind. His heart sickened, worried when she noticeably blinked back the hurt.

"Stop staring," Lynden warned in a low whisper. She draped herself onto him, as if they arrived as a pair, and he hooked his arm around her waist. "You don't give a shit."

Panic rose sharply within him. He was on the verge of an emotional breakdown, never experiencing such shame nor exposure to such debased behavior in his life. Lynden sauntered next to Coal as they trailed Mack. Coal was relieved that she did not unzip her jacket nor remove her hood. His eyes jumped between the people massed around them and the dingy floor at his feet.

He could not distinguish gender for many in this room, which made him more distraught. The androgynous culture elevated his social anxiety unlike any other shock to date. In the underground, it apparently was a highly desired trait.

A woman with pink hair caught his eye from across the room, a slow smile spreading on her lips, flaunting a color that matched her hair to perfection. It was a soft pink, like cherry blossoms. Unlike most of the people who presented themselves as women in this room, the woman in pink held a soft femininity that appealed to Coal immediately. Her creamy white skin shimmered despite the shadows, and dark eyes, flirtatious, laughing almost, invited him over and made promises in a single glance. Coal's heart thrummed loudly and he swept a look to Lynden and then to the flashing lights over her head.

The walls were covered in flat screens, flashing images unfit for any eyes. One particular video created a discomfort so grand, Coal gasped in astonishment. Mack shot a look over his shoulder and shouted over the noise, "Rule 34. Keep your head down, *dokyun*. We're almost out."

"Oh my god!" A female cried out from a nearby group, and a woman in a tight, low-cut black dress fell onto Mack. "Where have you been?"

"Dreaming of you," Mack said with a subtle smile, then looked away as if disinterested. "You're far better than any fantasy, though."

"Where's Corlan?" She let out a sigh and casually looked around, delivering a lazy, flirtatious for Mack once more. "Is he here?"

"Nope. On Mars."

"He is out of this world. You're such a tease." She smiled appreciatively. "I've missed you."

"I know."

The woman laughed again, a coquettish sound that grated against Coal's nerves.

"What happened to your eyes?" She stuck out her bottom lip.

Mack considered Coal, then issued a dramatic expression for the woman, as if he was suffering greatly. "I fought a bad man. Don't worry, I took care of him."

"Poor Mack. Let me kiss you and make you feel better." Her fingers trailed up Mack's chest to his face and drew him down, but Mack slapped her on the arse and said, "Not now.

Later." With a wink he kept walking and the woman let out a frustrated huff and stormed off.

"Dreaming of her?" Lynden snorted. "Wow. Do you even remember her name?" Mack slid her a mischievous glance and kept walking. "God, you're a winner, Mack."

He smirked. "Don't kill my sexy *henshin*."

"Don't worry. I don't have to. You're doing a pretty damn good job of it yourself."

"Whatever, Rainbow. I'm the King. I just let Fillion think he is so as to not destroy his fragile ego. I'm a good friend like that."

His face remained serious, but his lips twitched and Lynden could not hold in her mirth and laughed. Not a mocking laugh, but a genuine laugh of amusement. Mack's face softened with the sound and he tugged on a red strand peeking through her hood. She continued to chuckle, but it halted abruptly when spotting the woman with pink hair. Lynden's body tensed into haughty coolness and she pushed Mack forward. He tossed a casual, inspective glance in the woman's direction, his eyes darkening. In his typical laid-back way, Mack ambled forward until he reached a metal door, acting as through nothing was amiss. Coal knew otherwise, but not why.

Another room opened up, featuring high tables and chairs with unusually long legs. People sipped drinks, their low chatter barely audible over the music, the same sounds from the previous room.

"You passed the first circle of hell," Mack said, shrugging his eyebrows.

"No, I do believe that was the second."

Mack laughed. "Different inferno."

"Most assuredly."

"All other rooms are unicorns, kittens, and rainbows in comparison." Mack paused in front of another door. "Noobs rarely make it past the Den of Iniquity."

Coal lifted a corner of his mouth, to hide his trembling, and said in a dry tone, "A celebration is in order then."

"Let's kick some cage-fighting ass. Betting money on you. Don't disappoint."

"Go," Lynden said, pushing past Mack into the next room.

They passed through several doors and rooms, each one with its own flavor of fetish or purpose. The farther they went in, the more industrious the rooms became, people working rather than playing. An engineering room piqued Coal's interest the most, and he wished to observe the mechanics and diagrams. But Mack was on a mission and, therefore, so were they. The quiet of these rooms eased Coal's growing nerves, but the experience was short-lived.

Our Sire's age was worse than our grandsires'. We, their sons, are more worthless than they; so in our turn we shall give the world a progeny yet more corrupt.

— Horace, "A Progeny Yet More Corrupt," Book III of *Odes*, circa 20 B.C. *

Fundamental to the tournament was the idea of chivalrous and romantic conduct. A knight selected a lady; beautiful and preferably married to a husband of slightly higher rank. In her honor he would fight.

— "The Medieval Tourney," National Jousting Association, nationaljousting.com *

CHAPTER TWENTY-EIGHT

A tall, lean man—at least, Coal thought he was a man—no, maybe a woman?—with very pale skin, shoulder-length black hair and equally as black eyes waltzed into a room as if floating. The person's eyes lacked pupils, a shocking and creepy appearance that sent cold tingles up Coal's spine. A long coat with a high collar covered his or her body. Coal panicked even more with the lack of physical cues as to gender.

Was it human?

"Mr. Ferguson, you requested me?"

"Mel, I have a proposition."

The otherworldly being gestured toward three chairs in the corner of the room. They walked over and Mack indicated with his head for Coal to take a seat. Lynden, playing her part, slinked onto Coal's lap, with a bored yet flirtatious expression, and returned her attention to the other men. Unable to bring himself to look at Mel, Coal focused on the small, seemingly private room.

Dark, rust-tinged pipes patterned the ceiling in a grid. Three of the four walls were painted black. The last wall boasted a dark red. As Mack spoke, the otherworldly being studied Coal, with nary a blink nor movement of any kind. It was if this person fed on Coal's fear, enjoying the elevated blood pressure and throbbing heart rate.

"So," Mel said with a soft, smooth voice, a voice not too high, not too low. "You wish the underground to crack the sealed files and erased cyber activity of the world's leading Corporate King." Slowly, Mel's head swiveled in the direction of Mack. "What protection do we have against your target?"

"None." Mack eased back into his chair, and crossed his arms over his chest. "Nobody does, regardless of the situation. I could do this myself, but I'm a nice guy. I like to help out my community. Corlan will make it well worth the risk. And, separate from Corlan's offer, I will hire the best cracker as an additional cryptographer for my father's team—with full benefits and set-up housing, of course."

"Very generous of Mr. Ferguson."

"Like I said. Community player."

"Yes, your father is a valued patron of the Open Source community."

Mack did not comment. Rather, he activated his Cranium and fingers commanded the air. "Sending you the proposal right now."

A white hand lifted, the nails long and painted black, and Mel brushed the air with graceful strokes. A few seconds later, Mel stared into space, the black eyes moving back and forth. "Double it, three-quarters up front."

"No, a tiered plan as outlined. Gov docs cracked earns the money indicated; social media cracked, another sum. Only those who accomplish their task get a cut. I'm not paying for a hacking field trip. No full disclosures. And everyone involved will sign legal statements, drafted by my lawyer, agreeing to not dox the target family with their findings. They'll disappear if they do."

"Corlan agrees with such drastic measures? Does not sound like his way of handling situations."

Mack offered a cocky smile. "Doesn't really matter, now does it?" He sniffed and leaned back in his chair. "Deal?"

"Tiered plan, double the monetary values outlined." Mel stared at Coal.

"One-and-a-half times the set values."

"With a non-refundable retainer." Mel's tongue slid over fang-like teeth with a wicked smile, and Coal shivered. At this point, Coal had decided that Mel was either Satan himself or one of his lead demons. He resisted the urge to cross himself. Perhaps they really had descended into Hell.

"Of course." Mack pushed off the back of the chair and leaned on the table. "Quarter as promised in the proposal."

"Third."

"Twenty-eight percent. Shit, I'll throw in another half-percent for kicks and giggles."

"And him." Mel's smile widened while staring at Coal.

Mack shifted his angle on the chair and contemplated Coal as if inspecting him for the first time. "He'll be there. Draken is part of my team. My cousin from the UK, works at New Eden Enterprise's London office, and will be our insider to decode the info."

"London underground?" A faint smile lit Mel's thin lips. "Interesting." Black eyes stayed on Coal, then flicked to Mack. "Any other … talents?"

"Terrible singer. God, all musical attempts will make your ear drums commit suicide." Mack shook his head as if it was indeed a great loss, and Mel remained unmoved. Coal tried not to laugh, especially when Mack flew a deadpan look his way. "But," Mack dragged the word out for emphasis. "He's a well-known cage fighter in his parts."

"Excellent. I wish for a show."

"Of course you do. We're happy to oblige. Draken is a bit jet-lagged, but he'll put on a good show."

"Draken…?" Mel inquired, black eyes riveted onto Coal.

"Smyth. Draken Smyth." Coal steadied his voice and tensed his muscles as he dipped his head. "At your service."

"And your companion?"

Coal placed both arms around Lynden's waist. "Rainbow Leigh, my personal assistant."

"Mr. Smyth," Mel began, "I will agree to Mr. Ferguson's and Mr. Jayne's proposal to involve the underground in a collaborative hack against a certain high-profile individual provided you *entertain* me."

Coal licked his dry lips and pushed out a confident, "Yes, I understand."

"Miss Leigh, I insist you sit with me during the fight. Shall we?" Mel rose from the chair as if formed from the thick, dark air of the room. "I look forward to your exhibition, Mr. Smyth." The demonic-looking being held out an arm to Lynden, who accepted with a sensual smile, not a trace of fear in her movements. Mel looked down at her. "How is your brother Corlan, dear?"

With head lowered, Coal walked behind Mel and Lynden down a long hallway, ignoring the conversation. Cheers and angry shouts rumbled, growing in volume as they neared a door at the very end of the narrow passageway. The door opened before they arrived, and a young man dipped his head as Mel entered, as if he knew the pale being approached.

Bodies blocked Coal's view from the doorway so he looked up, following a persistent deafening noise. Large vents in the ceiling forced cooler air into the space. Their sound mixed with the crowd's vociferations and with the loud music, and Coal wanted to cover his ears. But he remained impassive, appearing bored.

As he entered, a person bumped into him. Coal stumbled to the side, staggering into another, who flipped him off without looking his direction. Coal swept his vision across the undulating heads and skimmed over the server racks caged along the perimeter of the room. Metal bars formed a fence from the crowd and a walkway before each cage. The walls and ceiling were painted black, brightening the thousands of computer eyes, in shades of blue, white, red, and yellow, winking from the racks.

Two cages loomed at the center of the room, divided by a gaming deejay. Each cage housed an intricate virtual gaming apparatus. A fight was in session, and Coal paused and watched the holographic avatars above the cages, displayed by twin Imigicasts. The vivid colors popped against the black, the three-dimensional aspects so real it was baffling. Two young male opponents interacted in a jungle theme, towering high above the rainforest floor in wattle-like treehouses. Suspension bridges connected different spaces, and the players battled on one of them. The bridge swayed, and one of the fighters nearly lost his balance, making the crowd gasp. Coal felt a tug on his chains and he whipped his head in their direction to find Lynden pressed against him.

"This way," she shouted with an arched eyebrow, nodding in the direction he should have walked. "I thought we lost you."

"My apologies," he shouted in reply.

"Nervous?"

"No, of course not." He offered a charming smile and her face softened.

"I'm terrified."

"Of Mel?"

"A bit. More for you."

Mack's faced emerged behind Lynden's as he squeezed through the agitated crowd, his hair fairly glowing beneath the strange lighting. "Come on. Time to prep." He looked at Lynden. "Miss Leigh, Mel is waiting for you."

She rolled her eyes. "Eww. Not into half-deads."

"Just sit and look pretty for them, nothing else. You're not their type either." Mack shifted his attention to Coal. "It's their way of honoring you, by putting your 'personal assistant' on display."

"I see." Coal paused, confused. "*Their* type? Are we not talking about Mel?"

"Neutrandrogyne transgender."

Coal understood the pieces of each word, but failed to comprehend the whole meaning. Another time, he thought. "Lead the way."

Lynden gripped a chain dangling from his pants and they pushed through the crowd. Mel waited by a gate, and they slipped into the walkway between the metal bars and server cages, bypassing the crowd as they walked the periphery of the room. The deejay, who sat elevated upon a small platform, tipped his head at Mel.

A man with a shaved head approached. Bluish-white glowing tattoos, in a continuous intricate design of multi-colored electronic grids, decorated the man's entire head, even his face, down his neck and arms and, Coal assumed, his entire body. It was as if he materialized from a circuit board, even more so when he noticed how the tattooed man's eyes shone light blue under the strange dark lamps. Mel lifted a long, lithe finger at Coal and the tattooed man gripped Coal's sleeve and nudged him forward. Lynden followed, still holding to a chain, as Coal was led to a waiting pen by one of the gaming cages.

"Mel tells me you fight?" The man's deep voice boomed over the music, fans, and cheers with ease. Instead of replying, Coal simply offered a curt nod. "Did you bring your own gear?"

"No."

"You know the drill."

Coal turned to Lynden, unzipped his bulky jacket and handed it to her. She accepted, her face unreadable with exception to her lip ring, which she nibbled as she waited patiently. With smooth movements, Coal pulled his shirt off and draped it over his jacket. Then, he removed his shoes and pants, afraid to meet Lynden's eyes, although he wore shorts designed for such events. Still, he had never been so undressed before so many. Nor before her. Their gaze collided anyway, and her hazel orbs held his. After several beats, she pulled her eyes away from his to admire the elaborate tattoo of a Japanese dragon slithering up his left arm and curling over his shoulder and across his chest.

Coal lowered close to her face and, as quietly as possible, asked, "Do you have a token I may carry into battle, My Lady?"

She arched an eyebrow and regarded him as if confused by his question. Then, without further hesitation, her fingers untied the black ribbon around her neck. Her hands shook, the only part of her that relayed any definable emotion, as she retied the shiny trim around his wrist in several knots. A shy smile touched her lips for a brief moment, before it relaxed into the usual emotionless expression. Lynden flicked the black and red strands hanging over his eye.

"My money is on you, Mr. Awesome."

"I fight for you, Lyn." He exhaled a shaky breath. "There are many injustices, but I wished for you to know that a man fights in your honor."

Her mouth parted as her eyes glossed beneath the dark lighting. The openness pulled Coal in, and he found her emotional display quite fetching. She leaned forward, resting her hands on his upper chest, and his muscles tightened under her touch. Then, her lips found his and her hands slipped around his neck. For a few seconds of bliss, the world completely disappeared. The affection was unexpected, but he reasoned it was part of the act they all performed. Their mouths continued to embrace as they communicated their need of each other, a need for comfort, a need for reassurance, a need to be known. As Lynden pulled away, she kept her eyes to the ground, and said, "I hope you win."

Her eyes flashed to his for half a heartbeat, right before she spun on her heel and sauntered over to Mack and Mel. Coal attempted to process her comment, but his mind was far too distracted. The spooky being extended a hand to Lynden and helped her rise to a plush seat that overlooked the arena from the side. Pupil-less eyes fixed on Coal, canine's bared, as Mel situated beside Lynden.

Creeped out, Coal rolled his body toward the glowing tattooed man, who began to apply electro-sensor patches to various parts of his body. He knew from videos, and explanations from Ignis, that these patches would release electric pulses to his muscles and stimulate the feel of punches, kicks, and other injuries sustained from fighting.

Nerves fluttered and raced through his body, and he tensed and relaxed his muscles. The energy trickled from his upper body, kick-starting his heart, and traveled down his legs. He started to jump on the balls of his feet as he swept an uncertain gaze over the crowd. The current game ended and the winning cage blazed with white lights as music pumped in celebration. Coal used the opportunity to study the man he would fight, a small smile forming upon noting his opponent's unremarkable build.

The tattooed man tapped Coal's right foot and he lifted it off the ground. With a dab of adhesive, the man applied a flat tracker to the sole of Coal's boot and helped him back into it. Then he did the same to the other foot. Next, Coal was offered a small pair of goggles, which suctioned to his eyes and strapped around his head. Once the man confirmed it was snug, he slapped Coal on the shoulder and led him to the open cage.

The lights doused and the room blackened. However, the goggles showed Coal a clear path to the circular treadmill he would stand upon. The disc—its diameter the length of two men—lay upon the ground, its edges curved upward. Arms protruded out from the disc and angled back toward the center, supporting a padded ring that would ensure his physical body did not hit pavement should he fall to the virtual floor. No matter how many times Coal studied the gaming apparatus, his mind transformed the machine into a dead spider upon its back, legs curled toward its belly. The disturbing image did not help his anxiety.

Nearly five weeks ago, he awoke in linen garb and tinkered in a Forge to build and provide for his community. Now, he walked into an entirely different enclosure, directed by high technology, to entertain a different community in order to provide for the one he left behind. The thoughts racing through his mind were baffling.

Trackers on his soles connected to the computer system and a confirmation screen appeared through the lenses of his goggles. He closed the arm of the apparatus, which circled around his body. Coal looked around and noted four drones hovering along the ceiling to record and build a three hundred-and-sixty-degree view of his body. A red light appeared, and he stood still as they scanned him from head to toe. A few seconds later, their signals turned green.

Lights flashed on and the deejay announced Coal—Draken Smyth—and his opponent, Kenzo Suzami. Coal bowed to pay his respects and threw his arms out when the screen went black. Breath slowly escaped through clenched teeth as he waited. The roar of the crowd competed with the heartbeats pounding in his ears.

"Fighters, are you ready?" The deejay's voice filled the room, and Coal bowed toward him. "Time to get served!"

A green light blinked in the corner of Coal's vision. The next thing he knew, he was in a desert. His breath came in quick and sweat started to form on his forehead—and he had not even battled yet. He was a hammer, and the opponent an anvil. He would not be so easily conquered, he chanted in his mind. This was not real. Nothing about this moment was real. He was not truly in danger. "I am awesome," he muttered under his breath.

Coal skimmed over his environment. A crumbling sandstone temple towered over the landscape in the near distance. Its ancient beauty filled Coal with awe and he blinked, disbelieving. Around the temple, monolithic statues shot up like spires. Others rested on their sides, chunks and bits unearthed in the sand. Various sized gears protruded sporadically from the ground. He tilted his head and studied the metal objects, unsure of why copper, bronze, and nickel gears were necessary in such an ancient civilization.

Not seeing Kenzo, he moved toward the temple. The virtual sand issued a resistance and the sensors on his legs pulsed in response. Soon, the dark entrance yawned. He hesitated a moment, then stepped into the ruins with equal parts courage and wariness. Steam hissed to his right and Coal jumped, his vision clouding with the thick vapor. He stepped back and, when clarity returned, examined the intestines of a machine. Copper pipes ran across the walls, and valves released spurts of steam at different joints. A strange hum purred in the distance, but he could not ascertain from what direction.

Why did an ancient temple contain pipes and steam mechanics?

Was the temple a machine itself?

He did not have much time to dwell upon such an enigma. The sensor patches came to life and pain shot through his jaw. His head flung back with a snap. The muscles in his stomach cramped next and he gasped for air. Through the haze, he locked onto a fist disappearing into the cloud of steam. Now he was pissed. Coal rotated to his left and side-stepped back, fists up at face level. Kenzo emerged from behind the cloud, his lip curled in satisfaction. Bright yellow hair was arranged in sharp spikes all over the fighter's head, drawing Coal's attention. But not for long. The young man threw another punch and Coal instinctively blocked.

A fist flew his direction. He ducked to the left to avoid another hit. He kicked, but misgauged the distance and bypassed his opponent entirely. The virtual system was a slippery concept. He fought air. Yet the pain begged to differ. Heaving for breath, both men circled away and studied each other.

A valve hissed and released another cloud of steam. Kenzo darted his eyes to the source of sound, all Coal needed. He seized the distraction and delivered an upper-cut to the jaw, making solid contact. The yellow-haired man's body went rigid. Coal swung another punch, connecting to the side of Kenzo's face. Spit flew from Kenzo's mouth as he staggered back a few steps. The goggles lit up on the sides confirming the hits. The visual distraction hurt Coal's eyes and he winced. Sensors in his hands pulsed and rewarded him with pain. Coal grit his teeth. Jumping on the toes of his boots, he flexed his hands and shook it out.

Ready for more, he balled his fists. Coal's upper body tensed as he arced another blow toward Kenzo's stomach. As Coal rotated, the muscles across his torso and back rippled, tight and coiled. Kenzo twisted his body at the last second. But Coal could not halt the momentum. With a crunch, his hand collided with the man's hip bone. Fire spread through Coal's arm and he recoiled. The intensity stole the air from his lungs. Sweat broke out over his entire body in a cold flush. His hand still flexed, though, and Coal released a relieved sigh.

Dazed, he failed to block Kenzo, who grabbed Coal's head. Surging through the pain, Coal counterattacked. They grappled with each other in a lock, neither able to reasonably inflict injury on the other. Then Coal remembered a move he saw in one of the videos and fell back toward the ground, pulling Kenzo down with him. His grip tightened round Kenzo's neck as he rolled behind the man. Inexperience, however, stinted his too-slow if graceful maneuver, and Kenzo broke free.

They jumped to their feet, arms and fists at the ready. Steam hissed and billowed from several valves. Vapor filled the room. Kenzo's form disappeared from sight. Wary, Coal moved backwards out of the shadows and into the false sunlight. The mist gleamed and sparkled, and Coal squinted against the glare.

Tearing through the cloud, Kenzo charged with a loud growl. Coal held his position and glowered, lifting a corner of his mouth. Right before collision, Coal feinted left and then dodged right, grabbing Kenzo by the arm in the confusion. The man screamed as Coal flung him across the courtyard with a hard yank. Yellow hair flew in a streaking blur, and his flailing body crashed into a pile of long, thorny sticks.

Quick and nimble, Kenzo jumped back to his feet. It was such an unnatural response that Coal simply stared, unmoving. A stupid mistake. Before Coal could blink, Kenzo grabbed a large stick with a wicked grin and swung at Coal's head. Unable to move away fast enough, Coal arched back until a hand touched the ground and his face was perpendicular to the cerulean digital sky. It was if time slowed, his core muscles and thighs hardening, burning with strain each second. The stick glanced over his head in a rush of air and a thorn sliced across Coal's cheek. The sensors pulsed and flared as his back rolled to a straight position. His fists lifted in defense as he angled his body to the side. A sticky sensation ran down his face. He almost lifted a hand to inspect. But it was not real. Nothing was real. Anger surged through him and he clenched his jaw.

Poised for another hit, Kenzo lifted his staff. Tiny spots of blood flecked the man's body from the thorns. The stick swooshed toward Coal's shin in a sharp cut. He sprang up in a leap, the staff swiping the air beneath his feet. He hit the ground running and dashed to a nearby fallen statue.

Coal grunted as he jumped high off the sand and landed firmly on top of the sandstone structure. Every muscle was taut and coiled for action. Kenzo joined him and pieces of the statue crumbled beneath his feet as he sought balance on the unstable monument. Still, the stick remained clutched in the man's hand. Coal looked around.

What were his options?

He did not know. There was nothing but sand and statue. Desperate, he did the only logical thing that came to mind. In a swinging arc, his boot kicked Kenzo's hand and dislodged the staff. Sand moved, as if hungry, chewing, taking bites, and the stick was devoured within seconds. Kenzo scowled with fury, but Coal was terror-stricken.

The sand lived?

Kenzo leaned over the edge with one final look and spit at the sand. Then, he sharply turned Coal's direction, slipping on the statue with his abrupt movements. Coal capitalized on the moment, marching over and kicking him hard in the gut. The man fell off the statue, arms open wide, and slammed into the sand with a solid thud. Living sand or no, Coal was determined to end this fight. He pivoted on his heel and launched from the statue and fell onto Kenzo with a growl of his own. After a small struggle, Coal had him pinned. Adrenaline coursed like liquid fire, his head buzzing with battle fury. He was the hammer. Kenzo was the anvil. Coal struck Kenzo across the cheek, then pummeled his face, delivering one solid blow after another.

Blood spurted from Kenzo's nose and dribbled from his lips. Within seconds, dark red oozed and gushed down the man's chin and neck. Coal pushed away. Kenzo maneuvered onto his knees and slowly crawled away, the spit and blood sizzling on the sand. Coal stared at his hands, drenched in blood, and at Kenzo's dripping face—the visuals taking hold of his mind despite efforts to block them. He did not recall this level of reality when studying the videos, and his stomach sickened. No time to reflect.

A whirring sound sliced through the air. Coal's head snapped up. His eyes locked onto a metal disc whizzing toward him at great speed. He ducked and nervously sucked in his bottom lip as the gear entrenched itself into the sand behind him. Coal snatched up the gear and raised it above his head as he had seen in illustrations of Greek disc throwers, flexing his muscles as a show of intimidation. Kenzo's eyes widened and he took a single step back. Coal hurled the bronze gear with a loud grunt. A smug grin widened on the man's face, and he easily moved out of the gear's trajectory. Inflamed, Coal looked around for another object to throw.

Laughter taunted him. Coal shifted his focus to the bloodied man just as another gear carved the air. Coal dove to the side and ploughed into the sand. Pin-prick sensations tingled across his face. A deep, guttural growl surfaced as he picked himself up. But Kenzo rammed into his body, knocking the breath from him. Electro-sensors flared and his muscles spasmed. Coal groaned.

The young man straddled Coal's body and pinned his arms. Coal drew a breath and head-butted him in the chin. Bright red spittle dotted the air. Kenzo bared his blood stained teeth, then spit in Coal's face. Fear fired through Coal in hot waves and he pushed and twisted to roll away. But his strength was draining with each electro-shock. A shadow crossed Coal's face as Kenzo lifted a chunk of crumbled statue. He shoved the young man just as the statue remnant bludgeoned Coal in the side of his head. A red light flashed in Coal's goggles as sharp pain lanced through his skull and down his spine. He let out a scream, his body arching in pain. He lashed out to throttle Kenzo, but his arm glitched, blinked, and faded from the scenery as the rock crashed into his head once more.

The words "Critical Hit" flashed across the screens.

The goggles returned to normal vision just as he was plunged into darkness. Coal pulled the virtual equipment off and shook the sweat from his head. His chest heaved for breath as his muscles twitched. It was not real. Nothing about that world or its dangers was real. But the pain still shuddered through his body until queasiness settled in his stomach. Coal opened the arm of the apparatus and walked from the circular treadmill, hoping he would not retch. He approached the cage door, which opened as he neared. The tattooed man shook his hand and led him back to the waiting pen.

People shouted his handle, but all Coal wished to do was dress and sit down to gather himself. Lynden approached him, her steps unsure as if she now feared him. The very notion conjured more shame. He had failed to beat his opponent, which he expected for a first attempt at anything. But his pride would not allow him to properly face the woman for whom he pledged to fight. Nor could he digest the humility of failing to secure Mel's blessing for the collaborative hack. As if to add insult to injury, the spectators continued to chant his name. He cringed.

"Why do they call my name?" Coal finally asked Lynden, chancing a glimpse of the crowd. "I lost the fight, did I not?"

She twisted the ring on her thumb and looked anywhere but at him. "Fights aren't always about winning or losing."

Distressed by her answer, Coal pushed his eyebrows together, thankful that the dark lighting hid his embarrassment.

The tattooed man peeled the sensors from his body, pulling at his skin and removing fine hairs. The discomfort was minuscule compared to the spasms still wracking his muscles. When finished, he took his clothes from Lynden's hands and dressed, trying to keep his hands from shaking with adrenaline. Coal lifted the hood of his jacket far over his head and hid his face from the spectators who reached out and touched him as he walked past, shouting praises and adoration.

A wild look blazed in Mack's eyes as he shrugged his eyebrows and bit down on his tongue suggestively at Coal. Confused, Coal fixed his eyes back to the ground. He followed Mack and Mel along the walkway and out of the server room, fatigued yet still pumped. They traveled down the long hallway and back into the small, private room.

Coal slumped into a chair and Lynden cozied into his lap for lack of a seat. They avoided each other's eyes, only increasing his awareness of her. He thought of their kiss, and tried to stop. Nor could he look away from the exposed, freckled skin resting against him. She fingered the black ribbon around his wrist and he released a sigh. His entire system caught fire under her touch. In a moment of weakness, he brushed the hair from the back of her neck and planted a light kiss on the dragon tattoo perched below her shoulder. Lynden stilled, then wove her fingers with his.

He wished to pull her to himself and indulge in her softness, to feel something gentle and feminine while the adrenaline of battle still coursed through his veins. Such thoughts increased his shame and he cleared his throat and rested his head against the back of the chair as his eyes tracked the pipes along the ceiling.

"Mr. Smyth," Mel said in—their—eerily soft voice. "You are a beautiful fighter. Watching your body in motion was like watching living art. A *pleasure* the crowd experienced as well. I can only imagine how you must fight when not jet-lagged."

Coal tried not to gape in surprise. Somehow he managed, "Thank you," in the rush of relief.

"Mr. Ferguson, I accept your offer of one and a half times the set values and twenty-eight and a half percent retainer." Black eyes moved to Mack. "Message me your preferred team and bring the retainer within two days to finalize plans. We'll collaborate on October twenty-ninth, right after midnight." Mel rose from the chair and glided across the floor directly toward a black wall. Without turning, they said, "Please send Corlan my greetings." Then the otherworldly being disappeared into the wall.

Coal gasped. Mack leaned forward and whispered, "It's a trick wall. An illusion." Mack then whooped and gripped Coal around the bicep with a small shake, and Coal flinched. "It's going to happen."

"You are welcome." Coal flaunted a charming smile, hoping it covered up his fear and discomfort.

"What the hell are you talking about? Mel couldn't keep their eyes off my legs. Business skirt for the win." Mack winked and jumped from his chair, striding toward the exit.

Several hours later, Coal crawled into bed. He pressed his face into a pillow to stifle a sob and wrapped his hands around his stomach. There were images he could not unsee. Pain that could not be unfelt. Shame that would forever burn his soul.

Grief claimed him and upwelled all the agonizing emotions he had been attempted to tamp down. His mind conjured images of his loved ones in response. Norah's face smiled at him, then Joel's. Ember took his hand, his sister's brown eyes gazing at him with worry. Blaze and Corona waved, gleeful at his sight, and oblivious to how much he had changed. His father placed a large hand on his shoulder and squeezed. It was Oaklee's image that finally broke him, however, and he clutched the pillow as his body convulsed. He would spend her sixteenth birthday participating in a collaborative hack.

A soft touch brushed his hair from his forehead and he looked up to find Lynden leaning over his bed. "Hey, Mr. Awesome," she whispered. "I heard a sound and thought it was you."

He rolled to his side in order to see her better. "Please do not tell me to tough—"

"Shhh."

She gently brushed her fingers through his hair again. In smooth, graceful movements, Lynden slid beneath the covers and curved her body against his. Coal's breath shuddered and he wrapped an arm around her waist, burying his face into her hair. Back home, this would be considered one of the highest forms of scandalous behavior, her reputation only saved through marriage. Here, right this moment, the chaste intimacy soothed his pain and sparked a small flame of hope. He pulled her tighter against himself.

Lynden was right. Until now, he never had to emotionally survive, and he needed her. Perhaps she sought the safety and consolation of his embrace as well.

Their shared warmth lulled him and, eventually, Coal fell asleep with her secure in his arms. Later that morning, he awoke to an empty bed, confused, and wondered if he had dreamed the moment. So many experiences of this world were not real, a bitter truth that persistently ached inside of him. Especially as he attempted to orient himself once more. Still unsure, he looked down at his wrist and ran a finger along the black, shiny ribbon.

Your love has wrested me away from me,
You're the one I need, you're the one I crave.
Day and night I burn, gripped by agony,
You're the one I need, you're the one I crave.

I find no great joy in being alive,
If I cease to exist, I would not grieve,
The only solace I have is your love,
You're the one I need, you're the one I crave.

— Yunus Emres, 13th century A.D. *

CHAPTER TWENTY-NINE

Wednesday, October 28, 2054

New Eden Township, Salton Sea, California

The hour of rest had descended upon the biodome nearly a quarter of an hour prior, leaving the fields and surrounding areas empty. Oaklee rambled through the meadow toward The Forge to shelve her heckling combs.

Today, she had spent most of the afternoon brushing through bushels of fiber for other village spinners. Older apprentices worked nearby and utilized a brake to crush the outer stem of the flax straw and a scutching board to remove loose pieces of chaff still clinging to the newly freed fibers. Occasionally, she would pause in her work to inspect and instruct as needed. The pounding rhythm still echoed in her head. The younger apprentices had gathered at her feet and corded the fresh, carded fiber. Although not necessary, it gave their small hands an occupation which, in the end, enabled the spinners to draft the prepared fibers with more ease.

Without a wheel, Oaklee had been relegated by the head spinner, Mistress Katie, to the duty of overseeing the apprentices. It was an employment she did not mind so much. As such, she had remained available as the apprentices properly stored the partially processed flax linen and larger tools until the morrow. The only remaining task now involved her heckles, which she carried in a work basket. Several of the iron tines on her finer comb had become misshapen and a small number had broken off completely. Oaklee made a mental note to mention the needed repairs to Connor over evening meal.

The back walls of The Forge ran beneath her fingertips as she caressed the mud surface. The Orchard lay a stone's throw away and she stared wistfully toward the knotted branches and beyond to The Rows. The wheat fields in the main dome had been felled with success, and the reapers moved to the Mediterranean biome as a select group of villagers winnowed the first harvest. Traces of the sweet, earthy fragrance still carried on the bio-wind, but it waned more and more each day.

Although the reaping rhythm was established, her brother dragged his feet into their apartment every evening. He maintained a ready smile despite the ever present dark circles beneath his eyes. Laurel would perch next to him on a chair, lean her head on his shoulder, and fill his ear with the latest gossip among the children.

Ember, ever quiet and resourceful, prepared a tumbler of hard cider from the Great Hall for Leaf before each hour of rest, as well as a bucket of water with fresh hemp wash rags so he might freshen before evening meal. Their gazes lingered on each other as Ember moved about the apartment, both careful not to steal attention from Laurel's birdsong chatter. As weary as Leaf was, he never interrupted their sister. Instead, he would further indulge her by asking questions and making comments about her stories.

In three weeks, Laurel would begin an apprenticeship with the Herbalist, and the evenings would be filled with new adventures and stories. Joannah was kind and carried thoughtful wisdom, and Oaklee was grateful her sister would study under such a respected woman in the community.

After soaking up attention from Leaf, Laurel flitted Oaklee's direction, skipping merrily across the wooden planked floor. With a kiss upon Laurel's forehead, Leaf would continue toward his room to rest and refresh. Oaklee savored these moments and often thought of mother as she sat quietly in a corner with Laurel to provide basic lessons on sewing or knitting. She was Laurel's age when mother passed away, but the tucked-away memories unfolded with each stitch. Especially when she praised her little sister or guided her with additional lessons as mother had for her half a lifetime ago.

A month had passed since her father and Norah had died. Although their home would never be the same, nor their community, Oaklee drew comfort from the new patterns and traditions they had established together. Touches of grief afflicted her in some moments, but it no longer carried her away. The swaths of mourning cloth that had shrouded her life unraveled layer by layer and, to her amazement, a different woman slowly emerged. Girlhood almost seemed an entire lifetime ago.

The strained atmosphere of the community continued to build, however, and she worried that a flood of angry protests might wash away the remaining remnants of peace. Since the Moores and Carsons left, an entirely new tension plucked at the taut, fragile state of New Eden. Neighbors turned on each other, hissing and spewing hateful words to one another on the village paths and in the Great Hall. A small pocket still demanded Skylar Kane as King and Aether, but the vast majority supported her brother.

The day Leaf drew a line in the fields with expectations of love and peace and granted permission for people to leave without shame or judgment, he earned the community's respect. Leaf, however, carried the guilt upon his sleeves, unable to cope with the fact that two families had actually left. He and Jeff had escorted both families personally to The Door with Scrolls in hand. Her brother, then, disappeared for the remainder of the day, only returning before Laurel headed off to bed.

Since that fateful day, Skylar remained hidden from the community, and many speculated he was behind the rumors as a form of vengeance. Oaklee, however, could not believe Skylar capable of such malicious behavior. Timothy, his wife, and their daughters showed at every meal and community event, and Timothy laughed and charmed those in his company with his jovial nature. For some time, Oaklee had been wary of the former Wind Element's behavior, especially toward their family. But now, she thought him akin to a snake—something she feared—and she avoided him at every opportunity. Sadly, her fear of Timothy trickled to Skylar, even though she did not judge the Son of Wind. She simply did not know how to interact with the awkwardness of unresolved conflict.

For Skylar's sake, she was grateful some did not shy away as she did. While delivering processed flax to Mistress Katie the other day, she discovered Fillion outside the Kane apartment. Oaklee had ducked behind a tree and listened as Fillion asked Skylar to join him for a walk. The Wind Element accepted with reluctance, and only with a hood over his head to hide most of his features. Before she departed, she heard Fillion say, "I get it. My community judges me because of Hanley. Being a political son is a shitty life. You can't hide, though. It only feeds the rumors."

Oaklee smiled with the memory, moved by Fillion's compassion as he drew Skylar out of the shadows. Since the day the two families departed the community, Fillion had risen as a visible leader. Rather than shrink away from accusations, both he and Leaf had established a time following evening meal in the Great Hall for residents to sit and process their fears and grief. As the New Eden Enterprises representative, Fillion was able to reassure many of their legal rights and allay their unfounded fears of the future. Jeff sat beside Fillion to further confirm the Outsider's statements.

Several times she had overheard villagers ask Fillion to use his magic to connect to their loved ones. But he refrained, kindly, with explanations that even though he was the Son of Eden, his magic had limitations and "summoning" was one of them. Messenger Pigeon was never offered as an alternative, a decision the new Elements agreed upon as the first generation already knew of this option and had chosen, from the beginning, to not exercise it. Emotions were simply too high and erratic, Leaf had explained. It was best to wait until the Second Phase and use the time they had now to establish trust between the community and new leadership.

Through it all, a confidence glowed on Fillion's countenance, a confidence she found alluring. He was a far different man than the one who had entered New Eden. Then again, she had changed much as well. Everyone had.

Over the last week, she and Fillion had grown comfortable together in casual conversation over meals and at the apartment. Often, he would sit beside her after evening sessions with the community and watch her hands work with one project or another, asking detailed questions about the process of her task. She had come to realize that his mind loathed the idea of rest and needed constant stimulation.

She, in turn, would listen to Fillion and Leaf debrief their evening sessions and pluck at ideas. Oaklee enjoyed Fillion's philosophical speeches, never tiring of his ability to reform thoughts, ideas, and long-held beliefs as if clay and he the artist, applying pressure here, carving away there, and pulling apart and fusing together pieces to make a new whole. His voice shifted from soft to biting, from warmth to a burning cold. With eyes closed, she was convinced his voice reflected a soul that was the very source of the wind, one that gently caressed topics or gusted personal convictions with passion. Often, Fillion would ask her to contribute her own thoughts, a consideration and level of respect never given her by another before. Leaf would listen to her responses with a small, proud smile, further bolstering her own confidence.

Both she and Fillion were ever so careful to establish physical distance since the day she sought his comfort. Though, if she were honest, she coveted his touch. Longed for it. Lately, she fell asleep to thoughts of what it would be like to know his love and love him in return. The forbidden thoughts shocked her, trepidation curling itself around her mind and heart. She did not wish for such intimacies, feared them actually. Curiosity still tempted, nonetheless.

Her mind was quickly running away from her, and she suppressed a sigh. Oaklee pulled her fingertips from The Forge's wall and tucked a strand of hair behind her ear, attempting to think of other things. But she could not. A deep voice rumbled nearby, just as she was about to round the corner, and Oaklee finally startled from her thoughts. She scanned the meadow and confirmed that nobody could see her. Eavesdropping was highly inconsiderate. Nevertheless, she pressed her body to the wall and listened upon recognizing her brother, although she could not make out his words.

"What sign shall I deliver?" Skylar asked, his voice hopeless. "All I have is my oath that I am not behind the rumors nor have I encouraged such sentiments. I am not your enemy, and I am honored to kneel before you, My King."

"Sky," Leaf sighed, "Please. We are alone. I grow weary of titles." Silence ticked to the rhythm of Oaklee's heartbeat. Her brother continued, "I am frightened, my family…"

"No harm shall come to them."

"You speak with such assurance."

"I speak as one who knows our community. They are confused, but I am unable to believe they would physically harm women and children."

"The community is far too influenced by fear and has already demonstrated irrational and dishonorable behavior." Leaf cleared his throat. "Fillion's team shall explore our concerns."

"You once asked me if I ever wondered how young men our age live beyond these panes." Skylar's voice cracked. "I replied that I did not, but it is not true. I know we are far different, and that truth shall destroy our generation. It already is in the process of doing so. We were never meant to survive on Earth."

They grew silent once more and Oaklee tensed as she considered Skylar's words. They were never meant to survive on Earth? The mystery of those words spooked her. Immediately thinking of Coal, she stole a glimpse of the geodesic sky as if the fractured panes held the answers. Another secret weighed upon her to consider, and the sudden heaviness exhausted what remained of her energy this day. She could not endure more changes, most especially after securing her footing upon the new path she trod. And what did her brother mean by Fillion's team?

"No matter what Fillion's team unearths or confirms," Leaf said, calm, steady, "I shall always remain your family, Sky. You stand upon your own merit. You are my brother."

"Leaf—"

"I shall not allow fear to destroy our home." The passion in Leaf's voice moved Oaklee with a surge of pride. "This may have begun as an experiment, but this is my life, and my mother and father both died so I may have it. They will not have died in vain."

"Spying?" a soft voice whispered into her ear. Oaklee jumped back and spun toward the source with a hand upon her chest. Fillion leaned a shoulder against the wall, placed a joint in his mouth and puffed, exhaling a thin stream away from her face.

"Of course not," she whispered back with an indignant huff, and lifted her chin. Shame burned through her at being caught, but she refused to entertain him.

"Nah, not your style. You prefer the more covert, stealthy approach of demanding information."

"I do no—" she replied louder than she intended and clapped a hand over her mouth. Fillion struggled to hide a smile, taking the basket of heckling combs from her hand.

"I'll put these away for you so you can get back to *not* spying," he said with a wink, the bored look on his face giving him away. He pushed off the wall and turned the corner toward Leaf and Skylar, tipping his head as he walked by them.

Irritated with Fillion's nettling, she clenched her fists and trailed after him, breezing by Leaf and Skylar without acknowledgement. From the corner of her eye, however, she noted the confused expression on her brother's face. But she continued to march toward The Forge. Narrowing her eyes, she opened the large doors, pausing only briefly for her sight to adjust.

Fillion continued to smile in that annoying, arrogant way of his, but did not acknowledge her entrance. He fidgeted with a sheet draped over a large object. Perplexed, she placed hands on hips and glared at him lest her irritation give way to another emotion entirely. Still, he ignored her. She took heavy steps to announce her presence, had he not noticed previously, and waited until he was impelled to look her way.

"Come to demand an explanation? The stomping was very sneaky. I'm impressed." His face remained inscrutable, but his eyes glinted with merriment.

"The meadow was empty," Oaklee said. "How did you come upon me?"

"You're not the only spy in New Eden." He looked away and picked at the sheet to hide his amusement. "But you're definitely the most formidable."

"Hardly. Where did you come from?"

"A ninja never reveals his secrets." Fillion stiffened and provided a quick, tight bow and uttered words in a language she could not understand.

"Pray tell, what is a ninja?" He just stared, quirking an eyebrow as if throwing the question back at her. Losing patience, she placed hands on hips once more, watching his

body shake with a low, quiet laugh. "Why do you enjoy vex-
ing me so?"

"I like sparring words with you." She pursed her lips
with this comment. "But mostly, you're cute when you're
mad."

"I am—" Her eyes grew wide and her mouth slackened
in disbelief. "I beg your pardon?"

"Granted. Although, I think you should really beg your
brother's pardon."

She sucked in an angry breath. "Fillion Nichols!"

He laughed and attempted to puff on his joint again, but
covered his mouth with the back of his hand in amusement,
instead. The joint dangled loosely from his fingers, and wispy
smoke danced until it disappeared into the shadows. Their
eyes found each other and his face relaxed as he took a step
toward her, blinking slowly to flirt with her temper.

Oaklee backed up, gasping when she pressed against a
workbench. The fire crackled and flickered amber hues across
his face, highlighting his dashing features. She leveled her
gaze, however, refusing to appear enfeebled, even though her
legs grew unsteady the closer he came. If he kissed her, she
feared she might actually faint. But, oh, how she hoped he
did!

When their toes touched, he whispered, "May I walk you
home?"

"Yes," she barely breathed in reply.

She should have said no to hold strong to her ire, but the
way he looked upon her melted every protest she possessed.
Her response pleased him, a reaction that should make her
cross. Instead, it pleased her as well.

A tiny smile touched the corner of his mouth and he
puffed on his joint. With suave movements, he pivoted on his
heel and strode toward the door.

Never had she given permission for a young man to escort her home until this moment. She did not possess romantic notions, or so she continued to reason within herself. Although, she was not the same young woman who once made

such firm declarations. Girlhood faded into the memories that existed before her father died. Even her tempestuous nature had dimmed considerably. Oaklee removed her apron and attempted to smooth her hair, blowing at the flyaway strands framing her face.

The door creaked open and Fillion held it for her as she slipped through and into the twilight of evening, lacing her cloak as she walked. Skylar still stood in the shadows with Leaf, hood covering his face, and she attempted to appear natural as she stepped onto the main pathway toward the forest.

"We'll meet you at the apartment," Fillion called over his shoulder.

Leaf squinted his eyes as he looked between them. "Take the path along the village." Oaklee turned several shades of red when her brother delivered a subtle warning look as she did not have a proper chaperone.

"Is Laurel still at the Hansens?" she asked with a shaky smile.

"Ember fetched her already." Leaf bowed to her. "I shall see you at home *shortly.*" He said the last word with a pointed look at Fillion.

"Yes, Your Majesty." She curtsied and studied Skylar as she said, "My Lord." Skylar dipped his head, and she was unsure if it was to honor her in return or to further hide his crestfallen features.

The biodome was strangely quiet this evening. Not even a bio-breeze touched the leaves or inspired the trees to dance. The forest, however, blushed with the heat of autumn's ardor. Such passions swept away her imagination and the magic infused her thoughts. A canopy of reds and oranges blazed above their heads as they edged the woods and walked beside the apartments. The serenity of their surroundings wrapped around her and a contented sigh passed her lips.

A young lad, chased by two others, ran by and the cool air of their wake caressed her skin. She rubbed her arms, preoccupied with her thoughts and her surroundings, and unwittingly gained Fillion's attention. His face was unreadable yet tense, and he studied her eyes as if in search of direction. He looked so lost, so young, a lad in search of safety and comfort. She had thought him older than Leaf, but in this moment, his youthfulness baffled her previous perceptions.

"This may seem a strange question," Oaklee began. "But, what is your age?"

"Seventeen."

"Truly?"

"Truly." A small, humored smile played across his features. "Older than you thought?"

"No, My Lord. Much younger. I thought you at least five-and-twenty or so."

"Sorry to disappoint you."

"I am not disappointed," she replied softly, turning her head toward the forest and securing her cloak tight around her shoulders. "It is a comfort to know we are closer in age. When do you turn eighteen?"

"March."

"I turn sixteen on the morrow." Oaklee focused on the leaf-littered floor, embarrassed by her nervous banter. It felt childish to volunteer such information.

"Truth or dare?"

"Pardon? What a strange question." He waited for her reply, his eyes begging her to choose. "Very well. Truth."

"If you could have anything from my world, what would it be?"

"China silk in the shade of wood violets." Oaklee smiled into her shoulder. "I have read that silk is luxuriously soft and shimmers under candlelight as if the surface of water." His face remained unreadable. "Do you possess a garment made from silk?"

"My sister and mom have silk dresses."

"Perhaps it is a silly request as I am sure there are ever so many exotic sundries to choose from," she said, fidgeting with the edge of her cloak.

"No, it suits you."

Oaklee sighed. "To own a silk garment with matching ribbons in such a pretty color would be a lovely extravagance." She hugged her arms over her chest and swayed back and forth. Fillion regarded her with a faint smile, and she instantly felt ridiculous for her confession. His dark mahogany strands gently stirred in the breeze and she creased her brows. "Your hair is different from when I saw you through the portal. How is that possible?"

"Hair dye, like how you color linen or wool."

"Really?" Oaklee's eyes widened in wonder and she looked at his hands, touching his fingertips. A jolt of pleasure pulsed through her with the contact. Nevertheless, in a clear voice, she continued, "And your nails are no longer black."

"Just paint."

"I feared you had contracted a horrible Outsider disease, which blackened your nails and streaked your hair blue." Fillion burst into laughter. Oaklee rolled her eyes and waited for him to finish, raising an eyebrow in mock irritation. "I suppose the piercings and the ash around your eyes did not indicate savagery?" A fresh wave of laughter rolled through him. "Fillion!"

"Savagery?" he said while attempting a straight face. He puffed on his joint to hide his smile. "God, that made my night."

"I was terrified of you."

He touched her forearm and leaned in close to where she stood and whispered, "Still terrified?"

She replied in a breathy whisper, "No, My Lord." A distraction was needed before she was reduced to a puddle at his feet. Lost for direction, she blurted, "Truth or dare," cringing with what she had done.

"Dare," Fillion answered quickly with an impish grin.

"Oh." Oaklee looked around for inspiration. "The proper answer is truth."

"Not with those two choices."

"I am not familiar with this diversion." She knew he was grinning in that irritating way of his. "I *dare* you to answer this," she said with a slight lift of her chin. "If you could possess any profession, which would it be?"

"Musician." He lifted the hood to his cloak and studied the apartments. "I've played classical guitar since I was five. Part of a youth orchestra once, too. I own a few guitars, from a traditional six string all the way up to a twenty string."

Oaklee bit down on her lip nervously. "What, pray tell, is a guitar?"

"Similar to a lute and guittern."

"Shall you play for me sometime?"

He lifted both shoulders and looked away once more. "Sometime."

"And do you also sing?"

"Maybe."

Oaklee studied his hand as he lifted the joint, and contemplated the magic he wielded and imagined the music he created. Perhaps this was why he often leaned against the wall near the musicians during Sunday feasts? And why he tapped his fingers against his thigh or on a table? His answer was rather astonishing and insightful.

Enjoying their camaraderie, she asked, "What does your name mean?"

"You ask a lot of questions."

"Oh, is it your turn? My apologies."

"Just kidding." He slid a sly look her direction. "I don't think my name has a meaning."

"I have thought of your name—"

"You think of me?" That teasing smile reappeared.

"Your *name*," she said with a huff. "I believe it is Old French for son."

His expression sobered and his eyes glinted with a multitude of thoughts once more. Silence followed and Fillion puffed on his joint, eyebrows drawn together. They continued their stroll along the apartments and Willow nibbled on her bottom lip nervously. Had she said something upsetting? His moods had a tendency to swing at the blink of an eye, similar

473

to her, actually. It was refreshing to be in the company of someone who was acquainted with strong emotions.

"Willow." Fillion paused and stared at the fiery path of leaves. When he spoke again, his voice strained and she barely heard him. "Why did you reject Coal?"

The question was most unexpected, and she fidgeted with the ties of her cloak. "He was restless," she said, "and wished for adventure, and I knew I would never be enough for him."

He whispered, "You love him?"

"Yes," she said. "But not in the way I believe you are asking."

Fillion nodded his head, his eyes still focused upon the path. "Mack shares that he's fitting in pretty well. Thought you'd like to know."

"He is happy?"

"Yes." Fillion finally looked at her, concern darkening his countenance. "Seems he has a thing for my sister, too."

"A thing?"

"Um … affection."

"Truly?" Oaklee slowed her steps as the muscles in her stomach clenched. For a moment, anger coated every thought. She touched her lips and turned her head away from Fillion, confused. In a soft voice she continued, "Thank you, My Lord. Your sister is blessed if she returns his affection. He is a good man." Then, she lifted her chin and picked up the pace of her walk. After all, she was the one who refused him, nor did she possess romantic inclinations for the Son of Fire.

Fillion studied her profile. "I was worried." He released a nervous breath. "I wasn't sure if I should say anything."

"You are kind to concern yourself with my welfare."

"I'll always be concerned for your welfare." His face darkened once more. "You're part of my inheritance, remember?"

"You are part of mine as well, Son of Eden." She stopped and faced him. "We are bonded."

He flinched. "We should keep walking."

Their footfalls shuffled the leaves and, on occasion, Fillion would lightly kick up a flurry. A strange and uncomfortable silence brewed between them and Oaklee failed to ascertain why his mood shifted once again. She peered at him through lowered lashes and asked, "Have I offended you, My Lord?"

"God, no." The anguished look on his face did not match his sentiments, so she stepped in front of him. "Willow, please." His eyes reddened and he tensed his face again.

A family stared at them through their window and Oaklee lowered her head to maintain propriety and said, "I do not think little of you for your position or mine."

"How are we to do this?" He threw his joint down on the ground and rubbed it into the brittle leaves. "I wish I was just a boy and you were just a girl and our lives added up to only that—just us. But we're not, and there can be no us. Ever. It'll *never* work. I'll *never* be around. Our relationship is nothing but *nevers*. You're essentially my employee, right? But, until then, you're Hanley's and he … he…"

"Come, My Lord. We have an audience."

Oaklee resumed a leisurely pace along the path and warmed with thoughts of his declaration. The village path looped through a small copse of trees and she slowed her pace, relishing the privacy the alcove afforded.

At that moment, something caught Fillion's eye and he walked away a few steps. Crouching down, he lifted a leaf and stared at a tree frog, angling his head to get a closer look. How had he seen the small, camouflaged creature amongst the fall foliage? With a single finger he stroked the back of the frog, then carefully replaced the leaf atop the small amphibian once more.

The dichotomy of his personality never failed to intrigue her. One moment he used vulgar language and behaved with flippancy. And the next, he showed respect and wonder to some of the smallest details of life. He oscillated between not caring and caring too much. Fillion slowly stood, and stared out into the woods.

"Have you ever wondered how this world feels so real when it's all fake?"

"How can I, when I have never known any other world?" Oaklee folded her hands in her lap and straightened her posture. "Am I fake to you?"

His shoulders sagged with a heavy breath. "That's not what I meant. God, I wish I hadn't tossed out that joint." Fillion scuffed at the leaves until the earth emerged. "Why does everything have to be an illusion? We are born into a world and into a culture we have no control over. From our first breath we have zero control, right?"

"Yes, in those ways, I suppose."

"What we can't control defines us, shapes us, makes us, breaks us, torments us." Fillion looked up at the geodesic sky. "I'm rich. I'm worth so much money it's asinine. People want me because of my price tag. And if they can't have a piece of me, then they want to be me, idolizing my every move. I did nothing to earn that money. Nothing. Yet, I'm defined by it. And I'm going to die one day, just like the unlucky bastards who've eaten scraps from a commercial compost bin their whole life. Who assigned that value system? Who decided that I'm more important than the person who lives their life hungry and cold?"

"I cannot say, My Lord." Oaklee nibbled on her bottom lip as she watched him struggle. People live entire lives hungry and cold? The very thought grieved her conscience and she swallowed back the guilt of living such a plentiful life. The Outside world seemed frightening to her, yet again.

"I'm trapped," he continued. With distracted movements, he snapped a twig off a tree and rolled it between his fingers. "I know I own my life, but I feel like I have no control. None."

Fillion finally looked at her again. Intensity shone from his eyes as he searched hers. "All I want is you," he whispered. A delirious rush stilled the air in her lungs. "I want to be with you, kiss you until you can't think straight, then kiss you some more, and argue with you until life has the last word. But it never matters what I want. Ever. This," he said, gesturing at something between them, "is an illusion. It's a dream, not reality. Like New Eden."

Sensations fluttered through her body and she grew faint at the mere thought of kissing. "We are not an illusion, My Lord," she somehow managed to say. Oaklee fidgeted with the strings of her cloak once more and said, "I welcome your pursuit."

He closed his eyes tight and dragged his fingers through his hair. Slowly, his eyes opened and he peered up through the branches. "I just don't know how to do this." His voice cracked as he spoke. "Any relationship I pursue with you will end in pain, for both of us. I couldn't live with myself if Hanley harmed you because of me."

She knew of what he spoke, having overheard Fillion and Leaf discuss their predicament during a few late-night evenings. Clenching and unclenching her fists, she blurted, "You are not responsible for your father's actions!"

"This affects more than us," Fillion said softly. "The community needs your family. I'm making this choice for you and New Eden."

"Ridiculous," Oaklee spat. "Hanley places my family in his Legacy and then punishes us for existing? I struggle to comprehend how he could be so heartless as to reduce my family to the equivalent of slaves. For who treats another with such cold indifference, as if they are property to do with what they will?"

"You exist because of Hanley, never forget that. The second gen is the product of human manipulation," Fillion said, more derisively than she expected. "You're a character to entertain scientific theories. Everything about your life is built on lies. I tried to tell you and Leaf this before."

"Well, I refuse to cower before Hanley." Oaklee flared with indignation and clenched her fists once more. "Your father shall not manipulate my home anymore."

A bitter smile curled Fillion's lips. "He's not my father. He's my employer."

Oaklee had never heard of a child denouncing their parentage. Her eyes rounded as she considered the implications and his confessions. Heartbroken, she laced her fingers with his; and he stared at their knotted hands. "The day you arrived in New Eden," she began softly, "you asked me to grieve for both of us. Do you remember?" He nodded. "If I could, I would steal your pain. You are worth every sorrow and hardship I would endure."

A single, angry tear crawled down Fillion's cheek and he quickly wiped it away. "Everything about you," he whispered, "is beautiful."

"Fillion Nichols, your name is carved into the boughs of my heart. I am yours, and *nothing* shall ever alter this truth."

His entire countenance reflected serenity as her words sank in, like that of a weary traveler who had, at long-last, crossed the threshold of his home after a lifetime in search of where he belonged. She did not wish to cry—tired of all the tears, actually—but she was moved by the honor of being his refuge. However, the sense of belonging disappeared a moment later, eclipsed by confusion.

"God, Willow," he choked out. "You're the *only* reality I wish I knew." Fillion tensed and his face hardened with angry tears once more. "But I don't know how to gain control to make it happen. Hell, I'm not sure how to keep New Eden from project shutdown. I promised Leaf. In a moment when I was emotionally wrecked, I gave Leaf my oath that Hanley wouldn't lay a finger on his family." Fillion shook his head. "I can't control Hanley. Shit, I don't know how to control my own life."

"You do not break an oath by trying—"

"You're going to hate me one day." Fillion drew in a shaky breath.

Oaklee's mouth slackened. "How could you say such a thing? You accuse me of cheapening you with false pledges when I have only proved myself faithful to you."

"I don't know what to do!" He shouted and tossed the twig. "I can't give you what you want! I can't give myself what I want! And I'm going out of my freaking mind!"

"Please, do not be angry with me. I could not bear it." Their atmosphere around them tightened, a taut string ready to snap with the slightest provocation. Gently, she lowered the hood hiding his face and he tensed even more. "I desire predictability," she continued. "But I belong to a future I cannot control, either. I am subject to the winds of change, which gusts entirely from the cardinal direction of New Eden Enterprises.

"You are my prince," she said, breathless, fingering her father's token tucked into his belt. "One day, when owner, you shall be my King. I am confused as to why, with such power, you are unable to make a reality of your choosing?"

"Because any power I get from Hanley is an illusion, even ownership of all this." He gestured to indicate the bio-domes. "I've been manipulated and groomed my whole life. I'm a tool, and it will be under my ownership that New Eden will disband. Ever thought of that? I get to be the bad guy, and Hanley walks away on top." Fillion moved away. "But if you have ideas, don't hold back."

Oaklee studied the way the evening light dappled across his features as his eyes roamed the wooded trail. Ideas swirled inside her head and she attempted to concentrate. Although, with the intensity of emotions storming around him, it was difficult. Then, with a start, she stepped before him. "Is there a way for your mother to meet Leaf before the Second Phase? If your mother truly held affection for my father, then surely she would not allow any harm to come to our family. It was my father's dying wish for my brother to seek Della, actually."

"What ... what did you say?"

"I wonder if there is a way for your mother—"

"No, I heard you." His eyes widened. "Damn. That's brilliant. She's here at N.E.T. according to the latest message on your brother's Scroll." He stared at Oaklee in awe and she blinked with modesty, focusing her attention on a lacy, brittle leaf upon the forest floor. "I should have thought of that." He continued in a droll tone, "You make me stupid. It's an ongoing problem."

"You are far from stupid, My Lord. I admire your intelligence." She twirled a strand of hair as thoughts pulled her even deeper. "Perhaps your *employer's* power is simply an illusion, and he has accomplished nothing more than fooling you into submission. For how can one man truly control so much?" She lifted her eyes. "I am *real*, a truth he shall never bend. Nor can he control our affection. Do you feel the invisible thread that stitches our lives together?"

"Yeah." A timid smile tugged on his lips as the toe of his shoe pushed leaves around aimlessly. "It's like quantum entanglement. What happens to one is experienced by the other. Regardless of time and space." He paused a beat. "Even death."

"The son of Della and the daughter of Joel." She stared out into the forest to hide the blush and whispered, "Our relationship is meant to be full of forevers, not nevers." Oaklee folded her hands at her waist and squared her shoulders. "So, how do you plan to seize control and make your own reality, Dungeon Master?"

"You're a brat, you know it?" A corner of his mouth lifted.

"You like it," she replied, hoping she sounded like him.

"I do. It turns me on. *You* turn me on." Fillion bit his bottom lip and she lowered her eyes. "Be warned, though. Once you start thinking of me, there'll be no saving you."

Oaklee rolled her eyes as he quietly laughed. "Perhaps I do not wish to be saved."

"Damsel in distress much?" He lifted an eyebrow.

"Only when I am with you."

"What?" He laughed. "Ouch."

"It is a trouble most welcome." Warmth threatened to suffuse her face and neck with her wanton behavior. Nevertheless, she maintained a level gaze.

A gentle breeze swept by, feathering strands of dark hair across his eyes. The often rumpled tresses had grown in the last month, a look she found rugged and handsome. After a few long heartbeats, he leaned close, hovering dangerously close to her mouth. "Distressed?" he asked in a seductive voice, his body nearly touching hers.

Her heart faltered with the soft tones, and she grew faint as his breath whispered longings to her lips. The energy, so often present between them, crackled and sparked. She waited for him to kiss her, her body demanding more breath with each heartbeat, and still, he did not. Distressed indeed, she mused to herself. She would not allow him to win so easily, though. Nor could she live with herself should she succumb to swooning. The very thought irked her more stubborn sensibilities.

"Do not flatter yourself, Dungeon Master," she riposted and sauntered past him and out of the trees. Once upon the path, she whipped his direction with a celebratory smile.

He relaxed into an aloof posture and moved toward her as if a predator on the prowl, slow, careful, the sleek confidence and smug satisfaction an intimidating vision to behold. When he reached her, she drew to full height and refused to back down, even though every part of her quivered with his nearness. And he knew it. But he only stared, unmoving, his body perfectly still as if lying in wait.

She grew weary of his arrogance and sighed with impatience, a sound that set him in motion. He leaned forward until his warm breath tickled her ear. In gritty tones, he whispered, "Run." A shiver of delight shuddered through her as he straightened. And his slight, imperious grin widened into something altogether wicked. Then, he pounced.

Oaklee squealed and bounded out of his grasp. Without a moment's hesitation, she scooped up a handful of leaves and threw them in his face. The autumn flurry bought her a small measure of time, and she dashed down the trail, her laughter escalating with anticipation. He eventually passed her, sticking out his tongue and laughing at the angry look she threw his way. When the stairway leading to her apartment appeared around the bend, Fillion grabbed her hand and sprinted off of the trail and into the forest. Oaklee giggled as he leaned her against a yew tree, the long, lacy boughs dipping to the forest floor.

Their eyes locked, chests heaving, and then he kissed her laughter until she was truly breathless. Fervor swelled and pulsed as his lips moved across hers. He buried his hands into her hair, gripping fistful of strands, then trailed finger tips down her neck in whisper-soft motions. A warm drizzle of emotion, sweet like honey, poured over her in a languid, tantalizing flow. His caresses were soft and yearning, his kisses tender and provocative, and Willow surrendered every beat of her heart to him.

The memory of his breathy whispers to drink up and drink fast danced across her mind. Their stolen time was precious. It was a thought Fillion apparently shared, and Willow swayed when he broke away, completely and utterly drunk on him. Each limb tingled and her head swam as she marinated in one pleasurable rush after another. Her legs eventually grew unsteady, and she fell back against the tree in reverie, succumbing to the lightheadedness that claimed her entire body.

Fillion blinked, slow and lazy, unable to hide from his eyes a similar intoxication, and said, "Just like kissing the surface of the sun."

His thumb brazenly grazed along her bottom lip and her eyes slid shut, weighted by pleasure. This was the very definition of bliss, she decided. His body shifted closer, his breath pulsing with hers, just as a bird nearby flapped noisily off of a branch. Her eyes flew open. Fillion whipped his head toward the path, and the hand cupping her face dropped back to his side.

"We should start walking."

She sighed with resignation. "I feel as though my legs might fail me." A ghost of a smile teased his lips with her confession. "Do not let it go to your head," she said.

"Say it."

Willow shook her head while restraining her mirth. He leaned forward until they were eye to eye, a mischievous gleam in his steady gaze, irritating her.

"Say. It."

She loosed a heavy sigh and lifted her chin. "I am distressed."

"Pretty much." She pushed him with a harrumph and flounced out of the forest and back onto the path. Fillion grinned and jogged after her, weaving his fingers with hers. "The feelings are mutual," he said, ending with a wink.

Oh, how that smile destroyed every effort to remain strong! Nevertheless, Willow cast him a sidelong glance. "Once you start thinking of me, there will be no saving you."

"Perhaps I don't wish to be saved."

As soon as the words left his mouth, he sobered, and the anguish he expressed earlier returned. She squeezed his hand and he squeezed back, but both avoided eye contact. They walked a small ways in thick silence when a yellow leaf, perfectly golden, spiraled through the air, as if nature honored her—honored them. Fillion reached out and plucked the leaf from its graceful descent and brought it to his lips. Then, he placed the golden token into his pocket.

Under the linden tree
on the heath
where we two had our bed,
you might find both beautiful
flattened flowers and grass.
At the edge of the wood in the valley,
tandaradei,
The nightingale sang beautifully.

I came walking
to the meadow,
where my sweetheart had come.
There I was received
oh honored woman!
So that I forever happy was.
Did he kiss me? A thousand times!
Tandaradei!
Look how red my mouth is!

There he made
in joyful haste
a bed of flowers for us both,
that must still cause a knowing smile
to those who find it in their path,
and see the spot, where, on that day,
tandaradei,
My head among the roses lay.

How shamed were I if anyone,
God forbid, would know
that he had romanced me!
There we two lay,
but that was known
to none except my love and I,
and the little nightingale,
tandaradei,
who, I know, will tell no tale."

— Walter von der Vogelweide, "Under the Linden Tree," 12th century
A.D. *

CHAPTER THIRTY

Portland, Oregon

T he car rolled to a stop and Coal fidgeted in his seat. The blindfold dug into his skin. But he remained still, even when a gift he pocketed for Lynden, prior to their leaving Seattle this afternoon, poked him through the jeans.

Since they had reached the Portland train station, he had been subjected to one of Lynden's games. He could not refuse, though. The vulnerability in her eyes while she brimmed with nonchalant excitement—she had truly perfected the art of bored playfulness—silenced the protests that nearly fell from his tongue.

A hand touched his thigh and traveled to his knee, and his skin startled into goosebumps. "We're here," Lynden said into his neck. She lifted her head from his shoulder and fussed with the blindfold on his eyes, tightening it even further, then moved away from him. Although he was blindfolded, Coal closed his eyes, his entire being pulsing to life under her touch. "Wait for us," she said to the town car driver. "We'll only be an hour. I'll make it worth your while."

"Yes, Ms. Nichols," the driver responded, and Coal could almost see the man bobbing his head with eager anticipation of the monetary reward.

"All right, Mr. Awesome. Keep your head down."

"Do we jump onto the road?" He offered a charming smile.

"Nope. We crawl."

He remained motionless for a moment. "You wish for me to crawl across the road? Are you mad?" When she didn't reply right away, he pressed his lips together. "Surely there is another way to journey toward this intrigue you play."

"Maybe. It'll cost you, though."

"Name your price."

She touched the black ribbon still tied around his wrist. "I ask for a favor."

"Now?"

"No, whenever."

"I see." A slow smile crept up his face. "You are a tiresome faerie, but I will consent."

"Walk," she replied simply, as if bored already.

Coal kept his head down and exited the car, squinting against the light, even through the blindfold. He had been shielded from light so long, his eyes had grown far too sensitive.

"Do you still wish to remain in my world?"

"Yes," he breathed in reply, almost irritated.

"You might be wishing for a lifetime of regrets." She took his hand and led him a few steps before his shoe touched a curb. He lifted his foot and continued beside Lynden on the sidewalk.

"The same could be true about returning to New Eden."

"Last chance. You sure?"

"Lyn, what is this about?" Frustrated, Coal tugged on the blindfold, but she grabbed his hand. "I have not looked upon a single thing since Union Station."

She flicked the strands of hair falling over his covered eye. "I didn't want to make it harder on you and just realized my idea may be sucky like that."

"I have blindly followed you thus far, and for a second time no less." Coal crossed his arms over his chest. "How will I then convince you that I *wish* to remain in your world? Shall I fall upon my knees and plead my case until I receive your benevolent mercy?" His arms fell back to his sides. "I grow weary of this question."

Lynden released an annoyed sound from the back her throat rather than verbally reply. But a few seconds later she said, "Look, I've traveled a lot. Visited many places. Still, nothing compares to home. When you go back to New Eden for your goodbyes, you'll understand what I mean." She caressed two of his fingers like she wished to take his hand, then pulled away.

A car whizzed by and the wake of its passing made their garments rustle against their bodies. She remained quiet, and he refused to play to her insecurities. After a few, long agonizing seconds, her fingers, cold to the touch, grabbed the edges of the blindfold and pulled it over his head. Her hands hooked around his neck as she lowered her arms, and she nibbled on her lip ring. Their eyes locked and he remained unwavering, holding his ground until she looked away.

"Ready?" She dropped her arms and focused on a light blue house, austere in appearance compared to Lynden's and Mack's homes. The neighborhood was quaint, dotted with trees and small flower gardens. A waist-high, white posted fence framed the modest yard, with a gate beneath an arbor covered in a giant tangle of vines. "This is the surprise."

"A house?" He turned her direction with confusion.

"Your grandma's house."

Air left his body as the shock settled in his gut. "My father's parents died several years ago."

"Your mom's mom."

His eyes widened and he blinked back the surprise, slowly turning toward the blue house. "I have family here..." Elation, fear, and relief curled their way through him as his mind struggled to comprehend the moment. "I contain no adequate words." Coal swiveled toward Lynden and lifted his hand to caress her cheek, and decided last minute to pull away, suddenly feeling shy. "You possess the loveliest heart."

Lynden nibbled on her lip ring again and gently took hold of the chain dangling across his thigh. "Come on, Mr. Awesome. We don't have much time."

They walked through the gate and were approaching the front landing when the door opened. An older woman, with reddish gray hair, greeted them with a cautious smile. First, her eyes rested on Lynden. Small, wrinkly hands brushed across the simple clothing, clinging to the older woman's frail, wiry frame, as she ironed out imaginary imperfections while appraising the younger woman by his side. Coal forgot that Lynden was viewed as quasi-royalty, referred to by the world as the Eco-Princess. Warm brown eyes traveled his direction and rested upon his face next. She placed a hand to her chest and remained very still.

"Coal Hansen?" Her voice carried a genteel element, soft yet confident, reminiscent of Ember.

"Yes, Madam." Coal bowed, feeling a light thump against his thigh as Lynden released the chain. "It is a great honor to meet you."

"Your voice... You sound so British. Not what I was expecting."

She had not seen his interviews?

Beckoning with her hand, his grandmother said "Please, come in."

They crossed the threshold into her home and Coal studied the clean, mostly empty space. A scratched dining table with two mismatched chairs nestled against a wall near the kitchen. The entry shared location with the living room, showcasing a single blue divan, a weathered end table, and a small Imigicast. A tear in a back cushion of the divan revealed a white, cottony substance, and Coal felt a lump in his chest. Digital pictures lined the walls, images fading into other images every few seconds. Dark curtains draped to the floor and were pulled tight against the remaining traces of evening light.

His grandmother flitted across the room and toward the kitchen in a dither, over what he knew not. "Make yourself at home. You want a pop? I have Coke or root beer."

"Sure. I'll take a Coke," Lynden said, glancing around at the sparse furnishings.

"Have a seat on the couch." Before they could even sit, her voice rang out from the kitchen once more. "Coal, do you want a pop?"

"Water, please." He sipped a carbonated beverage once and shuddered with the memory. Coal lowered onto the couch, realizing, with shame, that he did not know his grandmother's name. He turned toward Lynden and whispered, "What shall I call her?"

She lifted an eyebrow. "Grandma."

"No," he laughed softly. "I do not know her first name." Just then, his grandmother entered the living room, handing him and Lynden their beverages.

"Thanks, Sarah."

"Of course, Ms. Nichols."

Flitting across the room again, she grabbed a chair from the kitchen and began dragging it toward the living room. Her thin arms shook, the chair landing with a soft thud onto the carpet when she lowered it to catch her breath. Coal thrust his glass of water into Lynden's hands and strode to the nook area, taking the chair from her hands.

"Allow me," he said simply. She released the chair and he carried it effortlessly toward the old, worn divan. "Please, sit beside Lynden and I shall enjoy this seat."

"Next to Ms. Nichols?" Her eyes grew wide, and she swept a nervous look around her house.

"I don't bite." Lynden nearly rolled her eyes and leaned back against the divan, holding out the glass of water to Coal.

"You have a beautiful home. The couch is very cozy."
Lynden patted a spot next to where she sat.

"Thank you," Sarah responded, quiet, dubious. She sat
beside Lynden and met Coal's waiting gaze. "I can't believe
you're here."

"Nor I." Coal smiled kindly, chancing a look at Lynden.
"Ms. Nichols surprised me when she called yesterday."

"Yes, she is quite fond of surprises."

"I wish I was available sooner, but I had to work. I'm
afraid to miss a day. I guess it worked out, though, since Ms.
Nichols had school." She chuckled nervously, staring at her
hands.

Silence fell upon them like a gentle weight. Coal sipped
the water, his attention roaming back toward the digital photo
frames on the wall. Captured memories, both happy and formal, greeted his curiosity as unknown faces and family smiled
from the digital surface.

What was it like to possess such a wealth of reminders
when those you love are gone?

Many times Coal wished he possessed photographs of
those he left behind and lost in New Eden, believing it would
comfort the ache. And yet, sometimes, he wondered if it
would only increase the longing. Perhaps fading images protected the heart and allowed it to continue on.

"That's your mother," Sarah volunteered as a picture surfaced of a young woman with light blond hair, similar to his
own, and bright blue eyes. "She had what I called 'wounded
critter' syndrome. Her heartstrings were easily pulled and
she'd give the shirt off her back to help another. Such a compassionate soul."

"My older sister, Ember, is similar in nature." Coal
smiled politely as his fingers fidgeted around the cup and he
shifted in the chair.

"She met your father at the Emerald City Comicon, and
they married three weeks later in Vegas." Sarah lost focus as
she stared past Coal's face. "I was so angry with her. Such a
foolish, dumb thing to do. But she met someone as impulsive

and spontaneous as her." A quiet laugh left the elderly woman and Coal took another sip on his water.

How did one reply to such a statement?

He knew not.

"Connor looked like a puppy dog, happily trailing behind Cami everywhere she went," she continued, her voice growing distant. "I thought for sure my daughter was a rebound relationship. I heard he had a nasty breakup a few months before with another young woman, named Brianna, I think. Anyway. I was convinced the wounded critter syndrome had finally ruined my daughter's life." Sarah's gaze traveled back to Coal. "And, too, I believed she was star-struck. You see, she watched 'Eco-Crafting Eden' religiously and Connor was a King in that. That's why they met. He was part of an exhibition at Comicon."

Coal stiffened and Lynden shot him a worried look.

"Cami was insistent, though. They were in love." Sarah studied Coal's face, her sadness etched into every wrinkle. "A year after they married, she signed up to join New Eden Township. Connor didn't want to. He made it known that he had no desire to be part of his friend's 'latest scheme' and wanted to move on with his life, to be part of the real world." His grandmother cast a nervous glance toward Lynden, then continued. "But, like a puppy dog, he trailed after Cami into the biodome when he found out what she had done, and I never saw my impulsive, caring, fun-loving daughter ever again."

Coal placed the glass of water onto the carpet and took his grandmother's hands in his. "She and my father were very much in love from the stories I have heard. He still mourns her death to this day." He studied their hands, one large and calloused, the other soft and wrinkled. "I wish I knew her. There is not a day that goes by where I do not ponder the woman who lost her life so I may have it. I carry shame over my birth, even though I know I am not truly at fault."

"What a beautiful thing to say." Sarah squeezed Coal's hand and let go, and tensed against the forming emotions. "I see her face in yours. Maybe it's her soul."

"I shall hold such comforting thoughts close to my heart," he whispered.

"Tell me about your sister?" Sarah asked, wiping away a tear. "You are twins?"

"Yes. Ember is kind to a fault, always wise, insightful, and fiercely protective. Often I am surprised when her temper emerges when defending someone she loves." Coal gently laughed. "We are nothing alike. She is shorter than I, with curly, strawberry blond hair. We do share eyes, noses, and the famed Hansen dimple, though."

"Oh, yes." His grandmother laughed, a lovely sound once more reminding Coal of his sister. "Your father could charm a snake with that smile." Coal grinned and Lynden lowered her eyes, playing with the ring on her thumb. She angled her head toward the kitchen while casually sipping on her Coke. Sarah looked over at Lynden, then back at Coal. "If you're anything like Connor, it's probably a necessary form of protection."

Coal smiled wider. "Indeed."

"Do you have any other pictures?" Both Coal and his grandmother turned to Lynden.

"Yes. Let me get them."

Sarah eased out of the divan, pausing to get her bearings. Coal came to a stand in response, years of training as a gentleman springing into action out of habit. His grandmother gave him a curious look and then padded across the living room, disappearing down a hallway.

When alone, he chanced a look at Lynden and said, "Rather trite, but *thank you*."

A small, bashful smile broke through the aloof countenance. "We need to leave in a half-hour," she said, taking another sip of her Coke. He nodded and rose from his seat once more when his grandmother returned.

"Sit down," Sarah said, dismissing him with a wave of her hand. "Don't fuss over me. Here."

A strange, rolled up device was offered to him. He curled his fingers around the furled metal. "What is this called?"

"A Scroll. They've been obsolete for almost as long as you've been alive, but all my pictures are on there and I'm too lazy to move them over to a cloud file. Feel free to email any photos to yourself."

He pushed the button and it unclasped and flattened out onto his lap. This was a piece of technology he was not familiar with. Nevertheless, he recognized the power button and pushed it. A screen lit up and he marveled at how it curved and rippled with movement. The start screen stared back at him a few seconds later and he handed it back to Sarah so she could enter her password.

"Just swipe 'camihansen,' one word."

A wistful smile touched his lips as he obeyed the instructions.

Was his grandmother alone?

Did she have any other family?

Once he passed the security screen, he looked up for direction.

"Select the 'gallery' icon. The pictures will appear next."

Time passed in a merry blur as he eventually squeezed between Lynden and his grandmother on the tiny divan, scanning through her large collection of photographs. She shared stories and memories, and he soaked them up until he was so full he feared he would overflow with a multitude of bittersweet emotions. He especially loved seeing younger pictures of his father, and those of The Elements as well. Lynden rose from the divan sometime later, and Coal swallowed against a sudden tightness in his throat.

"Hey, we need to get going. Volo Rail waits for no man." Lynden looked to Sarah. "Sorry. We have another appointment."

Coal offered his hand to help his grandmother stand. "May I visit you again?"

"I would like that. Cami was all I had left in the world."

The number of divorces and broken families never ceased to shock Coal. "We are family," he said, covering her hand with both of his. "I shall make way to Portland again and see you."

They stared at one another and Coal felt awkward, never having much practice in the art of goodbyes. In a moment of courage, he folded the small frame of his grandmother into his arms and held her close. With stiff, awkward movements, he pulled away and strode toward the door and out into the front yard. The town car driver opened a door for Lynden, who slid into the backseat. Coal lifted his hand in farewell once more. A strange ache in his chest persisted, even after the driver closed the door and Coal had settled beside Lynden. Partings and distances were still difficult concepts for him to digest and, sometimes, he wondered if they always would be.

The car rolled away a few moments later and Coal released a pent-up breath. Lynden fell against the door and stared out the window once they were alone, careful to keep her distance from him. In a way, he was grateful. His mind and heart were too full, and he desired to think over the stories and pictures in solitude.

The sun lowered behind the foothills and cityscape just as he and Lynden arrived at Union Station. The old brick building served the original rail station as well as the new high-speed rail. Bronze and coral glinted off the tinted windows of the magnetic levitation train, reflections of a sleepy sky chasing its celestial pillow to the other side of the world.

They boarded the maglev in silence and sauntered toward a private cabin. She had reserved the cabin when purchasing their tickets that morning under a pseudonym and paying entirely in cash, ensuring the media was not alerted of their whereabouts. So far, the plan had worked. The thin metal door slid closed behind them, and she slumped onto a seat against the window, placing her forehead onto the glass, just as before. He watched her, grabbing a pole near a seat when the train took off. Within a minute, they traveled at high speed above the landscape on a twin track.

The city, trees, and setting sun whirred by at, what felt like, the speed of his pulse, and he whispered, "Lynden," and realized he had spoken his thought aloud. His heart and head were full of her, a growing affection that consumed him night and day. In fact, the swelling emotions felt close to a form of insanity at times. She lifted her head from its resting place and peered at him. Their gazes collided and she blinked, the veneer of indifference falling away for a moment.

Coal studied her face, enjoying how the light reflected tiny flecks of gold in her hazel eyes. Faint freckles danced across her skin; and he thought of how Norah often proclaimed to her children that freckles were the product of faerie kisses, especially to Mist who boasted many. Today, Lynden's hair was down, the bright, colorful strands caressing her shoulders, the tips curled ever so slightly. She considered him once more, before returning to meditate while gazing out the window.

"Motion sick?"

"Heart sick," he replied, focusing on his fingers. The charcoal stains had nearly faded. Black still tinted the skin around his nails and some of the more stubborn grooves in his fingerprints. Willing courage, he finally said, "This afternoon is a gift I shall cherish all of my days. I do not know how to properly thank you."

"Then don't." Lynden studied him. "Sometimes words ruin everything." She offered a quick smile, then leaned against the window and closed her eyes.

Seconds passed by quickly in tandem with the landscape, simultaneously feeling slow and forced. Individual trees blurred into each other until they formed a giant green mass. Serious gray clouds to the west threatened weather, drowning the blue sky before making good on such promises.

The maglev was thrilling, especially when buzzing over the cities and between buildings, and at an impressive speed of three hundred miles per hour. Now that they traveled over the open countryside, the speed accelerated to five hundred-and-fifty miles per hour. Which meant nothing to Coal other than they were traveling in haste even quicker than before. At least two stories above the ground, they flew over the landscape quicker than one could blink.

Coal released a quiet breath. His thoughts were poor company. A strange tension hung in the air, and he wanted to engage Lynden in conversation to ease the discomfort. How he longed for her, content with even the smallest morsel of interaction. Anxious, he slipped a hand into his pocket and touched the gift he had brought along, troubled as to when to present it to her, a dilemma he had pondered since yesterday.

"I feel peckish," he finally said to break the silence.

Lynden opened her eyes with blasé irritation, an emotional response he knew was entirely in jest. "God, you're always hungry. If I'm not saving your sorry ass, I'm feeding you. You're worse than a dog." She looked at his feet. "At least you're wearing shoes."

He shrugged sheepishly. "I fear I am far too indebted to you for any hope of repayment."

She rolled her eyes. "Yeah, no kidding. And, you still owe me a favor."

"Shall I order us dessert? Perhaps chocolate will act as a first installment toward my debt."

"No, I'll order us something. It'll be a surprise."

Coal sighed. "Please tell me a blindfold is not involved."

"A blindfold is not involved."

"Any transforming strawberries or poisoned apples?"

"What's wrong with transforming strawberries?"

"Nothing, but a man should be prepared."

"Oh please. Toughen up." She stuck her tongue out at him and he tapped her nose until she drew away and shouted, "Knock it off!" making him laugh.

"Toughen up," he goaded.

"Whatever."

"Does this surprise involve chocolate?" He grinned comically, begging her with his eyes.

"What's with you and chocolate?" He remained silent, offering a cherubic expression. Lynden exhaled and slid down in the seat as if her very being had deflated, while exhibiting the most impressive unimpressed look he had seen yet. "Fine. It involves chocolate. Stop your whining."

"Excellent. Then I consent to this next surprise."

"I think you just duped me."

"*Moi? Non Mademoiselle.*" He bowed gallantly. "I am but your humble servant."

"You're so full of shit." A hint of a smile touched her red-painted lips and Coal grinned in reply.

A few minutes later, a waiter appeared at their cabin door with a tray boasting two bowls of a solid yet creamy white mound, dusted off with a glittering brown substance and curls of chocolate. Lynden left a tip, then released a tiny squeal as she bounced onto the bench seat with her bowl.

Cold seeped into Coal's fingers, and his attention shifted from Lynden to his bowl in astonishment. "What is it called?"

"Ice cream, and it's topped with hot chocolate mix."

"Truly?" Coal examined the dessert more closely.

How could something be both cold and hot?

"I have never tasted ice cream before."

"What? Weird." Her eyes rounded in disbelief. "How have you not tried ice cream?"

He quirked a smile. "I blame you."

"Shut up."

"We do not have ice in New Eden and only goat's milk for cream."

"I feel sorry for your childhood." Lynden wrinkled her nose. "Take a bite already."

Coal obeyed and the cold, creamy substance coated his lips and tongue in a sweet balm. His head fell back as his senses drowned in a mystical transcendence. "Ecstasy," he sighed. Lynden grinned and spooned another bite into her mouth. When finished, which he accomplished with much gusto, he said, "I could drift away in eternal bliss."

While enjoying another bite, she somehow managed, "I ran out of chocolate syrup one night." Covering her mouth, she continued, "Out of desperation, I sprinkled my ice cream with hot chocolate mix and fell in love. So. Damn. Good."

"Indeed."

"I want to plant my face in the bowl and lick it clean." Instead, her bowl clanged as she stacked it on top of his on an empty chair. "Nervous about tonight?"

"No, I desire answers. I left to find information, and I have been doing a rather poor job thus far."

"Information on what?"

Coal released a heavy breath. "Now my turn for surprises. Come, sit beside me."

"Um, OK."

"I wished for you to know before it was revealed this evening."

"Are you a woman?"

He rolled his eyes and slid her a humored look. "Yes, actually. Do I make for a handsome young woman?" Lynden's eyes roamed over him, and he lifted a corner of his mouth. "Perhaps I should wear a skirt akin to Mack's."

Lynden burst into laughter. "Nah, you'd give Mack a complex. He's too fond of his legs to be showed up by yours."

"True. Although, I do enjoy watching him preen."

"Oh god. Don't remind me." She sauntered across the small space and lowered next to him, leaning her head onto his shoulder and draping her legs over his. Every muscle tightened with the feel of her against him, but he feigned ignorance of her presence in order to focus. "Tell me," she whispered, and Coal cleared his throat and attempted to focus once more.

He powered on his Cranium and brought up a message screen. With a steady finger, he swiped the first message: *We may not speak aloud of such information.*

She nodded and so he continued, sharing of how the Watson siblings were alive, and she stilled. In as few words as possible, he shared all the background he had regarding Fillion and Hanley. The message ended with his fear that her mother was ignorant of everything and he did not wish for Lynden to be with the hack tonight, extending heartfelt apologies for not sharing sooner.

"Holy shit…" Her head popped off his shoulder and she jumped to a stand. Her normally pale complexion turned ashen and she assessed him, as if afraid he was jesting. Lynden bit her fingernails for a few seconds, then she sat and erased his message, swiping one of her own: *Is my brother OK? He's seen Willow?*

"Lyn," Coal said, and she positioned herself on the seat to better see him. When she lifted an eyebrow in a nervous gesture, he found courage and whispered, "She's Oaklee."

Her eyes slowly widened as the information registered. "Oh my god." She stood up and paced the cabin, eventually looking at him. "Why didn't you tell me sooner?" He reached for her hand but she swatted him away. "Don't touch me. I'm so pissed off at you! And Mack! And Fillion! Assholes. All of you."

"I was honor-bound. Believe me, I have wanted you to know for so long." The Cranium was still on, so he maintained a steady position. However, his eyes remained fastened to Lynden, tracking her movements.

She collapsed beside him and pointed to the screen, her face a mask of emotion. "Answer the question."

Yes, Fillion has seen Willow. Concerned, Mack sought me out to ensure Willow was of a sound mind as your brother holds affection for her.

"So weird. God, that's got to mess with my brother's head. Uber creepy. I always thought Fillion needed a girlfriend. He mopes around too much. But this is just…" She cringed and looked at Coal. When he showed no response, Lynden sighed and leaned back against the seat, staring up at the ceiling. "Is this why you want to remain in my world?"

"No, of course not. Contrary to popular belief, I am not petty, nor impulsive." Coal turned his Cranium off then leaned back on the seat next to Lynden, their faces inches apart on the back cushion. "I would go mad if I returned to New Eden indefinitely. I cannot get my fill of wide open spaces or mountains. Or transforming strawberries. I have recently added ice cream to this list as well." He playfully lifted a corner of his mouth and she rolled her eyes. "I enjoy experiences such as riding a speed rail or traveling by car. I find technology fascinating. And, I hope to help people. Perhaps your father could employ me to do something meaningful for those who are destitute." He blindly took Lynden's hands and drew slow circles on the back of her fingers with his thumb. "Not to mention, I would sorely miss your surprises."

"Nah, you'd get over them." She lowered her head.

"What is that look for?"

"I was just thinking of Fillion." Lynden nibbled on her lip ring. "Freaking out for him." She twisted the ring on her thumb, then rolled so her back was flat against the seat. "Coal?" She shifted focus to the floor and slouched forward, tilting her head away from him. "Do you think you could ever … love … a girl like me?"

"I already do."

"Not like a friend or a charity case." She reddened and turned toward the door. "Never mind. Forget I asked. Dumb girl moment. I didn't mean anything by it."

All her emotions were hidden behind a mask of indifference within a blink of an eye. Coal clenched his jaw with a small surge of frustration, tired of never being believed. Grieved, as well. That she would believe a man, who honored and respected her, would not do so for any other reason than obligation or pity.

With a single finger, he took a risk and boldly caressed her jawline and neck. "You are magic to my senses and I am bewitched," he whispered, his eyes following the paths he made along her smooth, soft skin. "My thoughts are consumed by you."

Lynden gaped at him and he met her stunned expression. "Are you messing with me?" Her entire body froze in fear.

"I adore your freckles and your laughter. I am thrilled when swept away by your imagination and sense of adventure. You bring an excitement to everyday life that I find attractive. But most of all, I am completely taken with your affectionate and generous nature." He paused a beat, then whispered, "I am in love with you."

"Coal—"

"I am most sincere, nor would I ever trifle with your heart. I have been falling for you since the moment you brought me to life upon your lawn." He drew close, his hand positioned against her leg, and her breath quietly hitched with his nearness. It was such a strange response coming from Lynden that Coal felt encouraged. "I ache for you," he whispered against her mouth, cradling her face. "And long to make *you* happy." She leaned into his hand and closed her eyes as his lips fell onto hers in hesitant, curious touches.

An incoming call notification echoed in his head just as their kiss ignited. The computer voice announced the caller and Coal jerked away from her and muttered, "*Merde!*" A pained expression flashed in her eyes and she looked away, wiping her mouth as if trying to remove the evidence of their confessions. "I am sorry," he said and she stiffened and began to rise. Coal grabbed her hand and blurted, "Your father is calling me. I am not displeased with you. Please, do not leave." She lowered back onto the seat, but refused to look at him. Coal closed his eyes and tapped the device strapped to his ear and said, "Coal Hansen."

"Is this a good time?"

"Yes, of course, sir." He flicked a worried glance at Lynden, then focused on his fingers. "How may I be of service?"

"You are needed back at N.E.T.," Hanley replied, his tone casual but business-like. "I'll send my private jet in the morning. John will take you to the airport and accompany you."

"Is something amiss?"

"No, nothing to worry over." Coal winced with the fake sound of reassurance in Hanley's voice. "I'll fill you in with all the details once you get here."

"I see." Coal's heart plummeted to his stomach. "Anything else, sir?"

Hanley chuckled. "Relax. Everything will be just fine. Be sure to pack everything you own, though. See you soon."

The line disconnected and Coal turned off his Cranium, yanking it off his head. Lynden waited in the awkward silence. "I am returning to New Eden on the morrow—I mean, tomorrow."

"Press junket?"

"He asked me to pack everything I own," Coal said, gritting his teeth. "John is fetching me in the morning."

"Oh." Lynden's eyes glistened and she delicately sniffed, sharply turning her head to the side. With a quick push, she stood and ambled toward the window seat, crumpling upon the bench, and pressing her forehead to the glass.

A dark cloud filled the atmosphere of the cabin in her wake, rivaling the ominous weather that dressed the sky. Rain pelted the window, streaking upward with the momentum. Perched in the bench seat, Lynden curled up even more when she quickly wiped away an errant tear. Then another. Coal did not know what to say or do, heartache stealing every breath he possessed.

Did he not have at least two months left in The Exchange?

They traveled to Mack's apartment in silence. The tension ratcheted tighter until they did everything possible to avoid eye contact or physical contact. The elevator opened to Mack's apartment and they shuffled inside with funereal steps. Confused, they tarried when the young man was not present to greet them as planned.

Lynden tapped her Cranium and tramped toward the floor-to-ceiling window. "Where the hell are you?" Her body deflated slightly. "Really? OK. No worries. Yeah." She turned around a second later and met Coal's eyes with a flat, dispassionate expression. "Got it. Bye." Fingers brushed across the silver device, but her eyes never wavered from his. Electricity crackled in the air between them and Coal's pulse spurred into a gallop. "He's at work still. Problem with an overseas client or something. Wants us to meet him at TalBOT Industries in two hours."

The words barely left her mouth when the room dissolved and faded away as their lips crashed and hearts collided in mutual anguish. She tasted of sweetened cream and chocolate and he deepened the kiss, pressing her into the large glass window until he was not sure where his body began and hers ended. It was if they floated into the twilight, drifting toward their wishing stars until they were so full of each other the only option was to fall. And he was falling hard, unable to contain the rush of loving her.

Warnings from his upbringing flared in his mind, especially when Lynden removed his shirt and unbuckled his belt, then his pants. But he ignored each and every voice. A more honorable man would behave differently, he knew. Perhaps he was stupid, foolish, and acting with insensitivity. Everything within him felt reckless. The pain from their impending separation demanded he eliminate all distances now. But, more than that, he needed her. Longed for her. Wished to be known by her in a way no one else had ever known him.

They stumbled over to the divan and lowered onto the cushions, breathing each other in, indulging in one fervent kiss after another. Their bodies moved in a slow dance, arms and legs entangled in a rhythm created by their melding lives; and Coal was sure he died a thousand deaths with each rise and fall of their blended pulse.

He buried his face into her neck and whispered, "I love you," and she found his mouth, kissing back her reply with equal ardor. Every beat of his heart yearned for the passion to forge a new version of himself until she emerged, intricately and irrevocably fashioned into the infrastructure of his soul.

This moment was nothing like the evening when they almost hooked up before knowing each other. Nor, like any of their previous kisses. Heat had always existed between them, but this was beyond shallow stirrings. The intimacy was unfathomable beauty, an inferno of emotion and sensation, and he fell more in love with each echoed pulse, each breath given and taken, and every touch shared.

Now, he understood why a man should never take what is not his to have. It was not necessarily about being outside the bond of marriage. Rather, he held in his arms the soul of another, one whose soul made love to his, a bond that would linger far beyond this shared moment.

The room darkened, save for the ambient light from the city filtering through the window. Coal reflected upon the darkness of night far above the horizon, the shadowed hues untouched by the city below. Here, the sky twinkled, alight with the flecks of tiny, scintillating stars, and his heart made endless wishes to remain beside Lynden and never leave.

Lynden's head rested upon his chest, her steady breaths soft whispers across his skin. He caressed the silky strands of her hair, refusing to fall asleep to bliss' lullaby. His fingertips slid along her tresses until they made slow trails along her shoulder blade, drawing constellations with the freckles as if stars upon her skin. Guilt crept into his thoughts and nibbled at the corners of his happiness, but he did his best to ignore the remorse. Never had he felt so in love nor so loved in return, and he did not wish to be robbed of a single moment.

Remembering his gift, he reached for his pants on the floor and pulled out a string of small, copper linden leaves from his pocket. He clasped the bracelet around her wrist as gingerly as possible. Nevertheless, she awoke with the movements. Lifting her arm, she studied the dangling piece of jewelry before adjusting her position to better see his eyes.

"Where did this come from?"

"I made it for you."

"You made this? For *me*?" Her eyes rounded even more. "The project you were working on in the garage?"

Coal nodded his head as warmth filled him. "They are linden leaves."

Her eyes noticeably glossed, despite the shadows, and she blinked, whispering, "It's beautiful." She rested her head upon his chest once more and joined his gaze out the window. "Making wishes?"

"Yes." Then in playful tones, he said, "But if I share my wishes, they will not come true." Coal ran his finger along the inside of the copper bracelet.

Hazel eyes lifted from the wristlet to meet his, a flirtatious smile curving her lips. "I don't know how to properly thank you."

"Then do not," he whispered, pulling her on top of him and cupping her face. "Sometimes words ruin everything." Their lips touched—warm, soft, and thrilling—and he wrapped his arms around the small of her back. His heartbeat throbbed audibly in his ears, his pulse desiring to synchronize with hers once more. He quietly moaned, murmuring, "You render me useless."

"You were already completely useless." She took his hands and pinned them above his head, pressing her nose to his. "That's why I need to save your sorry ass all the time." She sat up and threw a small, decorative pillow at his face. With an impish giggle, she attempted to move away. But Coal was quicker. He pushed the pillow away and tumbled her beneath him. She squealed, rolling her eyes when he grinned in triumph, and said with a scoff, "Hot alien boy and earthling girl. We're so cliché."

"Hot?" Coal smiled, amused. "Well, I am the Son of Fire." She groaned, a cross between annoyance and humor. "We still have yet to ride ponies or pick flowers."

Lynden grinned, then pressed her face into his arm as she laughed. When she recovered, she said, "At least you don't have a smoldering gaze. That'd really be cliché."

"I should work on that, then." He lowered to kiss her, but she put a hand to his mouth and stopped him.

"We need to meet Mack."

"He was late. It is only fair that we extend the same courtesy, no?"

"We'll give Mack nightmares if he finds us like this. Do you really want to be responsible for that?"

"Tempting," he said with a charming smile. "I shall risk it, if you are willing?" Instead of answering, she flicked the black and red strands falling over his eye, nibbling on her lip ring, and he sobered. "Are you well?"

"Yeah, of course." She turned her head toward the window. Several emotions flitted across her face, until she asked, "Do you ... regret... Shit, I've gone all school-girl." She took a deep breath. "I don't want you freaking out. I couldn't handle it."

"I am yours, My Lady, body and soul," he replied softly. Fear curled in his stomach when her face grew more serious, the sensations gaining strength when she refrained from replying. He whispered, "I would never wish to hurt you in any way."

"You're the first person ever to love *me*." She placed her hands on his arms and reluctantly met his eyes. "I'm not afraid of being used. I'm used to it. What I'm terrified of is being loved and found not good enough in the end. Especially by you." Her breath shuddered, as if holding back tears, and she turned her head and stared at the ceiling. "I've never been good enough or essential to anything."

The pain of her words cut him. He knew to what she referred and another weight pushed against his chest. Coal lowered his body and lay on his side next to her, pressing his face to her cheek as she stared up above, her eyes sheening with restrained emotion.

"Lynden," he whispered, and felt the light, flutter of lashes as her eyes closed. "You will always be too good for me and I will always endeavor to deserve you. I am your knight and you my fair princess. I shall fight to reclaim your heart over and over again, for you are essential to me." She shifted to her side and faced him, a tear slipping down her cheek and across her lips. Coal brushed a light kiss across her mouth, her lips still tantalizingly warm and swollen. "I am not leaving you," he said with a reassuring smile, fingering the bracelet. "It may be a year before I may legally return, but I will. All that I am, all that I will ever be, is yours to have, My Lady."

"Did you say the same things to her?"

"Pardon?"

"I'm afraid I'll end up like Oaklee."

Coal stilled, unsure he heard her correctly. The words replayed in his mind and shame burned hot with her accusations, more so when her head rolled away from him. He sat up in swift, jerky movements. Draping his arms over his knees, he looked toward the window, attempting to rein in the onslaught of thoughts and emotions that speared his conscience.

Had she used him?

Had he misinterpreted her permission earlier?

Too crushed to remain in Lynden's presence, Coal stood and retrieved his clothes. With his back turned, he dressed quickly. Fury lit a fire inside of him and it flamed into a roaring blaze, his body numbing from the intensity of pain. He went into the kitchen and poured a glass of water, taking his time to allow her privacy. She appeared in the doorway a few moments later with heavy movements, and he maintained an averted gaze.

"Ready?" he asked, his voice tight and even.

She attempted to mask her feelings with a cold, aloof posture and expression, but could not. "Coal—"

He slammed the cup down and water sloshed over his hand and onto the counter. Lynden jumped back startled, her face draining of all color. "You are not a mere dalliance for me until I return to New Eden," he said through clenched teeth. "And I am wounded that you believe I would lie in order to gain intimate favors. I would never take advantage of a woman in such a way, most especially *you*."

Angling through the doorway, he brushed past her and toward the elevator. The doors opened and he stepped inside, staring at the ground as she entered. Lynden lifted her hood and wiped away an occasional tear, crossing her arms tight across her chest. Back rigid and shoulders straight, he stood enclosed within metal and glass, falling through the night toward the ground, as if trapped within a modern shooting star.

Once more, was his heart's one desire folly?

Several times since his emergence, he had felt like the little blue fish in the aquarium that gasped for air. But for the first time while traversing the Outside world, Coal felt akin to the little brown fish belly up in the corner.

ELEMENTS

Adams: What is something you've learned about New Eden Township that was unexpected? Or have you?

Dr. Nichols: For me, it is that by age fifteen, the youth are emotionally capable of integrating with adult society. This is a hypothesis I have longed to prove for many years. Socially throughout the ages, most young adults have been treated the same as their adult counterparts by working, taking care of the home, and starting families. The Postmodern Era changed this ideology and, instead of building careers and homes—as teenagers have done since the first civilization—they are referred to as children. I fear this has psychologically impacted whole generations. The youth are willing and capable. But society holds them back, and there are no communities in place to help them fully transition to functioning, actively participating adults. In New Eden, the idea of a teenager does not exist.

Adams: Very interesting. Didn't Fillion finish his education at fifteen and enter the workforce shortly thereafter?

Dr. Nichols: Yes, this is true.

— Dr. Della Jayne Nichols and Jennifer Adams, *Atoms to Adams Daily Show*, October 15, 2054

CHAPTER
THIRTY-ONE

Thursday, October 29, 2054

Seattle, Washington state

A loud, slow beat echoed from beyond the metal barrier to the Den of Iniquity, and clashed with the rate of Coal's pulse. He stared at the door until his eyes stung. Mack and Lynden flanked him on either side, equally as somber and tense.

Fingers touched his, and he moved his head toward Lynden as she took hold of his hand. He debated whether or not to pull away, confused as to her desire for connection. But when her fingers shook, despite his enveloping hold, he let out a slow breath. Regardless of how she hurt him, his vows of protection were made in earnest. Nor would he wish for her to feel afraid. So, he entwined his fingers with hers, even though doing so felt as though a sword slashed through his heart.

The door opened and Coal immediately pointed his focus to the concrete floor. With a single, large step forward, he entered, pulling the dark hood further over his face. Mack angled through the throngs of people with ease, flashing a smile here and a wink there. Lynden tucked her other hand into the pocket of her tattered jacket and regarded the chaotic whirl of limbs and laughter as if it were the most disinteresting sight she had ever beheld.

"Hey, Coal," said a smooth voice at his side. He looked up and met dark eyes. They blinked, eyelashes fluttering in a coy yet unassuming way, the allure and gesture both feminine and girlish. "Nice to finally meet you."

Soft, pink hair shimmered under the dark lighting, curling up at chin length. A black, satin ribbon cut through her cherry blossom tresses, tied into a bow. The mix of pink and black continued down her body, with a pink ribbon latticed down the front of a black, lacy corset. Her skin was so creamy white it seemed unnatural, most especially when he noticed how her body possessed strange tremors and mildly jerked. Coal stiffened, unsure if she was human, and his heart rate kicked into a gallop. Lynden cursed next to him, tightening her hold on his hand.

"Rainbow has kept you all to herself," she said in sultry tones, her light pink lips forming a pretty pout.

"Come on," Lynden said as she stepped forward, yanking one of the chains that dangled from his side. They had to keep up the show, despite his and Lynden's conflict, rubbing more salt in an already blazing wound. He scanned the room for Mack, who appeared to have been swallowed whole by the bacchanalia. Dismayed, Coal wrapped his arm around Lynden's waist and pushed her the opposite direction of the unnatural woman.

Was she a high-end android?

Or was she perhaps sick?

How could one present such perfection in form, but move with glitches?

"Leaving so soon?" With a playful smirk, the woman slinked between him and Lynden and hooked her thumbs into his belt loops. "Now, where's your sense of fun? I can push you around, too, if that's your style."

A slow, seductive smile formed on her lips. Dark eyes laughed at him as if he were the most humorous man she had ever met, as well as the butt of every joke. Coal stepped back in a panic, bumping into a man.

Or was it a woman?

They pushed him back with colorful language, and Coal fought back the urge to punch a wall. He was already fuming, overstimulated by the mere thought of this room. But interacting with it billowed the fire already roaring through his veins.

"Ignore her," Lynden said with quiet disgust. She attempted to pull him forward, but they were blocked once more.

"Always so uptight. Ruins a fun party. But then again, that's what you're known for, Rainbow. No skills. Always needing to run home to daddy or your brother. Pathetic," the woman purred, a haughty expression stealing her soft features for a moment. "That's why the whole world is laughing." She turned to Coal. "You've read the celebrity gossip. You know what they say about her. Nothing special. No talents. Not pretty like her parents or brother. No friends."

Lynden remained expressionless, her body a black hole of emotion. Coal knew the words wounded her deeply. Still, she held her ground. A sinking feeling filled his chest. She really did believe *he* would eventually see her the way everyone else did—unworthy of his affection and good opinion. Nothing special. And he had been worried about attacks on his own sense of honor. The air in his lungs burned as a new layer of shame fell upon the multitude of emotions battling within his heart and mind. A few people nearby overheard the woman's statement and started laughing, hurling jeering comments of their own at Lynden, and Coal's blood writhed with anger.

"Loosen up more, sweetie," the unnatural woman continued. "Learn what it means to have a good time. Right?" She turned and asked Coal in a saccharin voice, pressing her body against his, and in such a way her breasts appeared bare against his jacketed torso. "I'm Pinkie, by the way, if you didn't know already." Hands slipped under his coat and shirt and touched his skin. "I'll be a way better friend to you than she'll ever be. I have skills. Talents. I'm unforgettable." The last word left her mouth with a flirtatious wink, her fingers shaking slightly as they inched upward toward his chest. He gripped her hand and stepped away.

"Please refrain from touching me, Madam." Coal dropped her hand. "Nor will I permit you to speak ill of Lynden in any way. I assure you, she has far better skills than you could ever dream of possessing, including kindness and compassion." Pinkie rolled her eyes and looked at her friends with a derisive smile. "While you stand here and mire her character among peers, knowing the trauma she suffered, she has chosen to say nothing against you. Nor has she ever in the time I have known her."

With a firm grasp on Lynden's hand, he gently pushed Pinkie to the side, forcing his way through the crowd, and marched forward, fury fueling each step. People swore at him and flipped him off. A few attempted to pull him into their activities, making his skin crawl with each touch. But he pressed onward.

The hollow, empty faces around him and Lynden flashed different colors when the music changed and as new lighting danced around the room. Grieved, he studied Lynden once more and she reluctantly met his eyes. "I am ashamed of my outburst earlier," he said. She blinked shyly and shifted on her feet. "Please—"

Mack barreled toward them, his gaze frantic, widening even more when catching Coal's eye. "What happened? One moment you two were there and the next, poof, you disappeared."

"Pinkie happened," Lynden said, her voice weak. "Let's go."

"God, I'm so sorry, Lyn," Mack said, his face tensing even more. "I thought you were right behind me."

"It's nobody's fault. Now, come on. Get me out of this place."

"Roger, roger," Mack replied with a salute.

Mack grabbed Lynden's other hand and led them through the crowd, ignoring every woman who approached him, even those who knew him by name. Layers of disgust settled on Coal and he wanted to vomit. To him, these individuals were animals, regarding one another without care or thought for another's humanity. Or their own.

When they entered the next room, Coal turned to Lynden and asked, "Are you well?"

"Yeah. Never better."

"Lyn…"

She stopped walking and faced him. "I'm fine."

"No, you are not."

"What Farm Boy said." Mack flicked a glance over his shoulder, before turning around.

Lynden cracked a shy smile once more and fingered the copper bracelet, slowly meeting Coal's eyes. "Thanks for what you said to Pinkie."

He tucked a soft yellow strand of hair behind her ear, and ignored the strange look Mack flung his direction. "I have only ever been honest with you. Yes, I had pledged myself to Oaklee once, but never with the sentiments I pledged to you. Nor would I make such intimate promises to you if I were bound to her."

"What if she changed her mind while you were gone?"

"She would never wish to hurt me and, like a fool, I placed her in a position to either break my heart or break her own by agreeing to a relationship she did not desire." Coal cleared his throat and stared at the ground. "Any hope I felt was of my own manufacturing."

"I don't want to be a rebound." Lynden twisted the ring on her thumb and shifted on her feet.

Coal thought of his grandmother's story of his parents. "You truly believe I have used you as a fix for my wounded pride?"

"Maybe. No," she said with a heavy sigh. "It's stupid, I know."

"No, it is not stupid. You have valid concerns and, like the insensitive fool I am, I rushed in without proper care for your feelings. You have suffered long enough and deserve my respect and my understanding, not my pride." He reached for her hand and thought better of it.

"I love you, Lyn," he said, almost desperate. "Never have I felt so completely about another as I do about you, and I am at a loss as to how to convince you that my affections are in earnest." He ran a finger along the black ribbon tied around his wrist. "And I hoped, believed, you loved me, too. I would have never allowed anything to transpire between us otherwise. You know that much of me to be true." Lynden nodded her head, her face shifting from emotional detachment to distress and back to indifference. "Perhaps I am selfish and insensitive at times, but I am not shallow." Coal studied her eyes for several heartbeats and whispered, "Am I wrong to assume you care for me?"

"I love you so much it scares me," Lynden answered quickly, tears welling up in her eyes. "I'm just... It's just..." She sighed, deep and long. "Don't break my heart, Coal Hansen. That'd be worse than anything I've ever endured."

"I would rip my own heart out first," Coal said, resting his forehead against hers. He wove his fingers with hers, begging her to believe him with his eyes. "Forgive me, please?"

She smiled and brushed a chaste kiss across his lips in reply. Then, she rolled her eyes. "You still need to work on that smoldering gaze, Son of Fire."

He tried to restrain a smile as he intensified his gaze, knowing it was comical at best. "How about now, *mon joli petit dragon?*"

"Really? We've already reached the relationship status of 'pet names'?" She laughed, the tinkling sound like magic, bewitching him once more. "God, we move fast." After a few seconds, she looked over at Mack. "Your legs look especially nice tonight. Black is totally your color."

Mack pulled his eyes away from Coal and raised his eyebrows at Lynden. "Damn. I thought so, too. Glad I'm not the only one who noticed." He struck a melodramatic pose in his kilt and Coal burst into laughter. "Don't mock greatness," he said to Coal, wagging his eyebrows.

"I never mock *greatness*," Coal quipped.

"Smart-ass."

"You provided the qualification. I simply agreed."

Mack continued forward, lifting up both hands and flipping him off. When they reached the next door, he turned to Coal. "Smoke?"

"Yes, actually. I could use one."

They lit up and continued walking. Mack measured him every now and then with the same expression of perplexity. As they paused by another door, Mack straightened his shoulders and narrowed his eyes as one does before saying something rather important. He cleared his voice, to signal further attention and to appear official, and said, "Welcome to the other side."

"Pardon?" Coal studied the room, confused.

Mack rolled his eyes. "No, *dokynn*. Manhood."

"Did you injure your head this evening?" Coal asked with a lopsided grin. "I think this is the real reason for your tardiness." He dragged on the cigarette and opened the door, but they all remained fixed where they stood.

"Shit. Is that any way to say 'thank you'? Where are your manners, Farm Boy?"

Coal exhaled smoke and leveled his eyes at Mack. "I am a gentleman. My manners are impeccable. I exude class and charm wherever I am, regardless of company." He bowed and gestured to the doorway, saying to Mack, "Ladies first."

Mack went ahead through the door, lifting his kilt as he went to scratch his bare ass with his middle finger. Coal laughed despite Lynden's loud groan and protestations that Mack was gross. She eventually gave Coal a push, and he attempted a straight face. But one mischievous look from Mack and he was rolling with laughter all over again.

"He's got the man giggles bad," Mack said to Lynden. "Good job."

"Oh my god," Lynden blurted. "You two stop now before I kill you both."

"Sorry, Rainbow. I couldn't help myself." Mack winked and tugged on a strand of her hair.

She remained impassive and in a cool voice, said, "You're dead, Mackenzie."

"It was a good life." He placed the hand holding his cigarette onto his heart and melodramatically drew breath, closing his eyes tight as the smoke rippled toward the ceiling. Coal and Lynden watched him, both restraining smiles, and he eventually squinted open one eye and asked, "Can I do one last hack first? For good times?"

"I suppose," she relented. "Make it quick, though."

Mack flashed Coal a suggestive look, placed the cigarette back into his mouth, then pivoted on his heel and walked through the door. "Best. Day. Ever!" Mack sang as he jumped in the air, clicking his heels together, promptly giving a young man he passed a high five. The stranger watched Mack, baffled, then carried on as if he was not randomly slapped in the hand by a man who trotted along in a skirt.

"You two are slower than a LAN connection. Hurry it up. The caffeine in my system is about to climax," Mack hollered over his shoulder, and they picked up their pace and followed him through the underground's labyrinth of rooms and passageways.

The crowd's thunderous boom from the cage-fighting room rumbled through the narrow hallway, then faded as they turned a different direction. Nevertheless, Coal's pulse throbbed with the memory, a mix of adrenaline-fueled pleasure and lingering trepidation as he remained on the lookout for Mel, as if the otherworldly being could materialize from any wall. But they never showed.

Another nondescript metal door loomed and he and Lynden paused in front as Mack touched his Cranium, his fingers flying through the air. Directly above was a rather bright overhead light, a sparse fixture one usually only saw around doorways. Unlike other areas of the underground, the floor contained no trace of puddles, nor did the ceiling weep onto the walls. In fact, this area appeared downright posh comparatively. Nevertheless, the dank air shivered through Coal's body and he rubbed his partially gloved hands together, jumping up and down lightly upon the balls of this feet.

"Last chance to back out," Mack said to Coal. "You could go to prison for this."

"The Watsons deserve real answers," Coal said. "The Rows cannot speak what Joel, Claire, and Norah have taken to their graves. Nor will I abandon my family. An entire generation within New Eden may be affected by what we discover, including my brother and sisters."

"The Rows?"

"Where we bury the cremated remains of our loved ones." Coal lowered his head and blinked. "The trace elements of those who died sustain the living."

Lynden's eyes widened in horror. "Yuck."

He did not have a chance to reply. With a high-pitched screech, the metal door opened, grinding against the floor. A woman with cobalt blue hair inspected him, then rolled her attention onto Mack. Her mouth widened in a slow, wry smile and she nodded her head in a curt greeting.

"You're late," she said simply. "The team's assembled."

The woman turned and marched away from the door. Her shirt, the color of freshly tilled earth, dipped low down her back, revealing an extravagant tattoo of a phoenix rising from ashes. Green eyes took in their full measure, a spirited spark twinkling from their depths and directed at Mack. Then, golden brown eyebrows lifted in a gesture of impatience.

Spurred by her look, they stepped into the room, and Coal felt relieved when the temperature rose several notches. At least a dozen people inhabited the generous space. A few sat at tables, others in large, stuffed chairs, and a couple stretched out on enormous cushions. The walls and ceiling were black, and the furniture was various shades of gray, choices Coal now knew were to brighten screens and ease eye strain.

Just as his thoughts began to wander, all eyes shifted over their privacy screens and studied their small party. Coal offered a polite smile and bowed his head.

"Who'd you bring?" The woman with blue hair gave a passing glance to Coal and Lynden, raising her head to better see Mack.

"This is Rainbow Leigh."

The woman studied Lynden a few seconds. "I can tell you're related to Corlan."

"His sister," Mack volunteered.

"Knew it. Only seen you online before."

Lynden raised an eyebrow.

"And this is Draken Smyth, my cousin from the UK."

"Oh yeah. I know all about you." She sized him up, as if seeing if he were truly human. It was annoying, but a common response by most when realizing who he was.

Mack had explained that many people in the underground took handles, especially within the hacker communities. Many were ordinary names, used on their fake IDs and legal online personas. Some, however, used nicknames, such as Lynden. People, of course, knew who she was. The whole world did. But being referred to by a handle created a desired sense of anomaly. Everyone in the underground wanted to escape something, and so it was a well-guarded tradition. Unlike most, Mack typically went by his real name since he represented TalBOT Industries, even in the underground. The

Open Source community proved a valuable pool of talent when hiring out. When hacking, however, Mack used one of his alternate identities.

"Draken, Rainbow," Mack said. "This is Amanda. She's our social media guru-slash-hacker, our token rowdy Canadian, and the one I lean on to keep people on task." Mack bent down and pecked a kiss on her cheek. "If I wasn't in love with Corlan, I'd run away with her." He formed his hands into a heart and pretended it pumped from his chest, mouthing the words, "I heart Amanda."

Amanda laughed, a friendly sound that eased the tension coiled into every muscle of Coal's body. "I'm twice your age, Mack."

"I like older women."

"You like all women."

"True." Mack shrugged as if she just unearthed the greatest secret and, in the end, it proved disinteresting.

"All right, enough flirting. Let's get to business."

Mack whispered loudly to Coal and Lynden, "Dominatrix."

"I heard you," she said with a tiny, amused smile. "That's what I get paid for. So either sit your ass somewhere and connect to the forum, or get out of my way."

"I need to warn you," Mack said to Amanda, while puffing on his cigarette, "I've had way too much caffeine."

She eyed Mack with a comical look of long-suffering. "Great. So, debrief us before you system crash." He opened his mouth and she lifted a hand in front of his face. "One more thing. Did you set up a cloud with all known files and links yet?" Mack nodded. "OK. Shoot."

Without further encouragement, Mack launched the plan after introducing everyone in the room to Coal and Lynden, using their handles. Deciding to lounge on one of the oversized cushions, Coal and Lynden downloaded new encryption software. Then, they connected their Craniums to the group forum. After a quick lesson, he and Lynden swiped their first posts, both registering that they were ready to work as information moderators for the collaborative hack. Lynden would peruse hacks involving her parents and John, and Coal would sift through gleaned tidbits and discoveries on New Eden and those inside.

The hack officially began a few minutes later. Mack set up office near Coal and Lynden, and from there met with each individual privately. Coal could not help but overhear some snippets of information, pretending to read through the new threads as he watched Mack.

"How's your daughter?" Mack quietly asked Kev, a man in his early twenties with dark green choppy hair and several facial piercings.

"Still sick. Small improvements." The government hacker lifted a single shoulder in a weary shrug.

"Sorry, mate." Mack slid a small pouch under the table. "Hey, take this and get her something special, OK? Use the extra to pay for the medical bills." Kev took the pouch and slumped forward, leaning his elbows on the table while covering his face. "I have a special job for you." The young man wiped his face and gave Mack his full attention. "Your focus is all legal, gov docs for Hanley. Birth cert, licenses, you name it. I trust you to keep your findings between us. No full disclosures. Not even on the forum."

"I understand."

Nadine was summoned next. Coal studied her lavender colored hair, most intrigued by her two different eye colors— one more traditionally hazel and the other a dark brown. She planted a solid kiss onto Mack's mouth and then eased into a chair, placing her feet up onto the table. Mack studied her a few seconds, a quirky grin on his face. "I heard your roommate left."

"Yeah. He hit me so I kicked him out." Mack's goofy smile fell just as Coal's stomach churned. Fidgeting with anger over her statement, Coal readjusted his position on the cushion and checked on Lynden, who read an old article and seemed unaware of the conversation. Mack caught his eye, but pretended to not notice, focusing on Nadine again. "I'm paid up through November, though," the woman said, the heel of her black combat boot swiveling side-to-side upon the desk.

"Shit. Are you OK?"

"No, but you know, one day at a time. Sober for two weeks."

"Really?" Mack's eyebrows shot up. "Alcohol or speed?"

"Shot my brains out and almost died. Neighbor found me. I'm done. It's been a nightmare, but I'm done. Got a patch from the rehab clinic and taking daily inhibitor shots." She placed her feet onto the floor and slumped across the table, resting her chin on her hands. "Thanks for including me. I need this. I owe you both. Big time."

"Nah, we'd do anything for you. You know that. Plus, you're the best hound I know. Corlan and I have a specific hunt for you. You got my private message?" She nodded. Mack passed another pouch under the table and Nadine took it, her thin, dark eyebrows pushing together in a baffled expression. "Use it for food, bills. Everyone deserves second chances, especially you." As she stood, Mack gently took hold of her arm and pulled her forward, whispering into her ear. She nodded, her face emotionless like everyone's, but her eyes clouded with unshed tears.

Everyone had a story. And everyone received a small pouch from Mack. Even Amanda. This was such a stark contrast to the Mack who negotiated with Mel, which Coal was beginning to believe was all for show. Control was the greater currency, Coal reminded himself. Mack had given Mel a sense of control in negotiations.

Coal's heart grew heavy with the pain and brokenness carried by each person reporting for duty. They were a community. He had been sure such a concept did not exist in the Outside world, fabricated only online but never in reality. However, as he listened in to each one-on-one and read the threads posted on the forum, he felt a connection to their bond. The computer underground was isolated and confined by society, branded as rebels, nobodies, and corporate cast-offs.

In some ways, it reminded him of New Eden.

Newfound respect for Mack burned within Coal, and he regarded Fillion's dearest friend a few more seconds before returning to his own work.

"Hey, look at this," Lynden whispered by his side. Coal removed the Cranium from his ear and leaned onto her shoulder to view her screen. "Kinda weird to see the three of them together in such a chummy way."

She pointed to a picture taken at a gala of some sort. Both Hanley and Joel appeared dapper in black suits, each man with an arm around Della's waist, who was resplendent in a strapless gown. Hanley smiled at the camera, holding up a sizable gold medallion in a case. But Joel angled his face toward Della, as if his smile were only for her.

"Are there comments as to the history of this image?" Coal asked.

Lynden scrolled up at the notes and stilled. "The Nobel Peace Prize award ceremony." She blinked a few times, concentration wrinkling her forehead. Then her eyes widened a notch. "Look. In the far background. There's another face looking directly at the camera. It's a little blurry."

"That is Timothy Kane," Coal said. "The Wind Element inside New Eden."

"Huh." Lynden made notes on the forum, flashing Coal a quick smile. He lifted his head from her shoulder and placed the Cranium back to his ear. "Oh. Look at these," she said. Coal chuckled and leaned into her again, Cranium back in the palm of his hand. "It's my Uncle Dylan and Joel," she whispered. "My mom and Timothy are in the far background."

Coal studied the bags and gear at their feet. "Before the mountain climbing trip?"

"Yeah, I think so."

"What is Timothy holding?"

"I don't know."

"Can you enlarge the image?" Coal asked.

Soon, the image took up the full screen, and he and Lynden squinted their eyes and stared at Timothy.

"I think," she said in a slow, distracted voice, "he is holding rope. Yep. That's what it is. See the coil looped around his shoulder? It's almost the same color as his shirt."

"How did Dylan die exactly?"

"The rope snapped—" She sucked in a sharp breath. "You don't think…"

"I really do not want to believe so. Timothy is quirky, a bit on the jolly side, and well-spoken. But I have never seen him as an aggressive man." Coal released a heavy sigh.

"Hmm…"

She swiped their discussion into the forum, linking her comments to the image while nibbling on her lip ring. Coal strapped on his Cranium and returned to the forum and read her notes. Then he poured over the links and images assigned to him.

"Eco-Crafting Eden" had become common reading material for him, an intriguing predecessor to his own birth place. So much so, that as time slipped behind a veil of predictable information, he grew weary of opening links, figuring it was much of the same. The more he read of "Eco-Crafting Eden," the more ashamed he became of his theatrical origins.

Was he a character, groomed and designed to be the man he grew up to be?

Or did he reflect the truest part of himself, without influence or aid from any environment?

He thought of Dr. Nichols' question at N.E.T.— whether he believed he was a product of his community— and paused for further reflection. Coal's inspection drifted warily from face to face and catalogued the technological wonders contained within this room. Still, he felt like the same man who emerged from the experiment, simply tempered by new experiences. The core of who he was had never bended to this world—nor the one he left. Perhaps he possessed a far healthier portion of self-respect than he realized.

With a heavy heart, he thanked Joel and Norah for their steadfast love and care, as if a prayer, relishing that their fingerprints stained his soul.

Hours passed, quicker than he realized when he glommed onto the time. Lynden pulled the Cranium from her head and rubbed her eyes. With a yawn, she turned toward Coal and curled into the crook of his arm. Her head rested between his chest and shoulder. He smiled into her hair, leaning his head against hers.

After a few minutes, he knew she had fallen asleep. Exhaustion tempted him as well. Still, he could not sleep if he wanted to. In a few short hours he would leave. These were his last moments with Lynden, and Mack for that matter. As if sensing his thoughts, Mack looked over his screen to Lynden, met Coal's eyes with a brief, friendly nod, and returned to his work. His fingers flew through the air, eyes narrowed in concentration.

Coal returned to his work as well, lifting his head and straightening his posture. The pictures of his father interested him the most. The King of Terraloch was far different than the blacksmith. At first, Coal was nearly convinced that his father may be the faction leader. Now, he knew the overheard comments were those of protection and defense, statements of concern and fear made while speaking with Brianna about how to handle such grievous conditions and possibilities.

For a moment, Coal paused and thought of how his father and Brianna had known a romantic relationship with each other prior to New Eden. Every so often, more so as he grew older, Coal contemplated how Brianna had delivered him safely into the world, only to become his step-mother when he was four years of age. And, to think, Brianna was Lynden's second cousin. Coal belonged to a small world, but never had it seemed so small and connected as when learning the backstory and relational history of those enclosed to those who ran N.E.T.

Was it difficult for Brianna to see Connor with another woman?

To deliver Connor's children, knowing they were not hers?

A new link, assigned to him, appeared on the forum and pulled Coal from his thoughts. He tapped on the attachment and rubbed his eyes, burning from sleepiness and mild eye strain.

Amanda had recovered a photo his mother had posted online after meeting his father at Comicon. The future couple leaned in close to one another, both smiling, with an image of Terraloch just beyond their heads and shoulders. The caption read, "OMG. Connor Hansen is way more hot in person. *dies and resurrects* Dreams really do come true." Beneath it, a couple days later, Connor replied, "You're way more hot in person, too. *pinches self* *still sees girl of my dreams*," with a winky emoji face. Coal needed a moment, feeling strange while reading his parents' public flirtations.

Pushing away the familiar guilt, Coal focused on the image itself. He had gathered from various posts that his father traveled and met many people during exhibitions. Nothing in this photograph indicated an initial interest or attraction on his father's part. Yet, they eloped three weeks later.

What was it about Coal's mother that sparked a connection in this moment?

Was she an escape from Connor's reality or commitments?

Perhaps she was someone he did not feel beholden to because of long-time friendships and shared history?

Through his groggy state, he returned to the forum thread to add notes and comments when a thought surfaced, making his heart race. In a few swipes, he asked the group to find a note from Hanley to Connor, private or public, requesting Connor's residency within New Eden Township, as well as Connor's rejection of Hanley's offer. A couple seconds later, Mack called Nadine over to join him at his makeshift desk. Over his privacy screen, Coal met Mack's eyes, who gestured with his head for Coal to come over as well.

Gently, Coal eased Lynden down onto the giant cushion and traipsed over.

"Hey," Mack said to Coal. "Nadine here is working only on the Connor and Hanley relationship."

"Lovely," Coal said, with a small dip.

"What made you think of that question?" Nadine asked, studying Coal's face. "Did you see something?"

"Yes, but not on the forum," Coal said and quietly debriefed the story his grandmother shared.

Mack paused a few seconds, then asked, "When did you hear this?"

"Today, when visiting my grandmother, Sarah Hiddleston. Lyn—Rainbow took me to see her at her home in Portland."

Mack's eyebrows shot up in that comical way of his. "No kidding."

"And Sarah is Camilla's mother?" Nadine asked, the sharp look returning to her eyes. Coal nodded, unsure of which eye to focus on—the hazel one or the brown one—deciding instead to check on Lynden's slumped over body. "Anything else?"

"Nothing of consequence," Coal answered.

"All right. Thanks. I'll get busy." Nadine stood and walked back to her plush, leather chair.

An hour later, Nadine sent a private message to Coal with a screenshot of an email Connor had sent to Hanley, politely refusing to join New Eden Township. When Hanley pressed for an explanation, Connor had not replied. Typical of his father, really. Connor only replied or divulged information as needed. Coal could almost hear his father explain that his reasons were not Hanley's affair.

Another private message came through from Nadine, this time of an email from Hanley to Cami, expounding upon the many benefits and opportunities in joining the biodome community. The owner continued with statements of how he knew she had always wished to be part of "Eco-Crafting Eden," and here was her chance, and all to benefit science.

Coal's mother had responded with eagerness, much as Coal's grandmother had shared.

A third message popped up, and Coal opened the screenshot, holding his breath. His father had berated Hanley for approaching Cami behind his back and obtaining her legally binding signature after Connor had made it known to Hanley the day prior that he wished to open his own weld-tech company and start a family. Hanley's reply:

> *The key to the future is in the past, Connor. I'll make you the town blacksmith. You prefer the old craft anyway. Just think, your children will be world-changers—and by emulating a simple life, the one you prefer. Right? This is what you want. Instead of living off-grid somewhere in the wilderness, like you tease, I'm giving you a real way to escape the neo-industrial revolution and just be you. Think about it. You'll come around. Plus, you're making your wife's dream come true.*

Coal tugged the Cranium from his head. No more notifications demanded attention, and the forum experienced a lull as several of the hackers left for personal breaks. Lynden's head rested in his lap again, and he brushed his fingers through her tresses, lost to his thoughts. They would need to leave soon, for Coal still had to pack his belongings and John would arrive within a few short hours. The ache he experienced earlier in the evening returned as he admired Lynden's serene features. Her sleeve dipped down her shoulder and the dragon tattoo peeked at him from beneath the folds.

Coal was about to wake Lynden when Kev approached Mack, and the nervous way Mack watched the man made Coal pause. The hacker knelt before Mack and handed him a Cranium, which Mack strapped to his other ear, tapping the one he was using. In the typical blank stare of those riveted to a holographic interface, Mack appeared trance-like as he scrolled through whatever findings Kev was showing him. "Holy shit!" Mack grabbed the Cranium and whipped his head in Kev's direction and whispered in such a low voice, Coal could not discern the words. The hacker nodded his head, his eyes moving Lynden's direction. Snapping out of his state of shock, Mack flicked a worried look at Coal as he walked over.

"She out?"

"Soundly," Coal said.

"Put this on." Mack's voice had taken an edge to it, the sharp points of each word digging deep into Coal's gut. When the Cranium was fastened securely, Coal looked up. "Not a word to her," Mack said. "Got it? It's safer if she doesn't know right now."

Coal nodded and moved his focus to the holographic screen and his eyes took in a document from the Federal Bureau of Investigation. "*Merde*," Coal whispered after reading the first few lines.

Hanley's real name was Hayden Kane?

Witness protection program at age four?

Whatever was this program?

Anderson Kane—Hanley's father—was a con artist?

Nausea swirled in Coal's stomach. Nevertheless, he continued to peruse the document, which gave a detailed account of how Anderson wooed women into matrimony who were listed as beneficiaries to large fortunes. At some point within the first four years of marriage—it differed in each relationship—he would poison the parents with food or beverage using medications they were already taking, mixing the drugs with other herbs or pharmaceuticals. Once his wife collected her inheritance, Anderson would clean out the bank account and disappear. Apparently, he went by several pseudonyms, complete with falsified identification and other official government documents. When investigators finally caught up to Anderson, he killed himself.

Coal pulled the machine from his ear and thrust it back into Mack's hands. The young man's face tensed into a fierce expression. "Fillion is going to freak," Mack said.

"Or it might empower him," Coal said, matching Mack's fury. "It would me."

Mack was silent for several long seconds before whispering, "You guys need to go, right?"

"Unfortunately."

"Hey, it's not going to be the same without you around. Just so you know."

Coal smiled. "I will return, Hulk Smash moves and all."

"Good." A sly smile returned to Mack's face and he wagged his eyebrows. "You should really consider a career in cage fighting."

"And give you cause to laugh at my suffering?" Coal's grin widened. "Business skirt for the win."

"Yeah," Mack said with a goofy smile. "All right, Farm Boy, let's get going before we start crying into each other's shoulders. And when I say we, I really mean you."

An hour later, Coal paid a cab driver and carried Lynden, who fell asleep again during the car ride home. Her soft, even breaths warmed his neck. He laid her in her bed, set the external alarm on his Cranium, then slipped into the covers beside her. He did not wish to sleep. Rather, he wished to memorize the feel of Lynden against him, allow her pulse to speak to his.

His movements to settle in woke her, and she rolled to face him, lacing her fingers with his. They studied one another in the dim light, words seeming trite. This farewell was worse than any he had experienced to date.

A shy smile touched her face and then her lips tasted his, hesitant, almost mournful, releasing the flood of emotions they both attempted to hold back. His kiss deepened to a seductive rhythm, longing to savor every second, and he slid his hands around her waist as she held his face. Time was soon forgotten, as their hearts slowed to a dimension all their own.

One of the highest forms of emotional intelligence is when an individual awakens to the pain of others and, in response, extends empathy and compassion. Their defense is no longer to remain inward, but they are instead compelled to become outward. It is their moment of social rebirth as they transition from a state of emotional isolation to a place where they recognize the bonds they share with others, an experience they could not grasp nor feel previously. In a culture that does not possess many physical communities, this is an even greater feat for the individual who defends the humanity in others.

— Dr. Della Jayne Nichols, "Chapter 9: Rebirth into Society," *Misery Loves Company*, 2047

CHAPTER THIRTY-TWO

New Eden Township, Salton Sea, California

Fillion perched on the windowsill of his bedroom. A chill settled on his face, the only part exposed to the night air. Well, and his fingers, which were stiffening from the cold at this point. For the last hour, he hadn't felt well and wondered if it was something he ate? Or nerves? Or heartache? The fresh air helped. Or maybe it was a placebo effect. Either way. Whatever worked. He had a lot to accomplish tonight before he missed an opportunity.

A willow oak leaf spun in his fingers, round and round, like his thoughts. He watched the yellow haze blur into the dark air, resolving to try and call again. Fillion tapped the device on his ear and whispered, "Cranium, phone Dr. Della Jayne Nichols." The outgoing signal popped in his head with an occasional chirping sound. She didn't answer. Again.

"Damn it," he muttered, and rubbed his eyes with the palms of his hand. "Make her pick up," he pleaded.

God, he really needed to stop talking to himself. It was getting old. Still kind of funny. But old. He'd try one more time and then take a break. Fillion tapped the device, including the recording feature, and repeated the process for the sixth time while the last twinges of hope faded. As the chirp echoed in his head, his mind formed shapes with the lines on the dome ceiling. Hexagon. A tessellation of hexagons. A parallelogram of sorts.

"Who is this?"

"Finally." He jumped off the windowsill. "It's Fillion."

His mom gasped. "Fillion? Is this a prank? If so, I will prosecute whoever this is for harassment. As of this moment, the call is being recorded and traced. This is a private number and—"

"Holy shit. A bit dramatic don't you think? Do you often get prank calls from people claiming to be me?" She remained quiet. Fillion pulled the window panes shut and closed the shutters. The candle in his lantern had burned down to nearly nothing, but a faint glow still stretched across his room. "Kill the recording switch." The tell-tale beep sounded. "Good. We need to talk. Are you with Hanley?"

"No." A choking sound filled his head. "Is it true?" she asked, her voice strained. "Is Joel Watson dead?"

"Yeah, I called you at one in the morning, several weeks later, just to break the news to you." Fillion rolled his eyes and clenched his jaw. She wouldn't ask how he was doing. It wasn't her way. "Are you somewhere private?"

She let out a heavy, shaky breath. "Yes. I am glad you called as I have been concerned about the stability of the project."

"For one nanosecond, can you pretend you actually give a damn about something other than your career or your love life? Like 'why the hell is my son calling me at this hour' kind of concern?" Fillion slumped onto his bed.

"You're angry, which is understandable. Life never turns out how we think or hope it will. Part of the process of deconstructing our illusions is experiencing anger over the loss of our previously known reality. It's an essential element in the cycle of grief."

Deconstructing illusions?

It sounded like she was talking to herself, not him. Maybe there was a "talk-to-yourself" gene that ran on his mom's side of the family. Still, a disturbed sensation ran up his spine. She didn't sound like herself. As much as he was annoyed with triangles, he knew her heart was truly hurting.

"Mom, Joel is really dead," he said in a soft voice. "His ashes are in the gardens."

Silence. Not even the sounds of breathing. She must have muted her end to hide the crying and spare his head. He waited patiently and stared at the shifting shadows on the ceiling. Minutes passed and still nothing. For a moment, he thought she hung up, but he checked the call screen and the line was still open.

"Sorry," she whispered, eventually. "Thank you for telling me." The professional, detached sound of her voice annoyed him, but he remained silent. "So, why did you call?"

"I have an opportunity for you," he said. "At two-thirty I'll be in the room with Messenger Pigeon. There's an airlock. I'm going to break the circuit logic so both doors can be open at the same time. Do you know how to enter the technosphere?"

"Yes, of course."

"And do you know where the airlock is?"

"Fillion, tampering with the project may result in failure. I am not about to place my career, or the sacrifices of those inside, on the hinges of whatever revenge attack you have planned against your father."

"Turn on the video feed."

"I am not suitable at the moment."

"Mom, please. I'm alone. I want to see you. It's been awhile." Fillion breathed in through his nose and released a slow breath. A holographic image of his mom wavered in front of him. He'd only seen her a few times without make-up. But, to him, it looked normal. After gazing at people in their natural state for a month, it almost seemed more beautiful to him.

She leveled an uncertain gaze his direction, her red, swollen eyes rounding as her complexion blanched. "You look so much like... Are you playing a cruel joke on me? Do you understand how much grief I have endured?"

"I'm not Dylan. I'm not Hanley. I'm not whatever or whoever you think I am." Fillion narrowed his eyes to hide the hot, angry tears that were forming. "You didn't know my voice, and now you don't recognize my face."

"Fillion—"

"Stop. No justifications." Fillion lowered his hood all the way. He needed to keep her on point before his heartache took over. "Now. The airlock. Here's your opportunity. I'm bringing two people with me who you need to meet. I can't stress that enough. You can ask them any questions you like, but under one condition." She arched an eyebrow. "You never tell Hanley of our meeting. Ever. For any reason."

"You're asking me to go behind your father's back?"

"Don't play cute. Like you never keep secrets from him. I've seen the video of you and Joel after Claire died. Hanley has no problems keeping things from you, either. I also saw a video of your reaction when Hanley told you Joel had died. "

She winced. "How—"

"The entire world is at my fingertips." A smug grin lifted the corners of his mouth. "I'm a genius, remember? Your prodigy, your gifted son, the one who was bred and raised to be the apex of humanity?" Fillion relaxed his face, allowing all the emotions to pool in his eyes. His mom had the decency to appear stung by his comments. "Do you agree to this condition?"

"Yes, I agree." She released a dainty sigh and touched her hair, as if she feared her fingers no longer transferred the ancient magic of eternal beauty. "Two-thirty, correct?"

Fillion's body deflated some. "See you then. Oh, and it goes without saying that you're to come alone. I'll hack the video feeds from N.E.T. and all other log entries to erase your activity." He disconnected the line and fell back onto his bed. "Cranium, block all incoming calls and messages from Dr. Della Jayne Nichols." The encryption key should block his number, but he wanted the extra precaution.

He lay still and closed his eyes tight. Breathe in. Breathe out. His hands were trembling. In a last-ditch effort to calm the river of emotions flooding through him, he relaxed his arms and hands on the bed, palms side up. Was this the corpse position? Fitting. "Namaste, loser," he mumbled to himself.

Since birth, the real zombie apocalypse had defined his life. The Anime Gen had spent their entire lives dedicated to acquiring brains and showcasing their intelligence. But none of that mattered. Society had killed them, exalting information above everything else while simultaneously turning them into objects of entertainment. And all for the purpose of gaining followers on the Net. Every tap and swipe validated or shared a stranger's fake existence, perpetuating the cycle of cyber-glamour. The Anime Gen were nothing more than products to be used and discarded, rated and reviewed. And for what? It was a meaningless, intangible community. One that pulled the wool over everyone's eyes to block reality— they were slaves to a corporate system.

He wouldn't stand for it a moment longer. Freedom to live and survive was a human right. He was the Son of Eden, a man of magic; and like the bedtime stories proclaimed, he understood the potential evils of the Outside world. The lies and expectations had tortured him for seventeen years. It was time to change things, beginning tonight. Willow's encouragement impassioned him and he would fight to defend a reality of his own making. One that had nothing to do with an image on the Net or corporate empire-building.

After a couple minutes, he resurrected from the bed. Trembling fingers slid the willow oak leaf back into his pocket, and the imagined connection he felt to Willow slipped away.

The dry sound of fire nest material replied when he pushed against the pouch hanging from his belt. He opened the tinder box and paused, angling his head as he studied the joints. One was loose. Normally he was precise, making them all the same and lining them up. Fillion groaned. He knew he was OCD. But still, how did he not notice this earlier? Probably too upset to notice anything. He picked up another joint and rolled it between his thumb and forefinger. It was looser than usual as well. "Getting sloppy," he muttered to the flickering shadows. Annoyed with himself, he pulled them out and re-tightened each one. Then, he packed a few, just in case he forgot to earlier, and blew out the lantern.

He had a habit of forgetting cigarettes, bumming them off of others. Not many to bum joints off of in New Eden, though. Especially after midnight. He was mentally rambling. Time to go. With a flip of his giant hood, he left his apartment and leaned against the back wall of The Forge. Leaf and Skylar were to meet him here and, together, they would go to the rainforest biodome.

The day the Moores and Carsons left New Eden, Leaf had sent a note to Hanley. Per protocol in The Code, Leaf supplied communications on permissions, and granted an open door for the two families to return when they were ready.

This shocked Fillion. If he were Leaf, he'd never want them to return. Especially as they may relay fearful descriptions of what they saw, escalating an already snowballing situation. But Leaf defended them, as they were part of his community. And as their King, he declared he'd go to any lengths to ensure they knew they were valued and welcome, and that New Eden was still their home. Fillion just stared, dumbstruck. Leaf had laid down his right to be offended. Instead, he wanted to fight for the people who had persecuted him. Crazy.

This is when Fillion knew. Love really did have everything to do with honor and little to do with romance. Until this moment, he didn't trust anyone or anything shackled to a code of honor. It was counter to everything he'd ever known or experienced. In the underground, he and Mack took care of their own, did what they could. Still, he had always viewed honor as the mark of weak-minded idealists. Door mats. Pushovers. But he couldn't be more wrong. To act honorably toward another, more times than not, required a hefty personal price.

"Oh. My. God." He said to himself. "I sound like a medieval hippie."

Fillion had to laugh. What the hell had happened to him? A few weeks ago, self-gratification was the answer to all situations and problems. Now, he took pride in laboring for everything. He'd built and repaired things for people, even cradles, volunteered during reaping, and assisted Leaf in reassuring people of their legal rights. The smiles of gratitude, the cries of newborns in a freshly hewn cradles, the smell of cut wheat, and the tears of relief, had stained his soul. Nothing fake about it. Hell, until New Eden, he'd never personally interacted with the dying or celebrated a birth. His hands sustained life. Unlike Hanley's, whose touch guaranteed a golden death. In order for Hanley to gain profit, glory and power, something had to die. Always. It made Fillion sick.

Someone in his family needed to pay for the crimes committed, and Fillion was willing.

This was Willow's home. And this is where she wanted to remain. He would make it happen, even though it would force him to face his greatest fears beyond the safety of these walls—and possibly cost him everything. Willow Oak Watson was worth every sacrifice. The heart she gifted him was not only a token of her, but all of New Eden Township, too.

Fillion let out a sigh and trained his thoughts back to his mission. He could think of her all night. Wanted to think of her all night. Persistent mental rambling was always the first sign of exhaustion, though. This didn't bode well. A queasy sensation stole his concentration for a moment. What was he thinking of originally? Oh, yeah. The Scroll.

The conversation on the thread confirmed Fillion's worries. Hanley made it very clear to Leaf that the families would not be returning. According to the Gamemaster, they had shown signs of mental instability and were undergoing evaluations. Whatever. In typical fashion, Hanley had made it seem like he was doing Leaf a favor. But Fillion could see through the charm. The families were mentally unstable because they declared that the Watsons were alive. Fillion was sure of it. So tonight, at Willow's encouragement, he'd introduce Leaf Dylan Watson to Dr. Della Jayne Nichols and hope it was enough to spin things back in their favor. If not, he'd force a second Watson Trial when he left New Eden.

Muffled sounds came from around the bend. Leaf and Skylar sprinted around the corner. Fillion lowered his hood. A wave of light dizziness passed through him and he shifted on his feet.

"Ready?" Leaf whispered.

"Sure."

"We need to run and not stop until we arrive," Skylar said. "There are rumors of private meetings this night."

Leaf dashed out first, followed by Skylar. Fillion bolted from the shelter of the Forge walls and into the exposed pathway of The Orchard near the village. His legs pumped as fast as they could, the muscles burning with the effort. Skylar cut through The Rows, and Fillion and Leaf followed. Eventually, they trailed along the biodome wall. Large boulders were stacked on top of each other like castle walls, covered in ivy and honeysuckle. The mouth of the South Cave loomed and Skylar disappeared first into the black hole, then Leaf, and then Fillion.

"I ... need ... a moment," Fillion barely got out. Shit, he felt weak. His chest heaved in big gulps of air. "Damn." Leaf chuckled, breathy, but far more in control than Fillion.

A groaning creak echoed off the cave walls and Fillion startled, snapping his attention to the large doors. Everyone froze. There was no time to run. He wasn't sure he could, anyway. Even if they did, they'd be running into open space. And they were enclosed, only so many places to hide. They could be chased in circles until the sun came up. In a few steps, he pressed himself against the wall next to Leaf and pulled his hood deep over his face. The crunch of footsteps on the compacted path grew louder and Fillion held his breath. Then, the footsteps stopped.

"Who are you?" Connor demanded. "State your business."

"Skylar Kane, My Lord."

"Leaf Watson."

Connor walked down their line until his eyes settled onto Fillion. With a faint smirk, Fillion morphed into cool detachment and met Connor's contemplative stare.

"What are you doing in the rainforest, My Lord?" Leaf asked, stepping forward. His voice took on a note of authority to match Connor's. Fillion relaxed a notch when remembering that the former Fire Element now answered to the exposed Aether. It was the same posture and tone Leaf used with him in Messenger Pigeon when trying to trump control—aristocratic, noble, peering down his nose.

The blacksmith moved in front of Leaf. "I would ask a similar question, Your Majesty. It does not appear you gather The Elements, as Ember and Rain are not in your company. Strange hour for business. Nor is it safe."

"Safe? Why do you feel I should fear my community?" Leaf removed his hood and waited for Connor to reply, but he did not. "I shall repeat myself. What brings you to the rainforest at such an hour, My Lord?"

"I heard it on the wind that Timothy was heading to Messenger Pigeon, and so I decided to follow." Connor shifted on his feet and held his hands behind his back.

"Heard it on the wind?" Fillion arched an eyebrow and studied the former Fire Element.

"Mere signals in the air, My Lord, as the saying goes."

Connor didn't flinch or shift his eyes or anything else to give himself away. But the double meaning and hidden information downloaded instantly. "Shit." Fillion scuffed the path, turned around, and rested his forehead against the stone. "Damn it!"

Leaf turned toward Skylar. "Did you know of this?"

"No, I did not." The distress in Skylar's voice was acute. "Your Majesty, you have my allegiance."

Fillion pushed off the wall. "What time is it?"

"A quarter to two," Connor replied quickly.

"And how long has he been in the hatch?"

"I would wager twenty minutes."

"Others with him?" Fillion lowered his hood.

"No, he travels alone."

"Did you learn anything? Or are you part of Timothy's plan?" Fillion stabbed his hair with trembling fingers. "Heard it on the wind that I was coming, too?"

"Ah, I see. Hanley is rather busy this night." Connor stepped in front of Fillion and said in a hushed tone, "I am unable to tune to your frequency." Resuming a normal volume, he said, "When I left, he was talking to your father and confirming that you are in possession of another Cranium. Apparently, your first one was disabled. Rather interesting piece of information, actually." The former Fire Element crossed his large, bulky arms over his wide chest. "Does he know?" Through the darkness, Fillion watched as Connor gave a gentle nod Leaf's direction.

Fillion shook his head "no" as subtly as possible.

Although it was an obvious exclusion to all others, Connor leaned forward and whispered into Fillion's ear. "He needs to, before Hanley messages him the details of who betrayed the Guild."

Not bothering to whisper back, Fillion asked, "And why would Hanley make a move like that? Blow cover over a Cranium? Yeah, right."

"Seems there is a hacker in our midst, My Lord." Connor created distance between him and Fillion again. "And I gathered from the conversation, a rather good one, too. Apparently, he wound up in trouble with the law and is serving a sentence in New Eden Township. Part of the punishment is to work off his crimes in the community. Is this correct?" The older man paused and studied Fillion, who remained silent. "Someone needs to the take the fall for assisting this hacker, especially after the first Cranium was intentionally disabled. Hanley now has a target."

Fillion quietly groaned. "If Timothy has a Cranium, which I'm guessing he does," he said, relaxing his posture, "why did he need to go to Messenger Pigeon?"

"There is a LAN cable to port into the Cranium," Skylar volunteered. "I am sure I do not need to explain the advantage of such a move."

"No," Fillion sighed. "I get it."

"I will not allow Hanley or my father to target anyone other than me." Skylar beseeched Fillion to agree with a single look. "I assisted Fillion. No one else." Although dark, Skylar stood closer to the cave entrance and a faint, silvered light touched his face. Fillion nodded his understanding and Skylar returned to a stoic expression, flicking a quick glance to Connor, who frowned slightly.

"How is it you are familiar with Outsider technology?" Leaf asked, turning toward Skylar. "So much so, you could assist the Son of Eden?"

Fillion cut in to distract Leaf. "Did Timothy and Hanley discuss anything else besides my criminal life?"

"Yes. The meeting was about an entirely different subject, actually." Connor walked over to Skylar. "Your father is determined to make you King. He was pleading your case, yet again, to Hanley, offering up information on Fillion to gain favor."

"A position I shall refuse should he win," Skylar said, the sad resignation pulling on the noble's features. "My father will not listen to reason nor respect my wishes."

"Indeed." Connor placed a hand on Skylar's shoulder and quietly asked, "Are you ... well?" The Son of Wind nodded slowly. After a few seconds, the former Fire Element dropped his hand and moved over to Leaf. "Did you receive a Curse Card by chance?"

Leaf's face remained steady, even though his eyes narrowed a bit. "I do not follow this conversation entirely. How is it you knew to follow Timothy?"

Connor cleared his throat and lowered his voice. "That information is irrelevant at this moment. Do you have the card, Your Majesty?"

"I do not answer to you." Leaf stepped forward. "I no longer trust you or Timothy, or Jeff for that matter. You placed a Death Card in my father's pocket without care or concern of how I might handle that discovery. Nor am I clear on exactly what evidence you possess that led to such a judgment concerning my father's death." Leaf stepped forward once more, and his voice dropped to a low, threatening sound. "You manipulated me into an elopement with Ember, using your daughter's reputation and my declaration to become the Earth Element as a means to motivate my response."

A frown pulled further on Connor's lips. "All necessary actions. Some I am not proud of, but ones that have only benefited you in the end." The former Fire Element inched closer to Leaf and said in a low, friendly tone, "I am not your enemy. When your mother died, and Joel learned of your future, he sought my protection. I swore an oath to guard your life. I have no allegiance to Hanley, Timothy, or Jeff. Only you." Connor knelt on the ground before Leaf and bowed his head. "My King."

A chill swept over Fillion as he watched the former King of Terraloch bow before the King of New Eden. He chewed on Connor's explanation, tapping his fingers on his thigh to a song running through his head. Still, each muscle tensed and Fillion clenched his jaw until a headache bloomed behind his eyes.

"Rise, My Lord," Leaf said in a strained voice. The young noble turned his head toward the door and away from view. "I can, perhaps, understand some of your choices. But I shall never understand how you could so carelessly regard your daughter."

"I was there when you were born, Leaf Dylan Watson," Connor said, almost tender. "For nineteen years I have watched you grow and mature into the fine man who now stands before me. Do you think I did not know it was you who left flowers for my daughter on her windowsill every month since she was twelve? When Skylar stepped forward, the flower offerings ceased." Leaf turned back toward Connor. "I also noticed how she stitched leaves, the same ones fashioned on your furniture, onto her wedding gown and trousseau garments, which she began when fifteen years of age. The Son of Wind may have held affection for my daughter, but he was obeying orders from Timothy, nothing more."

Skylar lowered his head and a pained expression flitted across his features for a moment.

"You threatened to confront me before the community for sullying your daughter." Emotions burned across Leaf's shadowed face. "She and I were both innocent. Yet, you were willing for her to suffer public shame, and for what, pray tell?"

"Her protection."

"You voted for me to leave!" Leaf covered his face with his hands. "You do not make sense. Nothing makes sense anymore."

"Yes, and in your absence she would have still been married to you and, thus, could not become another man's wife."

Willow's brother released an anguished groan and fell back against the cave wall with a resigned thump. Fillion bit the inside of his cheek as he watched Leaf struggle. It wasn't a sound of irritation. It was the sound of a man fighting while on the brink of giving up. Confirming his thoughts, Leaf said, "I am breaking beneath the weight of so many secrets and deceptions."

"Connor is right," Skylar said so quietly that Fillion almost thought it was mistake. "My father is delusional when it comes to gaining Aether status for me, it seems."

"God, I'm so tired of the endless vague comments from everyone." Fillion slid a glance toward Skylar. "Marrying Ember would never grant you Aether status. What's this really about?"

Skylar flinched, another rare crack in his typically stoic demeanor. "The rumor within Nobility holds that Hanley would appoint Ember over me in the event that a new Aether was needed. This, of course, assumes that The Aether was from Nobility and that Ember was not next in line to begin with, or me. Many speculated that perhaps Connor was The Aether." Skylar looked away and mumbled, "Ember is far safer with Leaf, even though his family is the target of a power struggle."

"That doesn't make sense," Fillion muttered.

Leaf lowered his hands. "You would never harm her."

"No," Skylar said with a sad smile. "I would not."

The two young nobles silently communicated with one another, and Fillion's stomach clenched. Is this why Skylar feared and obeyed his dad, even though he was legally a grown man, in both worlds? That would explain some of the weird behavior and comments from Skylar at times. Fillion suddenly understood. He felt the same way about Willow as Skylar did about Ember. Fillion would go out of his mind if Willow was harmed because he failed somehow. Or as a means to grant him power.

Fillion pushed off the wall in frustration and faced Connor. "You know, this information could've been useful, oh, I don't know, maybe five weeks ago." He glared at Connor and spat, "What the hell? You knew I was looking for information! What is it with people not getting that this isn't a game? This. Is. Real!"

"Yes, but you did not value nor respect your own worth then. So, how could I trust you to care about the worth of others? That, too, is real. I swore to protect Leaf. Yes, even from you, Son of Eden. Hanley would never commit murder, but he has no qualms about taking advantage of situations or adding to the chaos. And I suspect you are just as much a pawn for Hanley as Skylar is for Timothy, if not more so." Fillion stilled and creased his brows. His head swam with dizziness as goosebumps prickled the nape of his neck. "I am much relieved to know that both you and Skylar desire to walk an honorable path." Both Fillion and Skylar looked down at their feet, and silence thickened like a hot suffocating wind all around them.

Finally, Leaf cut through the awkward hush and asked, "Who, pray tell, entrusted the Death Card to you?"

"Della."

"I figured," Fillion said. "Well, I thought it was Hanley originally. But, after making an ass of myself, I realized it was probably my mom." Connor regarded Fillion with curiosity. "Why'd she give you the card?"

The crunch of gravel in friction with the ground echoed as the blacksmith shifted on his feet again. "She was quite convinced Dylan's death was not an accident and that Joel was meant to die rather than her brother. She was adamant, actually, especially when learning of Joel's inheritance. But she was afraid to push such feelings further. When Joel broke off the engagement after accepting a job offer from Hanley to oversee the humanitarian efforts in Africa for New Eden Enterprises—"

"Whoa. Wait. He accepted a job from Hanley first?"

"Yes, although Joel insists he sought employment with Hanley. You see, Della and I grew up together and enjoyed a close relationship, similar to Willow and Coal. Our mothers were best friends. Della trusted me to care for Joel." Connor paused and looked at Leaf. "And his family. She could not reconcile that Joel would leave her, as it was not in his nature. He was a fiercely loyal man."

"I still don't get why Joel was targeted back then," Fillion asked, narrowing his eyes. "What did he have that pushed others to be reckless?"

"Love." Connor dropped his voice to a whisper. "And the woman who held the key to the future."

"What?" Fillion slumped against the cave wall, ready to explode. A twinge of nausea rolled through his stomach once more. "Do realize what you just insinuated? You're saying my mom is the one with the power."

"Yes, that is precisely what I am telling you."

Then, Fillion stood to attention as a thought hit him sharply. "Oh god," Fillion whispered. "Theory of Reconstructing Universal Society and Trusteeship." He looked at Connor with wide eyes. "The T.R.U.S.T. patent and copyright."

"Trust?" Leaf asked.

Synapses started rapidly firing in Fillion's head as thoughts connected. He turned to Leaf and asked, "What did your dad always say to you?"

Leaf paled. "Trust is paramount in the biodome."

"Timothy will be coming soon, Your Majesty," Connor said softly. "I suggest you hide until he passes you by."

Leaf drew in a labored breath and schooled his features. "Yes, thank you, My Lord. Your *unexpected* assistance is much appreciated."

Connor placed a hand onto Leaf's shoulder as he said, "I am available to talk tomorrow should you desire to seek my company. I am happy to answer any question you carry." The older man offered a kind smile. "You possess your mother's strength and your father's heart. Do not allow your heart to surrender to anything other than your strength, Your Majesty."

Leaf dipped his head. "Norah shared the very same words."

"She was a wise woman and cared very much for you." Leaf and Connor's eyes locked. "Good evening time," Connor said with a bow. The crunch of footsteps resumed until Connor's feet found the soft grass.

A muscle twitched on the side of Leaf's face. "Let us hide on the west side of the cave." Fillion caught the Son of

Earth's eyes for a brief moment, before Leaf lowered his head once more.

They rounded the corner and hunkered down against the short lip of the outer cave wall. Fillion turned toward Leaf, but both Leaf and Skylar had their heads bent together in low conversation. Disgust snaked through Fillion as he thought of Timothy and Hanley. He needed to think of something else. Stat.

Restless, he lifted his head toward the fractured night sky. Not much to look at except lines, New Eden's version of cloud shapes. He examined his hands, marveling at how the wounds had healed up so nicely. Nothing to think about. What the hell? Now, when he had time to let his thoughts wander—nothing. A round of queasiness churned in his stomach. It had to be anxiety. He thunked the back of his head against the stone, closing his eyes.

Just when he was about to nod off, a noise, like whistling, echoed from the cave. His eyes jerked open. It was probably a light wind rushing through the cave. Fillion closed his eyes again as mild nausea returned. God, he felt awful. Just as he relaxed, the sound came again. Not wind. It was actual whistling.

He angled his head toward the opening of the cave. From the corner of his eye, he watched as Leaf and Skylar snapped to attention as well. The whistling grew louder, and Fillion cringed, the smug, cheerful sound reminiscent of Hanley whenever the Gamemaster cornered someone. What the hell? One of these days he needed to stop questioning hell and just accept that it is. He bit the inside of his cheek and rolled his head toward his brothers-in-arms. Leaf and Skylar both delivered worried looks his way, their bodies perfectly still.

"Almost out," he whispered.

The whistles softened as Timothy emerged into the open air of the biodome. Heavy, padded footsteps shuffled along the dirt path. Fillion leaned forward and peeked around the corner. A hooded individual faded into the night toward The Rows. When the tune dissipated, Fillion turned toward Leaf.

"It's safe. Let's go."

Fillion crept along the rock wall with awkward movements to ensure each step remained muffled. Jagged, rough points poked through the layers of wool and linen. He knit his brows together in irritation, swearing under his breath with another sharp jab. Then, black swallowed him into safety as he entered the mouth of the cave. He jogged down the narrow path and yanked open the large doors. After the others entered, he walked into the hot, humid air, wincing with the deafening noise.

"Let us move swiftly," Leaf said.

Once they reached the Dragon Bridge, Fillion ran his fingertips over the arched, scaled back of the railing. Ribbons of tepid, vaporous mist swirled and danced, as if the bridge was shrouded in dragon's breath. The magic threads broke and reformed when his fingers poked at the air.

He needed to rest a moment. Leaning over the edge of the bridge, Fillion tried to steady his rapid breathing. He felt weak and lightheaded. Maybe his blood pressure was too high. With resignation, he rested his forehead on the arched railing. "Get it together," he said to himself.

Leaf approached. "The hatch is open. Skylar already lowered himself into the room. Do you fare well?"

"No. But whatever." Fillion straightened his posture and offered a lopsided smile, lips trembling. "Let's get this over with."

"Is it your mother?"

"Nah, she doesn't bother me like Hanley does. I get pissed, but I don't get paranoid." Fillion sauntered by Leaf, who turned and matched his strides. "I'm dizzy and sick to my stomach. Must have been something I ate."

"We ate the same meal, and I fare well."

Fillion shrugged.

Leaf stopped and faced him. "Do you trust Connor?"

"Yeah." Fillion lifted his eyes. "I'm still not sure how he concluded that Joel was murdered, though."

"I can trust no one," Leaf said, the words muffled as he rested his face in his hands. "For no one is who I believe them to be." Fillion remained silent. What could he say? It was true. They were all role-players. Every single damn person in the dome. Even the unwitting second generation. "Fatigue has weathered my spirits to nothing." Leaf's hands crumpled to his sides.

"I'm sorry." Fillion sighed. "I really am."

"Thank you, My Lord." Leaf bowed. "I am humbled by your many sacrifices for my family." The Son of Earth pulled Fillion into an embrace and thumped his back, then plodded to the hatch with sullen steps.

"Sure." Fillion looked down at the damp, jungle floor. "I'll be there in a sec. Need to clear my head."

A few seconds later, Leaf disappeared down the hatch and Fillion glanced around the jungle. Birds and insects competed to be heard, their songs and insistent chatter annoying him. He wanted quiet as he organized all the known details to date. The cacophony in his mind clashed violently with the jungle. Still, he managed to finish incomplete strands of mental code. The facts built a script that ran an algorithm through his mind in search of hidden details.

As he lowered into the hatch, he looked up at the ceiling. Fractured, mosaic pieces of nightfall stared back at him, dark fragments of a whole. And, yet, every line and point was connected, despite the illusion of separation. What were the points of connection he was missing?

The minute I heard my first love story, I started looking for you, not knowing how blind that was. Lovers don't finally meet somewhere. They're in each other all along.

***

Sorrow prepares you for joy. It violently sweeps everything out of your house, so that new joy can find space to enter. It shakes the yellow leaves from the bough of your heart, so that fresh, green leaves can grow in their place. It pulls up the rotten roots, so that new roots hidden beneath have room to grow. Whatever sorrow shakes from your heart, far better things will take their place.

— Rumi, 13th century A.D. *

CHAPTER
THIRTY-THREE

kylar bent over the airlock with a stiff spine. Fillion paused to take in the scene. The cover for the buttons lay on the floor as Skylar studied the exposed electronic innards of the circuitry. A knife shook in the noble's hand as he fingered a rainbow of wires, resting the blade against a blue one.

Leaf stood in the corner and watched his friend with a curious yet pained expression. Fillion gathered that Skylar had blabbed about the Techsmith Guild. Better coming from Skylar, he guessed. At least the Son of Wind would guard Ember's involvement. At least, Fillion figured he would. Whatever. Games within games. So over it.

As Fillion neared the airlock, the Wind Element looked up from his crouched position with relief. "Whatever you do," Fillion said, "don't cut the red wire." Skylar panicked and looked back at the wire in his hand. Fillion lifted a corner of his mouth. "Just kidding." He chuckled and knelt next to Skylar. "Outsider joke."

"Shall I cut the blue wire and cross it with the white one, then?"

"Normally, I'd say let's cut the wires. But I don't want evidence that we've been here. I'll hack it and do a temporary software override. After we're done, I'll erase the log entries for any Guardian Angels standing watch."

"Far safer plan, My Lord. I did not relish the notion of possible electrocution."

"Nah, you'd enjoy it." Fillion held a deadpan expression. "Become one with a machine and feel its energy. The buzz is glorious. Everyone is doing it."

Skylar laughed, a rare sound. "I shall pass, thank you all the same."

A knock sounded and the muddy sound of his mom's voice called out his name. "I'm here," he hollered back through the panel. "Working on it. Five minutes, tops." Fillion pivoted on his knees toward Leaf. "Kill the lights?" Leaf flipped the switch and the room plunged into darkness.

Fillion tapped his Cranium and the user interface brightened the surrounding space. He found a place on the ground to sit a few feet back from the airlock and went to work. After a minute, the scanning software he and Mack created to communicate with non-Cranium technologies registered a hit. The Smart Tech comm center for the airlock pinged back and Fillion captured the frequency and hacked into the signal. In a few swipes, he reverse-engineered the encryption algorithm and deactivated the circuit logic. A hiss of depressurization cut through the silence, and Skylar opened the door.

"Give it a try," Fillion shouted. The clunk and grind of a handle rung through the chamber and a light breeze came through the hole. Fillion tapped the air on autopilot, his fingers trembling, as he locked the layers of holographic screens. Then he turned off the vid feed and switched the camera to record. "Lights," he said simply and scooted toward the open door as Skylar moved out of the way.

The airlock was sizable, at least three-by-three feet and four feet deep, and perfectly framed his mom. Her black hair shone in the bright lighting of the technosphere. Pale eyes that mirrored his own stared back at him with part curiosity, part irritation. She arched her eyebrow, as usual, when assessing an individual or expressing impatience. For a moment, Fillion waited for a reaction. Anything more than this. Most mothers, he was sure, would be showering their child with maternal exclamations of concern. But, no. She touched her hair and blinked, eyebrow still arched in anticipation.

"Before I introduce you to my companions," he began, "I have a question." He leaned into the airlock. In a softer tone he asked, "How are the Moores and Carsons? Especially the children?"

She brushed dark locks off of her shoulder and tilted her head. Lips, painted bright red, eased into a casual smile. "They are well cared for, if that is your concern."

"Not the angle of my question."

"The children show initial hesitation and respond with healthy and expected levels of anxiety when introduced to something new, especially technology. However, their curiosity and eagerness to learn turn any fears they possess into opportunities for education."

"Their parents?" Fillion maintained even eye contact.

The smile returned and she fingered a silver necklace as she formed an answer. "The parents are different. Their statements are consistent, but each adult, and child for that matter, exhibit signs of delusions. One moment the adults seem connected to reality, and the next, they make false claims and unreasonable demands at an emotionally heightened state that is concerning."

She straightened her head and rested her hands in the airlock. The professional facade disappeared and she stared at him in earnest. "Are you feeling well? You look pallid."

The air in his lungs stilled and his fingers gripped the edge of his cloak. She was worried about him? Because he entered New Eden? Or because he was mentally unstable? Or because others were listening? Maybe he was over-thinking things. He probably looked like shit. He sure felt like it.

"Lynden misses you." The mention of his sister's name pushed the air out of his lungs and he tensed. Before he could answer, she continued, "It's normal to relive fears through another's experience. Your concern for the Moores and Carsons demonstrates a learned empathy. You understand the shock of interacting with an entirely different world."

"Yeah," he mumbled. "Do I win a prize?"

"Since Grandpa Corlan passed away and the Watson Trial, you have continually expressed your anger through sarcasm and rude humor." His mom leaned in a little further. "I know these past few years have been difficult for you."

"Nice. Thanks for noticing." He shook his head in ill-humor. "Now you want to have this conversation? Right this very goddamn second? Well, let's see, the last time I saw you was probably eight weeks ago. Who knows when I'll see you again after my time here is up. So shoot. Fire away."

Della's mouth set in a tight line and he snapped.

Fillion slammed his hands onto the base of the chamber and shouted, "I'm so fucking angry!"

His mom didn't flinch. Strong reactions from people were probably nothing new to her. Still, he would be heard.

"And I'm hurt," he continued, his emotions congealing into solid and substantial thoughts. "My community rejected me and publicized my shame when I needed them the most. And my family exploits me and expects me to take it and react as if I'm a machine. Any acceptance I received was an illusion. It was always about how someone could use me for their glory or pleasure. I'm pissed that so many years of my life were wasted under the belief that I was nothing. Nothing!"

He gripped the edge of his cloak again. The incubus that confined his life to a black, rotting coffin had awakened. The warm, tantalizing breath of each oppressive lie whispered seductive promises in his heart.

But no more.

He was done with death and wanted to live.

"I'm finally understanding my worth and value. The real me is emerging." His vision blurred and the salt stung the tender skin beneath his eyes. "So don't tell me how to feel or what to think. You no longer have my permission."

His mom elegantly squared her shoulders and arched her eyebrow again. "Why am I here, Fillion?"

"I won't allow the lives of others to be deemed as nothing, either."

Fillion adjusted his position and locked eyes with Skylar. Without a single word, Skylar walked over and knelt on the ground and faced Della. The Son of Wind's face slackened and he drew in a quiet breath. Fillion rolled his eyes. Skylar's reaction was typical of most men when they saw his mom. Reduced to a stupor. Dumbstruck. Blood pumping at accelerated levels. It was gross. And she reveled in it.

"Dr. Della Jayne Nichols, this is Skylar Kane, Son of Wind and the newest Wind Element." He turned to acknowledge Skylar. "This is Dr. Della Jayne Nichols, wife to Hanley Nichols and the lead psychologist and second-in-command at New Eden Biospherics & Research."

"A pleasure, My Lady," Skylar said and bowed his head. "Your son is a quintessential part of our community."

Della regarded Fillion and returned her attention, part incredulous, to Skylar. "How does the community fare?"

"New Eden is in the midst of Harvest, which strengthens the community spirit." Skylar cracked a charming smile. "Our King and Aether is a fine leader."

"I have heard it on the wind that some are not satisfied with New Eden's leader."

"There will always be those who oppose even the simplest of matters." Skylar paused with a thoughtful look. "Heard it on the wind?"

"A saying from a former life. Does your father use this term?" Della blinked and tilted her head in a way some would perceive as coy. Fillion wanted to gag. "You are Timothy's son, correct?" She released a quiet laugh and Skylar shifted on his knees. "I must confess, you remind me a bit of my husband when he was younger." Her smile fell and a puzzling expression replaced the momentary amusement.

"My father still uses this term, My Lady." The impassive tone of Skylar's reply made Fillion smirk. His mom noticed and cleared her throat with a dainty sound, the same way Brianna often did when corrected.

"In your opinion," Della began again, "are there many who exhibit symptoms of depression or anti-social behaviors?" She wove her fingers together and rested her hands in the chamber.

"The residents of New Eden are hearty and healthy."

His mom's eyes brightened. "Are there any who show aggressive tendencies?"

Skylar silently questioned Fillion, who offered a faint smile of assent. "Only recently, My Lady. Our Aether has shown remarkable strength and steadfast wisdom in handling each incident."

"The Moores and Carsons say they will only return if you are King. They are unwilling to support the man who is claiming the position of Aether, for several reasons, the main one being they believe he suffers from deep mental afflictions. After several interviews, it appears your Aether may possess traits of isolation confinement and extreme environment syndrome. Are you familiar with this term?"

"Yes, My Lady," Skylar said, steady.

"You do not believe this man exhibits such traits?"

"He is of a sound mind, and I am proud to stand behind him as our leader."

Della rolled her focus to Fillion and drew her brows together as if wincing. Then she relaxed once more and touched the silver necklace. Fillion had never seen it before. It wasn't her usual style—simple, and modestly short, doing nothing to draw enough attention to her assets. Her movements created a breeze and a mild honey scent wafted their direction. Now his stomach was sick. Could she be any more cliché? Skylar, to his credit, didn't react. Instead, he remained poised and steady.

"Apparently, your father promised both families positions of esteem if they rallied in your cause," she said, hooking a finger through the silver chain. "You do not support your father's wish for you to claim a place on New Eden's once invisible throne?"

The normally rigid, straight posture Skylar carried deflated. Fillion's eyes bugged out, despite all efforts to contain a reaction. He figured it was Timothy who influenced the families who left, but to hear it confirmed? He studied Leaf from across the room. The dark shadows beneath Leaf's eyes deepened as he paled.

"I do not support any efforts to place me on a throne in New Eden, invisible or otherwise." Skylar lowered his head. "For I am not a thief."

His mom remained quiet and her eyes roamed over Skylar's bent form. "Of course not." Her calm, saccharine tone infuriated Fillion and he gripped the edge of his cloak, wanting to rip it—or something—into pieces. "Why did you believe I viewed you as a thief?" The plastic smile returned to her face. Fillion knew what she was doing. But before he could intervene in her attempt to twist Skylar's words, the Son of Wind lifted his head and spoke in a clear, strong voice.

"I did not, My Lady. Your original question was in regard to my reasons, not another's possible view or opinion." Skylar offered a charming smile, and Fillion almost laughed. "My apologies for any confusion. Allow me to rephrase. I shall not rob another of their birthright. If Hanley desired for my family to hold the status of Aether, he would have written my father's name in the Legacy instead of Claire Johnston." He bowed his head in a gesture of honor. "If you will excuse me." Skylar flashed Fillion a look and stepped over to the corner where Leaf awaited direction.

"I did not realize my interview was over. Why did he leave?" Della asked.

"Doesn't matter. In New Eden, it's rude to demand an explanation when someone excuses their presence from a room or conversation." Fillion relaxed his face to disinterest. "No status updates here. Privacy is a rare resource and respected."

"The established trust between individuals must be remarkable. To diminish curiosity or demands out of respect for another's privacy is a mark of strong bonds. Interesting." She tapped a finger against her red lips. "Coal is careful with Internet use and remains respectfully guarded. I wonder if introducing Internet culture would dramatically weaken the community's views on personal privacy with one another and thus weaken their bonds."

"You don't have any credible information gathered from the Techsmith Guild?" Fillion asked.

"Techsmith Guild?" Della lifted her hands from the airlock. "In New Eden?"

"I guess Hanley keeps many secrets from you." Fillion shook the hair out of his eye and clenched his jaw. In a few, brief sentences, he explained the plan and purpose of the Guild. Every so often, he would look Leaf's way. The Son of Earth remained still, as if a corner statue. His mom didn't blink, either, the intensity of her gaze growing as he continued. "Skylar is the leader of the Techsmiths."

"To test the socio-psychological functions of interacting with technology and Earth, as if an actual colony on Mars?" She pressed fingers to her temple and gently rubbed as she closed her eyes. "With real twenty-two minute delays?"

"Sums it up well."

Fillion combed his fingers through his hair, itching to grip the strands and scream. If Hanley could keep years of research from Della, what else was he hiding? Nothing Hanley ever did was what it seemed on the surface. There were always multiple plot points. What was the real reason for the Techsmith Guild? What was hidden? And did the real purpose have something to do with Joel's death? He could ponder these questions in length. But he needed to stay on track.

"You've met the leader of the Techsmith Guild and the one the Carsons and Moores desire as King," Fillion said. "Now, I want you to meet The Aether of New Eden Township." On cue, Leaf knelt beside Fillion and peered into the chamber.

A small scream echoed through the airlock. Della's hands, perfectly groomed and decorated in jewelry, covered her mouth to muffle the sound. Color drained from her face and she stared wide-eyed at Leaf as if he were a ghost. "Who ... who are you?"

"Leaf Watson, My Lady," Joel's son said with a half-bow. "It is an honor. My father spoke highly of you."

Tears glistened in his mom's eyes as she studied Leaf's face. "No. Not possible. I have seen Leaf Watson's death certificate. Investigations and a monumental trial confirmed his death, as well as that of his sisters, and ruled out any possible project negligence." She fingered the necklace around her neck. Fillion squinted his eyes to study the pendant. Was that a linden leaf? Calm and even tempered, his mother asked, "Were you close with Leaf Watson? Honoring his memory by emulating him is a common way to keep a loved one alive." Fillion knew this voice. It reeked of clinical stoicism and pretentious compassion. "His loss must have been traumatic for you."

"My father died in my arms," Leaf replied, his voice breaking as his body tensed. "I also held my mother's hand as she breathed her last. My sister, Laurel, cried without cease that day. Father was so grief-stricken, he refused to leave mother's side or allow others to enter our home for fear she would be removed. I held Laurel and Willow Oak all night long as I dipped a rag in goat's milk for Laurel to suckle. She was but four days old." Leaf wiped away a tear. "The day my father died, he reminded me of the time I cared for my sisters in his absence. Four hours later, as he struggled for breath, he urged me to gather Laurel and Willow Oak, leave New Eden, and seek out Della Jayne, a woman to whom he was once betrothed. He died as your name left his mouth, My Lady."

The professional demeanor shattered, and Fillion's mom released a sob as she covered her face. "No, no, no," she cried. Her shoulders trembled and she leaned her head on the edge of the chamber as a guttural moan shuddered from her small frame. It was unbearable to listen to and watch, and Fillion lowered his eyes.

The anger that consumed him earlier melted into pity. And before he realized what he was doing, he whispered, "Mom," with an outstretched hand. Tears stained her unnaturally youthful face and she gaped at his gesture. What the hell was he thinking? God, he was such a sap. And stupid. An idiot. They didn't touch. The whole world touched, but not them. Leaf's strength and story had emboldened Fillion, as it often did. Warmth flushed his body as he mentally prepared for her rejection. Through the haze of vulnerability, however, a thought hit him. Perhaps she was the same as him? Angry and broken. Maybe they'd both been played by the same Gamemaster?

Time dripped away like a well-worn torture device. Each second shouted a reminder of Della's request for Joel to kiss his children for her. Fear pooled in her eyes and fell down her cheeks as she timidly extended her hand. Their fingers touched and Fillion's body slumped forward as years of abandonment flowed from his mom to him and back in a complete circuit.

Although he was the one offering the comfort, it felt the other way around. This was a moment he'd longed to know for so long. Maybe she really did care about him? Her crying eased and she gave his fingers a light squeeze. A cold sensation tingled in his hand as she pulled away to touch the chain around her neck. She lifted the silver necklace and kissed the small pendant.

Leaf cleared his throat. "I have seen your and father's initials on the linden tree."

A heartbreaking smile touched her red lips. "The linden tree was Joel's engagement gift to me," she said, and flit a nervous look at Leaf. "He carved our initials into the trunk after I said 'yes'. When he announced his acceptance of Hanley's offer to join New Eden, I hired a company to dig up our tree and plant it inside the Township."

"We have a tradition, My Lady," Leaf replied. "When a man pledges his life to a woman, and she honors him by becoming his bride, he carves their initials into the very same linden tree. The trunk bears the marks of many lovers." A bashful smile touched Leaf's face and he blinked nervously. "Everyone in New Eden knows the legend of the first initials. My father often shared the story of the two star-crossed lovers, a man of the earth and humble circumstances and a woman of noble bearing and great beauty."

Leaf smiled shyly once more as he met Della's eyes. "It is said that when tragedy finally tore their love apart, the tree took pity on the maiden and wept. A small, silver linden leaf fell from the branches and magically formed into a pendant as a token of the young man's eternal love, which the maiden carried with her the remainder of her days."

Della touched the necklace once more. In a quivering voice, she said, "A letter from Joel arrived for me the week New Eden sealed its doors. This story you share was enclosed, along with this necklace." Silent tears slid down her face. Then she shook her head. "This is not possible. The courts verified the deaths of each of Joel's children."

Leaf pinched his brows together. "After mother passed away, father urged me to memorize several statements to verify my identity, a notion I found rather strange, but never questioned. He was most insistent that I was to relay a message to you, should ever we meet and he was not present for introductions."

Distressed, Leaf regarded Fillion and Skylar, lowered his eyes, and whispered, "As you know, my full name is Leaf Dylan Watson, Son of Earth, Aether of New Eden Township. Although I am not the son you miscarried after Dylan's death," Leaf said, his expression remaining steadfast, "I offer myself as your humble servant."

Della blanched with his words and let go of the necklace. "How did you... Oh my god." Her eyes rounded and she placed a hand on her throat. "I was fifteen weeks along, and we didn't want our families and friends to know before the wedding. We never told anyone. Not even Hanley knows." Tears gathered and fell down her cheeks as her face altered from expressions of horror to disbelief.

She peered at Fillion and quickly looked away. Della straightened her posture and brushed black strands off of her shoulder. She offered Leaf a worried smile. "The world believes you are dead. If your identity is revealed, it could place New Eden Township in jeopardy."

"Yes, I understand, and I have considered such consequences." Leaf raked a hand through his hair. "I am also aware that I am due a large monetary legacy. The scandal goes beyond my resurrection. Are the funds sufficient enough to assist New Eden in the event of contract losses?"

"To be honest, I have not seen the sum. However, I have gathered from my husband that it is a rather large amount of money." Della paused for a beat. "Are you prepared for medical examinations and court trials? Both would remove you from New Eden Township for a duration."

Without hesitation, Leaf replied, "I am prepared to do whatever is necessary to ensure the safety of my home and my family."

"Your family?"

"My sisters, Laurel and Willow Oak, and my wife, Ember Watson, Coal's twin sister."

"Strange," Della said, thoughtful. "Coal has not mentioned your family or even that his sister was married."

"Not strange." Fillion narrowed his eyes. "Obvious."

His mom regarded him for a split second and then returned attention to Leaf. "The Moores and Carsons have requested to return to New Eden, despite your Kingship. Did you perchance grant permission? I am assuming this is part of why we are meeting, beyond the *obvious*."

Leaf pulled the Scroll from his pocket and brought up the email threads. "I have been in communication with Hanley since the day they left." He handed the device to Della through the shaft.

Her lips formed a thin line as her eyes moved across the screen. Dark hair fell over her face as she swiped to the next page, covering the distress forming on her features. She looked up and locked eyes with Fillion, the hurt and betrayal showing in her sagging shoulders and mouth. "I will sign the release for the families to return to New Eden tomorrow. I cannot offer any guarantees, though, as Hanley could veto my command." Della said to Leaf, "If all goes well, you and Jeff both will receive a message of when to arrive at The Door."

An intense wave of nausea rolled through Fillion and he closed his eyes until it passed. A clammy sensation chilled his skin and he lifted a shaky hand, closed to a fist, and covered his mouth.

"Fillion, you really do not look well," his mom said with genuine concern on her face. "This has been a stressful..." She stopped and cleared her throat and looked away. "My apologies."

"I'm fine." Fillion blinked and let out a slow, measured breath. "Thanks for your help."

"May I have a word alone with my son?"

"Of course, My Lady." Leaf started to rise. "On behalf of New Eden Township, thank you. It is truly an honor to meet you." Leaf remained bent over to see her and dipped his head.

Red lips twitched into an uncertain smile. "Likewise. Although, I wish over better circumstances." She swallowed back the rising emotions. "My condolences to your family. Joel was the finest man I have ever known. His love changed me."

"His love changed many people." Leaf smiled and then rose from his crouched position. "We shall meet you above ground," he whispered to Fillion.

Fillion watched Leaf and Skylar leave, then turned back to his mom. "We're alone now. What's up?"

"Thank you for sharing with me your pain." Long, slender fingers toyed with the necklace again. "I am grieved…" His mom lifted a hand and wiped away a tear. "I know I have done a poor job showing you over the years, but the day you were born was one of the happiest days of my life."

Fillion tensed and looked away. He didn't know how to receive her words. Several festering wounds winced with pain and he swallowed back the rising anger and remained silent.

"I allowed fear over losing you—and Lynden—to mold my motherhood," she continued. "Fear is a master of shape-shifting and becomes what feeds it. Therefore, I did lose you. And lost myself in the process. But I am waking up."

His mom released a heavy sigh and wiped away another tear. "I never wanted any of this to happen. I had ideas, theories, and allowed my excitement to carry me away. But I never wanted my friends to suffer, or my family. This was not the plan, nor how I saw my future life play out. I have made decisions that I can never take back, and they will haunt me for the rest of my life."

He nodded his head and continued to bite his tongue. What could he say?

"You will need time to process that information." She cleared her throat in that dainty way of hers. "You are right, Fillion. You are not my brother or your father. I am pleasantly stunned by your courage and your sense of honor, two traits you possess that I am ashamed to have never noticed." His mom placed her hands onto the edge of the chamber and leaned forward. "Such strengths already reside within a person, but choices and situations showcase their presence. In your pain, you could have chosen to hide. Instead, you chose to protect others who might suffer like you have."

"I don't know what else to do," he said, lifting his shoulders. "I refuse to let Hanley win whatever game he's playing. He's brought me into it as a key player, and I'll be damned if he uses me to hurt others."

The heartbreaking smile returned, her thumb and fore-finger caressing the leaf pendant thoughtfully. "So Willow Oak Watson is alive... How are you handling being in her presence?"

"Peachy." Fillion bit the inside of his cheek.

"No PTSD hallucinations?"

"Like I said, I'm fine." He held onto the lip of the chamber as his head swam under a dizzy spell. His mom arched her eyebrow and studied his face. For some reason he confessed, "I love her." Maybe it was the nausea and light-headedness. Maybe just pure stupidity. Or perhaps he had turned into the corniest sap that had ever walked Mars and Earth—it was killing him. But regardless, the words were out before he could take them back.

His mom whispered the word "synchronicity" to herself, a distraught expression tensing her features. That was her on-ly reply, and not even meant for him to hear he realized. Still, it allowed him an opportunity to mull the idea internally. And god, knowing there was a clinical term for his brand of crazy only confirmed his freak status.

She dropped the necklace and leaned forward once again. Worry and sorrow creased her forehead and pulled at the lines around her mouth, as if she wrestled with remorse over his moronic confession. He braced himself. Her mouth opened to speak and then she sat back, an entirely different form of concern flitting across her eyes. "You really do look sick. You should get some sleep." She offered a troubled smile, looking away. "Call me anytime you wish to talk. OK?"

"OK. Thanks. I promise to think over everything you shared."

His mom dipped her head and averted her eyes once again. An awkward silence ensued. It was the same feeling he had when leaving Norah's room. He knew he needed to sever the connection, but didn't want to at the same time. He'd waited his whole life to feel real in his mom's eyes. But he also wanted to crawl into bed, his mind quickly slipping away.

"When you shut the door," he said, in a sturdy voice strange to his ears, "I'll reconfigure the circuit logic. I'll clean up the log entries to hide your activity, too." She nodded her head and smiled her goodbye, and started to close the metal door. "Wait." His mom paused and met his eyes. "Take care of yourself. Joel would want you to." After half a second, he whispered, "So do I." Her eyes welled up with tears and she smiled, the gesture warm and vulnerable.

They both looked away and shut their respective doors in slow, quiet movements. Exhaling loudly, Fillion fell to his back and closed his eyes. He needed to stay focused. He could crash later. At this point, he needed a system restart to refresh his emotional state. New thoughts uploaded at rapid speed. His sluggish brain was unable to keep up with the momentum. Forcing himself to keep moving, he unloaded his fire nest material and, within a couple minutes, lit up a joint. God, that first drag never got old.

As the smoke left his lips in thin wisps, he turned on his Cranium and reset the circuit logic. Then, he hacked into the Guardian Angel mainframe, perusing the log entries for the last twenty-four hours while he waited for his mom to enter the heart of the lab. Gave him time to smoke in peace, too. Biometric scanners recorded her trek across the property and through N.E.T., adding a new line-entry to the top.

While he waited, he searched through the previous entries. The word "air_lock" scrolled past and he halted, pushing the screen back up. Yesterday, the airlock was accessed via the technosphere mid-day. That night, it was accessed by someone in the hatch. His pulse raced with the possibilities, wondering if it was Timothy, Connor, or someone else.

With a groan, he closed his eyes tight. The act was a useless counter-pressure to the headache blurring his vision. And the pain only intensified with each thought his mind attempted to deconstruct and re-engineer into the machine that made up his mental faculties. His eyelids pushed open to a squint, determined to finish the job so he could fall into bed.

Fillion erased the new log entries when he was sure his mom was back in her room, and then closed out all the screens. With a last puff on the nub of his joint, he snuffed it out and swept the ashes to the corner of the room to hide evidence of being here.

Muscles ached with each movement and shook with weakness. Still, he managed to climb up the ladder to the waiting gazes of Leaf and Skylar. Rock back in place, they lifted hoods and began the long walk back to the village. At this point, the way he felt, it was tempting to curl up beneath a large leaf, allow the jungle to claim him, and call it a night. "Mind over matter," he muttered under his breath, the roar of the waterfall receding behind the thick, draping vines.

I believe in everything until it's disproved. So I believe in fairies, the myths, dragons. It all exists, even if it's in your mind. Who's to say that dreams and nightmares aren't as real as the here and now?

***

Surrealism had a great effect on me because then I realised that the imagery in my mind wasn't insanity. Surrealism to me is reality.
— John Lennon, singer and songwriter, *The Beatles*, 20th century A.D. *

CHAPTER THIRTY-FOUR

ach step drained Fillion's strength, and his muscles shook and burned with the effort. In The Rows he stumbled, face planting into the dirt. Gross. Was this a sign? Were the residents not lucky enough to make it to Project Phase Two trying to take him captive? The ashes of a Nichols in New Eden would be an appropriate blood price. Maybe then the dead would rest in peace. Fillion, too. A sound left his mouth when he rolled to his side, becoming louder when Leaf pulled him to his feet.

"Do you fare well?"

"No." Fillion's head felt heavy, but he found a spark of strength to lift it. "I think I need help."

"Of course." Leaf's face tensed, and he flashed a quick look to Skylar as he draped Fillion's arm around his shoulder and moved slowly. "Do you think you can travel to my apartment?"

"Yeah," Fillion said, catching his breath. He didn't want to be left alone. The weakness and sensations were starting to freak him out. Same with the direction of his thoughts. When the trio reached the forest, Fillion lifted a hand. "I need to stop. Set me ... down." Leaf lowered him and crouched by his side, face puckered with fear. Fillion's lungs pumped hard, even though they had walked at a snail's pace. "Skylar," he croaked.

"Yes, My Lord."

"I have ... a gift for ... Willow. In The Forge. Under ... a large sheet. You'll know it ... when you see it."

"You wish for me to fetch it?"

Fillion closed his eyes, then forced them open and found Skylar's worried gaze. The forest around them shifted and moved, a quick advance and a slow retreat, and Fillion shook his head. That was weird. Was he really so exhausted his mind was playing tricks on him? Remembering Skylar's question, he answered, "In her ... living room ... by morning. Surprise."

"It shall be done. Worry not."

"Thanks." With another shallow breath, Fillion looked to Leaf. "Let's go."

Leaf hefted him to a standing position and Skylar sidled up to Fillion's other side to help. They continued to edge along the village, Fillion's head lolling as lethargy set in. His mind began to tingle, like the beginning stages of a high. Occasionally, the ground beneath his feet would disappear and he seemed to walk across an obsidian river. The black, shiny trail was ominous and beautiful, and his feet trod over each rise and dip of the gentle, solidified waves with ease. But then, the image would fade and the leaf-littered path would return. Maybe he finally had slipped into insanity. How else could he explain it?

At the top of the stairs, Fillion's legs finally gave out and he nearly crumpled to the floor. Leaf and Skylar caught him and held him up, but his legs refused to move. God, this sucked. What the hell was going on with him? The next thing he knew, hands scooped under his legs and arms, and the nobles carried him into the apartment.

The sound of the door pierced through Fillion's head and he groaned, grimacing with pain. "Damn it. Did you ... make my head ... explode?" he asked.

"My apologies," Leaf said softly, but still, Fillion cringed.

"My Lord," a female intoned from the other side of the room. He thought perhaps Ember. "Is he injured?"

"No, he is sick and plagued by sudden weakness."

A pause. "Oh, the poor man! Where shall we place him?"

"In my parents' bedchamber," Leaf said.

The room tilted, then spun. The walls swirled and disappeared and faces contorted into horrific shapes. Fillion's stomach lurched and he gagged, sweat breaking out on his forehead. "I'm going ... to puke."

"Quick, the wooden tumbler on the cabinet," Leaf boomed, gently placing Fillion into a chair.

Within seconds, a cup was thrust in Fillion's hands and he retched. Stomach muscles cramped and squeezed with each heave until a slow fire spread across his waist. Weakness finally claimed him and his body folded in on itself, and he felt weightless as he fell from the side of a chair. Hands grabbed him and eased him onto the floor, where he remained. Light flooded the room as multiple lanterns and candles were lit, and Fillion closed his eyes against the brightness.

Thoughts became hazy and his mind soupy, but strangely fluid at the same time. It was as if he had ceased breathing and no longer struggled. Reality faded in and out until Fillion lost himself to the racing thoughts and swirling sensations.

A gasp sounded nearby and the clatter of footfalls rushed in his ears. The sound brought on a strong ache in his head, and he winced. Cool, soft hands touched his face and he opened his eyes to the blurry image of an otherworldly woman with pale skin, glowing in the candlelight, radiant hair that shimmered like threads of gold, and a white, flowing dress, edged in iridescent lace and ribbons. The garment was so beautiful he reached out and fingered the lace, and the angel's lips, red and full, parted in a wide-eyed expression. She leaned forward, dabbing his face with her sleeve, and her silky hair brushed over his cheek with the motion. Peace washed over him and he offered a shaky smile before closing his eyes once more.

"I'm ready, angel," he said, convinced he was dying. Strange thoughts flitted across his mind and his body began to shake. It began as small tremors, but soon he convulsed.

"Fillion!" the angel cried. Her voice was warbled and strangled, as if pained as she stood by and watched the life drain from his body. A cool kiss touched his forehead and a sigh left his quaking body. "Is he truly dying?"

"He grew sick in the rainforest until he could no longer stand." Leaf's voice seemed louder than usual and Fillion covered his ears and groaned. What was Leaf doing here? Fillion's mind disappeared behind a giant wall in a foreign land of images and sensations. Where was he?

"Skylar," the angel's said, her musical tones wrapping around Fillion. "I wish to call upon your services."

"Anything, Your Highness. I am your humble servant."

"Please fetch the Herbalist and the Naturopath."

Footsteps clapped on the wooden floor and Fillion groaned again, covering his head.

"First, let us move him." Leaf's booming voice elicited another stab of pain, ripping through Fillion's skull. Hands lifted Fillion from the floor and he felt as though he was floating, especially when a cool breeze caressed his warmed skin. Maybe he really was drifting through the air. Had he finally died? "The door, Ember," Leaf said and a loud creak transformed into the screeching sound of an old-school dial-up modem and Fillion cried out against the sharp stabs in his head. His stomach clenched and he dry heaved as a cool, damp sheen of sweat broke out over his entire body. "Almost there," he heard the man whisper. Where had Leaf gone? Did the Son of Earth disappear?

"In here?" the angel's squeaked, more like the trill of a bird. "Leaf…"

"Where else? He shall have peace in this corner of the house and this room provides the most space to care for his needs."

"I have not been in here since father died…" The angel's voice trailed off, followed by a sharp intake of breath.

"I shall fetch water and a rag," another female quietly said, causing barely a ripple of sound in the room. Still, bursts of blues and purples erupted in his vision and Fillion stared in wondrous awe at the ribbons of color her voice created in the air. He lifted a hand to touch one but it disappeared.

Fillion's body lowered into soft clouds, the fluffy, white layers proof that his life was ending. The mysterious hands released his limbs and, this time, he was sure that he was floating. "Where's the angel?" he asked, squinting his eyes. The words formed thick in his mouth and he slurred. Something wasn't right. He licked his lips. Had they swollen? They felt huge. The glowing woman with golden hair pushed past the man with the pain-inducing voice and leaned over Fillion's body. "Please," he asked in a mere whisper. "Sing for me. Before I die."

A smooth, earthy voice hummed a feather-soft tune near his face as fingers brushed damp hair from his eyes. She continued to hum, and then words, sweet and melodious, spilled from her mouth, and tears formed in his eyes. Her voice was the most beautiful sound he had ever heard and his heart grew faint as her image dimmed around the edges. His body began to shake again, convulsing violently, before his muscles eased and he rested upon the clouds once more. Her singing faltered, but then continued and something cool and wet dripped onto his face. He flinched with the rain and she stopped singing, even though the storm continued.

Fillion raised a shaky hand and wrapped his fingers around her wrist, pressing her pale hand to his cheek. "Don't stop," he rasped.

"His skin feels as though it is on fire," the angel whispered, angling her head away from him.

"That's because I'm in eco-hell," Fillion volunteered. His voice seemed detached and distant, yet blaring at the same time. "I'm burning because the sins of the father fall upon the son," he murmured.

"I am frightened." The sounds of crying waved from her body, and he felt each melancholy note lap against him. "I cannot lose another I love."

"I found a tumbler of water and a clean cloth," the other female said, taking his hand in hers. She leaned forward and studied his face, her mouth dipped in a frown.

Blues and purples blossomed before Fillion's vision once more. The walls crashed toward him and Fillion screamed, throwing out his arms to stop the attack. The angel and the other woman jumped away from the clouds and grabbed each other for support. The walls stilled and inched back, resuming their sentry positions. The sudden motion churned his stomach and his gut heaved. Hands forced him to roll to his side, but nothing, except a trace of bile, left his stomach.

"We need to cool his skin," the angel said.

"Willow, you should leave the room." The man replied in a dark, solemn tone. An ache rung through Fillion's head with this voice, and he moaned. "Ember can assist me."

"Don't send the angel away!" Fillion cried out. In a trembling whisper, he confessed, "I'm so scared. Oh god, don't leave me. Please don't leave. I don't want to die alone. I need you."

"I shall not leave you, my prince," the angel sang over him, and he smiled, closing his eyes.

"I'm a prince?"

"Yes," she whispered, her fingers running through his hair. "My handsome, infuriatingly witty, pigheaded prince."

He opened his eyes and tried to focus on her glowing face. "God, you're beautiful. It's painful." He watched, mesmerized, as his sigh caressed the soft skin of her face. Their eyes locked and he lost himself in her emerald depths, green and rich as a forest.

"I'm in love with an angel. How can I be in love with someone who's dead? Oh. My. God. I'm such a freak."

His body ached with the movement, but he couldn't stop the chortles that escaped his dry, parched mouth. The humor faded when a bright pain lanced through him. He choked, "We're full of nevers," as a forming sob tightened in his chest. Seconds ticked loud and ominous in his head. His clock would stop soon. Everything would stop soon. The pain. The bliss. The joy. The anguish.

Then, as if waking from a dream, his eyes fluttered open and logic caught up to his racing thoughts. Fillion gripped the clouds in a tight fist and tried to sit up, but couldn't. "Wait." With a start, he yelled, "Who are you? Where am I? Damn. Why can't I move?"

Golden drops fell down from the maiden's cheeks onto his, and he could almost see the metallic streaks sliding across his face. "I am Willow Oak Watson." The musical sound of her voice lilted with minor keys, the sorrowful tune like flaming coals on his already burning skin. Her words caught fire in the air and the ash snowed over his still body. "You are in New Eden Township, do you not recall?"

The glowing, ethereal image of the maiden warped and the gold bled away to reveal an emaciated, gaunt figure. Her sunken eyes dulled as they focused on him, her lank, dingy blond hair lying limp against her skull. Blue lips parted and, when she spoke, a foul smell permeated the room, like rotten, decaying flesh. Fillion screamed and tried to move away, but a heavy weight pressed him down.

"Fillion," the corpse said. She tilted her head with concern and his pulse raged with fear. "I shall not harm you."

"Go away!" he shouted, covering his face. "Get the hell away from me!"

"It is I, Willow," the corpse said. Her voice spliced when she spoke, as if her body, soul, and spirit replied in unison, the high and low sounds spooking his already terrorized state. "You shall be fine. Rest. I shall care for you, my prince."

"I don't want you here! And I'm sure as hell not your prince!" Weakened by the emotional outburst, Fillion whimpered, and his head rolled to the side. "I belong to no one." In a plea, he whispered, "I tried for so long to forget you. I can't save you, so go away. Stop haunting me!" With a clenched fist, he hit his head repeatedly saying, "Get out of my head! Get out of my head!" until shackles pinned down his arms to the clouds. How could something get chained to a cloud? The very idea mystified him and his thoughts reeled from the endless possibilities, never knowing clouds could be solid and forceful.

"Leaf," the corpse blurted in a sob and black, oily tears oozed from her eyes. "My heart is breaking. I cannot breathe."

"Fillion is not in his right mind. Do not take his words as truth. He knows not what he says." The deep voice sliced through Fillion's head as if razors, and his body writhed in response. "Perhaps you should leave the room until he requests the angel once more, *ma chère.*"

"No! I shall not leave him. I told him I would stay." Desperate, the corpse placed cold, decaying fingers on Fillion's cheek and leaned toward him. "Do you not recognize me?" In a panic, he tried to move away, but the heaviness deadened his arms and legs and he couldn't move. The stench of her nearness was overwhelming and Fillion recoiled as his stomach heaved, over and over again into a bucket that suddenly materialized.

"I don't ever want to see you again," he finally managed between ragged, shallow breaths. "Never. I want my sanity back. This is goodbye. Forever. Now leave and stay the hell away from me."

The black tears ran down her face and his skin sizzled and corroded when they landed on him. He screamed in terror and in pain, making her cry even more. The man with the painful voice came behind her and placed hands on her arms to lead her away. But the corpse fought, pushing the man away as she shrieked, her keening wails like a banshee. Others entered the room and circled the clouds he floated on, much to his relief. Then, a sudden panic hit him and he grabbed the arm of the man with the loud voice, and everyone in the room became still-frames in a paused video.

"Don't let them take me away."

"I do not follow," the painful voice replied.

Fillion cringed, releasing a soft moan. When he recovered, he whispered, "Put me in The Rows. Don't let them take me." Fillion turned his head to the side as a pang wrenched through his chest, tightening the muscles. He whispered, "Where'd she go? Why did she leave me?"

The man leaned forward so that their eyes connected. "You shall not die."

"I'm already dead."

In the last image he saw of the corpse, her legs had buckled and her shrieks silenced, and the man carried her limp body from the room. Finally, she was dead and would leave him alone. Now he could die, too. And in peace.

A woman rested her ear against his chest. And when she spoke, it sounded hollow and glitchy, as if digitalized. "Activated charcoal, quick. His pulse is weak." Fillion's body started to convulse again and his eyes rolled to the back of his head. "Skylar, hold him down." She said several other words to another woman, her image winking in and out of focus, fuzzing on occasion. But Fillion only heard one word before he drifted into a state of unconsciousness.

Poison.

Deconstructing illusions is an imperative aspect in the grief process. This is often the step known as the 'if only' stage. If only I had said this instead of that. If only I had not held so many grudges against this person. If only I would have slowed down and enjoyed my life more. Each time sorrows and hardships challenge prior beliefs and convictions, the individual is forced to reset the value system of his or her life. This stage inevitably brings to the surface the individual's greatest fears and strongest desires. Processing the polarity of dreams and nightmares becomes the very catalyst that deconstructs illusions and reprioritizes the many elements of the grieving person's life.

— Dr. Della Jayne Nichols, "Chapter 10: Deconstructing Illusions," *Misery Loves Company*, 2047

CHAPTER
THIRTY-FIVE

Willow awoke to her own voice crying out, "Do not leave me!" However, the raw edges of her plea were drowned out by a swarm of other female voices delivering commands in a nearby room. She blinked away the fog while taking in her parents' bedchamber, warmly lit by candles. Activity swirled around the bed as a body thrashed, fingers clawing and gripping the covers. From the dark shadows of the hallway she watched in horror, words and images drifting through her mind in a haze. Then, she remembered.

Fillion never wished to see her again, was terrified of her even. Why did he refer to her as an angel rather than by her name? Her heart twisted and writhed, wishing to weep and never stop, until she drowned in her grief. Another she loved was being taken—no—lacerated from her heart, each cut deep and unbearable. Although she knew Fillion was sick, and though Leaf encouraged her to ignore him, she could not forget Fillion's words. Despite all appearances, there was truth behind his wild responses, as if Fillion's apprehensions took shape and gave voice to his darkest fears. What if he died with such bitter sentiments as his final thoughts of her?

Air left her body, long and deep, and she hiccupped, a quick gulp to steady the enormous emotions whipping around inside of her. Arms tightened protectively around her back and arm, and that is when she noticed her position. Leaf sat upon a chair near the doorway, holding her slumped over body, which perched upon his knee, her head resting against his chest. The whoosh of his heart muffled the voices, but not enough.

A tiny sniff nearby startled Willow and she stilled. "Leaf, will he die?" Laurel's voice came as a squeak and Willow's heart lurched.

"No," Leaf replied in a whisper. "He shall rise renewed with the morning sun, you shall see."

"Did father suffer like him?" A small sob escaped from Laurel, and a tear silently trailed down Willow's cheek in response. Leaf held both her and Laurel on his lap, each sister upon a knee.

"Father passed on quickly, *ma chère*."

"Is father happy, you think?"

Leaf whispered in reply, "I believe he misses us as we do him. But I also believe he is happy, for he has reunited with mother and his soul no longer aches." Leaf paused as Laurel readjusted on his knee, and Willow felt Laurel's small fingers upon her back. Softly, Leaf said, "Both mother and father desired for us to know only happiness while they lived. I cannot imagine that their gift of love and joy departed with them. It is a gift we are to always enjoy, although difficult at times."

"I think so, too." Laurel bumped into Willow again. "I love you, Leaf."

"I love you, too, Laurel."

Another tear slid down Willow's cheek and she refocused attention to those caring for Fillion inside the brightly lit room. Joannah and Timna, the Naturopath, lifted Fillion to a sitting position as Ember leaned forward with a cloth. Skylar stood near the foot of the bed, preventing a clear view of Fillion.

In low tones, Timna turned to Joannah and said, "I think we should employ a modified Trendelenburg position to aid the hypotension. I fear he may aspirate, however, should he vomit once more. What is your opinion?"

Joannah studied Fillion with a thoughtful look. "Yes, I agree with you. We could take turns to stand guard through the night and roll him to his side should he begin to vomit."

"Your Highness," Timna said to Ember, "we need more pillows."

"You may use the chair pillows from the living room," Willow volunteered. All heads turned her direction in surprise.

"Willow!" Laurel said from behind her. "But you made those for father."

"Yes, and he would wish for us to assist Fillion."

Timna gave a brisk nod. "Very well. Skylar, My Lord, please fetch the pillows."

The Son of Wind began to move but halted his steps when Fillion moaned. "Skylar," he said, his voice weak." Call Mack."

"How, My Lord?"

"Cranium in pouch ... belt." A cough wracked Fillion and he dry-heaved once more into a bucket Joannah supplied. "Where's ... the ... angel?" Willow gasped and every muscle tightened. Those in the room shot a nervous glance her direction.

"He is lucid some moments," Leaf murmured close to her ear, "and falls away into delusions within a single breath. The hallucinations are waning more and more as the poison purges." Troubled by his words, she could not speak. Fillion suffered hallucinations? Poison? Instead, she nodded her head to acknowledge his explanation. "Do not allow his words to injure you," Leaf said. She nodded again, although she struggled to accept the encouragement.

Skylar marched across the plank floor, revealing Fillion, and her eyes widened. She expected her brother to remind her to avert her eyes and preserve Fillion's modesty and her own. But he did not. Perhaps his mind was too tired or preoccupied to notice. Ember and Joannah continued to support Fillion in a sitting position, his exposed chest heaving for breath. Candlelight warmed his paled, clammy skin and her eyes roamed over his bare arms and torso. The blanket bunched in his lap and slid off one leg as they maneuvered him. The rushing air in her lungs stilled when he moved, her eyes fixated to the show of sinew and muscle, never seeing a man so undressed, nor so decorated.

"I have your Cranium." Skylar moved in front of Willow's view. Embarrassed by her thoughts, she blinked several times and spun a small strand of hair to calm her flustered state. "Who is Mack, My Lord?"

"Allow me," Ember said. "I have assisted Mack recently, although he only knows of my Guild name."

"Leaf?" Willow lifted and twisted to see her brother's face. "What does Ember speak of?"

"I am as astonished as you," he said, eyes narrowing.

"Voice ... activated ... biometric start ... screen," Fillion groaned, the sound full of such misery that Willow tensed against a forming sob. Ember leaned toward the head of the bed and placed the Cranium to Fillion's ear, who said in a thin voice, "Cranium ... phone ... Mack."

Then Ember strapped the device to her ear and sat upon the bed, taking Fillion's hand in hers. "No, I am afraid not. This is Ember Watson, Coal's sister." She remained perfectly still. Joannah and Timna exchanged curious looks, but then busied their hands as before. "Yes, sir, unfortunately, there is a problem. Before I explain, please know that he is breathing well and interacting on a limited level; however, we believe he may have been poisoned." Ember lifted her other hand and caressed the back of Fillion's, the act so tender and compassionate that Willow could no longer hold back the tears. "Yes, he wished to speak to you. Do not be alarmed if he fades in and out of reality, for he is afflicted by hallucinations." In deft movements, she removed the Cranium and fastened it to Fillion once more. "Speak, My Lord. Your friend awaits you."

"Mack." Silence for several heartbeats. "Diagnosis site. Drag0nMaiden2038 is Ember." Another pause. "Take care … of Lyn … if … No. No leave. Don't. I'm … finally happy … floating on a cloud bed. See colors in … the air … angel gone … she'll come back … when I die." A longer pause. "Love you, too, mate… You're not … pathetic. Yeah. Peachy." Fillion lifted his arm, shaking with weakness before it fell to the bed. "For … you." Then his body went limp.

"He has slipped beneath consciousness once more," Joannah whispered. "Shall I apply smelling salts or shall we allow him peace?"

"Peace," Timna answered. "Skylar, the pillows please."

"Yes, Madam."

Ember plucked the device from Fillion's ear and placed it back onto her own. "This is Ember. Yes, sir, one and the same. Pleasure to officially meet you." She lifted a finger and tapped the device and then a finger danced through the air. "Yes, I have a browser screen." Her fingers flew around more.

Willow spun toward Leaf. His gaze was riveted onto his wife, though, brows deeply creased and mouth in a straight, thin line. Nevertheless, when he looked at Willow, she noticed in his pale green depths a marked pride toward Ember's actions despite the betrayal.

Skylar returned with the pillows and looked to Timna for direction. "Joannah, slowly ease Fillion down with me." When he lay flat upon the bed, Timna continued. "Skylar, use the bed and chair pillows to gradually elevate his legs, the feet supported the highest, and at least two or three hands high. Thank you, My Lord."

"The site says we need a small sample of blood," Ember said, directing her comment to the two women.

Timna removed a knife from her belt, poured a small measure of whiskey over the blade, then held it over a candle flame while Joannah gathered a clean linen strip from a medicinal bag.

"The Naturopath is sanitizing a knife," Ember reported to Mack. "Once we prick his finger, I simply align the blood sample beneath the holographic scanner? Thank you, sir. Yes, your directions are understood." Timna held the knife into the air for the pre-dawn chill to cool the blade. "It is true, Fillion does not wish for Outside medical attention. No, sir. A man and woman should always choose their path, in life and in death. I shall respect his wishes and Fillion trusts you shall, too." Ember closed her eyes with a pained expression. "I know, sir. I share your fear and grief this moment, and that of his sister. Rest assured that we care deeply for your friend and will do all possible to ensure his comfort."

"The blade is ready, Your Highness," Timna said to Ember. "Skylar, please hold Fillion down should he wake while we lance his finger. Joannah, please secure his arm."

With a steady hold, Timna opened Fillion's hand and selected a finger. Willow buried her face into Leaf's chest, same as Laurel. Yet her distress also demanded she watch. Peering through lowered lashes, Willow held every muscle still as if wielding the knife herself. Quickly and carefully, Timna sliced through the tip of Fillion's finger, which blossomed red before one could blink. Remarkably, Fillion did not move. Nary a sign of discomfort crossed his face. Ember maneuvered the blood offering, which pooled and dripped from his finger, to a desired location up high from the bed and tapped the air.

"The diagnosis scanner is calculating," Ember reported in a low, even voice. "The sample was acceptable and the screen is loading the results. You may clean him up, now." Timna wiped Fillion's finger and placed an ointment upon the wound and Joannah wrapped the linen strip, tying it off. "The first result: *psilocybe cubensis*."

"That would explain the hallucinations. I had my suspicions," Joannah said. The Herbalist looked toward Willow and Leaf. "Psychedelic mushroom, Your Majesty."

"Another result: *grayanotoxin.*" Ember lifted her eyes to Joannah's. "There do not appear to be any more potential toxins listed, only what the site declares as normal properties and chemistries."

"Did he ingest honey recently?" Joannah slowly met each pair of eyes in the room, to which most shrugged or shook their head. "It typically comes from a rhododendron or azalea bush known for its production of 'mad honey.'"

"Is it fatal?" Willow asked, unable to remain quiet.

"No, rarely fatal," Timna said, with a small smile of relief. "Although, it can cause bradycardia and hypotension, which would account for the low pulse and general weakness. It is most known for inducing vomiting and convulsions. He shall recover."

"The poor man," Willow said, coming to a stand, careful to not wake her sister, who somehow found sleep through the chaos. Resting her head upon the doorway, Willow wrinkled her nose with the pungent smell of sickness. Fillion's breathing had slowed to a restful rhythm, and her throat tightened.

Timna placed her middle and index fingers upon Fillion's wrist with a look of concentration. After a measure of time passed, she looked up and said, "The hallucinations might have influenced additional sickness depending on the sensorial effects he experienced."

Joannah rested a hand upon Fillion's arm. "I do believe the worst has passed. However, he is in dire need of hydration and salts."

"I shall wake Cook, if she is not awake already, and have her prepare vegetable broth," Skylar said. "Do you wish for her to brew a pain reliever as well?"

Joannah dipped her head. "Yes, thank you, My Lord." The Herbalist turned to Timna. "Shall I administer another dose of activated charcoal?"

"Yes, please."

"Did you hear the conversation, Mr. Ferguson?" Ember's finger slid through the air with an occasional tap. "Yes, you may rest easy. I sent your contact information to my account and shall call you if there are any changes. And worry not, I shall relay a message to Fillion to call you once he regains strength. Thank you for your assistance. Of course, sir. Farewell." With a final tap upon the device, she pulled the silver machine from her head and looked directly at Leaf, before lowering her eyes to the floor.

"I wonder if highly concentrated rhododendron and *psilocybe* hash oil were placed inside one or more of his joints?" Joannah asked, as if sensing the need to redirect the tension. "It is the only way to ingest either that I can conclude at the moment. Unless there are more modern applications involved that I am not aware of, which is, of course, entirely possible. Dried rhododendron leaves contain trace amounts of toxins and would not warrant such a strong reaction." Joannah turned to Timna. "Usually *psilocybe* loses psychedelic affects with direct heat, too, except when an oil."

Timna held a thoughtful look. "We do not have either of these ingredients within New Eden naturally."

"There is a hatch in the rainforest with technology that connects to the Outside world," Leaf said, his eyes solely upon Ember, "and an airlock, granting both parties a means for commerce."

"More neighbors have gathered outside, Your Majesty," Skylar said in a hushed, hurried voice, his eyes bouncing between Leaf and Ember.

"More?" Willow asked.

"Yes," Leaf replied. "They have come in a steady stream, many awakened by Fillion's thrashing and screaming. It appears news is traveling despite the hour."

"A crowd has gathered to keep vigil."

Leaf regarded Skylar once more. "Please tell those who have gathered that the Son of Eden shall make a full recovery and presently rests."

"Yes, Your Majesty."

With an easy rise, Leaf repositioned Laurel and carried her toward her room. A few moments later, he returned and peered in to watch Ember as she sat beside Fillion on the bed, stroking his hand while Johanna held his head up and spooned a small amount of black, shiny liquid into his mouth. The Herbalist pinched his nose while cleaning up the dark dribble that spilled from his mouth, and Fillion grimaced, then swallowed before opening his mouth for air with a slight cough. She lowered him back upon the straw mattress, and his head rolled on the pillow with a soft moan. But he remained unconscious. Joannah left a hemp rag bunched beneath his mouth to catch any residual drips or saliva, ensuring the linens were not stained.

"You should find whatever rest this night promises before sunbreak," Leaf said softly to Willow. "The matriarchs and village matrons shall arrive soon after first light to prepare you."

"To prepare me?" Willow knit her brows together.

Leaf leaned forward and kissed her on the forehead. "Happy sixteenth birthday, Willow Oak."

"Oh…" Her eyes widened and she placed her hands upon her cheeks. "I had completely forgotten." She studied Fillion once more, the covers drawn to his upper chest now. "I am afraid to leave," she whispered.

"He shall not die." Leaf frowned with understanding. "Nor does he wish to leave you. However, you both need rest."

"Yes, I am only in the way, nor is my presence desired," Willow said with a shallow curtsy, trying to not blush and doing a rather poor job of it. Leaf placed his hand upon her arm and she paused, looking up.

"He loves you. Those words were true," Leaf said. "Do you remember what father would often share?" She watched the flicker of candlelight upon the wall and clasped her hands together. Willow was not in the mood for one of Leaf's lessons, but she would oblige him. "Our feelings are real, they often become our reality, but they are not always based on truth. Many of Fillion's fears and heartaches became reality while under the influence of the hallucinogenic. And, for a while, he forgot the truth. He shall remember come morning and you shall see that all your worries were for naught." She provided a quick nod, feeling her neck and face suffuse with warmth. "Rest well, Oaklee."

"Willow."

"Indeed." Leaf raised an eyebrow. A hint of smile contrasted with the deep circles and lines of fatigue. "Rest well, *Willow*. It makes my heart glad that at least *his* company is preferred over that of a snake." She did not wish to smile, but could not help the pull on her lips with his words.

Just then, the entry door opened and Connor worriedly peeked inside. Leaf gestured for the former Fire Element to enter. Connor slipped in quickly and quietly shut the door. His heavy footsteps clacked across the wooden floor.

"The rumors are running wild," Connor said, glancing inside the room. "Will he fare well?"

"If you will excuse me," Willow said, lowering to a curtsy. Both Connor and Leaf regarded her with a bow, remaining quiet as she rose.

After one last glance, taking in Fillion's pallid complexion and matted hair, she backed into the hallway and trundled to her room. Connor and Leaf could debrief and deliberate with one another. She did not possess the fortitude to listen and relive the horror of this evening.

Collapsing upon her cot, she wrapped the wool blankets around her form until they felt like warm arms, holding her tight while her tears dampened the pillow and her mind drifted into fitful slumber.

A sudden bounce jostled Willow's body and she flew to a sitting position. A strong ache pounded within her head. She touched her forehead with a grimace, then relaxed her face upon seeing her little sister. Laurel slipped into the covers beside her with a large grin, her amber eyes sparkling.

"You gave me a fright," Willow said, placing a hand upon her chest. She fell back onto the pillow with a few more deep, measured breaths.

"Oaklee, you will not believe what is in the living room!"

"No?" She rolled to face her sister until they were nose to nose. "Shall you tell me, or must I guess?"

"Neither, you must come see for yourself." With a giggle, Laurel hopped from the covers and gamboled toward the bedchamber door. "Hurry!" Braids skipped to the beat of her sister's footsteps, the sounds echoing in Willow's head until her sister disappeared into the hallway.

"The little imp," she muttered to the morning shadows.

Sunlight peeked through the shutters and Willow released a tiny groan. Her eyes winced with pain, their swollen state a reminder of all the heartache and intense emotions of the previous night. She came to a sitting position once more, ensuring her nightgown draped over her toes, and luxuriated in the warmth. Then, after several groggy heartbeats, she forced her tired and achy frame into motion. Thankfully, her linen work dress fell over her chemise with ease—one less struggle—and she thus decided against a belt or brushing her hair in favor of traveling into the hallway to see this great surprise.

However, she was not prepared for the image that filled her vision. Willow inhaled sharply, her lungs gulping for air, reliving the shock over and over again. In a trance, she trod toward the corner of the living room where stood a magnificent spinning wheel. The sun's golden fingers stretched across the floor and nearly touched the wheel's warm finish. Still, enough light reached the corner to cast a magical aura around the simple, wood machine.

"Am I in a dream?" Willow asked, breathless. Laurel sat in a chair upon Leaf's lap, barely containing her glee. Her brother, however, met Willow's eyes with the same weariness she possessed. Nevertheless, a small smile appeared on his face. Incredulous, she asked, "Where did this come from?"

"Inspect the legs and you shall see."

Smiling, she turned toward the wheel and brushed her fingertips across the smooth surface and over each carved groove. Tingles of excitement shot up her limbs and through her body in sharp bursts of wondrous joy. She knelt on the ground, her exuberance overshadowing her fatigue. As if extensions of her fingers, her eyes caressed each carved and notched oak leaf, every scrape of a whittling blade. Willow nibbled on her lower lip, not sure if she wished to laugh, cry, or perhaps both.

Suspense almost became unbearable when not finding any clue as to the gift-giver after studying two legs. Her knees inched closer to the third leg and her body stilled. There it was, perfectly etched into the wood and her hand flew to her mouth. She snapped her focus back toward Leaf, and her brother's face softened.

Willow returned to the initials. Her fingers caressed the "F" with reverence before pressing into the leaf that formed from the tip of the last line in the "W," similar to her father's carved initials in the linden tree. A giggle emerged, followed by another, and her entire body soon shook with felicity.

As she looked more closely, she noticed salvaged parts from her previous wheel. A blend of the old and the new. Then, she spun the wheel and listened to the melodious whirl, the mechanical song stretching to every corner of the room.

She swiveled toward her brother with a wide smile and asked, "May I see him?"

"And break tradition?" His expression remained guarded, but she recognized the small twinkle in his eyes. "Hurry before the matriarchs arrive. I warrant you would not relish their chastisement."

Willow nodded her head, while grinning into her shoulder. Per tradition, a woman on her sixteenth birthday was to remain hidden until the evening celebration, most especially from potential suitors. With light, quick steps, she entered the hallway and paused before the bedchamber door. The wood groaned with the pressure and movement, and she cringed with the sound. Fillion, however, remained unmoving, his chest rising and falling with deep, peaceful breaths. The bed was positioned back to a normal state and pillows now rested behind his head.

Skylar stirred with her entry and came to a stand, blinking away the sleep. "Your Highness," he said, stifling a yawn.

Willow pulled her gaze away from Fillion's undressed state to Skylar, placing a hand to her throat. "Oh, I did not mean to disturb your rest, My Lord." Willow curtsied, and fussed with her unbrushed hair before turning her back to the bed out of modesty. "I shall return later."

"No, please. I shall step out momentarily to allow you a private moment."

"Really, that is quite unnecessary." And rather scandalous, she continued internally. What would her brother or the matriarchs say about her being alone in a room with an undressed man? Perhaps everyone was too tired and preoccupied to think of such things.

Although she knew better, her feet remained fastened to the floorboards when Skylar brushed past her. Dark circles lined his eyes and he reluctantly looked her way, guilt tinging every movement and gesture in his departure.

Once the door shut, she slowly faced the bed and took in Fillion's presence with unabashed curiosity. The covers swirled around him in dips and rivulets of shadows cast from the limited light, one of his hands clutching a fold. His waxen complexion seemed unnatural in the gray morning dusk, made more so by his pale lips; although, he possessed more color than a few hours prior. The dark hair had been washed and groomed, a faint shadow of stubble lined his jaw and mouth, and his skin glowed clean.

Willow approached the bed and bit her bottom lip as she admired his bare chest. Although she had seen glimpses of the upper male body on occasion, they were always fleeting and fraught with embarrassment. Now, she felt no shame, only curious reverence as she admired the limp and weakened form of the man who knew her heart as if it were his own. Faint definitions of toned muscle moved across his abdomen with each breath. The hand that clutched the blanket shaped his forearm with the intensity of his grip, and Willow's mouth parted in pleasure. He was the very definition of beautiful masculinity and she had to remind herself to breathe.

Gray wings stretched across his chest, drawing attention to his narrow, toned frame. The feathers unfurled as if the wings of an angel, and they appeared so soft and life-like that she reached out and touched one. Her eyes darted to his face to see if he responded to her touch. When he remained still, she allowed her fingertips to brush along his skin until they rested upon a human heart, shaded in black and white. Thorns wrapped around the organ and blood dripped from the center where it rent in half. "Your heart is broken," she whispered, "just like mine."

A sound echoed from the hallway and she snapped attention toward the door over her shoulder. Heartbeats ticked away in her head, and she sighed in relief when she and Fillion remained uninterrupted. Twirling a strand of hair, she studied him once more, conjuring explanations should he awake and find her reveling in his exposed condition. The cad would probably enjoy it, she mused, biting down on a smile once more. Never would mortification burn so hot, though. Still, she could not keep her eyes from soaking in the sight of him.

Celtic knots circled around his right bicep, similar to the carvings in the stairway leading to the second story apartments. Outlines of stars trailed from his upper chest, just beneath his right arm toward his stomach, growing smaller with descent.

Out of all the tattoos decorating his body, the one upon his left arm intrigued her the most. A tree, similar to the one engraved upon The Door, stretched from his elbow to his shoulder blade. Just like the feathers, it was remarkably life-like. The long, narrow leaves pointed in various directions, dotted by red fruit akin to pomegranates. The roots tangled into a Celtic knot, similar to the ones banded around his upper right arm. But what intrigued her most were the flames that licked the branches in swirls and curled over his shoulder, even singeing the tips of the wings on his left side. Whatever did it signify?

"Drink up and drink fast," she whispered to the morning air. Knowing she needed to leave, Willow bent and pressed her lips to his cheek. "Thank you for my gift," she whispered against his cool skin. "My heart is full beyond measure."

His face leaned into her touch and a soft, breathless sound left his mouth, his lips full and relaxed from sleep. "Anything for you, Willow," he rasped. Eyelashes fluttered open for a moment, tickling her skin, before shutting once more. "One day," he murmured, "I'll spin the tales … weave the stories together…"

The last word faded into the shadows of the room as he pressed into her touch even more. Slow, rhythmic breathing returned and she reluctantly drew away, straightening her posture, her pulse in a race with her thoughts. He had recognized her voice and sought her nearness. Whatever did he mean by spinning tales? A tremor began at the nape of her neck and jolted to her feet as she pushed away the confusion and grief that wished to take root, fury rising in replacement.

Weary and resolute, she lifted her chin and exited the bedchamber. Skylar rested against the wall with eyes closed. Upon seeing her, he tipped his head and entered her father's bedchamber, resuming his post as before. She continued into the living room, grateful when she found Leaf alone.

"Who poisoned him?" she demanded, taking a seat beside her brother.

In a low hush, Leaf answered, "Skylar and I are quite certain it was Timothy." He looked toward the entry door and back to her. "And that he is also the owner of the Curse Card."

"Curse Card?" Her eyes grew large. How is it she always forgot about this insufferable card? And yet, she continually felt the guilt of its existence. Willow thought over the inscription and shook her head with disgust. "How could a man be so cruel?"

"Yes," Leaf replied simply. "A thing and a person were damaged. That leaves only a place."

"But there are several places I love." Willow covered her mouth and stared at Leaf wide-eyed. "My tree. You do not believe Timothy would harm my tree, do you?"

"No, Hanley." Leaf closed his eyes, an anxious gesture, and rubbed his face with the palms of his hands. Upon noting the look of confusion she cast him, he explained, "The Curse Card is meant for Hanley. I heard him declare it personally." Willow's mouth fell open, but he held up a hand. "He claims that the spinning wheel was destroyed as a warning, for he spins the tales and weaves together all the stories."

The hairs on her arms rose as she recalled Fillion's words to her just now and she twisted toward the corner where the wheel sat. "Tell me you jest!" Willow clenched her fists and jumped to a standing position. "All this time I have felt responsible for the grievances befalling our home, Leaf Dylan Watson. I knew Fillion had met with Hanley. When did you personally do so?"

Leaf winced. "A fortnight ago. Hanley did not know I was present during his and Fillion's meeting." Leaf's eyes dimmed as he took her hand and kissed it, bowing his head as his shoulders slumped even further. "I did not intentionally withhold this information from you. Sometimes I become so consumed with various responsibilities, I simply forget. "

Willow sighed and withdrew her hand, turning her head to the side. "Why my spinning wheel? There are six spinners in our community." She lowered into the chair with stiff movements.

"Fillion believes you were specifically targeted because of your resemblance to mother."

"Dear Lord in Heaven…" Willow leaned her head against the back of the chair and closed her eyes. Then she popped forward with another thought. "I was under the impression that Hanley did not possess love for his son. Did not the Curse stipulate the person, place, and thing were objects of love?"

Leaf's face sobered even more. "A father could love his son for many reasons and still hold no affection for him."

"Truly?" Willow looked at her hands, resting in her lap. "Such thoughts break my heart even more, if that were possible."

"Aye, mine as well."

"Why would Timothy go to such lengths?" She asked, falling against the back of the chair once more. "Has he taken leave of his senses?"

"Perhaps." Leaf studied the door and window once more. "Fillion is rather convinced that Timothy was in line to be The Aether before our mother was given the official duty."

The anger rose within her once more and she seethed through gritted teeth. "He killed our father for power, destroyed my spinning wheel to deliver a message, deceived two families into leaving, created division in our community, tried to destroy your friendship with Skylar—then blame you for it—and harmed the future owner of New Eden Township…" She stood and began pacing, grunting with fury. "How shall I face that despicable man? He has never heard anything on the wind quite like the hurricane brewing inside of me!"

"We do not know if he killed father nor if he truly held the Curse Card, but the evidence thus far leans mightily in Timothy's direction."

"How could you defend him?"

"I am not."

"Perhaps we need to bring him before the community for questioning?"

"I refuse to publicly accuse a man outright as a means to satisfy my anger."

"No," Willow said. "You shall hide behind whatever glimmers of peace you fancy solves every problem. I, for one, believe diplomacy is no longer a path worth pursuing where *he* is concerned."

Leaf released a long, heartfelt sigh and stretched out his legs, rubbing his eyes once more. Then he stood with fluid motions and trudged to where she paced along the floorboards. Eventually, she stilled long enough to notice her brother's hardened features.

"You shall face him this evening, as you must, and you will hold your tongue," he admonished. She pinched her face in anger and her brother narrowed his eyes, his voice lowering even more. "This morning, following Mass, I shall give an account of Fillion's suffering. I worry that the residents shall panic upon learning that the Son of Eden was poisoned and by one within the community who surely conspired with one from the Outside. Do you realize how this shall fan the flames of the faction? And, of course, I shall have to reveal the hatch in order to justify my claims. But I must." Leaf paused and placed weary hands on hips. "Do *not* add to the load I must carry this day," he said firmly.

Willow gaped at Leaf with his insinuations and promptly turned her back to him, crossing her arms over her chest with a huff and an ill-humored chuckle. "Do not trouble yourself, *Your Majesty*. I shall refrain from publicly humiliating you. Please excuse me. I no longer wish to be reminded of what a burden I am, especially while processing information you have known for weeks!" Clenching her fists at her side, she marched toward the archway leading to the hallway with as much dignity as she could muster.

The front door opened just as her toe stepped into the shadows of the hallway and Willow halted her steps, internally groaning. Laurel called after her and Willow looked over her shoulder as several matriarchs and village matrons spilled into their apartment, followed by Rain with Ember close behind, carrying a copper basin.

"Good morning time, Your Majesty," Verna said with a slight dip toward Leaf. "Felicitations, Willow Oak." The head matriarch met Willow's eyes. "Shall we begin?"

Willow fidgeted with the folds of her dress and drew in a shaky breath. She look at Leaf who stood with his head down, refusing to meet the eyes of those gathered in their home, a muscle twitching in his jaw.

"Yes, Madam."

"Your Majesty, would you be so kind as to fetch heated water from Cook?" Verna asked.

Leaf bowed and left the apartment in quick strides, not even sparing a glance at Ember, who also directed focus upon the wooden floor. The door shut with a slam, and Willow flinched. Others, however, appeared ignorant of the tension.

Mistress Katie came forward and approached the spinning wheel, covering a gasp with her hand. "Your Highness, how lovely! From whom did you receive such a splendid gift?"

"My Lord, Fillion Nichols," Willow said, weaving a strand of her hair between two fingers as she turned away from the women. "He crafted it for me." The women exchanged looks, then broke into an assortment of reactions from giggles, excited chatter, to knowing smiles. But Rain offered a conspiratorial grin.

"We are glad to hear of his recovery," Verna offered softly, and regarded Ember with a frown. "Your brother shall investigate and ease our fears." Willow nodded, still averting her eyes. "Come, show us to your chamber and we will transform you into a vision that shall bring your young man to bended knee."

This very moment, the ground could reveal its dank, grave maw and Willow would willingly jump inside without hesitation. Instead, she faced her caretakers with a tight smile before she spun toward the hallway, heels digging into the floor as she stalked to her bedchamber.

Armed with toiletries, pots and pitchers of cold water, henna, leaves, flowers, and the stories that accompanied such occasions, the matriarchs and matrons poured into her room and settled in to their tasks. The clamor of activity grated on each of Willow's nerves and increased the pounding in her head, but she masked her emotions behind a veil of quiet stoicism. But, oh, how she wildly stormed inside!

As the women slowly undressed her down to her shift and bindings, Willow studied Ember's wedding gown, draped across the oak chest. Tonight, she would be presented to the community as a bride. However, the sight of this dress evoked entirely different thoughts and emotions of the day several weeks prior when one man left and another arrived. Goosebumps pricked her body as she shivered. A matron wrapped a blanket around Willow's shoulders with a kind smile, mistaking the chill.

Trepidation steadily increased as she pondered her father's absence this day. Come evening meal, her father would have escorted her through the gathering and stood beside her upon the stage. *He* would comfort her sorrows. *He* would understand how helpless she felt, allowing her to fight for those she loved. And *he* knew what it is was like to have a relationship full of nevers because of Hanley Nichols.

Instead, she must suffer her brother and his insensitivity. Ember came forward to retrieve her cast-off garments and met her eyes, her sister-in-law's mouth set in a thin line. It appeared the Daughter of Fire shared Willow's sentiments as well.

"Power is an illusion," Willow said softly.

Ember arched her eyebrow, her familiar small and mysterious smile forming in reply. "Indeed."

ELEMENTS

Modern as the style of Pascal's writing is, his thought is deeply impregnated with the spirit of the Middle Ages. He belonged, almost equally, to the future and to the past.

— Lytton Strachey, British writer and critic, 20th century A.D. *

This week's celebrity ship should be no surprise to anyone who has paid attention to the buzz the last few weeks. It looks like love is in the air for a certain Eco-Princess and her Martian guest. Thank you, Daddy! We sent our Cupid undercover to provide you, loyal followers, with a gallery of delectable images. Seriously. Just scroll through. Warning: Your screen might catch on fire. They're hot! Our favorite? When Lynden Nichols leads Coal Hansen blindfolded through the suburbs of Portland to meet what our sources say is his grandma. If that's not love, folks… And freaking adorable. And this almost-kiss? Enough to make even the sun melt. If all Martians look like the Son of Fire, then bring on the alien invasion. We give this ship a solid five stars. Not every day you can say someone's relationship is literally out of this world. Iheartotakulife wants to hear from you! What's your favorite picture? Do you ship Coal and Lynden? Comment below."

— RainyMonday0427, "Celebrity Ship," Iheartotakulife.com, October 29, 2054

CHAPTER
THIRTY-SIX

The muscles in Coal's jaw winced with tenderness as he clenched down once again. All day he had waited for something to happen, anything to justify why he had to fly out at first light. Now, it was evening, and he had yet to see Hanley or Dr. Nichols, and only visited with Michael on occasion. Nor had he seen the Carsons or Moores. Rather than wait in his room, he had decided to wander the building, eventually ending up in the main meeting room.

Shifting in his seat, his focus traveled back to the aquarium bubbling in the corner. The little blue and brown fish no longer haunted the glass box. Instead, happy, healthy fish swam in circles. Each minnow trailed a predictable pattern, blissfully unaware of their environment.

Could he become a fish once more?

He knew the answer to that question before he even asked it of himself. It was the same question he had asked himself the vast majority of the day. Still, as he studied his fingers, noting the telling absence of carbon stains, he continued to wonder.

The burn of longing to see those he loved pulled mightily upon his heart. But the ache of leaving Lynden felt as though shards of glass were embedded into his body. Each breath was tight and shallow, eliciting sharp stabs of pain from his stomach. And his gut already felt on fire with swirling, agitated motions.

When he left New Eden, his anxiety was steeped in a desire to fight. Curiosity was there, too. And soon, wanderlust had claimed his adventurous spirit. Today, the mere thought of returning to New Eden indefinitely caused his pulse to race.

Would he even fit in with his community anymore?

When he picked up hammer and iron, would he slip back into familiar routines with satisfaction?

Physically, he looked like an Outsider, even his vocabulary and speech patterns had changed. He was no longer of his world, but neither was he of this one. Rather, he was stuck in a strange form of purgatory until the moment Hanley decided to finally grace Coal with his presence and seal his fate. Literally.

Restless, Coal strode out through the large double doors and strutted down the hallway. In bondage pants—the metal loops and chains clinking with each step—a visual kei-inspired button-down black shirt, and combat boots, he clashed with the crowd of sterile, pristine lab coats. He emerged from New Eden as an anomaly in a tunic and breeches, and he returned as a different one. Now, however, he no longer felt shame with the stares and whispered conversations.

Warm light spilled into the hallway and he shifted attention from the bland walls and carpet to a large window. As he passed, he caught his reflection and searched his false self for answers. Platinum blond hair poofed in the very back while black and red strands draped across the front of his eye at an angle. A hooped bottom lip ring glinted in the light from the window. So, too, did a hoop in his nose. Small, black faux plugs in his ears competed with his naturally dark eyes. Coal lowered his head, distressed over his appearance. Yet, despite the changes, he only saw the man who, just weeks prior, inspected his full reflection for the first time in wonder.

What would Oaklee think when she saw him?

Would she forgive him for his behavior prior to The Exchange?

Could they still be friends?

How would she respond to his declaration of love for Lynden?

Was there a way to keep Oaklee and her family—his family—safe while living in the Outside?

The olive tree beside the kitchen garden swayed in a gentle breeze and Coal stared past his reflection to the Outside. Lifting his eyes, he settled upon the white, wispy clouds high above, their thin smudges painted across the azure atmosphere with fine strokes.

Michael had shared during their brief time this morning that Coal was to remain indoors. It was maddening. A trapped, confined feeling encroached upon Coal as when he first heard Michael's rule, and Coal's chest expanded with rising panic as his throat went dry. He forced his attention back toward the hallway, and then he was walking, not able to distance himself from the view fast enough. Still, his mind remained anchored to the wide-open landscape beyond the window, even as his feet moved swiftly upon the carpet.

Is this how the fear of confinement inspired one to feel and behave? He often wondered what comprised such an experience. Most especially as his entire life was enclosed to prevent this very unraveling of the mind. Although, he did not know of such a condition until after he left New Eden. Now, he felt akin to a caged animal, an expression he finally understood. Perhaps it was good he did not interact with others today.

The scent of pine and earth struck his senses and he awoke from his heated thoughts to find himself in the middle of the forested entry biodome room. A blue jay jeered from a branch and a small brook bubbled and gurgled to his left. Coal took in the familiar scene as hot tears prickled the back of his eyes. The gray, geodesic sky seemed to fall upon him and the trees pressed in, and Coal physically winced. Yet his heart soared with an overwhelming euphoria he could not describe, and he closed his eyes and allowed the scents and sounds of home to consume him.

For a moment, he swore he heard the clank of metal on metal as his father forged and repaired tools; and the soft, lulling hum of Oaklee's voice as she weaved through the trees; the bright laughter of his brother and sister; followed by the comforting pressure of his sister's hand upon his arm.

"Coal," a soothing, female voice said near him and his eyes snapped open to find an actual hand upon his arm. He jumped back, gulping in a large breath as he did so. Dr. Nichols stood beside him, dressed elegantly as usual. But her usual playful smile and inquisitive eyes remained impassive, worry burning behind her gaze instead. "I was looking for you."

"My apologies," he said, blinking rapidly as he attempted to calm his pulse. "I removed my Cranium an hour ago and left it inside my room."

"May we sit?"

Five weeks ago, he would have rolled his eyes at such a request. Now, he only complied. Looking around, he found a sturdy log just off the trail and gestured toward the makeshift bench. She sat down, crossing her ankles and tucking her legs to the side, her hands clasped tightly in her lap.

"How may I be of service?" he asked, angling toward her on the log.

"I just learned a half-hour ago that you were here." She brushed black locks from her shoulder, more self-conscious than coy. "We have been tied up in meetings all day."

"I see." He turned his head away from her to hide the offense. "Do you know why I am here?"

"Well, I believe Hanley plans to end the exchange."

"What if I do not wish to return?"

Her eyebrow arched and she regarded him a moment. "What would you do?"

"Perhaps New Eden Enterprises has a position I could hold?" Coal plucked a piece of wild grass and spun it between his fingers. "I will continue to act as a media front. Or perhaps I could become a liaison between the Township and N.E.T. during the Second Phase? I am willing to do both positions if that is what is necessary."

"Why is it you wish to stay?"

"I believe I would go insane if confined after knowing such an endless world." Coal met her eyes. "I am altered by this experience and fear I shall never want for a simple life again. Nor could I handle being isolated from the world."

Dr. Nichols studied him once more. "Understandable," she said, quiet and thoughtful. "I feared this response, actually. However, the government only allowed twenty-five years and refused to allot more time while New Eden Township was considered an experiment for Mars colonization. I worry for your generation."

"My Lady?"

She straightened her shoulders and brushed off invisible objects from her skirt. "Did you know of a Techsmith Guild within New Eden?"

"No. High technology exists inside the biodome?"

"Cranium technology and other high-tech devices and applications."

Coal watched the grass spin in his hands, his thoughts spinning equally as fast. "Who possesses such connection to the Outside?"

"Your sister."

The blade of grass stilled between his fingers. "I beg your pardon?" A memory hit him at once of sitting in the copper room with Hanley. *Have you heard from your sister?* Coal swore under his breath and grit his teeth.

"Yes. Ember has been trained as a communications director, proficient in several technologies, and ready to work as a liaison between Earth and Mars, should a colony truly exist on the Red Planet."

Coal came to a stand and tossed the piece of grass. "Who trained her for such a position?"

A slight frown touched Dr. Nichols' mouth. "Your father and Timothy Kane."

"Unbelievable!" Coal stomped away a few steps and peered up at the fractured sky. Rejection surged through him in agonizing waves. He refused to accept that his father would keep such a secret from him, nor allow Coal to participate in the Guild alongside his twin sister. Coal whipped his focus back to Dr. Nichols and clenched his jaw. "How did you come across such information?"

She blinked nervously and touched a silver necklace around her neck. "It came up in the meeting today. One of the reasons Hanley and I were not available." Her hand reached out and patted the log next to where she sat. Coal lowered himself once more and slumped forward, resting his elbows on his knees to support his head. "Skylar Kane is the leader of the Techsmith Guild," she continued. "The rest of the Guild members are from the village."

"I am at a loss for words," he said, tucking his head in toward his chest.

"Perhaps the world will not feel so small with this knowledge." Dr. Nichols rose from the log. "I will present your case to Hanley, but he makes the final decision and I fear, at this juncture, the decision has already been made."

"I refuse to be enclosed." Coal crossed his arms over his chest. He might sound like a petulant child, but he would not be bullied by a Nichols. They did not own his life, nor did they engineer him. He was the product of himself—his choices, his beliefs, his actions. "The Code states that anyone may leave at any time and for any reason."

"True. But if you leave, you must reside inside N.E.T."

"Then, I have made my choice. I shall take up permanent residence within the lab."

Dr. Nichols tilted her head and searched his eyes once more. "Why would you prefer the lab over your family?"

"Reasons that are my own."

"You have shared in several interviews that the expectation to marry young is strong." A sad smile touched Dr. Nichols' burgundy lips. "Do you fear if you return you will be required to marry?"

"That is merely one of my many concerns," Coal said.

"You cannot refuse to marry?"

"I could," he said. "But all a father or head of home has to do is declare that I touched his daughter inappropriately and I could be forced into a situation where I would be required to redeem the young woman's reputation before the community, or face banishment. As a gentleman, regardless of false claims, what choice would I have? I would leave her in disgrace, while I awaited project shutdown within the comfort of the lab."

"I am sorry," Dr. Nichols said, lowering her head. Her eyes sheened with tears again and she lifted a hand to delicately cover her mouth as she tensed. Several long seconds passed before she found her voice. "Have many been forced or swindled into a marriage they did not desire?"

"It is hard to say." Coal's gaze roamed over the forest and studied the patterned lines of the mosaic sky. "For no gentleman would ever defame his wife. I have witnessed three public demands for marriage in two years. How many happened privately? I am really not sure."

Coal shifted on his feet as he thought of Oaklee, and remorse clenched his gut, adding to the queasiness. At one time, he courted such trouble with the Daughter of Earth, her age the only block for Joel or Leaf to demand marriage. Yet Coal had secretly hoped for such a dilemma, one he would have willingly rectified. He had yearned to always remain bonded with Oaklee and could not conceive how another woman could ever take her place in his life. Stupid. So very selfish. Foolishness, indeed. But in his minor defense, after her father died, his fear was genuine and he thought only of her protection. He would go to the ends of the Earth to protect Oaklee. Although, no longer for romantic reasons.

The topic of marriage brought snippets of information from the collaborative hack to mind. He pondered the possibilities of Joel's disengagement to Dr. Nichols. With the recent development of Joel's financial legacy, it seemed clear to Coal that Hanley had a plan from the beginning.

Slowly, he locked onto Dr. Nichols' eyes, steady and even. "Being swindled into marriage exists regardless of world, does it not?"

Her expression remained fixed, but her complexion visibly paled with his question. Coal stood and searched her eyes for a moment, trying to set his anger and betrayal aside. He had struggled with whether to divulge his feelings to either Dr. Nichols or Hanley. However, as he faced Lynden's mother, the answer became clear. Coal had vowed to fight for Lynden's heart all the days of his life, and so he would.

"There are several reasons I wish to stay, some I have already shared," he said quietly. He sucked in his bottom lip momentarily. Finding additional courage, he whispered, "I am in love with your daughter."

The familiar arched eyebrow reappeared and her fingers immediately flew to the necklace. "Is Lynden aware of your feelings?"

"Yes, My Lady. She returns my affections."

"Coal..." Dr. Nichols' delicate features tensed in a pained expression. "It is not so easy. You see—"

The door opened and Michael popped his head into the room. "Dr. Nichols, Mr. Nichols is looking for you."

A small smile appeared on her face, one Coal knew was entirely fake, and she lightly fussed with her dark strands. "Thank you, Michael. Please accompany me, Coal?"

"He's in the main meeting room," Michael said, and Coal sighed. He had just left that room. With a nod of assent, Coal gestured toward the trail and followed Dr. Nichols, taking hold of the door from Michael. They traveled in silence. Upon reaching the large double doors, Michael turned and said, "I was just summoned by the Guardian Angels. I'll be back."

"You wished to see me?" Dr. Nichols asked as she sauntered into the room. Hanley sat in a corner seat, his fingers scrolling the air behind a privacy screen. "Della..." The older man paused when spotting Coal and a friendly smile replaced the professional facade. "Great. I was just going to ask my wife to find you. Please, have a seat."

"I prefer to stand, thank you."

"Yes, I'm sure you do. Just like your father."

"No, just like me. I am my own person and wish to be viewed as such."

Hanley considered him a few moments. "Of course." He shifted in his chair, tapped the Cranium resting on his ear, and then folded his hands over his knee. "Sorry I wasn't available earlier. Della and I were pulled into several meetings. Did she share?"

Coal looked at Dr. Nichols then back to Hanley. "She did share that you were in meetings today, yes."

Hanley leaned forward and smiled again, one that did not reach his eyes. "The Moores and Carsons returned to New Eden earlier today."

"Really? When?"

"Close to lunch time." Hanley eased back into the chair and crossed an ankle over his knee. "John escorted both family groups to The Door and reported that the families were welcomed back with embraces and well wishes." Coal flashed a surprised look toward Dr. Nichols, who remained stoic.

"After much deliberation," Dr. Nichols volunteered, "we decided it was in the overall best interest of the Moores' and Carsons' wellbeing to grant their request and return both family groups to New Eden. Although you have shown remarkable adaptability and comfort with technology, my observations after spending significant time with these families are that the township would best benefit from transitioning together, as a community, with aid from the Techsmith Guild."

"Techsmith Guild?" Coal asked, not sure if he should play along or not.

"Yes," Dr. Nichols replied simply. "The training those in the Guild received, as I shared with you moments earlier, is also to benefit the community's transition during Project Phase Two. It is long known in sociology that people learn best from their own."

Coal crossed his arms over his chest and studied the aquarium. The heaviness in his heart throbbed, growing as he recalled images of the rotting permaculture gardens. How would they thrive as individuals let alone as an entire community post-project? He shifted his focus from the fish to Hanley. "The world barely supports those my age. How shall the second and third generations find meaningful lives after project shutdown?"

"The details are not important at this moment, but there is a plan. Right now, there are other matters to consider."

"Are you at liberty to share, sir?"

"Your future."

Hanley lifted a friendly smile again. Coal's heart stuttered as each muscle froze in anticipation. Was this man a con artist like his father? The very thought terrified Coal, but he refused to cave in to the many thoughts wishing to reduce him to a useless shell. He needed to remain alert and guarded, but act as though nothing was amiss.

With a much shakier voice than he intended, he asked, "And do I, as your human experiment, have a say in my future?"

"Well, I am guessing you've seen too much and *know* too much to return." Hanley leaned forward. Coal licked his dry lips, feeling a cold sweat break out once more. "Am I right?"

Was Hanley implying he knew about the collaborative hack?

Or maybe he was concerned Coal would share other information with the Watsons?

Perhaps just that Coal has seen too much of the world?

The experiment?

Or that Coal would find a way to use technology inside the dome and broadcast the Watsons?

The latter thought had merit and Coal hushed his mountain of questions. Perhaps Ember could assist him with this, regardless of which world Coal resided in? "Yes," Coal said with a slight dip of his head. "You have expressed my own sentiments, which I shared with Dr. Nichols prior to meeting with you. In fact, I wished to seek employment at New Eden Enterprises or at N.E.T., perhaps as a liaison between this world and the biodome community during the Second Phase? I am willing to continue in public relations with the media as well."

"Perhaps." Hanley stood and walked toward the double doors and Coal held his breath. "I am unable to resume ongoing permanent guardianship of you in my home, though."

The air left Coal's chest in a relieved whoosh. "I am happy to reside at N.E.T., provided I am granted traveling rights to visit Seattle and Portland, and Lynden and Mack are granted permission to be my personal guests at the lab."

"Portland?" Hanley asked.

"Yes, I wish to visit my grandmother, Sarah Hiddleston." If that surprised the owner, he did not show it. Instead, Hanley stood before Coal with his typical unblinking stare and casual smile.

"And if I do not grant traveling rights or permissions?"

"Well, as you say, I have seen and know too much. Perhaps that grants me some leverage, no?" Coal lifted a corner of his mouth.

Hanley chuckled. "I like your fire, Coal. You have finally learned to harness it for your advantage. A confident, well-spoken man is someone I always respect." The owner smirked, more as an expression of humor. "And my daughter? Did you guard her well?"

"Yes, sir. She has discovered how essential she really is." Coal straightened his posture and cleared his throat. "It is an occupation I am most fond of, actually."

"Perception." Hanley allowed that word to rest before them a few moments. "I am glad you both have formed an attachment. It will be good press for New Eden and all Martians, present and future. The world needs to see you and all other biodome residents as fully human."

Dr. Nichols fingered her necklace with a shocked expression, the pain and hurt evident on each of her features as she met Coal's eyes. But, as usual, she remained quiet when Hanley had the stage.

"Your daughter is *not* an asset for business," Coal said, low and threatening. "And neither am I."

"So, now your feelings are not genuine?"

"I love her. But I shall not allow you— "

"Good. We'll talk more on this later. Come, Della," Hanley said, tipping his head to Coal as he stepped around him. Every muscle tightened as Coal grounded his feet and remained in place. He would not lose control in front of Hanley, nor Dr. Nichols. Glancing over his shoulder, Hanley continued, "You may have traveling rights to Seattle and Portland. I will personally grant you a stipend. As for Lynden and Mack, they may be your personal guests, provided they remain out of trouble."

"Thank you, sir," Coal said, unable to hold back a grin, despite the betrayal. The victory was small, but it was a movement in the right direction. "One more request, if I may?" Hanley tarried in the doorway and faced him with look bordering on boredom, as if to intimidate Coal from any further questions. But Coal was no longer afraid and pressed his case. "May I return to New Eden for a single day to give my farewells to my family?"

"Let me speak with Della and John, and I will get back to you."

"Much appreciated, sir." Coal bowed, grin still in place. Dr. Nichols paused in the door frame with a small smile and mouthed the words, "well done," then followed her husband out into the hallway. But as soon as the door closed, it opened again. Hanley and Dr. Nichols were ushered back into the room by Michael, who frantically looked at Coal. "My apologies," Coal offered and strode toward the door. "I was just leaving."

"Stay," Hanley said. "Go ahead, Michael."

"The Wi-Fi repeater is up or disabled in the room?"

"Up."

Michael sank into a chair and brought up a Cranium screen he did not bother to hide. With a tap, he selected the reverse screen option and then placed it on a chair to project onto a large whitewashed wall. "As you can see from the numbers, the CO_2 has climbed considerably inside the biodome in the last few minutes."

"Is it comparable to when there is a funeral pyre?" Hanley asked.

"No," Michael responded quickly, shaking head. "The nanotech panels are equipped to absorb and convert a large amount of carbon dioxide, as you know. I've never seen numbers like this before."

Hanley studied the incoming data, his eyes twitching back and forth as he read. "The oxygen sensors haven't kicked in?"

"We can initiate the emergency O_2 with your permission."

"Let's wait."

Michael's eyes widened as his skin turned a sickly shade of green. "But, sir, they'll suffocate."

"No. Jeff or The Aether would contact me if there was a problem. Or, someone would go to Messenger Pigeon. Are you sure the numbers are correct? Have the Guardian Angels verified this isn't the work of a hacker? Are all other software systems intact and reading properly?"

"A hacker?" Michael's eyes rounded again.

"Until I am notified by someone within New Eden that something has happened, we will do nothing." Hanley looked to Della. "Let's go have dinner. Coal, care to join us?"

Coal lifted the hem of his shirt to wipe away the sweat gathering on his forehead. His heartbeat thrummed in his ears, adrenaline pumping through his body. Hanley, on the other hand, appeared as if this was as worrisome as choosing between two favorite desserts. The very thought of all those he loved suffocating sent Coal into a wild panic.

"Oh, wow." Michael paled again and Della's mouth parted in a delicate look of astonishment. "The numbers flipped. Now the CO_2 looks healthy and the O_2 is increasing."

Hanley placed his hands inside his pants pockets. "Coal, has Fillion contacted Mack lately?"

"No, sir."

"But he has before?"

"Yes, sir."

"When was the last time you saw Mack?"

"This morning."

"And what were you doing?"

Coal paused a moment. "Hanging out, sir."

Hanley nodded his head and looked toward Della. "Let's go eat." As he walked out of the door, he said to Michael, "Tell the Guardian Angels they've been hacked and to contact the security team."

"Will do," the scientist replied, picking up his Cranium and practically flying out of the room.

"Coal, are you coming?" Dr. Nichols asked from the doorway.

"Go ahead. I shall join you shortly. I need to visit the restroom first." She smiled, the look more sorrowful than anything, and then exited the room.

A few minutes later, Coal fell onto his bed and stared at the ceiling. He needed to alert Mack and wished to tell Lynden the good news—minus the abhorrent confession by her father. However, Coal knew he would raise suspicion should he dawdle too long. He would call Lynden later. For

ELEMENTS

now, it was imperative Mack knew he was suspected of breaching the biodome's control system at Fillion's behest.

Blindly reaching over to his nightstand, Coal felt for his Cranium. Once his fingers curled around the device, he strapped it to his ear and called Mack.

"Hey, you're in or out?"

"Out," Coal answered. "I am pressed for time so please forgive my abruptness."

"Bit dump."

"Did you perchance hack into the control system for the biodome?"

"Uh, no. Why?"

Coal scanned his room, then explained the situation to Mack. "So, you have not spoken to Fillion?"

"Shit. No. You haven't heard?"

"Heard what exactly?"

"God, they really take honoring someone's delusional wishes seriously in New Eden. Holy shit. I had hoped they came to their senses and called for medical attention."

"Whatever are you implying?"

"Fillion was poisoned last night. The lucky bastard pulled through, thanks to your sister and some other folks. Joannah. Tim."

"Timna."

"Whatever."

"How did you hear of this?"

"Ember called me at four-something in the morning after you and Rainbow left."

"I see." Coal grit his teeth together. "So, the faulty data is not the work of you or your team?"

"Big. Emphatic. No. But I'll start investigating. Flipping numbers like that is a good indicator of a rush job. Hack doesn't know what he's doing. I'll isolate the idiot, don't worry."

"Thank you." Coal closed his eyes. "I need to go. Please tell Lyn I will call her tonight. I am not going in the dome, but there are conditions."

"Nice. Will do. This means I'll get to see your girly ass again, Farm Boy?"

"You are lucky I cannot punch you right now."

Mack laughed. "Later, mate."

They disconnected their line and Coal's mind buzzed with the news of Fillion's poisoning. However, he would remain quiet. If Fillion wished for his parents to know, they would by now.

At this moment, Coal would give anything to remain in solitude and forgo dinner with Hanley and Dr. Nichols. His body was on fire with a multitude of emotions. If a robot were nearby, it would probably ask Coal if he experienced dizziness or felt lightheaded as his blood pressure was most definitely elevated. Irritated, he rolled onto his side with a grim smile and studied the black box that housed Ignis. Coal needed to start moving.

Tucking the Cranium into his pocket, he rose from the bed and traipsed toward the door and continued toward the dining hall. The smell of food assaulted his senses and sharp pains exploded from his unsettled stomach once more. Nevertheless, he lowered into a chair opposite Hanley and Dr. Nichols and offered a companionable smile.

ELEMENTS

And as it turned out, oxygen was not the only problem. Biosphere 2 also suffered from wildly fluctuating CO_2 levels. Most of the vertebrate species and all of the pollinating insects died, while cockroaches and ants started to take over the place. The ocean eventually became too acidic and the internal temperature became impossible to control.

And just to make matters worse, the team started to experience health and psychological issues. The four men and four women left Biosphere 2 depressed and malnourished after nearly two years of isolation. Interpersonal relationships had regressed over the course of the two years, creating what the biospherians called a "dysfunctional family."

— George Dvorsky, "Why We Should Reboot the Biosphere Projects," *io9 / Gawker*, August 29, 2012 *

CHAPTER THIRTY-SEVEN

The community rose from their kneeling positions and the skittish, fidgety energy rippled through the gathering as before. Willow fastened her sight to a latticed window on the opposite end of the Great Hall. A lace veil covered her face per tradition, a ceremonial prop she was for once grateful to possess. Mortification permeated every ounce of her being and her head grew faint as she oscillated between holding her breath and breathing quickly to satisfy her pounding pulse.

Leaf gently grasped her hand and lifted it as he drew breath in order to speak loudly. Any words he was about to share dissolved, however, when the large hewn doors opened. Timothy strolled into the Great Hall, dipping his head in greeting and offering an apologetic salute to those who gathered upon the stage. Where had he been? His family was here. Willow was almost tempted to peer over her shoulder, where

The Elements sat, and see Skylar's reaction. Instead, she remained rigid, shoulders straight and back, and her head held high.

Leaf's hold upon Willow's hand tightened and then he spoke, his voice deep, carrying easily across the room. "It is with great honor that I present Her Highness, Princess Willow Oak Watson, Daughter of Earth, to the assembly as a woman within the community who is bestowed every lawful right and privilege within our Township."

Willow's eyes shifted to her little sister, who stood under the protective arm of Brianna at the front of the stage. Laurel's eyes shone bright with romantic fancies, her lips and cheeks pinked with girlish notions her young mind was no doubt indulging in readily. Corona tapped on Laurel's shoulder and they both stifled giggles behind hands.

In gentle motions, Leaf turned toward Willow and lifted the veil. Her legs buckled slightly, but she refused to faint. Leaf's eyes met hers briefly before averting them, and a muscle in his jaw tightened.

This was not a wedding ceremony, she kept reminding herself. It was simply symbolic. Young men also stood before the community upon their sixteenth birthday. They knelt and swore oaths to protect and provide. To Willow, however, the women's ceremony seemed so shallow—becoming objects to worship, mere ornaments to dangle upon the boughs of the community's core values. She tired of feeling judged, measured, and constricted, as if the success of their colony solely resided in a young woman's reputation, with marriage the only salvation against scandal.

Swathes of wool swished in a metered rhythm as Brother Markus came forward. Two of his fingers cut through the air in *signum crucis* as he said, "*In nomine Patris, et Filii, et Spiritus Sancti.* Amen." The community murmured an "amen" in reply.

Willow studied the wooden stage, turning the slats into knotty branches. If only she could spend her birthday in the sprawling limbs of her beloved tree instead of being trussed up and paraded before the community. At this moment, she was grateful Fillion was still in bed at their apartment and not witness to her shame. "Dear Lord in Heaven," she muttered with irritation under her breath, catching Brother Markus' attention.

The old monk bowed his head as his hands extended a wooden crucifix. "Daughter of Earth, today you stand before all as New Eden's bride and represent the holy sacrament of matrimony." Willow issued a glare her brother's direction beneath lowered lashes. Brother Markus, oblivious to their exchange, continued, "Family is the well of strength of our colony. For marriage strengthens community bonds and is an essential rite of passage our Township reveres and eulogizes. Therefore, this day we hold a feast in your honor, Your Highness, celebrating the union of all the lives who comprise our community."

Extending his arms, Brother Markus faced the gathering, who placed hands upon hearts and intoned the familiar benediction in unison: "May your future home be blessed with the riches of love, happiness, and the laughter of many children. Amen."

Now, Willow was ready to die, but not before giving her brother a piece of her mind for forcing her to go through with this nonsensical ceremony. Furious winds whipped inside of her and would need release before too long. Leaf had been in a reactive mood all day, however. She tired of being the target of his troubles. She had been biting her tongue, a rather difficult feat for her. Leaf simply refused to see reason, declaring that trust was a commodity that no longer existed within the biodome.

Following Mass, Leaf gave an account of Fillion's hardship to those present. From the stories Willow heard by women who visited her apartment throughout the day, the Township was horrified. And, as Leaf had feared, many had panicked, and neighbor turned on neighbor. For hours, she was told, people argued and cast blame. Even physical altercations had occurred. All the while, Leaf stood upon the stage and moderated the discussion until villagers and Nobility alike agreed that they should rally for justice rather than cater to dissension—the real enemy.

Sullen and broody, her brother seemed on the edge of fracturing. Perhaps it was the long night and lack of sleep, the constant flux of pressure and expectations. If not for these reasons, she would have pushed back with force against his patronizing responses already. The winds of change continued to storm, it seemed. This time, her brother hosted the gale-force winds—and everyone within the dome wilted beneath his challenging glare.

Willow exhaled slowly as she grew lightheaded once more. Nevertheless, she continued an elegant bearing before the gathering. Brother Markus lifted a weathered hand and drew a heart upon Willow's forehead, the symbol of life and death in New Eden. Ceremony complete, she ignored her brother's proffered arm and strode toward the stairs, itching to sit down and drink a goblet of wine.

"Please, Your Majesty," Timothy's voice rang out from the crowd and she stilled. "I wish to draw attention to a situation I encountered yesterday, concerning your sister."

Leaf squinted his eyes and shifted on his feet, the muscle in his jaw twitching with more regularity. "Let us speak privately, then."

"As a father of two daughters, I fear I would be doing the community a disservice by not addressing Willow Oak's reputation publicly."

Willow gasped and stared at Timothy, unable to form words or even a sound. He questioned her reputation? During her birthday ceremony?

"My sister's reputation is none of your concern, nor that of anyone in this room," Leaf replied, his tone low, threatening.

"If only that were true, Your Majesty. As Nobility, she more than most must uphold the traditions and values of our community, would you not agree?"

"You shall refrain from making further comment, Timothy Kane."

The former Wind Element eyed Leaf with a faint smirk. "You may bend traditions to suit yourself and your family. But by doing so, you mock those who do not possess such power to exact privileges at will."

"I mock no one," Leaf said in furious exasperation. "Nor am I responsible for the traditions you as well as other first generation residents created."

"Yesterday eve, she and the Son of Eden kissed. Are they pledged?"

Leaf's eyes winced as gasps and whispers circulated. "Once more, neither she nor I owe you or anyone else an explanation."

Shame thawed the fear gripping Willow's senses, and she clenched and unclenched her fists. Renewed and charged, she faced Timothy and opened her mouth to reply, but Timothy cut her off.

"Please, look in the eye those of the second generation who have married because of similar situations and tell them why your sister deserves clemency and special considerations?"

Leaf remained quiet and Willow's heart sank. Slowly, he faced her with a sorrowful expression and fear paralyzed her once more. Would he require her to marry as the final lesson on behaving as a lady should? Tears gathered in her eyes and she tensed her face, refusing to give Timothy the satisfaction. The Great Hall was deathly silent, and Leaf continued to regard her, the confusion evident in his eyes.

"It does not matter if Willow and Fillion are pledged," Skylar said by her side, and Leaf's face relaxed with relief. "Neither have broken The Code, nor any physical laws of the United States or the state of California. Some traditions are not healthy—as evidenced by publicly shaming a young woman on her sixteenth birthday."

"Traditions exist for a reason, son," Timothy countered in a lighter tone. "They keep order and peace within our community, knowledge that true leaders, such as yourself, understand."

The room murmured once more, but Skylar remained unmoved. "Father, I do not think—"

"Power is an illusion!" Willow spat.

"Indeed." Timothy smiled in a way to appear kind yet amused. "Yes, your family is well-versed in ruling behind an illusory curtain of power."

"My brother is honorable and revealed himself before the community to dissolve such illusions and ideology, and people punish him for it. Yet he does not *poison* people's good opinion nor *spin* tales to fan the flames of rumors and dissension." Timothy offered a faint nod and his smile grew and, in such a way, Willow knew he understood her deeper message. "You have no power over me or my life!" The injustice burned hot and she gripped the veil on her head and tore it off, throwing the ceremonial prop to the ground. "And neither do traditions that foster order and peace through fear and condemnation!"

Willow lifted her chin and marched off the stage. The gathering parted as she passed through, many bowing their heads in deference, some staring wide-eyed, and some pulling their children back as if her rebellion was contagious. A few weeks prior, Fillion declared that he was not afraid of New Eden's mob mentality and, at this moment, she realized that neither was she. This was her birthday. The willow oak beckoned for her to sit in its branches, and so she would. The community could celebrate without her.

With a dainty grunt, she yanked open the doors with every intention of flinging her long hair over her shoulder and storming away. Instead, she recoiled and blinked when smoke stung her eyes. Through the haze she saw the source and terror's chill oozed into her veins. Her chest expanded as she gulped in a large breath and shouted, "Fire!"

Flames licked up the side of The Forge and black smoke formed dark clouds beneath the dome ceiling. Shrieks and exclamations swelled behind Willow and her vision began to fade around the edges.

"Quick!" Connor boomed somewhere behind her. "Fetch any bucket or container you can find and form an assembly line from the well."

"Open the East and South Cave doors!" Skylar yelled.

People rushed around her and into the meadow, knocking into her. She braced herself as best she could, unable to move as villagers stampeded out of the Great Hall. Leaf pushed through, gripped her shoulders, and pressed her against one of the doors, shielding her body with his. They remained in this position until the threat of being trampled had passed.

"Are you well?" Leaf asked, easing away.

"This is my fault," she whimpered, heaving with the effort to hold in the urge to sob. "Coal left because of me, and now his family suffers and so does New Eden."

"Do not be absurd," her brother snapped. Willow turned her head to the side and clenched her jaw. "This has nothing to do with you and everything to do with Hanley."

Her eyes rounded and the blood rushed from her head. "Do you believe Fillion is safe?"

"I … I cannot say."

"He is alone, is he not?"

"Yes, I do believe so."

"Then hurry and restrain Timothy before he can do more damage."

"We do not know—"

"He is a snake and should be taken captive and formally addressed! Go and retain him now before he slithers away!" Willow nudged her brother in the shoulder, and he staggered back a step, but did not turn to leave. "This is not a time for diplomacy. You cannot reason with such a man."

"What if he is a pawn and we wrongfully accuse him?"

"What does Skylar believe?"

Leaf glanced over his shoulder toward his friend and furrowed his brows. A heartbeat later, he lowered his head and said, "Yes, Your Highness. It shall be done."

With a quick bow, Leaf trotted away, grabbing Skylar by the arm. Her brother signaled to other men nearby to join them in a tight circle. She could not hear the words her brother spoke, but his determination was unmistakable. Heads nodded and the small group dispersed and Willow released a breath she had not realized she had been holding. On his way back to where she stood, Leaf crossed his heart and she offered a weak smile in reply.

"Your Majesty," Jeff hollered as he jogged up to where they stood. "Shall I alert Hanley of the fire?"

"Only if the fire cannot be contained," Leaf replied quickly. "Please escort Willow to my wife. I shall return or send a messenger if we need to notify Hanley of our distress." To her he said, "Encourage the women and children to remain in the Great Hall. If they will not listen to you, have Ember speak."

Jeff bowed as Leaf stalked out of the Great Hall, but Willow remained against the door as angry tears finally gathered and spilled. "Come, Your Highness," Jeff said in a shaky voice. She took his arm and allowed him to lead her back toward the stage, where Rain, Ember, and Brianna had already gathered a crowd of women. Upon arrival, Jeff kissed her forehead with paternal-like affection, and sauntered off to a cluster of older men on the other side of the room.

Fidgeting with the folds of her skirt, Willow looked out the latticed window to the unfolding scene across the meadow. She could not meet the faces turned her direction and see what lay beneath their stares. Already, she felt responsible, as if somehow Timothy knew she would fight against his accusations and had, therefore, set up a preemptive punishment for resisting the traditions of the community.

Laurel wrapped her arms around Willow's waist and buried her face between the crook of her arm and her chest. She kissed her sister's cheek and resumed her watch out the window.

The grass around The Forge had caught fire, the flames bending to a bio-breeze as if bowing before its meal. It would consume and destroy, and her stomach tightened. What would happen if the fire reached The Rows? Did the bio-dome possess enough oxygen, or would they all suffocate? Did The Door open from the inside or only from the Outside? The worries persisted and Willow swiped away an angry tear, lest anyone see her cry.

"Tumblers of water and cider shall be placed on these tables over yonder," Ember said in a strong yet elegant tone. Willow looked to see where her sister-in-law pointed. "And on this side, let us gather herbs from the kitchen and prepare poultices for any burns or injuries sustained."

"I have freshly laundered linens, Your Highness," a kitchen maid volunteered.

"Wonderful, thank you, Killie." Ember smiled at the children. "Shall you tear strips for us?" The little heads nodded and Ember smiled wider. "Thank you."

"Come, lads and lassies," Cook said. "We can tear strips here while we nibble on ginger biscuits."

Laurel shifted her face to better see Willow, her eyes tinged red, and Willow's heart constricted. "Shall you fare well?"

"Yes, darling." Willow attempted a brave smile to bolster her sister's spirits. "Go, I shall fare well." Laurel peered out the window as her face pinched in distress. "Do not fret so," Willow whispered. "All will be well, you shall see."

Her sister bit her bottom lip, then whispered, "Did Fillion really kiss you?"

"Never you mind," Willow said, feeling herself blush. Her sister's eyes sparkled as her small frame released a melodious sigh. "Do not allow such fancies to carry you away."

"I am afraid I shall float to the other side of the room," Laurel said with a dreamy sigh. With a final embrace, her sister skipped over to Corona, who took her hand. Coal's little sister wiped away a tear and looked out the window, and Laurel draped an arm around her friend's shoulder and drew her close.

Once everyone settled into their respective duties, Willow said to Ember, "I shall assist the children." She watched Laurel and Corona amble over to Cook to fetch a biscuit and a hemp rag from Killie.

Rather than reply, Ember pulled Willow into an embrace and held her tight, stroking her hair. "You are not faithless," Ember said in gentle tones, pulling away to see her face. Willow lowered her eyes the stone floor. "I had overheard your comment to Leaf."

"But I do feel so faithless. The guilt is unbearable, even more so as I do not feel I have committed any wrongs." Willow sighed.

"For you have not."

Ember took Willow's hands. She opened her mouth to say more, but the doors opened with a loud bang and Willow squeaked, jumping back. She blinked several times, feeling foolish for her response. The Daughter of Fire resumed a regal bearing as Leaf marched into the building, his strides long and purposeful.

"Place him in this corner," her brother commanded.

Several men shoved Timothy into a chair, his face remaining passive. Skylar hung back by the door and intercepted his mother and sisters who rushed over in confusion. Grief welled up inside of Willow, twisting and aching in tight knots, as Skylar's mother wept in her son's arms as if Timothy was dead. Then, a wintry chill slid up the curve of Willow's spine and her eyes traveled back to Timothy. Lips tipped up in a smile, and the former Wind Element pinned her with a hard stare while being bound.

With a shudder, Willow pivoted on her heel toward the window and followed Ember's worried gaze. Buckets of water were tossed onto The Forge and nearby buildings in quick succession. But the fire appeared to gain strength, despite all efforts. Poor Ember, she thought to herself. How must it feel to watch one's family home burn?

Sudden angry shouts ricocheted off the stone walls, startling Willow from her thoughts, and she twisted toward the entrance. For a moment, Willow could not gather what was transpiring. A cluster of men had stormed into the Great Hall and grabbed her brother. Leaf was bound before he could respond, and hauled away. The men who were restraining Timothy sprang into action, but they were blocked by more individuals who swarmed the entrance.

Ember gasped and took off running, yelling, "Release him at once!" Henry, one of the larger men, held Ember as she thrashed against him. When her efforts failed, her sister-in-law's legs gave way and she sobbed, "Do not harm him! Please!"

"Leaf Watson shall be removed as Aether," another man proclaimed. The Great Hall fell silent, the roar of the fire the only sound. "Long live King Skylar, Aether of New Eden Township!" The group began to chant, their voices growing louder and louder.

Laurel ran over to Willow and pressed her face into Willow's side, her small body shaking with tears. "Is Leaf going to die like father?"

She thought of the conversations between Fillion and Leaf during the evening hours. Fillion had shared Hanley's threat that she and her siblings no longer existed, and that he would allow Leaf to play king for a short duration. "Pray for our brother's safety," was all Willow could manage. "You may use my prayer beads if you like." Laurel's fingers curled around the beads and small whispers pressed through her lips, and Willow drew her sister closer.

Skylar shouted, "I refuse! I serve our true King and Aether and shall never comply with these political games."

"But your father—"

"My father does not make decisions on my behalf. I am a grown man. Perhaps you should have verified on which side of the faction I resided before taking up his war."

"You are the true Aether," another proclaimed. "Leaf is an impostor!"

"Skylar," Timothy said in his usual jovial tone. "You were always meant to be The Aether."

The Son of Wind crossed his arms over his chest and peered down his nose at his father. "And, yet, our family's name is not written in the Legacy. This is what *you* want, not I."

"Son, you would turn on your own father? After all I have sacrificed to give this to you?" Timothy asked, and Willow sickened with the pitiful expression he tossed Skylar's direction.

"Silence! Your conniving words and deeds have caused enough damage. I am ashamed of you." Skylar tensed his face to hold back his emotions, then grew stoic once more before marching over and reaching for Ember. "Unhand her."

Ember backed out of the man's arms. "Do not ever touch me again, Henry Sparrow!"

"Forgive me, Your Highness." The man bowed with an uncertain look at Timothy.

"I shall never forgive you if any harm comes to Leaf," Ember said, choking on each word. "How could you behave with such unfeeling?"

"We do not wish to disband, Your Highness," Henry said firmly. "Timothy guaranteed our colony's protection with Skylar as King."

"Timothy has no power for such decisions or futures."

"He reassured us that he had the favored ear of Hanley Nichols, who listens to him regularly concerning New Eden."

Skylar's face grew fierce and he said, "Did you never think to discuss decisions with me as your desired King? Have I ever once come forward carrying my father's war banner?"

Henry dropped his head. "No, My Lord."

"What has become of our true King, Henry?" Skylar stepped before the middle-aged man and leveled a look, grim, serious, and full of warnings. Willow had never seen such passionate feelings from the Son of Wind.

"It would be best not shared before the ladies."

"Believe me when I say," Ember began, "that I shall ensure each person who has conspired against my husband this night shall be prosecuted." Ember drew herself into a rigid yet elegant posture, despite the angry tears that flowed down her cheeks. "Now, go and bring back the true Aether of New Eden or you shall deal with my fury!"

The men stood around, unsure of what to do. Then Willow watched in curious horror as Ember pulled from her pocket a metal device like Fillion's and placed it upon her head, bringing up a transparent screen. Ember's finger manipulated the air and the crowd gasped, equally stunned.

"How is it you know magic?" A young man from the second generation asked, eyes wide. He stepped back, as did others their age. The first generation stared at Ember with bafflement, however.

"Outsider technology is a craft in which I am well-versed, Saul. Please be advised that I am currently alerting the authorities. All I have to do is tap this call button and the police shall arrive. As you know, per The Code, a faction shall end the project. Those who lead and participate in such actions shall be tried for corporate sabotage."

"The police?" Saul asked, looking to the other men for direction.

"Those who enforce the law of the Outside government," Henry said, flicking a wary glance Timothy's way once more.

The former Wind Element shook his head with disgust. "You believe her?" he asked. "She quotes The Code and wields it as a weapon although she is not bound to it. Is this the leadership you desire for our colony? Our home?"

Skylar's eyes transformed into sharp knives as he stared at the group of men blocking the exit. Ignoring his father, he placed a metal device upon his ear and drew into the air. "I am ready to deliver a message to the Guardian Angels of

N.E.T. and inform them of the treasonous acts against the legal minority owner of New Eden Township. Simply give the command, Your Highness."

"Carl," Henry said, his tone cautious. "Fetch Leaf and the others, and return to the Great Hall." The young man dipped his head and ran through the small gathering toward the fires.

"Do we still have a quarrel to settle?" Ember asked, arching her brow.

"No, Your Highness." Henry knelt down on bended knee. "I humbly ask your pardon for my part in brewing and condoning dissension within our community. I beg for your mercy, although I am undeserving of it."

"My husband shall decide your fate, not I, unless I am forced to do so. In the meantime, I suggest you and your band sit and await his judgment."

Willow smiled as she beheld her sister-in-law's display of strength. Ember Watson made the most radiant Queen. So much so, even Laurel whispered, "Beautiful," as their older sister wiped away another tear while staring down the large group of men.

A shout of warning came from beyond the meadow, followed by a loud crack and groaning crash. Willow sucked in a loud breath. Out the window, she watched as the roof of The Forge fell, sending wild sparks spiraling through the night air. The orange glow burst with the renewed oxygen and more shouts were lifted in response. To Willow, it appeared as if New Eden had become a funeral pyre, and the shrouded deceit and betrayals were finally turning to ash.

ELEMENTS

There's a time when the operation of the machine becomes so odious, makes you so sick at heart, that you can't take part; you can't even passively take part, and you've got to put your bodies upon the gears and upon the wheels, upon the levers, upon all the apparatus, and you've got to make it stop. And you've got to indicate to the people who run it, to the people who own it, that unless you're free, the machine will be prevented from working at all.

— Mario Savio, free speech activist, in a speech at the University of California Berkeley, December 2, 1964 *

CHAPTER
THIRTY-EIGHT

Fillion sat on the edge of the cot and looked toward the doorway. Dizziness affected him every time he moved to a sitting or standing position. It was really annoying. But it would be even more irritating to fall down or black out. So, he sat. When the sensations passed, he slowly stood and waited.

He needed to piss—bad—and the lavatory was on the opposite end of the apartment. Ready to move, he placed his hands on the wall and shuffled across the floor. Damn, he still felt so weak. He'd never been so sick in his life.

In the living room he paused and turned toward the door. What was that smell? It was acrid and Fillion grimaced. Did someone die yesterday? The only way such a strong, smoky scent would reach the Watson apartment was if there was a funeral pyre. Spooky.

He resumed his journey to the lavatory, his eyes nearly rolling back in relief when done. Nothing felt as good as taking a piss or a first drag on a cigarette.

Now, he was ready to explore the source of that pungent smell. He needed to move and regain strength, anyway.

Back in the living room, he studied the spinning wheel and smiled. Then he trudged toward the entry door. A hazy, afternoon light spilled in from the window, wisps of light curling up from beneath the front door. Wait. Light didn't do that.

Fillion yanked open the door and gaped. Black smoke circled and danced through the air, covering the dome's ceiling in a thick, dark cloud. What the hell?

His legs were trembling, but he pushed himself to the end of the deck and scanned the forest. In the direction of the North Cave, the smoke was thin and the trees were greener. Toward the village— "Shit!" Had the village caught fire? With a start, he knew this was the last act for redemption according to the Curse Card. He swore under his breath and moved toward the apartment to alert N.E.T.

Once inside the apartment, he collapsed onto the edge of the cot and grabbed his Cranium off the nightstand. After he caught his breath, he brought up a browser screen and accessed his and Mack's cloud file. He scrolled through the contents until he found the folder on Messenger Pigeon. In a matter of seconds, he tapped the number, silently rejoicing when the outgoing signal chirped in his ear.

"New Eden Enterprises, my name is Ellie, how may I…" A girl Fillion had never seen before—maybe early twenties?—gawked slack-jawed through Messenger Pigeon's video feature. A new hire to replace whoever took over his night shift? She reared her head back slightly and closed her mouth. "Oh my god. Fillion Nichols?"

"Yes."

"For real?"

He rolled his eyes. "There's a fire." Fillion paused to breathe. "We need The Door opened."

"I'm sorry." She turned several shades of red. "But if you're Fillion Nichols, then The Door remains closed."

"What?" He closed his eyes for a moment, willing patience. "The fire will eat up all the oxygen and the residents will die. You want that on your head?" Dizziness hit him again and the room swam. But he pushed through the mental fog. "Open The Door!"

"Hanley Nichols, er, your dad gave instructions that you were not to leave New Eden Township." Ellie darted her eyes around the communications room. "The memo said you might lie to attempt release and that you were to speak directly with Mr. Nichols."

Fury rushed through his veins. "Patch me through to Hanley."

"One moment. Stay on the line." The woman concentrated on a screen away from the video camera as her fingers tapped and danced through the air. Fillion closed his eyes. God, he was so weak. Walking outside had drained him. "Mr. Nichols, this is Ellie Hunter from Comm in Seattle. A young male connecting through Messenger Pigeon, tagged at New Eden Township, claims to be your son." Her focus shifted to Fillion, then back to her other screen. "No, he appears to be using a Cranium." Her eyebrows drew together with skepticism. "Yes, Mr. Nichols." Fingers tapped off-screen and then eyes, brimming with distress, studied him. "He says if you are truly his son, you'll know how to connect with him without using Messenger Pigeon."

"I'm not lying. There's a fire." Fillion silently pleaded with her and, after several long seconds, said in a softer voice, "Please, open The Door. There are hundreds of people who could lose their lives, including children."

Hesitancy flashed in her eyes. "I'm so sorry. I can't open The Door for you." A sad but friendly smile touched her lips. "Hopefully another will connect through Messenger Pigeon to report the fire."

Fillion hung up without a reply and released a slow growl. Rage pulsed through his limbs and he gripped his hair and pulled. After a few seconds, he brought up the Cranium's user interface and accessed his profile through the admin screens. Yes, make it public to everyone on his contact list. Yes, take a profile picture. He brought the Cranium in front of him and flipped off the camera with a cocky smile, then strapped it back to his ear. UI admin screen backup. Yes, show profile picture and information to blocked users. Yes, show GPS location. No, don't notify users of profile changes. Apply. Save. Done. He swiped out of the admin screens and said, "Cranium, phone Hanley Nichols."

An outgoing ping echoed in his head as he trudged down the hallway, leaning on the wall for support. When he entered the living room he held on to the chairs.

"I warned you that everyone at N.E.E. and N.E.T. knows not to open The Door for you. Nice profile picture, by the way."

"There's a fire," Fillion said through shallow breaths. "I swear." He opened the front door and walked onto the deck.

"Michael," Hanley said in a muffled voice. "Do the Guardian Angels have new reports on the CO_2 or oxygen levels?"

"Let me check," came the distant reply of the scientist.

Fillion reached the railing. "Turn on your vid feed," he said, selecting the reverse camera feature. Black smoke billowed near the East Cave, and orange flames played peek-a-boo through the forest skyline.

"All biomimicry vitals now look solid," Michael said in the background. "No new changes since last check."

"Either someone hacked the sensors," Fillion replied to Hanley, "or it's an inside job. I'll show you."

"If anything changes, Michael, you'll find me in my room." A long pause followed and Fillion closed his eyes as his legs shook. He was so dehydrated. "Now we're alone," Hanley said. "I see it."

Fillion returned back to the main vid cam and stared at Hanley. "Open The Door before we lose all our air."

"Are you sick?" Hanley raised both eyebrows.

"Poisoned yesterday. Someone laced my joints with something they received from outside the biodome." Fillion slid against the wall and leaned his head back. "I'll give you one guess as to who."

Hanley didn't answer, instead he asked, "Why didn't someone notify N.E.T. yesterday?"

"I asked them not to."

"Suicide mission?"

"Want to know why no one ever leaves for medical treatment?" Fillion drew in a labored breath. "The fear of separation is stronger than the fear of death." Hanley leaned back in a chair with a bland expression. "Death makes life richer. People here would rather die and 'return to their trace elements to sustain the community that sustained them,' than leave and possibly never see their loved ones again. Or be prevented from returning to a life that gave them purpose and meaning. Ironic, right? Death reveals the true elements of life."

"You still call that Stockholm syndrome?"

"Partially." Fillion glared at this dad. "Open the damn doors!"

"No."

Incredulous, he shouted, "What?! Are you mental? You want us all to die? Me?" Hanley remained unmoved. "Wait," Fillion pushed himself up as his eyes grew wide. "You knew this would happen." Hanley let out an irritated sigh, but didn't blink or verbally confirm or deny. God, he hated this game. Fillion didn't have the energy to guess what Hanley was thinking. Or, what Fillion believed Hanley wanted him to think. So, he'd change the subject. "What was your meeting with Timothy about the other night?" Fillion smirked.

Hanley chuckled and shook his head with ill-humor. "Paranoid? The poison may still be symptomatic."

"I know all about the Techsmith Guild."

"It was only a matter of time."

"Time…" Fillion's thoughts blared with sudden warning. "The fire is a distraction," he mumbled to himself. The sick feeling in his stomach intensified. Maybe the biomimicry vitals were correct and Hanley had pre-thought out a solution to any potential structural fires. Of course he did. Who wouldn't? Or a hacker messed with the results. Or both. No wonder Hanley didn't seem ruffled by a fire.

A Gamemaster ponders the hidden. Was Fillion poisoned by his own flesh-and-blood to remove any potential involvement or disruption in a coup? Several weeks ago, he would have demanded to be released to a medical facility for treatment. Not anymore. But Hanley didn't know that.

Fillion grimaced with anger. "What are you doing to Leaf?"

"Again, I think the paranoia is playing with your mind."

"How do you know the poison causes paranoia? God, there's a fire in New Eden. You confirmed that you saw it." Fillion blinked rapidly as panic seized him. "It's not in my head so stop trying to persuade me that it is. If you won't open The Door, then I'll do it." He raised his hand to end the conversation but Hanley's voice stopped him.

"Wait. Think through this decision." Hanley leaned forward in his chair. "Do you realize what an emergency evacuation would do to the project? To all the people who have only known a sheltered life? The world is vast and enormous compared to their confined existence."

"What the hell is Timothy going to do to Leaf?!"

"Timothy? You can't accuse a man of foul play simply because he has meetings with me."

Fillion's eyes rounded. "So you admit it. He had a meeting with you."

"I've had meetings with all of The Elements."

"What is planned against Leaf?"

"Fillion," Hanley said with a sad smile. "I'm sending in a medical team to remove you."

"No!" Fillion grit his teeth. "Stop deflecting and answer the damn question! If Leaf dies, I'll press charges against you. I know too much already and you know it." Hanley's eyes winced. Subtle, but Fillion was looking for a sign and zeroed in to every nuance of body language and inflection of speech. "Open The Door to keep me silent or get hauled back into court."

"Have you experienced hallucinations in addition to the paranoia?"

"Really? Playing that card on me?" Fillion glared at Hanley, pressing his lips together in a tight, thin line. "I'm giving you ten seconds to answer my question or I'm shutting down New Eden Township."

"If you do, everything will be lost. People have sacrificed twenty years of their lives for this project. And for what? Do you really think they would throw all of that away over one man?"

"The one man who has written to you to return the Carsons and the Moores to New Eden?" Fillion bit the inside of his cheek. "That's the kind of man you want to sacrifice? He would do anything for his community and they know it. Apparently, so do you."

"If *you* were truly community minded, *you* would realize that what is best for morale is to ensure success at all costs." Hanley touched the side of his head in a dramatic gesture. "Think for one second. Use that gifted brain you have to defend *reality*. Project failure would immediately displace everyone and they would be thrown into the Outside world with no transition. What do you think Project Phase Two is for? N.E.T. doesn't have capacity for a mass exodus. The community would have no protection from the media."

"Oh please. You have enough money and power to make anything happen." Fillion grimaced and clenched his teeth. "Like I'm supposed to believe you never thought through an emergency mass exodus plan? Yeah, right. You have a protocol for everything."

In a soft, kind tone, Hanley asked, "What would Leaf want?"

"Truth." Anger burned in Fillion's chest and he yelled, "Leaf would die for noble reasons! Nothing about this situation is noble or honorable."

"No? Any financial disaster that befalls a subsidiary of New Eden Enterprises directly affects our good in the world." Fillion groaned and rolled his eyes, but Hanley continued. "Think of all the countries that are dependent upon our family, Fillion. Countless nations owe their economic and agricultural health to N.E.E. This is not just about Leaf. It is a much larger picture and many people are affected. Is this the legacy you wish to leave the world?"

"My legacy?" Norah's deathbed words and blessing whispered to his soul. "Your hate for Joel runs deep." Fillion took in a deep breath, feeling light-headed. "You won in the end. You got the girl and legal access to her theory. Nations bow at your feet. Money is nothing to you. You're the King of the Green Movement and the global economy's Corporate King."

"Genius status does not make you right." Hanley narrowed his eyes. "You are a hot-headed fool. Be warned, if you try anything, I will take you to court for corporate sabotage."

"No you won't." A cocky grin stretched across Fillion's face. "You spent my entire life grooming me for whatever plot twist you have planned for the world. Plus, I'll just press charges against you as well."

"Are you admitting that perhaps I did sire a son more powerful than myself?" Hanley laughed, the derisive, mocking sounds meant to belittle Fillion. But Fillion held his ground despite his rapidly declining mental, emotional, and physical state.

With disgust, Fillion said, "If I'm more powerful than you, it's only because your power was only an illusion to begin with." He formed one last arrogant smile, shrugged his eyebrows and said, "Game over."

He swiped the air and ended the call, drawing in deep breaths. Time was limited. Hanley knew Fillion was about to hack and so he needed an attack plan against any counterstrikes Hanley may prepare. Flood their mainframes? Maybe.

"Cranium, phone Mack," he murmured as he brought up N.E.T.'s mainframe. His finger brought up layer after layer of information as his eyes scanned for the path of least resistance.

"Fillion?"

He flicked his eyes to his friend. "I need your help. Emergency."

"OK." Mack's face darkened as his eyes traveled over Fillion's face. "Glad you're alive."

"Sorry, mate. I'm freaking out right now. There's a fire. Like a huge fire and Hanley refuses to open the doors. I think something is going to happen to Leaf."

"Shit. Can you breathe?"

"Yeah."

"Good. Coal called me over an hour ago and shared that the CO_2 and O_2 numbers spiked, then flipped roles. I've been trying to isolate the hacker, but can't find him."

"Yeah, I think there's a hacker involved, too. Did you try the Techsmith Guild handles?"

"Just started investigating it as an inside job."

"Well scratch that for now. I want a temporary distributed denial of service attack launched at N.E.T.'s system," Fillion said, closing his eyes for a moment. Dizziness hit him once more. Breathing in the smoke probably wasn't helping. "I'm shutting down the dome and Hanley knows it. Need a distraction. Release the stranglehold when you see the biodomes go live again."

Mack held his Cranium straight and turned his head to the side. "Hey, Amanda and Kev. Nadine and Blue still around? Yeah? OK. Ping them to return. Corlan has a side job for us. We need to launch a zombie apocalypse and infect N.E.T.'s servers in a flash-flood attack. Don't touch the biodome's system, only the lab's. All hands on deck. Whoever you can find. Have a virus handy or do we need to build one?" Mack faced Fillion again. "Amanda is on it."

"Thanks, mate." Fillion offered as shaky smile. "I need to go. Probably won't see you for a while. I'm sure I'll go to prison for this."

"No matter what, remember that I'm your one and only bitch," Mack deadpanned and Fillion chuckled. His friend sobered and said, "Take care of yourself, OK? No more heroics. I'll come visit you."

"Yeah. Peachy."

"Oh. Wait. I need to share something. Going to the privacy cell." The scenery around Mack moved and Fillion bit the inside of his cheek, waiting for Mack to reach the conference room. "OK. So, Kev uncovered some serious shit."

Fillion listened as Mack shared the details on Hanley and Timothy, his heart skipping a beat as it tried to restart again and again. Now wasn't the time for a mental breakdown. But god. He really was the son of a killer—from a line of them. The shock transitioned to rage and Fillion knew, more than ever, that his decision to temporarily shut down New Eden was right. It was time to push back and in a way that hurt. Fillion wasn't responsible for the world. He was only responsible for this one. Nobody was allowed to burn down his kingdom before he did. Nobody. So, he'd have the final word. Fight fire with fire.

"You gonna be all right?" Mack asked.

"Give Kev a bonus. I need to run."

"Sure." Mack's mouth tipped up in a lopsided smile. "Hey, wait. Did you kiss her?"

"Like a boss."

"Well done, sir. OK. Go have fun. Make good choices!" Mack said in a humorous voice. "God, kids grow up so fast."

"Shut up," Fillion said through soft laughter. "Catch you later."

They stared at each for a few seconds, offering one last smile, then Fillion's screen went black.

Fillion waited a few seconds and stared at N.E.T.'s system, watching the infection spread until their computer system was zombified. His friend was a freaking wizard. Hanley was probably shitting his pants. Now, to focus on his job. He slid a glance through the railing slats to the fire, watching the orange flames. The fire looked larger and Fillion's pulse kicked up a notch.

First order of business: sprinklers. After crafting an algorithm to search for keywords, he found the manual override and turned on the emergency water system. A large groan echoed through the biodome, as if the machine shuddered. Then, the fractured sky sputtered, followed by a heavy spray of drops. A roaring sizzle hissed from the village and a large plume of gray smoke billowed behind the forest. Cheers went up. It sounded like they were banging on pots and pans, too, and Fillion smiled.

Inching up under the eaves, a wall of water fell off the roof and plopped onto his shoulder. There was no help for it. His finger flew through the air and swiped in another keyword until he found the code for the operating system. Fantastic. A wicked grin stretched across Fillion's face. He studied the strings of code, reading and reading, until he found a plausible glitch. Furiously swiping, he programmed the biodomes to shut down for a short duration, initiating emergency evacuations and opening up all doors, but keeping the sprinkler system on.

This was it. He tapped the approve command and the biodome instantly went dark. He never realized how much soft light the reflective panels emitted at night, even on a moonless night. A strange, flat silence cut through the plink and plop of rain drops, almost hurting his ears. Then, a red light gradually brightened from the dome ceiling and a generic female-sounding computer voice spoke instructions in soothing tones.

"THIS IS AN EMERGENCY NOTIFICATION. PLEASE EXIT THE BIODOMES AT THE NORTH ENTRANCE IN A CALM AND ORDERLY FASHION. MEDICAL TEAMS ARE ON STANDBY. I REPEAT. PLEASE EXIT THE BIODOMES AT THE NORTH ENTRANCE IN A CALM AND ORDERLY FASHION."

The computer voice paused and Fillion closed his eyes. The N.E.T. ninjas could find him when they combed through the domes for stragglers. Right now, he was too damn tired to function another second. The emergency evacuation message repeated once again and Fillion tapped his Cranium closed and bunched up against the wall, steadying his breaths. Water spilled off the roof in sheets next to him. He hoped Leaf was safe, and his family. That was the last thought he had before passing out.

That a peasant may become king does not render the kingdom democratic.

— Woodrow Wilson, 28th President of the United States, 20th century A.D. *

ChAPTER
ThIRTY-NINE

Several women busied themselves pouring tumblers of water and cider, while others prepared poultices. Children tore strips of hemp cloth in the far corner. The atmosphere strained until taut, slowly fraying with the tension. The creak and groan of chairs and busy hands seemed like shouts over the quietude of panic. Not even Timothy spoke anymore. His intolerable arguments and persuasions were finally ignored by all, even by Henry. Still, people remained busy, as if doing so instilled a sense of normalcy. To Willow, this was the very definition of insanity.

She paced behind Ember and Rain, who sat before the small band of men responsible for turning the community against itself. Nearby, Corona and Laurel held each other. Their little arms tangled around each other in mutual grief and fear. Treading toward the girls, Willow paused, struck by how much Corona resembled both Fillion and Coal in this moment. Dark hair and light, clear eyes, a dimpled frown beneath the classic, straight Hansen nose. Even her expression of conveying intensity of thought and feeling through slight, knitted brows and the way Rona rolled in her bottom lip as a nervous gesture, was every bit Fillion and Coal. Unnerved, Willow spun the opposite direction and continued her agitated patrol.

One step. Another step. Move. Breathe. If she sat and attempted cool composure, she feared she would crumble into fragments, incapable of being pieced back together. The storm inside her raged with furious gales. Emotions whipped around despite her fatigue. It was as though she slowly crept toward a shuttered existence while the world around her moved at unnatural speeds.

"The Wi-Fi is down," Skylar muttered. Willow's steps faltered as her heart jumped with the sound of his voice. The flying pages Ember and Skylar had ever-present blinked, then changed to a soft shade of blue. Skylar tapped the metal device on his ear, and the otherworldly light disappeared. A strange, unsettling quiet fell over the biodomes simultaneously with his movements. Ember lifted an eyebrow in question. "The generators have hushed," he said.

Then, the miraculous occurred—bio-rain. She heard the familiar groan before the sputter. Willow, as well as others, rushed to the nearest windows. Within a heartbeat, the fire hissed in protest and the community cheered. Some even took to dancing in the meadow, lifting buckets and pots, banging them together in celebration. A loud cheer erupted from the Great Hall as well and Willow laughed. She could not help but share in the unexpected burst of joy.

The smiles fell, however, when the ambient light from the dome ceiling winked out, and their world became pitch black. An eerie hush settled in the Hall. She held her breath, afraid to move. The candles in the Great Hall flickered more noticeably than before, glinting in the panes. And the stones warmed in richer hues of amber, colored by the fires that had spread to other buildings in the village and outlying areas of the meadow and Orchard.

The dome did not remain black for long, though. A glaring, red light spread in a grid across the dome ceiling. It was as if the heart of New Eden broke open and dripped blood. Even the splashes and streaks of bio-rain tinted red across the glass panes. Willow shuddered and took a step away from the latticed window. A woman's voice, unnaturally magnified, began to speak and Willow clapped her hands over her ears with a cry.

"THIS IS AN EMERGENCY NOTIFICATION. PLEASE EXIT THE BIODOMES AT THE NORTH ENTRANCE IN A CALM AND ORDERLY FASHION. MEDICAL TEAMS ARE ON STANDBY. I REPEAT. PLEASE EXIT THE BIODOMES AT THE NORTH ENTRANCE IN A CALM AND ORDERLY FASHION."

"Who is that?" a young woman shrieked. "How did she amplify her voice to such a volume?"

Skylar turned toward her and said loud enough for all to hear, "An emergency broadcast system. *She* is a computer and will continue to speak on repeat, I am sure."

"Oaklee?" Laurel screeched as she paled. "We must go Outside?"

"I … I am confused. The instructions seem to imply so."

"But what about Leaf?"

Ember met Willow's eyes, the fear behind her dark brown depths asking the same question.

"Leaf trusts us to lead and guide the community. He may be delayed for the very same reason," Rain offered weakly. "He is safe, I am sure of it."

Henry lowered his head as apprehension flashed in his eyes. The man was unwilling to share what the other men were charged to do with Leaf. Timothy had only smiled when asked. To Willow, receiving no answer was worse than hearing the truth, for her imagination was more than capable of forming its own conclusions. Playing with her mind was one thing. But playing with her heart, still scabbed over from grief, was entirely different.

Fists clenched, she marched over to Timothy and asked, in a low growl, "What have you done with my brother?" The slow smile crept along his face once more and he stared at her unblinking. "Tell me now!"

"Is this your illusory attempt at power?" He asked simply. Timothy tsk-tsked and shook his head. "I spent nearly thirty years of my life building toward this future. One you cannot even begin to perceive. I do not answer to a mere slip of a girl, especially a human product programmed to become psychologically conditioned to her environment. How does it feel to be *cursed* by science?"

"You are a monster!" she spat. Heads whipped their direction and bodies stilled. Shaking with rage, Willow slapped him. Sharp gasps circled around her, but she ignored everyone. The smile on Timothy's face only grew wider and her self-control snapped. Willow hurled toward him with a guttural scream and clawed at his face. All thought left. The only emotion present was black emptiness. Thin, pricks of blood and red scratch marks surfaced on his face. Yet, the smile remained. He had robbed her. He had destroyed her family and her home. "Tell me where he is!" she screamed over and over again.

Hands, warm and gentle, pinned her arms at her sides with an embrace from behind. "Your Highness, please," Skylar whispered near her ear. "Oaklee." Willow fought against Skylar, hot tears streaming down her face. "Please, Willow Oak Watson of the Wood," he quietly pleaded once again. It was her childhood nickname that dispelled the storm and the winds of injustice died to a low moan, matching the one she released. "I shall rectify this," he said for her ears alone. "And we shall recover your brother."

Then, she was turned over to the waiting arms of Rain.

"Timna? Joannah?" Skylar began again. "Please bring aid to my father."

Willow peered over Rain's shoulder at Timothy. The man's face remained calm. Shame burned through her as thoughts returned. Although the anger had demanded justice, it could not be considered honorable to attack a bound man. She was sure of it. Inspecting her fingernails, bile rose and her legs grew weak. What had she done?

"Henry," Skylar said, strong, firm, "I suggest you aid the Watson family or I shall ensure your family is permanently banished while you are tried as an accomplice for harassment and assault."

"My Lord." Henry paled as he stood with a bow and quickly pivoted toward the door in anxious, jerky movements.

"THIS IS AN EMERGENCY NOTIFICATION. PLEASE EXIT THE BIODOMES…"

Willow cringed against the blaring noise. The sounds of weeping, mostly the children, closed in all around her. Murmurs began as low whispers and quickly escalated into shouted debates. The Daughter of Fire moved through the distressed crowd to the stage. Her lips trembled and her eyes skipped around the room. Seeing Ember so shaken brought shadows to the edges of Willow's vision and she gulped in a large breath. Then another. Breathe, she reminded herself.

"We must leave," Ember said in a loud, but tremulous voice. "All shall go save Timothy. He shall remain here bound to the chair and shall be removed by the Guardian Angels."

"Please!" Emily Kane directed at Ember. "Have mercy."

"I am being merciful, Madam." Ember descended the stage and took Emily's hands in her own. "My heart grieves for your family. I am so very sorry to ask this of you, for I know my own heart would break into infinite pieces if in your position." Ember placed a trembling hand on Emily's cheek with a look of compassion. "I cannot allow Timothy to be freed."

Emily lowered her head and moaned, low wails shaking her body. Skylar turned his mother toward him and she wrapped her arms around his neck and buried her head into his shoulder. "I shall care for mother. Windy?" The eldest of the two sisters approached Skylar with skittish movements and silent tears. "Please take Gale's hand and hold onto the back of my cloak so we do not separate."

"Yes, My Lord," Windy whispered with a small dip.

"For those who supported Timothy's faction, go to your families." Ember's words echoed in the quiet-stricken room. "When all has settled, I trust each of you to behave as honorable men and come forward, confessing your deeds to His Majesty."

"Yes, Your Highness," several answered with sweeping bows.

"We cannot leave!" Laurel cried out. "How shall Leaf find us?"

"Lady Rain is correct, sweetling," Ember said, wiping away a tear. "Leaf expects us to lead and guide the community. We gave oaths of honor to do so before all of New Eden." Ember lowered to eye level with Laurel. "Leaf shall find us. I have a hunch, and—"

"And you are rarely wrong."

"Indeed." Ember attempted a brave smile, but Willow noted the strain in doing so. Rarely was not the same as never, and she tensed.

A short duration later, the Great Hall emptied, many with the prepared supplies, and they hurried toward the village. Chaos had seized the biodome. People dashed across the meadow in search of loved ones. Names were shouted in panic. Hands pushed. Shoulders bumped. Bodies were in constant motion. Laurel jumped into Willow a few times, clutching fistfuls of fabric. Edgy and wary of the whirring shadows seemingly coated in ash, the sisters clung to each other. It was as if the community had become leaves tumbling in the wind. Cast off from the mother tree toward an unknown future. Twirling about without control.

Bio-rain continued to fall, seeping through the wedding dress. Willow rubbed a hand over her arm as she shivered. She held Laurel's hand, her eyes jumping from face to face in search of Leaf. But she could not locate his sturdy build nor crown of curly brown hair. Droplets ran down her face and into her eyes, and she brushed away the rain in furious motions.

The Forge lay in a heap, steam wafting past the thrumming rain in thin ribbons. Willow's heart lurched at the sight. Memories of Coal—hair and skin gilded before the forge's fire, hammering over the anvil—dropped like rain through her mind and evaporated in the thick film clouding the village. Connor, Brianna, and their two littlest stood before the remains. Their silhouettes sharp against the low, amber glow produced the illusion of chimerical beings from mythology.

The crowd gawked and keened before the rubble. Some fell to their knees and covered their heads. Some grabbed the arms of others and whipped them around with hopeful expressions. Scattered and afraid, people moved in and out of focus. Faces burned red beneath the red light. Mud-splattered clothing and hair hung in damp clumps. Black smoke wafted between and round each person. It was as if even New Eden's dead had been called from the ashes, rising to haunt the biodomes.

Her mind continued to leap from image to image to the rhythm of her galloping pulse. Ember broke free and reunited with her family, becoming a dark angel against the sparks and dying fires. Willow averted her eyes from those who openly stared at her and Laurel as they passed. She was helpless, just like them. If Willow and her sisters did not find Leaf, she would rather exit with the Hansens. And so she waited. The very thought constricted the muscles in her stomach, but she refused to crash. She refused to grow sick with grief, though the suspense was addling her senses. At times, she swore her brother's voice lifted above the whirlwind of shouts, wails, coughing, and hissing steam; and she startled each and every time, even now.

"Willow Oak!" A deep voice called from behind.

She closed her eyes, attempting to find nature's music to comfort her grief-stricken state—a silly notion, really. She was on the verge of declaring herself delusional. Her eyes were stinging from the caustic air and she coughed. But the voice persisted and called her name once more. So she turned toward the sound.

She whispered, "Leaf," in disbelief and bit down on her knuckles to stifle the forming sob. Shocked statements of concern and cries of alarm sprung up from those Leaf passed in the hazy darkness, assisted by Henry. Blood and bio-rain streamed down her brother's face, the blood flowing from a laceration on the side of his head. His left eye had swelled, made more pronounced by the dark bruise that had begun to form. Then, she noticed he walked with a limp. When close, Leaf turned to Henry and spoke, but she could not hear him. The man bowed and walked away, head hung low and shoulders dramatically slumped forward.

"Willow. Laurel," their brother said, a catch in his voice.

Willow rushed to him, and he staggered back a step when she wrapped her arms around his neck. Laurel squeezed into their tight embrace and Leaf circled his arms around them both. "I was so scared," Willow said over and over again. "I thought they had killed you."

"I fare well, *ma chère*. I am but a little roughed up. I shall recover."

"Willow attacked Timothy!" Laurel said, eyes rounded with the memories.

"Laurel!"

"Well, you did. He refused to say where you were, Leaf, and Willow slapped him and scratched his face." Her sister beamed at her with a form of pride. "She fought for you."

"I am most ashamed of my actions."

"He wished our family harm," Leaf said quietly, clearly uncomfortable. "Although violence is not recommended, do not hold onto the shame."

Willow pulled away and studied her brother. "What have they done to you?" Leaf pressed Laurel to his side with a slight shake of his head. Understanding the cue, Willow asked, "What is happening?"

"I believe the project has been shut down."

"No!" she cried, the panic finally breaching her attempts at composure. "I refuse to leave our home!" The horror leeched into her bloodstream and a scream formed in her gut, slowly worming its way up. But it never released. The anxious, crawling feeling tormented her for several heartbeats until she thought she would go mad. "I shall not take another step!"

Leaf covered his face with his hands and his fingers lightly plowed down his cheeks. "Willow Oak," he whispered and stopped. Her name was spoken with such sorrow, such misery, her heart began to weep, although her eyes remained dry. "Please." His eyes brimmed with pain and fatigue. The shadows on his face grew darker as he surveyed the destruction and heartsick people.

"I am terrified," she said.

"I am as well." A weak half-smile appeared, a gruesome look with the blood dripping down the side of his head. "I could benefit from your indomitable spirit this moment." Before she could reply, his gaze traveled over her head and fixated on another. His chest rose and fell, as if he held back a flood of emotions. "Please excuse me," Leaf said, akin to a whispered ache.

Willow and Laurel pulled away as Leaf hobbled toward Ember. Awash with fear and confusion, the community drew closer to Leaf. He only had eyes for Ember, though, and she for him. Dread knotted Willow's stomach, uneasy with the desperate looks and frenetic motions of the villagers.

Before he reached his wife, the crowd converged on Leaf, and Willow shrieked. Hands flocked to touch him. Fingers tugged at the tattered hem of his tunic and sleeves. They shouted his name as a plea, begging, crying. Many chanted for him to have mercy on them. She was confused by their request at first. But quickly, Willow realized the foundation for their hysteria was the same as that of her very own apprehensions and sentiments.

For a horrifying moment, Willow feared the community would trample Leaf and Ember in their frenzy. However, men stepped forward and pushed the crowd back, with orders to give berth so their King could speak. Ember ran into Leaf's embrace, pressing her face to his chest. People did not struggle long against the self-appointed guards. But they were coiled tight, ready to spring into action, eyes darting around, feet shifting.

"What happened to you, Your Majesty?" asked Kyle, a fellow gardener and one of the self-appointed guards. His wife, who had assisted in the Great Hall, pulled a hemp cloth from a basket and handed it Leaf, who pressed it to his head wound.

Her brother's eyes roamed over all the soot-covered, rain-soaked residents, and shouted above the roar of the bio-rain. "I was assaulted when I refused to abdicate power, with threats that the violence would continue until I relented or I no longer drew breath."

Sharp gasps circulated as eyes widened in horror. The whites of each eye appeared ghostly in the dark smoke, ghoulish images that elicited a shiver through Willow's body. Laurel snapped her eyes to Willow's in fright, returning attention to their brother when he continued.

"My wife negotiated for my release, I understand. The attackers resisted, however, determined it was a trick. They only relented when the biodomes shut down, followed by Henry Sparrow's announcing that the faction, led by Timothy Kane, had lost." More cries of alarm rippled through the village as the news spread. "Those responsible are returning to their families per my command. I shall pass judgment once our community resumes as before."

Kyle placed a hand upon Leaf's shoulder. "I am beyond grieved. If there is anything we can do for your family, Your Majesty, you have but only to ask."

"Thank you, sir. I am honored by your kindness." Leaf dipped his head, his face tensing with emotion. "New Eden! Please hear me! I wish for everyone to ignore the emergency message and return to their homes. We shall not disband this night, nor will I allow the poor choices of a few to ruin the future of many. I shall personally leave the biodome and meet with Hanley Nichols and fight to defend project continuation."

Willow's heart stopped. She knew this was not the time to challenge her brother nor give in to her darkest fears. Still, what if he never returned? What if Hanley finished what others had started this evening? She looked around at all the faces, who gazed at her brother with respect. Tears of relief streamed alongside the bio-rain on their cheeks. Her parents had died in service to their community. She could not lose another she loved as a sacrifice for New Eden.

The protests and groans from her soul were overwhelming. But it did not matter how she felt. She knew the truth, although acceptance of such knowledge slayed her. With unsteady legs, she stepped forward and took Leaf's hand, imparting whatever remnants of her indomitable spirit remained. His shoulders relaxed and he squeezed her hand in reply, with an appreciative look her way.

Kyle turned toward the community and shouted, "I speak for our Aether! Please gather your families and return to your homes. I repeat. Return to your homes! Do not exit! Our community shall not disband this night." Pockets of cheers erupted in a slow-moving wave as the news traveled through the gathering. The gardener said to Leaf, "Focus on settling your wife and sisters before you leave. I shall appoint others to assist me in caring for any needs that arise."

Leaf blinked back emotion. "I am humbled, sir. Thank you."

Kyle bowed and then trotted through the village, ushering small groups toward the apartments. The mysterious voice echoed through the domes again, and many ducked and raised hands to their ears, looking around wildly for the source.

Willow's heart throbbed as her mind wandered toward the Son of Eden. Was Fillion safe? Did those from Timothy's faction assault him while he was alone and vulnerable? A slow panic began to rise, making her wish she could dash to the apartment and find him. But the crowd was thick, and fear gripped her at the thought of running off into the forest without protection. She willed herself to be patient, telling herself they would be home soon.

Squinting against the burning air, Willow studied the dome and shivered. Red light saturated the growing pools of water near her feet, sanguine sprays erupting with each droplet. Dark shreds of smoke cut through the air despite the rain. The scathing orange glow of embers glared back at the stares of passersby with the memories of their fiery destruction.

New Eden had transformed into a nightmare—a haunting, shuddersome sight to behold. Perhaps it was what Fillion uttered in his delusional state: an eco-hell.

The willow is my favorite tree. I grew up near one. It's the most flexible tree in nature and nothing can break it—no wind, no elements, it can bend and withstand anything.

— Pink, musician, 21st century A.D. *

CHAPTER FORTY

It seemed akin to a lifetime before they reached the stairs leading to their apartment; and Willow thought surely her heart would burst from suspense. Within a few steps, she and her siblings managed access to the stairs and raced into their home, Lea limping close behind.

Their apartment was dark. They paused in the living room, breaths shallow. What if others wishing her family harm laid in wait? Carefully, Willow wended her way toward her parents' room, her sisters and brother on her trail. The door to her father's bedchamber was left open and she stilled. Her entire body shivered, beyond the cold seeping through her skin.

"Fillion?" she whispered, entering the pitch black room.

"Yeah." A weak reply. "In bed."

His voice quavered and she could hear his teeth chattering. Her hands, trembling but sure, reached out and blindly felt along the edge of the bed until she found his body. He shook, despite the covers, which were damp.

"Are you bleeding?"

"No," he whispered. "I passed out on the deck. In the rain too long. Couldn't find dry clothes. Too weak to rummage through Leaf's room." He sucked in a shuddering breath. "Is Leaf OK?"

"I am well enough, My Lord."

Fillion's breath hitched, as if catching on a sob. "I wasn't too late."

The obnoxious, loud voice sounded instructions once more and Willow sighed heavily. They remained quiet as the unnatural woman issued her commands.

When the voice silenced, Leaf asked, "Are you well, My Lord?"

"Yeah. You have no idea how relieved I am to hear your voice." Fillion adjusted his position on the bed. "I turned on the sprinklers and shut down the dome."

"Ladies, I wish for a private word with Fillion, please."

Willow contemplated resistance. But Ember tugged her hand and she filed out of the room behind her sisters. They groped along the walls until they reached the living room. Ember found her way to the cupboard and began striking a fire nest in a stone bowl. Each silent in their tasks, they roamed around the living room until all of the candles and lanterns were lit. The bio-rain continued to thunder upon the deck, and Willow peered out the latticed window to the world she no longer recognized.

Eventually, the bedroom door opened and Leaf emerged, his haggard steps thumping across the floor. She fixed her eyes toward the chamber, hoping to glimpse Fillion. Leaf approached as if every bone in his body ached. She could not say farewell to her brother. How would she bear it?

Leaf knelt and opened his arms to Laurel, who ran into his waiting embrace. Her small frame quaked with sobs as she clung to him. Their brother whispered into her ear. She nodded, knotting her arms around his neck one last time before pulling away. An affectionate smile warmed his ghastly features and he cupped their sister's face and kissed her forehead then her nose. Slowly he stood, and his face grimaced with pain, his breath hissing through his teeth.

Next, he stood before her and his eyes filled with tears. "Be strong and resourceful, Willow Oak," he whispered. "I shall return." He crossed his heart then pulled her into a tight embrace. In her ear, he said, "An Outsider medical team will probably arrive to fetch Fillion. Do not fight them. Let him go, *ma chère*. It is not the last you shall see of him." He wiped away a tear crawling down her face with his calloused thumb.

"I understand." A faint, rueful smile pulled on her lips. "And, despite my protests, I have actually always preferred your company to that of a snake." He laughed and she could not help but smile fully in response.

"You pay me a great honor."

"Do not let it go to your head, Leaf Watson."

They smiled at each other a heartbeat longer, and then he shifted Ember's direction. The Daughter of Fire stood in the corner, lashes lowered and head dipped toward the ground. Her posture remained straight, however. Ember's elegance and refined beauty remained evident, despite the sopping dress and damp tresses.

In a few quick steps, Leaf gathered his wife in his arms and kissed her as if they were the only two people who existed. Perhaps, in this moment, they really were. Willow no longer blushed, understanding the agony and sense of completeness in such moments. Their younger sister giggled daintily behind a hand. Nonetheless, silent tears continued to make trails down her flushed cheeks.

No words were spoken between Ember and Leaf. No whispers in her ear or his. Their kiss slowed and they held each other as if memorizing the beat of each other's heart. With a final kiss, Leaf pivoted on his heel, issuing one last look over his shoulder before shutting the door.

The flames dancing upon the wicks momentarily bent with the soft breeze. In melancholy beats, the iron ring sang against the hewn wood, fading to nothing. A bewildered hush fell upon her home. Willow watched her sisters, who stood where Leaf had left them. How could they move? It was as if doing so would dissolve the last moments that were now just memories. Ember met her eyes, the panic rising in their dark brown depths. Laurel's soft cries lanced Willow's heart, and she broke through the spell of shock and grief and scooped up the girl.

She held her sister and let her weep, refusing to promise her sunshine, laughter, or another moment with their brother. The only goodbyes they had ever known were deaths. At age eight, her sister had known many hardships. But this one was different.

Laurel whimpered as the tears eased, her heart continuing to weep even as her body grew fatigued. The emotions soon gave way to sleep, the rise and fall of Laurel's body fitful and troubled. Ember—with deadened eyes and wan complexion—reached for Laurel and carried their younger sister to her and Leaf's bedchamber, quietly shutting the door behind her.

For a few moments, Willow simply stood. Shadows of bio-rain and tree branches swayed upon their red-tinted walls, hypnotizing her. Lightheaded, she gripped the edge of the cupboard. Breathe, she told herself once more. But it was difficult even to do something as mundane and automatic as that. She needed to start moving before her mind completely slipped away.

Willow grabbed a candleholder and trudged toward her chamber to change into dry clothes. The hallway filled with the soft glow of the candle's flame. The floorboards creaked and groaned beneath her feet. Just as she passed Ember and Leaf's bedchamber, a light tap sounded from the front door. Startled, Willow squeezed the iron holder. Slowly, as if in a trance, she approached the door, opening it a crack. On the other side, a stranger met her frightened gaze.

"Miss, is Fillion Nichols here?"

His accent was undeniably Outsider, with his quick speech mannerisms and clipped words. The hollow, empty feeling in her chest permeated every part of her body with his question.

"Yes, sir," she whispered in reply. Willow opened the door all the way. A man and a woman stood beside him, boasting bizarre hair colors and wearing similar fashions of form fitting tunics and breeches, as well as a white cloak with sleeves, edged in sky blue. Women wore breeches in the Outside? Most shocking was Canyon Daniels' presence, and she stiffened.

"Leaf bid me lead them to your home, Your Highness," Rain's brother said.

"Thank you, Canyon." He bowed, shooting one last anxious look at the Outsiders before disappearing down the stairs. She turned back to the strangers and, in a small voice, eked out, "Please, come in."

They entered, carrying a litter, each shifting with obvious discomfort as they looked around the family's apartment. Water dripped and pooled where they halted, adding more puddles to the others that dotted the planked flooring of the main room. Eventually, the trio rested their eyes upon her. They studied her mud-soaked clothes, soot-splotched face, and stringing wet hair, taking in her full measure with careless disregard, as if she did not possess dignity or feeling. In response, she angled her head to the side and lifted her chin.

"My name is Seth, and this is Corey and Andie. We are Guardian Angels at the lab." He extended a hand and she stared at it, drawing her brows together.

"Have I offended you?" she asked meekly.

"Uh, no, not at all, miss."

She considered the outstretched offering once more. The act seemed barbaric to Willow, as he presented no meaning to his gesture. What man asked for a woman's hand without proper explanation or clear motive? Nervous, she flit her eyes to his, then turned away and trundled toward her father's room.

"Follow me," she said simply.

Another step, another snap, and pieces of her heart trailed behind her like bread crumbs. Her thoughts grew more dark the closer she came to Fillion, until the grief painted everything black—each stone in the archway, the path down the hallway, the abyssal hole in her heart.

Entering her father's chamber, she said, "My Lord, you have visitors."

"Willow?" he asked, eyes-widened at her disheveled state. His ashen features appeared gaunt despite the warm glow of candlelight. Fillion gradually moved to a sitting position and looked past her to the doorway and she watched as the air visibly left his body. "Damn it. I told Hanley not to send in a medical team. That bastard."

"We have orders, Mr. Nichols."

"And if I resist?"

"Law enforcement is just outside The Door."

"Shit." Fillion lifted his troubled gaze toward hers. "I'll be OK."

She furtively looked toward the Outsider and then studied her own fierce grip on the candlestick. "Yes, My Lord."

Fillion glared at the Outsiders and barked, "Give us five minutes. Shut the door on your way out."

"Mr. Nichols—"

"Now!"

They stared at her before departing, clearly communicating their disapproval. She flushed under their scrutiny, feeling stripped of her pride once more. Fillion was a prince of their world and what was she, really? A pretend princess in a game designed for science.

When the door shut, Fillion elevated his shoulders a notch. Gingerly, he coaxed the candlestick from her hand and placed it upon the nightstand. Pushing off the bed, he stood on shaky legs, swaying slightly. He gripped the edge of the bed until the spell passed. Willow placed her hands on his forearms for extra support and a corner of his mouth lifted for half of a heartbeat. Once regulated, he drew her into a loose embrace and smoothed away a wet strand of hair from her eyes.

"Why are they ordered to take you?"

"I broke the law. Again. I'm in a helluva lot of trouble," he said. "Probably going to prison."

A sob formed deep in her chest and her body tensed with the effort to remain in control. "I shall not survive the heartache of losing another I love. The pain…" She hiccupped with the effort to not weep. "The pain is unbearable. My heart is breaking for you."

His eyes rested on the candle. "I don't know where or how. Not even when," he whispered. "But I will see you again. I don't want a relationship 'full of nevers' with you."

"Spin the tales and weave the stories together, My Lord. Make a reality of your own."

He softly bit down on his bottom lip and took her hand in his. Maintaining a downcast posture, he cleared his throat. "Wait for me?"

"I would wait an eternity for you."

A vulnerable, boyish smile warmed his face. It was just as heartbreaking as the first time she glimpsed it several weeks prior when saying farewell through the portal. Gray eyes wandered over Ember's wedding gown with an expression akin to humility. The wet garment clung to the curves of her body. But she did not blush, nor look away from his imploring gaze.

The invisible thread stitching their lives together pierced her heart and looped the final knot with his. The tempo of his breathing altered just as much as hers; and she knew he felt the strange energy, too.

The tips of his fingers traced along her face and combed into her hair. He tilted her head up toward his and lowered until their lips caressed in a gentle slow dance. The touch was beyond intimate, as if their hearts were handfasting, each beat a whispered pledge and promise. Dressed in a wedding gown and alone in a candlelit bedchamber, it was easy to pretend she was his bride; and her pulse quickened with such heady thoughts. His breath became hers. His kisses akin to poetry, sonnets of love and loss, of passion overflowing with unspeakable beauty. But, as usual, they needed to drink each other in and drink fast, their stolen time precious.

Overcome, she pressed a hand to his heart and whispered against his lips, "*Voici un témoignage de mon affection, conservez-le bien.*"

He covered the hand with both of his, and whispered in reply, "*Korekara zutto, ore no jinsei wa anata no mono desu. Zutto eien ni sasagemasu.*"

The door opened a crack and she jerked away from Fillion's embrace, heart racing. "We need to leave, Mr. Nichols."

A muscle twitched in Fillion's jaw once more. Silence stretched unbearably. Then he issued a curt nod. She watched as they moved him onto the litter. As they draped a blanket over his body. His eyes closed for a moment. Images of her father's corpse being carried out of her family home to burn upon a funeral pyre scraped across her mind. The scream worming in her gut clawed upward. Still, it refused to emerge.

The hungry floor reached up with greedy fingers to claim her if she crashed. Whispering her name with promises of no pain. Willow shoved fear's voice out as far away as possible, her vision fading as the blood rushed from her head. This pain was beautiful. This misery an experience she did not wish to forget. For he was worth it. He needed to know that someone would grieve his absence. Tears shrouded her cheeks as she quietly wept, holding back the urge to double over and keen.

The Outsiders gave instructions that Fillion was to remain hidden due to "media" clamoring outside the gates. Before his face disappeared beneath the odd, metallic sheet, Fillion met her eyes and slowly blinked. Those otherworldly eyes never missed beat, often trailing after her with keen intelligence, as if she were a cipher he needed to solve. And, at times, they provided glimpses of the man behind the pain and derision. But, in this moment, he looked upon her as if she were the light of day after a long, dark night.

Then, he was gone.

The scream dug its claws through her chest until it broke free from her raw, blistering pain in a heart-shattering wail. With each gulp, each breath, she filled her lungs with the altered atmosphere of her fractured community. It would become a part of her, sustain her. But, right now, it burned as if a thousand fires.

Ashes to ashes. Dust to dust. Nothing was exempt. Not the leaves. The air she breathed. The water dripping from the bleeding sky. Nor her heart. She curled her fists tight, nails digging into her palms, as another doleful scream scorched through her body, unable to stop the dirge.

There are reports that the famed biodome city, New Eden Township, is under emergency evacuation. The gates are heavily armed with law enforcement and the scientific compound jammed wireless signals, preventing drones from capturing images. Management has commented that the scientific compound is under cyber-attack by what they believe to be a human rights hacktivist group. So far, it appears only one resident has emerged—a young male, believed to be sixteen to twenty years of age. But drones and journalists are unable to verify any details at this time. Shelve this newsfeed for continual coverage and up-to-date information. We'll provide more details as they come in.

— Jack Arthur, "Attack on Mars: A War of the Worlds," *The Associated World News*, October 29, 2054

CHAPTER FORTY-ONE

I t seemed like hours since Fillion left the Watson apartment. But it had only been minutes. His mind was fading again. Weakness flirted with his stamina long before his goodbye. Talking to Willow had drained what remained of his battery life, and he barely kept it together. The emotional toll was too much to quantify. So he didn't. For once.

Before leaving, N.E.T.'s equivalent of a search and rescue team covered him with a thermal nanotech blanket. Almost immediately warmth infused his skin, slowly making its way to his core, regulating to his needs as his biometric stats changed. And. God. Never had heat felt so glorious. For a blessed moment, he didn't have anything to rant about. Not even the metallic pitter-patter of raindrops crashing against the blanket. OK. So, maybe he did.

Fillion's eyelids sank shut as his body lulled to sleep with the light jostling and heavenly warmth. The crunch of footsteps echoed in his ear, reminding him of the rush of wheat hulls in his pillow. And he smiled. Wait. He liked that sound? Whatever. His mind was rambling. Not a good sign. At least the mental tangents kept his thoughts focused on something besides Willow. That was a slippery slope he couldn't navigate right now. A fight with Hanley awaited him at N.E.T. There was time later to process his and Willow's separation and officially shut down.

"Mr. Nichols, we are about to cross through The Door. Per instructions, we are to keep the thermal sheet over you until you are safely inside the lab. Media drones and journalists are hovering at the gate. Do you understand the instructions?"

"Roger, roger," Fillion murmured. Life was a bit soupy at the moment. He felt so weak—the antithesis of manliness. There was no help for it. Still, anything that allowed his body to continue to draw warmth was a reasonable plan to him, even at the cost of his ego.

"Here we go."

The footsteps became softer, padded. Fillion figured they had left the biodome. A sharp pain lanced through him with this realization. He didn't want to leave. In fact, he would be content living there the rest of his life. What would his mom have to say about that? Socially, Fillion had already suffered from isolation and confinement. The ever-watchful eyes of the media created an extreme environment. Although the biodomes closed in on him, the ceiling seeming to drop more and more each day, he would still rather be part of that world. Would still rather be with Willow, and with Leaf.

She'll never be yours.

What was Hanley really saying? Like his employer could stop him from having a relationship with Willow. Yeah, so the world thought she was dead. So what? Miracles happen every day. Harming her or Leaf wouldn't magically erase their existence. There was a different message in that simple statement. And Fillion began to worry. His mind was in no state to ponder the hidden, though.

Gasps and exclamations grew strength like a wave. Then the sounds crashed over him. What the hell? It must be the media, Fillion reasoned. He heard his name in the digital cacophony. Alarmed, he tried to move to sneak a peek, but his arms wouldn't budge. Did they strap him down? Shit. Must have happened when he was taking his fill of Willow for the last time. Panic filled him with the loss of control. He hated being at the mercy of others. Fillion released a string of swear words and thrashed. Still, the men continued forward, pausing only before what Fillion guessed were security stations and doors.

The shouts gave way to a gurgling creek and a jeering blue jay. Then those sounds quickly disappeared, and there was nothing. A quiet voice might pop up here and there. But really, there was zero sound. Super creepy. He heard doors open and then the gurney was placed on top of a table.

"Close your eyes, Mr. Nichols. The light is bright." Fillion obeyed as the blanket was rolled away from his face. Slowly, his eyes squinted open and he stared at the two men who had removed him from New Eden. "Welcome back to Earth, Mr. Nichols. My name is Seth and this is Corey. We're going to help you get ready to see your father. How are you feeling?"

"Pissed," Fillion said with a glare. "Remove the straps now."

"Yes. Only to help you change your clothes," Seth said. "Officer McKee is on the other side of this door. Please be advised that if you try to leave, he is under orders to subdue you, by whatever means necessary. After you're done dressing, he'll escort you to your father."

"Fantastic." Fillion rolled his eyes. "Got it. Now, remove the straps." Once removed, they eased him up to a sitting position and Fillion closed his eyes. "I need some water." Corey dashed to the other side of the room and filled a cup from the sink. Damn. A sink. That sparked an idea. "Is there a shower nearby?"

"Sure, Mr. Nichols. There is a suite prepared for you." Seth smiled politely. "Once you are ready to stand, we'll help you get there."

Fillion took the cup of water and gulped the cold liquid, grimacing with the aftertaste. "This water tastes like shit."

Another patient smile. "City water."

"Let's go. I want to get this over with."

Forty-five minutes later—thanks to a clock (he could really kiss time pieces)—he was dressed in a fresh tunic and breeches, which was weird. But whatever. At this point, he was grateful for the small connection to New Eden. Everything stank. It had this weird chemical smell he couldn't place. He decided it was the scent of unnatural living. No herbs. No earth. No tallow candles. The overhead lights would be the death of him. The intensity hurt his eyes.

When declared ready, Brent—Officer McKee—chained his ankles and cuffed his wrists behind his back. Shame burned through Fillion. Nevertheless, he kept his head high. He was a prince and would stand tall. But, damn. Hanley was a mind job. First taking care of his needs, then reminding Fillion who was in charge just in case he decided to get too comfortable.

Brent kept a hand on Fillion's arm the entire way to the Faraday cage meeting room. It was strange being touched so much. He actually enjoyed having his body to himself. The rules were strict in New Eden. However, Fillion felt in control of himself, something he'd never known until then.

For a moment, the hallway tilted as his body regulated. And his legs shook, too. But damned if he'd black out. He needed to remain sharp.

An officer opened the double doors. Brent walked Fillion through without a break in stride. For Fillion, each step took great effort, especially with the restraints. Inside the room, Hanley sat in a chair and sifted through paperwork on his Cranium.

"Thank you, Brent," Hanley said as he looked past his screen. Fillion sank awkwardly into a chair and kept his head lowered. "You are excused."

Fillion looked up at the officer. "Remove my restraints."

"You may go," Hanley said again.

"I refuse to talk unless these cuffs are removed." Fillion's body leaned to the side. "I'm too sick to punch you again anyway."

"Remove the bindings around his wrists." Hanley tapped on his Cranium and shifted in his seat with a pointed look. "Ankles remain."

Soon, Fillion's wrists were released and he brought his hands to the front and instinctively rubbed where the cuffs had been. Brent then left the room. When the door clicked shut, Fillion slid a glance at Hanley. They inspected one another in thick silence.

"Where's mom?"

"Taking care of an issue that popped up."

Fillion figured Hanley spoke of Leaf. Rather than reply, he continued to stare back at Hanley, who was buffering. Hanley shifted slightly in his chair. Buffering time was over.

"From the time you were little, I always thought you had more passion in your little pinky finger than I have ever possessed. One day, you'll surpass even my deeds." Hanley watched Fillion closely. "The funny thing about passion is that it can burn with destruction, too. Do you even grasp what you have just done? Thirty years, Fillion. Thirty years!"

"I know who you are."

Hanley chuckled. "You forgot?" He leaned forward in his seat and studied Fillion's slumped posture. "The poison may have affected your mind for a brief period."

"No," Fillion said, taking in a steady breath. "I know who you are, Hayden Kane." All emotion fled from Hanley as he eased back against the chair. Fear flickered on Hanley's face for a brief moment and Fillion continued. "Son of Anderson Kane, half-brother to Timothy. Grandma Esther went into witness protection when you were four years old. No wonder she was a weird, hyper-anxious woman. Your father was a famous con artist and serial killer who ended up taking his own life when caught by police. What were you? Six, seven years old when that happened?"

"How many others know?"

"Doesn't matter." Fillion closed his eyes with another breath. "Yet."

"I suppose this is the moment when I cower at your feet and you make your demands?"

"If you insist."

A smug smile formed and Hanley crossed his legs, resting an arm over his knee. The posture was one of casual confidence and Fillion straightened as much as possible in his chair. The movement caused another dizzy spell and objects in the room spun for a moment.

"What is it you want?" Hanley lifted his eyebrows, as if humored. "Nothing changes the fact that you still have to ride out your sentence. There may be charges of corporate sabotage, too. Over four hundred people will be displaced due to your stunt if the domes do not return to full function soon. You think you are a hero? They will need to get vaccinated and go through stringent medical exams. Of course, mental evaluations as well. And I am sure they will be singing your praises the entire time."

Mustering strength, Fillion flashed an arrogant smile. "None of that is necessary."

"Health regulations." Hanley remained unblinking when Fillion lifted a shoulder in a single shrug. "State law."

"Unless you meet certain criteria by the morning news, you'll get doxxed. I know everything. Including Dylan." Fillion paused and placed his head on the back of another chair.

"Such as?"

He knew Hanley was baiting for information. The patronizing tone fueled another round of fury and Fillion wanted to punch something. Someone. Instead, Fillion said, "You'll announce that during the fire inspection your team discovered that the Watson siblings were alive and a quick DNA test confirmed Joel and Claire Watson as their parents. Timothy Kane, suffering from ICE, among other things, confessed to irrational and aggressive behavior toward the Watson family. It began as jealousy over placement in the Legacy, and progressed from there. If you don't, after doxxing you, I'll start a second Watson Trial so the world knows the truth about your project negligence. Not to mention, how you tampered with the experiment's evidence."

Fillion swallowed, his dry throat aching. "I'd always heard of a long-con. But shit, this is talent," he said sardonically. "'Image.' 'Perception.' Gross. The world is wrapped around your finger. Did Timothy agree to give up Aether status for your master plan to get Joel's money? Or did you double-cross your own brother?"

Hanley's smile fell and, for a blink of a nanosecond, he actually looked distressed. "You plan to press charges?"

"I will if you refuse to assist Leaf and his family." With shaky fingers, Fillion brushed dark strands out of his eye to better see Hanley. "Because the second gen never signed The Code, they didn't hold harmless New Eden Enterprises or any of its affiliates. If I were you, I'd do whatever possible to pacify Leaf over the murder of his father, the falsified deaths of he and his siblings, the harassment toward his family, and the attempt made on his life. The media would love to finally see you taken down in court."

Appreciation curved Hanley's mouth. "Clever. I am not too proud to acknowledge a masterful game move when I see one." Hanley was far too accommodating and a queasy feeling, separate from his recovering stomach, settled in Fillion's gut. Then he remembered. The first phase was always charm. "And the money?" Hanley asked.

"What do you think? It's rightfully Leaf's," Fillion said, rolling his eyes, "who is willing to negotiate for the permanence of New Eden Township. If you amend The Code to allow permanent residence status, Leaf will relinquish the funds to New Eden Biospherics & Research." Fillion touched his Cranium, which thankfully left with him from New Eden.

He brought up the document, then held out the Cranium. "Here."

Hanley took the device and perused the notes and desired changes. Over the screen, he met Fillion's eyes and said, "They wish to permanently reside in a biodome?"

To better clarify, Fillion said, "They wish to reside in the biodome city of New Eden Township."

"Of course they do."

Did Hanley agree? Unease dripped into Fillion's thoughts. God, his mind was still too hazy. "So, you'll not harm the Watsons, and you'll let those who choose to remain in New Eden, stay?" Fillion rolled his body to an upright position with a heavy breath.

"Let me make a deal with you." Hanley removed the Cranium and folded his hands into his lap with a sharp look. "If I let those who signed The Code remain in a biodome as their permanent residence, you will call off your hounds. Their choice, of course. Doxxing me damages our entire family, including your sister." Hanley brushed at something invisible on his pants. Fillion tensed, knowing an accusation was coming. It always did at this point. "You want the world to know that killing is in your blood? Isn't that what they used to call you? Son of a killer?"

Heartache seized Fillion, and he looked at his hands. Fingers, jittery and in need of an occupation, picked at the leather on his belt. Voices from his past hurled insults at him all over again. Their cruel words pushed against the tender wounds. An image of Willow layered in his mind and Fillion willed himself to stay focused. His mind needed to stay sharp.

Weary of the emotional games, Fillion pinned Hanley with a hard stare. "Do you agree to acknowledge the Watsons publicly?"

"A whole generation who has never seen a mountain or a rainbow stretch across the blue sky." Hanley crossed his arms across his chest with another satisfied expression. "I knew you were the perfect solution."

"What the hell does that even mean?" Fillion groaned and sank further in his chair. "Never mind. Stay on point. Do you agree to represent the Watson family?"

Hanley chuckled. "And if I agree to everything else but this?"

"I have a video of someone at New Eden Biospherics & Research meeting Leaf through the airlock. It will be released to the world, discrediting the reputation of the experiment and those who run it."

"I see." Hanley covered his mouth with his hand in a thoughtful pose. Hazel eyes darkened as he considered Fillion's words. "I will agree to reveal the Watsons to the world and protect them only if you honor the engagement and marry Akiko."

"What?" Fillion stood up, and his head swam. "No way. I'm not a pawn to be married off. Consider yourself doxxed and discredited." He looked toward the door and shouted, "Officer McKee!"

"Go ahead. If I fall, then so do you. And if you fall, then so does New Eden, including the Watsons. Where would all the families go then? Everyone is a pawn on a chess board, awaiting your move, Son of Eden." Hanley raised his eyebrows.

Ember's voice drifted back to Fillion. Had Hanley drilled these same words into the Techsmith Guild? Nausea swirled in Fillion's stomach and a cold sweat broke out on his forehead. "So it's my fault if the project fails? If you take out The Watsons? Here's my official response to that." Fillion lifted both hands and flipped off Hanley. "You swindled and terrorized an entire family, but the demise of the ninth Wonder of the World rests in my hands. Yeah, you're not a bad guy at all. I finally see your point, *Hayden*."

"If New Eden Township is shut down, I will issue a restraining order against you and you will never see the Watsons again, including Willow Oak…if they survive shut down that is."

"You can't issue a restraining order on behalf of someone else. When the project is shut down, I'll see them if I want."

"They were born in a lab and are the result of an experiment. The U.S. government recognizes me as their legal guardian, regardless of age. Their rights are limited."

"What? Shit, you can't be serious."

Fillion crumpled into his chair. "This is why the second gen never signed The Code," he whispered to himself as the epiphany stabbed him over and over again. "They never had to." A sharp pang tightened his chest as his heart broke and Fillion gasped with the pain. Tears brimmed and his vision grew cloudy. "I'm inheriting human property. Oh god. You made me a slave owner?" He swiped an angry tear away. "Frankenstein laws can't apply to them. Impossible. They're not genetically engineered."

"Transgenerational epigenetic inheritance through psychological conditioning is the correct terminology."

"You're so disgusting." Fillion wiped away another tear. "Does mom know?" Hanley just stared with a droll expression. A knock sounded on the door.

"Come in," Hanley said in a light tone.

"Sir." Officer McKee issued a brief look Fillion's direction. "I heard my name?"

"False alarm, Brent. Our apologies."

Michael and John squeezed past the officer. The scientist looked around the room with large, rounded eyes. "Sorry to barge in, but the biodomes are fully operational again. The motors revved back to life ten minutes ago and the lights just turned on. The emergency switch reversed. There was a glitch in the computer software. The Guardian Angels are now preparing a patch to the operating system to fix the problem. The fire has burned out. Oxygen levels are fine. Better than our atmosphere, actually. And the N.E.T. servers are no longer under hacker control."

A small, proud smile taunted Fillion from the across the room. Hanley maintained a level gaze with Michael, but Fillion knew the smile was for him. Fillion couldn't believe the man appreciated his move. No, he didn't. They were back to charm.

Hanley shot Fillion an enlightened look, then asked Michael, "And the people?"

"The state confirmed we are free to let the people remain." Michael noticed Fillion and turned white.

"Does the state require that they meet health regulations?"

John lowered into a chair next to Fillion and answered, "I spoke with the surgeon general and she said it is your call, since the residents will probably remain enclosed until project shutdown."

"Then we'll skip it." Hanley looked at Fillion with a smirk. "Della still in a meeting?"

"Yes, Dr. Nichols and her team are ready to help those traumatized by this event. A few psychologists are preparing to enter New Eden for a short duration with your permission."

Hanley locked eyes with Fillion, then turned to John. "We're going to amend The Code and begin Project Phase Two immediately." Then he turned to Michael. "I will go with Della's lead."

Michael nodded and looked at Fillion again. "Medical is outside the door when you're ready."

"How are you?" John studied Fillion.

"Sick." Fillion swallowed back a wave of grief. "I was poisoned. Yay me." He met John's eyes. "Hey, sorry about taking your Cranium."

John smiled at him with genuine concern. "No worries."

Fillion tensed to hold back more tears. "Is it true?"

Jeff's cousin tilted his head and looked him over once more. "Lynden? She's fine. Recovered well. You'll be all right, too. We'll take good care of you before you're moved to a corrections facility."

"Uncle John, tell me it's a lie." Fillion sucked in a quick breath. Panic was rising and his heart rate became erratic.

"The second gen, are they really human property?" John lowered his eyes and shifted uncomfortably in his chair. "Oh god." Fillion slumped over and his body shook, no longer able to hold back from crying. "I can't. I just can't," he managed, heaving with the pain. "Did ... did the first gen know this?"

Hanley relaxed into a look of compassion. The fake emotions further insulted Fillion and he clenched his jaw. With a brief look at the floor, Hanley said, "They willingly enclosed their families."

"What the hell kind of answer is that?"

Fillion stared at the man who had sired him. The man whose father was a notorious con artist and serial killer. The man who tricked good people—his own friends and family—into an experiment to create slaves for science, something Fillion once said in sarcasm, never even getting an inkling he was actually right. All this time Leaf had suffered, but the position of Aether was a joke. What power did Leaf really have? It was an illusion. Joel's son had partial ownership in a company that owned him. Hanley essentially owned Leaf's share. In a couple of years, Fillion would, as majority owner. Probably another reason Hanley duped Timothy. Rage pumped through Fillion until he couldn't hold it in any longer.

"I hate you!" he shouted at Hanley. Fillion stood on unsteady legs, made more so by the chains. Every muscle in his body tensed and his face contorted in rage and grief. "Did you hear me? You sick, twisted bastard. I hate you!"

"Think of all you could do for them, Fillion."

Hanley rose from his chair and walked toward where he stood. Perhaps to others, Hanley appeared gracious and sympathetic this moment. The pathological liar didn't fool him, though.

"You really are the perfect solution."

"Perfect solution for what?! What are you going to do to them?" Fillion's eyes widened. "Holy shit, what am I going to do to them?"

"You're bonded to the community. They trust you, Son of Eden. What is the story? Oh, yes. A man of magic, one who will save them from the evils of the Outside world." Hanley offered a kind smile. "You are predictable, Fillion, from your overactive mind to your bleeding heart." Hanley paused and the smile widened. "Did you perchance discover what was real?"

Another intense pain stabbed Fillion, weakening his body, and he started to fall over. Arms wrapped around him and held him up. But Fillion pushed the person away, screaming to leave him alone. He just wanted to fall and keep falling and shatter into a million pieces.

"The poison may still cause hysteria and paranoia," he heard Hanley say to those in the room. "His PTSD triggers have not been repressed either. He needs sedation."

Another pair of hands touched him and Fillion fought back, knocking over a chair. Shouts echoed off the walls as people rushed into the room. Fillion was thrown to the ground. Through the haze of faces and voices, Fillion locked eyes with Hanley. A sharp prick in his upper arm made Fillion wince and he snapped his attention to the woman leaning over him. She started to speak but he couldn't hear a single word over his own screaming. Fillion thrashed, fighting the sensations until a heaviness settled over him and the room undulated with the faintest movement.

"I think we have reached an agreement," Hanley's soothed from above. Fillion opened his eyes to the fuzzy image of his father, the features of Hanley's face eclipsed by a bright light overhead. Nevertheless, he knew the smile didn't reach Hanley's eyes. It never did. "I expect you to fulfill your end of the bargain." His dad angled his head away. "Michael, I need PR. We have an announcement to make. Leaf still with medical?"

Fillion turned his head and stared at the whitewashed walls through the arms holding him down. The world dimmed and Fillion fell into the dark atmosphere of his head. The black air didn't possess expectations. It absorbed everything and reflected nothing. His body hovered over reality until it blurred into the shadows of his mind. Death was welcome, and he surrendered to the throbbing ache in his heart.

"You will make an excellent Gamemaster one day," Hanley whispered in his ear. "But do not ever forget that this game is over *only* when I say so."

Everything went black.

ELEMENTS

Biosphere 2 was built in 1991, to see if man could build a contained environment which they could live in, without the aid of the outside world. It was bringing the dream of seeing new worlds to Earth, taking the first steps towards a future in which humans could expand onto new planets and new frontiers; and to this day it is still a picture of science fiction brought to life. Biosphere 2 did something incredible at that time—it showed us that we had no idea what we were doing. Not enough oxygen, not enough food ... they couldn't do what they set out to do, and for some this was a disappointment and a failure. This stance, however, is based on a misunderstanding of the scientific method. No scientist always gets the results that they want, but an experiment is not a failure if something new can be learned.

— AB Raschke (aka Waitingforrain28), "Biosphere 2: Bringing Science Fiction to Life," pathofthenightborn.wordpress.com, October 18, 2012 *

CHAPTER FORTY-TWO

Tuesday, November 17, 2054

New Eden Township, Salton Sea, California

ight weeks had passed since Coal last found her in this position. Oaklee lay upon her stomach, ankles crossed with feet swaying back and forth through the air. A willow oak leaf twirled in her hand. Something always had to spin in her fingers. Coal smiled as memories of their times together came flooding back. He leaned against a tree across the forest path from her; she was oblivious to him. Her focus was riveted on Laurel, who ran and jumped with the other children by The Waters.

Unlike the adults who were rebuilding the village—and trust—after the Great Fire, the children were building dreams, fighting battles forged from their imaginations, and laughing. They were not as wary of the strangers as their older counterparts, or so he was told at the lab. The world for these younger ones was simple and beautiful.

Scientists and psychologists now lived inside New Eden. The second wave of colonists had arrived. The community welcomed the new residents, he was told. Many still suffered trauma from the events that unfolded three weeks prior. Most, however, had recovered with renewed vigor to remain an enclosed community.

The new colonists marveled over the children of New Eden. The youngest generations were like faerie creatures to them, embodying antiquated ideas and lifestyles that seemed more like myth and lore to the Outside culture. Coal worried that N.E.T. would rush to introduce technology. But the Outsiders were far too enamored with the children to introduce anything that could ruin the magic. The rest of planet Earth was locked into a system where even children were part of a corporate machine that groomed their minds to be complacent workers and co-dependent upon technology. But not here.

Coal did not need to see Oaklee's face to know she watched with wistful longing. He felt it, too. Especially when a bio-breeze disturbed the trees and set the leaves to dancing. The green and gold offerings spiraled their ballet through the air, much to the delight of the children. Oaklee's legs stilled as she watched the leaves, her feet poised in the air, a fern ring gracing one ankle.

"To be young and carefree again."

Startled by his voice, Oaklee flew to a sitting position and clutched the long, golden leaf to her chest. The fright on her face dissolved to astonishment as she found his eyes. Time slowed and he visibly noticed the moment when air returned to her lungs. It was followed by the fountain of tears that usually accompanied such moments. She studied his hair, then traveled to his piercings, followed by his clothing, and lastly his eyes once more.

Pushing off the tree, he made eye contact with Michael, who stood a few trees down the path, a required escort for "safety" reasons. Although Coal understood the larger message—he was not be trusted alone in New Eden—he was grateful for the gift of spending a day with family.

"Please stop looking at me so, My Lady. I shall not shatter, no more made of glass than you," Coal teased. She rolled her eyes and hid a giggle behind her hand. He smiled playfully to hide his nerves. "I am still the same, see?"

"You are most certainly not the same," she finally said, wiping away an errant tear. The musical sound of her voice stilled his heart for a moment.

"No?" he asked, raising his eyebrows. "Drat."

"But neither am I."

They stared at one another for several seconds until Oaklee patted a patch of earth next to where she sat. He lowered himself to the ground and plucked a piece of grass, spinning it between his fingers. The silence stretched between them, and strangely, he did not mind. For weeks he had dreaded this moment. Even now his stomach was a jumbled mess of sensations. Still, she was his friend, and had promised to remain his friend even as he departed New Eden after foisting himself upon her.

"Coal," Oaklee said, shy, uncertain. She looked away and fumbled with a strand of hair, twisting and unraveling the golden threads upon her finger. "I am ashamed of the names I called you. I have carried such tremendous guilt since your departure. You are not a stupid man, nor insensitive." A bashful smile lifted a corner of her mouth as she cast him a mischievous look. "Although I might argue you are impetuous and perhaps a fool at times."

He laughed and her smile grew wider. How he had missed the radiance that glowed from her countenance when earning such smiles. But his heart no longer turned such exchanges into promises or longings. "I am every bit a fool, which consequently makes me rather stupid and insensitive some moments. You were not wrong about me."

"You do not resent me?" she asked, her tone dubious. "I shamed you before the community with false accusations. How do I even begin to apologize for such behavior?"

He whispered, "I could never resent you." Coal chanced a look at her. "Your heart was broken and your suffering made me feel so helpless. I could not save you, could not rescue you from the pain, nor make it right. Most of all, I feared I would fail to protect you." He cleared his throat and looked away. "It is I who apologizes for forcing your heart in a direction you never desired to go. I was dishonorable and ungentlemanly."

"Coal—"

"I love you, Oaklee. You are my heart." She lowered her head with a becoming blush. "But I am not in love with you. You are my dearest friend."

Her head whipped up and her mouth parted. Then, she threw herself into his arms. Coal nearly fell back with the force, a rather unexpected feat considering her small size compared to his. Oaklee buried her face into his shoulder and wept, and he held her. This is what she needed so many weeks ago and he had failed her. Her forgiveness was humbling and he wrapped his arms around her back and pulled her tighter against him. The breeze rustled the leaves once more and golden leaves fell all around them, landing with whispers of new beginnings. It was their fate, their destiny, their endless cycle of life, death, and rebirth.

A cheer from the children brought them back to the moment, and she slowly pulled away from him. Her gaze touched upon his hair and piercings once more, offering a shy smile. "The look suits you. Very handsome, actually."

"Are you suggesting I was not before?"

She scoffed with playful irritation. "Begging for more compliments are we?"

"Never would I dream of such a socially outlandish thing to do."

"No, you are class and charm itself."

"Naturally."

Oaklee noticed Michael and her brows drew together in that subtle way of hers once more. "I have seen him before."

"Yeah, he is Hanley's personal assistant and managing scientist at N.E.T. I enjoy his company at the lab, where I reside now."

She tilted her head as her eyes questioned him. "Did you enjoy your travels and adventures?"

"Mostly." Coal watched the blade of grass spin in his fingers. The carbon residue was now a memory, much as his former life. He shot a quick look at Michael and whispered, "I am not allowed to return to New Eden. Although, I did wish to remain in the Outside world." He flicked a glance her way to watch her reaction, but she merely appeared as though that was not surprising news. "I have bargained some freedoms for myself. I may visit the community twice a month, or for communal feasts or ceremonies, should I choose. But always under the supervision of someone from N.E.T."

Oaklee nibbled on her lower lip a few seconds, then fell back upon the leaf-littered grass with a sigh, her arms tumbling to her side as long, golden hair spilled all around her. With a single look, she issued an invitation for Coal to join her and he tossed the blade as he eased down into a bed of grass and leaves. They turned their faces, noses inches from each other, and smiled.

"Now," she whispered, "Tell me everything. From the very beginning. I especially wish to know of Mack and Lynden." Oaklee said *her* name with softness, as if she knew his secret already.

"What if someone comes upon us in the grass in such a scandalous position?"

"I do not fear New Eden's mob mentality," she whispered, a catch in her voice. Coal did not know how to reply, deciding instead to smile his understanding. Oaklee gave him a slight push. "If you only have one day, you shall have to begin quickly for I do not think I can wait until your next visit for any details you fail to provide."

He laughed and her face relaxed, as if memorizing him. To her credit, she treated him as if he had not changed, although he knew he looked drastically different. "Well, when I arrived in Seattle, it had begun to rain..." He continued to share how he met Lynden and Mack, how he earned his nicknames Farm Boy and Mr. Awesome. Oaklee smiled and laughed; tears formed when he shared of fears and hardships; her face grew tense as he described cage fighting and the underground.

As she listened, his heart stuttered. This is what life was like before expectations to marry, before Joel had died, before they ever dreamed that one day they would become intimately acquainted with the Outside world—become intimately acquainted with the Nichols family.

"Lynden seems rather spirited," Oaklee said when he finished.

"Yes, she is fond of surprises." He rolled to his side and supported his head with bended elbow. His pulse throbbed in his chest, the rhythm uncomfortable. Nevertheless, Coal gathered courage and whispered, "I am in love with her."

Tears glistened in Oaklee's eyes and she cupped his cheek. "She is a lucky woman to have your heart, Coal Hansen."

"Yes," Coal said with a small smile. "She is."

Oaklee laughed and rolled to her back, groaning when the mirth subsided. "You are such a rascal."

"At your service, My Lady." He dipped his head with a charming grin. He fell to his back and they watched the leaves fall, both blissfully enveloped by the companionable silence.

"Coal," she began again, hesitant. "When you see Fillion, please tell him that his Grandpa Corlan's chest was damaged by the fire as well as most of the contents." She moved her hand into a pocket and pulled out a stained rag mottled with dark spots and burnt edges. "Please give this to him?"

He took the rag from her hand and drew a quiet breath upon recognizing the embroidered oak tree. "Shall I deliver a message with your token, My Lady?"

"Tell him to guard it well."

"Coal, sorry to interrupt." Michael approached with a friendly smile directed at Oaklee. "We need to get back. Meeting with NASA."

Oaklee moved to stand and Coal quickly rose and offered her his hand. "I shall see you soon," he said. He tucked her father's token into his pocket.

"Yes, be not a stranger, Son of Fire."

She flashed him an impish look and he shook his head with a grin. With her hand in his, he bowed, meeting her eyes before he rose. With a final look, he pivoted on his heel and strode down the path with Michael.

Earlier he had visited his home and spent time with his father and step-mother. He had new appreciation and respect for his father, despite not being included in the Techsmith Guild. In a way, the exclusion no longer mattered to Coal. The Outside world had fashioned such an education, and Coal found he no longer cared for the reasons his father had in not including him. Their time together would be different now, and he did not desire wedges to come between them. His family had temporarily moved closer to the North Cave near the Watsons as they rebuilt The Forge and their home, along with other trade buildings in the village.

After catching up with his father, Coal had romped around with Blaze and listened to Corona share her many adventures with Laurel. His younger siblings touched his lip ring with curiosity. Corona marveled at the faux plugs in his ears, declaring her desire for pierced ears. This speech ended with her promise that she would wear any jewelry and baubles he wished to bring her from the Outside world.

How could he refuse a lady such a request?

His favorite moment, however, was when Blaze asked, very serious-like, if Coal's hair was burned in the Great Fire, which made Coal laugh. Coal explained that the Outsiders used magic to infuse fire into his hair. Blaze's small mouth parted with wonder and he stared at Coal's hair as if the strands might spark into a flame at any moment. Coal tousled the four-year-old's hair. "Just wait until you are known as the Son of Fire."

Before he visited his parents and siblings, and long before he sought out Oaklee, he spoke with Leaf and Ember. The media buzzed endlessly with the discovery that the Watson children were miraculously alive and heirs to a great fortune. Hanley fairly glowed with the positive press, using the Watsons to deflect, for the moment at least, investigations and human rights charges cropping up in the media. Leaf had visited the lab on several occasions since the Great Fire. The world still believed that a human rights hacktivist group temporarily shut down New Eden.

But Coal knew the truth.

He had watched from a window two weeks prior when Fillion was escorted to a police car for transport to a juvenile correctional facility, and possibly prison once he aged out of that system. Fillion was under further investigation for his role in the fires that stopped time, the moment when the past met the future. The rumors within the lab ran rampant. However, Coal knew no such findings would be made. Hanley avoided negative press for his family.

Timothy was removed the day of the Great Fire and, according to rumors, institutionalized for mental instability. Coal was unsure if this was Fillion's doing or Hanley's, but either way, it kept Hanley's identity hidden. Skylar showed signs of bereavement, as did his sisters. Regardless, the Son of Wind joined the rebuilding of the village. For their part, Windy and Gale brought food and water to the workers. But their mother took to her bed. Brianna and Ember visited daily, Leaf shared with Coal.

The men responsible for aiding Timothy and assaulting Leaf were sentenced to kneel an entire night in The Rows to ponder the lives and sacrifices made by all in the community, to reconnect with the value of life and loss. Following Mass, they each confessed their wrongdoings and honorably asked for New Eden's forgiveness, which was granted—but not without an honor price. Leaf asked for a show of good faith to regain their reputation and trust among their peers. Unanimously, the guilty had volunteered their labor to rebuild what was burned, to perform most of the grunt tasks, and to work clear through the hour of rest each day until completion. According to the Son of Earth, this appeased all and New Eden took her first step toward healing.

His visit with Leaf and Ember ended with Coal relinquishing the Fire Element position to Ember, who had acted as First Representative in their home since fifteen. His presence in New Eden would be sparse, a purgatory existence that, so far, suited him.

Memories of the day dissipated as he and Michael passed through The Door to Hanley's impatient look, and Coal clenched his jaw. This man was the source of so much anguish. Coal longed for the day when the world knew the famed Gamemaster was the ultimate pretender, the master of illusions.

"The Director of Mars Operations at NASA is eager to meet you," Hanley said to Coal. "Remember your job?"

"To guard your daughter?" Coal asked with a lopsided grin. Hanley responded with a bored look. "The liaison who speaks on behalf of the Martians, present and future? Yes, I have not forgotten my *new* role."

Hanley offered a humored smirk. "You are a dragon among men, Coal."

A few moments later, Hanley, Michael and Coal walked into a large meeting room and Coal flashed a charming smile. The scientists launched into their meeting with gusto soon after and Coal eagerly faded behind his thoughts.

He pulled out the rag gingerly stuffed into his pocket and opened up a fold. A golden willow oak leaf stared back at him. Oaklee had not noticed when he tucked it inside her father's token for Fillion to have. Somehow, he knew the Son of Eden would appreciate the sentiment. With a sigh, he placed the rag back into his pocket and then fingered the black ribbon tied to his wrist.

Rosa set a cup of water on the table before Coal. "Thank you," he said, looking her direction. She placed a mug of black coffee before a NASA official, but her lips pulled into a fluid smile with Coal's courtesy.

"The reports from New Eden Biospherics & Research show exciting breakthroughs. I am impressed with the results of the T.R.U.S.T. study," the Director of Mars Operations said to Hanley, acknowledging Dr. Nichols with a single nod. Coal attempted to appear natural and shifted in his seat. "What is the future for the human experiments?"

Dr. Nichols' eyes flitted to Coal's, her face tensing in subtle ways, guarded and remorseful.

"Human property laws allow a wide range of possibilities." Hanley leaned back in the leather chair with a casual smile. Coal's mind stilled as he attempted to process Hanley's comment. Human property? Who...? With a nonchalant look Coal's way, as if reading his thoughts, Hanley said, "The future of the lab-owned test subjects is, at present, to remain a tight-knit colony."

Coal's mouth fell open and he tried to recover as eyes moved his direction. His generation was the human property? Owned? He shifted his eyes to Dr. Nichols, begging for reassurance that he heard incorrectly. But she had physically withdrawn into a cocoon, similar to when learning of Joel's passing. Words screamed from his gut and turned to sawdust in his mouth. Never had he felt so humiliated. So debased. The plan for Lynden to make him appear fully human and desirable, and questions about being a product of his culture, suddenly took on new meaning—and his heart shattered.

"Coal Hansen?" the Director asked.

He swallowed against the pain. "Yes, sir?"

"NASA is eager to study your kind, Mr. Hansen."

Coal flinched with the non-emotional, belittling tone and lowered his eyes. "Thank you, sir."

"Your epigenetic imprint is already altered from living unconfined and interacting with Earth. But your colony is uncompromised."

"I do not follow, sir."

"NASA astronauts, who live in scientific habitats on Mars for short cycles, are programmed for Earth and will always be Earth-connected." The Director offered a polite smile. "After studying your kind, we'll know if human experimentation in the T.R.U.S.T. study has psychologically engineered DNA capable of fully detaching from Earth."

Coal blinked back the growing anger. "Detach from Earth?"

"New Eden Biospherics & Research may have unlocked the key to cultivating a Martian race."

Heat swirled and writhed in Coal's veins as shame burned his skin. Still, he would not allow another human to look down upon him or those in New Eden as nothing more than ideas and theories to manipulate and exploit. With a charming smile, he lifted his eyes. "I am happy to assist you in understanding my *people* and my world. Now, if you will excuse me." Coal stood and stared at Hanley briefly before intentionally meeting the eyes of every person seated at the conference table. Dr. Nichols stared into her cup of tea, gripping the handle. "This is New Eden's mandatory hour of rest, and I find some habits are harder to break than others."

He pushed out of the room and stormed down the hallway. Once in his room he collapsed onto his bed. "I am a dragon among men," he whispered to the darkness. One day, Hanley would understand such prophetic words. The residents of New Eden were not products of science. They were human beings with beating hearts and souls filled with dreams. In the meantime, as much as he hated this, Coal needed to contain his fire until he could ascertain Fillion's position and plans.

"Boo!"

Ignis lifted from his black box and materialized next to the bed. "Hello, Coal. You seem upset."

"Yes, I am bothered. I have a question."

"Of course."

"What are human property laws? And what legal rights do human property have?"

Ignis began to talk and Coal closed his eyes and listened, each breath more painful than the last. The holographic man moved from one subject to another. ...

"Human property are not allowed to marry free humans, and any offspring resulting from their coupling revert to the owning laboratory. This preserves any dysfunction in engineered genetics from integrating with uncontaminated DNA..."

"I have heard enough," Coal said. "I wish to be alone now. My apologies, Ignis. I shall call upon you later."

"I hope you feel better, Coal." With a wave, the hologram disappeared and the drone whirred back into its box.

Seconds ticked by and his room dissolved into the nightmare of his raging mind. He needed to move. Springing to a stand, Coal left his apartment and briskly walked down the hallways, though the various control rooms, and exited the lab. Outside, he lifted his eyes to the fading afternoon sky and the still invisible stars.

Did Lynden gaze upon the same sunset?

How many in New Eden looked upon their mosaic evening sky this moment?

Did his father know that he would sire slaves for science?

He could not imagine so. From Coal's discussions with Leaf, the first generation were stumped by their singularity in signing The Code. A sharp pang gripped Coal's chest. This is why Coal was not to be trusted in New Eden alone. Hanley knew Coal would learn of his generation's reality.

A cool breeze brushed along his flushed skin. He whispered his wish to the hidden stars, allowing the wind to carry his heart's desire to the heavenlies. The pomegranate tree in the courtyard rustled, the rushing sound moving through Coal as if the very breath of life. The song broke into chorus with another gust and a couple leaves broke free to dance in the approaching night.

He refused to be the brown fish belly up in the corner, or the blue fish gasping for air. Coal pivoted on his heel and returned to the lab and to the keepers responsible for his survival. "I am awesome."

APPENDICES

1. Author Notes

2. Hacker Terminology

3. Anime and Japanese Terminology

4. Additional Definitions

5. Translations

6. The Elements of YOUR Life: Blog Fun with Readers

7. Selected Bibliography

Read THE CODE at
www.jesikahsundin.com

.

AUTHOR NOTES

Oh, my goodness! You're reading my author notes! Does this mean my characters did their job and you enjoyed their story? THANK YOU dear reader for giving my book series a chance. *bows to you* I am honored by the time you gifted my novel, time that could have been spent in the company of an entirely different cast and world. Thank you! Thank you! Thank you!

Torrent reader much? If so, hello! Pleased to meet you. Soon after LEGACY was published, I was blown away by the sheer number of torrent links that cropped up all over the interwebs. As you know, Fillion and Mack approve of the Open Source community *wink, wink* Since you were bold enough to download a pirated copy, I am going to be bold in return. Please leave my novels a review on Amazon and/or Goodreads. Neither site requires purchase in order to rate and review products. Reviews are like currency to authors and this is a great way to pay it forward and support an artist. Thank you <3

Phew! What a process. Writing ELEMENTS was a loooooong journey. I set off empowered by conquering the newbie learning curve after writing LEGACY, completely ignorant of how much work and angst goes into the making of a second novel. It's kind of like going from one child to two. You start questioning things, like is it possible to love this one as much as the first? How do I manage my time equally between both projects? It was awkward at the beginning and I, in all my melodramatic glory, had some downright epic tantrums. Eventually, a rhythm was established, life carried on, and I had to laugh at myself. And yes, I do love this novel as much as the first. How could I have ever thought differently? ELEMENTS had demanded a different set of rules and TLC than LEGACY. But that's OK. I learned to have grace for myself and enjoy the ride. And, wow, what a ride it was!

For those who patiently waited for ELEMENTS to finish, even when I took nine months longer than anticipated, thank you. I finished because I'm richly blessed to have a supportive team that "gets me." They accept all my quirks. They forgive me when I space out in a conversation. Roll their eyes privately instead of in front of me when I ramble on-and-on-and-on-and-on about my story. Or when I spam their inboxes about my story. Sigh. I'm bad. They don't tell me to get a life. Or to have anxiety over real-people issues for once. Instead, they ask with excitement, "Is it almost done yet?" Or say, "Hurry up! I want to read it!" Half the time I know they're just being polite because I've been rambling on-and-on-and-on-and-on. How did I get so lucky? I'm deeply humbled by their unconditional support, encouragement, and love.

Cue the credits!

FAMILY

Myles Sundin: Husband, grantor of dreams-come-true, Technology Guru, and the BEST negative lead/bad boy character I've ever fallen in love with. Truly. None compare to you.

Myles, Colin and Violette Sundin: Pride-and-Joy x 3, infinite wells of inspiration, my biggest fans, and the best sources of giggles ever. I really do have giggly children.

Dennis, Adriel Nicole ... ahem ... Nicki, Penny, Bryan, and Myles Jr.: Thank you for you everything <3 I could make a list, but it would be infinitely long. There is absolutely no way I could have written both books without each of you. I have the best family ever! Special shout out to *Toby, Amy, Katie, Connie, Erik, Brandy, Kristin, Dirk, Cory, Jordan, Logan, Corinne, Kathryn, Darla, Debbie, Donna, Al,* and—ACK!—I'm sure I'm forgetting someone. Sorry!

FRIENDS (who made this project a reality):

Melissa Slager: Beloved friend to the two-decade power, best writing partner ever, Editor Extraordinaire, and inventor of Five Happies *clears throat* For book two, mine are: 1) Seabrook; 2) Apple Pie Moonshine in Neah Bay; 3) Hugo House; 4) Novel inspired coffee mugs; 5) #sugarpacket. And, on that last happy note: *A word is a portal to a thought or just a word, so choose wisely* #sugarpacket

Tracy Campbell: Fellow Nathan Fillion and *Firefly* fangirl friend, The Queen of "maybe this is an opportunity," Wednesday work partner, a coffee addict after my own heart, my introvert soul-sista (hamster bubble!), and the mother of Morgan, life-long best friend of my boys. Oh, and BTW, "I'll never see you again!" *waves dramatically*

Jennifer Newsom: My fellow Vulcan curly-haired, fair-skinned, freckled friend who fangirls over the shade as much as me, workout buddy, *flails small arms like a T-Rex*, epic science nerd girl and grammarian, coffee talk pal, my Typesetter-in-Shining-Armor (swoons!), and the mother of Olivia, best friend of my boys.

Katie Kent: Book-lover-movie-watching-music-listening-deep-talk-and-lots-of-giggles friend, a Searcher of Truth, *Outlander* fangirl and bearer of pocket Jamie Fraser (movie nights are not the same without him, btw), Spinner-Weaver-Knitter Mage of the Highest Order (it's magic to me!), Helpless Romantic *heart sigh* and one of my biggest promoters.

Timna Lansel, Jill Reasoner, Jocelyn Skinner, and *Corrina Lance:* You ladies rock! This entire year, each of you have brought me words of encouragement exactly when I needed it, or hugs, or coffee, or chocolate, or all of the above. I cannot express how grateful I am for your continual friendship and your support. I heart you! And, as a side note, I find your laughter infectious. Each of you. When you laugh, I have to laugh, too. Can't help it.

AUTHOR FRIENDS

CeeCee James (*Ghost No More* series), Selah Tay-Song (*Dreams of QaiMaj* series), Amanda June Hagarty (*Little Lacey* on Wattpad), Rob Slater (*A Deserted Lands* series), Joannah Miley (*The Immortal Game*), Mike Hartner (*The Eternity Series*), Mati Raine (*Archipelago*), Artis Fricbergs (*The Muskokans*), and Shannon L. Reagan (*The GearMaker's Locket*): I owe so much to each of you. Thank you for the writing community; the endless support; encouragement and feedback; the hand-holding when I walked around in a newbie fog; the many giggles; conference and book event memories; and our partnership. Authordom is complete with each of you by my side!

READER FRIENDS

To all my readers: Thank youuuuuuu! I love, LOVE, love interacting with you online. #ReadersRock

Jessica Jett, Hannah Miller, Andra "Anzu" Perju, Heather Padgett, and Becky (from Goodreads): Thank you for making this the best two years of my life! Your kind words of encouragement and fellow fangirling over all things books, music, and video games carried me through book two. I write for readers—no, friends—like you <3 Mwah!

BETA READERS (aka Team Jesikah)

Barbara Simonds, Ryan Peterson, Hannah Miller, Penny Sundin, Katie Kent, Jennifer Newsom, Jocelyn Skinner, and Selah Tay-Song: Thank you for polishing up my story and making me shine. I appreciate your bravery and willingness to be real and truthful with me. Because of your gracious service, readers everywhere will have a richer reading experience. THANK YOU!

MY COMMUNITY

Amalia Chitulescu: You are AMAZING. I love working with you! Ahem ...*bends on one knee* Would you be my forever Cover Artist? Thank you for lending your talent to clothe another one of my novels. The linden tree, stone bridge, biodome panes, and medieval Fillion are beautiful! Your digital illustrations truly are a form of magic...

Kiffer Brown and *Chanticleer Book Reviews & Media:* I am proud and honored to be part of the Chanticleer Family. Thank you for always making me part of the writing and conference scene!

Uppercase Bookshop (Snohomish, Wash.): Leah and Cheryl, you two are amazing! Thank you for displaying my book poster in your front window for as many months as you did, including me in your author events, and for all the great conversations. I LOVE volunteering in your bookstore whenever my schedule allows. My heart skips a beat every time I peruse your scifi and fantasy section. And—sorry, not done gushing yet—the new store location is beautiful!

Main Street Books (Monroe, Wash.): Emily, thank you sooooooo much for translating Fillion, Lynden, and Mack's language into the beautiful Anime language of Japanese. My family LOVES perusing your selection of Manga. And I always enjoy coming in and chatting up all things *Les Mis* and books with you. Thank you for being an epic part of this journey! *Arigatou gozaimasu!*

Village Books and *Cozy Corner Books* (Bellingham, Wash.): Bellingham seems to be where are all the writing magic happens in my life. Thank you for making me a part of your reader community!

Life is Good Cottage at Seabrook (Seabrook, Wash.): This cottage contains muses—I am fully convinced! ELEMENTS was completed within your walls, a feat that had taken nearly seven months to do. But within a few short days, I whipped out several chapters (I think four or five?). That has never happened before in my writing career. Besides being magic for writers (and probably other artists), your location, nestled against the woods and by the sea, was exactly what my soul needed for rest and rejuvenation. All the hearts go to you, Life is Good Cottage!

Leo Todd Website Design & Marketing: I loooooove my website. Thank you SO much for all the hard work and creativity involved in getting my info out there on the interwebs. I truly appreciate all that you have done for me and my family.

The Nest (Woodinville, Wash.): Beth Fetty, you're my hero. Thank you for coming to my rescue last summer and giving Violette a fun and awesome place to play while I was in the heat of writing. She still talks about *Frozen* camp <3 The Nest Drop and Play Center is simply the best! Your love and care for my children this past decade has sustained me through many hardships and times of renewal. Hugs & Kisses!

Jennifer Cook and *Claire Lalande*: Claire, thank you SO much for translating Leaf and Willow's language into the beautiful, romantic language of French. The Middles Ages comes alive in the biodomes with your help. Jennifer, your continual, unwavering support of *The Biodome Chronicles* through FrogskinU means the world to me <3 I appreciate all the communications between Claire and I, too. *Merci beaucoup!*

Mike and *Francesca Mesneak of Tapestry Church* (Monroe, Wash.): Your living example of God's love has changed the way I view myself and the world. Thank you for all the prayers and support over the years. I am beyond blessed to have you in my life!

Talbot Shoemaker: Um, I kinda borrowed your name for Mack's family's Smart Tech business: TalBOT Industries. Now you're immortal. That's cool, right? *grins innocently*

Traci & Jason Kaldestad, Diane & Jay Dillion, Shelece Nosker & Pat Garrett, Crystal & David Spurrier, and *Jill Reasoner:* Neighborhoods really can't get more epic than ours. We're pretty badass. I owe many productive hours of writing to each of you. Thank you for including this reclusive, quirky, geek girl as part of the neighborhood cool, even if I don't listen to country music or watch football ;-)

Morgan, Olivia, Xander, Abie, Cady, Geneva, Cameron, Cayden, Julion, Baby Jayce Oakley, Kiera, Hayley, Brody, Brynlee, DJ, Valerie, Sophia, Peter, Nathan, Evelyn, Jamie, Alice, Lia and Sera: Thank you so much for being part of Myles, Colin, and Violette's lives. I love listening to all your many adventures while I sit at the table inside or outside and write. You each bring smiles to my face every day! Remember, never underestimate your value and worth. It's immeasurable.

And now, time to get busy writing book three.
Tsuzuku…
(To be continued…)

HACKER TERMINOLOGY

HACKER – A hacker is an individual who breaches security in a computer system or computer network to capitalize on exposed weaknesses, for beneficial or nefarious reasons. Sometimes the term is applied to an individual with expert knowledge of computers and computer networks. A subculture now exists for hackers, formed by a real and recognized community known as the computer underground. This subculture of tech-savvy individuals has also developed a unique language and slang terms defined and collected in The Hacker's Dictionary (originally known as the Jargon File), which is searchable online.

A Lefty's Catcher Mitt – Net jargon for something people think exists, but doesn't. The term came from the anime show *Laughing Man (Ghost in the Shell)*, where a character owns a left-handed mitt inscribed with a quote by Holden Caulfield, title character in the novel *The Catcher in the Rye* by J.D. Salinger

Bagbiter – a person who always causes problems, is a whiner, and is never satisfied. Comes from the hacker term for a piece of equipment, hardware, or software that fails

Black Hat – someone who maliciously hacks into secure systems to corrupt or gain unauthorized information. The hacker subculture often refers to this person as a "cracker" rather than a "hacker"

Bletcherous (bletch) – disgusting, makes you want to vomit, usually in reference to an object, and rarely regarding people

Defragment (defrag) – an action to reduce the fragmentation of a software file by concatenating parts stored in separate locations on a disk

Faraday Cage – a grounded metal screen (usually copper) that surrounds a piece of equipment to exclude electrostatic and electromagnetic influences

Fatal Exception Error – an error that closes down and aborts a program, returning the user to the operating system

Glitch – a sudden interruption in electric service, sanity, or program function, sometimes recoverable

Gritching (gritch) – to complain; a blend of "gripe" and "bitch"

Kernel Panic – an action taken by an operating system when detecting an internal fatal error from which it cannot safely recover; also known as "the blue screen of death"

Loser – an unexpectedly bad situation, program, programmer, or person

Uncanny Valley – The hypothesis in the field of aesthetics which states that some humans feel revulsion or disturbance when robotics or 3D animation look and move almost, but not exactly, like natural beings

White Hat – someone who hacks into secure systems and instead of corrupting or taking unauthorized information, exposes the weaknesses to the system's owners so they can strengthen the breach before it can be taken advantage of by others (including **Black Hats**)

ANIME and JAPANESE TERMINOLOGY

ANIME / MANGA – Anime is a distinctly Japanese style of animation, while manga is the term for comic books that feature anime-stylized characters. Anime differs from American cartoons in that it is more often created for teens and adults with a range of topics that typically explore serious themes. It has been criticized by parents in the United States for discussing such taboo topics as teen suicide, violence, social rebellion, spiritual ideas, and sex. However, anime and manga include many genres, including romance, comedy, horror, and action, and feature several series for children, *Pokémon* being the most notable and successful in the U.S. Many video games, for general or mature audiences, feature anime-style characters and themes. In Japan, and even in the U.S., anime fans have formed a subculture with punk undertones emulating goth, emo, or cyberpunk movements.

Bishounen (bishonen, bish, bishie, bishy) – literally, "pretty boy" in Japanese, a term used to describe a young man—including those in anime, manga, and video games—who is notably beautiful and attractive

Bakayarō – dumbass, idiot, fool

Chikara – strength, power

Desu – Japanese for "it is," often said at the end of sentences to seem cute or unwitting

Dokyun – a derogatory internet slang term that spread from Japan's 2ch.net, which mostly means dumbass or idiot

Henshin – "to change or transform the body"; in anime and manga, this is usually when a character transforms into a superhero

Hikikomori – someone who purposely stays in their house all day long, isolating themselves from society, and who usually spends all their time on the Internet, playing video games, or watching anime

Jitsu – martial arts term for "technique" or "art"

Kono Yaro – translates to "that bastard"

Kusogaki – little shit, shitty brat, damn child

Otaku – in Japan, originally a very negative term to describe a recluse who has no life, usually because their world revolves around fictional characters, such as in anime and manga; in America, the word has been applied by anime fans as a positive term for fanboy/girl

Nakoudo – translates to "matchmaker" or "go-between" and is the person who contracts a marriage between the man and woman who hope to marry

Nettomo – slang term for a friend made on the Internet

Nosebleed – used by fans about someone whom they think is hot or exciting; when an anime or manga character has become sexually excited, it is portrayed with a sudden nosebleed

Yuinou / Yuinou no gi – translates to "betrothal presents" and is the ceremony where the groom and bride to-be swear their engagement publicly, followed by an exchange of gifts between the two households

ADDITIONAL DEFINITIONS

Cob – a type of structural mud made from clay, sand, water, and straw that is applied wet between stones or in clumps to form walls. Cob homes, shops, and barns became the preferred building type during the Middle Ages, especially in the British Isles. The mud structures reached the height of popularity with Tudor-style architecture made famous for its external geometric timber designs, stone or brick accents, oriel window boxes, and lead multi-lit latticed windows. This is the most commonly featured style of building in fantasy storybook villages.

Cyberpunk – a literary and visual media genre that takes place in a future or near-future Earth and is most notably known for the film noir detective-like qualities of the story, high technology (computers, hackers, robotics, artificial intelligence), and a degraded society. The world or place setting is typically regulated and influenced by large corporations and wealthy elite rather than traditional governmental bodies. The protagonist is usually a rogue/misfit, a loner in society with a dark past. The cyberpunk genre is prominently featured in anime and manga in Japan.

Dungeon Master (DM) – individual in charge of organizing and planning the details and challenges of a given adventure in the table-top role-playing game "Dungeons & Dragons." He or she also is a participant in the game, but their key role is to make all the rules and control the story, telling the player characters what they hear and what they see. The only part a DM does not control are the decisions/actions of the player characters.

Emo / Emocore – an alternative rock subculture influenced by the punk music scene that emerged in the 1980s, featuring lyrics about self rather than traditional punk themes of society. The Emo scene exploded in the 1990s with the indie rock grunge scene and popularity of pop punk, and was later brought back to mainstream teen culture in the early 2000s through the Internet social media site MySpace. Individuals belonging to this subculture have a unique and notable fashion, the modern looks and trends believed to have been influenced by the anime and manga subculture. The Emo's (sometimes called Scene Kids or Ravers) are described as being "emotive" in nature, giving rise to the idea that the boys possess more feminine traits and qualities than their non-emo counterparts.

Gamemaster (GM) – an individual who officiates and referees multi-player role-playing games (table-top or live action), sometimes with other Gamemasters. They arbitrate and moderate the rules, settle disputes, create and define the game world/environment, blend and weave player character stories together, and oversee the non-player character roles and influence in the story. The Gamemaster's specific job and function is unique to each game.

Live Action Role-Playing (LARP) – a style of game that transcends traditional table-top or video game role-playing into live action where people physically become a character and act out their role in a defined fantasy setting. A LARP must contain three consistent ideas in order to be considered true live action role-playing (expanded in more depth by larping.org): collaborative (a mutual operation where everyone understands they are a character and must work together toward a common goal); pretending (a necessary element for each LARP, such as the game world/space, weapons and characterization, to name a few); and rules (agreed upon by the community of gamers and refereed by Gamemasters but usually sustained by an honor system among players).

Mundane – an object or person that does not belong to the fictional game or setting, such as a cellphone in a medieval community, or the President of the United States in ancient China. In the LARP and role-playing subculture, mundane also refers to one's "real" life versus his or her character life/world.

Visual Kei ("visual music" or "visual system") – an alternative rock music movement in Japan that features band members who typically try to emulate a unified androgynous appearance. They embody unique makeup, hair styles, and clothing that is punk in nature with mainstream success and influenced by Western concepts such as glam rock, goth, and cyberpunk. Some argue that Visual Kei is no longer about a music genre but about a subculture of individuals who reflect this fashion style and trend.

TRANSLATIONS

"Coal, nice to finally meet you. *Je vous souhaite une cordiale bienvenue en touchant le sol de la terre pour la première fois.*"
Translation: *I extend a warm welcome as you walk Earth for the first time.*

Coal regarded the man warily, surprised by the welcome to Earth in French. *"Acceptez mes humbes remerciements pour l'invitation et l'experience,"* Coal said. Although he felt insulted by the insinuation that he was an alien to their land rather than a neighbor, Coal thanked him for the opportunity nonetheless.
Translation: *My humble thanks for the invitation and experience.*

There were far too many questions, Coal internally quipped. Instead, he voiced the loudest of them all in French, too ashamed to ask in English before John and Michael. *"Est-ce que mon père a donné son autorisation finale?"*
Translation: *Did my father grant final permission?*

"Fillion," a male voice whispered. Warm air pulsed near his ear, followed by a firm shake. "Fillion."

"Koroshiteyaru mae ni hotto ite!"
Translation: *Go away before I kill you!*

Fillion squinted and lifted his head. "What?" With a groan he fell back onto the pillow and sighed when the sound of wheat hulls rushed in his ears. "*Hanarete ikanakereba, umarete kita toki o koukai suru zo!*" He had been dreaming in Japanese. Reality was a bit soupy at the moment.
Translation: *Leave me alone or you'll wish you were never born.*

"*Arigatou gozaimasu.*" Fillion wanted to roll his eyes with the shaky sound of his voice.
Translation: *Thank you.*

"Yeah. Same to you." Unable to resist, he gave a shallow, tight bow and said, "*Yoi ichinichi o.*"
Translation: *Have a nice day.*

Mack pulled open a drawer from a nightstand positioned against the bed and removed a large, thin book. "Read and write?" Mack asked. Coal grit his teeth against the insult.
"*Bien sûr, idiot, et en trois langues différentes!*"
Translation: *Of course you idiot, and in three different languages.*

He straightened the cloak around her shoulders with a sad, distracted smile. "Your indomitable spirit has encouraged me these past few days." Leaf slipped Fillion a quick look, but said to her, "*Je suis fier de la femme que tu deviens.*"
Translation: *I am proud of the woman you are becoming.*

"Indomitable? Really, Leaf Watson." She blinked with embarrassment. Nevertheless, her brother's words of pride touched her heart. "*Père serait très fier de toi, cher frère.*"
Translation: *Father would be most proud of you, brother dearest.*

Lynden accepted the sticks with a tight head nod and said, "*Arigatou gozaimasu.*"

"*Dou itashimashite,*" Selah replied.
Translation: *Thank you / You're welcome*

He tried to restrain a smile as he intensified his gaze, knowing it was comical at best. "How about now, *mon joli petit dragon?*"
Translation: *My lovely little dragon*

Overcome, she pressed a hand to his heart and whispered against his lips, "*Voici un témoignage de mon affection, conservez-le bien.*"
Translation: *Here is a token of my affection, guard it well.*

He covered the hand with both of his, and whispered in reply, "*Korekara zutto, ore no jinsei wa anata no mono desu. Zutto eien ni sasagemasu.*"
Translation: *"I now see that you have always owned my life, and always will. I give it to you."*

ELEMENTS of YOUR LIFE
BLOG FUN WITH READERS

The Biodome Chronicles presented an opportunity for a couple additions to the cast in book two. In an effort to create a fun and memorable character, I requested help from my readers. Yep, YOU dear readers!

In the blog titled, "What is your favorite color? No really?" (May 2014), these were the questions I asked:

1) What is your favorite color?
2) What is your nervous habit?
3) Do you like to walk barefoot? Or prefer shoes?
4) Night Owl or Early Riser?
5) Time Management Guru or Procrastinator?
6) What is a random fact about you?

Here were the replies I used:

Jessica Jett (via Goodreads)
What is your nervous habit? *Biting my lip ring.*
* Used for Lynden.

Anzu (via Goodreads)
What is your nervous habit? *Constantly turning my thumb ring around.*
* Used for Lynden.

Leylan (via Goodreads)
Do you like to walk barefoot? Or prefer shoes? *Definitely barefoot.*
* Used for Coal.

Barb (via Goodreads)
What is your nervous habit? *Wiggling my feet.*
* Used for Nadine, the hacker in the underground who wiggled her feet/combat boots on Mack's desk, and for Lynden, who often swung her legs/feet when sitting.

Lynne (via Goodreads)
What is your nervous habit? *Humming.*
* Used for Oaklee, especially when she leaves the Great Hall to wander alone at night. Coal refers once to wanting to hear her hum, too.

Kalliopeia (via Goodreads)
What is your favorite color? *Violet.*
* Used for Oaklee, the shade of silk she desires if she could have anything from the Outside world.

Bipasha {is eviscerated by fiction} (via Goodreads)
What is a random fact about you? *I'm heterochromic. Hazel and Dark brown.*
* Used for Nadine, the hacker in the underground who focused on the Hanley and Connor relationship. Coal noted her two different eye colors.

Francesca (via blog on my website)
What is a random fact about you? *When in a crowd, I have a social limit. When I'm done, I am DONE talking to people.*
* Used for Fillion and Oaklee, who were both often "done" talking to people, especially when in or before a crowd.

Melissa Lee (via blog on my website)
What is your favorite color? *Blood red.*
* Used for Lynden, often referenced by Coal who admired the "blood red" chunk of hair that swooped across her eye.

Jennifer Newsom (via my Facebook page)
What is your nervous habit? *Recite my favorite passage from* Dune *in my head: "I must not fear. Fear is the mind-killer. Fear is the little-death that brings total obliteration. I will face my fear. I will permit it to pass over me and through me. And when it has gone past I will turn the inner eye to see its path. Where the fear has gone there will be nothing. Only I will remain."*
* Used for Lynden and Coal. OK, so I took some liberties here (please don't hate me *Dune* fans). The message given in this beautiful passage became Lynden's mantra to "toughen up" and "You are awesome."

Megan Jacobson (via my Facebook page)
What is a random fact about you? *Hmmmm... I like putting hot cocoa mix (powder) on vanilla ice cream if we don't have other chocolate sauce.*
* Used for Lynden, her surprise dessert for Coal during the maglev train scene.

I had a great time while building characters that utilized random and unique ELEMENTS of you <3 Thank you for the fun!

SELECTED BIBLIOGRAPHY

Paolo of Certaldo, 14th century merchant and writer. Quote from William Kremer, "What medieval Europe did with its teenagers," BBC News, http://www.bbc.com/news/magazine-26289459 (March 23, 2014)

George Dvorsky, "Why we should reboot the Biosphere Projects," io9/Gawker, http://io9.com/5938855/why-we-should-reboot-the-biosphere-projects (August 29, 2012)

Dave Funk, "LARP Definition." LARPing.org, http://www.larping.org/larp-definition (accessed November 13, 2013)

Robert. T. Gonzalez, "Why the Mars500 mission doesn't prove we're psychologically capable of a trip to Mars," io9/Gawker, http://io9.com/5855888/why-the-mars500-mission-doesnt-prove-were-psychologically-capable-of-a-trip-to-mars (November 3, 2011)

AB Raschke (aka Waitingforrain28), "Biosphere 2: Bringing Science Fiction to Life," Pathofthenightborn.wordpress, https://pathofthenightborn.wordpress.com/2012/10/18/biosphere-2-bringing-science-fiction-to-life/ (October 18, 2012)

Jesikah Sundin is a sci-fi/fantasy writer mom of three nerdlets and devoted wife to a gamer geek. In addition to her family, she shares her home in Monroe, Washington with a red-footed tortoise, two gerbils, and a collection of seatbelt purses. She is addicted to coffee, laughing, Doc Martens... Oh, and the forest is her happy place.

Discover the worlds and characters
of *The Biodome Chronicles* at:

www.jesikahsundin.com

CPSIA information can be obtained at www.ICGtesting.com
Printed in the USA
LVOW11s2231220316

480330LV00001B/21/P